# ICE BROTHERS

## SLOAN WILSON

AVON
PUBLISHERS OF BARD, CAMELOT AND DISCUS BOOKS

AVON BOOKS
A division of
The Hearst Corporation
959 Eighth Avenue
New York, New York 10019

First Avon Printing, February, 1981

AVON TRADEMARK REG. U.S. PAT. OFF. AND IN
OTHER COUNTRIES, MARCA REGISTRADA, HECHO EN
U.S.A.

Printed in the U.S.A.

TO THE MEN OF THE GREENLAND PATROL
   1942 –1945

Forgotten now and little honored then, but still
They'll never have to wonder if they're men.
                              S.W.

# Author's Note

This is fiction based on historical fact. Boston beam trawlers were used by the United States Coast Guard on the Greenland Patrol during World War II. At least one German weather ship was captured by the Coast Guard in Greenland waters. There were many rumors about German weather stations being established on the east coast of Greenland and of German submarines being refueled in the fjords. The author is still not sure how much truth was in them.

I have used the names of real places in this novel, though the characters and their actions are imaginary. The names of the ships except for the *Dorchester* are also imaginary, although I have made them sound like the Eskimo words which were used by the Coast Guard for trawlers.

Although this is not an autobiographical novel in any narrow sense, I did serve as an ensign aboard the U.S. Coast Guard Cutter *Tampa* on the Greenland Patrol in 1942. A year later I served as executive officer and finally, for a brief time, as commanding officer of the American trawler *Nogak* on the Greenland Patrol. Our sister ship, the *Natsek*, was lost with all hands, though near Labrador, not on the east coast of Greenland. The incident of the German officer dropping the liqueur glass was told to me by Gerda Klein, author of "All But My Life." It happened to her when she was a young girl in Poland in 1939.

The drama in this novel is pure fiction, but I have presented Greenland exactly as I remembered it. It is apparently true that memories of Greenland, like the bodies of people who are buried there, last forever. This book was written in 1979, thirty-six years after I left Greenland, but I did not have to do much research in the libraries.

—Sloan Wilson

# ICE BROTHERS

# Part I

# CHAPTER 1

The people on Fieldstone Road in Wellseley, Massachusetts, celebrated the bombing of Pearl Harbor with an enormous party. Of course the families there were well aware that war is a terrible thing and they kept saying that to each other, but they were excited, even exalted because hate for a common enemy who is a long way away can make people feel almost ennobled. The radio did not make anything clear, except that the United States had been wantonly attacked and was going to war. "We're off!" Mark Kettel said, as though the war were a horse race or a long-awaited trip.

The first thing most of the people on Fieldstone Road did was to telephone all their relatives. Families gathered. Neighbors came in, drinks were mixed, and within a few hours the street looked as though a wedding, not a war, were being celebrated in every house.

Paul Schuman drove up to his father-in-law's house shortly after dark. He had spent that weekend working on his father's old yawl which was moored off the end of a pier at a deserted shipyard in Quincy. He had not turned on the radio, and at six-thirty that Sunday evening, he was one of the very few people in America who had not heard the big news. Wars between nations were the farthest things from his mind, which was entirely preoccupied with a small, and to him a most mysterious war with his wife, which had caused him to spend a dismal weekend alone. On the drive from Quincy to Wellesley he was trying to make up his mind whether he should just surrender and buy peace with Sylvia at any price, despite the fact that he felt he had been entirely in the right throughout this latest argument.

But wasn't any man who thought he was entirely in the right during a fight with his wife on dangerous territory? Sylvia was young and pretty and loved parties—certainly

3

he should find no fault with that. Her father was a banker who somehow maintained his modest level of prosperity even in the Depression, and it was hard for her to understand that her young husband didn't have a dime which he didn't earn or hustle in some way while trying to get through college. Paul and his brother, Bill, spent a lot of time working on their family's ancient yawl not just because they loved sailing, but because they were running her as a fairly profitable summer charter boat. And though he was somewhat ashamed of it, Paul spent many evenings playing bridge and poker at fraternity houses and yacht clubs because he had found that it was surprisingly easy for him to make money at cards simply by staying sober.

That all made sense, but the fact remained that Sylvia was not a girl who was accustomed to waiting around home alone, filling her time with vacuuming rugs or reading. She had been going to parties and college dances since her early teens, and as she said, she didn't think that getting married meant she was supposed to turn into a nun. Her two brothers and Paul's brother, Bill, often served as her escort when Paul was not available, and what could be wrong with that?

Plenty was wrong with it, Paul reflected darkly, for once she arrived at a party, Sylvia played the familiar part of the belle of the ball as exuberantly as she had before their marriage. He never was sure who brought her home, often in the early hours of the morning, and when he asked questions about what she had been doing, her answers were at best evasive. Her girl friends appeared to be giving a great many very late parties to which no men were invited and there seemed to be a great many very fine old movies which were shown only at midnight.

Paul was a jealous husband and a suspicious one, with or without reason, and he knew that this made him ridiculous, a fact which did not improve his temper. He also worried about his wife because she sometimes drank too much at cocktail parties, and she drove their ancient Ford roadster with the same joyful recklessness which won her so much admiration when she danced. She was, as she boasted, a very skillful driver, just as she was a very good dancer, and this scared him most of all. Sylvia was one of those who just didn't think accidents could happen, not serious ones, and not to her, anyway.

Sylvia was a handful—her own mother said that, had

4

been saying it for years, and many young men, Paul ruefully thought, had agreed. She was fast and she was wild, had been ever since the age of sixteen, ever since Paul had known her. If he had wanted a nice quiet girl, he should have fallen in love with someone else. He had always known that, but compared to Sylvia, all other women seemed to him to be only half alive.

As she grew older, she would quiet down—he had always been sure of that. And she really wasn't anywhere near as fast and wild as she liked to pretend and as envious gossips liked to say—he had always been sure of that. Sylvia was Sylvia, and since he could not stop himself from loving her and couldn't change her, he would have to learn how to live with her in some kind of peace. Lecturing her and trying to lay down the law did not help. The righteous, he had learned, often have to sleep alone.

As he drove through the quiet streets of Wellesley, Paul wished he could buy some flowers as a peace offering for his wife, but all the stores were closed. He needed a gift for her—gifts she always understood better than words, even if they had no real value. Trying to think of something available on a Sunday night, he remembered some new foul weather gear he had bought for the boat at a sale some days before and had left in the trunk of his car. It included a yellow southwester hat, and she always loved headgear of any sort. She would laugh, perch it saucily on the top of her head even if it didn't fit, and for a little while at least, all their troubles would be forgotten.

When Paul approached his father-in-law's driveway, he was surprised to see a lot of cars there. The old Plymouth station wagon owned by his older brother-in-law, Mark, had been left on the edge of the lawn, where no one was supposed to park, and the new Buick convertible which his younger brother-in-law had just bought stood at the end of a line of vehicles in which he recognized those belonging to a variety of uncles and aunts. The thought occurred to him that Sylvia might still be so angry at him that she was thinking of leaving him and that a whole family conference had been called to consider the situation, as had been done when Mark's wife left him. Certainly his differences with Sylvia were nowhere near that drastic, but Paul still felt nervous as he got the yellow hat out of the trunk and approached the front door. After all, if Sylvia was feeling hurt, and if her relatives had gathered for whatever reason,

5

she would be unable to resist the temptation to get sympathy and support from them. She would tell her version of their arguments, which would have very little to do with the issues as he perceived them.

When Paul gloomily opened the front door, holding the yellow hat, he was surprised to see what appeared to be a large cocktail party in progress, and he was completely astonished when Sylvia, looking beautiful as ever and much more excited by his arrival than usual, rushed up and embraced him, hugging him with more fervor than she had displayed in weeks. He left the hat on an umbrella stand by the door and forgot it.

"Oh, *Paul!*" she said. "We've been trying to get in touch with you!"

"What's happening?" he asked.

"My God, haven't you heard?" Mark said, coming up to offer him a martini. "The Japs bombed Pearl Harbor. We're going to war, buddy boy! We're off!"

# CHAPTER 2

That was an incredible moment, one he was to try to analyze many times for years afterward. Sylvia and a lot of other people were trying to talk to him all at the same time, but suddenly they seemed as voiceless as actors in a silent movie. The fight he had been having with Sylvia suddenly appeared ridiculous, the causes and issues entirely forgotten. He had a sense of everything being swept away, this house full of excited people, his college, the boat on which he had been working, and most of all, Sylvia herself, who now stood with her arms around him as though she expected to dance. Already they all had been torn from his life, and in their place was this new thing, war. As Mark had said, they all were going to go to it, as though it were a dance of some kind. They were off. Soon, perhaps in a few weeks, he would be dressing up in a uniform. He didn't know anything about war, except what he had read in *All*

*Quiet on the Western Front*, descriptions of horses trying to run on shattered legs and men trying to hold in their intestines with their hands. The thought terrified him, but of course he wouldn't be in the army, he would be in the navy. He then had a quick vision of himself as the captain of a destroyer in the act of torpedoing a battleship. This was followed by a sense of absurdity and futility—since he had dropped out of the naval reserve to get married and to make money in the summers instead of going on training cruises, he probably would be unable to get a commission. For him the war would be swabbing decks and saluting classmates who had had enough brains to stick with the ROTC. And before that, war would mean being shipped off to some training camp. War would mean saying good-by to Sylvia for years, maybe forever. Then he had a vision of himself returning to her, his sleeves covered with gold braid, his chest bedecked with medals. He knew this fantasy was ridiculous but his errant mind kept elaborating on it. His gaunt face would be tanned and scarred just a little at the corner of his mouth. He would explain that he got that scar while ramming a Japanese aircraft carrier, and she would kiss him with the intensity he always hoped for and rarely got. Absurd, absurd! War is hell, Sherman had said, and he was sure that it wouldn't turn out to be a movie starring him like Errol Flynn. He had the sensation of sinking in a cold sea, being dragged down by a sinking destroyer.

"You won't have to go right away," Sylvia was saying. "They said on the radio that students will probably be allowed to finish college."

After hugging him, she stood holding his arm as though to prevent his being whisked away. He resented the news about being allowed to finish college. He might be able to accept war either as death or as a chance to become a hero, but finishing college seemed an anticlimax. He had an urge to enlist immediately, not as an act of patriotism so much as a dramatic necessity. Absurd or not, he wanted to be a hero *now*. By leaving Sylvia he would win her. A devoted Sylvia was the prize offered by war. This was crazy, of course. He accepted a drink.

"Hell, I bet the whole damn thing will be over in six months," Mark said. "Those little yellow bastards can't fight!"

"Don't be ridiculous," Erich, Paul's father-in-law, said

7

from the back of the room, where he was sitting hunched over a radio. Turning the machine off, he stood up. "Don't forget," he said in his deep voice, "that we will also be fighting the Germans."

"Hell, they're so busy fighting the Ruskies that they don't know where they are," Mark said.

"Maybe," Erich said. "Perhaps this is not the time to remind you, but everyone in this family has German blood. The only pride I have left in that is the knowledge that Germans are never easy to beat. Get ready for a long war."

"I, at least, am German only on my father's side, and his father left Germany because he saw that everyone was going crazy there," Lucy, Sylvia's mother, said. "We're all Americans now, thank God."

Erich did not answer. Slowly he sat down and hunched over the radio again.

"I think I'll go upstairs," Paul said, sounding oddly normal to himself. "I have to get washed up."

He started toward their apartment on the third floor, hoping that Sylvia would follow. She did. Their private war forgotten, they hurried to bed, and never before had the love-making been so good. War in its very first stage, at least, was not exactly hell.

Long after she had gone asleep, Paul sat staring at the curtains which moved slightly in the draft from the window, as though someone were standing behind them. The north wind whistled around the eaves of the old house, and rattled the shutters. He wondered what a storm like this would be like aboard a ship at sea. Since boyhood he had prided himself on being good with boats, but he was only a summer sailor, he suddenly realized, and had no idea what the North Atlantic in December could be. The more he thought about it, the less he wanted to find out. At heart he was probably a coward—everyone was afraid, he had read, and bravery consisted in the ability to conquer fear. Whether he had this ability he could not guess. The moaning of the wind grew more and more mournful, more terrifying when he pictured what it must be like on the open sea. He put his arm around the warm shoulders of his wife and hugged her closer. Never before had he been bold or thoughtless enough to start making love to her when she was asleep, but the rules of peacetime were already disappearing and he did not restrain himself. When he realized

8

that she was helping, the world, however briefly, was his. Despite his exhaustion, he still could not sleep when it was over. Suddenly the first real meaning of the war to him became clear: there would be an end to love-making. Erich was undoubtedly right when he said it would be a long war. His mind was suddenly full of a newsreel he had seen which had shown pictures of young German sailors marching in a training camp. A superior race, the Nazis called themselves, and it made him feel really odd to think that his blood was just as "Nordic" as theirs. If they were superior, he was too, but he didn't feel very superior as he thought of all those Germans who were now training to shoot at him. Millions of them had already been fighting for years and must be pretty good at it by now. But he would be good at it too, if they didn't kill him too soon— despite his fears, he had some inner certainty of that. And despite the abject loneliness that he was sure he would feel as soon as he left Sylvia, he realized that he was eager to enlist, to get on with this whole enormous drama which had just begun for him. With all the experience he had had on boats, and his two years of ROTC, maybe he could find a way to wangle a commission in the navy or the Coast Guard, which in time of war was just about the same thing. It would take years, of course, but maybe he actually could get command of his own ship before the war ended. Why was that so important to him? Did he still think he could end up the hero of some crazy war movie?

Paul didn't know, but he made up his mind to make some telephone calls in the morning to see if he could possibly get a commission. After all, it wasn't just a matter of pride or absurd dreams of glory. Officers got paid a lot more than enlisted men, and he had a wife to support, didn't he?

# CHAPTER 3

Before Paul got a chance to call anyone in the morning, his brother, Bill, telephoned him.

"I'm going to join the army air force," Bill said exuberantly. "That's where the real action's going to be! What are you going to do?"

"I don't know yet," Paul replied.

"Listen, I've got an idea for you. I hear the Coast Guard is going to take over a whole bunch of yachts for an offshore patrol. If they took the *Valkyrie*, they'd fix her all up, and they might let you go as skipper. They'd probably make you a chief boatswain's mate. You'd get good pay and you'd probably get back to Boston every week or so."

"Why don't you do it that way?"

"Hell, I don't want to fight the Germans with an old yawl. Give me a P-38. You were always the great sailor in the family anyway."

"I'll check into it," Paul said, but he already had decided that he too did not want to fight the Germans with an old yawl, despite the attractions of the scheme.

"Just don't get yourself drafted, boy," Bill concluded. "I hear the infantry ain't good for the health."

"I'll see what I can do," Paul said, and he envied the apparently carefree bravery with which his brother was planning to join the army air force. The only thing that scared him more than the thought of being machine-gunned in a muddy trench was the vision of crashing in a burning plane. Putting on his best blue suit, he drove to the Boston headquarters of the Coast Guard.

This day, Monday, December 8, 1941, the streets and sidewalks were crowded with people and the bars were overflowing. Long queues, some of them stretching around a block, stood before each recruiting office. Every car, store and bar had a radio turned on loud to await news, and the sound of music was mixed with an excited babble of voices.

Paul could not get anywhere near the district office of the Coast Guard. For half an hour he stood in a line that stretched over the top of a hill, seemingly to infinity. Gray-haired men with the collars of old pea jackets turned up around their ears stood in that line, middle-aged men, some of whom were kept company during the long wait by their wives, and many boys who looked too young to be out of high school. They were almost all unusually cheerful and joked about the possibility of the war being over before they got a chance to enlist. Their breath frosted in the cold December air, and some of them danced little jigs to keep warm. A good many carried bottles and were quick to offer a swig to strangers. When a pretty girl walked by on her way to a nearby office, a few of the men whistled. A tall thin man in a trench coat which looked much too thin for that weather called, "Come join up with me, baby!" Instead of sticking her nose in the air and hurrying away, she gave him a brilliant smile and blew him a kiss. The long line of men applauded, clapping their mittened hands together as loudly as possible. To this she responded with a pretty curtsy just before disappearing into a doorway and the crowd cheered.

The long line appeared to move hardly at all. Halfway up the block a stout man dressed in a Chesterfield coat and wearing a homburg hat tried to cut into it and was jovially rebuffed by a short man in a brown leather jacket.

"You push ahead of me, Jack, and you won't have to wait for no war. You'll have one right here!"

The crowd laughed, and with hasty apologies the well-dressed man hurried to the end of the line.

All this was interesting, but Paul soon grew both cold and bored. Reasoning that he might do better with telephone calls, he ducked into a bar. Long lines stood there, too, both in front of the two telephone booths and at the bar itself, but here it was at least warm. A jukebox blared in the corner: "Beat Me, Daddy, Eight to the Bar." At the crowded tables men and women sat drinking and talking intently to each other. They leaned against each other, touched a lot and held hands—the atmosphere was certainly a lot sexier than it ordinarily was in a Boston pub at ten o'clock on a Monday morning. When three chief petty officers, resplendent with gold hash marks, walked in, a

11

place was immediately made for them at the bar. Many people offered to buy them drinks and asked them if they knew what damage had actually been done by the Japs at Pearl Harbor.

It took Paul only about twenty minutes to get to a telephone booth. He was not surprised to find that he got a busy signal when he called the Coast Guard office, and settled down to a routine of repeating the call about every two minutes. He was surprised when his fourth call got through. Figuring that he would get nowhere if he asked to speak to the busy recruiting officer, he told the harried girl who answered the telephone that he wanted to speak to the district Coast Guard officer. After a series of buzzes, a weary male voice said, "Lt. Christiansen speaking . . ."

"Are you the district Coast Guard officer?"

"I'm one of his assistants. Who is this?"

"My name is Paul Schuman. I'm the master of a charter boat and I've got three and a half years of college, two in the Navy ROTC. Can I get a commission in the Coast Guard?"

"You should be talking to the recruiting officer."

"I know, but nobody can get through to him. I just thought you could tell me if I have a chance, and maybe you can mail me some forms or something."

Lt. Christiansen laughed. "You sure know how to expedite," he said. "I bet you'd make a good supply officer."

"I want to go to sea. I'm good with small ships."

"You are, are you? Give me your name and address. I'll send you the forms."

"Paul Schuman, Two-oh-nine Fieldstone Road, Wellesley, Massachusetts."

"Well, you're lucky," Christiansen said. "At least you live around here. We've got people from all over sleeping in men's rooms and railroad stations."

"I guess that must be quite a problem."

"You said it, boy. I got my own wife and kid in a hotel that costs more in a week than I make in a month."

An idea hit Paul then. He didn't know whether it sprang from the milk of human kindness, from the practiced opportunism of his older brother, or from a lesson he had learned in some odd, reverse way from his father. Instead of simply sympathizing with Christiansen, he said, "If you want an apartment, I can find one for you out in Wellesley."

"How are you going to do that?"

"Like you said, I'm an expediter."

Christiansen's voice suddenly turned sharp. "Look, I can't do anything for you because of this except send you some forms. But if you can find me an apartment near this crazy city, I'd sure appreciate it."

"It will only take me a few minutes," Paul said. "Do you have a telephone number it won't take me half the day to reach?"

In a clipped voice Christiansen gave him a number and abruptly hung up, perhaps in confusion. Putting another nickel in the telephone, Paul called Lucy Kettel, his mother-in-law.

"Mother," he said, using the appellation she wanted, though it never seemed natural to him, "I just met a young Coast Guard officer who can't find an apartment around here for his wife and child. You must know plenty of people with big houses. . . ."

"Well, I don't know anybody who wants to *rent* . . ."

"There's a war on. Isn't it our patriotic duty to help servicemen?"

"I know, but I don't know anyone who wants to take a stranger into her home."

"Let's face it, it would do me some good if we can do this guy a favor," Paul continued. "He's an assistant to the district Coast Guard officer and I'm trying to get a commission. As an officer I'll get maybe five times the pay I'd get if I enlisted."

There was a pause before she said, "The Hendersons have an apartment over their garage. It's been empty since their chauffeur quit. They're not planning on hiring another."

"Please call them right away," Paul said. "I'll call you back in five minutes."

"How much rent will these people pay?"

"The guy's a serviceman. Tell the Hendersons that this is a matter of patriotism. Maybe the guy can pay fifty a month, not much more. Call right away. There's a crowd trying to get into this phone booth."

Actually, the people waiting in line did not seem restless. They all had drinks in their hands and were watching with appreciative interest a sailor who was giving his girl such a hearty and prolonged embrace that he would have been evicted from the bar in peacetime.

While he waited five minutes Paul sat with the receiver

13

to his ear to show he had a right to remain in the telephone booth. Finding that he had no more nickels, he conquered a feeling of waste and inserted a dime. His mother-in-law answered immediately.

"The Hendersons say they'll take him if you'll absolutely vouch for his character."

"I vouch for it. How much rent do they want?"

"They'll need sixty a month if they're going to pay for the heat."

"It's a deal. Give me their name, their address and their number."

This time Paul had to put a quarter into the telephone, an extravagance that hurt him deeply. Christiansen answered immediately.

"This is your expediter," Paul said. "I got you a garage apartment in Wellesley. Nice section. Sixty bucks a month, heated. Do you want it?"

"God, do I want it! I was going to send my wife and baby back to New London. I can't thank you enough!"

"Just send me the forms and answer me one question," Paul said. "If I have all the qualifications, what happens? What's the timetable?"

"You'll take a twelve-hour examination in navigation and seamanship at M.I.T. on February second. If you pass that, you'll be wearing an ensign's uniform by April. What's the address of this apartment?"

Paul gave it to him and added, "It's only about a block from where I live. If you have any trouble give me a call."

"Is the place furnished?"

"Yes," Paul replied, though he wasn't dead sure. "Anyway, it will be easy to get everything together. The Hendersons are nice people."

He didn't really know the Hendersons, but he figured they must be nice people if they were friends of Lucy and Erich.

"That's great," Christiansen said. "Look, everything's so jammed up around here that it would be days before we got your forms in the mail. I'll stick them in my pocket and bring them to the Henderson house tonight. Drop in maybe at about seven and we can have a drink."

And so that was the way Paul got a commission in the Coast Guard as quickly as he did. There were a few people

14

who said he used pull and political pressure, but all he did was to get a guy an apartment and study like hell for six weeks to pass the twelve-hour examination.

The speed with which Paul made all these arrangements bewildered Sylvia. All her classmates, after all, were planning to finish their college year before entering the service. "You'd think you just can't wait to leave me," she said reproachfully in their bedroom one night after they had made strangely unsatisfactory love.

"You know that isn't it at all."

"Well, what *is* it then?"

He found it difficult to give an answer except to cite patriotism, which he knew would be mostly a lie. He wanted to help defend his country, all right, but he wasn't really in such a great rush to get out there where the shells were flying and the hurricanes were blowing. No, the truth was that naive though it might sound, there was a lot of joy involved in getting a commission. For one thing, he found that temporarily, at least, he would outrank his condescending older brother. While training to be an army air force pilot, Bill would be an enlisted man, while as an ensign Paul would be the equivalent of a second lieutenant. If they ever met in uniform, which Bill's assignment to flight instruction would probably make unlikely, tall Harvardman Bill would have to salute his miserable little Boston University brother. It was obviously wrong to feel glee about that, but Paul did anyway.

It was also true that the war, whatever horrors it might hold for him, was getting him away from a lot of things he hated. Most of all, his own confusion about his marriage, his career and everything else. This confusion, he realized, was by no means entirely Sylvia's fault. It had started, so far as he could understand, when he was fifteen years old and his family had moved from the big house in Boston to the cottage in Milton. The old yawl on which he had spent the happiest summers of his life had been left under cover in the shipyard and had not been sold only because his father was insulted by the only kind of price she could bring during those Depression years. Right before his eyes, his father changed from a big exuberant stockbroker and yachtsman to a hesitant old man who sat all day in his "studio" puttering with paint brushes or whittling chains out of wood. His business failure was never discussed by the family, and this silence increased its terror.

Paul and his brother, who was three years older, reacted to this debacle in different ways. Bill got a football scholarship at Harvard, earned his degree in only three years, and got a scholarship at the business school. Big, brash and self-confident, Bill never even gave the appearance of working hard to win his victories.

What Paul did at the age of fifteen was quite different. He hated athletics and his studies at Milton Academy and, when he could not get a scholarship, was the first to suggest that he go to the local high school. The only thing he really loved was boats, and he spent a lot of time helping his father to paint and varnish the old yawl to prepare her for a customer who would appreciate her already antique grace. He also loved girls—hopelessly. Almost as far back as he could remember he had been secretly infatuated with one or another of the girls at his school or at the Boston Yacht Club.

When he was sixteen Paul discovered something else he liked: money. Money was such a tortuous subject in his home that like failure and sex, it could never be discussed openly. The discovery that he could actually make money himself instead of asking his mother for quarters came to Paul as a revelation and a liberation.

He made his first dollar, ten dollars in fact, when he varnished the combing of a Wee Scot at the yacht club. He had simply been trying to make himself valuable as a crew, and he was astonished when the owner gave him a ten-dollar bill. The first thing he did after that was to put a notice up on the club bulletin board offering his services. During the summer he had all the work he could do, and that fall he got the idea of taking spars, oars, and rudders back to his garage and cellar for refinishing.

Soon he found that he could sell magazine subscriptions, wash cars, and sell magic tricks at school for more than he paid for them. Later he discovered that he could sell clothes from a local tailor to his classmates. There was no mystery about money—there was an infinite number of ways in which it could be made. He started a savings account.

"You take after my father," his mother said proudly. "He was always a wonderful businessman."

The trouble was that Paul wanted to make money without becoming a businessman, which seemed to him to be a very boring fate. When he was sixteen he came across a book by Warwick Tompkins, who took college boys on long ocean cruises aboard the *Wanderbird*, a stately old pilot boat, and at the Boston Yacht Club, he actually met Irving Johnson, who was doing the same thing with the clipper-bowed schooner *Yankee*. Here were men who were sailing the world and getting their crew to pay the expenses! They were adventurers who found ways to make money by doing exactly what they wanted during their best years instead of spending a lifetime at dull jobs with the hope of escape during their old age.

Because of these men Paul began to dream and his dreams seemed to him to be practical. Somehow he would earn enough money to fix up his father's old yawl, and would find college students to serve as a paying crew during short summer cruises. After he graduated from college, he would take such a crew around the world, just like Warwick Tompkins and Irving Johnson.

When Paul's older brother realized that it actually might be possible to make a little money running cruises to Gloucester, Nantucket, and Provincetown, and that the old yawl was a wonderful place for parties, he helped, and their father was also delighted to find a way to avoid selling the *Valkyrie*. They made the first stage of Paul's dream a family project, and he rarely discussed the later stages he had in mind with anyone.

Except Sylvia. When he first met her, she was sixteen and he was seventeen, and he had the old yawl moored off the end of the yacht club pier while he and his brother were readying her for their first cruise to Nantucket.

"Is that your boat out there?" she asked when he rowed the dinghy to the float.

"Yes," he said with the deep pride which the old yawl always gave him. At sixteen, Sylvia was already a vividly pretty young woman who usually danced with the older boys and she never before had paid any attention to him. She was wearing a green bathing suit and he was afraid to look at her for more than a moment.

"Could that boat cross an ocean?"

"You bet. I'm going to sail her around the world."

Tossing up her chin, she laughed. "When?"

"As soon as I get out of college," he said, although he had not yet graduated from high school.

She grinned, and there was that wildness in her eyes

which seemed to make anything possible. "Will you take me with you?"

"It's a date," he said. "Would you like to go out and take a look at her first?"

He was aware from the beginning that Sylvia did not know anything about boats and scorned the discomforts of the sea, but he sensed that she was an adventurer, a rebel like him. The first hour she was aboard the *Valkyrie*, she went scampering up the rigging and stood poised on the crosstrees, balancing with one hand on a shroud.

"Be careful!" he shouted.

"Come on up! I can see the whole harbor."

Much as he loved boats, he had always been afraid of heights, but he mustered the courage to climb the rigging and stand on the other side of the crosstrees. The view was indeed grand up there fifty feet above the deck if he didn't look down.

"Have you ever dived from here?" she asked.

"No!"

"The top board on the club tower is almost this high."

"But here you might fall before you got clear."

She smiled and there was that look in her eyes again when she said, "I dare you!"

"Don't, I—"

Before he could say more she launched herself into the air and swooped toward the metallic surface of the water, her arms outstretched. His mixture of anger and admiration turned to fear when he realized that she was not really a very good diver. She hit much too flat, and when the explosion of foam fell around her, he saw her come slowly to the surface, looking wounded, out of breath and scared. Forgetting his own safety, he jumped, pushing himself off the rigging more effectively than he could in a dive. Plummeting into the water a dozen feet from her, he swam rapidly toward her. She had recovered her breath and was laughing.

"You looked so funny," she said. "All the time you were falling, your arms and legs were moving as though you were trying to climb up!"

He had been angry at her and totally unable to resist her. That's the way he had stayed, year after year.

One of the confusing things about Sylvia was that despite her wild ways, she was in certain matters very conventional.

18

In public she played a teasing game, but in private she was scared and angry when he tried to go beyond a kiss. When at the age of seventeen he couldn't stop himself from telling her that he loved her, she said she loved him too, but her family would be furious if she paid too much attention to any one boy. They were, she pointed out with perfect logic, much too young even to dream about getting engaged. If he had any idea of getting married even in the distant future, he should start thinking of doing something more substantial with his life than sailing an old yawl around the world.

He realized that if he seriously wanted to pursue his dream, he should forget her, but that was impossible—when he came right down to it, he had to admit that even if he had to take a dull job, life with Sylvia offered more excitement than even a voyage around the world without her. When he failed to get into Harvard College he felt terrible, especially since he knew that she went to almost all the dances there. He enrolled in Boston University instead of Columbia, which had accepted him, because he couldn't stand the thought of leaving her.

Paul's brother, Bill, often made fun of his obsession with Sylvia.

"You're going to get nothing but trouble from her," he said. "Right now she's a cockteaser, damn near the queen of that whole sorry tribe. In a year or two she'll start putting out, but not for a poor slob like you who's been running after her forever. She'll put out for some guy she thinks she can't get any other way, some smart bastard who won't fall for her line of crap."

Paul hated his brother for saying that but was afraid that he was right. He also suspected that Bill might have some hope of being the smart bastard he'd described. Bill never asked Sylvia to go out, but he often cut in on her at dances, and prided himself on insulting her whenever possible.

"Sylvia, you're not as pretty as you think," Bill said one night when Sylvia arrived at a yacht club dance, resplendent in a new silver evening gown.

"I bet you say that to all the girls," she replied with a smile. "Good old Bill always has a surly word for everyone."

"Ah, but my insults are sincere," Bill said. "You can't accuse me of saying things I don't really mean."

19

At this point Paul cut in on them.

"Take her, she's all yours," Bill said, and strode away with a laugh.

"I apologize for him," Paul began.

"Don't bother. Your brother thinks that insults are charming. He's doing his poor best to please."

In her eighteenth year something seemed to happen to Sylvia. She lost much of her self-confidence. Perhaps she found that the precocious exuberance which had brought her so much attention in her early teens didn't work so well at the big coming-out parties to which she was invited because her parents had managed to get her on the proper lists, despite the fact that she had not made a formal debut. Boston society had a way of putting down the daughters of the newly rich, especially when they weren't so very rich, and Sylvia's manners were not calculated to impress the old guard. Instead of toning herself down, she became more flamboyant than ever. It was at this time that she began drinking so much at cocktail parties that Paul began to worry about her. Once she fell while trying to climb up on a marble coffee table to demonstrate some sort of dance, and the laughter was not entirely friendly as Paul helped her out to his car. She cried all the way home.

Maybe more important things happened to Sylvia during her eighteenth year than discovering that not all the doors in the world were open to her, Paul sensed. Perhaps she had her first real love affair and was severely hurt by it. She never mentioned such a thing, but there were weeks when she didn't see Paul, pleading that she was ill or had other engagements. His brother, Bill, as usual had something hurtful to say.

"I hear Ted Barrington is taking her out. He's a real cocksman. I bet he's breaking her in."

Ted Barrington was a varsity football player at Harvard and the son of a famous Boston lawyer.

"Ted took me out just once and we didn't do anything but go to the movies," Sylvia said when Paul asked her about him. "He's a bore and a snob. I hope I never see him again."

Paul was already learning that one either believed Sylvia or one did not, but there was no point in questioning her. One either loved her or not, and he did, although he often wondered whether he really liked her. And there was one result of the mysterious loss of confidence she suffered which delighted him; more and more she began to depend on him and to spend more time with him.

In the summertime she often went as cook on short cruises aboard the yawl, and in the fall when no more paying passengers could be found, they often spent their evenings alone together on the boat. Paul did not find it easy to seduce her, but impossible not to. When he first took her to bed he felt he was claiming her for himself forever. No matter what precautions they took, she was terrified of getting pregnant, and she admitted that it was that continuing terror more than anything else which finally made her want to get married.

Everyone Paul knew tried to talk him out of marrying Sylvia. He himself realized that they were of course too young, and that maybe they were almost as crazy as Bill said they both were, but his obsession with her continued and was strengthened by other feelings. He was afraid he would lose her. Now that she had graduated from high school and had more or less dropped out of the round of parties which had sustained her so long, Sylvia had begun to think of marriage as a salvation. He suspected that if he didn't marry her, she would soon take up with somebody else, almost anyone who would marry her. There was something pathetically vulnerable about her. Bill said it looked as though she was having a nervous breakdown, and maybe she was coming close to that. Paul wanted to protect her. He realized that a desire to protect a pretty girl must be regarded somewhat sardonically, but it was true that she obviously needed someone to take care of her.

Paul was aware that the circumstances of his wedding were not auspicious. Her family was almost as much against it as his own, except that they possibly understood her better, and were glad to see her get settled, even though they didn't approve of her penniless choice. Almost all their friends assumed that she was pregnant. The whole little ceremony in her father's living room was subdued, almost shame-faced, with nothing like the excitement which followed the news of Pearl Harbor.

Yet Paul was happy and Sylvia seemed happy for about six months, before she was overtaken by a terrible restlessness. She couldn't get used to the fact that Paul had to work much of the time. Once more she wanted to go to parties—as a young matron, the wife of a man who came from an old Boston family, even if he had no money, she

21

regained some of her self-confidence. Her brothers, who had seen her moping about the house, encouraged her. She just went out with old friends and relatives, or that's the way it started.

Where it was ending, Paul was not at all sure. The truth was that his entire past became more and more confusing the more he thought about it, and until now his future had been even more bewildering. But this new thing, war, made at least the immediate future clear. He would be a Coast Guard officer. Whatever else the war did to him, it would get him away from home for a few years and give both him and Sylvia a chance to grow up, almost as though their marriage had never taken place. When he came home, maybe a hero, for heaven's sake, they might have changed enough to work out a way of life they both wanted.

"There's a war on," he said to Sylvia when she questioned his haste. "I might as well go and try to get it over with. College just doesn't seem to make much sense to me anymore."

Late in March Paul felt elated when he got a letter from the Coast Guard which formally commissioned him and told him to buy his uniforms. A long list of required equipment, including a dress sword, was enclosed, but no money for the purchases. Officers were expected to buy their own uniforms, and the Coast Guard had not yet got around to deciding that swords were unnecessary for World War II.

After a moment of thought, Paul called his mother in the nearby town of Milton, explained the situation and asked if he could borrow five hundred dollars. Because he almost never asked her for money, she was surprised, but after a short pause, said, "For that purpose we can always find a few dollars. We're so proud of you, Paul! Come out and see us as soon as you get one of those uniforms on. It's been ages since we've seen you."

He was ashamed of himself for visiting his parents as seldom as possible. That was one of the bad things about him, along with getting married before he graduated from college, dreaming about sailing around the world instead of getting a good job, and not wanting to live a respectable life in the suburbs. Still, the image of himself which looked at him from the mirror of the military tailor did not seem like such a disreputable young man. This Coast Guard ensign with the close-cropped blond hair appeared much too young for the broad gold stripe on his blue sleeves, but he didn't look like a villain either. When Paul put on his new cap with the gold strap and the big gold eagle, tilting it to the proper angle, the young officer in the mirror looked as though he might actually belong aboard a ship.

The tailor agreed to turn up the cuffs of one pair of pants immediately. The dress whites and the sword which his list called for would take a few days to get. Soon Paul was driving to see his parents.

The small, brown-shingled cottage would have appeared shabby if it had stood on a suburban street, but in its country setting surrounded by a grove of pines it had a certain charm. His mother, Rachel, a big blocky woman dressed in shaggy tweeds, had been watching from the window and opened the front door before he touched it.

"Paul!" she said. "How beautiful you are! I feel I should salute!"

Never before had he received such approval from his mother and he did not quite know how to handle it. When he hugged her, her tweeds felt as rough as a burlap sack, and she pulled away before he could kiss her big broad cheek.

"Come see your father," she said. "He's in his studio. His work has been going very well lately and he's been hard at it all week."

His father, or the father she presented to him, was almost entirely a work of fiction, he realized with the strange new ability to face facts which his commission had apparently given him. Charles Schuman actually did no work, had not done any for at least ten years. After going broke and losing his job in a brokerage house in 1929, he had retired on the slender income his wife had inherited, and had taken up painting. At this he was a genius, according to Rachel, but he was so ahead of his time that galleries and art museums didn't understand him. For about two years Charles had experimented with cubism and many kinds of abstractions. When his work brought him neither money nor praise, he busied himself with woodcarving, furniture repair, fishing and hunting. As a mild-mannered man who at least had weathered failure in a family where that was the worst of all crimes without going crazy or taking seriously to drink, he was worthy of respect, and Paul wished that his mother could let his sons love him for what he was instead of pretending that he was a hardworking artist whose genius would undoubtedly be recognized after his death.

Charles's studio consisted of a back porch which had been glassed in, and which was heated by a pot-bellied coal stove on which an aluminum coffee pot steamed. Near the door stood an easel with a half-finished abstract painting, black and red lines leading to a huge sphere which had only been sketched in. The painting had not been touched since Paul's last visit a month ago. This large canvas acted as a screen, behind which Charles was sitting in an armchair near the stove. He was carving a long chain from a pine two-by-four. This was something which he did very well. The part of the chain which he had finished and which lay coiled at his feet, was as flexible and perfectly formed as its iron counterpart.

"Paul!" he said, getting to his feet. "Or should I call you captain?"

His father was a stout man as tall as himself, almost six feet, and Paul couldn't understand why he persisted in thinking of him as small. He was wearing a tweed sports coat, a black turtleneck sweater and baggy gray flannel trousers. His long silvery hair and his craggy long-nosed face with heavy dark eyebrows enabled him to play his assigned role as a distinguished artist convincingly, whether he really wanted to or not.

Paul shook his father's hand heartily—they never hugged. Rather embarrassedly Charles took a pipe from his pocket and began to stuff it.

"Your grandfather would be proud of you," he said. "He always wanted me to go in the navy. I tried, but my bum ticker ruled me out. How long will it be before they send you overseas?"

"I expect my orders anytime now. I don't actually know where I'll be stationed."

"He's in the Coast Guard, not the navy," Rachel said. "They may keep him right in Boston."

"During wartime we're part of the navy," Paul said. "I've already put in for sea duty."

"Well, you're better qualified for it than most," Charles said. "It's nice to think that the old *Valkyrie* did you some good. Bill thinks we should junk her now. Did he tell you that?"

"He's talked of it."

"He's even got a buyer. Three thousand dollars we're offered. Jesus Christ!"

"Now, Charles, you mustn't take on about that," Rachel said. "The *Valkyrie* has served her purpose. She's given us all a great deal of pleasure for years and she's an old lady. Everyone has to die sometime."

"Three thousand dollars for a sixty-foot Lawley yawl," Charles said. "The buyer is the Katstein Metal Works. *Sic Transit Gloria.*"

"I say we're lucky to get the three thousand," Rachel said. "Who'd look after her after Paul goes? Who knows how long this war will last?"

"I guess I have to vote for selling," Paul said. "She's got some rot in her, Dad. There won't be much left of her in two or three years."

"Let's talk about something cheerful," Rachel said. "How about some tea, and I've just baked an apple cake."

"While you're getting that together, I'd like to show Paul the model I'm making in the basement," Charles said and led the way down a steep, rickety stairway.

This cellar was far different from that in the orderly house of his father-in-law. One corner was filled with a jumble of unstacked firewood, another with coal. They had to pick their way through broken chairs and tables to get to the workbench, where tools lay everywhere but in their racks. The half-model of the *Valkyrie* which Charles had carved from a piece of mahogany was as smooth as flesh. Paul was touched by the fact that both his father and father-in-law had spent hours making models of the old yawl.

While Paul was running his fingers over the graceful model, Charles produced a half-empty pint bottle of scotch from a tool drawer.

"Your mother doesn't think that this stuff is good for my ticker, but a snort now and then never hurt anyone. Here's to your new career. I bet you're good at it."

Passing the bottle back and forth with curious urgency, they finished it. Then Charles took two big cigars from the tool drawer.

"Your mother can't stand the smell of these, but I like one now and then," his father said. "We have to be careful, though. The smoke can go right up through cracks in the floor and make her sick."

An armchair with a broken arm already stood in front

of the furnace. Charles pulled a diningroom chair with a split back up beside it. Sitting down, he opened the furnace door, lit his cigar and blew the smoke into it.

"Sit down, son," he said. "This way we won't bother anyone. Sometimes it's good just to sit and smoke a fine cigar."

Ten minutes later his mother called them for tea. She had set out her best Spode china and a variety of cookies, as well as apple cake. An alcohol flame burned under the silver teapot in gimbals which she had inherited from her grandmother. On that winter day not much light came through the pine trees and the gray curtains at the windows. The armchairs and tables in the room had been designed for a much larger house and made this cottage feel cramped. Silver frames showed pictures of Bill in academic dress as he graduated from Milton Academy, Harvard, and the business school. There were no pictures of Paul, but then he had never graduated from anything except the local high school. On the walls were photographs of both his grandfathers, both successful businessmen, and both looking the part. A scrapbook containing newspaper clippings and photographs which Rachel had garnered from her career as president of the Federated Garden Clubs of America was on a coffee table in front of the couch. Over the fireplace was a large painting of the *Valkyrie* under full sail on an improbable blue and waveless sea, one of his father's first efforts. Silver loving cups which Bill had won at tennis, golf, and swimming lined the back of a sideboard. They, like the silver tea set, had all been recently polished. This was really a trophy room, not a livingroom, Paul thought. The sideboard with its candles looked like an altar to success, every little success the family had ever known to make up for the big ones which had been for so long lacking. Paul was sure that soon a photograph of himself in uniform would be added to the collection.

"How's Sylvia?" his mother asked suddenly and dutifully.

"She's fine," Paul said.

"It must be hard for her to have you going away," Rachel added.

"I'm sure she's very brave," Charles said.

"I think I better go to her now," Paul said. "She hasn't seen my new uniform."

"There's just one more thing," Charles said. "This man

Katstein will want you to sign some papers and show him over the boat if he's really going to buy it. When can you meet him?"

"Better make it as soon as possible. Like I said, I expect my orders any day now."

As Paul hurried toward his car, his mother said, "Wait just a minute. I want to take your picture. I'll have it enlarged and send a copy to Sylvia."

He stood almost at attention while she fussed with her box camera. Brushing aside a nasty premonition that this was probably the photograph which would appear in the newspapers when he got killed, he forced himself to smile at his mother's command. When the shutter had finally been snapped, he gave both his parents a hasty kiss, climbed into his car, and with supreme self-discipline did not allow himself to speed out of their driveway as though pursued by demons.

# CHAPTER 4

As Paul drove home to show his new uniform to his wife, he could not get out of his mind the picture of his father sitting in a broken chair in the cellar puffing cigar smoke into the furnace. He had always loved his father with an intensity which made him want to cry when he thought about him too much, but he also had done his best, he realized suddenly, to make himself the direct opposite of him. One thing Paul never wanted to do, one thing he had avoided since the age of fifteen, was to take money from his mother, or any woman. As a matter of fact, he could have paid for his own uniforms. While he was driving away from his parents' house, he began to wonder why he had presented his mother with this bill when he had handled all others himself. Did he somehow resent the fact that she always had tried too hard to drive him toward equaling all the conventional successes of his brother, and now that he had a commission for her to boast about, was he meanly trying to charge her for it?

Perhaps there was an element of that, but he was also worried about his ability to continue the token rent he insisted on paying to his father-in-law for the apartment and the allowance he gave to his wife to enable her to buy clothes. An ensign's pay was mighty fine compared to that of a private in the army or an apprentice seaman, but it wouldn't stack up very well against the income of an accomplished campus hustler. Paul wondered what the opportunities for bridge and poker would be in the service. Aboard a ship he would have to be careful, but he might get a chance to visit a few officers' clubs.

Paul tried to forget his financial worries as he parked in the driveway of Erich's house and hurried to show his wife his new uniform.

"You look lovely!" Sylvia said, "but you don't look like my husband." Then she burst into tears. After calming her, he took her to see a movie, a war film in which Errol Flynn mowed down whole armies.

When they got home Sylvia's mother told him that his father wanted him to call.

"I got hold of this Mr. Katstein," Charles said. "I also talked to Bill. Bill is handling the details. All you have to do is sign the master papers and give the keys to Katstein. The bastard will meet you aboard the boat at nine in the morning."

"Okay," Paul said. That didn't seem much of a reply to make to the momentous news that the *Valkyrie* actually was to be sold to a junkman, but no more words would come.

Paul arrived aboard the *Valkyrie* an hour early. In the morning fog the graceful hull of the old yawl looked almost ready to sail around the world. This, he told himself, was no time for nostalgia and sentiment. He should pack his personal belongings. There were few—a moss green sweater which Sylvia had left there on her last summer visit, his .30-.30 shark rifle, a cheap sextant he had bought but never actually used. The thought occurred to him that he might take the binnacle and perhaps some of the cabinet doors with their diamond-shaped leaded panes before the buyer saw them, but suddenly he realized that he didn't

28

want any dusty souvenirs, parts of a corpse, following him around from house to house for the rest of his life. This old yawl, aboard which he had learned to sail and where he had, for better or for worse, wooed and won his wife, was in no danger of being forgotten.

The teak decks were covered with grime, and there was some small pleasure in the thought that he would never have to scrub them again. Going below, he lit a fire in the shipmate range for the last time and poured himself a shot of rum. Once he had told his brother that if they ever did have to sell the yawl to the ship breakers, he would polish her up and deliver her, under full sail. Suddenly he felt old. He had no more impulses at all to undertake a gesture of that kind.

Before long he heard the chugging of a diesel engine close by. Going on deck he saw a small harbor tug emerge from the surrounding fog. Black tires had been hung from her rail as fenders. As she nosed alongside, these squeaked against the white topsides of the yawl and Paul almost yelled in protest before he realized that now of course a few marks wouldn't make any difference. A seaman on the bow tossed him a line and as he made it fast to a cleat on the yawl, a thin man in a camelhair coat which looked odd in these nautical surroundings stepped from the pilothouse of the tug and climbed nimbly aboard.

"I'm Katstein," he said. "You Paul Schuman?"

"Yes."

"Your brother showed me this vessel about a month ago. I just want to make sure she hasn't been stripped."

"Nothing has been taken."

"All the inside ballast still there?"

"All of it."

"We can get on with the papers then. There's no use wasting your time or mine."

They went down to the cabin, which was warm enough now to kill the musty odor. The papers, which had been kept in a drawer of the chart table, were so damp that they were hard to sign.

"I guess that's it," Katstein said, giving him a receipt for the documents which he already had prepared, and a certified check made out to Charles R. Schuman for three thousand dollars. "This is the way your brother wanted it handled. Is it okay with you?"

"It's okay with me."

"I'm going to tow her over to my yard right away. I don't want this place to be sending me any bills."

"Okay."

"She's a beautiful old vessel," Katstein said, running his hand over one of the leaded glass cabinet doors. "They don't make 'em like this anymore and they never will again."

"I suppose. Do you want a drink, Mr. Katstein?"

"Don't mind if I do. I suppose you think I'm stealing this ship from you, don't you?"

"No one has offered us a better price."

"The day of these old vessels has gone. No one can afford them these days, even if there wasn't a war on. If it's any consolation to you, she won't be making anybody rich. There's not enough lead here to bring more than five grand, and I have to get rid of the hull and melt the stuff down."

"I wish you luck."

"Maybe they'll use the lead to make bullets. It sure would be nice if this old keel finished Hitler, wouldn't it?"

The vision of the old yawl's keel sailing through the air into Hitler's face and smashing the dictator shook Paul. He poured himself another drink and refilled Katstein's glass.

"I guess it would be nice," he said.

"Well, I've got to get going," Katstein concluded. "Will you help us cast off these lines?"

Paul had already placed the personal belongings he had collected on the painters' raft. Still carrying his glass of rum, he got aboard the platform. Placing it by the rifle, he paddled ashore. Leaving his possessions on the raft, he walked to the end of the pier and on a signal from the seaman aboard the yawl, let the stern line fall. Slowly he walked around to the end of the other pier and released the bow line. It took several minutes for the men aboard the yawl to coil these heavy lines. Then the tug made a chuffing sound and started to move the old yawl into the mist which shrouded the harbor. At this distance the white hull of the *Valkyrie* again looked almost new and in the fog her slender spars seemed endlessly tall. Paul watched until the swirls of mist completely obscured her. He tried to think deep thoughts about his youth disappearing into that fog, but they seemed phony as hell. The wind from the harbor was cold. He walked rapidly back to the raft and stood staring at the junk he had gathered there. Why save a rusty rifle when the Coast Guard would give him big guns soon enough? Why have a sextant that was little better than a toy? Paul kicked these items overboard with his right toe and they sank silently into the muddy waters. Only the moss-green sweater and the glass of rum were left. The rum he did not kick overboard. After taking a sip, he studied the glass as though for the first time. It was a cut-glass tumbler, part of a diminishing set that had been aboard the yawl ever since he could remember. It was strange to think that this was the last of the *Valkyrie* that he had left. The glass would make a good souvenir, but after draining it, he lifted it high above his head and, on impulse, threw it down on the raft. Instead of smashing, the heavy tumbler caromed off the wet wood and sank intact, indestructible to the last. Picking up the moss-green sweater, Paul hurried to his car without a backward glance.

# CHAPTER 5

Only a few days later, on April 2, Paul received his orders by registered mail. It was not an impressive appearing document. Mimeographed on pulpy paper with blanks filled in a heavy hand with green ink, it said:

From: Commandant, U.S. Coast Guard Headquarters, Washington, D.C.
To: Paul R. Schuman, Ensign, USCGR
Subject: Order to active duty.
1. You are herewith ordered to active duty.
2. You shall proceed immediately to the First District Office of the U.S. Coast Guard in Boston, Mass. for assignment to duty as executive officer of U.S. Coast Guard Cutter *Arluk*, and transportation to that vessel.
3. In view of the proximity of your home to the First District Office, no travel allowance is granted.

"Well, they must think pretty well of you if they make you executive officer of a ship without a day of training," Erich said when Paul showed him the paper.

"I don't know what it means," Paul replied. "I think I'll call Chris and see."

"Proceed immediately means that you've got twenty-four hours," Christiansen said when Paul read him his orders over the telephone. "You better come up to the apartment tonight at about seven. I'll find out what I can about the *Arluk* and let you know."

"Twenty-four hours!" Sylvia said. "What are we supposed to *do* when we only have twenty-four hours?" She looked very much alarmed, as though he might expect to spend that entire time spinning like a lathe with her in bed.

"I'll have to pick up the uniforms I ordered," he said. "Maybe we ought to run over and see dad and mother."

It was not hard to do the things he felt he ought to do because he couldn't think of much that he really wanted to do. The idea of driving off alone somewhere with Sylvia crossed his mind, but they had grown so mysteriously tense that without admitting it, they were afraid to be alone together. The worst thing in the world would be to have a fight just before parting and without knowing exactly why, they both felt one brewing.

Their tension increased when they drove to the military tailor and picked up the gear he had ordered.

"What on earth do you need a sword for?" Sylvia asked, as the clerk showed him this glittering object in a black scabbard with gold trim. "Does the Coast Guard expect you to fight submarines with that?"

"I think I'm just supposed to use it in dress parades," he said. "Anyway, it's on my required list."

The truth was, he loved his new sword with its shining, delicately etched blade and gold handle, a sword which was part of a commissioned officer's equipment, not just a costume piece or an antique. The fact that Sylvia regarded the sword as a joke annoyed him. When they got home, she asked him to show the sword to her family, and they insisted that he put on the elaborate belt with a big gold buckle which came with it. When he could not figure out how he could adjust the belt to prevent the scabbard from dragging on the floor when he wore it, everyone roared with laughter. Paul's face turned red, and taking the sword off he put it in its tan leather carrying case.

"Paul, where's your sense of humor?" Sylvia asked.

"Damn it, I don't see anything very funny about this whole damn war, and I guess the sword is part of it," he said. "All right, it's ridiculous—let's let it go at that."

"That whole list of stuff they made you buy is ridiculous," Sylvia said. "Are you really going to wear those dress whites with the epaulettes on a ship?"

"They gave me a list and I bought the stuff. So it's funny. The whole war is one damn big comedy, at least to the spectators—"

"That's not fair," Sylvia said.

He knew she was right, but still he did not want her to laugh at him and his military regalia. Damn it, he was going to leave her soon, maybe forever, and he was going to have to try to be the executive officer of a ship, even if he was only a college boy and a summer yachtsman. He ached to be taken seriously by his wife, if by no one else. He wanted her to weep for him, not laugh.

But Sylvia often made jokes when she was nervous, and maybe she was afraid of trying to live up to too much drama. Even when she tried to be serious, she couldn't manage it.

"I won't make any more jokes about your sword," she said. "When the war is over, it will make a nice souvenir. We'll hang it over the mantelpiece, and you can tell our sons how you killed millions of Germans with it. I can just see you when you're an old man, stabbing away at the air, showing your sons and grandsons how you did it."

That day went slowly for Paul. Somehow they were afraid to make love and afraid not to and when they did, they found themselves trying to act out much more emotion than they felt. Then Sylvia started to talk about all the girls he would meet in every port. In her way she was obviously trying to be brave, and Paul was ashamed of feeling that he somehow had already left her. His mind was full of questions about the *Arluk*. What kind of ship was she, and where would she operate? And why, as Erich had pointed out, had he been made executive officer, the Coast Guard equivalent of first mate, without a day of training? Although he had scored well in the twelve-hour examination on navigation and seamanship, he was all too aware that he knew nothing about such details as gunnery, communications, and service procedures. Without thinking about it, he had assumed that he would be given some sort of training, either afloat or ashore. The thought that he was immediately to be given such a responsible position aboard a ship of whatever size was a little flattering but very scary. He wondered and half hoped that Chris would find that a mistake of some kind had been made.

Sylvia did not want to go with him to Chris's apartment. She was uneasy there partly because the Coast Guard lieutenant's manners seemed abrupt to her and partly because Katherine, Chris's Swedish wife, nonchalantly nursed her baby in the livingroom even while guests were there. Without even bothering to keep a blanket draped completely over her huge bosom, Katie just sat there and chatted with the men while her baby sucked and fondled her breasts. Sylvia had never seen anything like this. She was angry at Paul when he said that he thought the sight of Katie nursing her child was beautiful and that he admired her for her lack of prudery. They had had a big fight about that, and about what was good taste and what wasn't. After that Sylvia never wanted to go to Chris's apartment again.

So precisely at seven o'clock Paul presented himself at Chris's door alone. Looking a little strained, Chris gave Paul and Katie a drink of scotch. Then he said, "You better go into the bedroom, Katie. We've got top secret stuff to discuss."

Katie withdrew, carrying her baby.

"I don't know whether this is going to come as good news to you or bad news," Chris said. "The *Arluk* is a brand new Boston beam trawler we've just taken over. She's being fitted out for the Greenland Patrol."

"Do they really want me to be executive officer without any training at all?"

Chris shrugged. "Once you've qualified for the stripe, you're not supposed to need training. That's crazy of course, but we just are getting more ships than we are qualified officers. The skipper will break you in."

"Greenland," Paul said. "I have no idea what that's like except that it's supposed to be cold."

"You can say that again," Chris said with a grin. "In the interior, it goes to a hundred and ten degrees below zero. You're lucky. On the coast it's rarely worse than fifty below."

"I guess I better take my tropical whites."

"Hell, in the summer it often gets to sixty or more above there, and you may not be there in the winter. They may bring the trawlers back to Boston before the worst weather really sets in."

"That's a comforting possibility."

"I haven't told you the worst part yet," Chris said, refilling his glass. "These trawlers aren't really Coast Guard cutters—they're just fish boats. And the captains they're getting for them are nothing like regular Coast Guard officers, because what they have to be is ice pilots, and we don't have enough of them to put aboard small ships."

"Who are they getting?" Paul asked.

"Gloucester fishermen, even some Norwegians, Danes, and Icelanders we've made into American citizens. Old explorers, sea hunters, anyone who's been on an Arctic expedition, old Greenland hands—there are a few around who love the place, believe it or not—the idea is to grab anyone we can who can get a ship through Arctic ice, and who understands the weather conditions up there."

"What's so bad about that?"

"Some of these guys are wild men. We're getting drunks, queers, and Captain Blighs who still want to flog a man they don't like. Of course we're weeding out the worst as soon as we can and there are a few really great officers in that crazy gang, but I have no idea what kind of a skipper you're going to get. The *Arluk* hasn't been assigned a commanding officer yet. She won't be ready to sail for another month, and there's nothing but a warrant boatswain and a skeleton crew aboard her. And now an ensign—you. You'll be in charge until we find a skipper for her."

"Are you serious?"

"Don't worry—you'll just be tied up in the yard. The personnel officer doesn't pay much attention to me, but I'll do my best to see that you at least get a skipper who can speak English."

"That would help."

There was a brief silence while they both drank.

"At least no one will be shooting at me in Greenland," Paul said. "Compared to the assignments a lot of guys will be getting, Greenland may not be so bad."

"I wouldn't be too sure about that," Chris said. "There may be German submarines up there. During some times of the year, at least, those fjords, especially on the east coast, would be an ideal place for tankers and subs to rendezvous. Ever since the Germans took Norway and Denmark, they've had plenty of ice pilots who know that region like their own backyard. Greenland is Danish territory, you know—the Danes have been up there forever."

"What else?" Paul asked drily.

"Plenty else! The Germans have long-range planes which can patrol the east coast of Greenland. And they're always sending weather ships up there—they need to know Greenland weather just as much as we do, to make forecasts for the bombers in Europe. It's only a matter of time before they try to establish weather bases in Greenland, just the way we have. It takes maybe five men to man a weather base, instead of at least thirty for a weather ship. I bet that we're going to have a big job stamping out their weather bases."

"Anything more?" Paul asked.

"Plenty more. You've got a lot of floating mines in Greenland, some maybe left by subs, and more that have been brought by the currents from Europe. And at least one big German battleship has come within sight of Cape Farewell, the southern tip of Greenland. Don't get the idea that you're going into some backwater, far away from any possibility of action. You're going to have to keep your eyes peeled up there all the time."

"I'll remember that."

"Let me be honest with you," Chris said. "Greenland is a fascinating place—I've been there. The worst part of your assignment is that you've got a trawler. Those ships can't carry any real armament and they couldn't get out of their own way in any kind of action. The only reason that we're sending them up there is that they're about all we've got, except for a few icebreakers, that can handle ice."

"Well, I asked for a small ship."

"You've got one—there are plenty of tugs bigger than those trawlers. And you're going to have a nonregulation skipper of some kind, probably a good ice pilot, but those guys don't often turn out to be what you'd call an officer and a gentleman. To tell you the truth, I wouldn't blame you if you tried to have your orders changed. That can sometimes be done."

"How?"

"Get the skipper of some other ship to ask the personnel officer for you. I have a friend who's got a hundred-and-sixty-footer down in the Caribbean. She's a real Coast Guard cutter and he's a real Coast Guard officer. At least you won't freeze to death down there. Want me to see what I can do?"

"No," Paul said. "Thanks a lot, but I wouldn't really feel right about that. Anyway, you've got me all curious about Greenland."

"Good," Chris said with a booming laugh. "I doubt if I could have swung it anyway, but I wanted to see if you'd go for it. I think you have the makings of a real Coastie. Katie, come out here and rustle up some chow. Let's give the condemned man the best meal we can!"

"I have to get home," Paul said. "Sylvia is waiting for me."

"Well, you hurry right on along then," Chris said. "And my advice to you is, get all the screwing in you can before you head north, because you won't get much in Greenland unless you learn to catch an Eskimo, and that ain't as easy as you've probably heard tell."

# CHAPTER 6

At the district office early the next morning Paul was told that the *Arluk* was being outfitted in a small yard in East Boston. He took a taxi there. It was a windy day and though the April sunshine was bright, there was no warmth in it. Paul was wearing his brand new blue greatcoat with shoulder boards emblazoned with his proud single gold stripes. It seemed a rather theatrical getup and he fought a feeling that he was all dressed up to go to a costume ball of some kind. As the taxi drove along the waterfront, he saw that the many shipyards which ringed the harbor were crowded with great gray aircraft carriers, sleek destroyers, freighters, vessels of every kind. So many acetylene torches were being used that each yard appeared to be celebrating the Fourth of July.

Finally the taxi turned down an alley and stopped at a

wire gate. As Paul got out of the car a petty officer in a pea coat with the collar turned up to protect his ears stepped out of a sentry box and saluted him smartly.

"What ship, sir?"

This was the first time anyone had saluted Paul and also the first time in his twenty-two years that anyone had called him "sir." The petty officer was at least twenty years older than he, a heavyset man who slightly resembled his father. Paul felt ridiculous and the thought crossed his mind that the man might be mocking him, but his expression was dead serious.

Sort of brushing the visor of his cap in a casual return of salute, Paul said, "The *Arluk*, thank you."

"Identification, sir?"

Paul had not yet been issued a card, but his orders sufficed.

"She's lying right at the end of the south pier, outboard of the *Nanmak*."

The fact that nonsense syllables had apparently been used to name these vessels somehow seemed an appropriate part of this Alice-in-Wonderland adventure. The taxi man dragged Paul's footlocker and his sword in its leather case from the trunk of the car. Dissatisfied with the quarter tip Paul gave him, he gave a burlesque of a salute, said, "Thanks a lot, *sir*," and roared off. His contempt somehow struck Paul as more reasonable than the respect shown by the petty officer.

"I'll have your gear put aboard for you, sir," the petty officer said.

"Thank you."

Paul strode through the gate in the wire fence, feeling that now he was really entering the service. Eager to see his ship, he walked fast. This yard was building sub chasers and a row of the sleek craft stood on the ways. An old four-stack destroyer obscured his view of the south pier. The bright lights of welding and cutting torches made him blink and the sound of riveting guns and air hammers made it difficult to think. The smell of the harbor at low tide filled his mind with memories of the *Valkyrie*, and he half expected to see the old yawl, but by now she existed nowhere at all, and she didn't belong in this time and place anyway. When he passed the high bow of the destroyer, he saw two beam trawlers moored at the end of the pier. Because Chris had told him they were no bigger than a tug, they looked much larger than he had expected. They were, perhaps, no more than twice the length of the *Valkyrie*, but were so much beamier and higher that they probably had more than ten times the tonnage. There was no real comparison between them and the old yawl. The trawlers looked like huge bulldogs, while the yacht had been a toy poodle.

The trawlers were also much more handsome than Paul had expected with the beauty of strength instead of grace. Their high, flared bows looked as though they could punch into the highest seas without danger. Their well deck amidships was only about four feet above the surface of the water, but the sterns were high and handsomely rounded. The only things streamlined about the ships were their short oval smokestacks, which were tilted aft at a rakish angle. They had short stubby masts and heavy freight booms. The ships had been freshly painted with irregular patterns of light blue and white, ice camouflage. There was an air of excitement about them which stemmed from the fact that these little vessels had the ability to live in Arctic seas and ice which would sink thin-skinned destroyers and most of the other ships which towered over them.

The two trawlers were so alike that one resembled a mirror image of the other, but as he walked closer, Paul saw that the inboard vessel already had a stubby cannon on her foredeck, a steel platform for antiaircraft guns amidships and racks of depth charges on the stern which workmen were in the process of adding to the *Arluk*. Before a wooden gangway that led from the pier to the *Nanmak* Paul hesitated. There was a whole rigamarole about boarding a Coast Guard or navy ship which he had read about in a copy of the *Watch Officers' Guide*, which Chris had given to him and he supposed that he better try it. As he reached the rail of the ship he paused, saluted the quarterdeck (although why he should salute a deck he had no idea), and said to a young seaman who was lounging by the rail, "Request permission to come aboard."

The seaman looked at him oddly and said, "Come ahead. You want someone aboard here or the *Arluk*?"

"The *Arluk*." The decks of the ships were of bright new pine—apparently these vessels had just been built. Picking his way through a tangle of hoses, lines and piles of stores which had not yet been stowed, Paul climbed over the rail to the *Arluk*. He didn't bother with saluting the quarterdeck this time, but seeing a short, stout old man in a knitted blue watchcap and a khaki parka, he said, "Permission to come aboard?"

"Why come right ahead," the man said with a pronounced Maine accent, and his ruddy face broke into a surprisingly sunny, almost childlike smile. "You ain't our new skipper, be you?"

"I guess I'm supposed to be the executive officer," Paul said, sounding pompous to himself, and added his name.

"I'm the boatswain—Seth Farmer. We don't have what you'd call real officers' quarters aboard here, but I'll show you your bunk."

He led the way down a steep companionway near the stern to a dimly lit compartment, all white wood with two bunks on each side and a table in the middle. As they entered, an ensign in his mid-twenties who was lying in the forward, starboard bunk looked up from the book he had been reading. He had a thin, melancholy face, thick glasses and a hooked nose, which gave him an owlish, scholarly appearance.

"This is Mr. Green, our communications officer—he just came aboard about an hour ago," Farmer said. "Mr. Green, this is Mr. Schuman, our new exec."

"Pleased," Green said, and began to climb out of the bunk. Because the deck above the mattress didn't quite give his tall frame sitting headroom, it was difficult for him to do this gracefully. He bumped his forehead and had difficulty untangling his long legs from a blanket before he stood up, a gaunt, stooped man six feet, two inches tall who had been described as resembling a "Jewish Abe Lincoln."

"Glad to meet you," he said, shaking Paul's hand firmly. "This is my first sea duty. I'm afraid you'll find I have a hell of a lot to learn."

"It's my first day in the Coast Guard," Paul said with a rueful laugh. "How about you, Mr. Farmer?" He wasn't quite sure whether to be so formal in the use of names, but the watch officer's guide had demanded it.

"Well, I wouldn't say that this is exactly my first sea duty," Farmer replied, his Maine twang somehow making it obvious that he had spent at least thirty years sailing the oceans of the world, "but I don't know much about the Coast Gad. I've been a fisherman all my life. I sort of came with this vessel, you might say, like the trawl winch.

They're taking off the rest of the fishing gear, but I guess they're going to leave me aboard."

"I'm glad that we've got somebody who knows what he's doing," Paul replied, deciding that honesty must be the best policy. "I've been to sea a little, but to tell the truth, I'm just a summer sailor, and I have just about everything to learn about a ship like this."

Farmer's smile illuminated his curiously innocent round, ruddy face.

"That's the way things go in time of war—first you get the job and then you learn how to do it. There will be plenty to keep you busy, but you young fellers look smart enough to catch on fine before long. You want a cup of coffee?"

"That's just what I want," Paul said.

"We don't have a skipper aboard this hooker yet, and we don't rightly have an engineer, but we got the damnedest, finest cook I ever seen afloat. They say he used to be some kind of a real fancy hotel chef before he joined up, and I believe it. He's been baking this morning and I can hardly wait to see what he's going to come up with this time."

Green said nothing but listened attentively and smiled. As Farmer led the way to the galley in the forecastle, Green followed, hitting his head on the hatch on the way out and laughing ruefully at his own ungainliness.

The forecastle was a low-ceilinged, V-shaped compartment about thirty feet long with three tiers of bunks on each side for the thirty enlisted men who would make up the crew, and a long, V-shaped table in the middle. Around this table about a dozen young seamen now sat, greedily grabbing fresh blueberry muffins from large platters. In the door to the adjoining galley a short man about forty-five years old stood in a white apron. He wore a tall white chef's hat, which even Paul knew to be outlandish aboard a trawler or a Coast Guard cutter. When he saw the officers he grinned in a curiously obsequious but sly way and in a thick foreign accent said, "What will it be, gentlemen? Blueberry muffins, apple cake or cherry tarts? Don't tell me. I'll fix you a selection."

Without being asked, a seaman poured coffee from a big pot on the table into white mugs for the two ensigns and the warrant boatswain.

"We need more milk, Cookie," he called.

"Get it yourself," Cookie replied haughtily as he ap-

41

peared with a tray of pastries which would have graced the fanciest of restaurants.

"I never seen anything like this aboard any vessel of any description in my whole life," Farmer marveled as he helped himself to a cherry tart. "Where did you learn to cook like this, Cookie?"

"Where?" Cookie replied, drawing himself up to his full height of five feet, six inches, which bent his chef's hat against the overhead. "Where did I learn my profession? Why in the best hotels of Switzerland, of course, in the Cordon Bleu in Paris, and at the Ritz-Carlton here in Boston. And after all that, this Coast Guard makes me a *third-class cook!*"

"Now don't you worry about that, Cookie," Farmer said. "As soon as we get us a skipper aboard here, we'll all recommend you for a promotion just as quick as the regulations allow. As far as I can see, you ought to be a regular admiral of cooks if they rate them up that high."

"Thank you, sir," Cookie replied with an almost Oriental bow. "I shall always try to please." Still bowing and smiling in his sly, obsequious way, he backed into his galley and disappeared.

The enlisted men had fallen silent at the approach of the officers, but now a coxswain who looked and talked like a bright college boy, said to Paul, "Sir, are you going to be stationed aboard here?"

"It looks that way."

"Are we going to Greenland?"

"I guess that's supposed to be a secret, isn't it?"

"Well, we figure from the way this ship is painted and the way they're beefing up the bow with steel plates and all, it sure doesn't look like we're headed for the jungles of New Guinea," the coxswain said and everyone laughed.

"You might say that," Farmer said, "but the way the Coast Gad does things, they might send an icebreaker to New Guinea after all."

More laughter.

"Sir," the coxswain continued to Paul, "did you see the news this morning about Greenland? It was in the *Record*."

"No. What is it?"

"The *Northern Light*, sir, she captured a German weather ship just five miles off the east coast of Greenland. They had a regular battle, but when our planes came in, the Germans gave up."

42

Paul wondered whether Chris had known that when he discussed the German interest in Greenland weather.

"They had a picture of the German ship in the paper," the coxswain continued. "She's a trawler just like this, but much bigger and she carries a long gun on the bow, something like a five-inch fifty-one, much bigger than any of our trawlers have. She's got big antiaircraft guns mounted all over her. The papers don't say how much of a fight she put up, but you know the *Northern Light* is just about the biggest cutter we have. I was aboard her just a couple of months ago. She carries two five-inch fifty-ones and two three-inch fifties, along with about six twenty-millimeters. If the *Northern Light* had to radio for planes to beat a trawler, that must have been some tough ship."

Well, Paul thought, Erich had said the Germans wouldn't be easy to beat.

"That's interesting," he said. "I'll try to get a copy of the paper."

"Sir," the coxswain persisted, "do you think this means the Germans will give up on Greenland weather, or just come back with ships that are even better armed?"

"I don't know," Paul said carefully.

"I do not believe that the Germans can give up on Greenland weather," Green said, speaking for the first time. His voice was very deep with a New York edge to it, maybe a hint of a Brooklyn accent. "Without a knowledge of Greenland weather it's impossible to make accurate forecasts for Europe."

"Why is that, sir?" the coxswain asked.

"To oversimplify it, Greenland weather moves east, warms up, and that's what Europe gets two days later. I'm no meteorologist, but I've read a lot about it."

"Thanks, sir. Are you going to be stationed aboard here too?"

"They tell me I'm to be the communications officer."

"Thank you, sir. When do you think we'll be getting our skipper?"

"Before we sail, I hope," Green replied without a smile, but there was a glint of humor in his deep-set eyes.

Paul hardly heard him. He was imagining a German trawler much bigger than this one being outfitted in some Danish or Norwegian yard with enormous guns. Her crew would be made up by experienced sailors, Germans like his own ancestors, but men who knew the Arctic, not a bunch of novices. Such a ship might be heading for Greenland just as the *Arluk* started north. In what fog-shrouded ice floe would they meet and what would happen?

Feeling restless, Paul excused himself and starting forward, began a minute examination of the ship. The high bow had been reinforced with sheathing of stout oak planks and steel plates. There was a small gun platform on the forecastle head, but no gun yet. The bridge ran the full breadth of the deckhouse, but was not more than six feet deep. There was an engine room telegraph, a wooden ship's wheel, a magnetic compass, pigeonholes for signal flags and very little else—no fancy modern equipment or naval gadgetry. A door with a new metal sign saying "Commanding Officer" stood open at the afterside of the bridge. After a moment of hesitation, Paul stuck his head in. There was a bunk, a big chart table with a stool and another door that had been newly labeled "Head—for C.O. only." The cabin was painted white and trimmed with varnished oak. It was Spartan enough, but Paul imagined the pride he would feel if he ever actually deserved to occupy that space. Dreams of glory! It would be years before he even deserved the job he had. What kind of a man would appear to occupy this stark but somehow royal cabin in the days immediately ahead? Chris had warned him that some of the ice pilots chosen for such jobs were real wild men. Why didn't they make a man like Farmer a captain instead of a warrant boatswain? Farmer somehow gave the impression of knowing everything in the world about going to sea, and he certainly was no wild man.

Continuing his walk aft, Paul saw that the name of the ship had been painted in white letters on the blue smokestack. Some wag had dipped a brush in white paint to add the word "Just" in front of it, so that it read, "Just Arluk." It was funny, but the scrawled addition subtracted from the trim appearance of the new paint job, and it seemed to Paul to disparage the ship at a time when they should be building pride in her. What the hell did *Arluk* really mean, anyway?

"Hello there."

The voice, with a slight Scandinavian accent, came from the wing of the bridge of the adjacent trawler. He looked up and saw a rather elegant appearing gray-haired man in a blue uniform with the two stripes of a full lieutenant.

"I'm Hansen," this officer said. "Are you the *Arluk*'s new skipper?"

Flattered by the idea that he at least looked as though he could be the captain of such a ship, Paul said, "I'm the new exec. We don't have our skipper yet."

"I'm the skipper here," the lieutenant said. "Would you like to come over for a drink?"

Paul climbed over the rail and to the bridge of the *Nanmak*, which was almost exactly like that of the *Arluk*. Hansen shook his hand warmly and led the way to the captain's cabin, which was the same as that of the other ship, except that it now boasted a clean sheepskin rug, dark blue silk curtains at the portholes, a damask bedspread, the framed photograph of a beautiful woman on one bulkhead and what looked like an original Audubon print of an Arctic hawk on another. Paul was happy to note that a sword just like his own hung in brackets over the bunk.

"It's a little fancy, but I like it," Hansen said. "My wife fixed it up. Where she found the print of the hawk, I don't know. *Nanmak* means 'hawk' in the Eskimo language, you know."

"It's great. Do you know what *Arluk* means?"

"The hunter—a very proud rank in the Eskimo culture. I don't know who named these ships. Some admiral's wife, I suppose, but she did a good job."

From a rack in a cabinet over the chart table Hansen took a decanter half full of a colorless liquid and two small tumblers of heavy cut glass much like those which had been aboard the *Valkyrie*.

"The Coast Guard has all kinds of regulations against liquor aboard these vessels, but they'll have a hell of a time enforcing them with us old ice pilots," he said. "Do you like Aquavit?"

"Very much," Paul replied, though he had never tasted the stuff. His first sip stopped him from being a liar.

"Well, here's to the hawk and the hunter," Hansen said. "My, that does sound dramatic, doesn't it? From the look of that German trawler they captured up there in Greenland, I must confess that I'm beginning to feel more like a sparrow."

The man's Scandinavian accent was mixed with British overtones. His small hands looked soft and were neatly manicured. He seemed to fit neither Paul's conception of an old ice pilot nor of a wild man.

"I was up at headquarters talking about that German trawler," Hansen continued. "It's all supposed to be top secret, but she gave the *Northern Light* fits. That German gun control system is something. She landed her first three shots on the bridge. Killed the skipper and a dozen men."

"Why did she give up?"

"The *Northern Light* was lucky. A whole flight of P-38's was right overhead on a practice run from Narsarssuak. They came down like thunder and blew the whole superstructure, guns and all, right off the German. That picture in the paper is from one we found aboard. The idea is to keep the Krauts guessing why she quit."

"That's interesting."

"I've been trying to figure what we should do if we run into a Kraut like that," Hansen said. "With the popguns they're giving us, we wouldn't have a chance at shooting it out. I figure I'd radio for planes and try to keep the hell away from him. The trouble is those big North Sea trawlers can do twelve knots to our eight."

"What's your answer to that one?"

"If we can keep our eye on the big picture, I suppose, our job will be done once we call the planes down on him. If they sink us before they get theirs, it won't matter much to anyone but us. I would sure try to lead them one merry chase among the icebergs, though."

Hansen laughed, apparently with genuine merriment. "Are you from the Coast Guard Academy?" he asked.

"No, I'm just a reserve officer. To tell you the truth, I haven't had a damn day of training and I'm so green I scare myself."

"At least you know you're green and that's a good way to start. My exec is an Academy j.g. He's never seen more ice than you'd find in a highball glass. I'm supposed to make him an ice pilot, but for some reason he thinks he already knows ten times what I do."

"Do you mind if I ask how you got to be an ice pilot?"

"I'm a Dane and I was brought up in Greenland—my father was in charge of the cryolite mines there. We owned fishing boats and I brought a small trawler with me when I came over here. I've been more or less reared in the ice pack."

"They ought to get you to give a course at the Academy."

46

"There's not much anyone can teach about ice—you just have to work in it. You'll catch on fast enough."

Paul was suddenly overwhelmed by the amount of knowledge he was supposed to catch on to so fast. Ice was only the beginning of his ignorance. He actually knew almost exactly nothing except how to pass written examinations. He was essentially a fraud and should be arrested for impersonating an officer. Suddenly he felt dizzy and finished his Aquavit in a gulp, hoping it would steady him.

"Want another?"

"I'd like one, but I have an awful lot to do."

Hurrying back to the *Arluk*, he stood near a huge mechanical winch which he knew nothing about and tried to think how he should begin the vast learning process which was required of him. How does one begin to conquer almost total ignorance? With determination he began examining the winch simply because he was leaning against it. The anchor winch on the *Valkyrie* had been about the size of his head and had been on the bow. This machine was a mass of cogwheels the size of a small automobile and it was located in the waist of the ship, far away from the anchors. The chain aboard the old yawl had been about the size of his thumb; this chain was as big around as his arm. It led over a racheted drum which was connected to several big cogwheels. There were three long, heavy levers and a panel with buttons and dials like the instrument board of a motorcycle. No matter how closely he studied it, Paul had no more idea how to run it than if it were a locomotive.

"That's a trawl winch," Farmer said with his nasal twang, walking up behind him. "Practically nobody in the Coast Gad or navy ever seen one like it. This here winch will practically lift up a sunken battleship. Want me to show you how she works?"

"Please."

An hour later Paul knew how to operate a trawl winch. It was the only part of the ship he did understand, but it was a start.

After teaching him the mechanism of the winch, Farmer said, "Do you want to make up some kind of list about who spends what nights aboard here and who goes ashore? I got the crew divided into three watches, but this is the first time we've had three officers."

"I guess we can just take turns."

"That's okay with me. I don't mean to put myself forward, but I've been stuck here for five nights running and I got a wife in Gloucester."

"Then take off. Mr. Green and I will take tonight and tomorrow."

"I already talked to Mr. Green about that. Maybe you ought to have a few words with him. He seems kind of worked up about it."

Paul found Green in the wardroom, as the cabin where the officers slept was called. He was sitting at the table with his head in his hands and his long face looked more morose than ever.

"Mr. Schuman," Green said, jumping to his feet. "I have to talk to you. Mr. Farmer asked me to take the deck—to be in charge here tonight. I have to explain to you that I don't know a thing in the world about ships. There's been some terrible mistake. It would be immoral of me to take responsibility for something I don't know anything at all about." There was a pause before he wearily added, "Now I know you're going to ask me how in the world I got a Coast Guard commission and why I wear a gold stripe."

"You took a twelve-hour examination," Paul said.

"No. I didn't even have to take an examination. I am an electronics specialist. I graduated from Brooklyn Tech, R.P.I., and I was working for General Electric. We were doing a lot of work for the navy. When we got in the war I wanted to do my bit, and I tried to get a commission in the navy. They didn't want me, but told me to try the Coast Guard. They took me as soon as they saw my record. I assumed they were going to put me in charge of installing radar or big communications systems, but suddenly I'm communication officer on a fishing boat bound for Greenland. There's no more equipment here than a third-class radioman can handle, but they told me at Headquarters that now I'm commissioned, I'm supposed to be a regular deck officer, not just a specialist. I'm not trying to rat out, but how can I take responsibility for a whole ship and a *crew* yet, when all I know about a ship is that the sharp end is supposed to be called the bow? I know we're just lying at the dock, but what if they wanted us to move? What if there was a fire? I could be court-martialed for gross incompetence, so I'm *telling* you I'm incompetent now!"

48

"You shouldn't feel too bad about that," Paul said. "We're all beginners. We're all in the same boat."

"Very funny. How the hell are we going to get this thing to Greenland or even across the harbor?"

"Our skipper will be an expert. Mr. Farmer knows a lot and so do some of the petty officers. The real reason they commissioned men like us is that they figure we're smart enough to learn fast."

"I don't even know how to start learning. The most boat I've ever been in was a rowboat in Central Park."

"I can give you some books to start you off. Or maybe you could get your orders changed if you want. I know a guy up at the district office . . ."

"No!" Green said fiercely, bringing his fist down on the table. "They sent me here and I'm not going to beg off. I'm not going to pretend I know something I don't know, either. If they want to keep me here *knowing* I don't know a damn thing about anything except electronics, that's up to them. I won't go begging off."

"That's good," Paul said. "Tomorrow I'll give you some books and show you what to do if a fire starts. Have you got a wife ashore?"

A look of pain crossed Green's face, but was quickly controlled.

"My parents have come to see me," he said. "They're waiting for me up at a hotel. I haven't even called them because I don't know what to say."

"You can go ashore now and you'll probably have every third night for a couple of weeks at least. Be back at eight in the morning."

"Yes, sir. Or am I supposed to say, 'Aye, aye, sir'?"

"Just have a good time."

Nathan walked slowly from the shipyard and waited on the street, hoping to get a taxi. He dreaded going to see his parents because he knew they would talk about their latest attempts to get news of his wife, and after more than two years of trying, Nathan knew that there was very little chance of that, and if they did get news, it was almost certain to be more than he could stand to hear. On August 14, 1939, his wife, Rebecca, had gone back to Poland to try to get her parents out. She had arrived in Warsaw only a few days before the Nazis had invaded Poland, and had

49

not been heard from since. No member of her family had been heard from since.

For two years Nathan had tried to persuade the United States government and the Red Cross to try harder to trace his wife, and he had even tried to go to Poland himself, giving up only when the British authorities convinced him that the last thing his wife would want would be for him to follow her into prison or death. For the past six months Nathan had forced himself to accept her probable fate, and the only emotion left to him was a need to fight the Nazis, which this very unmilitary man was now trying to do as best he could. Nathan never talked about this. Somehow talking about it with people who couldn't share his depth of feeling would seem to him to be a kind of desecration of his wife. What had happened was too terrible to be discussed. Even his mother and father did not understand this. If they had understood, they could not have kept giving him assurances that Rebecca "must be" all right, and hiring more and more lawyers who promised they had ways to get news of her. . . .

When Nathan could not find a taxi on that waterfront street, he was almost glad for the excuse to delay seeing his parents. Slowly he walked the many blocks to the Plaza Hotel. When his mother embraced him and his father gave him the quick, affectionate hug he remembered so well, he was genuinely glad to see them, but then they started talking about a Free French lawyer they had found who had real connections with the Underground all over Europe, and even with people who had access to people who had access to Nazi authorities who for a price could find who was in the concentration camps.

Nathan listened quietly, aware that his parents were too old or too vulnerable themselves to give up hope. They still lived on the pretense that everything was going to turn out all right, and perhaps conditions in Poland were not as bad as they had been painted, one never knew what was propaganda and what was truth. Rebecca was a very resourceful person with great inner strength, and they were sure that she'd find a way to pull through.

Perhaps they did not really believe this but were afraid that *he* needed the reassurance to go on. After making it seem almost certain that good news about Rebecca would soon be forthcoming, they asked Nathan about his new assignment aboard the *Arluk*.

"Do you like it?"

"I like it fine."

"What kind of a ship is it?"

"I'm afraid that's a military secret," he said with a smile.

"And the captain, do you like him?" his mother asked.

"We don't have a captain yet. The executive officer is a nice guy."

As soon as possible Nathan left his parents, saying he had to report for duty before ten that evening. His feet were sore from the many blocks he had walked that day, but he was far too restless to remain still. After walking around the Boston Common, he rented a room in a small hotel and fell into a deep sleep with dreams he did not remember when he awoke, but which had caused him to twist his sheets into ropes.

After telling Green to go ashore for the night, Paul had stood watching the tall, stooped figure walk away from the ship. Nathan was a strange one, Paul thought—a man who obviously had great troubles, great weaknesses as an officer, but a kind of depth that made Paul feel curiously shallow. In a way this made Paul resentful, but there was a quality of rueful honesty about Nathan that he also respected. He seemed to be an intelligent man only a little older than himself, the only one on the ship Paul could think of as a potential friend in any meaningful sense of the word. And he obviously knew even less about running a ship than Paul did. In this respect, he and Nathan were certainly in the same boat, but now was not the time to worry about that. Seth Farmer walked ashore with a wave and for the first time Paul found himself the only officer aboard a Coast Guard cutter.

Briskly he walked around the deck. It was getting dark. Bright lights and cutting torches were reflected on the murky waters of the harbor. The din of ship construction continued ashore, but there was no sound aboard the *Arluk*. Locating several coils of fire hose on the sides of the deck house, Paul wondered how he would get pressure on them in case of an emergency. After trying three watertight doors, he found the way to the engineroom and descended a steep flight of shiny metal steps. The size of the diesel engine astonished him—it looked as though they had parked a locomotive in the bowels of the ship. In the dim light he saw a young machinist's mate sitting in a chair reading a comic book. The boy put it down guiltily and stood up when he saw Paul.

"I'm just looking around," Paul said. "If there were an emergency and I called for pressure on the fire hoses, would I get it?"

"Sure, sir."

"Thanks." Big deal, he thought, feeling pompous.

Next Paul walked to the bridge, where he found a quartermaster sitting on a stool, studying a girlie magazine.

"In case of an emergency, how would I sound a fire alarm aboard here?" he asked.

"This switch is for the general alarm," the man said, pointing to the bulkhead near the wheel. "We're just supposed to sound that and shout fire."

"Thank you."

Well, *that* procedure at least had not turned out to be very complicated. What should he do next? On a shelf in the bridge he saw an ordinary telephone. He had, he remembered, promised to call Sylvia as soon as he knew what was going on.

"Is that a shore phone?" he asked the quartermaster.

"Yeah, but it goes through the district switchboard, and they won't put through private calls."

"Where's the nearest phone ashore?"

"There's a little bar across the street. . . ."

"I'll be back in a ten minutes."

As he walked across the shipyard he was sure that by leaving the ship, he was committing a heinous breach of regulations. If the ship blew up while he was gone, he would achieve the unique distinction of being the first officer in the long history of the Coast Guard to be court-martialed on his first day of active duty. On the other hand, he had promised his wife that he would call her as soon as possible. It would be cruel to delay much longer and the idea of regulations which defied common sense made him angry.

The nearest bar was a big smoky room crowded with shipyard workers, sailors and their girls, all of whom were talking so loudly that even the jukebox could hardly be heard. There was only one telephone booth, which stood in a dimly lit corner at the back of the saloon. As Paul approached it, he saw that it was occupied by a burly gunner's mate and a buxom blonde who certainly were not telephoning anyone. The dawning realization that they were actually making love standing up in a telephone booth filled Paul with an odd mixture of disgust and admiration. It didn't seem right to stand there staring at them, and he certainly did not think it would be wise to tap the gunner's mate on the shoulder and ask if he could use the telephone. Turning to the bar, Paul ordered scotch. Before he finished it, the couple came out of the booth, looking happy if rumpled, and he hurried into it. Sylvia answered at the first ring.

"Paul! I've been dying for you to call. What's happening?"

"Well, I got on the ship and everything's going fine. It looks like I won't be going anywhere for a few weeks, and I should be able to get home about one night out of three."

"Wonderful. Are you coming home now?"

"I have the duty now. Tomorrow or maybe the next night. I'll let you know as soon as I can."

"Oh, Paul, I miss you so. I've been going crazy alone here. I'm sorry I've been so bitchy and terrible!"

"Honey, you've been fine, Wonderful."

"No, I've been crazy. It just hit me today that you're going away for a very long time, months, maybe *years*."

"We'll have a few days together."

"None of this seemed real to me until you actually left. Paul, this may sound crazy, but I wish I was pregnant. I want to have a baby while you're gone. Hurry home and help me with my problem."

This sudden passion bewildered Paul, and he felt a tingling sensation in his groin that was almost enough to make him take a taxi to Wellesley immediately, despite Coast Guard regulations. No, that really would be all wrong. Sneaking away for a few minutes while he had the duty was bad enough.

"Tomorrow," he said. "I should be able to get home around six or seven."

"That seems like ages. Paul, something's happened to me. I feel the way I did that first night for us on the boat. The hell with the future. We only live once."

"That's right. Look, I had to sneak away to make this call and I have to get back to the ship. Tomorrow night!"

"I'll be waiting. We'll have the house to ourselves. Dad's taking mother to the symphony. I'm going to give them tickets."

"Great."

53

"I love you, Paul. I'll prove that to you."

"I love you too," he said, and forced himself to hang up. While he hurried back to the *Arluk*, he tried to imagine why one day of loneliness had worked such a considerable transformation in Sylvia. Was she afraid of losing him forever, and was this her effort to keep him, or did she really love him as much as she had said? No matter—she was still in character. Sylvia had always been the most unpredictable person he had ever known, and now he could hardly wait to get home to her.

As he climbed across the *Nanmak* toward the *Arluk*, he saw that there was some kind of disturbance at the gangway of his ship. Two men were grappling with each other while a third tried to separate them and all were shouting. Naturally something would have to happen during his brief run ashore!

Boarding the *Arluk*, he saw that two seamen were now holding the arms of Cookie, who was struggling and yelling. The Swiss chef's fury was so great that his voice was incomprehensible. Suddenly Paul realized that he was speaking German, a language Paul had learned both from his father and at college.

"Now, my friend, what's the matter?" Paul asked in German.

"Tell those bastards to let go of me," Cookie yelled in German.

"Let him go," Paul said to the two seamen in English.

"He'll go wild again," the taller seaman said. "He's crazy."

"Will you quiet down if they let you go?" Paul asked in German.

"I'll kill them if they don't. I'll shit in their soup," Cookie said in German.

"What the hell kind of language is he speaking?" the taller seaman asked.

"He's talking Swiss. Let him go. He'll be all right."

The seamen took their hands from Cookie's arms. He stood limp and trembling. Suddenly he sat down on the deck.

"You have to realize my situation," he said in German, sounding curiously calm and reasonable.

"Explain it to me," Paul said in German.

"How come you're talking German?" Cookie said in German. "Are you a fucking Nazi?"

"I'm talking Swiss the same as you are," Paul said in German.

"Well, you look like a goddamn Nazi. Have you any identification?" Cookie said, suddenly switching to his broken English. Paul realized that he was not only crazy, but drunk. It also happened that he did not have any identification on him. His orders had been taken by the quartermaster.

"Never mind that," he said in English. "What's all the trouble here?"

"I insist on seeing your identification," Cookie said in English with dignity. "You look like a Nazi and you speak perfect German."

Figuring that the man was so drunk that he wouldn't know the difference, Paul took a card showing that he was a member of the Boston Yacht Club from his wallet and showed it to him. Cookie blinked at it in the dim light.

"All right, you're not a Nazi. Try to understand me. I'm a *chef*. I'm not a goddamn sailor. There's no reason why I can't go ashore when my work is done."

"Mr. Farmer assigned him to the third watch," the taller seaman said. "Tonight the third watch has the duty."

"You goddamn ignorant bastard!" Cookie yelled in German. "I'll shit in your soup."

A bright floodlight suddenly illuminated the well deck. It came from the *Nanmak*, and looking up, Paul saw a tall, husky lieutenant j.g. standing on the wing of that ship's bridge looking down at them. He looked aloof and his voice was disdainful when he said, "I thought you might want to see what you're doing."

"Thanks," Paul said, and to Cookie added in German, "You're too drunk to go ashore tonight. If you don't quiet down and go to your bunk, we will have to lock you up."

"You've got no place to lock anyone up," Cookie said in German.

"I'll find a paint locker," Paul said in the same language. "Be good, Cookie. We are trying to take care of you."

"If you lock me up, I won't cook," Cookie said in English.

"Cookie, we all have to follow regulations."

"Then I'll follow the regulation Coast Guard cookbook. If you go by the book, so will I. How will you like that?" Cookie started to struggle to his feet.

"Cookie," Paul said, reaching out a hand to help him and putting his arm around him. "We all know that you're the best cook a ship ever had."

"I'm not a cook, I'm a *chef*."

"You're the best chef a ship ever had. Even the French Line never had a chef like you. I want to take care of you. Now let me help you to your bunk. Tomorrow we'll get this matter of standing watch all straightened out . . ."

Grumbling alternately in English and German, Cookie allowed Paul to help him to the forecastle. Struggling free, he went to the galley, took a quart of gin from a flour bin, dusted it off, took several swigs, and carried it to the bottom bunk nearest the galley door. Paul helped him to climb in and took off his shoes. Cookie half sat up in an attempt to finish his gin and passed out, leaving the open bottle on his chest. Paul grabbed it before much spilled, took a swig himself, located the cap on a galley counter and put the bottle back in the flour bin.

When Paul emerged onto the brightly lit well deck, the husky officer was still standing as though at attention on the wing of the *Nanmak*'s bridge.

"You can put your light off now," Paul said with irritation, and stopped himself from adding, "Show's over."

"Do you mind if I come down and talk to you for a minute?" the officer said. The bright light stayed on.

"If you want," Paul said.

The officer went into his pilothouse and soon emerged on the well deck of his ship, where he leaned on the rail without coming aboard the *Arluk*. He had a broad, freckled face and his eyes looked pink.

"You're a reserve officer, aren't you?" he said to Paul.

"How did you guess?"

"You've got to learn how to handle enlisted men. You can't just stand there arguing with them like that, lowering yourself to their level."

"What would you have done?"

"Put the man on report and have him carried to his bunk. Find a way to lock him up if necessary and have him taken ashore to a brig in the morning. No fuss."

"Then you'd lose the damnedest cook there ever was."

"It's easy to get cooks," the lieutenant said disdainfully. "You have to learn to maintain discipline. One incident like that can spread."

"Thanks for your advice. Now would you mind putting that light out? It hurts my eyes."

"Men rarely cause trouble in a brightly lit place," the officer said. "Better leave it on for the night to prevent a recurrence." He went into the wardroom of his ship.

Paul couldn't think of any regulation which might allow him to shoot out a light on another man's ship. Muttering to himself, he went below to his own wardroom. A steam radiator hissed and it was much too hot. After opening the portholes, he sat down at the table and looked around. It was a bleak, stuffy little room. How many years would he have to spend in it? And why, oh why, hadn't he done what Sylvia wanted, and stayed in college till June instead of hurrying to join up? If he'd done that, he'd have three more whole months to live with his beautiful wife in their little apartment under the eaves of that old colonial house, the memory of which already seemed distant and Utopian. Before his classmates even got in the service, he'd probably be dead, sunk in an Arctic sea by some monstrous German ship.

Almost crying with homesickness, self-pity and regret, Paul climbed into his bunk and quickly slept.

# CHAPTER 7

In the morning Cookie seemed alert and energetic as ever, though his eyes were red. As soon as Paul appeared at the table in the forecastle, Cookie brought him freshly squeezed and iced orange juice, croissants, coffee and a mushroom omelet. Paul did not have a chance to do justice to this repast before he heard a fearful thumping on deck and a rising babble of Southern voices.

"Watch out thea, son. What kind of a mothah fucka is this here crazy fishboat anyhow?"

The voices sounded black to Paul, but the men were all white. He got the impression that dozens of sailors, all dressed in soiled and rumpled blue uniforms, were throwing sea bags to the deck of the *Arluk* and jumping aboard. They were led by a fat chief machinist's mate with gold hashmarks up to his elbows.

"What's going on here, Chief?" Paul asked, still wiping his mouth with his handkerchief.

"All these here men have been assigned to this ship," the chief said. "It sure looks like somebody don't like us Southern boys."

"Where are you all from?"

"Well, we was all in the brig, and this son of a bitch from personnel came through this morning and picked all us Southern boys for the Greenland Peetrol."

"Well, I ain't no Southern boy," a burly gunner's mate whom Paul recognized as the man he had seen with the blonde in the telephone booth said in a New England accent. "You guys are all from the *Cayuga*, ain't you?"

"So what if we are?"

"Well you guys been fucking up ever since you got into port. You the guys that cleaned out the Silver Dollar Bar, ain't you? And ain't you the guys that chased that old tassel girl right out of the Crawford House into the street and around the block? Well, they *told* us all that if we fucked up again we'd land on the Greenland Patrol. They're making an ex-ample out of us. You must have fucked up again last night, just like I did."

"We just got tossed out of the Old Howard," the chief machinist's mate said. "We didn't cause no damage."

"You chased the girls on the stage again. I heard about it. We all fucked up and here we are, ex-amples on the Greenland Patrol."

There was a rising chorus of moans and protestations. Paul was suddenly aware that the aloof lieutenant j.g. was out on the wing of his bridge again, disdainfully watching him.

"All *right!*" Paul said angrily as sea bags bounced all around him and the confusion mounted. "Quiet! You men fall in here on the well deck. I want no more Chinese fire drill. This may look like a fish boat, but she's now a United States Coast Guard cutter. All *right*. Attention!"

Now that they were all lined up at attention, Paul had no idea what to do with them. He decided to give them a speech, pretending he was a marine sergeant in the movies, or maybe a captain in the Foreign Legion.

"All right, you men are brig rats. We'll forget that. All we care is how you act from now on. And if you foul up again, you won't go back to a nice warm brig. We got other ways of handling foul-ups on the Greenland Patrol. Try us and you'll see. Now I'll have bunks assigned to you men. Your first job will be to clean up yourselves and your gear. And do it quietly. The first man who raises a racket will get the first taste of how we handle things on the Greenland Patrol. At ease. Fall out!"

Noticing that Farmer had come from the wardroom to see what was going on, Paul added, "See that these men get settled, Mr. Farmer, and take no nonsense from them."

"Aye, aye, sir," Farmer said. "Come on, boys, and I'll see you get bunks."

Paul walked to the wardroom, clicking his heels hard on the pine decks. Green was lying in his bunk studying a copy of *Knight's Modern Seamanship* which Paul had lent to him. "What the hell is going on up there?" he asked.

Paul sat down at the table and suddenly broke into laughter. "I don't know," he said. "A bunch of guys from the brig came aboard, and I had to straighten them out. I don't know if I'm Captain Bligh, Errol Flynn or Sergeant York, but it seemed to work."

Paul's bravura act did not work for long, however. The new members of the crew were old Coast Guard hands, and they soon recognized him as a raw reserve officer, Green as a man who knew even less than Paul did about ships, and Farmer as a nice old fisherman who cared nothing about military discipline. When the officers tried to get them to scrub the decks, wash down interior bulkheads and stow the mountains of gear that were constantly being shoved aboard, they cheerfully began the tasks and abandoned them as soon as the officers turned their backs. They bickered constantly with each other and the yard workers, engaged in frequent scuffling matches, carried beer cans and pints of whiskey in their pockets and kept the ship in shambles. Green simply retreated to his bunk, and Farmer sat on the bridge sorrowfully shaking his head. Paul kept yelling at the men more and more and always got instant obedience that lasted only for an instant.

"I don't know what to do with them," he said in exasperation to Green. "Do you suppose we could send them all back to the brig?"

"The guys ashore know better than to take them,"

Green replied morosely. "I keep dreaming of the ship sinking. It used to be a horror dream, but now I've begun to look forward to it. At least the noise would stop."

Just as Paul was about to go home to his wife and leave the mess to Farmer for a night, two of the newly arrived machinist's mates had a fight in the engine room. This was no prank—they fought with ballpeen hammers. One was knocked out and both were blinded with blood before they were parted. By the time Paul got them on an ambulance and figured out the legal procedures, it was far too late for him to go home and he was too exhausted anyway.

"What happened?" Sylvia wailed when he finally got to a telephone.

"I couldn't begin to tell you. Top secret. I'll be home as soon as I can, dear. I don't know when. I'm beginning to think that fighting the Germans and the Japs will be the easiest part of this war."

The next day was the first really warm sunny one that spring. After being urged by Mr. Farmer, all hands washed clothes and hung them on the rigging and rails to dry. All the bedding was also hung out to air. The ship looked like a gigantic laundry rack.

Paul had no warning that their new commanding officer was to come aboard that day, and no inkling of what kind of a man he would turn out to be.

Clifford P. Mowrey, who for decades had been known to regular Coast Guard officers as "Mad Mowrey" (a name with which he often introduced himself), arrived at the gate of the shipyard where the *Arluk* lay, in a black Buick convertible driven by a middle-aged grass widow he had met the night before at the Essex House bar. On that surprisingly warm April afternoon he wore his khaki uniform with the two-and-a-half gold stripes of a lieutenant commander on the shoulder boards and four rows of multicolored campaign ribbons on his chest. He was fifty-two years old, with a head that looked sixty and a body that looked thirty. His short gray hair had been dyed an improbable shade of inky black, and what there was of it was carefully combed. He smelled strongly of perfumed hair oil and shaving lotion. He had a big beefy face with the battered red nose of a retired prize-fighter—he had, in fact, once been light heavyweight champion of the navy's China fleet. His false teeth seemed unusually white in his red face and gave him a sharklike, if dazzling, smile. He wore dark glasses. His neck was so short and thick that it hardly existed at all between his massive, high sloping shoulders. He had no pot belly and no waistline—his body was almost a perfect cylinder, but his thighs were still muscular in his tight khaki pants and his legs were unusually long. He wore the cuffs of his trousers tucked into the tops of highly polished brown jackboots. In his right hand he carried a nonregulation overseas cap made of golden sealskin with the Coast Guard insignia attached. He put this on at a rakish angle after kissing his driver good-by. He marched through the gate with the cocky strut of a drill sergeant.

When the sentry saluted and said, "What ship, sir?" he returned the salute with precision, said, "I know where I'm going," and brushed impatiently by. The sentry had been told always to ask for identification, but he didn't dare.

While all this was going on, Paul was standing on a steel gun deck that had just been installed forward of the bridge of the *Arluk*. Four shipyard workers were welding this to some heavy steel cones about four feet high, the pedestals of 20-millimeter antiaircraft guns. The sparks from their torches were shooting into the blankets and clothes drying on the rail and an unruly group of seamen and machinists' mates was loudly objecting. To reply to their accusations, a stout welder took off her mask, revealing a mass of dark red hair. Realizing for the first time that she was a woman, the crew gathered around, giving loud catcalls and whistles. The woman yelled indignantly at them in a high, piercing voice, and amid much laughter a machinist's mate invited her down to the engineroom for activities which, he said, would be much more helpful to the war effort than welding. The woman started to swear, the men began to laugh, and Paul began to yell, "Quiet, silence!" but no one paid the slightest attention to him.

At this moment Mowrey stepped between two blankets that were hanging from a clothesline over the rail, and like an actor stepping through a curtain, jumped to the well deck, his jackboots making a sharp report on the pine decks which was heard above the pandemonium. Everyone turned toward him and there was instant silence. Mowrey stood almost at attention, the sun gleaming on his dark glasses and gold accoutrements. His haughty gaze traveled from the bow, where underpants flapped on the railings, over the motley crew amidships, to the stern, where more

61

shirts and blankets flapped on every rail and line. He said nothing, and his silence, which became more and more tense as it continued for a full minute, was more effective than any disgust he could have voiced. When he finally spoke his voice astonished everyone because it was deceptively calm, even pleasant, and he gave a strange smile, which was somehow both sweet and ominous.

"Is the executive officer aboard?" he asked.

Snapping out of a kind of trance, Paul hurried to him and saluted. "I'm the exec," he said. "Paul Schuman."

Mowrey returned the salute gravely. "I am your new commanding officer. Bring the men to quarters and I shall read my orders."

"Quarters, quarters!" a coxswain started to yell without being asked, and the cry was repeated throughout the ship. Men poured from hatches. They formed three lines on the well deck and they looked like a bunch of pirates, Paul realized suddenly. Because most of their clothes were drying, many of them wore dirty dungarees and no shirts. The knowledge that they were now assigned to the Greenland Patrol had caused many of them to start beards which were new enough to look thoroughly disreputable. They stood uneasily, scratching their arms and blinking into the bright sunlight.

"Attention," Paul said.

The men stiffened into uneven lines. Farmer, who stood in the front row, kept rubbing his chin nervously. At this moment Green walked from the wardroom. He had been studying *Knight's Modern Seamanship* most of the night and had been asleep when he heard the men yelling "quarters." Uncertain of what this meant, he had simply put on his rumpled blue uniform and without bothering to shave, was ambling forward. His tall, stooped, gaunt figure looked the very antithesis of everything military as he leaned against the big winch to watch the strange proceedings. Mowrey stared at him unbelievingly for an instant, but looked away without saying anything. There was another long minute of tense silence.

"At ease!" Mowrey finally barked.

The shoulders of the men slumped a little, but they still looked anything but at ease.

"My name is Clifford P. Mowrey. I shall now read my orders."

Taking a crisp envelope from his coat pocket, Mowrey extracted a piece of paper and read in a deliberate monotone: "To Clifford P. Mowrey, lieutenant commander, United States Coast Guard. From, Commandant U.S. Coast Guard, Washington, D.C. Subject: Order to active duty. Paragraph one: You are herewith ordered to active duty. Paragraph two: You are herewith assigned as commanding officer of U.S. Coast Guard Cutter *Arluk*. You will proceed immediately to District One Headquarters, U. S. Coast Guard, for transportation to that vessel. Immediately upon arrival aboard, you will assume command."

He folded the orders with great deliberation, put them back in the envelope and pocketed it. For perhaps thirty seconds he silently looked up at the sky, like the minister hoping for divine inspiration.

"This morning," he said in his oddly casual, pleasant tone, "I spent about two hours at the district office going over the personnel records of every man aboard this ship. I know everything about every one of you that the Coast Guard knows."

There was another long silence during which he seemed to stare directly into the face of every man present.

"Now some of you already know and you all will soon find out that I am widely known as 'Mad Mowrey.' Don't let that scare you. Actually, I am a very reasonable man. You can be sure, at least, that I know my business. I've been at sea steadily since I was twelve years old, when I went as a cabin boy on a fishing schooner. I've put in twenty years with the navy as a chief boatswain's mate and in the First World War the navy made me a lieutenant. Later I went in the Coast Guard. I know the Arctic as well as any man alive except the Eskimos. You'll be safe with me if you do what I tell you."

There was another long pause.

"If you don't do what I tell you, you won't be safe," he said mildly, and flashed them his sharklike, but curiously charming smile. No one dared to smile back. Mowrey looked at the sky and then his eyes focused on the new steel gun deck. The workers there hastily retreated.

"Now let me tell you a little about Greenland," Mowrey continued pleasantly. "It's not the terrible place you've heard—I'd rather be in Greenland than anywhere in the

63

world. It's God's country and it's a *man*'s country. Though you don't think it, a sailor can have one hell of a good time there, better than anything you can find here."

He paused again.

"But the Arctic is also the most dangerous place for ships in the world, even when the Germans aren't there, which they are—don't make any mistake about that. The Arctic is a great place for sailors who know exactly what they're doing, and a great place for everyone else to die."

This time he paused only a moment before adding, "Now I don't want to die and I don't think you do, not yet anyway. Even old as I am, the thought of dying makes me mad. That's the real reason why they call me 'Mad Mowrey.' And because the thought of dying makes me mad, inefficiency makes me mad, ignorance makes me mad and a lack of discipline makes me mad. A filthy ship makes me mad, it makes me madder than hell."

As he said this, his face suddenly turned truly ferocious. His blunt jaw jutted out and his ice-blue eyes seemed to shoot fire.

"If I took this ship to the Arctic the way she and her crew are now," he continued, "she wouldn't last a month, even if the Germans didn't find her. I don't think you young fellows want to die any more than I do, so don't complain when I whip you into shape. You may think that the Greenland Patrol is the worst thing you can get and that you'll just be transferred if you foul up, but there are worse things I can send you to, like small shore installations in Greenland where even the Eskimos won't go. I'm warning you that I'm looking for an example and I've got just such a shore installation all picked out. The district personnel officer has promised to cooperate with me. If you want a transfer, you'll get it fast. On the other hand, if you cooperate with me, we can make this into a happy ship and a safe one."

His expression turned pleasant again as he continued. "I want to get up to Greenland as fast as possible. We're needed up there—some of those colonies of Eskimos and Danes haven't had supplies all winter. More than that, the first ships up there this spring will get the best assignments. The last will get weather patrol, steaming in a circle in the middle of Davis Straits for thirty days at a time, drawing the subs with steady radio signals. If you want that, delay me."

The men looked scared. They shifted their feet uneasily.

"There's no way I can whip this ship and this crew into shape fast by being a nice guy," Mowrey said quietly, but his face was now stern. "Hate me all you like, but remember that I'm saving your lives. All leaves and liberty are hereby cancelled aboard this ship until further notice. If you work with me, you'll get one, maybe two nights ashore before we sail, if you don't, you'll get none. It's time for learning your jobs, not liberty. That goes for the officers as well as the men, everyone except me. I'm the only one who already knows his business."

There was one last long pause during which he stared stonily at the men before he finally hissed, "Dis-missed!"

Silently the men shuffled toward the forecastle.

"Come with me," Mowrey said to Paul and led the way to the pilothouse. For a moment he stood by the wheel staring at the new gun deck and the gun pedestals. The yard workers reappeared and began to weld ready boxes for ammunition into place. After watching them a moment, Mowrey strolled out on the new steel deck with Paul following and examined the pedestals.

"Is this welding job finished?" he asked a burly workman.

"Yes, sir."

Moving with astonishing speed, Mowrey placed his back against a rail and delivered a vicious kick to the midsection of one of the gun mounts. It came loose and toppled over with a loud clatter.

"I don't want no gun mounts I can kick off," he said mildly.

"Yes, sir. That one hadn't really been inspected yet."

Without reply Mowrey walked back to the pilothouse with Paul following meekly. Standing moodily by the wheel again, Mowrey took a cigar from his breast pocket and lit it. There was another long minute of silence.

"Mr. Schuman, you're a college boy, not a ship's officer," he said suddenly in his curiously pleasant voice.

"Yes, sir."

"I looked at your papers, but I forget. Did you go to Yale or Harvard?"

"Boston University, sir."

"They're all the same to me. You look like a Yale."

Paul said nothing. He was not tempted to laugh.

"So what I get for officers here is a Yale, a Sheenie and

a fisherman who's never been farther north than Georgia Banks and who's too old to learn."

Still Paul said nothing.

"After we sail, I can run this ship alone night and day for maybe a month, but I'm not as young as I used to be, and sooner or later I'll tire. By that time you better be able to stand a watch and handle the men."

"Yes, sir."

"Don't count on Mr. Farmer. There's two kinds of sailors: one goes on local knowledge, and the other goes on the knowledge of how to run a ship anywhere. Fishermen go on local knowledge. Get them out of their own territory, and they ain't much better than lubbers. And no fishermen ever knew how to handle men on a long voyage."

"Yes, sir."

"And we can't count on Greenberg. I don't know how he ever got in the service in the first place."

"His name is Green, I believe, sir. He has no experience at sea but he seems very intelligent to me."

"You ever hear of a Sheenie sailor?"

"Well, none that I can name at the moment. I'm sure there have been many."

"I never seen a Sheenie sailor, except for yeomen and supply officers. Tell Greenberg he's our supply officer, along with communications, and when I give him a list of things I want, I want all of it fast, even if he has to steal it."

"Yes, sir."

"Now Yale, I want you to remember one thing. I've got no hope for Greenberg and no hope for Mr. Farmer, but you I just might be able to shape up. Six months from now I have to send in a fitness report on you. If you've shaped up, I'll make it good enough so you just might get a command of your own inside of a year—in time of war, things move fast. But if you fuck up, I've got a job already picked out for you. You'll be in command of a Quonset hut so far north that they won't even think of looking for you until the war's been over for a year, if they remember you then."

"Yes, sir."

"Now you can start by getting this ship cleaned up. If the men have to dry clothes and bedding, they can rig lines ashore."

"Aye, aye, sir."

"And clean up that stack where the name of the ship is. *Arluk* means hunter—get somebody to paint on a picture of an Eskimo throwing a harpoon. And over the name of the ship I want the Coast Guard motto. Do you know what that is?"

"*Semper Paratus*, always prepared," Paul said with a smile.

"Well, it ain't *semiparatus mañana*, like it looks this ship should have painted up there now. Put up the Coast Guard motto and under that put my *personal* motto in red letters: DON'T FOUL UP HERE."

"Aye, aye, sir!"

"Now, *git!*"

The men jumped to the task of taking in their laundry, but one seaman had been sent ashore for supplies, and his garments continued to flutter from a rail on the forecastle head. Before Paul could have these taken in, the general alarm rang, a Klaxon horn which throbbed with ear-splitting urgency. For the first time Paul heard the shrill call of a boatswain's pipe aboard that ship, followed by the hoarse call, "Fire drill, fire drill!"

There was a disorderly scramble for the hoses which Mowrey watched sardonically from the gun deck. When they finally got pressure and were directing thick jets of water into the bay, he strolled to the well deck, took the nozzle of one hose from the crew and directed it toward the offending bits of laundry on the forecastle rail, sending them spinning into the harbor.

"Secure from fire drill," he said pleasantly.

# CHAPTER 8

Captain Mowrey did not allow any of his officers or men to go ashore that day even to go to a telephone. Instead he arranged to allow each man to make one short call from the telephone on the bridge. To make sure that no military secrets were divulged, he sat on a high stool near the telephone, smoked a cigar and sardonically listened. It was while he was placing his call to his wife that Paul realized that his admiration for Mowrey was mixed with sheer hatred.

"Hello, Sylvia?" Paul said.

"When are you coming home?"

"I can't. Not for weeks maybe."

"Why?"

"I can't explain now and I may not be able to call again for days."

"What's going on?"

"Sylvia, there's a *war* going on—that's just about all I can say."

"Are you mad at me? You sound so angry."

"I'm not mad at *you*! I'll call as soon as I can. Don't worry about me—I'm in no danger at all—"

"I love you," she said.

"I love you more than I ever have in my life," he concluded, and hung up.

"That's nice," Mowrey said, licking the end of his cigar. "That's *sweet*. Now if you want to save your ass for your lover-girl, get it below and put it on a chair. I want a clean copy of a watch, quarter and station bill right now."

As soon as Paul finished one task on that memorable first day under Mowrey's command and tried to steal enough time for a cup of coffee, he heard his captain bellowing from the bridge, "Yale! Yale! Send that bastard Yale up here!"

Green had it easier, because as supply officer he was often sent ashore, but many of the items which Mowrey demanded that he get, such as a standby gyrocompass and full sonar gear, were simply not issued to trawlers. When he reported this to Mowrey he got such a brutal tongue-lashing, all couched in the most vile anti-Semitic language, that his long mournful face went pale, and he developed such a tremor in his fingers that he put his hands in his pockets, which infuriated Mowrey all over again.

"I'll try, I'll try," Green kept saying, and stayed ashore as much as possible, though Mowrey demanded that he spend his nights aboard.

Farmer was the only man on the ship who did not seem in the least affected by Mowrey. He just smiled when the captain called him "that farmer" and went about the ship cheerfully doing the best he could.

Most of the trawler captains ate in the forecastle with the other officers and men, but Mowrey dined alone in his cabin, big ship style. The first night Cookie carried up a tray with a dinner which included a choice steak with mushroom sauce, delicately whipped potatoes, fresh vegetables that he had purloined during a visit to the kitchen of the Ritz-Carlton Hotel and a selection of French pastries which he had made himself. Mowrey was malevolently staring at Cookie's tall chef's hat when he removed the inverted bowl covering his repast. He was, as a matter of fact, on the point of grabbing his nonnautical headgear and pitching it overboard when he realized that he was being served no ordinary Coast Guard meal. After tasting the steak, he reached into a drawer, took out his sealskin overseas cap and put it on his head.

"Cookie, you and I are the only two men aboard this ship who have earned the right to wear nonregulation hats," he said.

"Yes, sir," Cookie replied. "I work hard all day to fix food like this, and chefs are generally allowed to go ashore every night, while we're in port, of course. Is that all right with you, sir?"

"Cookie, as long as we all get food like this, you can go ashore whenever you want, but if the quality of the grub falls off, you're restricted."

"Yes, sir!"

Cookie tried the first salute of his life and hurried happily back to his galley.

Mowrey disapproved of the watch, quarter and station bill that Paul drew up and demanded that it be corrected that very night. Paul had no idea how late it was when he finally fell into his bunk, too exhausted even to commiserate with Green, who lay in his bunk, staring up as though he were a corpse. Farmer was already asleep, snoring contentedly.

A little before three in the morning, the three officers were awakened by the howl of the general alarm and the shriek of the boatswain's pipe, which was followed by "Collision Drill, Collision Drill!"

"Oh *my!*" Farmer said, sitting up and rubbing his eyes.

"The bastard, the bastard, the bastard!" Paul said, putting on his trousers.

Green said nothing, but his lips moved a lot.

On deck Paul found complete confusion while half-dressed men dragged a heavy collision mat from the hold. The weather had turned cold again, and a light rain was falling. Wearing a parka, Mowrey stood on the wing of the bridge with a glass in his hand. He was smiling happily. On the wing of the *Nanmak*'s bridge the young lieutenant with the broad freckled face was also watching, and also smiling. A young machinist's mate who had got his hand caught in a watertight door came on deck holding it against his chest and whimpering. Green took him below.

"If this were a real collision, I figure we'd be about a hundred fathoms down by now," Mowrey said. "Speed it up, girls! This is the big game!"

A week went by with more drills at every hour of the day and night. When the 20-millimeter guns arrived, Mowrey expressed amazement that Paul did not know how to assemble them and ordered him to learn immediately. While Paul was working with guns, and some men from the yard on the complex mechanisms, he noticed that Mowrey was standing on a wing of the bridge blinking a signal light on him.

"Did you want something, sir?" he asked, wiping some grease from his face.

Mowrey said nothing but the light continued to blink. Getting the idea at last, Paul said, "I'm sorry, sir, but I can't read blinker lights yet."

"I can see that," Mowrey said pleasantly. "If you could read what I just called you, you'd be after me with a monkey wrench. I want you and Greenberg to practice blinker lights at least an hour a day."

"Aye, aye, sir," Paul said, and bent over the jigsaw puzzle of the guns again.

It wasn't the work, the exhaustion, nor even the fact that he was not allowed to go ashore long enough to telephone his wife that bothered Paul. It was not even the necessity of working harder than he ever had known he could without the slightest hope of praise or relief from criticism that tormented him. The worst part of the ordeal was the growing conviction that he could never please Mowrey, that he could never change himself from a college boy to a skilled Coast Guard officer in a few weeks, months or even years. One thing he learned quickly was that there was nothing of the fake about Mowrey. His contempt for his officers and men was not feigned for a purpose and his promise to arrange horrible assignments for those who failed to shape up was probably no idle threat. Paul became obsessed with the fear of being assigned to some tiny weather station or supply depot deep within the Arctic Circle, where he might be left for however many years the war lasted.

Sometimes when he was too tired to sleep, Paul lay in his bunk planning how he might explain to Mowrey that it really was not his fault that he had been a college boy, not an old Greenland hand, when the war started, and that he was really working as hard as any man could to make up for his lamentable deficiencies. This sounded reasonable, but he realized with shock that Mowrey was not susceptible to this kind of logic. The truth was, he suspected, that Mowrey hated him for reasons which had little to do with his inefficiencies. The classic, justified anger which a mustang who had taken twenty years to earn a commission felt for a reserve officer who had won his almost overnight was undoubtedly a large part of it. If Mowrey, as he said, had started his career as a fisherman's cabin boy, he might have developed a healthy or unhealthy hatred for anyone, especially a college boy, who appeared to be rich, "upper-class," and soft while mysteriously being given most of life's luxuries without effort. If Mowrey felt this way, he might really enjoy torturing his "Yale" for a few months before finally crushing him with the worst, most humiliating assignment he could devise.

Perhaps I'm going paranoiac, Paul thought, but there was at least a horrifying possibility that this dark diagnosis of his situation was right.

Paul's confusion was increased by the fact that he continued to admire Mowrey as much as he hated him. There was no doubt whatsoever that the man was fast turning the *Arluk* from a shambles into an efficient Coast Guard cutter. Mowrey was much easier on the enlisted men than on his officers and most of them clearly respected, almost loved him. They worked hard and cheerfully for him, and as a reward, many of them were already being allowed regular liberty ashore.

Perhaps he was just being ridiculously oversensitive, Paul told himself. Farmer, after all, endured his share of insults without apparent resentment, and though Green looked tormented, he grimly tried to do his duty without a

71

word of complaint. In a way Paul almost envied Green, because he could rightfully blame Mowrey's crazy anti-Semitism rather than his own weaknesses for most of the abuse he got. If Green were transferred with a bad fitness report, anyone who thought about it would know that almost no Jew could get along with Mad Mowrey, and Green would not have to spend the rest of his life questioning himself.

The hell with it, Paul always concluded. As Sherman said, war is hell, but I didn't understand that this is true even when we're thousands of miles away from any foreign enemy.

About ten days after Mowrey came aboard he made such a complete ass of himself that for once Paul did not have to wonder who was right and who was wrong. Immediately after dinner that memorable night, Mowrey got all dressed up in his best blue uniform and went ashore, presumably for the night, as he usually did, but on this occasion he returned shortly before midnight. To the astonishment of the quartermaster on duty, he had a woman with him, a buxom blonde in a bright green coat. "Tell Yale I want to see him," he said and went to his cabin with his friend.

"Captain wants you," the quartermaster said, shaking Paul awake, and slyly added, "You're going to get a little surprise."

Paul was indeed astonished to see Mowrey pouring a scotch for a blonde who was sitting on his bunk in the sacrosanct commanding officer's cabin.

"You wanted me, sir?" he said, trying to keep his face expressionless.

"Yale, I want you to meet Helen here. Helen, this is my Yale, a good boy if I can whip him into shape."

Helen giggled and said, "Pleased."

"Pleased," Paul said.

"Yale, I want you to rouse up Cookie. Tell him we want scrambled eggs, sausages and coffee."

"Aye, aye, sir."

"Then I want you to go to the bar across the street. Bring me four bottles of cold beer and a pack of cigarettes. What kind do you want, dearie?"

"Luckies."

"She wants Luckies." Taking out his wallet, Mowrey gave him a five-dollar bill.

72

"Is that all, sir?"

"Hurry it up. I want the beer."

"Aye, aye, sir."

Cookie cursed in German when Paul awoke him, but suddenly cheered up when he learned that he was to get food for the captain.

"Right away, right away," he said, and began to get dressed.

Paul hurried to the bar, suddenly jubilant at the thought that he would at least get a chance to telephone his wife.

"Paul!" she said sleepily after the telephone had rung several times, "Where are you? Where have you been?"

"I'm still in Boston," he said, and suddenly poured out his whole story, ending with his present errand.

"Oh, Paul!" she kept exclaiming. "I'm so sorry. What can we *do?*"

"We can't do anything, but I had to tell you. Damn it, now I've made you worry."

"I was even more worried, not knowing what was happening. Look, if he has his girl down there, why can't I come aboard?"

"I'm not an ice pilot," he said wearily. "They'd crucify me. I wouldn't bring you aboard that ship for anything anyhow."

"Paul, I've got to see you soon somehow. I've never wanted you so much. When I think of all the times I said no to you, I want to shoot myself. I'll never say no again."

"That's a dangerous promise. Look, I'll see you tomorrow or next day. I'll tell him it's a family emergency."

"You won't be lying!"

After hanging up, Paul ordered a double scotch for himself. He was damned if he was going to hurry back with the bastard's beer, he thought at first, but reflected that he better please him now if he wanted to wangle some leave the next day.

When Paul got back to the ship with the beer and the cigarettes, Mowrey was waiting for him on the gun deck. He had a glass of whiskey in his hand and was by now obviously drunk.

"Yale, where the hell have you been?" he bellowed.

"I came as fast as I could."

"The hell you did—you were hanging around that bar for half an hour!"

As Paul stepped to the well deck of the *Arluk*, he saw

that Hansen, the captain of the *Nanmak*, was standing by his rail listening and watching. Hansen gave him a weary smile, shrugged and spread out his hands in a gesture of helplessness. For this support Paul was intensely grateful.

Paul gave Mowrey the beer, the cigarettes, and his change.

"Anything else, sir?" he asked.

"That's all for tonight, Yale!" Mowrey said thickly. "For once you did your duty. Get the ship cleaned up early tomorrow morning. We're going out to compensate the compasses."

That meant another day would go by before he could see his wife. Paul walked wearily to the wardroom. There he found Green sitting at the table, looking as dejected as they both felt.

"He had me up to his cabin too," Green said.

"Why?"

"He wanted music. That comes under my responsibilities as communications officer."

"What did you do?"

"I gave him music. We have a portable loudspeaker."

There was a pause while Green lit a cigarette. "I'm worried," he said at last.

"Well, he may be a crazy bastard, but he said he'll keep us alive and I bet he will, if any of us really want to live after a few months of this."

"The question is whether he can keep himself alive," Green said. "I'm serious."

"What do you mean?"

"Can't you see it?"

"See what?"

"If Captain Mowrey were just a terrible bastard who was also good at his job, we could stand it. The trouble is that he's also an alcoholic. I don't know how long we'll be able to count on him."

"Oh, hell, he's probably been drinking all his life like that, but he's always done his job well, everybody says."

"Alcoholism is a progressive disease. Haven't you ever heard that?"

"How does it apply to him?"

"I'm no doctor, but my father is. I've seen plenty of alcoholics in my time and I know the symptoms. Indoors and out Mowrey always wears dark glasses. The capillaries in the skin of his face have burst. He's got a sun lamp which he uses to try to cover that up. I saw it in his cabin. His nose should also give you a message. And his smell."

"He smells mostly of shaving lotion."

"Alcoholics often use a lot of that."

"What do you think will happen?"

Green shrugged. "It's hard to tell. He may hold together for a long time, or he could just collapse in any number of ways. Watch out for him if he runs out of booze in a place where we can't get any more."

"Jesus," Paul said. "We've got the Arctic to look forward to, the Germans and a drunken skipper!"

"I keep telling myself that we're lucky compared to plenty of people in Europe," Green said. "That's the truth of it, after all. I hope I didn't get you all upset. I just had to talk it over with someone."

# CHAPTER 9

The blonde went ashore at a little before five in the morning. To Paul's astonishment, Mowrey came to the forecastle for breakfast at seven. Except for the fact that his hand shook on his coffee cup, he showed no sign of wear.

"We're going to get this bucket under way for a few hours at least today," he said to Paul cheerfully. "The compass adjuster is due at nine. You can call the men to mooring stations as soon as he comes aboard."

As they pulled away from the wharf and maneuvered through the crowded harbor, Paul admired the ease with which Mowrey handled the heavy trawler. A drunk he might be and a bastard he certainly was, but how long would it be before Paul could equal his skill?

The compasses needed a lot of adjustment, and it was late in the afternoon when they returned to their wharf. Mowrey immediately went ashore and Paul did not get a chance to ask him for a few hours of leave that night. He was disconsolately standing on the gun deck watching the sun go down over the harbor when Hansen came out on the wing of his bridge. "Mr. Schuman, it's a nice evening, isn't it?"

"It sure is."

"Would you care to come over and have another drink with me?"

Paul eagerly agreed. Hansen was so different from Mowrey that he found it difficult to believe that both were old Greenland hands, both ice pilots. The Dane had added a painting to the bulkhead of his elegant cabin. It showed a glacier, a river of silvery ice flowing to a black sea between tall mountains of rust-colored rock that had been molded so smoothly by the wind that they almost resembled flesh.

"My wife painted that some years ago," he said. "It catches a lot of the feeling of Greenland, I think. Will you have Aquavit or scotch this time?"

"Aquavit."

"Good. We'll make a real Greenlander of you yet—that's what most of us drink up there. Here's to good luck to both of us. I guess we'll need it."

They drank. Hansen had peculiarly large, dark eyes. He seemed a very gentle man. In all the days of lying alongside his ship, Paul had never heard him raise his voice, but no one ever questioned the fact that he ran an efficient ship. Apparently there was more than one way of handling a crew.

"I've been having a little difficulty with my executive officer," Hansen said, leaning comfortably back in his bunk while Paul sat on the stool in front of the chart table. "He's a good man, but these academy fellows think that a trawler is just about the worst possible assignment and most of them don't fit in. I think he wants to get just about a month of ice experience on his record. Then he'll be requesting a transfer."

"Who will you get to replace him?" Paul asked, his heart beginning to beat faster.

"That gives us something to think about. I see you working day and night over there for my old friend Cliff Mowrey, but he's kind of difficult to please sometimes. He has the reputation for changing officers a lot. I wouldn't want to try to steal a good officer from him, but if you should want or need a transfer, perhaps some of my friends in the personnel office could work something out. Good execs are mighty hard to find these days."

Paul's jubilation and relief knew no bounds. He had, indirectly at least, been called a good officer by an ice pilot! He was not just a miserably incompetent college boy!

"Captain Hansen, I can't tell you how much this means to me," he said, his voice absurdly eager.

"Now wait a minute. There's a lot to think about. I've come to understand a lot more about our probable assignments in the last few days. Cliff has been yelling to get ballast for his ship and they won't give it to him. I on the other hand loaded ten tons of lead today without even asking for it. Does that mean anything to you?"

"They want him to carry heavy cargo and they want you to do something else," Paul said after a moment of thought.

"Right! You catch on fast. That fits in with a lot of things. Cliff knows the west coast of Greenland as well as anyone. That's where they have most of the settlements and installations which have to be supplied. I on the other hand probably know more about the east coast than anyone they've got."

"And that's where the Germans probably are."

"Right. When they started loading me with ballast, I thought at first that they might be intending to send me on weather patrol, but they don't really need ice ships for that. Today I received some quite extraordinary information which makes me think different. It's so secret I don't want to burden you with it. Suffice it to say that I'm going to get some special equipment which makes me think I'm going to be chasing German weather ships or ships trying to build weather stations ashore. You must consider even that top secret."

"What happens if you catch a German? Are they giving you bigger guns?"

"You can answer that yourself. These ships won't take bigger armament. More than that I shouldn't say, except I don't regard this as a suicide mission. Dangerous, of course, but by no means hopeless."

"I see."

"Of course I know I haven't made everything exactly clear. I'm not supposed to tell anyone this much, but I wanted you to have enough information to make a decision if the question of a transfer comes up for you."

"How soon would you want me if all this works out?"

"About a month after we get to Greenland. These academy men like to get a few weeks of ice experience in their record."

"Captain Hansen, from my own point of view, I can't think of anything in the world I'd want more than to be on your ship."

"Think about it," Hansen said. "The *Arluk* is going to have much better duty, more interesting and less dangerous. I can't promise you all those Eskimo dances and Danish dinners. You don't know how they celebrate the arrival of a supply ship!"

"I'd like to find out, but, I guess it's no secret—Captain Mowrey doesn't seem exactly pleased with me. Will I be disloyal if I say he's not an easy man to serve under?"

"Perhaps, but that won't exactly be news along the waterfront. Turn all this over in your mind. We'll talk it over when we get to Greenland."

The sense of hopelessness which had been filling Paul for days disappeared entirely. He was eager to tell Sylvia that the captain of another cutter, an ice pilot, actually wanted him on his ship, but realized suddenly that this subject should not, could not be discussed with his wife. What was the choice, really? Wasn't it between a safe, interesting job with a crazy skipper he hated, or a dangerous job with a sane captain he liked very much? He knew very well what advice Sylvia would give him, and the thought of a powerful German ship looming out of the fog with her guns all zeroed in on him made him wonder what he really wanted for himself. At any rate he would have many weeks to make his choice. The wonderful thing was that it seemed he had an escape from Mowrey ready if he needed one.

Two days later the *Nanmak* left the yard for Norfolk, Virginia, where she was to be fitted with special equipment before sailing north. A week after that the *Arluk* got orders to start for Greenland the following Thursday, April 30. Paul was so involved in the frantic last-minute preparations, and Mowrey continued to discipline him so severely that he got only one night ashore to see his wife, a fact which made Chris shake his head in dismayed disbelief.

That one last night with Sylvia under the eaves of the old colonial house was wonderful, of course, and also so troubling in many ways that Paul simply could not allow himself to think of it now. He was so tired and so keyed up

78

when he came to Sylvia that their love-making was nothing like the fantasies both of them had had. She too was tense and full of a strange sense of failure. The truth was that they spent part of their last night crying in each other's arms like heartbroken children, but there had been more to it than that, and Paul simply could not allow himself to dwell on this joyful, painful meeting and parting at a time when his head was full of dozens of lists of things he had to do immediately to get the ship ready to sail. As he told Sylvia when he kissed her good-by, the only thing they should remember was that they loved each other and that there certainly was no doubt about that. If a night of passion at a time of crisis was not always what it was cracked up to be, that was nobody's fault at all, he told himself, but he was afraid to say that to her. Instead he told her that he loved her so many times that it began to sound ridiculous and added that she was the most beautiful girl in the world and was getting prettier all the time. Just before he left she said, "Paul—I guess I should ask you for the registration of the car. I never get stopped, but you can't tell."

He took the paper from his wallet and handed it to her. "Be careful," he said. "Be careful! Take care of yourself." Then he ran.

# CHAPTER 10

The *Arluk* sailed from the shipyard at seven in the morning. It was a rainy, windy day, cold for spring, but nowhere near as cold as it soon was going to be, Paul reminded himself as he buttoned his parka under his throat. The departure from the wharf was as undramatic as it could possibly be. Two bored yard workers cast off their lines and hurried back into the warmth of the sheds without a wave or a backward glance. Mowrey gave three short blasts of the ship's surprisingly high, unauthoritative air whistle as he backed into the harbor. The seamen who were not on watch hurried below to get coffee as soon as they had stowed the lines.

While Mowrey conned the ship, Paul stood on the starboard wing of the bridge watching the familiar coastline and islands of Boston harbor slip by. How many times had he sailed out of this harbor aboard the *Valkyrie?* It occurred to him that this voyage might end disastrously for him and that he might never see Boston or the U.S. again. This thought seemed absurdly melodramatic and he dismissed it.

"Yale, tell Cookie to bring me a cup of coffee," Mowrey said.

Paul relayed the message to the forecastle by telephone. When Cookie appeared with the coffee, Mowrey ducked into his cabin and shut the door. When he reappeared a moment later, the smell of whiskey rose from the coffee cup, almost as visible as the steam.

The bay was relatively calm, but soon after they left the lightship, they encountered big swells rolling in on their starboard beam from the broad Atlantic and the trawler began to roll. First a pair of binoculars slipped from a shelf in the bridge where Paul had carelessly left them.

"Don't you know that ships roll, Yale?" Mowrey asked.

Next Mowrey noticed that some big reels of cable which were part of their deck cargo had not been lashed in place securely enough and were starting to move.

"Get Farmer and secure that damn stuff before it carries away," Mowrey said. "What's the matter with you people? Can't you do anything right the first time?"

By the time the reels of cable were secured, the ship was rolling with greater violence than the old *Valkyrie*, with her deep keel and sails, had ever rolled. Cookie suddenly appeared in the forecastle door and shouted, "Mr. Schuman, everything's going crazy down here!"

Everything was. A dozen young seamen lay moaning in their bunks and one had vomited all over the deck. Cookie had never been to sea, and had had no idea of how to stow the galley. Paul realized that he should have foreseen this. Now pots, pans, broken dishes and open cannisters of flour, sugar and rice pursued each other back and forth across the galley deck. Astonishingly, Cookie was not in the least seasick. He was just furious.

"Get me some men to clean this up!" he shouted to Paul. "Such a mess is no job for a chef!"

Paul appointed three men who didn't look too seasick to the cleaning detail. Trying to help with the drums of wire cable had left his hands cold and he hurried aft to the wardroom to get gloves. Green was sitting on the edge of his bunk vomiting into a bucket. Books and boxes of writing paper which disgorged their contents were sliding back and forth on the cabin sole. The smell of sickness was strong.

"Where did you get the bucket?" Paul gasped and before Green could answer, dashed for the head. He had never been seasick aboard the old yawl, but he felt as though the convulsions of his stomach would never stop now. Seeing a bucket behind the head, he grabbed it and staggered toward his bunk. The wardroom telephone rang before he could sit down.

"Yale, is that you? Come up to the bridge! I didn't tell you to lay below, did I?"

Carrying the bucket with the handle hooked around his arm, Paul walked toward the bridge. As he climbed up the steps to it, he had to pause, clutch the railing as the ship gave a particularly vicious roll, and retch into the bucket again.

"What have you got that bucket for, Yale?" Mowrey asked pleasantly as Paul entered the pilothouse. He was holding his cup of whiskied coffee in one hand and a cigar in the other. The tobacco smoke, the fumes of booze and the odor from another bucket in which the helmsman had been sick were overpowering. Paul retched into his bucket again.

"I don't mind anybody being seasick as long as he don't miss any duty," Mowrey said with a great show of tolerance. "By the time you get to Greenland, you'll either be over it or near to dying. Some go one way, some the other."

Sipping from his cup, he smacked his lips and took a puff from his cigar. "The best cure for seasickness, I find, is a glass of warm gin with a cunt hair in it. Too bad we don't have the ingredients handy."

Both the helmsman and Paul retched into their buckets simultaneously. Glancing toward the sky, Mowrey cleared his throat and sang, "Roll, baby, roll, roll, baby, roll. You never can roll too much for me."

"Did you ever hear that song?" he asked Paul.

"No."

"They used to sing that on the vessels when I was a kid. Man, do you realize that Greenland is right up there over our bows? If the weather holds we'll be there in a couple of weeks. I can just smell them Eskie girls now." Looking up, he began to sing again: "Them Eskie girls don't take no baths and they wash their hair in piss, but they have a way of loving that no man ought to miss."

"Did you ever hear *that* song?" he asked Paul.

"No!" Paul said and retched into his bucket again.

"They used to sing it on the vessels when I was a kid. Man how I used to love to go to Greenland when I was a young feller like you. I could do it justice then. Man, I remember the first Eskie girl I ever had. She'd never seen a white man and she was so *de*lighted with what I had that she called her mother in to see it, and damned if she didn't call *her* mother. The daughter, the mother and the grandmother all just had to try me."

Paul was sick again.

"Now don't get the wrong idea. Them Eskies ain't whores. They're just the most *natural* people on earth. They're little bitty women and they do love a big white man."

"Do their men mind, sir?" the helmsman asked.

"The men don't mind a bit! There's no such thing as jealousy in an Eskie. They know that there's always enough ping-ping to go around. You know what ping-ping is, Yale?"

"I can guess."

"You guess right. You just ask for ping-ping and nobody's going to be mad at you, unless you're near some big settlement where the damn Christers have ruined everything."

"Boy!" the helmsman said.

"Why, I can take you to places where the women will knock you down trying to get to you first. They're always afraid of inbreeding up there. That's why they love a stranger so."

"When will we get to that part of Greenland?" the helmsman asked.

"That depends on our assignment, boy, but you can be sure of one thing: we're going *north* and that's the right direction. We're going to God's country, *man's* country, ping-ping land! We're going where the summer is just one three-month day. We'll run out of night before long. Do you realize that, Yale?"

"I've never seen it."

"I'll show you polar bears that weigh a full ton and men who can kill them without a gun."

"How?" the helmsman asked.

"You'll see. They got more than one way. I'll show you sheep that eat fish. I'll take you on a dog-sled race that will make any horse race look tame."

"It sounds fascinating," Paul said, swallowing in an attempt to contain his nausea.

"And you'll eat like you never ate before. Reindeer steak! Bear paw! Ptarmigan, Arctic shrimp and seal liver! You ever ate salmon and cod raw? The Eskies think the best part of a fish is the eyes and they're right!"

This time Paul and the helmsman both retched so hard that they couldn't hear what their captain was saying. Mowrey took the chewed butt of his cigar from his mouth and licked the tobacco leaves into place.

"Curl your toes up when you get sick that bad," he said. "That way you won't spit your guts up."

"Thank you," Paul said.

"Yale, you may not think it now," Mowrey continued with a chuckle, "but if you're any kind of a man at all, you'll love Greenland. After you've had an Eskie girl, all the others seem half dead. Once I get you up to Greenland, you'll never want to go home again."

# Part II

# CHAPTER 11

The first three days that the *Arluk* was at sea, Paul was so seasick that his mind worked hardly at all. He had plenty of company. Nathan Green was soon so weak that he barely had the strength to cling to a rail during his watches and stagger to his bunk below, where he lay clutching his bucket as a drowning man might hug a life preserver. The only enlisted men who were not seasick as the unballasted trawler with her heavy top load of guns rolled in a steady easterly gale, was the collection of old Coast Guard reprobates who had been sent from the Boston brigs to the Greenland Patrol as an example to other incorrigibles. The spectacle of all the nice people proving to be helpless while the foul-mouthed bums boisterously took charge suddenly seemed to Paul to be the essence of war. The only capable sailor who also appeared to Paul to be a halfway decent human being was the old fisherman, Seth Farmer, whose strongest expletive was, "Oh, *my!*" but who remained as cheerfully healthy aboard the violently rolling trawler as though he were standing on the rockbound coast of Maine.

At eleven o'clock in the morning when they were four days out of Boston, Sparks received a coded message from "Commander, GreenPat" to the *Arluk*. He typed it on yellow paper, clipped it with a carbon copy to a board and carried it to Nathan, who was still lying in his bunk hugging his shiny galvanized bucket. With a groan Green untangled his lank frame from his blankets, extricated himself from the bunk, and staggered to the table, where a sudden lurch of the ship almost threw him before he grabbed one of the chairs that had been bolted down, and eased himself on to it. Dully he stared at the message which the radioman handed to him. It began, "XWLV YQOP NVEO RPOQ" and went on like that for five lines. Feeling that it appeared about as sensible as everything else that was happening to him, Nathan initialed the carbon, gave it back to the radioman, and staggered to the door of a safe which had been built into the bulkhead. Before he could get the combination out of his wallet while holding the clipboard under his right arm, the rolling of the ship threw him against his bunk, where he bruised his knee but hardly noticed it as he grabbed for the bucket he had left in his blankets and used it.

"Can I help?" Farmer asked from his bunk, putting down a well-thumbed copy of *The Saturday Evening Post*.

At that moment Nathan was willing to accept almost any help, but he had been severely warned by Mowrey that only a commissioned officer, not a warrant officer, was entitled to handle codes.

"The only fucking thing your commission makes you good for is paperwork," Mowrey had said, "so don't load it off on nobody else."

"I can get it," Nathan gasped, propped his bucket into a corner of his bunk with a pillow and returned to the safe. An hour-long lecture in communications which had been his sole training as an officer had taught him to use a strip board with numbers and letters which looked like a child's game. Clinging to a chair with his long legs, he hunched over this board, pushing the paper strips back and forth with the eraser of a pencil. No matter what he did, nothing made any sense, but when he finally realized that he was using the wrong cypher, he found himself spelling out the following message on his board:

Your orders to proceed directly to Narsarssuak Fjord hereby canceled. Proceed immediately by most direct course to Argentia, Newfoundland, there to await orders to join convoy for Greenland.
                                    Commander GreenPat.

Proud of decoding his first message, Green started toward the bridge without bothering to have it typed. As he staggered up the steps to the pilothouse, he saw Paul white-faced and clinging in an apparently fond embrace with one of the 20-millimeter antiaircraft guns on the gun deck. The two men exchanged grins of desperation as Nathan grabbed the rail of the bridge and retched over the side before opening the door to the pilothouse. He found Mowrey sitting on a stool near the wheel smoking an extremely foul briar pipe, which made gurgling noises.

"Greenberg, what the fuck do you want up here?" Mowrey demanded.

"I have just decoded a radio message for you, sir," Nathan said and handed the clipboard to the captain before grabbing the engine room telegraph to prevent himself from being thrown to the deck by the lurching vessel. Guns, the burly telephone-booth lover, grinned, took a piece of chewing tobacco from his pocket, and bit a piece off with brown teeth.

"Now what the fuck is this?" Mowrey said as he accepted the board. After glancing at it, he crumpled the paper in his fist, hurled it to the deck and exploded.

"I bet that bastard Hansen did this! I knew he wouldn't let me get up there first! He's been up there sucking ass at Headquarters, and now he's going to have me sitting with my thumb up my ass at Argentia until it's time for all the real shit jobs to be handed out. Well, I won't stand for it. Did Sparks acknowledge receipt of this fucking thing?"

"I believe so, sir. I mean, that would be normal radio procedure—"

"You're supposed to be communications officer aboard here, and you tell that son of a bitch not to acknowledge receipt of *any* message until you decode it and I see what it is. Just keep them repeating it until you figure it out. Now, goddamn it, you've got me trapped. God knows how long we'll sit in Argentia while that bastard Hansen waltzes up there ahead of us and grabs off all the supply runs. I should have punched that bastard's head in while I had the chance. Christ, I've known that slippery queer for years and I should have known he'd figure out a way to shaft me up the ass one way or another!"

Mowrey walked to the door of the pilothouse, opened it and sent the offending clipboard sailing into the sea. Then he went into his cabin, quickly drew a course on a chart with his black parallel rules, and bawled to the helmsman, "Come left slowly to two eight eight, goddamn your eyes."

"I am coming left slowly to two eight eight," Guns replied cheerfully.

"Greenberg!" Mowrey yelled as Nathan tried to duck out the door of the pilothouse.

"Yes sir?"

"If we get our ass sent to the fucking east coast of Greenland looking for fucking Kraut battleships, or out on weather patrol as sub bait, maybe you'll get smart enough not to acknowledge any messages before we know what the fuck they are. Jesus, I thought you Sheenies were at least smart enough to cover your own ass."

"I'm sorry, sir."

"Get the hell out of here! Sweet Jesus, how can I fight a war with nothing but a Sheenie and a Yale for officers? At least don't stand there and make me look at you! I don't have any officers at all aboard this ship. All I've got is a fucking bucket brigade!"

Scuttling below as fast as possible, Nathan used his bucket again before sinking exhausted into his bunk. Gradually he realized that Newfoundland must be much closer than Greenland and that soon the violent motion of the ship might stop for a few days at least. Regardless of what terrors the delay might bring them, the prospect of even a few hours of relief seemed to him to be an unexpected chance to escape a disease which seemed worse than death.

The shore of Newfoundland was completely hidden in banks of fog, which soon made it difficult for the men on the bridge to see even the snub-nosed three-inch gun on the bow of the ship. They knew they had entered the broad, funnel-shaped mouth of Placentia Bay only when the hideous rolling of the ship gradually began to ease. Paul, who had always anchored as soon as possible when fog interrupted his cruises aboard the *Valkyrie*, watched Mowrey with admiration as the old sailor sat watching the flashing light on the dial of the fathometer and confidently gave the helmsman changes in course. What, he wondered, would he do if he suddenly found himself in command? Afraid of blundering onto invisible rocks, would he anchor here where the pilotbook said that fog often continued for weeks or even throughout the spring and summer months?

As the bay narrowed and the water shoaled, even Mowrey appeared tense as he stood on the port wing of the bridge staring through the fog into nothingness. Once he called for the engine to be stopped and they glided silently through a slight groundswell. Paul heard nothing but the lonely cries of invisible sea gulls, but Mowrey said, "I hear breakers about a mile to port. Bring her right slowly. Ahead slow."

About twenty minutes later Paul heard a terrifying high hum in the void ahead which rapidly built to the throbbing of huge engines and the rush of water.

"Something on the starboard bow!" the lookout yelled.

"Left full rudder," Mowrey said. "Ahead full. The bastard won't hit us anyway. If he's going that fast in this shit, he's got radar."

Almost as soon as he had spoken, the bow of a destroyer loomed from the fog ahead, and suddenly the long, low hull of the powerful ship was only three hundred yards abeam of them. Near the top of her short mast a screen which looked like wire mesh slowly revolved.

"He's got radar all right," Mowrey said. "You'd think they'd give it to the Greenland Patrol, but before we get it, every admiral's barge will have a set, even in the goddamn South Pacific, where they never get fog. The Coast Guard is part of the navy in time of war until it comes time for getting the new stuff."

"The radar they have in production is still pretty primitive," Green said. Now that the ship was no longer rolling heavily, he already sounded and looked like a new man.

"What do you know about radar?" Mowrey barked.

"I helped a little with some of the R and D at General Electric."

"Then I don't wonder that they say that the thing never works once you get to sea," Mowrey said. "Come right to course three two zero, damn it. Ahead half. And lookouts, keep your eyes peeled! If you don't have radar, you got to have eyes, ears and brains. No wonder they give it to the navy. That's the only way those poor bastards can find their way around."

As they reached the narrow end of the bay, they suddenly emerged from the banks of fog, finding themselves surrounded by a stern landscape of rocky cliffs and granite hills which rolled back from the sea, not much different in shape from huge ocean waves. Ahead of them loomed the great naval base of Argentia, a collection of perhaps a hundred great gray ships of all kinds, both merchant and navy, anchored and moored to wharves which spread out from a city of Quonset huts and hastily erected warehouses. A blinker light on a steel tower by the edge of the harbor flashed at them.

"Captain, he wants our identification," Flags, a blond young signalman called from the port wing of the bridge.

"What does he think we are, a fucking submarine?" Mowrey replied. "Tell him we're the U-2 out of Hamburg, Germany. Tell him we're looking for his biggest aircraft carrier."

"Do you really want me to say that, sir?"

"Christ, just send him identification signals and request berthing instructions. Sooner or later you bastards are going to have to learn to shit without asking me how to wipe your ass."

The lights flickered for what seemed to be a long while before Flags said, "Proceed to small ship wharf and moor outboard minesweeper *Redbird*."

The *Redbird* proved to be a trawler much like the *Arluk*, except that she was navy, not Coast Guard, and was painted gray. She was moored at the end of a narrow slip between a refrigerator barge as big as a warehouse and a nest of Canadian corvettes. The confined space and an outgoing tidal current which swept through the harbor like a fast river made ordinary maneuvering impossible.

"Put three big fenders on the port bow and get the number two line out fast when I give the word," Mowrey called in the curiously pleasant voice he used when he wanted really instant obedience.

"Aye, aye, sir," Boats, a red-headed boatswain's mate who had boarded the ship just before it left Boston, answered and began coiling a heaving line in his hands.

To avoid losing control of his ship in the swift current, Mowrey approached the stern of the *Redbird* at a speed which struck Paul as incredibly reckless. Seeing the *Arluk* approach at such close quarters with a bone in her teeth, an ensign aboard the *Redbird* gave a shout of alarm which brought a dozen startled men to her rail.

"Mind the helm now," Mowrey said in an even more pleasant voice as the bow of the 300-ton trawler seemed about to crash into the minesweeper. "Right full rudder." After a pause that seemed endless as the bow of the *Arluk* swept across the length of the *Redbird* with almost no space to spare, he added, "Stop the engine. Back full. Get out number two. Shift your rudder."

The *Arluk* suddenly squatted, spun and settled gently against the minesweeper with almost a sigh of content.

"Get out lines four, one and three," Mowrey said. "Stop the engine. Move lively now, lads. In a current like this, you have to get lines out fast."

The Coast Guardsmen on the bow and well deck moved like a well-drilled football team, but one of the navy men was slow to make a line fast to a bitt.

"Boats, go aboard that bird and show that lad how to make a line fast," Mowrey said with genial tolerance.

"We've got it," the ensign aboard the *Redbird* said. "Jesus, for a while there, skipper, I thought you were going to cut us right in half."

"You can't move a ship slow in fast water, sonny," Mowrey said. "Yale, come here. Get Flags."

"Aye, aye, sir," Paul said.

Mowrey led the way from the wing of the bridge into the pilothouse.

"Now you two fucked up once and I'm going to tell you once," he said in his sweetest voice.

"What did we do, sir?" Flags asked.

"I suppose you don't know either, do you, Yale?"

"I thought everyone did fine, sir. I thought it was a great job of tying up."

"Yale, this is a United States Coast Guard cutter tying up alongside a navy ship in a naval base. What the fuck was the matter with our flag?"

"Flag, sir?" Flags asked.

"A United States Coast Guard cutter flies her ensign at the gaff of her signal mast while under way, and at her stern staff while moored. The moment our first mooring line is made fast, I want the ensign snapped down from our signal mast and another ensign snapped up on our stern staff *simultaneously*."

"Aye, aye, sir," Flags said.

"Another thing. Flags, do you know what the third repeater is?"

"It's a pennant we put up when you go ashore, sir, to show that the commanding officer is not aboard."

"You got it, Flags," Mowrey purred. "Now, I want that third repeater snapped up the moment my foot leaves this vessel when I go ashore, and I want it snapped down the moment my first foot touches the deck again when I come back. Do you understand?"

"Aye, aye, sir."

"Just by watching a vessel's flags every man in the harbor can tell whether she's a taut ship," Mowrey said. "Now, they don't call me Mad Mowrey for nothing. If you fuck up just once more, Flags, you'll stand your watches in

93

the crow's nest for a week, and it will be damn cold up there when we get to Davis Strait. And Yale, it's your job to make sure that Flags does his job. If he fucks up again, I'm going to put a notation in your fitness report that you're no good at the detail of ship's routine. It won't take many notations like that to get **your** ass shoved ashore in the worst job they can find."

"Aye, aye, sir," Paul said.

"But sir," Flags protested, "how will I be sure when you're going ashore and just when you're coming back?"

Mowrey gave a genial grin. "There will always be a man on watch at the gangway, won't there? You rig a flag halyard where he can reach it fast. You're a petty officer, ain't you? Don't you know how to train your men?"

"Aye, aye, sir," Flags said. "I'm sorry, sir."

"You'll learn, sonny," Mowrey said, and gave the boy what appeared to be an affectionate pat on the cheek, except for the fact that his huge fist became a hand only at the last moment. "Now I'm going ashore to the officers' club. This once I give you warning."

The third repeater, a white triangular pennant with a black stripe across the middle of it, snapped to the yard of the signal mast a few seconds later, just as Mowrey jumped from the rail of the *Arluk* to the deck of the *Redbird*. Paul smiled. The whole rigamarole was ridiculous, of course, but he was beginning to feel almost in spite of himself that there was a certain beauty in it.

# CHAPTER 12

When Paul went to the wardroom, it was so quiet that something seemed to be wrong. The throb of the engine, the creaking of the wooden hull and the clicking of every small, unsecured object in lockers and drawers as the ship rolled, all this had of course stopped, and now the wardroom was silent as a library, an impression that was increased by the activities of Seth Farmer and Nathan

Green. As he did immediately upon arriving in any port, the old warrant officer was writing his wife a long letter on a pad of lined paper. Nathan was taking books from three big cardboard boxes and was storing them on every available shelf and in lockers.

"Where did all the books come from?" Paul asked.

"I bought them just before leaving Boston, but never got a chance to unpack them," Nathan said. "Feel free to use them if you want."

"What kind of books be they?" Seth asked, peering over his steel-rimmed spectacles.

"Kind of a varied lot. They have lists of books people would want on a desert island, but I picked my own. I found a lot of stuff on Greenland up at Goodspeed's. The skipper got me curious."

"I wouldn't take him too serious when he talks about Greenland," Farmer said mildly. "I always been told there ain't nothing there but rocks and ice."

"It says on the dust jacket of one of the books that Greenland has been called both the Land of Desolation and the Land of Comfort," Nathan said. "Except for Eskimos, it was first settled by Eric the Red way back about the year nine hundred, but all the Norse colonies just disappeared after about five hundred years. No one knows why. I'll tell you more after I read the book."

"Let me borrow it when you're done with it," Paul said. "Can you guys hold down the ship for a few hours if I go ashore to look around?"

"Sure," Seth said. "Ain't nothing here but a navy base. If you'll mail my letter, I don't want to go ashore at all."

"Now I know how to sound a fire alarm, I guess I can stand a watch in port if no one wants the ship moved," Nathan said.

"If they want the ship moved, I guess any of us would have to call the skipper from the officers' club," Paul replied. "I have an idea we'll always be able to find him there."

After showering, changing into a clean uniform and polishing his shoes, Paul went on deck. The sun was still shining brightly near the horizon and he was momentarily confused when he glanced at his watch and saw that it was a little after nine in the evening. On the way north from Boston he had been too sick really to notice the lengthening days. Now there was a strangeness about the gradual retreat of night which gave him an old-fashioned sense of adventuring which he had not felt since first going aboard the *Arluk*. As he stepped from his ship to the *Redbird*, he saluted his quarterdeck with studied casualness and found himself wishing that there was a little pennant which could be run up when the executive officer left the ship. Absurd, absurd! For days he had been too sick even to think about smoking, but as he climbed a hill between two rows of Quonset huts, he felt in his breast pocket and found a cigar he had bought in Boston. Before meeting Mowrey he had always smoked cigarettes, and it was odd to realize that he was in some ways already starting to copy a man he detested so much. Still, it was fun to walk cockily along in the bright northern night waving his cigar with authority. He was twenty-two years old and was already the executive officer of a United States Coast Guard cutter on the Greenland Patrol. If he could get over his seasickness and learn fast, he might get command of his own ship inside of a year. In wartime things move fast, Mowrey had said.

Paul did not have to walk far before he found the officers' club. It was a big Quonset hut and so crowded that there was small chance of his running into Mowrey, he was glad to discover. A triple line of officers at the bar was keeping a half-dozen Filipino bartenders busy and perhaps a hundred more officers were drinking at small tables. At the back of the room were several long, rectangular tables at which officers were playing cards. Tobacco smoke swirled up to the domed ceiling of the Quonset hut and a jukebox blared, "Don't Sit Under the Apple Tree With Anyone Else But Me."

For a few moments Paul stood staring at the men at the cardtables. The green felt tablecloths were littered with poker chips. Paul strolled toward the bar. His cigar was making him feel slightly dizzy and he left it in a large can full of smoking cigarette butts. After buying a glass of ginger ale, he walked toward the cardtables. At two of them men were playing with coins as well as chips, but at a third many of the officers had stacks of bills as well as chips in front of them. Paul waited silently until a lieutenant commander lost a big pile and left the table in disgust. Moving forward, he put his hand on the empty chair and said, "Can you use new blood in this game?"

Naval officers, Paul soon discovered, do not ordinarily

play poker much better than fraternity boys do, and most of them made the same ridiculous mistake of drinking while they gambled for fairly high stakes. At the end of two and a half hours Paul had made almost three hundred dollars and was wishing he had arranged for a telephone call to summon him from the game. After deliberately losing twenty-three dollars, he glanced at his watch and said he had to get back to his ship before midnight. There was some grumbling but no real objection as he cashed in his chips, pocketed a profit of slightly more than two hundred fifty dollars and quickly left the table.

At the bar Paul paused to order a double scotch. In the sea of men around him he saw two young navy nurses sitting surrounded by commanders and captains. They were nowhere near as pretty as his wife, but one of them had a figure plump enough to fill out even her stiff navy uniform attractively and their high excited laughter sounded beautiful. It had been only about five days since he had seen Sylvia, but somehow it seemed a century, and he was suddenly aware that it would be months, maybe years before he again saw his wife, or any woman at all, probably, except the Eskimo women, who really would not interest him, he was sure, even if he had not really meant his vows to be faithful to Sylvia forever, as he most surely had. He was not going to have a woman for years, maybe never again if he got killed, he thought with a sudden flood of anger and self-pity. The plump nurse's throat looked so good as she tossed up her chin and laughed! Even if a man were not bound by a vow to remain faithful to his wife, what chance would he have as an eternal transient in places where there were at least a thousand men to each woman? War, despite its adventurous aspects, meant no sex, no sex for years and years. Like Sherman said, "War is hell."

When he had won at gambling in Boston, Paul often had bought a new dress or a little bracelet to surprise Sylvia with, and such presents had often put her into a delightful mood. Now he had no idea what to do with the money except mail it home to her or hide it under his mattress aboard ship, neither of which seemed to make gambling even worthwhile.

When he arrived back aboard his ship, Paul found that both Nathan and Seth had gone to sleep. Stripping to his underwear, he crawled into his bunk. Seth's soft but irregular snoring irritated him and he was too tense to sleep. The memory of the young nurse's throat and bosom as she laughed plagued him and to get his mind off it, he began to let himself think of his wife. His last night with Sylvia in Boston was still too painful and complex to contemplate directly, but he had many other memories of her which still brought pleasure. Lying sleepless during the brief hours of an April night in Newfoundland, Paul thought about the good days with his wife.

They were at a football game on a cold October afternoon. She was wearing a muskrat coat which her father had just given her, "fake mink," she called it, but it was glossy and warm and when she turned the collar up, it came above her ears, framing her delicate chin. Their side was losing badly, and the crowd all around them kept booing and cheering and jeering.

"Get me out of here," she said suddenly. "Let's go to the boat."

A lot of other people were leaving early. They had to walk through a jostling crowd, and when they finally got to the car, they were caught in a traffic jam for almost an hour. A boisterous party was making the yacht club even noisier than the streets. All this was good, because when they finally rowed out to the yawl and climbed up on her decks, the almost complete silence was like a blessing.

"Maybe we should stay here forever," she said.

It was cold below decks. The crumpled newspapers which he put into the galley range were so damp that he had to blow into the stove to start a fire, but the kindling wood blazed up fast, and there was that sharp smell of burning pine. The little cabin heated up quickly. She took off her fur coat and tossed it on a bunk. She was wearing a moss-green cashmere sweater and a brown tweed skirt.

"Would you like a cup of tea?" he asked.

"No," she said, "I think I want to make love."

Never before had she been so open with him. He rushed to embrace her.

"Only not so fast," she said. "Maybe we ought to have that tea."

He put the kettle on after adding more wood to build up the flames. She stood by a porthole looking out.

"Come see," she said.

The sun was turning the still waters all around them to burnished copper, which slowly turned to gray. He lit a brass lamp over the cabin table. When the water boiled he made a pot of tea and she laughed because his hand trembled when he handed her a cup.

"I think you're as scared as I am," she said.

"There's nothing to be scared of."

"I keep telling myself that."

For a few moments they sat like a serious old couple sipping their tea in silence. The yellow lamplight flickered on her face. Getting up, she took his cup and carried it with her own to the galley sink. When she came back, she put her arms around his neck.

"I want to learn to be good at this," she said. "I haven't been very good at it, have I?"

"Good enough for me. You've just been scared."

"You promise you won't make me pregnant?"

"I'll do everything I can."

"Let me see you put the damn thing on."

On the few occasions they had made love before this, she had always averted her eyes, pretending that she did not know what was happening. At first he was embarrassed to have her watch him, but then he found that her open interest excited him. When she started to help him pull the contrivance all the way on, he had to beg her to stop, for fear that the game would be over before it started. The fact that she was still fully dressed while he was almost nude made him feel pleasurably perverse. He pulled her to him and she held up her hands in a gesture of surrender while he took her sweater off, and then the rest of her clothes. In the flickering yellow lamplight her full breasts and narrow waist looked like a scene from a blue movie.

"You lie down first," she said. "This time I want to try different things."

She was, he realized, more curious than passionate—she was allowing herself to satisfy her young lifetime of questions. She was, perhaps, not as confused as he was, not as bewildered by conflicting currents of desire, "true love" as he imagined it should be, honest lust and honest poetry. That night she was simply like a child with a new toy, and though in some sense that shocked him, it also delighted him.

"I want to try it every which way," she said. "Now don't hurry."

He lasted through perhaps fifteen minutes of experimentation, but when she knelt over him with her magnificent

99

breasts wagging only a few inches in front of his eyes while she eased herself down on him, that was the end of the first round. She laughed like a child winning a wrestling game. "I knew you couldn't hold out for long," she said.

At the time he had been hurt and perhaps a little scared by the realization that she certainly was having fun, but that this was not exactly the grand passion he hoped to inspire and which she inspired in him. In his lonely bunk aboard the trawler in Newfoundland, he now forgot that reservation, and remembered only how beautiful and eager she had been.

She was like a child—a beautiful woman with the face and spirit of a child, and maybe that was why he loved her so much. On that last night together when almost everything had gone wrong, he should have realized that she had never grown up. In the middle of dinner she had announced that she wanted to buy a house and fix it all up while he was gone.

"Where will we get the money?" he had said.

"Daddy will lend it to us. He says a house would be a good investment."

"But we can't be sure we'll want to live anywhere near here when the war is over. I might get a job anywhere."

"I wouldn't think of living anywhere else but Wellesley," she said. "Paul, don't you understand that I need a house to keep me busy when you're gone? I don't want just to live at home like daddy's little girl again. I want my own place. If we're going to have a baby, we're going to have to have a house, and I might already be pregnant."

He tried to understand and felt guilty for thinking that she was silly and self-indulgent. On his last night with her she wanted to discuss colors for walls and fabrics for rugs. Her mind was so intent on all this that any other conversation was impossible. For her his ship and the ordeal ahead of him simply did not exist, and she obviously did not want to hear about it. Her own immediate future was all that interested her. Despite all her passionate talk, and her interest in sexual experimentation, he began to suspect that she had not yet grown up enough to love anybody or to think much of anyone else. Which was when he started to get drunk—

But all this was nothing to think about now when memories of the good parts of his life were necessary to get him through the bad ones. Dismissing the memories of that last night with her, he went back to that evening aboard the *Valkyrie*, when after winning the first wrestling match, she had decided to see just how many times she could make him perform. That had been a childish game perhaps, but he dearly wished he could play it with her again. With startling recall, he could almost smell the sweetness of her sweat in the dark cabin of the *Arluk*, and hear her little cries.

Lying in his narrow bunk aboard the ship, Paul hardly had to touch himself to spend his solitary passion. At almost exactly that instant the general alarm began to clang, and he heard the boatswain's pipes shrill call, followed by Boats's hoarse voice yelling, "General quarters drill! Man and train all guns, and bring ammunition to the breech, but do not load."

"Oh, *my*!" Seth exploded as he always did at such times, and Nathan mumbled beneath his breath as he pulled on his pants. Usually Paul was the first from the wardroom during surprise drills, but under the circumstances he waited until the others had gone before changing his underwear and putting on his uniform. It was only a quarter to four in the morning, but when he scrambled to the deck, he found that the Newfoundland dawn was already bright. Mowrey was standing on the gun deck, a glass in his hand and his voice thick when he shouted, "Hurry it up, girls, or we'll be sunk before you ever get to your guns. Where the hell have you been, Yale, down there jerking off in your bunk?"

## CHAPTER 13

When the drill was finally over, Mowrey ordered Paul to the bridge.

Paul found his captain sitting on his stool, holding a glass which by its color and smell appeared to be full of undiluted whiskey.

"I see you playing poker up at the officers' club," Mowrey said. "Did I give you permission to go ashore?"

"No sir, but I assumed I could set watches. Both Mr. Farmer and Mr. Green wanted to stay aboard."

"You better learn to assume nothing and never set foot off this ship without getting my direct permission," Mowrey said quietly, looking off in the distance over Paul's shoulder. "See them ships coming in?"

Two big, gray passenger liners were standing into the harbor, their signal masts aflutter with brightly colored flags and pennants.

"They look like troop carriers," Paul said.

"What flags are they flying?" Mowrey asked sweetly.

"Sir?"

"Just take the white one there and the blue square in it, or the red one with the white stripe. What letters of the alphabet do they signify?"

"I don't know, sir. I'll start studying signal flags right away."

"You won't go ashore until you know them, and if you don't learn them damn soon, that will go in your fitness report."

"Aye, aye, sir."

"Have you been practicing blinker light with Greenberg, like I told you to?"

"When we were at sea, sir, I'm afraid we were both too sick for that."

"*That* will look good on your fitness report. Practice blinker lights for at least an hour a day with Greenberg—he at least knows Morse code."

"Aye, aye, sir."

"And I want you to teach him navigation for at least an hour a day. He don't even know the book part of it."

"Aye, aye, sir."

"I want you to take star sights, sun sights and moon sights right here at the wharf and let me see your computations."

"Do you want us to take actual sights?"

"Well, sweet Jesus, I don't want you to hold your thumb up to your nose and pretend."

"I mean, sir, we can't see any horizon from here. How can we take sights?"

"Is that what you're going to tell me when we're in the

102

ice pack? 'I mean, sir, we can't see any horizon from here, so how can we take sights?' "

"What do you want me to do?"

"Read up on artificial horizons. Try the bubble sextant. It's under the chart desk."

"Aye, aye, sir!"

"What's that planet up there in the sky now?"

Paul looked up and studied the morning sky, in which just one planet glowed.

"Venus, isn't it, sir?"

"Sweet Jesus Christ! If you don't know, look it up, don't guess! It's Mars. Can't you see that it glows red?"

"Aye, aye, sir. I'll read up on identifying planets."

"If you can't identify any planet I point to inside of twenty-four hours *that* will go in your fitness report."

"Aye, aye, sir."

"Now get the hell off the bridge. I was in a good mood until I had to look at you. How the hell do they expect me to run a ship with nothing but a farmer, a Yale and a Sheenie?"

"I'm supposed to teach you navigation and we're supposed to practice blinker lights," Paul said to Nathan when he returned to the wardroom. "Do you want to try to get some sleep first?"

"I don't think I can get back to sleep now," Nathan said, "but let's have some coffee."

Cookie had climbed back into his bunk, but he had left a big pot of coffee on the stove and a platter of fresh Danish pastries on the table in the forecastle. To avoid waking the sleeping men in the surrounding bunks, they took their heavy mugs of coffee to the hatch over the well deck and sat on the canvas cover, looking at the big troop ships, which were mooring on the other side of the harbor.

"I suppose they're going to England," Nathan said.

"Or Greenland. I hear they're sending a lot of construction workers up there to build airfields."

There was a pause before Nathan said, "I wonder how long it will be before this whole goddamn war is over?"

"I always think of four years," Paul said. "That's about the length of time most of our wars seem to last."

"Four years. . . ." Nathan gave a sigh of profound sorrow.

103

"Of course we probably will get home way before then," Paul said. "Have you got a wife waiting for you?"

Slowly Nathan turned his face from the troop ships toward him and Paul was shocked by the look on it.

"I'm married," Nathan said and seemed about to add more, but took a sip of his coffee instead. "Do you want to start on signaling or navigation?"

They started on the signaling, with Nathan sending Morse code very slowly to Paul, but after only a few minutes Mowrey ordered Paul to his cabin to bring the charts up to date with some Notice to Mariners bulletins he had just discovered. Nathan climbed to the flying bridge, the only place on the ship where he could usually be alone, and stood leaning against the mast. Overhead Mars glowed brightly in a deep blue sky. Nathan knew what planet it was—in his youth astronomy had been one of his passions. When he was about fifteen he had built a three-inch telescope and mounted it on the flat roof of his father's house in Brooklyn.

Now Nathan could almost smell the tar of that roof on a hot summer evening and hear the pigeons cooing in the nests he had built for them when he had been even younger. Homing pigeons! Becky at the age of fifteen had been even more fascinated by them than by the telescope. He had helped her to carry two pigeons to her apartment in a carefully pierced cardboard box. They had released them in her backyard and how she had marveled when they had flown straight home, a distance of almost four blocks!

"If I raised some, we could send messages back and forth."

There never had been a time when he had not known Becky. Her parents had been friends of his mother and father, though they were so different that even as a child, Nathan had not been able to understand why. Nathan's father was a doctor, a poor man's doctor, and his mother served as his receptionist and nurse, though she had no formal training. The doctor's office, which occupied almost the entire first floor of their house, was usually full of sick people, and at all hours of the night his father was called to hospitals and to the homes of the dying. Nathan remembered his house as a kind of crisis center. The conversation of his parents, even at the dinner table, was full of tales about the complications of childbirth, the sudden

104

deaths of heart patients and the slow deaths of those with cancer. His parents were usually exhausted, and as a boy he sometimes felt that they were the only two people in the world who were attempting to save a dying city.

But Becky's household was entirely different. Her father was a professor of the Slavic languages at Brooklyn College, where he apparently had few duties, for he spent most of his time at home reading and writing. His wife also spent most of her time reading, though she found time to cook elaborate meals and keep their apartment spotless. Even Becky at a very early age spent most of her time reading, and they all often read to each other and laughed over funny passages or discussed difficult ones. The house was always quiet, and the people in it moved in a leisurely manner compared to the frantic pace of Nathan's parents. No one in that household was mad at anybody. The professor and his wife, who were considerably older than Nathan's parents, had come from Warsaw to Brooklyn fairly recently, and they retained the detached amusement of highly educated foreigners about American political issues and controversies of the day which often made Nathan's parents argue stridently when they weren't talking about people being born or dying.

Almost nothing appeared to irritate Becky's mother and father, and even at sixteen, she was curiously serene and sunny in a world which to Nathan was almost entirely frantic and stormy. She even liked Brian Murphy's Christmas display.

Brian Murphy's annual Christmas display always infuriated Nathan's father and everyone else he knew. Murphy was a successful electrical contractor who owned a new house on a double lot in a predominantly Jewish neighborhood near Nathan's home in the Flatbush section of Brooklyn. Starting in early November, Murphy put together such a garish Christmas display of his own making that his house looked like a carnival. At least a dozen Santa Clauses, some life-size, crowded his front lawn and his rooftop. Driven by electric motors, some of these kept raising their hands in greeting or just sat rocking, supposedly with mirth, but they looked to Nathan more like old men in terrible pain. On Murphy's front porch there was a crèche with eerie life-size plaster people with vacant, staring eyes. Worst of all, the whole double lot blazed with blinking colored lights, and loudspeakers blared Christmas carols interspersed with Santa's ho-ho-ho's. During Murphy's many Christmas parties, the lights and the loud music continued until the early hours of the morning.

Among Murphy's neighbors was a fierce old friend and patient of Nathan's father whose wife was chronically ill, and who always had trouble sleeping. After an argument, he sued Murphy for disturbing the peace, and a whole neighborhood war started with all the obvious ugly undertones. Petitions were taken from door to door, and Nathan's father appeared as a witness in court to say that his patient's health had suffered. Murphy won the case anyway and celebrated by building a sled with life-size reindeer which rocked and blew steam or smoke from their noses on his rooftop. Spotlights played on this all night.

"Isn't that awful?" Nathan said when he and Becky were walking past the display, and he was astonished when she laughed and said, "Why? I think it's sort of marvelous."

It turned out that Becky actually knew Brian Murphy and liked him, as she knew and liked almost everyone in the neighborhood. Murphy was an electrician who was extremely proud of his creations, and felt that he was defending his religious freedom. Most of all, he was an unappreciated artist, and when Becky introduced Nathan to him he spent an hour explaining the complex mechanisms which produced all the motion and the smoke. Embattled, pugnacious and naively proud, Brian Murphy was nothing like the devil whom Nathan's father had described. Nathan had suddenly realized that Becky lived in a world that was entirely different from the one in which he had grown up, much less frightening and more hopeful. He loved her world and he loved her.

They were childhood sweethearts, too shy and restrained to make love. They were married while he was still a graduate student, in the spring of 1936, and she supported him by working as a secretary at Brooklyn College. They were both surprised when only a few months after their wedding her parents decided to go back to Poland. Although they had never complained, they apparently had never really been happy in America, and now that their daughter was settled in the new country, they decided to go home again.

Becky startled Nathan by asking if he would like to move to Warsaw, where, she said, her father could get him a good university position. She appeared to understand his refusal, but she was depressed for a long time after her parents left, and talked a lot of visiting them, which their slender budget made almost impossible. In 1938, she began trying to persuade them to come back to New York, and for a year they kept up a running debate by mail. One reason that her father wanted to stay in Poland was that he had an invalid mother and two sisters there. Becky kept trying to devise plans which would make it possible to bring them all over.

Her obsession with her family in Europe hurt Nathan. She tended to subordinate everything else to it, and persuaded him to turn down a good offer from the University of Michigan because she said, "We could never get dad to go up there." Oddly, Becky did not seem unduly worried by the rise of Hitler, and she went to Warsaw in 1939, not so much to rescue her father from the Germans, as from his mother and sisters, who, she had become convinced, were holding him in Poland almost against his will.

"I think it may be dangerous to go back there now," Nathan said.

"Come on! You don't really want me to bring them all back anyway. Admit it!"

He couldn't bring himself to admit it, but they both knew she was right, if only because he suspected that she would spend most of her time with her family if they settled nearby. They were tense together a lot of the time after that, and argued about almost anything but her family.

"If you love me, you won't try to stop me," she said when she decided to go to try to bring her family home, and there was no answer to that. He took her to the boat, and waited on the dock blowing kisses at her as she stood in the crowd on the promenade deck. A lot of people had thrown paper streamers as the tugs started to push the ship away from the wharf. Standing there alone he had suddenly realized that life without her even for a few weeks was going to be awful. Cupping his hands to his mouth he yelled, "Bring them all back, I *want* them here, bring them back, damn it . . ."

She gave him a smile of immense gratitude. Then a fat woman who was throwing paper streamers jostled her away from the rail.

He never saw Becky again. He remembered the mournful tooting of the tugboats, the smell of the harbor and the circling gulls as he watched the ship out of sight. In retro-

spect it seemed that he had a premonition that he would
never see her again. . . .

The gulls were still with him, circling around his head as
he stood on the flying bridge of the *Arluk* in Argentia two
and a half years or what seemed like several centuries later.
Then he heard Mowrey bawl, "Yale, where's that goddamn
Sheenie? I've got some new codes here that have to go in
the safe."

Closing his eyes for a moment to help blot out the past,
Nathan climbed down the ladder to the bridge.

"I'm right here, captain," he said.

For a week the *Arluk* waited in Argentia while Mowrey
drilled his men and indignantly sent messages to every
authority he could think of, requesting reasons for the
delay. He got no answers, but on the eighth day, the quartermaster on watch reported that "Captain Hansen's
trawler" was steaming into the harbor. Their sister ship,
Paul saw as she came to moor alongside, proudly carried a
metallic crescent device atop her mast for radar.

"Jesus Christ, that bastard Hansen copped a radar set
for himself," Mowrey exploded. "How come they give one
to him but not us? I know they figure the silly bastard can't
find his way without it, but damn it, he's not headed into
more fog than we are."

Hansen moored his ship alongside the *Arluk* without any
of the daring, flash and risk-taking which Mowrey had
displayed. He just came in bucking the fast current very
slowly, put out a bow line at leisure, and winched his stern
around. The operation fascinated Paul because he thought
that he could duplicate it himself.

"Hansen, you handle a ship like a fucking old lady,"
Mowrey growled from the wing of his bridge.

"I'd rather do that than handle one like a madman,"
Hansen replied with a smile. "How are you, Cliff?"

"How many asses did you have to kiss to get radar?"

"I didn't even put in for it. Don't get too envious. The
damn thing was great for two days and then quit."

"They'll probably be able to fix it here for you," Nathan
said.

"Maybe. I radioed ahead and they didn't sound too sure.
The damn thing is so new they don't have many techni-
cians, and those they got are all tied up with navy stuff."

"I'll look at it if you want," Nathan said. "I've done a little work on radar."

"You'll be saving our lives if you can fix it—maybe literally," Hansen said. "I got an idea they gave us the damn thing for a purpose."

Paul had always been curious about radar, which then was the newest and most hush-hush of developments, and accepted Hansen's invitation to come aboard with Nathan. Even Mowrey was curious enough to come along. The radar set was a huge metal box with a round piece of glass in the front of it, much like a porthole. It filled one end of the pilothouse.

"Looks like you got sort of the Adam and Eve of radar," Nathan said, inspecting the box closely. "I didn't know they put anything this primitive into production."

"They were going to give us a smaller one, but the navy grabbed it. The guys in Norfolk said they didn't know how long this thing would work, but we were lucky to get anything at all. The subs and the aircraft carriers have top priority on this stuff."

"Can your radioman give me some tools?" Nathan asked. "I'll have a look at it."

Paul watched him while he unscrewed metal plates. Aboard the *Arluk*, Nathan had always struck him as nice, intelligent in some abstract way, but completely incompetent and bumbling when it came to anything nautical. With tools in his long, slender fingers Nathan's whole manner changed. He moved briskly and with apparent enjoyment as he began examining the complex mechanism inside the box with a flashlight.

"It's nothing but a damn radio," Mowrey said and went back to the *Arluk*.

"Your basic problem is that this set has no real protection against vibration and dampness," Nathan said. "It was never designed for marine use. Probably there are one or more shorts. I hoped nothing is burned out. Did they give you any spare parts?"

"Not a one," Hansen said grimly. "We wouldn't know how to use them anyway."

Nathan reached for a voltameter and began the tedious job of testing scores of connections.

"You obviously know what you're doing," Hansen said. "God, I wish I could get you assigned to this ship!"

Nathan straightened up and for the first time Paul saw a smile erase that look of profound sorrow on his long, narrow face.

"Captain Hansen, if you could arrange that, you would be saving *my* life," he said. "I can't tell you what it's like to be on a ship where there is no way for me to be useful."

"I was going to talk to Cliff about Paul here," Hansen said. "There's just some small chance that I might be able to make some sort of a deal for both of you."

The two officers stood watching for perhaps half an hour while Nathan worked on the radar set. Finally he twisted some knobs and the little porthole in the box suddenly glowed with an odd green light around which a pencil line of brighter light turned like a big second hand on a watch.

"You've fixed it!" Hansen said.

"Temporarily, I'm afraid."

Nathan adjusted more knobs. The moving line of bright light began to trace a strangely glowing outline of the surrounding harbor on the glass.

"God, imagine what that thing would mean in a fog or at night if you were chasing someone or being chased," Hansen said fervently.

"I wish I could promise you that you'd have it for long," Nathan replied. "I'm afraid this set will be constantly going out and will always need tinkering. I can at least give you a list of spare parts you can order."

"What the hell good will they do us if we have no one who has any idea what the hell is going on inside that box?" Hansen said. "It's ridiculous to leave you on a ship which has no radar. I'm going over to see Cliff."

Hansen found Mowrey in his bunk aboard the *Arluk*, half sitting with his shoulders against two pillows. He had a glass in his hand and spoke thickly, a fact which did not surprise Hansen at all.

"Do you mind if I come in to talk over some problems of state?" Hansen began.

"Take a load off your ass, Wally," Mowrey replied, pulling up his legs to make room at the foot of his bunk. "I'll get you a drink."

From a drawer under his bunk within reach of his arm he took a bottle and a glass.

"If you want water, you can get it at the head," he said.

Hansen accepted the glass, went to get water and sat down on the stool near the chart table.

"I want to talk to you about the possibility of trading some officers," he said. "You've got a radar specialist but no radar. My communications officer is a guy who just made ensign after ten years as a quartermaster. Want to swap?"

"So you want my Sheenie," Mowrey said with his sweet grin. "What else do you want?"

"Well, my exec graduated from the Coast Guard Academy last year. He's never seen ice, but except for that he could easily run a ship like this himself. To sweeten the deal, I'll trade him for the guy you call Yale, and you can get some sleep at night."

"So you want my Sheenie *and* my Yale. Do you want my cook too?"

"I'd like him, of course, but I know you'll never let him go. How about it, Cliff? I'm sure we could clear it with Headquarters if we both approved and we'd both be a hell of a lot better off."

"What happens when I get radar? You're not the only one who can kiss ass for a thing like that."

"I think you know, Cliff, why they gave me radar. You better hope you don't get it."

"You mean they have more fog on the east coast than on the west coast?"

"I think you know it's not fog that has me worried."

"You guess there's no chance of us getting Germans on the west coast? Everybody thinks they're on the east coast, so why wouldn't they come to the west?"

"I think you understand the logistics of the situation. You're too big a man to be a dog in the manger, Cliff."

"Now don't call me no dog. Mad I might be, but the last man who called me a dog still can't bite apples."

"You know what I mean."

"Maybe, but I always say you can't get a better supply officer than a Sheenie. My Yale ain't much good, but at least he's not a smart-ass like all them Academies."

"I'll trade you one for one or two for two, any way you want. The guy with the radar should have the radar specialist. Even Headquarters could see that."

"Headquarters ain't going to do a damn thing with my officers without my approval. You know that."

111

"I think I know you too, Cliff. Crazy like a fox is what I always said. What else do you want to sweeten the deal?"

"Maybe some of your lead ballast if I'm interested at all. We was rolling thirty-five degrees in no sea hardly at all. You got a diesel engine in your motorboat?"

"Yes."

"They gave me gas. We might do some swapping around. Let me think about it."

"When will you make up your mind? They're liable to shove us out of here tomorrow."

"The first stop for both of us will be Narsarssuak, I'm sure. We'll see each other there before you go your way and I go mine."

"The paperwork will take time. Look, Cliff, if they're going to send me after a German weather ship, I don't want to go without radar. The Krauts are sure to have it. How else do they have such good fire control?"

"They got other kinds of range finders. Now don't get your ass in a swivet, Wally. You can't come on here and buy me out like this was a candy shop."

"We all will await your pleasure," Hansen said wryly. "It's quite conceivable that a good many lives and the success of a whole mission could depend on it."

"Wally, don't try to hurry me just because you're afraid to sail without all the newest gadgets going for you. I told you I'll let you know. I just want to think on it!"

With a sigh Hansen put the glass of whiskey, which he had hardly touched, on the chart table and left. Mowrey tossed off the scotch, put the unwashed glass back in his drawer and settled down for a nap.

Hansen immediately asked both Paul and Nathan to his cabin. After explaining the situation, he said, "Cliff has always enjoyed the sensation of having power over other men. I think he will toy with us for a few weeks."

"Do you think he'll finally let us go?" Nathan asked.

Hansen shrugged. "Ordinarily he gets a kick out of just being contrary," he said. "This time I may have a trump card. Before I sail I'm going to try to arrange to pick up about a dozen cases of scotch. That ought to sweeten the deal."

"This all makes me feel that I'm a little like a slave on the block," Nathan said with a smile, "but it's the first time that anyone in the service has ever wanted me. I feel like a wallflower who's being asked to dance."

112

"Do you understand that my mission is probably going to be a lot more dangerous than Cliff's?" Hansen asked.

"I've heard a lot of scuttlebut, but I think I get the general trend. To tell the truth, I don't think anything could be more dangerous for me than the feeling that I'm simply of no use in this war at all, no damned good."

"Christ, it's not your fault that they put a radar specialist on a ship without radar. Paul, how do you feel about all this, now that you've had a chance to think it over?"

"All I'm ever going to get out of Mowrey is a bad fitness report and the worst assignment he can find for me, no matter how hard I try," Paul replied. "I'll be glad to take my chances with you."

"I hope that Cliff lets us work it out and that you both won't be sorry."

Paul still was not sure how he really felt about requesting a transfer. Sure, the idea of an endless tour of duty with Mad Mowrey seemed unbearable, but the thought of chasing some huge German icebreaker with six- or even eight-inch guns wasn't too attractive either.

And there was also the nagging feeling that there was something wrong in this maneuvering. Mowrey was a tyrant, but that was the luck of the draw. Shouldn't he shut up and stick it out and get *on* with it ...?

# CHAPTER 14

The next afternoon the two trawlers got orders to sail to Greenland, there to wait at the edge of the icepack for the troopship *Dorchester*, which they were to escort through the ice to Narsarssuak Fjord.

The two sister ships took on fuel and cleared Argentia harbor at a little before ten on a sunny northern night. Mowrey was in a rage, for Hansen, presumably because his ship had radar, had been put in charge of the operation, despite the fact that Mowrey outranked him.

"Follow me at a distance of one thousand yards," Hansen blinked with his signal light as they steamed abreast out of the bay.

"Follow me!" Mowrey growled to Paul. "Follow me! The bastard always did think he was Jesus Christ!"

Defiantly Mowrey stayed abreast of the *Nanmak* for several miles before falling, almost by accident, into her wake.

As they approached the broad Atlantic they could see the fog banks lying across the mouth of the bay like an endless range of snow-covered mountains. Soon the *Nanmak* appeared to dissolve in the mist ahead and once more they could hardly see their own bow. Since whole convoys might be expected to be heading toward Argentia, Mowrey told the quartermaster to sound a blast on their air horn every two minutes, and reduced his speed. Only a few minutes later they could see Hansen's signal light blinking from his invisible ship only a few hundred yards ahead in the fog.

"No danger of collision or of navigational error now because my radar is working fine," Hansen signaled. "Resume speed of eight knots. Cease whistle signals."

"He's like a kid with a new toy," Mowrey grumbled. "If he thinks I'm going to trust my ship to him and his goddamn magic box, he's crazy." Nevertheless, he soon told the quartermaster that they might as well save compressed air on the whistle and gradually build up to eight knots, the top cruising speed of those trawlers.

As they emerged from the bay, Paul, Nathan and many other men aboard waited with a kind of horror for the vicious rolling to begin again, but the North Atlantic fooled them by remaining curiously quiet, leaden in the fog. Enlivened by the hope that they might actually be getting their sea legs, Paul and Nathan took sights with a bubble sextant whenever they could see the dim outline of the sun in the fog and worked them out in the wardroom. Nathan, Paul discovered, quickly learned how to use the logarithmic tables which had been devised to make any knowledge of spherical trigonometry unnecessary for navigators, but he was a highly trained mathematician and embarrassed Paul by asking questions about theory, then answering them himself.

After they had been at sea only about twenty-four hours, the ships received a radio message which gave the positions of enemy submarines that had been detected by radio direction finders or aircraft. After Nathan decoded the message, Paul plotted them on a small-scale chart. Two of the submarines were near the Straits of Belle Isle, near which they were to pass.

"Hell, no submarine is going to waste a torpedo on no goddamn little trawler," Mowrey said. "They're waiting for troop ships and tankers."

Still both Nathan and Paul imagined German submarines lying, perhaps only a few thousand yards away, whenever they stared into the veils of fog. Were the men playing chess, reading girlie magazines, writing letters home and listening to music on the radio, the way the crew was in their own forecastle? Despite the name of the *Arluk*, the submarines were really the hunters in this war and almost everyone else the quarry. It was the captains of the submarines who could decide whether to attack, to hide or to run, and whatever they did, the odds were always in their favor at that stage of the war. If Paul's distant forefathers had not emigrated to America, might he now be a professional in command of a really lethal weapons system, instead of a novice on a fishboat? His moment of envying the Germans did not last long, for he remembered a history professor at Boston University saying, "When all is said and done, Germany is a nation of only about eighty million people which has chosen to fight England, all the rest of Europe and Russia, a total of something like a half billion people. Their initial successes have been remarkable, but of course they are mad and will eventually die the death of a mad dog."

Still the question remained, Paul mused as he stared into the fog, of whether the mad dog would kill him before it was killed. The moan of a rising wind in the rigging and the mournful disembodied cries of seagulls hidden by shrouds of fog, all seemed to be whispering premonitions of death, and the breath of the north was getting colder.

Paul and the other men did not have long for morbid musings. As the trawlers entered Davis Strait, they ran into their first real Arctic gale. The fog was ripped off the ocean like a dirty sheet and all around them lay jagged seas, a nightmare of boiling, constantly heaving mountain peaks. Ahead of them the *Nanmak* disappeared entirely in every trough. The 3-inch gun on the *Arluk*'s bow was smothered in white water every time they finished one of their rollercoaster descents before shaking free and shooting up toward the sky like an express elevator. During these ascents there was a dreadful sucking noise under the bow, as though the ship herself were in frantic need of air for one last convulsion.

Although it was May, spray froze on deck and those few men who could walk at all hung frantically to hastily rigged lifelines. Every man aboard, even the old brig hands, was seasick, except Mowrey, who continued to smoke his cigar on the bridge, Boats, the rather sardonic chief boatswain's mate, one second-class machinist's mate, Seth Farmer, who volunteered to stand watches in the engineroom because fishermen know engines as well as deck work, and in defiance of all odds, Cookie, who stood cursing amongst his flying pots and pans, but continued to prepare gourmet food for anybody who could face it.

For both Nathan and Paul "seasickness" was not a term anywhere near drastic enough to denote the disease that beset them. The moment the gale hit they were turned into zombies or less than that, for their corpses could not walk but could only crawl up to the bridge, cling to a rail for four hours of semiconsciousness, then collapse in a bunk which offered blessed oblivion most of the rest of the time.

Paul found that he cared about nothing whatsoever, not even about staying alive, never mind clean or dry. It was always daylight now, and when he glanced at his wristwatch, he had no idea whether it was ten in the morning or ten at night. When the general alarm shrieked, he went skidding out on the frozen decks expecting to see a submarine preparing to gun them down and was not really much relieved to see only a small iceberg which Mowrey was considering a fine opportunity for gunnery practice. Paul was also not either surprised or angry to discover that the retching men on the violently rolling and pitching decks could not hit the iceberg until Mowrey steamed almost close enough to touch it, and then the *Arluk*'s guns, which had seemed so lethal in silence, succeeded not in demolishing the iceberg, but only in sending up small splashes of chips.

"If you boys can't learn to shoot, you better start writing condolence letters to your mothers right now," Mowrey said as he ducked into his cabin to pour whiskey into his coffee mug.

Nathan, if possible, was even more out of it all than Paul was. He could keep neither food nor liquid in his stomach, and his already thin face appeared to age twenty years in a week. His tall gaunt body was bent forward like that of an octogenarian. When he staggered on deck in the regulation garb for general quarters, a .45 pistol at his belt, a life preserver and a tin hat, he looked like a cartoon figure of wretchedness which was made even more ridiculous by the bucket he clutched.

"Don't worry, boys!" Mowrey said as Nathan painfully crawled up the steps to the bridge, sprawled on the deck as the ship took a particularly vicious lurch and slowly pulled himself up, clutching a rail. "Germany has Hitler and all those Prussian officers, but we've got Greenberg on our side. Greenberg, here, is our secret weapon. He may not look like much now, but wait until the going gets really tough!"

It is doubtful whether Nathan even heard him. He was intent on recovering his bucket, which had escaped his grasp and was now rolling noisily back and forth across the pilothouse. Managing to trap it with his foot without falling, he grabbed it, his lips spreading to a thin desperate grin of triumph before he retched into it.

Neither Paul nor Nathan had any idea how many nightless days went by before the general alarm again brought them from their bunks. This time they saw a big horned mine bobbing almost in their wake—the lookouts had failed to see it and they had almost hit it. After wasting a good deal of ammunition, the men on the 20-millimeter guns finally hit it and it exploded, producing the first roar of German violence that the men of the *Arluk* had ever heard.

"Captain," Nathan gasped, "just as a matter of technical curiosity, did Hansen's radar pick up that thing?"

"Hansen's radar quit about two days ago," Mowrey replied with apparent satisfaction. "Since we now know it was invented by guys like you, there's no reason to be surprised."

Even with an understanding of Mowrey's growing madness, Paul still found it difficult to accept the fact that the captain's anti-Semitism now embraced radar, which correctly or incorrectly, he assumed to be the work of Jewish scientists. It wasn't long before Mowrey was referring to radar as "Jewish magic," or "The Jew Box."

Shortly before they reached the coast of Greenland, the gale moderated. Paul immediately felt better, but Nathan had been so weakened that he still could get out of his bunk only long enough to stand his watches.

Paul's first glimpse of Greenland came at four o'clock one bright morning when he climbed onto the bridge to start his morning watch.

"There she be!" Mowrey said as though he were bestowing a personal gift. "There lies Greenland, sixty miles dead ahead."

At first the long ridge of mountains was hard to distinguish from the clouds on the horizon, but then one peak stood out against a steel-colored sky, a black silhouette, majestic but full of distant menace. Paul remembered Nathan saying he had read that Greenland had been called both "the Land of Desolation" and "the Land of Comfort." There certainly did not seem to be much comfort promised by those stark mountain peaks, but he did feel some strange new excitement in them, perhaps an echo of probably phony tales he had heard about "the clarion call of the north."

Paul was still studying the distant mountains, which appeared to change shape as they merged with clouds, when Nathan staggered to the pilothouse.

"Captain," Nathan said to Mowrey, "I have them repeating a radio message which I have decoded. They are getting quite angry because we don't acknowledge it. Captain Hansen has already acknowledged his—it's addressed to both of us."

Mowrey took the clipboard from him and read the message. It said, "German weather ship detected by radio operating in vicinity of Angmagssalik Fjord, Greenland east coast. *Nanmak* will proceed to investigate immediately. *Arluk* will stand by according to original orders to escort *Dorchester* to Narsarssuak Fjord."

"Well, good-by Wally," Mowrey said. "Sure, acknowledge it. We won't have that bastard giving us orders anymore."

Both Nathan and Paul stood on the wing of the bridge watching as the *Nanmak* changed to a southeasterly course. Lost amongst the whitecaps, the blue and white ship was almost invisible. It was strange to think that the *Arluk* was a sister of Hansen's ship—in a way it was just like looking at oneself, seeing oneself as little more than a chip lost in the Arctic sea and sky. Suddenly the signal light on the flying bridge of the *Nanmak* blinked briefly.

"He says good luck," Mowrey said. "Return the sentiment. That won't cost us nothing."

While the lights exchanged their brief farewells Nathan said, "They didn't even give me a chance to fix his radar for him again. I'd give a lot to be with him."

"Yeah," Paul replied, but he wasn't sure what he felt or thought except that stupid old adage about being careful not to jump from the frying pan into the fire. He stood watching the *Nanmak* until she was out of sight, and there was nothing but sea, sky and the distant mountain peaks.

# CHAPTER 15

After standing his watch, Paul slept, the usual druglike effect of seasickness expunging even dreams. When he came back on deck hours later the view of Greenland was much more dramatic. To his surprise the great mountains were smooth red granite with only a few patches of snow. Glaciers like white rivers pushed to the sea between them. These, however, were not the sights that excited Paul. Spreading out from the coast for miles was the Greenland ice pack. It was nothing like anything which he had ever seen or imagined.

If Paul had tried to visualize it at all, he had thought of flat cakes of ice jammed up. This was a vast city of ice castles, towers and crystal ramparts, all thrown together as though by some cataclysmic earthquake. Like the ruins of fortifications which some forgotten gods had erected at the dawn of time to protect the coast of Greenland, row upon row of these spires and sloping walls, some of them hundreds of feet high, stretched as far to the north and south as the eye could see. The crumbling ice palaces were astonishingly varied in color. Glittering blues and greens of all shades made the white background look anything but drab, and the sun, which was now low on the horizon behind them, gilded some of the snowy slopes, and made them glow in many tones of gold, bronze and even rose. This was not the most spectacular aspect of the ice pack. The sea in front of it was almost black, and huge combers rolling in from Davis Strait smashed themselves against the outer ramparts, sending spray high in the air and jostling the smaller icebergs together, causing a thunderous gnashing of teeth, a grinding roar which would make any sailor but a seasoned ice pilot turn his stern to it and run. The constant jostling of the icebergs in the outer walls which took the brunt of the surf produced a broad band of crushed ice which undulated on the dark waves just to seaward of the breakers, a writhing white serpentine barrier which somehow was most terrifying of all.

"Lord God!" Nathan said as he clung to the rail of the bridge and his ravaged face was transfixed.

"We call it storis ice," Mowrey said with grim satisfaction, as though he had created this miracle himself. "Do you think you could pilot a ship through that, Yale?"

"Not right now, sir," Paul said.

Mowrey changed course to parallel the ice pack at a distance of about a mile, called for slow speed and went to his cabin to refresh his coffee mug. Nathan and Paul continued to study the ice pack, as did Flags, Guns, who was at the helm, and Boats.

"Where do all those icebergs come from?" Flags asked with awe. "How do they get made like that?"

"I've been reading a little about it," Nathan said. "Apparently Greenland is shaped like a gigantic saucer with rocky mountains forming the rim. It's real cold in the interior, but warmer than you'd think around the coasts because of the Gulf Stream. In the interior, I guess, it almost never stops snowing, and you've got a mound of snow there damn near two thousand miles long, eight hundred miles wide and something like ten thousand feet high.

"It really is a big factory for producing icebergs," Nathan continued. "The weight of the snow on top of that big mound compresses the snow on the bottom to ice and drives it out through mountain ravines at the edge of the saucer. Those rivers of ice are the glaciers—we can't see them move, but you can't see the hour hand of a clock move either. When the ice rivers hit the sea, which has been warmed by the Gulf Stream, huge chunks break off— they call it calving, and that's a pretty graphic term when you come to think of it. Then the relatively warm wind over the sea takes over and sculpts the icebergs into all those shapes. The warm currents melt their bottoms too, and every once in a while, they turn over. Both the currents and the winds keep changing their shapes."

"Thank you, sir," Flags said. Most of the enlisted men had regarded Nathan's gaunt, bent figure with contempt, but now there was a note of respect in the young signalman's voice.

Paul was interested in Nathan's explanation of the ice pack, but he was concentrating on the problem of how a ship could be worked through such barriers without being crushed, ground to bits in the outer rim, where the smaller icebergs were being smashed together. When Mowrey reappeared, he watched him carefully to see what miracle he could produce. After draining his cup of "coffee," the old ice pilot went to the wing of the bridge, squinted through the vanes of a gyrocompass repeater and called, "Stand by to take down some bearings, Flags. The highest peak on our starboard bow is 148 degrees. The notch in twin peaks is 028 degrees. A big round mound is 152 degrees."

When Mowrey went to the chart table in his cabin to plot these bearings, Paul said, "Do you mind if I watch you, sir?"

"Won't do you much good," Mowrey growled. "You get to learn to identify these peaks on the chart. The Danes and the Eskies have given names to all these mountains which no one can pronounce, but I know 'em when I see 'em."

The lines which Mowrey drew on the chart crossed in a very small triangle about fifteen miles off the spot marked Narsarssuak Fjord. Turning to a radio direction finder in a corner of his cabin, Mowrey flicked a switch, donned headphones, and turned a horizontal wheel back and forth. Returning to his chart, he plotted another bearing which came about five miles from his triangle.

"Well, we're about here all right," he said. "Now how many days do you suppose that bloody troop ship will keep us waiting?"

The timing of the operation proved more precise than anyone aboard the trawler had hoped. After the *Arluk* had waited off the edge of the ice pack for only about six hours, a bright signal light blinked on the edge of the western horizon. Flags read the message: *"Arluk*, we have you on our radar. Stand by for us five miles off pack."

"At least the son of a bitch knows better than to get too

close," Mowrey said and rang up full speed as he headed toward the flashing light.

A sleek gray destroyer materialized on the horizon, and was quickly followed by the boxy shape of the much bigger troop ship, *Dorchester*. As they quickly closed the distance separating them from the *Arluk*, Paul studied them through binoculars. The destroyer zig-zagged around the *Dorchester* at high speed, her bow sending up arcs of white water that flashed in the sun. Bristling with guns, the destroyer looked lean, tough and mean, a strong contrast to the *Dorchester*, which was nothing but an old passenger liner, despite her gray paint and an incongruous-looking gun on her bow. The troop ship slowed as the *Arluk* approached and lay wallowing in the groundswell, obviously as unwarlike as some great beachfront hotel which had unaccountably gone adrift. The rails on her many decks were lined by soldiers and construction workers, who stared at the tiny trawler, perhaps astonished that such a miniscule ship could survive in this Arctic sea, and grateful for the lumbering hulk on which they stood. A rising wind moaned through the complex rigging and radio aerials of the old liner, a curiously ominous dirge.

At the time Paul, of course, had no way to know that the *Dorchester* would be sunk the following year near this spot with the loss of hundreds of lives, including those of the four chaplains who gave their life jackets to other men, but the old liner looked so helpless and out of place on the edge of the ice pack with her hundreds of soldiers waving like a holiday crowd that even then there was an aura of doom about her.

"They got no business sending an old liner like that up here," Mowrey growled.

The deep-throated whistle of the *Dorchester* gave a melancholy moan of greeting to the *Arluk* and another in farewell to the destroyer which dashed southward as soon as she had delivered her charge to the trawler. Paul drew pride from the knowledge that the lethal-appearing destroyer, with her thin plates and great screws set so far from her keel, would be able to survive the ice pack no better than the trawler could be expected to survive her kind of war.

Mowrey cut across the bow of the troop ship at the *Arluk*'s full speed.

"Get on your blinker light," he said to Flags. "Say,

'Follow me a distance of two thousand yards, speed eight knots.' "

While the lights were still flashing Mowrey closed with the ice at about a 45-degree angle. When he was just near enough to study the configurations of the pack, he changed course to parallel it.

"Now, Yale, do you think you can keep her going like this, no closer and no farther out?"

"Yes, sir."

"I'm going aloft. Station three seamen to relay my orders."

Buttoning his parka tightly, Mowrey lumbered over the well deck to the rigging of the cargo mast. With surprising agility he clambered up the ratlines until he embraced the mast near its truck. There he paused for a moment before hoisting himself into the barrel-like crow's nest. Standing there like a priest in his pulpit, he lit a cigar before studying the ice pack through the binoculars which had been swinging from his neck.

"There are no leads within sight," he called. "Bring her a little closer."

The edge of the ice pack, Paul saw, lay in bays and points like a rocky coastline. For about two hours they followed it until they reached one bay which appeared much deeper than the rest.

"Flags," Mowrey called, "tell the *Dorchester* this: 'Lay to here. Go no closer to ice but stay within signal distance. Wait for me.' "

The seamen stationed to relay his orders did so, but the captain's voice was so loud that this was a useless exercise. While the lights were still flashing, Mowrey swiftly came down to the deck and stamped up the steps to the bridge. Before ordering a change of course, he went to his cabin and quickly emerged with a newly filled coffee mug.

"Come right slowly now," he said to the helmsman. "Ahead half."

As they entered the ice cove, the sea became much calmer and they cut through the undulating white area to find smooth black water stretching for several hundred yards to what looked like the entrance to a river. The icebergs near the mouth of this lay quiet, for the grinding, smashing sounds came only from the outer edge of the pack. Proceeding more slowly, Mowrey explored this river, which twisted between ice peaks that towered far higher than the masts. The lead was perhaps a hundred yards wide at the mouth. Occasionally it broadened into small sounds, but it grew narrower as they continued to follow it, and finally they saw that one gigantic iceberg, which was more than a mile long, separated it entirely from the red granite mountains beyond.

"Well, that's the end of this one," Mowrey said, lighting a fresh cigar. "Stop the engine, right full rudder. We'll go back and see what else we can find."

As soon as they again reached the open sea, Mowrey told Flags to signal the *Dorchester*: "Follow me at distance of two thousand yards, speed eight knots." He began again to parallel the pack, and as the troop ship fell into his wake like an obedient Great Dane following a mouse, he spat over the side.

"Now, Yale, I'm supposed to teach you to be an ice pilot," he said after taking a sip from his mug. "The first thing is, be patient—sometimes you have to spend weeks looking for a lead, but one will always open up sooner or later. That ice ain't nowhere near as stationary as it looks."

"Yes, sir."

"Now finding a lead and following it is the easy part. The hard part is knowing when the pack is going to close in on you and crush you like a bloody sausage in a meat-grinder."

"How do you tell when that's going to happen, sir?"

"Watch the current, watch the wind. You can get a feel of the way the pack is moving by the way it bunches up where the water is shallow enough to ground it. The only thing I really trust, though, is my balls. When they start to ache, I get the hell out."

"Yes, sir."

"That's why nobody can train ice pilots fast. They can teach their heads, all right, but it takes years to train their balls. And a guy who has hardly no balls at all never can learn."

Mowrey smiled sweetly at Paul when he said this. Then he drained the contents of his coffee cup and ducked into his cabin again.

They searched for two days before finding a suitable lead, and even that one was so clogged with small icebergs at the narrow end that the *Arluk* had to push them aside to make a channel wide enough for the *Dorchester*. When all was in readiness, Mowrey steamed back to the edge of the

124

pack and signaled to the troop ship, "Follow me as closely as possible. Speed dead slow."

Suddenly the whole operation looked easy. The *Arluk* led the way through a channel which twisted gradually enough for the big ship to follow. Some of the icebergs dwarfed even the troop ship, and her decks were crowded with men who stood with as much awe as though they were entering a cathedral. The great vessel edged through the narrows which the trawler had cleared, but just when the captain of the *Dorchester* sounded a mournful blast of his whistle in apparent panic, they emerged into a broad black sound which separated the ice pack from the steep red mountains.

"We'll have clear sailing now," Mowrey said. "Tell the bastard that our speed is eight knots and to keep well astern. He's keeping so close it looks like he wants me to hold his bloody hand."

For two more days they steamed south between the ice pack and the mountains. The water was as calm as a mountain lake and Nathan spent his off-duty hours quickly reading through books on navigation and seamanship which he had bought in Boston, as well as several volumes on Greenland.

"If we get another few days of calm," Seth observed to Paul, "I think that Mr. Green is going to know everything in the whole world. He's apt to be giving the skipper himself lessons before long."

The wind-polished, rust-colored mountains of Greenland, too gale-swept to hold earth or much snow, never mind trees, rose in tiers to the ice cap, which was hidden by clouds thousands of feet above the sea. This coast was spectacular but changed so little as they paralleled it that the men of the *Arluk* soon began to take it as much for granted as they had the sea. Only Seth Farmer stood on the wing of the bridge studying it, even when he was off watch. As Mowrey had surmised, Seth was not much good with chart navigation, but he had almost a photographic memory when it came to coastlines. His boast was that if he had been to a place once, he could always get back.

When Paul came on watch at four in the morning of the third day since entering the ice pack, he found that they were well into Narsarssuak Fjord. He had had no clear idea of what a fjord was and was astonished to find the ships following what appeared to be a narrow river in the depths of a grand canyon. Upon studying the chart he realized that the fjord was several miles wide, but the mountains towered so high on all sides of it that they dwarfed everything, making even the big troopship look like a tiny toy lost in the Arctic wilderness.

In most places the mountains rose almost vertically from the fjord. There were a few bays surrounded by gently sloping land, some with low points which separated into groups of islands as they approached. Near one of these they saw a flotilla of kayaks heading toward them, their ivory-tipped double-ended paddles flashing in the sun.

"Eskies!" Mowrey said, ordering the engine to be stopped. "I was afraid the damn army had chased them all away."

Three of the kayaks approached the trawler, while the others headed for the *Dorchester*. The delicate craft looked exactly like pictures which Nathan and Paul had seen in the geography books of their youth, and so did the occupants, small, broad-faced Oriental-looking men in parkas made of skin and fur. They grinned broadly as they approached the *Arluk*. On the foredecks of their kayaks they carried ivory-tipped harpoons, inflated bladders to float their prey, and one of them had a dead seal about four feet long. Standing on the well deck Mowrey shouted at them and they looked astonished when they realized that he was using a few words of their language. Their grins growing even broader, they came almost close enough to touch the ship.

"Cookie!" Mowrey yelled. "Bring up some tins of coffee, tea, sugar, milk and Spam."

Soon a busy trading session was in progress. In exchange for the food, the Eskimos handed up ivory beads, walrus tusks, a spiraled narwhale tusk and, at Mowrey's insistence, their seal.

"Good as young beef any day," Mowrey said as he tossed the seal to the deck at Cookie's feet. "Cook it like steak and save me the liver."

"Do you expect me to butcher that thing?" Cookie asked recoiling in horror.

"I'll butcher it for you. Save all the ivory you can get, boys. The army and navy will give you cash or booze for it."

When the crew produced cartons of cigarettes, the Eskimos found more walrus tusks in the bottom of their kayaks. Looking astern, Paul saw that the men on the *Dorchester* were lowering buckets on long ropes to conduct their trading.

Finally the Eskimos spread out empty hands to show that they had no more to sell. Mowrey smiled and said, "Ping-ping?"

Immediately they all broke into gales of laughter which was so infectious that the men aboard the ship joined in.

"Ping-ping, ping-ping!" they all repeated in delight. Then, pointing toward the head of the fjord where the ships were heading, the oldest of the Eskimos, a man with a wrinkled face and brown stubs for teeth, said, "No ping-ping." Extending his arm toward the islands abeam, he grinned and said, "Ping-ping, *all time* ping-ping!"

Everyone laughed but Mowrey.

"I thought the army would move them miles from the big base," he said. "I bet the brass would hang us higher than the moon if we went ashore at them islands. We ain't going to have no fun until we get about four-hundred miles north of here."

Giving Paul the easy job of piloting the ship up the unobstructed fjord, Mowrey tied the tail of the seal to the cargo boom, got a sharp knife from Cookie, and proceeded to butcher it. Rolling up his sleeves, he attacked the seal as though it were a mortal enemy, but his big hands were expert enough to roll off the skin as though it were a garment. Newly relieved from the helm, Guns watched him with admiration.

"Damn, skipper! Can you strip an Eskie girl that easy?"

"There ain't nothing an Eskie girl can't do without stripping."

"You reckon we're really going to find some Eskie girls?"

"If they ever let us get away from these bases, we will. Course, I never had a crew this big up here. There were only about a dozen of us on the vessels, and a lot of them were Christers who didn't even go ashore."

"Damn," Guns said, "if I don't find me a woman of some kind pretty soon, I'm liable to take after one of them seals. That red meat looks pretty good."

"You wouldn't be the first to fuck a seal," Mowrey said as he cut a huge steak off a flank. "You better make sure the bugger is dead, though. They can bite like crocodiles. I had a friend who put a bag over the head of one, and she bit

127

right through it. It's a hell of a lot easier to fuck a holy roller virgin than it is a seal."

Nathan, who had been half listening to this while he admired the scenery, wearily went below and picked up one of his books on Greenland. "The Eskimos," he read, "are a gentle people who need protection from white men."

# CHAPTER 16

The *Dorchester* moored at a new wharf to unload her troops. The *Arluk* moored nearby. The army base and airfield did nothing to satisfy any curiosity the men of the *Arluk* had about the mysteries of the north. The rows of Quonset huts were so familiar that for a moment, Paul wondered whether he had ever left Argentia. This thought reminded him of the poker hands he had won and he wondered whether they played cards at the officers' club here.

"Captain, can I go ashore for a few hours tonight?" he asked Mowrey shortly after they had moored at a long, low wharf beside a Norwegian freighter.

"You can after you see if there's any mail for the men, after you discharge our cargo and load anything they got waiting for us here. I'm going ashore to see when the hell they're going to let us start north."

Much to the disappointment of all hands, no mail was waiting for anyone aboard the *Arluk*, despite the fact that letters from the States came in every day aboard planes. Boats, who had left Boston while his wife was momentarily expecting a baby, swore softly.

"I bet Headquarters has forgot all about us," he said. "Talk about the legion of forgotten men!"

"As soon as I can get ashore I'll try to straighten things out," Paul said. "Let's get this hold unloaded."

Nathan checked packing cases off an invoice as their cargo boom swung them ashore to waiting trucks. Most of their cargo consisted of bales of winter clothing and boxes of radio equipment, the lightness of which had contributed to the instability of the ship. Near the bottom of the hold were several boxes of spare parts for radar sets at the airbase.

"Damn, I don't think these would have fit Hansen's old set, but I sure would have liked to have tried to work something out for him," Nathan said. "To think I was sitting here on all this equipment, while that poor guy goes off with a busted set."

"I wonder where he is now," Paul said.

"From what I've read, he's probably trying to work his way through the ice. They say the ice is a lot worse over there. That's one big reason why all the big settlements are on the west side."

Paul had a quick mental image of Hansen's trawler caught helplessly in ice which a big German icebreaker might get through easily enough. Well, he could call in aircraft. How long would the planes take to get there? Suddenly, he was glad that he had no more to worry about than Mowrey's insults. Perhaps it was wise, after all, not to try to change the hand that the fates dealt to him.

When he called the operations officer from a dockside telephone, Paul was told that a new cargo for the *Arluk* was still being assembled, and that inquiries about their mail had been radioed to Headquarters. Since both Seth and Nathan were interested only in getting some sleep, Paul set off for the officers' club with a clean conscience.

Or almost a clear conscience. The idea of winning at poker and bridge from rich, often spoiled fraternity brothers and from the people who hung around yacht clubs had seemed to him to be cause for more pride than shame, but the concept of a Coast Guard officer, the executive officer of a cutter on the Greenland Patrol, acting as a card sharp with his brother officers did bother him a little. Of course, he was not really a card sharp because he never cheated, but so few of the people who played poker or bridge really studied the games seriously and so few even bothered to stay sober enough while they were gambling to remember what cards had been played that he knew he was taking advantage of them. But now he had a reason for trying to win all he could: when he mailed the money he had won in Argentia to Sylvia, he had said he would try to send more for her house if his luck at cards held. When she had first mentioned it, the thought of her father lending her money for a house in Wellesley had not exactly thrilled him, but now he understood what the building of a home meant to her, and he was enthusiastic, especially when he imagined the greeting she would give him when he returned, maybe in only about six months. It was the job of a husband to keep his wife happy, wasn't it, and if his "gift" for playing cards well helped him to satisfy some of her desires, why feel guilty about it?

Whatever reservations Paul had about the morality of preying on his fellow Coast Guard officers stopped bothering him when he realized that the club at this base was frequented almost entirely by army air force officers, many of whom were majors and colonels while still in their twenties, and almost all of whom had wallets swollen with flight pay. As the evening wore on and the stacks of chips in front of him grew, Paul also realized that the people at this club changed too much with in-going and out-going flights for a hustler to be recognized, no matter how many nights he won. Apparently convinced that their lives would be short, many of the baby-faced majors and colonels gambled with reckless abandon. This airbase, probably all Greenland officers' clubs, were absolute heaven for a man who really understood poker and bridge.

Before that eight-hour poker game was over, Paul had won close to nineteen hundred dollars. With his pockets full of rolls of twenty-dollar bills, he went back to the ship to devise a package for mailing it home, a task which was made much easier by the fact that he had designated himself the naval censor aboard the *Arluk*.

His thoughts of mailing the money and soon going back to win more were rudely interrupted, however, as he started across the wharf to his ship. Five trucks were just beginning to disgorge an avalanche of foodstuffs for transportation in the *Arluk*'s hold. Mowrey himself was supervising the loading.

"Where the hell have you been, Yale?" he bellowed. "I lit a fire under the operations officer and we got our cargo. The folks all up and down this whole coast, clear up to Thule, haven't had supplies all winter. I bet even the dogs are starving. Get your ass aboard here, Yale, and make ready to get under way."

The loading of the cargo did not go anywhere near as speedily as Mowrey wished and there were seemingly endless delays while they waited for medical supplies and heavy generators which had been requested by settlements they were to visit. When the hold was full, drums of diesel oil were stowed on the well deck and on top of these they lashed crates of odiferous dried fish which the Greenlanders needed for dog food. It was May 18 when they finally got their orders to sail, and by this time the ship was "loaded up like a tinker's wagon," Mowrey said. Even the confusion of a miscellaneous deck cargo did not dampen his high spirits, for his orders were exactly those he wanted and which he had feared would be given to some other vessel. The *Arluk* was to sail as far north on the west coast of Greenland as the ice conditions permitted, stopping at each native settlement and Danish village to deliver supplies. From Narsarssuak Fjord to Thule, far above the Arctic Circle, the distance was only about fifteen hundred miles, a voyage of little more than ten days in open water, but not much of that could be expected in the ice pack, which might make many of their ports of call inaccessible for weeks. Mowrey knew that his superiors would not be surprised if the voyage lasted six weeks, two months or all summer. The prospect of escaping military bases and returning to the unspoiled parts of Greenland which he remembered so well made him almost genial and most of the crew reflected his mood.

Paul's spirits were improved too when he found, soon after leaving the fjord, that Mowrey was seriously training him to pilot the ship through ice, a step he probably would not take if he expected soon to carry out his threat of transferring him to a shore base. In addition to standing his regular watch, Paul was told to remain on the bridge with the captain as long as he could stay awake and observe the way Mowrey twisted and turned through leads in the great jumble of icebergs, a process which made ordinary navigation by dead reckoning impossible. To keep track of their position it was necessary to keep identifying on the chart each mountain peak and bay which came into view, and to take frequent bearings. When a lead they were following narrowed and came to a dead end, it was sometimes possible to place the bow of the ship gently against a crack between two small icebergs and gradually increase the revolutions of the trawler's big propeller until the barrier parted like a great white gate and let them through. Suddenly released from the grip of the ice, the *Arluk* sometimes lunged ahead and would have crashed into the next iceberg if the engine were not stopped or reversed at precisely the right instant. Sometimes two or three long Arctic days and sunny nights were needed to shoulder their way from one lead to another, but the process fascinated Paul so much that he needed only two or three hours of sleep before returning to the bridge. Mowrey gave him no compliments and during the first week always jammed the ship in the ice to wait motionless during the brief periods that he himself had to sleep. When, on the eighth day, he retired to his cabin and let his executive officer pilot the ship toward a distant mountain peak for a full hour without supervision, Paul felt as though Harvard had just granted him a doctoral degree. Even the fact that the captain shouted at him worse than ever when he returned after a brief nap did not dim his sense of accomplishment.

For Nathan Green time passed much more slowly. Although he stood the twelve-to-four watch, Mowrey made sure that he was never alone on the bridge and considered him too incompetent to pilot the ship even under supervision. Still, when Nathan discovered that on this voyage the ship almost never left the ice pack and that the water amidst the icebergs was as calm as a small mountain lake, his release from constant seasickness made him feel as joyful as a condemned man upon receiving a pardon. Full of a new sense of contentment, he stood by the rail while Mowrey or Paul conned the ship and admired the spectacular scenery, which changed from minute to minute less because of the motion of the vessel and of the icebergs, which drifted slowly in currents and winds, than because of the strange atmospheric conditions which made Greenland resemble a vast stage with gauzy curtains, veils beyond veils in constantly changing patterns of light. Coming to the bridge from his cabin one rosy midnight, Nathan saw a row of sparkling white icebergs like the skyline of a city silhouetted against a pink cloud which at first looked solid enough to be a wall of quartz. As he stared in awe, a sudden gust of wind dissolved the cloud, revealing a range of naked mountains which now glowed a deep burnt orange against a lavender sky. What looked like a bank of snow at their base gradually turned into a luminous mist which blew away, revealing the entrance to an enormous fjord. Heavy pewter-colored clouds hung over that great canyon and delivered a narrowly localized snowstorm which was slanted by the wind into a diagonal pattern of gray and white, a translucent nearly transparent curtain through which the rising half moon shimmered. As the sun rose higher above the range of mountains, the surface of the sea, the ice and the land were momentarily turned almost crimson.

"Good God," Nathan said to Mowrey, who was taking a bearing on the entrance to the fjord, "I don't know whether it looks like heaven or hell, but it sure doesn't look like any earth I've ever seen."

"Do you know what it looks like to me?" Mowrey asked, lighting the stump of his cigar. Before waiting for a reply, he added, "The entrance to that fjord looks like the biggest damn cow's cunt I ever seen."

Nathan winced, angry at himself for giving Mowrey the satisfaction of shocking him. "Well, captain, I guess that's one way to look at it."

As his days of idleness passed, Nathan began to feel more and more guilty about his status as little more than a passenger aboard the ship. He had read all the textbooks on navigation and seamanship he could find and was quite capable of using the bubble sextant, but Mowrey wouldn't let him near the chart table to plot his lines of position. Nathan was so hungry for some useful work that he rushed to help Boats and a gang of deckhands when they were picking up a crate of dried fish that had broken and spilled onto the deck. As Nathan used his bucket to help shovel the fish into burlap sacks, Boats put a heavy hand on his shoulder.

"Sir, don't you know that officers ain't supposed to do work like this? This is my job."

Finding himself apologizing for trying to be useful, Nathan ambled aft and stood by the depth charges on the stern. Seasickness had been the worst physical agony of his life, but at least it had acted like a drug to dull other pains. The grumbling of the propeller shaft under his feet and the seagulls swooping over the bubbling wake astern suddenly reminded him of the Staten Island ferry, aboard which he and his wife had often ridden during their brief marriage.

Becky. For two years now he had, for the sake of his own sanity, tried not to think of her any more than possible, and he still never talked about her to anyone. They had had only nineteen months together before she had gone to Poland to get her parents. In the two and a half years that had followed, Nathan's grief had taken many forms. After having been forced to realize that there was no way to get information about her, he had tried to join the Canadian air force. Unable to pass the rigid physical examinations, he had accepted an offer to work on defense contracts at General Electric.

Immediately after Pearl Harbor, he had tried to join first the navy, then the marines and finally the Coast Guard. The idea of going to war to win personal revenge against the Nazis had struck him as futile, but still compelling. War was disciplined hatred, after all, and who had reason to hate the Nazis more than he? Despite his distaste for melodrama, he had imagined himself using his knowledge of electronics to sink Nazi battleships, landing in France and striding across Europe to rescue his wife.

Instead, he had landed aboard a trawler in Greenland where he was considered too ignorant and inept to give a simple order to the helmsman. And instead of working, however indirectly, to defeat the country which had swallowed his wife, he was spending weeks on end as a passenger, admiring the beautiful scenery. The fact that he at times found himself enjoying his leisure and his fantastic surroundings made him feel more guilty than ever.

About ten days after leaving Narsarssuak Fjord, however, Nathan did find a job for himself. It began when Sparks came out of the radio shack and said, "Sir, I'm picking up a message that might be from the *Nanmak*, but they're sending it in Morse much faster than I can read it. Do you want to see if you can get it?"

Since the age of fifteen, Nathan had been a ham radio operator, and he had no trouble in jotting down the coded signals. He was so curious about the activities of the *Nanmak* that he hurried to decipher them as though they were an urgent message for his own ship.

The message was addressed to "Commander GreenPat" and was from Hansen. The first part of it had been sent before Nathan had been called to the radio shack and was not repeated, despite the fact that heavy static made reception difficult. The message was sent as fast as possible and kept as brief as possible to give as little help as possible to radio direction finders aboard any German ship in the vicinity, Nathan realized. When deciphered, the message said: ". . . visibility almost zero. Proceeding slowly through heavy ice. No radio activity detected. Have discovered, however, four red marks on ice which look like copper antifouling bottom paint. Deduce that some ship has been this way since last snowstorm. A course of zero four eight brings us from first of these marks to others, which were discovered in circular search pattern. One soft flat berg has been ploughed through, leaving channel sixty-two feet wide indicating passage of ship much bigger than trawler. Probably icebreaker making much better speed than us, but am tracking."

Nathan wondered how it must feel to be a hare tracking a hound. If fog continued to reduce the visibility to zero and if the German had functioning radar, he would locate the *Nanmak* long before Hansen could see him. Perhaps the rush of incoming shells would be the first proof Hansen would get that the Germans were nearby. If only I were there, I probably could get that old radar set going for a little while and could at least give Hansen a chance to maneuver, Nathan thought. He was surprised and pleased to discover that he genuinely wished he were there. The thought of dying did not bother him anywhere near as much as the knowledge that he was useless in this battle that he wanted so much to fight.

Going to the bridge, Nathan found Mowrey standing beside Paul while he shouted orders to the helmsman.

"Captain, I copied a message from the *Nanmak* to GreenPat," he said. "We're not involved, but I thought you might want to see it."

Mowrey took the clipboard from his hand and quickly read it. Handing it to Paul, he said, "Looks like Wally is making himself into a hero. That little bastard always was smart. I bet he's holed up in the ice pack drinking that Aquavit of his and dreaming up all kinds of messages to make himself look good. One thing you can count on is that Wally Hansen ain't going to catch up to no Kraut icebreaker. He's too smart a squarehead for that."

When Paul read the message he couldn't deny his first feeling was gratitude that he was safe on the west coast of Greenland, instead of aboard the *Nanmak*. Which undoubtedly meant that he was a coward. But he couldn't feel too ashamed of that. After all, he had Mowrey. Who

135

was to say which was more dangerous—a mad dog or a German?

"Keep copying anything sent to or from the *Nanmak*," Mowrey was saying. "I want to see what stories Wally invents next to keep Headquarters happy."

# CHAPTER 17

The *Arluk*'s first port of call was Godhavn, which Mowrey hoped to reach in about a week, but it was more than two weeks before they wove and bucked their way through the ice pack to that rock-rimmed harbor. As they approached a low stone wharf, a flotilla of kayaks surrounded them, and a crowd of fur-garbed Greenlanders lined the shore.

"Let's give them a show," Mowrey said, and began tooting the air horn, which had sounded insignificant in Boston, but which echoed off the surrounding hills of Godhavn with satisfying authority. The natives seemed impressed.

"Flags, flash the searchlight," Mowrey said. "Guns, see that growler over there?"

"Growler, sir?"

"For Christ's sake, a growler is an iceberg so small it's awash in any kind of sea. See it? Try to hit it with the starboard twenty-millimeter. There ain't nobody you can hurt over in that direction."

"Aye, aye, sir," Guns said with enthusiasm. He always loved to fire the gun, and never before had he had an audience of civilians.

The Eskimos were startled when the big twenty started its rapid barks and directed a fiery arc of explosive shells at the blue mound of ice floating near the entrance to the harbor, but realizing suddenly that this was a show for their benefit, they jumped up and down in more lively fashion than ever, shrieked their laughter and clapped. Egged on by the enthusiasm of his audience, Mowrey stopped the ship and turned her enough to bring the three-inch gun on the bow to bear on the target. The gun crew loaded and fired as rapidly as they could, and though the shells missed their target by twenty-five yards, the short cannon made a satisfying series of explosions which echoed through the surrounding mountains.

"Give them a star shell," Mowrey said.

The sun was low enough in the sky to make the burst of the star shell brilliant against the opposite horizon, a display spectacular enough to make a fitting climax to the show.

"That's enough now," Mowrey said. "Mooring stations!"

As the first lines were secured to the wharf, Mowrey continued to tutor Paul. Because the tide here could fall thirty feet and because ferocious squalls often swept Greenland harbors, where the cold air from the ice pack met the warmer waters from the Gulf Stream, the normally simple act of tying up a ship was something of an art. While the deck force labored to double up their longest and heaviest dock lines, almost everyone else aboard the trawler changed into their best uniforms for a night ashore. The liberty party was assembling on the well deck, where they joked with Eskimos on the wharf, when a tall, thin old Dane approached the ship. His appearance was startling because he wore a gray business suit and a spiffy Chesterfield coat which looked as though he belonged in London or Boston, not in a crowd of fur-clad Eskimos. In heavily accented English he asked whether he could talk to the captain and Mowrey jovially beckoned him to the pilothouse. Soon they disappeared into the captain's cabin and Flags was dispatched to bring ice cubes, a commodity which Mowrey never used.

They did not stay in the cabin long. When they came out Mowrey no longer looked jovial, and the Dane hurried quickly ashore.

"Bring the men to quarters," Mowrey said to Paul. "I got to talk to them."

Paul passed the word and soon the shrill whistle of the boatswain's pipe sounded. The men who lined up on the well deck looked entirely different from the crew to which Mowrey had read his orders in Boston. Primed for liberty and disciplined by almost two months with Mowrey, these sailors stood at attention like a well-drilled company of marines. Even Nathan, who was looking forward to visiting a native settlement, had put on a well-pressed uniform and stood rigidly at attention. Only Farmer had remained himself. In his old khaki parka, he leaned against the winch and smoked his pipe.

"At ease," Mowrey said as he stood in front of the men. He had put on his blue uniform with the four rows of campaign ribbons and his short, improbably black hair was slicked down under his sealskin overseas cap, but he himself did not look at ease and his voice for the first time sounded unsure.

"Men, I have bad news," he began. "That Dane who came aboard is the *bistera* or governor of this place. He says they've had trouble from the crews of other ships and the Danes have passed a law for all Greenland. Nobody can go ashore here except on official business."

A loud collective groan came from the crew.

"Sorry, but I can't do nothing about this," Mowrey continued. "Too much army and too much navy is up here these days, not right here, but farther south. Too many Eskie girls got knocked up and got the clap, so now we're all restricted by order of the Danish government and our government backs them up. If I let you go ashore, it'll be my ass."

"Can't you find some official business for us?" Boats asked.

"The Eskies are going to carry supplies themselves—all we'll do is set their stuff on the wharf. Best I can do is set up a beerbust for you on the wharf, but the governor is going to make all the Eskies clear out first."

More groans.

"Farther north things may be different," Mowrey continued. "The law is the same for all Greenland, but there are places where there will be no Danes to watch us. I feel for you men and you can be sure I'll do everything I can for you. Dis-missed."

Before the men could engage him in conversation, Mowrey headed for his cabin. "Come," he barked at Paul.

After closing the door of his cabin, Mowrey sat on the edge of his bunk and Paul perched on the stool before the chart table.

"Of course what the man really said was, the officers could go ashore, but not the enlisted men. The Danes are throwing a shindig for us. Want to go? It will be official business."

Paul, feeling guilty, said he would.

138

"That farmer can't go because he ain't a commissioned officer and I don't want that Greenberg along. Not tonight. Just tell them you got official business."

"Mr. Farmer never seems to want to go ashore much, but I know that Mr. Green is looking forward—"

"I don't want no Sheenie with me. There will be a dinner and a dance and God knows what. You can't tell what that Sheenie would do. Anyway, I can never relax with him."

Paul said nothing, silence being the strongest show of protest he could make. The thought that Mowrey could not relax with Nathan after vilifying him for weeks fascinated him. Somehow that feeling was understandable, even reasonable, for although Nathan never replied to the insults heaped upon him, there was such contempt in his deep-set eyes whenever he looked at the captain that relaxation would have been difficult.

Mowrey left to Paul the job of telling Seth and Nathan that they would not be permitted ashore. Seth had already started to write one of his endless letters to his wife and did not appear to mind, but Nathan was studying a brief vocabulary of Greenlander words which he had found in one of his books.

"Sorry," Paul concluded. "To be honest, the skipper said he can't relax with you. I've been trying to figure out what the horrible meaning of that is."

"The offender never forgives," Nathan said with a wry grin. "Hell, I couldn't relax with him. If this is just going to be some kind of a party the Danes are giving for him, I'd just as soon not be there."

Holding his list of Eskimo words, Nathan went to the well deck and leaning on the rail, smiled and said something which sounded like "Oskos" to a row of Greenlanders who were solemnly admiring the ship. Apparently it meant "Hello." They immediately grinned and crowded as near to him as they could, laughing and talking in a combination of three languages—their own, Danish and English. Their blood, Paul observed, was as mixed as their speech. A few of the people on the wharf were the short, solid, copper-colored Orientals of the north, but despite the fact that they all wore fur clothes, some looked Scandinavian, and others represented every possible mixture of the two races. In their laughter and their enthusiasms, they were all pure Eskimo as they pointed to the sky, the wharf, the ship, the sea and articles of their clothing to give Nathan the proper words. And Nathan's craggy face, which seemed permanently cast in lines of melancholy and sorrow, reflected their humor and their joy. His interchange with them came as a relief after the constant bawdiness of the captain and the crew whenever they came into contact with Eskimos.

Seth came forward to supervise the opening of the hatches and the unloading of supplies. To save space the crates and boxes had been fitted into the hold like a huge jig-saw puzzle, without much regard for putting the crates designed for the first port of call on top. When Mowrey, who was watching the operation from the gun deck, realized that everything in the hold had to be rousted out and examined to find the pieces assigned to this place, he said, "Mr. Farmer, you can't throw supplies into a hold the way you throw mackerel into a fishboat. When are you going to look at that uniform you're wearing and realize that you're in the Coast Guard?"

For the first time Mowrey's criticism flustered the old fisherman. His face turned a deeper shade of russet red and he stuttered a little when he said, "Sorry, sir. I j-j-just do the best I can."

Ordinarily Mowrey would have given Paul hell for the inefficient stowage of the cargo, on the theory that the executive officer was responsible for whatever went wrong aboard the ship. The shifting of his wrath to Seth, in addition to his recent efforts to teach Paul as much as possible about the running of the ship, made Paul realize that his status had changed or was in the process of changing from scapegoat to protégé. Perhaps his being chosen as the only officer allowed to go ashore that night with the captain was further proof of that. The thought filled Paul with strongly contradictory emotions; relief, renewed ambition, pride in learning to do his job well, and also a disturbing sense of disloyalty to the others, especially Nathan. In the unending war between the captain and the other officers, he had always felt one with Nathan and Seth. Now was he supposed to change sides?

Although it was six-thirty in the evening when the captain and Paul went ashore, the sun was still high in the sky. As soon as they walked off the wharf and around a stone warehouse on the shore, a great many Eskimo dogs began to bark, and soon they were surrounded by a pack of about thirty of them, which growled and bared their fangs with all the ferociousness of a pack of wolves about to attack. Paul, who had never been afraid of dogs, was terrified as one huge gray beast with eyes that looked yellow pressed forward and snapped its great jaws only a few inches from his ankles.

Paul tried to say something soothing, and he put his hand out to pat the snarling animal.

The big dog crouched for a spring and was about to take off Paul's hand when Mowrey exploded.

"Back off, you sons of bitches!" he roared, and to Paul's astonishment, growled and roared more like a lion than a man.

The dogs cowered and retreated a few yards, but formed a circle around them. Mowrey stooped, and though there was no small stone in the frozen mud under their feet, he straightened up with an exaggerated pantomine of throwing and gave more roars. The pack of dogs turned tail and ran.

"Lesson one," Mowrey said with grim satisfaction, "sled dogs are not pets. The Eskies treat 'em rough and don't even feed 'em much when they ain't using them. Sled dogs will kill you if you fall. They kill kids all the time up here. The Eskies look at that the way we look at car accidents."

"I see," Paul replied, still finding it hard to believe.

"You got to talk to a sled dog in his own language," Mowrey continued. "And one thing they know is to run when it looks like a man is throwing a stone."

After passing a sod warehouse, they saw the village ahead of them. Paul had half expected to come upon a collection of igloos or primitive huts, such as he had seen in schoolbook illustrations, and was surprised to see what appeared to be a toy village, about a dozen miniature cottages and a church, all painted brick red with white trim.

"The Danes bring in wood for construction," Mowrey explained. "It's expensive and so is coal, so they keep everything small."

A half dozen children dressed as Greenlanders, but with faces of varying cast and hue, greeted them with a fine mixture of shyness and exuberance, laughing but keeping their distance. The youngsters led them toward the largest of the houses, which had neatly painted white shutters and gingerbread trim, but was no bigger than a two-car garage. The frozen mud around it had been raked during a thaw and looked curiously neat compared to the lane which they

141

had been following, a stony path littered by dog droppings, heaps of cans and other trash awaiting a thaw for burial. On this bright spring night the temperature was not much below freezing and there was no sting in the soft wind from the sea, but it was cold enough to rob dirt of any odor. The only smell in the crystal air was the acrid tang of soft coal burning in small stoves so carefully tended that almost no smoke came from the stone chimneys of the little houses.

As they approached the biggest house, the front door opened and Peter Anderson, the tall Dane who had boarded their ship, came out to greet them. When he had boarded the *Arluk* to lay down the law about enlisted men coming ashore, he had appeared stern to the point of hostility, but now his whole manner had changed and he was the deferential host. He ushered Paul and Mowrey through a vestibule so small that Mowrey had to edge his great shoulders sideways through rows of sealskin parkas hanging on the walls into a livingroom which was only about twelve feet square and which looked even smaller because it was crowded with eight Danes, all of whom looked enormous with their heads almost touching the ceiling. They were all wearing their best European clothes, and the three women had put on dark silk dresses like short evening gowns. One of these women was maybe sixty or seventy; one was about thirty, blonde and pretty, if a little gaunt, and the third was a fat, round-faced woman who could have been twenty-five or forty-five, and who wore a low-necked gown which she apparently had bought before gaining much of her weight. The top halves of her huge breasts bulged from this in a way that might have struck Paul as grotesque in Boston, but he had already been away from women long enough to make the display almost unbearably attractive.

Peter Anderson gave formal introductions. None of the Danes was proficient at English, but all knew a few words. The fat woman's name was Hilda. She had a circular, curiously babyish face above her triple chins and spoke in a high childish voice, interspersed with giggles, which made her startling bosom quiver in its tightly buttoned black silk bindings. Paul was wryly amused at himself for considering her beautiful and charming. He was disappointed when she appeared to have eyes only for Mowrey, who was, after all, much older than she, and whose beefy, old fighter's face had always struck Paul as exceedingly ugly. But he was still the captain.

The old man, Paul saw with surprise, possessed a brand of social charm which he never displayed aboard ship. He was courtly, formal without being unfriendly, and curiously dignified as he accepted the biggest armchair in the crowded room and smiled at the people who passed him drinks, canapés, and sat in a semicircle around him to pay court. Here, after all, was the commanding officer of the long-awaited supply ship, an American fighting man whose strength, wisdom and courage somehow appeared to be boundless. These Danes, who had lost their own country to the Germans, and some of whom had come to Greenland as refugees, treated him as an oracle, as well as a savior. As soon as the drinks (a kind of sweet warm martini which would have horrified Paul in Boston but which now tasted marvelous) were passed, everyone asked Mowrey his opinion of how the war was going.

"Now it's not going to be hard to take them Nazis," Mowrey said with a casual tone. "We can do it fast or we can do it slow. The thing is, we can take them with less loss of life if we take time for a big buildup first and the proper strategy. No one wonders whether we can beat the Germans. It's like killing a mad dog. First you have to get yourself a net and then you want to put it over his head without taking any chance of being bit."

This assessment of the military scene seemed well received. Hilda edged the invisible little chair under her so close to the captain that her great bosom almost rested on his knees. Which caused Mowrey to take off his dark glasses, a most unusual gesture, and to pat her shoulder affectionately. She in turn handed him a square of toast with a particularly succulent piece of smoked salmon.

No one paid much attention to Paul, a slim junior officer standing at the back of the room. The good-looking blonde woman was apparently Anderson's wife. She passed a platter with strips of salt cod and smoked salmon to Paul and filled his glass, but when he asked her if the winter had been hard, she smiled in confusion and said, "I have no English." Even so, she seemed to understand the captain and laughed whenever he made a joke.

Soon a buffet dinner was served, largely native foods, Anderson explained, because they had long ago used up most of their supplies from Europe. There were several kinds of fish, all of them delicious, seals' liver which tasted like good calves' liver, bear meat, which was stringy, and ptarmigan, which was much like quail, although smaller. Newly-baked bread took the place of potatoes, and canned tomatoes which almost had to be spooned up like soup were the only vegetable. For dessert there was a variety of baked goods which gave the phrase "Danish pastry" new meaning. A sweet, homemade wine which had been made from raisins was served with the meal, but Mowrey stuck with tumblers of the warm martinis, which he tossed off with gusto.

Anderson apologized for being able to serve neither coffee nor tea. Except for one remaining pitcher of the martinis, he could offer nothing more to drink.

"Why hell," Mowrey said, "I got a dozen cases of booze consigned to you down at the ship, and we got plenty coffee and tea. Yale, run down and have the boys bring up just enough for tonight right away. The booze is locked in the lazaret. I haven't told no one about it."

Shifting in his armchair, Mowrey took a key on a big ring from his pocket and handed it to Paul. "Hurry along now."

After the stifling little room, the cold air felt good. Paul's wristwatch told him that it was a little before ten in the evening, but the sun was still high above the polished backs of the dun-colored granite mountains. Still unable to take eternal daylight for granted, Paul felt odd as he walked back toward the ship. When the pack of dogs suddenly leaped from the shadow of a warehouse, he roared at them Mowrey-fashion and made throwing motions. "Get out of here, you sons of bitches!" There was great satisfaction in seeing them retreat. He was getting to be almost an old Greenland hand, he thought. Well, at least he was not a man who could be cowed by dogs.

Nearing the ship, he saw a line of Greenlanders carrying heavy crates and boxes from the wharf to the warehouse. When he saw their faces, he realized that they were all women. The men, who were dressed in similar furry clothes, were taller, and they were standing with folded arms, watching the women work and giving instructions. Boy, I wonder what Sylvia would think of that, he thought with a grin. All evening he had not thought of Sylvia, and the memory of her trim figure made the fact that he had

144

been spurned by the fat Danish woman that evening seem funny. As the old general had said, war is hell.

Anxious to leave a port where they were not allowed ashore, the deck force was continuing to unload cargo. As Paul boarded the ship, he saw Nathan standing like a solitary sentry on the flying bridge, a lone figure in a parka outlined against the sky. On impulse he climbed a ladder to speak to him. Absorbed in thought, Nathan did not hear him approach.

"You're not missing much of a party," Paul said.

"I'm glad I didn't go. We copied a message from Green-Pat to the *Nanmak*. I just decoded it."

"What's up?"

Nathan looked and sounded excited. "My God, nobody's sure what's going on, but our monitoring stations have picked up all kinds of radio signals on the east coast, all the way from Cape Farewell up to practically the damn North Pole. For days there was complete radio silence, and now there are German signals from seven different sources."

"What the hell can that mean?" Paul asked.

"The bastards know we're after them, with planes as well as the *Nanmak*, so they're trying to confuse us with decoys, I think."

"How would they do that?"

"GreenPat isn't sure. The visibility cleared considerably up there just before the signals came through. Maybe they have a long-range plane circling and sending signals."

"Maybe," Paul said. "Do the signals all come at once from different places?"

"Mostly no, but they do sometimes. The Krauts could have dropped recording devices or even floated them from balloons. They could have landed small shore parties all up and down the coast—"

"Or they could have a whole fleet of icebreakers and trawlers up there," Paul said.

"That's right. We've got three PBY's patrolling the area right now, but the visibility comes and goes. Paul, if they do have more than one ship up there, wouldn't we send more ships? Isn't there a chance that they'd take us off this milk run and send us up there?"

"I guess," Paul said, and was ashamed of not feeling sufficient enthusiasm. The thought of one heavily armed German icebreaker had been bad enough. How about sailing into a whole fleet of them?

Nathan obviously felt no such hesitancy. "God, I'd like to get into that brawl," he said. "If they could put me aboard the *Nanmak*, I could at least fix the radar. I doubt like hell if all those German ships have radar yet. If we had it we might be able to call the planes down on them without even having them sight us."

"If the weather was good enough for planes," Paul said. "What did Hansen have to say about all this?"

"Nothing. He just acknowledged the message. He's trying to keep radio silence as much as possible."

Paul wondered what Hansen must be feeling as he sat in his well-furnished cabin plotting German radio signals all around him.

"If the weather gives them a break, the planes ought to find what's going on up there before long," Nathan said.

Paul was not so sure. If any ship was painted white, she would be difficult for even low-flying planes to see in the ice floe. Certainly the Germans would be smart enough to jam a ship between two big bergs, cover her decks with snow and blur the outline of her guns with large sheets of white canvas. In his own mind he had rehearsed such steps if his ship were ever the quarry.

"I guess we'll just have to wait and see," Paul said, and remembering his errand, went to the lazaret in the stern of the ship. Mowrey always wanted him to hurry, but never more than when he was sent out after booze.

The lazaret was a large storage compartment, the after end of which had been partitioned with heavy wood and a door with a padlock. Inside there were many stacks of cases of whiskey, gin and vodka, each marked with the name of a port. Mowrey himself had supervised the storage of these goods, and the boxes for this port were on top. Paul had planned to ask a couple of deck hands to help him to carry the heavy cases, but it seemed suddenly wrong to ask men to lug liquor to a party which they could not attend. After putting one box of twenty-four bottles of scotch on the deck, he returned to lock the door. For a moment he could not find the padlock, but after locating it between two floorboards, he put it in place, snapped it shut and pocketed the key.

The case of scotch was clearly marked, HAIG & HAIG. As he climbed from the lazaret and picked it up, Flags and one of the seamen laughed somewhat bitterly.

"Good party, sir?" Flags asked.

"If you like Danes fat as whales," Paul replied with a grin, and shouldering the heavy box, walked to the gangway at the well deck. First Boats and then a dozen seamen solemnly snapped to attention and rendered statuesque salutes as the executive officer with the big box of scotch on his shoulder passed.

"Shit, guys," Paul said. "This is for the Danes. It's part of their consignment. They paid for it."

"Aye, aye, sir," Boats said. "First time you ever did stevedore work, sir?"

"Look, I'll try to get the skipper to break out some beer for you guys in the morning. I'd give you this booze if it were mine."

"Sure you would, sir," Boats said with a smile. "We know your heart is in the right place, sir."

Feeling ridiculous, Paul hurried to the Dane's cottage. He was halfway there before he remembered that he was supposed to bring tea and coffee too, but he doubted whether they would be missed.

In Paul's absence the party had livened up. The table and chairs had been pushed into a bedroom and people were dancing to a scratchy record of "You Are My Sunshine." In the center of the room Mowrey had stretched his arms around all of Hilda's quivering charms. The two of them were enjoying the dance without bothering to move their feet much. "By God, you finally made it!" Mowrey said when Paul carried the case of whiskey into the room. Taking the heavy box off his shoulder, he ripped it open with one swipe of his heavy hand and handed it to Anderson. The Dane's thin blonde wife appeared almost immediately with a tray full of glasses and a pitcher of water. As the whiskey was being poured, the spring of the victrola began to wind down, drawing the words of "You Are My Sunshine" into a mournful moan. Striding across the room, Mowrey cut it off. "Let's make our own music," he said. "How about a song?"

With his arms still around Hilda, Mowrey started with, "Let Me Call You Sweetheart," the title of which everyone chorused, though no one knew many more of the words. The Danish national anthem came next, followed by "The Star Spangled Banner," "America," and "God Bless America." After a short pause for refilling glasses, Mowrey started on "One-Eyed Riley." Few people understood the words, which he did not pronounce clearly, but they rec-

147

ognized the fact that the song was bawdy and cheered lustily. The blonde woman passed a platter of codfish strips which had been salted so heavily that they produced a burning thirst. Anderson opened another bottle of whiskey.

Standing at the back of the room, Paul drank his share. It was hard not to contrast this revel with the predicament of the *Nanmak*, now ringed by enemy radio signals. Suddenly it seemed inevitable that the *Arluk* would soon be sent to help her. The thought that this might be his last party crossed his mind and seemed more gloomily realistic than melodramatic. Hilda's breasts jiggled magnificently as she attempted to dance with the captain. Now the victrola was playing Italian opera.

Paul's legs began to ache and the floor felt strangely comfortable when he sat on it. A thin bald man who explained that he was a doctor joined him. He carried a bottle of whiskey and kept both of their glasses full while in broken English he described the medical problems of the Eskimos. They suffered a great deal from tuberculosis, from venereal diseases, and from what white men call childhood diseases. Most died before they were forty. Eskimos melt like snow once white men arrive in great numbers, the doctor said almost casually. They can't handle alcohol. Sugar rots their teeth, and they exhaust their game supply soon after getting guns. It takes only a few years for their best hunters to become drunken beggars.

This news deepened the brown of Paul's mood. The Eskies were dying and probably he himself would not last long. Finishing his drink, he lay down on the wonderfully comfortable floor and napped. When he awoke sun was still streaming through the lace curtains at the windows. His watch told him it was a little after three, and he was suddenly unsure whether that was three in the morning or afternoon. Most of the other people were now sprawled on the floor. Mowrey was sitting with his back against a wall and his arm around Hilda, who was stroking his face. Mowrey did not react. His mouth was slightly open, and when the victrola stopped, Paul heard him snoring lightly. Hilda caught Paul's eye, and moving surprisingly fast on her hands and knees, crawled over to him. At that time and place her method of locomotion did not seem in the least surprising. Her great bosom swayed attractively in front of her.

"The captain, he no hold liquor good, you say?"

"I say," Paul replied, and folded her into his arms as she sprawled by his side. The room was so full of tobacco smoke that his eyes stung. Some of the Danes had left and those who remained were asleep, as far as he could make out in the dim light. Hilda kissed him, her lips blubbery and soft, her breath coming hot and hard.

"No men here," she said. "No men for very long time."

"It must be tough."

"You beautiful boy."

"You're beautiful too."

Certainly she seemed that at the time. He buried his face between her breasts.

"You come my place," she said, stroking his hair.

They had difficulty standing up. It was hard enough for him to get on his feet, but almost impossible for her, and when he tried to pull her up, she won the tug of war and he found himself sprawled on top of her. After kissing some more, they crawled to a window ledge, and using that for support got to their feet with only two heavy falls. Her hand hit a whiskey bottle that had been left on the windowsill and sent it clattering against Mowrey's feet. Awaking with a grunt, the captain kicked it away. With much laughter and more embraces, Paul and Hilda put on their parkas in the vestibule and staggered out into the eternal sunlight. Holding each other up, they had not walked more than a hundred yards toward the nearest cabin when Mowrey came staggering after them. He had put on his parka but had not buttoned it, and in his hand he carried a bottle of scotch.

"Goddamn it, Yale, where are you going?"

"I'll see you aboard ship before long."

"Damn your eyes, come back here! Are you stealing my girl?"

"I'm just helping her home."

"Christ, she can get home alone. Come here! I want to talk to you."

Paul hesitated.

"Come here!" Mowrey thundered. "Goddamn it, that's an order!"

"Better go," Hilda said. "Maybe tomorrow." Letting go of Paul, she staggered toward her little house.

Mowrey waited, taking frequent sips from his bottle. He was swaying as though he were standing on the deck of a ship in a gale, and sat down in the frozen mud suddenly as Paul approached.

"Give me a hand, goddamn it," he said. "Lesson one: don't take the skipper's girl. Lesson two: don't fuck no Danish girls. They make trouble. Stick to the Eskies. There will be plenty of them farther north."

They staggered toward the ship. Suddenly they were surrounded by sled dogs. Perhaps sensing the weakness of the stumbling men, they pressed close, snapping viciously, and retreated only a few yards when Paul and Mowrey roared at them. Throwing motions and even clumps of frozen mud hurled in their direction did not break up the circle the dogs formed around them. In a rage, Mowrey charged the lead dog, swinging his bottle. Only then did the dogs slink back to the shadows of the warehouse.

"You can't let them know you're scared," Mowrey said. "Christ, let's take a breather. They'll let us alone now."

Clambering to the top of a granite knoll, he sat down and took a sip from his bottle before passing it to Paul. The knoll commanded a view of the wharf, the ship and the harbor beyond, which glowed copper in the sun. A crowd of Eskimos and sailors were milling around on the end of the wharf near the ship. There was a lot of shouting and singing, but at the moment that seemed simply logical to Paul on this night of partying. Mowrey did not seem to notice.

"Christ, I can't drink the way I used to," he said. "When I first came up here, I could drink for *weeks* without passing out."

"When did you first come up here?" Paul asked.

"Christ, I was on a salt banker when I was just a kid. We fished just a few miles off shore here. We had a man bad hurt and we put in to find a doctor."

"Things must have been different then," Paul said, taking a gulp of whiskey. Somehow the stuff seemed to have lost its kick. It tasted like warm water, but his head was spinning.

"The Eskies were really Eskies then. Not many fucking Danes around. No fucking laws and regulations." There was a pause while Mowrey drank and stared out over the iridescent harbor. "I was just a lad the first time," he said. "Then when I was sixteen, I went in the navy. After the war, the first damn war, they didn't want me, but when the Coast Guard started to fight the Rummies, they wanted me. I fought Rummies for about five years. You'd catch one, turn him in and then the judge would let him go. The Rummies was all driving Cadillacs, and all I had was a broken-down Ford."

"It must have been tough," Paul said, accepting the bottle.

"It took me five years to figure it out. Then I quit and got me a Rummy ship. Had friends in the right places and did right well till they killed Prohibition. Then I went fishing again. Came up here and bought cod and furs sometimes. Ran arms down to South America. Had all kinds of rackets, but things got tough, I didn't know what the hell to do, but then the war started back up again . . ." Mowrey sighed with apparent relief. "I guess we better get back to the ship," he said.

The noise of the Eskimos and sailors making merry at the end of the wharf increased as they approached. Groups of people were singing, dancing, shouting and a few were fighting. Almost all were carrying bottles. In the shadows near piles of stores couples were grappling and it was hard to tell whether they were wrestling or making love. As they reached the fringes of this crowd of more than a hundred celebrants, Mowrey and Paul did a kind of double-take.

"Jesus Christ, they're all drunk!" Mowrey said, dropping his own bottle. "Where in hell did they get the booze?"

"I better check the lazaret," Paul said, and ran to do so.

The lock of the liquor locker had been broken off, and no sign of the bottles remained except empty cartons. When Paul went to report this to the captain, he couldn't find him. Suddenly Mowrey burst out on the gun deck from his cabin.

"Christ, they took every bottle I had!" he shouted. "I'm dry!"

There was panic as well as rage in his voice. A few of the men on the wharf stared at him, but the writhing crowd continued to celebrate. From the forecastle Cookie staggered, his tall chef's hat crumpled on his head.

"Don't blame me, captain!" he said. "I tried to stop them. They just broke in and handed out bottles to everyone."

"*Who?*"

"Everyone! They all stole and gave to everyone else. They're all guilty, every last son of a bitch."

151

"Who has the deck here?" Mowrey roared. "Where's Farmer and Greenberg?"

"I think they're asleep, sir. They tried to stop it, but there wasn't nothing they could do."

"Yale, get those bastards up here," Mowrey said, his voice suddenly turning dangerously sweet. "Greenberg was the senior officer present. I'll have to figure out whether to nail that Sheenie's balls to the mast or send him to Portsmouth for twenty years."

Paul hurried to the wardroom. He found Seth and Nathan in their bunks. Seth had his eyes closed, but Nathan was reading a book.

"The skipper wants you," Paul said to Nathan. "He's mad as hell. What in Christ's name happened?"

Nathan put down his book and sighed. "After you left with the case of whiskey, I went to sleep and so did Seth. When all the yelling woke us up, they had already broken into the booze and the party was already going full blast. We tried to stop them. No one would even listen. Have you ever tried to stop a crowd of about a hundred drunken Eskimos and sailors?"

"Why didn't you call the skipper or me?"

"He told us not to go ashore," Seth said, opening one eye. "I figured it was an emergency, so I went up there. The skipper was asleep with a bottle in his hand and you were rolling around on the floor with a fat woman. I said to hell with it and came back to the ship. You were having your fun, so why couldn't the boys raise a little hell too? There was no way to get the booze away from them anyway except to shoot them. So I figured that we might as well let the thing run its course."

"There really wasn't much we could do," Nathan said. "As soon as they got their hands on the booze, they were completely out of control."

"You better try to explain that to the skipper," Paul said. "God help you."

"I'll go too," Seth said. "By God, if he takes me to court, I'll tell them I figured that what's good for the captain must be good for the men."

Nathan was obviously nervous as he put on his coat to go to the captain, but Seth for the first time looked indignant. Paul followed them to the well deck, where Mowrey was standing, steadying himself with his hand on the cargo boom.

"Do you call yourselves officers?" he bellowed. "Where the hell were you when all this started?"

"We was asleep when it started," Seth said. "And after it started, we couldn't stop it."

"Farmer, you couldn't make a baby take its thumb out of its mouth. What have you got to say, Mr. Greenberg? You were legally in charge of this ship."

"Mr. Farmer told it right," Nathan said, his voice little above a whisper.

"What do you mean, you couldn't stop them? If they disobeyed direct orders, that was mutiny. Did you give direct orders?"

"I asked them to cut the noise and put the liquor back," Nathan said. "Most of them didn't hear me."

"To what individuals did you give a direct order?"

"I don't know, sir," Nathan replied softly. "It was a very confused situation."

"You *don't know!* Obviously you collaborated with this gross breach of discipline."

Mowrey slurred these words, but he was beginning to act surprisingly sober.

"He's no more guilty than I am," Seth said. "I figured it was an emergency, captain, so I went up to get you. I found you. You weren't in no shape to do nothing about it yourself. Bring us to court and that's what will come out."

There was an instant of silence during which Mowrey suddenly smiled, his best sweet smile, and his voice was sweetly reasonable when he finally replied.

"So, Mr. Farmer, you are something of a sea lawyer," he almost cooed.

"Facts is facts, sir. If you're smart you'll just let this thing run its course and forget it."

"How thoughtful of you to give me advice. Thank you, Mr. Farmer. I know you want to help me to run this ship efficiently. Now, Mr. Greenberg, do you have any advice for me?"

"No, sir."

"Mr. Schuman, I want you to log what I have to say now. Mr. Farmer and Mr. Greenberg are herewith charged with gross dereliction of duty, negligence, incompetence and insubordination. They are also charged with cooperating with enlisted men, names presently unknown, who breached our cargo and committed grand theft. They are also charged with aiding and abetting a mutiny. Both officers are hereby relieved of all duties. They are ordered to remain in their cabin until our return to a base where they can be transferred ashore for a court martial. Yale, I want that written up in the log right away. Then show it to me . . . Now Greenberg and Farmer, listen and listen well," Mowrey said.

Letting go of the cargo boom, he forced himself to stand very straight. His voice thickened. "You may think you got me by the balls because I went ashore and got drunk. That's not as bad as letting the whole crew go crazy. When this thing comes to trial, the judge is going to pay attention to just one thing. They don't have many ice pilots. They got plenty of deadheads like you two. If it's a question of hanging you two or hanging me, you guess what they're going to do. Now go to your quarters and stay there till I say to come out. Your food will be brought to you. Dismissed!"

The two walked silently aft. Mowrey, followed by Paul, climbed to the bridge. Mowrey stood staring at the men ashore, many of whom were still singing and shouting, though others had seen his return and were gathering into subdued little groups.

"Yale, see if you can find me a member of the black gang sober enough to run the engine. Find Boats and send him to me. If he's too drunk, get any boatswain's mate."

Among the crowd of people who were sobering up and staring at the ship, Paul found both the chief machinist's mate and Boats. They ran to the captain. A few moments later the shrill sound of the boatswain's pipe cut the still air. "Mooring stations," the boatswain's mate shouted. "All hands to mooring stations."

Perhaps a third of the men on the wharf hurried back to the ship. A third kept on with the drunken singing and shouting and about a third lay in the shadows, passed out or busy with the Eskimo women. Going out on a wing of the bridge with a megaphone, Mowrey said to Paul, "Give one blast of the whistle."

The unexpected shriek of the air horn produced instant silence on the wharf.

"Now hear this," Mowrey bellowed through the megaphone. "This vessel is going under way and leaving this wharf immediately. All who do not come aboard now will be abandoned here and reported missing without leave. The Danes will lock you up in a warehouse. Carry your

154

mates aboard if you give a damn about them. You've got exactly two minutes. Boats, single up the lines."

About half the sailors on the wharf ran to leap aboard the ship while the others carried limp bodies to the gangway. The Eskimos suddenly ran. When the entire crew appeared to be aboard, Mowrey said, "Yale, check out every corner of that wharf and see if anybody is left."

Paul found one unconscious seaman hidden between two crates of canned goods and had him carried aboard. The last of the Eskimos had fled, and the dock was deserted.

"All hands seem to be aboard, sir."

"Bring the men to quarters and call the muster. Have the men sound off for friends that can't."

This was done. The entire crew was present and accounted for.

"Yale, do we still have any cargo for this port aboard?" Mowrey asked.

"It's all been unloaded, sir," Paul said after checking with Boats.

Mowrey spat in the water to observe the direction of the current. "Take in all lines but number two," he said. He waited impassively on the wing of the bridge while the lines were brought aboard. "Left full rudder. Ahead slow."

When the stern swung away from the wharf he said, "Shift your rudder. Stop the engine. Back slow."

A crowd of Eskimos now came back to the wharf to watch the departure of the ship. Mowrey gave them three blasts of the whistle and a few clapped their mittened hands.

Paul had guessed that Mowrey would anchor in the middle of the harbor, but instead he began to thread the intricate channel that led to the sea and the ice pack. Disdaining a broad lead that paralleled the shore, he slowly followed a narrowing channel into the ice floe. Gently he wedged the ship between two icebergs which were slightly larger than the vessel.

"Finished with the engine," he said. "Set the morning watch, and everyone else can turn in. Yale, send Cookie to my cabin."

Almost immediately Cookie appeared. He had put on a clean apron and a freshly starched hat. Mowrey ushered him into his cabin and shut the door.

"Cookie," he said, "I need a drink. They took all of mine. Do you have any left?"

155

"Only two bottles, sir."

"Bring me one. I'll pay you back. We'll get more before long."

"Aye, aye, sir."

Paul did not hear this exchange, but he guessed at its nature when Cookie dashed out and almost immediately reappeared with an awkward package wrapped in newspaper. Mowrey took it and shut the door of his cabin.

Paul went to the washroom. Seth had gone back to sleep, but Nathan was sitting at the table, writing a letter.

"Don't worry," Paul said with patently false cheer. "This thing will blow over one way or another. I haven't logged it and I won't unless he remembers and gives me a direct order."

"At least it might get me off this ship. They need ice pilots. Maybe they'll come to realize that they also need radar specialists. Aboard a ship with radar, I hope."

"They're sure to realize that," Paul said, and wished he felt as sure as he sounded. If Mowrey wanted to do harm to Seth and Nathan, he probably would succeed. The game, after all, was being played in his ballpark. Paul's head ached and he felt violently ill. After rushing to the head, he lay down in his bunk, feeling as dizzy as though the ship were in a violent storm. His last thought before sleeping was that he should feel lucky, that probably any man aboard the *Nanmak* would be glad to change places with him. Or would they . . . ?

# CHAPTER 18

When Paul woke up, the endless sunlight of an Arctic spring was flooding the wardroom. His watch said it was a little after eight o'clock, and with that oddly continuing disorientation concerning time, he wasn't sure whether it was morning or evening. Of one thing he was certain: he had the great-grandmother of all hangovers, the symptoms of which included a throbbing headache and a strong sense

156

of impending doom. After the sunlight stabbed his eyes once, he closed them again. Slowly the dismal events of the preceding night came back to him.

Some of it was still mercifully obscure to him, but the two worst results were clear. Nathan and Seth were "in hack," confined to their quarters pending a court-martial, and *he* had been ordered to write the charges against them in the log, a seemingly trivial task which could have dreadful effect, for once an event had been written in the log it could never be forgotten. Feeling sicker and sicker, Paul reviewed what he had learned about logs. There were two of them, a rough log written in pencil as events took place and signed by each officer of the watch, and a smooth log, a cleaned-up copy of the rough log, which he himself wrote in ink every night. Both were official documents, but the rough log, he had read, was considered the more important when investigations were held. It was against the law to make erasures in the rough log or to delete passages in any way. Every few months both logs were sent to Washington, where they were apparently preserved forever, like the final scrolls of the recording angel himself.

For these reasons Paul had written nothing in the log about Nathan and Seth, thus disobeying a direct order from his commanding officer. The idea of disobeying Mowrey had never before really occurred seriously to him, and the thought of the old man's wrath when he reviewed the log, as he did every day, now frankly terrified Paul. Soon, no doubt, he would find himself joining the others in hack, awaiting court-martial. Paul started to sweat, but he suddenly realized that there might be some safety for all of them in numbers. If Mowrey asked Headquarters to court-martial all three of his officers, he himself would look crazy, wouldn't he?

And there was more to it than that. A board of investigation would discover that every officer and man aboard the ship had been drunk on that ill-starred, sunny night, except for Nathan and Seth, the only two who were presently being punished. If they were to be disgraced, wouldn't some action have to be taken against all the enlisted men and petty officers who had broken into the liquor locker and stolen part of the cargo? And Mowrey himself had been drunk when he had taken such drastic action against Nathan and Seth. Was an executive officer wrong in refusing to carry out an order given by a commanding officer who was obviously drunk? How would the fact that he had been drunk himself affect a legal decision?

Obviously the best thing that Mowrey could do would be to forget the whole episode, wake up and laugh it off. Paul had been counting on him to do that when he neglected to make the entry in the log, but perhaps he had underestimated the vengeful aspect of Mowrey's character, the unreasoning hatred he had for Nathan and the curious contempt he seemed to have for Seth. If "Mad Mowrey" was really going mad, as he sometimes appeared to be doing, because of his vast consumption of alcohol or the growth of lifelong diseases of the spirit, a board of investigation should in normal circumstances pin most of the blame, at least, on him, but there was nothing exactly normal about this first year of the war. The Coast Guard, Paul realized, was an old-boy network, like the other services. As a mustang, Mowrey had not ranked high in it, but he certainly ranked far above the thousands of incompetent reserve officers whom the old boys were trying to sort out. As Mowrey well knew, the acute shortage of ice pilots gave men who knew the Arctic well a kind of immunity to ordinary rules and regulations. In time of war, anything which worked fast had to be done. The commander of GreenPat probably would not bother to undertake a long investigation of the doings of a trawler's drunken night in a tiny Greenland village, and he was unlikely to waste the time of his senior officers on the endless procedures of a court-martial which could end only by making everybody look bad. The practical, pragmatic course of action for "Commander GreenPat" was simply to forget all legal charges and transfer the officers whom Mowrey didn't like to some other unit. If it was necessary to find some rotten assignment for the reserve officers to keep the old ice pilot happy, that could easily be arranged. It might be wise to make an example of reserve officers who made trouble with the old hands, who couldn't fit into a military organization smoothly. If Nathan and Seth were transferred to some tiny supply depot or weather station deep in the Arctic wastes, they would have no opportunity to complain or to make recriminations. Even in peacetime, any member of the service was by honor and law bound to accept any assignment given to him, wasn't he?

The more Paul thought about it, the surer he was that this was the way the whole mess would be resolved. Nathan and Seth would get fitness reports bad enough to block future promotions or reassignment to any meaningful job. And if he himself tried to protect them by refusing to write their troubles up in the log, or even by trying too hard to present a case for them while talking with Mowrey, he might easily end up by joining them. It would, after all, be just as easy to transfer three reserve officers as two. If he demanded some sort of hearing, he guessed that few of the enlisted men aboard the *Arluk* would testify in his favor. To save their own skins, they would want to avoid a full investigation and would back the most powerful man aboard the ship.

Paul felt sick. Opening his eyes and squinting in the bright sunlight, he saw that Seth was still in his bunk, but Nathan was sitting at the table writing something. What would happen if Nathan turned out to be a sea lawyer and stubbornly demanded an investigation, or formally pressed his own charges? If it had to be proved that the captain was drunk, it would have to come out that Paul had not exactly spent the night as a teetotaler. Probably the Danes would be called as witnesses.

Suddenly Paul was angry at Nathan and Seth. There was no great crime, after all, in going ashore to get drunk, as the captain and he had done, but Nathan and Seth had been on duty aboard ship, they had stayed cold sober, and still hadn't been able to control the crew. If they had gone to sleep early and had awakened to find themselves in the midst of a drunken set-to they might have just given up, once they had found that the skipper and executive officer were drunk ashore, but Paul knew that Nathan, at least, was just not that weak. No, Nathan sympathized with the enlisted men, felt it was unfair to deny them a party while the officers had one ashore, and probably turned a blind eye and a deaf ear to the theft of the booze at the start. Perhaps he hated Mowrey enough to get some kick out of the revenge of the enlisted men. Maybe he liked seeing Mowrey's crew fuck up after all the old man's attempts at discipline. If the whole ship was to be disgraced and punished after treating him so harshly, maybe Nathan would take pleasure in the revenge.

As he thought about this, Paul's anger built. Nathan was always so goddamn righteous, so long suffering, so *put* upon! Sure, Mowrey didn't like Jews and made no secret of it. That was wrong, ugly, but wasn't Mowrey maybe a little justified in his contempt for Nathan as an officer? Openly ignorant of everything nautical, basically disdainful of everything military, eternally seasick and a thinly disguised intellectual snob, Nathan wasn't really all that much of an asset to the ship. If as an electronic specialist he'd been assigned to a trawler as a wartime mistake, he could have had the guts to fight for a transfer instead of making a virtue of being so damn passive, couldn't he? *Passive*— that's what Nathan was, when faced by a crew difficult to control, a storm at sea, or an overaggressive commanding officer who was egged on by passivity. If they had to battle a German icebreaker, Nathan might also be too passive to return gunfire effectively. His passivity could be the death of himself and of all of them. Already, by allowing the crew to run riot, he had brought a kind of disaster on everyone aboard. And then he began to shake his head and pull himself up short. Jesus Christ, what was he doing . . . ?

Yet this was not really a fair interpretation, Paul realized as his anger peaked. Nathan was undoubtedly doing as best he could in a situation which was nearly impossible for him. His passivity was really part of his courage, his refusal to give up and beg for a transfer. He was doing everything he could to learn an entirely new profession, and if the captain would give him a chance, could soon become an effective officer, Paul was sure. Part of Paul's anger was fear and guilt, fear that Mowrey would kill him if he tried to stand up for his friend, and guilt because he was tempted to side with strength and turn against Nathan.

Pulling a pillow over his face to shield his eyes from the sunlight, Paul tried to go back to sleep. He had just succeeded when a messenger came to announce that the captain wanted to see him on the bridge "right now."

As Paul hurried to put on his clothes, Nathan said "Good morning" in a curiously normal voice.

"Is it? I got to go face some Mowrey music."

Nathan shrugged, a habitual gesture, and began to write in his notebook.

Paul wondered whether he was keeping a private record of events which he planned to submit to a court of inquiry. Oh, quit it, he told himself. The guy has a right. Wasn't his pique mostly self-serving? And wasn't his stuff about Nathan's passivity and fitness as an officer mostly rationalization to take him off the hook with his own conscience if he did what Mowrey wanted? Why did he imagine that Nathan was plotting some kind of revenge? The man had never threatened that.

Without taking time to shave, Paul splashed his face with cold water, dried it on a dirty hand towel, and hurried to the bridge. Mowrey was alone there, hunched on a tall stool by the wheel. He looked pale and for once he was neither smoking or drinking.

"Where the hell have you been?" His voice was still strong.

"Sacked out."

"I've been standing watch here myself most of the night. Remember, you and I are the only commissioned officers on duty now. I'll take the eight to twelve. We'll give Boats the twelve to four and you take the four to eight."

"Aye, aye, sir."

"Bring me the log. I want to see what you wrote about Greenberg and Farmer."

Paul took a deep breath. "I didn't write anything, sir."

Mowrey flashed his sweet smile. "Didn't I tell you to log the charges?" he said softly.

"Captain, I was very tired, and I'd been drinking too. A lot was going on. I just plain forgot."

"You say you'd been drinking too. Are you implying that I was drunk?"

"Captain, I'm not throwing stones. We were both drinking."

"Maybe so, but I've been standing watch right here all night. At least a dozen enlisted men can testify to that. I made notes about the weather every hour in my own hand. Before that, I broke up the party and got the men aboard all right. I took the ship out the channel all right. Who's to say I was drunk?"

"I don't know, sir. But if we have an investigation, you'd have to court-martial just about every man aboard the ship. Can't you just forget it, sir? Can't you just write it off as a bad night?"

Mowrey gave another sweet smile and his voice continued to be sweetly reasonable. "Sure, a nice guy might forget it. But the cargo was breached and about fifty cases of booze were stolen. They weren't my property. They were consigned to the Danes all up and down this coast. When they don't get the booze they ordered and paid for, they'll complain to the authorities. Now do you want to be the one to explain that we just had a bad night?"

"Couldn't we replace the booze, sir? It would be better to take up a collection for that than to get everybody court-martialed."

"Do you have any idea how much a bottle of booze is worth up here, even if you could find fifty cases of it?"

"Sir, I could find it and I could get the money," Paul said desperately. "Believe it or not, I've been pretty good at getting things done when I had to—"

"Why, Yale, maybe you could buy booze at the North Pole. But even if you could, what would you do with officers who can't control the men?"

"I think I'd give them one more chance. That would be better than giving the whole ship a bad name. Any investigation would do that, wouldn't it, sir?"

"When I prove that an ensign and a warrant officer couldn't stop the men from running wild while the ship was moored to a wharf and I was ashore on official business, my name won't be hurt much," Mowrey said mildly. "I'm already on record with complaints about the quality of the officers assigned to me. My ass is covered. All I got to do is write up a report and hang somebody. That will be a hell of a lot easier than trying to replace the booze."

"Why? If I could do that?"

"Yale, the only place to get booze up here is army bases. They get a hundred dollars a bottle there. That's twenty-four hundred dollars a case for two dozen bottles. How much would fifty cases come to?"

Mowrey's hand shook a little as he took a pencil from his breast pocket and a scrap of paper from his wallet. "A hundred and twenty thousand dollars," he said. "Can you take up a collection and raise that?"

"Jesus Christ," Paul said. "Look, if we bought the booze legally, it would only be a few hundred dollars. Fifty cases! That's not so much."

"And how are you going to buy it legally?"

"I don't know yet. Maybe there's another way. What if we say we loaded the stuff onto the wharf and it was stolen by the Eskimos. After all, they drank their share."

"So we blame it on the poor Eskies. Do you think the Danes would go for that?"

"Can't we say we dropped the booze overboard by accident while trying to unload it? A cargo net broke. There's not a man aboard who wouldn't testify to that."

Mowrey smiled again. "There's one thing that Headquarters would never believe, and that's the loss of booze by accident. I'd rather try to sell them the idea that the whole damn ship just took off and flew. No, Yale, we have to hang someone, and if we have to hang someone, why not hang the two officers who couldn't control the crew?"

"Mr. Green may not be so easy to hang," Paul said quietly.

"What does that mean?"

"Captain, Mr. Green is not stupid. He may figure that he and Mr. Farmer shouldn't have to take the rap alone. After all, they're the only ones who stayed sober. I don't think that they feel they did anything wrong—"

"So they can throw dirt in our faces. Headquarters is not going to court-martial the entire crew. They're not going to take me off this ship because they don't have a replacement. Greenberg and Farmer they can hang and maybe you, if you take their side."

"Couldn't we just transfer them, sir? Wouldn't it be easier?" Paul was getting desperate.

"I've thought of putting Farmer in a supply depot and Greenberg on a weather ship that would keep him out in Davis Strait almost all the time, but how is that going to help us to explain the loss of the booze? There's no way out of hanging someone."

Paul was fresh out of ideas, said nothing.

"Farmer we might let go," Mowrey continued. "He can stand a watch and he's not bad on deck, except he can't handle men. But Greenberg was the senior officer aboard. He had the duty. There's no way I can save him, or ought to."

"You know, sir, maybe no one could control those men once they got going. And if he was asleep when it started—"

"Do you think it would have happened if I'd been aboard?"

"No, sir."

"Would it have happened if you had been aboard?"

"I don't know, sir. I suppose I would have yelled a lot but—"

"I bet you would. You were beginning to shape up, Yale. Too bad you've fouled up now."

Paul flushed. "What do you mean?"

"You disobeyed my direct order to log charges, or you were too drunk to carry it out. I don't plan to bring charges against you, Yale, but how can I give you a good

163

fitness report? And how can I keep you aboard here or recommend you to any ship? You're seasick as soon as we hit open water, and you're not reliable in port."

"I had an idea I was getting better, sir."

"So did I for a while there. And I might give you one more chance. First of all, log the charges against Greenberg. Leave Farmer out of it if you want. It will be a little easier to hang just one man. One more thing. They not only stole from the cargo, they got into my cabin and took my personal supply. Almost two cases. Since you say you can get booze at the North Pole, try it. We'll be at an air base before long. Your cooperation with me might change my mind about you."

Before going to his quarters, Paul went to the forecastle for a cup of coffee. He drank two before going to the wardroom to see Nathan, who was still sitting at the table writing in his notebook. He glanced up as Paul came down the companionway, his narrow, craggy face looking more mournful than ever.

"How's the captain?" he asked.

"Oh shit, Nathan. He wants to hang you."

Nathan shrugged and said nothing. Seth sat up in his bunk. "I suppose he wants to hang me too," he said.

"No, I guess I talked him out of that." Which was true, Paul felt, and he wanted to get credit for it. In his mood he needed all the credit he could get.

"Good for you," Nathan said wryly.

"You can fight him," Seth said. "By God, I'll back you up."

Nathan shrugged again. The silence seemed to hum.

"Are you going to ask for an investigation?" Paul asked.

For the third time Nathan shrugged, a nervous reflex with him. *Not* indifference, Paul now realized. "When you come right down to it," he said, "he can't charge me with anything except incompetence when it comes to handling men, and I've got to admit there's truth in that. Knute Rockne, I'm not. So hang me."

"He can block your promotions," Paul said. "He can get you a lousy assignment."

"Well, Paul, I never exactly had any career ambitions in the service and as for getting a lousy assignment, what could be worse for me than this?"

Nathan was certainly not crushed the way he himself

would be in such circumstances, Paul realized with admiration. And he also suspected Nathan was putting on just a bit of a show of bravado to make Paul feel less guilty about writing him up in the log, as he knew he had to do.

That day Farmer was restored to duty, but Greenberg was kept confined to his quarters, where he lay in his bunk reading night and day. He did not complain and for a while Paul was able to tell himself that he was just shrugging the whole thing off. Maybe he even was glad that he could spend his time with his books instead of standing watch on the bridge.

That's what he told himself until two nights later when Seth had the watch and he went to the wardroom with a cup of coffee and a sandwich for Nathan. He found the tall, gaunt man lying in his bunk, his hands covering his face. Nathan tried to hide his eyes in his pillow, but his shoulders shook and his sobs could not be muffled.

"Christ, get out of here!" he said. "I'm all right. It's just that I feel so fucking *useless*. The Nazis are taking over the whole goddamn world and I'm not even allowed on deck on my own goddamn ship."

So much for passivity and not caring. Paul wanted to die.

# CHAPTER 19

Although Nathan had technically been removed from duty, he continued to decipher messages. Because Sparks could not copy the fast, brief reports which *Nanmak* sent in Morse code to Commander GreenPat, Nathan soon took to sneaking up to the radio shack to do so. If the captain guessed that this was going on, he did not object. The whole crew was bored with the *Arluk*'s slow passage through the ice from one port where the men were not allowed ashore to another, and they eagerly awaited information about the far more dramatic struggles of their sister ship, aboard which many of the men had friends.

Much of the news from the east coast of Greenland appeared to be mysterious. Several sources of German radio signals, some of which frequently moved, were often detected over an area of a thousand miles. No one was sure whether this meant the presence of many German ships, aircraft, shore stations or decoys of intricate design. Red paint streaks on the ice were not the only tangible evidence of the German presence. While following those tracks, the *Nanmak* picked up an empty bottle which had contained Polish vodka. The Germans, like the Americans, were usually careful to sink all trash in weighted sacks. Mowrey, however, apparently felt some guilt about empty booze bottles, and Paul had occasionally seen him sneak one over the side without bothering to weight or break it when he thought no one was looking. The possibility that some man aboard the German ship had a similar problem gave Paul a peculiar feeling. Like they said, war made strange bedfellows ... and in strange ways. ...

The ice floe was closer to shore and more tightly packed as the *Arluk* continued north on the west coast of Greenland. Mowrey soon hoped to reach a fjord almost exactly on the Arctic circle where a small air base was being built for emergency landings, but a narrow lead they were following suddenly closed around them and for the first time they were really stuck in the ice, unable to budge an inch in any direction.

"What do we do now?" Paul asked.

"Wait," Mowrey said grimly. "This time of the year, it always breaks up sooner or later."

The captain did not look well. He was pale and sweated a lot, even in the chill wind on the wing of the bridge. His hands sometimes shook so much that it was hard for him to handle the binoculars, and if possible, he grew more irritable every day. Even Guns and Boats, who had been his favorites, couldn't do anything to please him.

Lying in his bunk in the wardroom, Nathan heard the captain's voice rise almost to an hysterical pitch one afternoon when he found that a line which as an extra precaution was used to lash the depth charges in place when they were in ice had become loose and frayed.

"Guns, you're about to blow us all up if you can't learn to secure those charges properly," Mowrey shouted. "Ice can knock them loose. In this stuff we couldn't get out of their way. We'd be blown sky high."

"Those charges are on safe, sir," Guns replied. "They couldn't—"

"Safe my ass! Don't you try to tell me . . ."

On and on he raved. "Yale, come here. Put Guns on report. I want him restricted for thirty days for gross incompetence and insubordination."

"Is the captain drinking much these days?" Nathan asked when Paul returned to the wardroom.

"A little, but I don't think he has much left."

"Has he got *any* left?"

"Cookie was bitching that he bummed some from him, and the crew is complaining that he's dipping into some beer we're supposed to be saving for them if they ever get ashore, but I think he's almost dry. I think he's trying to take himself off it. That's probably what's the matter with him."

"He probably still has a few pints stashed here and there, but the bastard probably is trying to taper off. Does he have the sweats and the shakes?"

"Some."

"I think you're going to have a problem, Paul. When he really has to quit, he'll be going through hell. He's been drinking enough for the DT's."

"What will happen if he gets them?"

"Wildly erratic behavior, hallucinations, convulsions, maybe death."

"Jesus Christ! He wants me to get some booze for him when we hit the next port. I hope I can."

"Drugs can help him if he gets too bad. I checked the medical chest. There's enough morphine there to last him a few days."

"Do you think it will really come to that?"

"I don't know. Alcoholics are unpredictable. Maybe he can sweat it out. I hope *you* can."

When the ice pack finally freed them, they followed more narrow leads which led them around in a twenty-mile circle before they found open water. Mowrey spent much of his time shivering in his bunk, wrapped with blankets, despite the fact that a steam radiator kept his cabin stifling. When the tension within him became unbearable, he went to the hold, opened a case of beer and sat gulping the stuff in the dark until he calmed down. When he felt weak, he was almost embarrassingly complimentary to Paul, calling him the fastest learner he had ever met, promising to give him the best possible fitness report and a letter of commendation as well. When he felt strengthened by a dozen cans of beer, however, he often turned on Paul, sometimes with no excuse whatsoever. After watching Paul con the ship through the ice for an hour, he suddenly said, "Christ, I hate to think that you're a Coast Guard officer."

"Why?"

"I just can't stand your looks. You look like a fucking little kid."

"I guess time will take care of that."

"A rich kid. Have you ever worked for a living in your life?"

"More than you think."

"You look like a girl. I bet you fuck boys."

Paul did not dignify this comment with an answer. Putting the binoculars to his eyes, he studied the ice ahead, where the pack curved out from the shore. Gulls flew overhead, dipping and wheeling with unexplained exuberance.

"Have you ever fucked a boy?" Mowrey persisted.

"For Christ's sake, I'm married."

"You didn't answer my question."

"Call me anything you want, but I'm not a queer."

"You're not a real sailor either. You'll never be one."

"Why do you say that?"

"You don't have the balls for it. You got no sea sense. And the men have no respect for you."

"I'm sorry if that's true."

"How can they have confidence in a fucking baby chick?"

Paul was tempted to ask, "How can they have confidence in a drunk?" but he clamped his mouth shut and picked up the binoculars again. Apparently Mowrey read his mind. "I'm a ten times better sailor drunk than you are sober."

"No doubt," Paul replied, staring through the binoculars.

"You can butter me up all you want, but when it comes to your fitness report, I have to be honest."

"No doubt."

"If I give you a good report, they are liable to give you your own command. You couldn't handle it."

168

"Not yet."

"Not ever."

The enlisted men reacted to Mowrey's stealing the beer being saved for a shore party by stealing it themselves. Perhaps Mowrey was muddled and guilty enough to think that he alone was emptying the big chest where the cases were kept. The screws in the hasp of the padlock were wobbly after having been taken in and out so often, but he did not seem to notice.

Yet Mowrey continued to be surprisingly effective when he was really needed. Four days before they reached the mouth of the fjord where the air base was being built, fog rolled in. They continued in the open sea until they figured that they were abreast of their destination, then headed into the ice pack, following any eastward lead. After turning and twisting for hours, Paul had no idea where he was. Occasionally the fog lifted a little, but there was nothing to see except icebergs and the reddish brown mountains, all of which seemed to look alike in the distance. The sun, the moon and the stars were all obscured in the haze overhead. For hours Mowrey stood on the flying bridge, a blanket wrapped around his shoulders to help keep off the wind.

"See that point of land broad on the starboard bow?" he asked Paul finally.

"Yes, sir. I'm not sure if it's a point or a fog bank."

"It's a fog bank over a rocky point. Go around it and you'll find the entrance to the fjord."

"How can you tell?"

"Sea sense. You either got it or you ain't. Can you take over now?"

"Aye, aye, sir."

Mowrey went down to the hold, where he drank the last of the beer. The discovery that finally it was all gone almost panicked him, but he had held in reserve a bottle of pure alcohol from the medicine chest. That would keep him together until he reached the air base, where there was bound to be an officers' club. He could get enough to drink there to last him until Paul found a source of major supply. The boy could do it, Mowrey was sure. He'd better.

While Paul worked the ship into the mouth of the fjord, Mowrey remained shivering in his bunk. The fjord itself was almost entirely clear of ice. On the chart Mowrey measured the distance, figuring that they had forty-eight miles to go to reach the base. After ordering the chief to give them all the power he could, he told Paul to call him when they reached the base. Downing the last of his medicinal alcohol, he settled into his bunk. It had been a near thing, but he had rationed the last drops of his booze exactly right.

The waterfront of the base under construction had few wharves, and those were crowded by big freighters and troop ships which had brought construction workers. The signal tower flashed a message to the *Arluk*, ordering her to anchor out in the fjord. When Paul told Mowrey this the captain jumped out of his bunk and studied the chart. "Christ, this isn't a secure anchorage," he said. "It's too deep and no real holding ground."

"The fathometer gives one-hundred-thirty feet," Paul said. "We've got plenty of chain for that."

"You won't if you get a foehn wind," Mowrey said. "Anchor, but stand sea watches. Lower the boat. I got business ashore."

The launch had never before been used. It was a brand new motorboat twenty-five feet long, and Boats had kept its paint and varnish gleaming. Its two-cylinder gasoline engine refused to start, however. While two machinist's mates worked on it, Mowrey paced the well deck cursing inefficiency, badly trained machinists, and especially Paul.

Finally the engine started. Mowrey leapt aboard, shouted for the coxswain, told the nearest seaman to get aboard and raced for the shore, not forgetting to make sure that the third repeater fluttered to the signal yard as soon as his feet left the deck of the ship. Taking the helm himself, he steered around the bow of a liberty ship and landed at a pontoon dock. Telling the men to stay by the boat, he hurried ashore. The first man he saw was a sentry standing at the gangway of a troop ship.

"Do you know where the officers' club is?" Mowrey asked.

"Never been there, sir," the man replied with a grin.

Mowrey charged up a muddy road that led up a steep hill. Quonset huts were everywhere, but few people were in sight. It took Mowrey a long time to locate the officers' club, and when he did, he found that it was closed. A sign said that it would open at five o'clock. Mowrey, who had lost track of time, saw that his watch said it was a little after two o'clock. My God, it must be two o'clock in the morning, and that's why the base seemed deserted. He

170

walked around in a daze until he thought to ask directions to the chief petty officers' club. This was a Quonset hut like the rest, but there were lights on in it. The door was locked, but it opened after he banged on it.

"We're closed, chief," a black steward's mate said. "We're just cleaning up."

"I just got in here aboard a ship and I'm frozen to death," Mowrey said. "I been standing watch all night. How about a drink?"

Zipping open his parka, he took out his wallet and gave the steward's mate ten dollars.

"Well now, I guess we can accommodate you in an emergency," the man said.

A chief steward's mate and two others were drinking at the bar. The man who had admitted Mowrey asked what he wanted.

"A double scotch."

"We ain't allowed to serve doubles here," the man said. He seemed to take a long while fussing with the bottle, the glass, and ice. Mowrey had left his parka on to conceal his rank and he was sweating profusely, despite the fact that he also had the shivers. His hand shook so badly that he had trouble getting another bill out of his wallet. The black steward's mate took him all in at a glance.

"We got a law against doubles, but I don't know no law against triples," he said, and poured a highball glass half full of whiskey.

"Bless you," Mowrey said fervently. "May the Lord be with you and with your spirit."

The first swallow of the whiskey took the edge off the panic that had been building in him for days, and the first three swallows really began to dissolve it. His sweat stopped running and his hands steadied.

"I guess I'll have another one of those," he said. The steward's mate had not taken his hand from the bottle.

Before leaving the ship Mowrey had tied a rubber hot water bottle from the medicine chest to a button of his uniform, leaving it hanging inside his coat. He had used this contrivance for this purpose many times before, and it was not difficult to pour every other drink into it. When he left the chief petty officers' club two hours later, he had spent the fifty dollars in his wallet, but the hot water bottle was full and so was his belly. He walked back to the boat with confidence. One way or another, he would manage to leave this port with enough booze to last six months. Never again would he subject himself to the terrors of withdrawal. He felt as though he had just escaped from a sinking ship.

While the captain was ashore, the men aboard the *Arluk* complained bitterly about being kept aboard. The fjord was like a narrow mountain lake, with the water mirroring the clouds, and they could see no reason for standing sea watches at anchor here. When Mowrey finally returned, no one said a word as he climbed aboard. Flags lowered the third repeater and walked stonily to the forecastle.

Mowrey went to the bridge, sat on the stool by the wheel and lit a long cigar.

"Send Yale here," he called to Boats.

"I'm here," Paul said, coming from the wing of the bridge.

"I got three things for you to do when they open up ashore," Mowrey said. "Talk to the harbor master and find a place to moor this ship, or at least a safe anchorage. That's number one. Number two is find a way to buy beer for the men legally. Get them admitted to some enlisted men's club in there, or at least find them a recreation field. They deserve some liberty." He said this in a voice loud enough for the men on the gun deck to hear, and there was a loud cheer.

"Now come into my cabin," Mowrey said.

He lay down in his bunk with his parka still on while Paul sat at the chart table.

"Let's face it, we got to get some booze aboard here, at least four cases. We got a long voyage ahead of us, and when we're done, we'll probably be sent to the east coast to help Wally play tag with the Germans, from all I hear."

"That seems possible."

"I ain't ashamed to admit it. I'm like a diesel engine—I can't run without fuel. If anybody don't like it, they can get themselves another ice pilot."

"I understand."

"How long will it take you to get four cases of booze? I mean the big cases with twenty-four bottles."

"That will take money, sir, maybe seven thousand dollars or more."

"I don't have no money left, no more than I need myself. A smart man like you can find a way to promote some booze."

"That may be almost impossible without money."

"That's up to you. Yale, today I'm going to write up two fitness reports on you and sign them both. One will send you to a supply depot in some godforsaken fjord and the other will get you a command of your own inside of a year, probably this ship when I move on. If you can't come up with the fuel I need, I'll transfer you with the bad report immediately. If you get the fuel, I'll send the good one. If you're that resourceful, you'll deserve it. How about it? Is it a deal?"

"I don't know, sir—"

"Isn't your career worth four cases of booze, no matter what they cost?"

"You change your mind a lot, sir. I'm not sure I could count on you, even if I could get the booze."

"I'll give you your good report already signed. You can mail it yourself. I'd make a damn fool of myself if I tried to deny it. The comments will be written in my own hand."

"That's kind of you, sir. I have one more request."

"What's that?"

"Drop the charges against Mr. Green and give him a good report."

"Oh for Christ's sake! How can I drop charges that have already been logged?"

"Log books have often blown overboard, sir, especially from small ships in rough waters."

"You son of a bitch, is that Sheenie doing something nice for you?"

"Sir, I'm going to need lots of money for the booze and I hope to get about half of it from him."

"Why not all of it? God, you are smart. Sheenies always have money. Why didn't I figure that?"

"Will you drop the charges and sign a good report on him?"

"How are we going to square the theft of all that booze if we've got no one to hang?"

"Report that we delivered it," Paul said with a straight face.

"The Danes will deny that!"

"Nobody ever believes anybody when they talk about booze up here. Headquarters will forget the whole thing if we're doing a good job at sea. They're not going to drag a ship off the Greenland Patrol just to argue about a few cases of booze. Complaints will be made and the papers will be lost in the shuffle."

"Well, you're probably right. If Greenberg is coming into this thing, how about making it six cases of booze? Sheenies can always get money if they need it."

"We'll get as much as we can. Is that all, sir?"

"Take the boat whenever you want to get supplies and I'll stand watch here. You're a smart boy, Yale. I knew that the minute I set eyes on you."

Nathan gave a bitter laugh when Paul told him about the deal Mowrey was willing to make, but he offered to go halves on "whatever we need to keep the old man from going over the edge." Paul jumped into the boat at nine o'clock that morning to go ashore and make the best deal he could. He had no idea where to begin to try to buy four cases of liquor at a Greenland air base, or where he could get his share of the money.

# CHAPTER 20

The wrong man to approach in a search for booze in quantity would be a bartender in an officers' club, Paul decided. Bartenders were approached far too often and had no power anyway. What he wanted was the man in charge of the officers' club or the man who supplied him, or the man who brought the booze into the port in the first place.

The best way to buy something illegal is to start with a legal deal, Paul instinctively felt. It was legal for a ship's officer to try to buy beer for a shore party for his men. The man who sold him beer legally might be willing and able to sell liquor if enough money were involved. The first thing Paul wanted was a price. When he knew how much he had to pay, he'd try to find a good poker game and maybe he could work the whole thing out without loss for both himself or Nathan. His ability at cards was one thing in which Paul had genuine confidence.

The commander at the harbor master's office told him where to find the supply officer who handled beer for the whole base. He was an army captain, a beefy-faced man by the name of John Ansak. The matter of the beer was easily settled, once Paul promised to have it delivered to his men ashore, not aboard the ship. No cash was involved in this. After signing the requisition forms, Paul said, "I'm on a small Coast Guard cutter. We're headed on a long voyage, clear up to Thule and Etah."

"At least there are no Krauts up there," Ansak said, leaned back in his swivel chair and lit a cigarette.

"We'll probably get to the east coast too," Paul continued easily. "Anyway, we have a long voyage ahead. It will be months before we get to any officers' clubs."

"Tough."

"Any chance of buying a little booze to ward off the chill?"

There was a quickening of interest in Ansak's blue eyes and Paul knew that at least he was not in for a moral lecture or a discussion of laws and regulations.

"How much booze do you want?"

"Four big cases, maybe six."

"A hundred dollars a bottle is the going price up here if you can find the stuff. When you hit it lucky, you can get a twenty-four-bottle case for two grand."

"That's a lot of money."

"Of course that's for whiskey, gin or vodka. I can get you sweet stuff for less. They send a lot of cordials and liqueurs up here that don't go so good at the clubs."

"What do they go for?"

"About half the price of whiskey, but the sweet stuff has just as much kick. I've drunk it myself so much I've come to like it."

"Could you find me six cases?"

"Of the sweet stuff, yes. That will be twelve hundred dollars a case, seven thousand, two hundred dollars."

"Can you make it six thousand cash for the lot?"

"Six and a half grand. Can you pick it up at the warehouse or do you want it delivered?"

"We're anchored out in the fjord. I can bring our boat into any wharf, but we don't have a truck. I'll need maybe twenty-four hours to get some cash. Will you take an officer's personal check on a stateside bank?"

"It will be his ass if it bounces. What kind of a boat do you have?"

"Just a twenty-five-foot launch, but it will take six cases easy enough."

"Is it in good shape?"

"Brand new. Why?"

"I've been looking for a boat. We don't necessarily have to make a cash deal."

"Can't you requisition a boat?"

"Not for recreation. The guys at the base like to go fishing. And they've moved all the Eskies to a settlement across the fjord. Some of the guys like to visit them."

"You want me to trade the ship's boat?" Paul asked incredulously.

"You could say it sank and requisition a new one."

"I don't know how long it would be before we could get one."

"What else have you got to trade?"

"A little ivory we got from the Eskies. Not a hell of a lot."

"Do you carry cargo?"

"Yes."

"Let me go over your manifest. Maybe you got something we need."

"Like what?"

"Radios. Electric heaters. Small generators. Steaks. The guys don't live too good up here. We can use anything that would make us comfortable."

"There are three generators in our cargo, but the Danes would raise hell up the line if we didn't deliver them."

"Say they were never delivered to you. Manifests are messed up all the time and nobody ever bothers to straighten them out. There's a war on."

"I'll think about it," Paul said, wondering if he really meant it.

After arranging for the *Arluk* to moor alongside a freighter at the wharf and for the crew to be admitted to a recreation hall, Paul got in the motorboat and went back to his ship. He found Nathan, who was still confined to his quarters, reading in his bunk.

"I can get the booze," he said. "Six and a half grand for six cases, or we can trade for it."

"Trade what?"

"They want our boat or stuff we can steal from the cargo."

"Our *boat*? That's supposed to be our lifeboat for God's sake! And we'll need it whenever we're anchored out. Would you really trade our only boat for booze?"

"They also want generators. We have three in the hold. We're supposed to take them to a weather station somewhere near Thule."

"You'd trade them? That would be sabotage. The weather station probably couldn't operate without them."

"If we can't trade, they want six-and-a-half grand."

"I'll pay my half if they'll take a check. Can you come up with cash?"

"I have about twelve hundred dollars," Paul said, remembering his winnings from past poker games. "Maybe I can get the rest."

That afternoon Paul went to the officers' club as soon as it opened. The bar was crowded, but to his surprise, he found no one playing cards.

"Our C.O. cracked down on gambling hard," a lieutenant commander told him. "Too many guys were going bad into debt. If you want a game, go up to the barracks where the civilian construction workers hang out. They got games going there around the clock, but hang onto your shirt."

The construction workers were playing at round tables made out of huge wooden reels which had held steel cable. A half dozen poker games and two blackjack games were in progress in the back of a bunkhouse which smelled of kerosene, tobacco, and stale sweat. As soon as Paul walked in, a burly bald man at the nearest table asked him if he wanted to take a hand, and Paul regarded his eager hospitality as a bad sign. Most of the men wore dirty khaki trousers and no shirts over their gray winter underwear. Few had shaved since coming to Greenland, and they were a piratical looking lot. Cash was used instead of chips, there were no limits and the betting appeared reckless.

They were playing ordinary draw poker. At the beginning Paul played very conservatively, a decision which was easy because he was dealt uniformly poor hands. He had a feeling, unusual for him, that this was not his lucky night. The men were drinking only beer, and they sipped little of that. They were too intent on their cards to talk much, but Paul guessed that they were friends who had played together a lot. Obviously they were old hands at cards, casually observing all the rules, written and unwritten. The burly bald man handled the deck almost too deftly when he dealt, but not smoothly enough to be making a point of it. When Paul was dealt four tens, he bet for the first time, was raised by a hundred dollars by the bald man, called him and lost to his four queens.

After paying for his loss, Paul said, "Thanks a lot. This is too rich for my blood," and stood up. The men laughed and urged him to have another try, but he left the building without comment. He didn't know whether his luck was bad, whether the others were cheating, or whether they simply were more skillful.

His failure to win at cards depressed Paul. As he crossed the decks of the freighter alongside which the *Arluk* was moored, he saw a large Coast Guard cutter going alongside a wharf nearby. She carried many boats, gigs, motor whaleboats and small landing craft. Suddenly possessed by an idea, Paul went aboard her and asked to talk to the executive officer. When he identified himself as the executive officer of the *Arluk*, the executive officer of the cutter, a tall urbane Academy lieutenant commander, asked him to his spacious wardroom for a cup of coffee. The officers of the big cutters, Paul sensed, thought of the men on the converted trawlers as orphans, but they apparently admired them for enduring so many hardships. The lieutenant commander was sympathetic when Paul said that the *Arluk* had lost her only boat and hated to head north without one.

"Hell, we can sign a boat over to you and draw a new one when we go home next month. What happened to your boat?"

"Got crushed in the ice. We sent it ahead to scout out a lead, and two bergs just closed around it like a vise. Splintered it. We were lucky to get the men off."

"Boy, that ice can be a bitch! Glad to help. What kind of boat do you want?"

"A motor whaleboat would be fine," Paul said, reflecting that those craft were stronger and roomier than the light launches issued to the trawlers.

"Do you want to take it right away?"

"We're supposed to head north pretty soon, I think."

"I'll have the papers made out and get the boat lowered.

178

While you're waiting, would you like some ice cream? I understand you can't get it on the trawlers."

"Great," Paul said. "Do you have strawberry?"

Once he got the motor whaleboat, there was a good deal of fast footwork he had to do to complete the deal. Although Ansak was delighted to get the launch, he refused to give honest booze for it and they finally settled on six cases of the sweet stuff. Mowrey was appalled by the thought of drinking triple sec, crème de menthe, and crème de cacao endlessly, but the cartons included a lot of Southern Comfort and various kinds of brandy which were acceptable, and all of it was high-proof stuff. The idea of trading the launch for booze and getting a *better* boat in the bargain appealed to Mowrey mightily.

"Boy," he said to Paul, "you deserve the best fitness report I can give you. I wish you'd been with me in the bootlegging days. We'd both be millionaires."

The enlisted men soon learned about the deal and were also full of admiration for Paul, especially when he promised them two cases of the booze to be consumed at the next beer bust ashore. The skipper wouldn't mind giving up some of the green crème de menthe, he figured.

Nathan was pleased by the arrangement too, though he said it made him feel damn strange to get his freedom and good reputation back in exchange for a crooked deal involving a bunch of lousy booze and a stolen boat.

"If I'd made the deal myself, maybe I wouldn't feel so bad," he said. "Paul, I still figure I owe you. After all, you arranged everything. You got me off the hook. Three grand or so would be a small price."

"Come on, Nathan . . . I'm not out a cent, and you were getting a raw deal."

"Well, I owe you one," Nathan said. "I owe you a big one. Someday I'll find a way to pay you back."

Warmed by the admiration of the captain and all the other men aboard his ship, Paul was happy for the first time since joining the service. It seemed probable that within a year Mowrey would be transferred to one of the hundreds of bigger ships which were being built every month, and with his blessing, Paul would become the captain of the *Arluk*, a position which he somehow felt to be a unique honor and proof of his worth. Of course Mowrey

179

could always change his mind, but, Paul figured, it would be hard for him to contradict the glowing fitness report which he had signed without dating, and which Paul now kept hidden with his money, folded between the leaves of *Knight's Modern Seamanship,* a large volume which he kept in a drawer under his bunk.

The question of whether he actually could navigate the ship safely without Mowrey did not scare him as much as it had at the start of the cruise. The captain was letting him maneuver the vessel around wharves now, as well as in the ice, and Paul was beginning to look at his sextant as a trusted friend. It was still difficult for him to find his way in the ice pack along the mountainous coast on the many days when fog obscured the sky, but he was beginning to realize that some of Mowrey's magical "sea sense" was simply familiarity with waters he had often sailed. The more Paul saw of Greenland, the easier the job of piloting would become. The question of whether he would be capable of taking the ship to the east coast to help Hansen look for German ships scared him too much to think about much. The radio messages which the *Nanmak* and Commander GreenPat exchanged told the same old story of their sister ship pushing slowly through heavy ice and poor visibility in pursuit of radio will-o'-the-wisps, paint marks on the ice and assorted bits of trash. It was possible, Mowrey said, that the Germans had given up on weather ships after losing one of them, and were making their observations entirely from long-range aircraft. Nathan pointed out that it was impossible to tell much about the wind from an aircraft, but even he acknowledged that the Germans might have found a way to do that, perhaps with the help of balloons.

After the *Arluk* left the air base and headed north for the small village of Upernavik, Nathan had a strange feeling that nothing was going to change much. The fact that the sun never set created a sense of timelessness. The scenery of the ice pack and the distant rust-colored mountains was spectacular, but except for shifting veils of cloud, always the same. Often they spent days jammed in the ice, and Mowrey, happy with his endless supply of Southern Comfort and assorted brandies, spent more and more time in his bunk, leaving the operation of the ship up to Paul. No one was in a hurry to go anywhere. Sometimes they stopped the ship to drift in clear water while the men

180

fished. The cod were so thick that it was unnecessary even to use bait. Seth showed the men how to lash hooks together to make jigs, and men soon learned how to snag fish in great quantity. Cookie invented dozens of ways to prepare fresh cod, and Farmer salted down barrels of fillets. When it became clear that they were not going to spend much time in port, and even less in places where the enlisted men were allowed ashore, Mowrey gave permission to give a few parties for the men off watch while the ship was jammed in the ice. Paul stood on the well deck, with the men washing down strips of salt cod with beer and green crème de menthe as gulls circled all around the surrounding mountains of ice, swooping in occasionally to claim morsels of fish tossed to them by the men. On such occasions Flags often played the harmonica, and the men sang to the plaintive tones of "The Wabash Cannon Ball" or "You Are My Sunshine," which somehow seemed the theme song of the Greenland Patrol.

As spring drifted into summer, the weather never seemed to change much, the intense blue of the sky obscured by fog near noon when the sun was hottest, but clear most of the rest of the time. Despite Greenland's reputation for being eternally cold, the men often worked in shirtsleeves when there was no wind.

The only person who seemed impatient with this changeless life was Nathan. "Damn it, shouldn't we get to Upernavik, drop our stuff and go on with the run?" he asked Paul.

"The skipper says there's no point in hurrying. From Upernavik we're supposed to go to Thule, and he says the ice won't open up there until July. Hell, Thule is less than nine hundred miles from the damn North Pole."

"I never thought the war would be like this," Nathan said. "All we do is drift around."

"Don't be in such a hurry to get shot at."

Nathan smiled, but he did not appear amused and soon went to the radio shack, where he spent most of his time trying to garner news about the *Nanmak*, and other news about the war in Europe and the Pacific.

Before reaching Upernavik, they received orders to stop at a small Eskimo settlement about a hundred miles to the south of that village, which had run out of dog food.

"Dog food!" Nathan exploded. "People are fighting for their lives and we're off to deliver *dog* food."

"That's as important as gas to these people," Mowrey said. "They don't go nowhere without it. Maybe the Eskies here will be the real thing, without a lot of Danes watching over them."

This settlement lay in the center of a large bay, which was shaped like a horseshoe, instead of a narrow fjord. The water lay as smooth as polished steel, and there were only a few icebergs inside the embrace of the rocky points. No wind blew as they approached, and smoke from the sod huts which Nathan studied through his binoculars rose straight up to ash-colored clouds, behind which the eternal sun glowed like a small pile of embers. The still air was much warmer than usual, and the men unbuttoned their parkas. Mowrey returned to his bunk after identifying the settlement, and Paul felt confident as he approached the shore slowly, keeping an eye on the fathometer. When the bay shoaled to fifty feet, he stopped the engine and waited for the vessel to glide to a stop before dropping the anchor. Just as he was about to give that order, Mowrey appeared on the bridge beside him.

"Hold it," he said. "Wait a minute."

Through the binoculars Mowrey studied the gravel beach ahead. "You seen any kayaks?" he asked.

"No, sir."

Lowering his glasses, Mowrey stared all around and inhaled sharply several times.

"I don't like the weather," he said, tapped the barometer, inspected the wet and dry thermometers on the wing of the bridge, and returned to his cabin to study his chart.

"We won't anchor," he said. "Bring her up to full ahead. Course one-three-eight."

"Where are we going, sir?"

"Tell Boats I want all our mooring lines and spare anchors rousted out on deck, especially the stern anchor. On the double. See to it. I'll take over here."

While the deck force hurried to carry out these orders, Paul returned to the bridge and watched with astonishment while Mowrey paralleled the shore of the bay, staying terrifyingly close to the high rocky cliffs, which towered over the ship. Finding a tiny bay within the bay, not much more than a cleft in the rocks behind a small granite knoll, Mowrey stopped the engine, reversed it, and briskly executed a complex maneuver. After dropping both bow anchors, he backed the ship into the cleft of the rock. Placing the stern with fenders against a granite slope, he sent men scrambling ashore to place small anchors in any crack they could find. With these, he secured the ship in a spiderweb of mooring lines. While he was still using the winch to take up the slack on the bow anchor chains, Paul heard a roar like the approach of an express train. The onslaught of the wind was so sudden that he didn't even see it come across the bay. He was blinded by a shrieking gale which beat the surrounding water to a froth and sent sheets of heavy salt spray across the decks even in that snug niche. The ship trembled and reared like a demented horse in a stall. Some of the men were blown off their feet and rolled across the deck, while others clung to rails. Even shouts could not be heard. The canvas cover of the new whaleboat suddenly ballooned and took off like a huge flapping bird. Ducking into the pilothouse, Mowrey turned on a clear-view screen, a whirling glass disk set in a big port. With that deflecting the sheets of spume he could see over the bow. Peering over his shoulder, Paul saw that the wind had whipped the water in the bay into rapids of white water which were going out like a rushing tide, leaving a seething caldron of rock and whirlpools behind.

Almost as soon as it had started, the hurricane, tornado, or whatever it was, died. The sea rushed back into the bay, swirling. The pewter clouds overhead parted, and the sun shone warmly on the dripping decks and the bewildered men. It was cold. The temperature had dropped thirty degrees.

"Boats, any damage done?" Mowrey called.

"Just the boat cover, sir, as far as I can see. What the hell was that, sir?"

"Wind," Mowrey said sweetly, and lit a long cigar.

"Is there a name for it?" Paul asked with awe.

"Foehn wind. Do you want a lesson in Greenland weather?"

"Yes, sir."

"Well, only a few miles back there, hidden in fog and clouds, is the ice cap, thousands of miles of ice piled up ten thousand feet above sea level. The temperature sometimes goes more than a hundred degrees below there."

"Yes, sir."

"Now here, only three or four miles away, we have the sea, warmed by the Gulf Stream and the sun. Right now you got a surface temperature of fifty-two degrees, despite all that floating ice. So you got a temperature difference of maybe more than a hundred degrees in a few miles. Cold air is lots heavier than warm air. Usually all that heavy cold air just sits on top of the ice cap, but sometimes something moves it and the edge of it falls into the warm air like a bloody Niagara Falls of melted lead. That shoves all the air at the bottom of the ice cap out, and you get wind like an explosion. The first gust is usually warmer than what went before and what will come after. Foehn wind means warm wind."

"How did you tell it was coming, sir?"

Mowrey flashed his sweet smile. "Sea sense."

"There must have been signs."

"My balls ached."

"Any other?"

"There were no Eskie kayaks out. They had carried them all up from the beach. There were no birds anywhere. Didn't you notice that?"

"No, sir—"

"The temperature and the barometer were going *up* like crazy. Then my cock began to twitch, and there was sure no tail around to cause that, so I knew we were in for it."

"That's something, sir."

"Just sea sense. Do you know what would have happened if you had been in command of this ship and had anchored out in that bay?"

"We would have been lost, sir. Dropped on the rocks and then flooded or smashed on the beach."

"You're fucking A. Many a ship has gone that way."

Ducking into his cabin, Mowrey poured himself a half tumbler of Southern Comfort. After taking a swallow, he said, "Yale, do you think you can untangle this ship and anchor close to the beach?"

Paul had no small talk left in him. Only some respect.

# CHAPTER 21

The Eskimo settlement was a disappointment to all who had expected the kind of revel which Mowrey had so often described. True, no one was there to object to the enlisted men coming ashore, but there was nothing to see except about a dozen tiny sod huts surrounded by dog droppings, a litter of bones, racks for the drying of fish, and rusty tin cans. Paul was surprised to see how healthy, almost spiffy the people looked in britches of white bearskin and a variety of furry jackets. These Eskimos were of purer blood than those farther south. Their faces were the color of copper, and they were far more reserved as they greeted the men from the ship. They laughed with pleasure only when they saw the crates of dried fish for the dogs which the sailors carried from the whaleboat.

"Where the hell are their damn dogs?" Guns asked, looking around in bewilderment.

None of the Eskimos spoke any English, but with gestures they caused Paul to understand that most of the able-bodied people had gone off hunting and fishing with the dogs, and many dogs had died or been killed for lack of food. Only old people, children and two young mothers with babies were left in the settlement, and they soon withdrew shyly into their huts when they saw that more boatloads of men were landing.

Guns insisted upon trying to enter one of the huts. When Paul ordered him to let the Eskimos alone, the big gunner's mate said, "Damn, sir. I been dreaming of ping-ping ever since we left Boston. Now I got a chance for some, are you going to stop me?"

"Christ, Guns, those women are nursing babies."

"I like that. If they don't want me, I bet one of the old women will."

"Forget it. Take the boat back and get some beer. Anybody feel like a baseball game?"

Instead of reveling with the Eskimos, the men played baseball, drank beer and orange cordial. Mowrey did not come ashore at all. Nathan went back to the ship and returned with cans of corned beef, Vienna sausage and tea for the Eskimos. He was the only one who saw the inside of their sod huts.

"I can't believe it," he said to Paul later. "Those huts are about eight feet by six feet, and I can't even stand up in there. They've glued old newspapers and magazines all over the walls, maybe for insulation, maybe for decoration. Each hut had a galvanized tin tub full of rotting seal meat, guts and all. The only heat and light came from a whale-oil lamp. The children are beautiful and so are the women in their way, but so gentle and scared that only a real bastard would bother them."

"Maybe it was different when Mowrey was young."

"Or maybe he dreamed up his own Greenland."

Mowrey had said he would follow the men to the beach when the boat came back, but after studying the settlement through the binoculars, he retired to his bunk and his Southern Comfort.

After the deck force beat the black gang and radiomen at baseball and the last of the beer was consumed, the crew came back aboard, picked up the boat, and Mowrey headed for Upernavik. Although they only had a hundred miles to go, the ice had been jammed into a closely compressed ring around the bay and they had to fight their way out, making only about twelve miles the first day.

On the second day after leaving the Eskimo settlement, Nathan picked up a message from the *Nanmak* to Commander GreenPat. It was longer than those terse sentences which Hansen usually sent to avoid radio direction finders, and used the most secret cypher, instead of the ordinary operational codes. Nathan expected to find dramatic news and was startled when these words were spelled out on his stripboard:

"My exec has medical problem. Head of penis swelling to twice normal. Fiery red. He has not been circumcised. He indignantly rules out possibility of venereal disease. Has fever of one hundred and two. Please contact physician and advise. Hansen."

Sparks read the message over Nathan's shoulder, and it wasn't long before the whole crew was talking about the penis of the *Nanmak*'s executive officer. Amateur diagnoses ran the gamut from syphilis to cancer. Sparks put a copy of the message on the bulletin board in the forecastle, where baseball scores were usually posted, and everyone speculated about the treatment the base physicians would recommend.

Paul remembered the executive officer of the *Nanmak* with considerable distaste, but no one deserved to have his penis catch fire while chasing German icebreakers. He read the base doctor's reply, which came an hour later, with horror.

"Your patient sounds as though he has infected foreskin. Not dangerous in itself but can lead to complications. Suggest soaking in warm water and bandaging with vaseline. Take sulfa as described on bottle to combat infection. If infection continues and worsens it may be necessary to lance or in effect perform circumcision. This not difficult but painful for patient. Do you have full supply of morphine in your medical chest? Base doctor, GreenPat."

"My God, what if he doesn't have morphine?" Guns asked. "In that ice pack there's no way they could get the man off or take a doctor to him. They'd just have to slice the guy's pecker cold."

Nathan and Sparks stayed in the radio shack and kept twirling the dials to get Hansen's answer, but none came. There was a great deal of static which sounded curiously like the roar of a wildly applauding audience.

During the following day and the next, Nathan still could not get any messages from the *Nanmak*.

"Maybe he's been sending on some frequency that we aren't covering," he said.

"Hell," Sparks replied, "they got exactly the same equipment we have."

Soon they could hear GreenPat trying to contact the *Nanmak*. "CQ, CQ, CQ," the base operator tapped out monotonously, following with the trawler's call letters, DBPH, which he also repeated endlessly. After twenty-four hours, the radio telegraph was supplemented by a calm, disembodied voice on a higher frequency. Sounding almost bored, the high male voice repeated, "CQ, CQ, Dog Baker Pilot Hypo, do you read me?"

There was no answer but the strange roar of the heavens.

"His radio must have gone out," Nathan said.

"Maybe their generator quit."

"Both the main and the auxiliary?"

No one made any answer to this. At dinner in the forecastle that night the men ate in silence.

Soon GreenPat began sending signals to all ships near Cape Farewell and the east coast of Greenland to relay his messages to Dog Baker Pilot Hypo. The night was alive with messages from ships saying they were complying, but no word came from the *Nanmak*.

In the days that followed the men of the *Arluk* crowded around the open door of the radio shack when they were not on watch. Nathan and Sparks had some news to report. Three PBY seaplanes were searching the area where the *Nanmak* had last reported herself, but there was heavy fog and they could see nothing.

"I bet they send us up to join the search," Guns said excitedly. "What do you think, Mr. Schuman?"

"Maybe."

"Why can't we volunteer?" Nathan asked.

"They'll let us know if they want us," Paul said, and went to tell the captain of the latest developments.

"Keep me informed," Mowrey said thickly, as he had after each of Paul's news bulletins. He was still lying in his bunk, making a halfhearted attempt to conceal a glass he was holding under the edge of his blanket. For the first time he looked and sounded too drunk to be fully aware of what was happening. Paul hesitated.

"Captain, are you all right?"

"Fine, fine, fine."

"What do you think has happened to the *Nanmak?*"

"Maybe Wally is playing possum. Maybe he's onto the Kraut and wants to keep radio silence."

Mowrey sighed, brought his glass into the open and sipped from it. "Or maybe he's just gone missing," he continued. "Wouldn't be the first."

"Do you think the Germans got him?"

Mowrey leaned over, took a bottle from the drawer under his bunk, and filled his glass before answering.

"There's lots of ways for a ship to go missing," he said with a sigh. "It could be fire or a magazine explosion. The ice could have closed in on him fast and hard, or a big berg could have turned over near him, squashing him. Sometimes a berg will have a big ice shelf under the water. When it turns over, it can lift a ship right up in the air and drop it. That's been known to happen."

188

"But Hansen knows the ice."

"There are a lot of floating mines on the east coast. They drift over from Europe. A plane could have got him, one of theirs or one of ours. Plenty of our fly-boys are trigger-happy. Or he could have found his Kraut weather ship."

Perhaps Hansen had blundered right onto a big German icebreaker in the fog, Paul thought. At first the enemy ship must have looked like an iceberg in the gloom ahead. Then it would materialize into the dreaded shape, the big guns slowly turning toward them.

"Do you think they'll send us up after him?" Paul asked.

"They'll throw everything bigger and nearer in first. That's a job for some of the fast new cutters." There was a moment of silence while Mowrey drained his glass. "Somebody will have to replace Hansen's ship," he said, allowing his head to fall back on the pillow. "That sure as hell could be us."

Gradually the men of the *Arluk* began to assume that their sister ship had been lost. They gathered in small groups and talked in whispers like people at a funeral. Only Guns was brash enough to try to make a joke about it.

"Anyway, I bet that bastard's prick ain't hurting him now. He probably was one man who was glad to go."

Nobody laughed and the men shot such angry glances at Guns that the big bearded man hurried to the forecastle for coffee.

It seemed strange to continue on to Upernavik as though nothing had happened, even stranger that nothing changed visibly all around them. The unsleeping sun still oscillated in its narrow arc overhead. The silent city of the ice floe spread all around them, glittering in many pastel colors, much as it probably was on the east coast, though Paul had heard that the ice was more closely packed there, and apparently there was more fog.

Upernavik was another neat little Danish colony with tiny wooden houses painted red and white. Mowrey stood on the bridge while Paul brought the ship alongside a wharf, but returned to his bunk as soon as the mooring lines were out.

"You go ashore and pay the courtesy visit," he said. "I don't feel like it."

Before Paul dressed to go ashore, a short, portly old

189

Dane in a fur parka came aboard. He looked rather like Santa Claus and his stern expression appeared out of place.

"Please to unload your cargo as soon as possible, and please to anchor out in the harbor if you wish to stay here. No one but the captain is to be allowed ashore."

"I guess you got the word from your friends at Godhavn," Paul said.

"We just want no trouble. Are you the captain?"

"I'm the executive officer. The captain is not feeling well."

"Then please to come to dinner to my house tonight. I am sorry we cannot accommodate the others."

"I understand. I'll be too busy to go to dinner. We'll just unload and get out of here."

While they were discharging cargo, Nathan informed GreenPat that they were at Upernavik and requested further orders. He hoped they would be told to go to the east coast, but instead GreenPat answered, "Wait at Upernavik until further notice. Arrangements being made for you to load Danish personnel and materials for establishment of weather base at Thule."

About half the crew appeared glad for this chance to remain out of trouble, and half were disappointed.

"I bet they just want us to finish up here before sending us to take the place of the *Nanmak*," Guns said to Paul.

"Maybe," Paul said. "It wouldn't surprise me."

After piling a heap of supplies on the wharf, Paul anchored the ship in the harbor without waiting for the Eskimo women to carry the stuff to the warehouses. The Danes' booze was of course missing from their consignment. If they had been more hospitable, he might have given them some of the sweet stuff, but to hell with them.

Ever since hearing about the loss of the *Nanmak*, everyone aboard the ship had been in a bad mood. The enlisted men fished, and followed radio reports of the fruitless efforts of the big Coast Guard cutters and the planes which were searching for the *Nanmak*. The days dragged into weeks.

"Maybe all those cutters and planes up there will flush out the Germans," Paul said to Mowrey.

Mowrey was still in his bunk and his eyes looked red, vacant and swollen. He had dropped and broken the last of his dark glasses.

"They won't find the German," he said in a newly feeble

voice. "Until the search is over, he'll just hole up in the ice somewhere and keep radio silence. When the cats have gone, he'll come out and play. He'll be waiting for us."

"You think then we'll be sent up there?"

"They'll have to replace the *Nanmak*. I have more experience than any of the other trawler skippers."

"Why don't they send us right away?"

"They won't need us till the big cutters have got tired of looking, and I guess the fly-boys want their Thule weather station. Seeing we're here . . ."

"Well, why don't they get us going?"

"I don't know, Yale. Do you still think I know everything?"

Some of the delay caused by the Danes who were to man the weather station came when they took a small boat off on some mysterious business of their own government, and their return was delayed by the ice. When they finally showed up in a husky little auxiliary ketch, they said there was no point in starting right away because heavy ice blocked the whole area. They asked Paul to bring the ship into the wharf, where they loaded a huge deck cargo of lumber for building the weather station and boxes of instruments and radio equipment. Two Eskimos who had been trained as carpenters were to accompany them.

It was August 3 when the *Arluk* finally left Upernavik, and she had not sailed more than thirty miles to the north before she became hopelessly stuck in the ice.

"Christ, if this doesn't break up soon, we could be stuck here for the whole damn winter," Mowrey said. "Pray for a hard north wind to break up this stuff."

But for days the weather remained calm. Mowrey remained in his bunk and the men painted the ship. For lack of anything else to do, they even chipped the anchor chain and painted the links with red lead. The only diversion came from seals, which occasionally surfaced in cracks between the icebergs, and a big mother polar bear with a cub, which often could be seen circling the ship on the ice, jumping and swimming from one iceberg to another. Guns wanted to shoot them and ran to the 20-millimeter whenever they appeared, but the presence of the cub made most of the men protective, and they laughed him out of it.

"What do you want to do, Guns," Sparks asked, "Paint a little white bear on the side of the bridge, the way the tin cans paint Jap flags for each plane they shoot down?"

191

Some of the men threw pieces of salt fish out on the ice for the bears, and before long the mother, leaving her cub safely behind, would rush up to grab these.

"If she gets hungry enough, she'll come right aboard the ship, and then you better watch out," Mowrey said from the wing of the bridge, where he was making a rare appearance. "It's happened plenty of times. Guns, break out a Thompson gun and leave it on the bridge just in case."

Nathan rarely left the radio shack, from which he reported with regret that no more attempts were being made to contact the *Nanmak*. The planes and the big Coast Guard cutters were sending in fewer reports of their search. Apparently they were already being ordered off on more urgent business.

At Mowrey's direction, Nathan regularly reported their position and their lack of progress to GreenPat. Usually he got nothing but an acknowledgment, but on August 11, he was told to stand by and soon received a message for the *Arluk*. Guessing its contents, he decoded it with eager fingers.

"*Arluk* will discontinue efforts to reach Thule. Take Danes and materials for weather station back to Upernavik. Proceed to Narsarssuak Fjord immediately with all possible speed to refuel and proceed to east coast. There you will search for *Nanmak* and maintain regular patrol."

"That's it!" Nathan shouted. "We're going to the east coast!"

"What are you cheering for?" Seth asked.

"Christ," Mowrey said when Paul gave him the message. "Well, I guess there's no help for it. Anyway, we ain't going nowhere until we get some wind to break up this ice."

It was strange to get such an order and still to be unable to budge. Guns and some of the deck force reacted by checking all the guns and oiling them. Some of the other men who had been most eager "to go where the action is" asked Paul if he could break out some booze for a celebration. When Paul went to the captain to ask him about this, he found that he had already celebrated or mourned so much that he refused to wake up for questions. Reflecting that once they broke out of the ice, they would probably have to sail thousands of miles before there was another chance for relaxation, Paul took some of the sweet liqueurs and helped Cookie to mix them with grapefruit juice to make a punch.

The party started merrily with songs and the harmonica on the well deck. First an argument and then a scuffle began between men who said they were eager for combat and others who said only a damn fool would want to go against a German icebreaker with a three-inch gun, but that stopped when Cookie refilled the big soup tureen which held the punch. At about eleven in the evening Paul went to the wardroom, where Nathan already slept. The sun was sinking almost to the horizon now, and the wardroom was surprisingly dark. Lying down, he quickly slept.

Paul was awakened three hours later by a blast of gunfire. Racing on deck, he saw Guns shooting the 20-millimeter at the polar bear and her cub, which were racing along the ridge of an iceberg about a hundred yards away. The tracer bullets were kicking up the ice just behind the cub. By the time Paul reached the gun deck, both the cub and the mother bear had collapsed, and the tracers continued to arch into the spreading red pools where they lay.

"Stop!" Paul kept shouting, but the steady gunfire deafened the marksman, and he did not stop until Paul clapped a heavy hand on his shoulder.

"I got 'em, I got 'em!" Guns shouted, and a drunken cheer came from the well deck.

"Get the hell to your bunk!" Paul said.

"What's the matter with you? Boats said I could shoot."

"I thought we needed a little target practice," Boats said, slurring his words. "We got to be ready, don't we, sir?"

Blasted from his sleep by the sound of gunfire, Mowrey groped his way to the bridge. "What the hell is going on?"

"Guns shot the bears."

"Oh crap, is that all?" Trying to go back to his bunk, Mowrey stumbled, and Paul had to help him, straining to lift his heavy body.

Standing on the bridge, Paul watched, stomach turning, as the Eskimo carpenters scrambled out on the ice with a long line. When they had made that fast to the mother bear, the men winched her toward the ship. She left a long trail of blood behind her. When the Eskimos returned carrying the cub, they too were drenched with blood, and in the golden rays of the early morning sun, their hands and faces looked lurid. More lines were used to hang the bears from the mast, apparently in preparation for skinning.

Paul went to the stern and stood looking out over the endless jumble of ice castles, from the tops of which a rising wind was blowing snow spume. If that wind kept increasing, it wouldn't be long before the ice pack broke up and freed them. How long would it take them to get to the east coast, and what were the chances that the Germans who probably had sunk the *Nanmak* were waiting for them? Then there might be more blood on the ice.

Suddenly Paul suffered from a dizzying sense of unreality. He was going to go hunting a German icebreaker, and all the *Arluk* had was a three-inch gun, two twenty-millimeters and a drunk skipper. Since Mowrey appeared to be sinking lower and lower every day, Paul would, in effect, be in command. Neither he nor his two sober officers really were more than hopeless amateurs when it came to fighting battles in the Arctic. How long could they expect to last?

Shaking his head, as though to clear it after a bad dream, Paul went back to his bunk. For what seemed many hours he lay there, his whole body too tense for sleep. The sound of a lot of shouting came from the well deck. For a while it quieted, but suddenly it reached a crescendo. Leaping from his bunk, Paul ran to the bridge, followed closely by Nathan. They did not have to ask what was happening. The mother bear had been skinned and her great red body lay in a pool of blood on the deck. On top of it Guns was pumping while a ring of men cheered.

"Jeez, I never thought I'd see a man fuck a bear," Boats said.

Nathan went to the rail, where he was sick. Paul went to the bridge and pushed the button which sounded the general alarm. Picking up the megaphone he returned to the gun deck.

"Now this is a fire drill! Break out the hoses and wash down those decks. Wash Guns down too if he stays there. If you don't get moving, I'm going to get a hose and wash you all down myself."

The men scrambled to their fire stations, and Guns, covered with blood, bolted for the forecastle. Soon the fire hoses were washing off the decks and causing the scuppers to run red with blood.

"Cookie, get two men to help you hack what meat you

can use off that carcass. Then I want the rest thrown overboard, Boats, all of it."

"Aye, aye, sir."

Within an hour the decks were clean and there was no sign of the bears except red streaks on the topsides of the ship under the scuppers.

"Secure from fire drill," Paul said.

Suddenly the decks were strangely quiet. All the men except those on watch on the bridge had disappeared.

"What are you going to do to Guns?" Nathan asked.

"Take the bastard to war, I guess. Maybe he's the only one of us who's really made for it."

# CHAPTER 22

As though it had been waiting for them to get their orders, the wind continued to rise and the ice pack freed them. Somehow Paul was becoming more and more superstitious, omen-seeking, full of dire premonitions. Blood on the ice, the wanton killing of the bears and the rape of the mother had been a very bad sign, and the willingness of the elements to let them go south after refusing them permission to go north for so long seemed part of a dark design. Mowrey's rapid decline to a trembling alcoholic seemed an even worse part of some inscrutable scheme for the destruction of the ship and all aboard her.

As he stood on the flying bridge piloting the ship through the broadening leads of the ice floe, Paul suffered more and more from a sense of doom. He had learned to love the strength of the trawler, her blunt power and ability to twist and turn as nimbly as a racing sloop, but the *Nanmak* had been a twin sister, and now, no doubt, she was lying a hundred or more fathoms below the icy surface of the seas, and crabs were probably feasting on the bodies of the men who had been trapped in the engineroom. The three-inch gun on the bow of the *Arluk* and the twenty-millimeters reminded Paul that their exact counterparts had failed to save the *Nanmak*, and were now pointing at fishes.

When Paul stepped into Mowrey's cabin to keep the listless old pilot informed of the progress of the ship, he recalled Hansen's cabin, the same compartment exactly, but all fixed up with curtains on the ports, the sword over the bunk, a sheepskin rug on the sole, a painting of Greenland, a print of an Arctic hawk, and a picture of his handsome wife on the bulkhead. Now the dark, sullen currents of the North Atlantic were ebbing and flowing in that cabin. Hansen's body would not be there, he would have been on the bridge in any kind of action. If he had been killed by gunfire, he might have been smashed to bits, or perhaps his body had been blown clear of the ship and was floating now in the ice floe, bloated and swollen, food for the gulls and sharks.

Paul's fists tightened. He was, he realized, even more angry than he was afraid. What was the point of sending a lightly armed trawler against the big guns of one or more German weather ships? Wasn't the United States supposed to be the most powerful industrial and military nation in the world?

The theory of sending a small ship to spot the enemy for planes sounded fine, but in the fogs of summer and the darkness of winter, planes were usually useless over the Greenland ice floe. And how could he, with no training at all and only five months of experience, outwit the Germans, who had at least made war their national business? . . .

It did not take the *Arluk* long to go back to Upernavik and put the Danes ashore with the Eskimo carpenters. As the deck force unloaded the lumber which had been intended for the weather station. Paul remembered the old phrase, "clear the decks for action." The crew worked fast and uncomplainingly. A rumor had started, or a possibility that was being fantasized into a conviction, that the *Nanmak* had sunk, but her crew might, indeed probably had escaped to make camp on an iceberg, where they were now awaiting help. Such things had often happened in the Arctic, Seth said. It was much more comforting to think of themselves as engaged in a heroic rescue mission than hurrying to replace a dead ship as a target.

After leaving Upernavik, Paul headed for the open sea. As they left the shelter of the ice pack, the ship reared like a startled stallion. Steadying on her southward course, she

196

continued to buck and roll, but the whistling wind on her stern gave her a speed of nine knots, fast for her. Nathan and half the crew were sick again. Paul felt queasy, but his fear and anger gave him both strength and control. Now that Mowrey rarely left his bunk, the men were depending on him, and he could not afford to look weak. Although he had to make a few quick runs to the head, Paul was able to give up his bucket and look confident on the bridge.

One thing a ship's officer cannot afford to be is honest, he realized with a sense of shock. He could not admit to the crew that he had never been more afraid in his life, not only of the Germans, but of the ice on the east coast, which was reputed to be much worse than here, and of the endless Arctic night, which would soon descend upon them. In Boston Mowrey had said that Headquarters had planned to bring the trawlers home before winter, but there had been no recent talk of that. With the *Nanmak* missing and one or more German icebreakers prowling the east coast, every ship available would be kept on station.

Constant daylight had been eerie. What would it be like to try to navigate in constant darkness? There were no radio beacons on the east coast and without radar the ship would be blind. Even the fathometer had stopped working. While bucking their way through the ice, they apparently had knocked off the metal dome on the bottom which transmitted its signals. The gyrocompass was becoming erratic, and although Nathan found ways to fix it, the machine had lost its aura of infallibility. There, practically on top of the magnetic North Pole, the magnetic compasses spun in bewilderment. What was he supposed to use to find his way through the black months in the ice—blind hope and intuition?

Perhaps the knowledge of the terrors ahead was what made Mowrey step up his drinking so much. As they rolled south, there was an hour of darkness at midnight. Mowrey celebrated it by climbing unsteadily to the flying bridge with a bottle of Southern Comfort which he no longer bothered to conceal. Straining through the gloom to keep watch for icebergs, he sang softly to himself, "One-Eyed Riley, One-Eyed Riley, Oh what a man was One-Eyed Riley. . . ."

For the next twenty-four hours Mowrey slept in his bunk, his slumber so deep that Paul listened carefully to make sure he was breathing. At noon he got up and prowled the decks, raising hell with Boats when he found that a painter of the new whaleboat had a frayed end. When Boats whipped it, Mowrey said, "Jesus Christ, didn't anybody ever teach you marlinspike seamanship? Bring me the ditty bag."

Squatting on the deck like the old boatswain he was, Mowrey fitted his hand to the leather palm, waxed his thread, poked it through the eye of the big sailmaker's needle with shaking fingers, and put a whipping on the line that was as handsome and intricate as embroidery. When Boats and the seamen admired his handiwork, he went on and whipped the ends of all the signal halyards, but for the third day he didn't even bother to ask Paul to show him the position of the ship on the chart.

That night Mowrey was sick and vomited in his bunk, not because of the violent motion of the ship, but because of too many sweet cordials. Paul did not want the crew to see their captain this way, so with towels and buckets of water he cleaned up the old man.

For a long time Paul had admired Mowrey, hated him and pitied him, all at the same time, but as he washed his uniform and blankets, he found himself just hating him. What right did a captain have to destroy himself at sea while constantly stressing the need for discipline in order to survive? And what right did the damn government have to enlist men and send them into battle aboard a fishboat with a crazy alcoholic for a captain? How was he, at the age of twenty-two, supposed to make up for all these errors?

Anger sustained him more than hope. After changing his own uniform, he took star sights. In the new twilight he could for the first time in months see the stars and the horizon at the same time. He had to leaf through two books to identify the stars and the unfamiliar tables of logarithms puzzled him for an hour, but his lines of position crossed in a tiny triangle which gave him a precise position. Nathan was better than he at the mathematics of navigation, but he had not yet learned the delicate art of bouncing a faint star on a dim horizon with the mirrors of the sextant. It was necessary for Paul to remind himself that after all, Nathan did keep the gyrocompass going for the time being at least.

When it came to celestial navigation, Seth was even more helpless than Nathan. As a warrant boatswain he was not expected to be an expert with a sextant, but how could the man have spent a lifetime at sea without bothering to learn to find his way around? Neither the Arctic nor the Germans could be expected to forgive ignorance. What, Paul wondered, would all these men do if he got sick, fell overboard, or decided to take a drink himself?

The sensation of being indispensable was frightening, but not entirely painful. It was better, at least, than feeling useless, as Nathan did, and as Paul had for so long.

As the ship neared Narsarssuak, where they would refuel for the final journey to the east coast, Paul wondered what he should do about Mowrey. If Paul complained to the operations officer about him, the base doctor would examine him and send him to a hospital. With the good fitness reports Mowrey had written under duress, Paul probably would be made captain and Nathan would be made executive officer. A completely inexperienced ensign would be sent aboard to be communications officer, and the ship could sail off to face battle in the long Arctic night without one man aboard who really knew what the hell he was doing.

The thought of this made Paul sweat, despite the cold north wind on the bridge. If he had a real sense of responsibility toward the men and a strong enough desire for survival, he should tell the operations officer that after no training and only five months of sea duty, he did not consider himself capable of commanding a ship headed for Arctic battle. No doubt the big brass would respect him for such an honest assessment of his own abilities, and would assign some experienced ice pilot to command the ship. He might not turn out to be a drunk, but probably he would ride Paul's ass and make himself as insufferable with young reserve officers as most old sea dogs did. The thrill of his newfound independence of spirit would be gone and again he'd have to live in fear of bad fitness reports and withstand constant insult. And if the new captain proved to be full of more bluster than common sense, a not unlikely prospect, the ship might not be much safer than under his own command. Paul was aware that he still didn't know much, but he was at least beginning to have some confidence in his own ability to learn.

Of course a third course of action was possible, perhaps the easiest of all. He would do nothing about Mowrey, revel in loyalty to him, remain actively in command of the ship, but profit from Mowrey's experience during the old man's sober moments. True, Mowrey would probably become more and more of a problem as his disease progressed, but by the time he finally sank into total oblivion, Paul might have had a chance to absorb a little more of his knowledge. Somehow it always appeared safer to do nothing, to leave his life in the hands of fate. If he had pushed hard enough to have himself transferred to Hansen's ship, after all, he would be dead. . . .

The north wind increased during the ten days it took them to reach the mouth of Narsarssuak Fjord. Paul had never really been to sea in a howling Arctic gale, and he was relieved to discover that both he and the ship could endure it without even a great sense of danger. Paul's stomach still would hold no food but hot bouillon and crackers with a little chocolate, but there was no more convulsive heaving, and he was strong enough to remain on the bridge almost all the time, napping as he sat on the stool, but alert enough to awake instantly when there was any change in the motion of the ship or the sound of the wind.

Although the wooden hull of the *Arluk* creaked and complained as she rolled her scuppers under, she always managed to rise to each mountain of water which rolled up astern and when she went rollercoastering into the great valleys of the sea, her blunt bow always rose triumphantly without burying the three-inch gun in more than foam. The heavy diesel engine rumbled without missing a beat, and enough men remained on their feet to man the controls and to keep lookouts on the gun deck and the flying bridge.

The acrobatic performance of the heavy trawler in the rolling seas would have been astonishing if it had been brief, but after a few days Paul began to take the ship's ability to survive for granted. He felt quite safe as he sat wedged into a corner of the bridge on his stool, which had been lashed to the bulkhead. The hissing steam radiators kept the bridge warm and the ports unfogged, even when the lookout on the gun deck was clapping his mittened hands together to maintain circulation, and cowering in the lee of a canvas-covered 20-millimeter gun.

Paul did not realize at first that the snugness of the bridge could foster a dangerously false sense of security. One night, during the brief hour of darkness, he was napping on his stool while Nathan, who had the watch, clung to a stanchion near the wheel, the wire handle of his galvanized bucket looped over his arm, his gaunt face like a mask of tragedy in the dim light from the binnacle. The roar of the seas and the wind outside had not changed in pitch for days, and therefore Paul was aware of it only when he had to shout to give orders to the helmsman. It had been more than eighteen hours since he had stretched out in his bunk and his eyelids felt heavy, but his hard stool felt curiously comfortable, and the hissing radiators warmed the bulkhead against which his back rested. As he dozed, his chin rested against the bulge of his parka, and sometimes he fell into a deep sleep for as much as fifteen minutes before starting and staring out the porthole into the darkness ahead. Little could be seen. Low-scudding clouds obscured the stars and a new moon, and there was only the dimly luminous flash of a breaking sea to prove that the glass in the porthole had not been painted black. Although he might as well have been blind, Paul was not unduly worried. In Greenland there at least was small chance of meeting other ships, and he had steered twenty miles to the west of the ice pack before turning south. While he dozed he dreamed of women, as he almost always did, of the few girls he had known before his marriage, of Sylvia, and disturbingly of late, of fat Hilda, who had had the redeeming grace of wanting him so much.

Suddenly something woke Paul up. He never knew what it was: a change in the motion of the ship, some new sound, or even divine intervention, but he came abruptly from a deep sleep to full alertness, stared through the port, saw a flash of white in the black sea ahead, and before he was even sure what it was, shouted, "Right full rudder!"

When the sleepy helmsman reacted slowly, Paul grabbed the wheel and frantically spun it with all his strength. Turning her side to the seas, the ship rolled almost on her beams ends. Losing his grip on the stanchion, Nathan fell, his bucket clattering on the deck, and the helmsman reeled against a bulkhead. Paul held the bucking wheel hard over until the ship rounded into the sea, where she plunged her bow through the crests, throwing cascades over the well deck. Nathan was pulling himself to his feet, hanging onto the engineroom telegraph. When Paul said, "Ahead slow," he adjusted the handle before the helmsman could reach it.

"Ahead slow," he gasped as the bell sounded. "What the hell is going on?"

Without answering, Paul opened the door of the bridge, pushing it against the wind with all his strength. Standing there he could clearly see the iceberg, so close and so big that it towered like a mountain above the ship. On the windward side of its base, where the ship would have hit it, the great seas crashed, sending spray fifty feet in the air, and there was a hollow booming sound. The ship had missed it by not more than a hundred yards. Her turning circle and momentum had, with the rush of the wind, brought them abeam of the monster, which now lay only about three hundred yards away, not far enough if there was an underlying wedge of ice.

"Left full rudder," Paul said, coming to glance at the compass. "Steady on three-zero-zero."

"Steady on three-zero-zero," the helmsman repeated. "Did you see anything, sir?"

"Lord God," Nathan said. He was standing at the open door staring at the iceberg, which was slowly receding into the night.

"Nathan, get the lookouts on the gun deck and the flying bridge in here."

"Aye, aye, sir."

Forgetting his pail, which continued to roll on the floor, he went out the door, his long arms seeking handholds. Paul picked up the clattering bucket, carried it to the wing of the bridge, and heaved it into the sea, much as Mowrey might have done, he didn't realize until later. When he returned to the bridge, Mowrey himself was standing in the open door to his cabin, unshaven and dressed only in his long gray underwear.

"What the hell is going on?"

"We almost hit an iceberg," Paul said. "Go back to your bunk, skipper."

"You been going ahead full. You got to slow down when the visibility is bad. Haven't you learned that yet?"

"I have now, skipper. Go to bed."

Grumbling, Mowrey shut the door. Soon Nathan came back, followed by the two lookouts. They all had been drenched by spray.

"Did you men see that berg?" Paul asked quietly.

"After you turned," one lookout said, and the other stayed silent.

"Nathan, you were the watch officer, and you two guys were the lookouts on duty. You fucked up. If I hadn't seen that berg in time, we would all be dead now because for whatever reason, you three men were not performing well enough to stay alive. There's nothing I can say to you that could make you feel worse than the knowledge of your own inadequacy ought to make you feel. Now go below. Nathan, send Seth and two lookouts who can stay awake up here."

"Aye, aye, sir," Nathan said. "I'm *sorry!*"

"I know you are. So?"

"I'll do better!" Nathan said and went below, his gaunt body bent against the wind.

"Tell Cookie to bring me a cup of coffee!" Paul called after him, and Nathan gave a small wave of acknowledgment.

When they were safely away from the iceberg, Paul went back to his southerly course, but he proceeded at slow speed until the first streaks of dawn allowed him to see a thousand yards ahead.

"Sir," the helmsman said, "maybe the *Nanmak* hit a berg like that. Maybe the Krauts didn't get her at all."

"Maybe."

"Could we have got off on the berg if we had hit?"

"Not in this weather."

"If there had been less wind and sea?"

"Maybe."

"Maybe they're waiting for us, holed up on some berg."

"Maybe," Paul repeated. "Mind your helm there. Don't let her yaw."

The excitement of the emergency had been almost pleasurable for Paul, but as he reached out for the coffee which Cookie brought to him, his hand was shaking so much that he spilled a little. They had come within only a few seconds of death, and had survived only by luck, or by divine guidance if one could believe in that. In the months ahead, how many more such emergencies would arise, and how long would it be before the law of averages killed them?

Paul's brain had long been aware of danger, but for the first time his heart now felt it enough to race. Death. On such a ship on such a mission with such a crew, death was a near certainty in the near future. If Hansen, with a lifetime of experience in the Arctic, had been unable to

203

survive in summer, what chance would Paul have in winter?

Death. The prospect of it did not fill Paul with as much self-pity as fury. Damn it, he hadn't yet had time for hardly any life at all! Twenty-two damn years, and the first ten of them he remembered hardly at all. The twelve years he did remember had been pretty well loused up by the Depression, the constant scramble for money and by legions of people, starting with his mother, who had kept yelling orders at him. In his present mood of depression, he felt that in his whole damn life, he could remember only about twenty good days. Loving Sylvia had been full of the pleasure of anticipation, but when he came right down to it, they had really not had many good nights.

The thing that made Paul angriest was the realization that throughout his brief so-called youth he had remained so stupidly *chaste*. Among his set at Boston University, he had enjoyed a raffish reputation, if only because he had married so astonishingly early, but the horrible truth was that in his whole life, he had bedded precisely three women, including his wife. One of these had been a crazy drunken girl who had been laying practically everyone at a fraternity party and the other had been a Radcliffe girl who said she loved him, but whom he had abandoned for Sylvia. His damned obsession with Sylvia, since the time she was sixteen years old, had robbed him of what should have been the best days of his short life. And marriage had not turned out to be the long sexual revel he had imagined it to be. A lot of it had been that mysterious tension and fights.

Since leaving Boston, Paul had fallen into the habit of romanticizing his marriage with Sylvia and his whole past. He had dwelt lovingly upon the few good nights he and Sylvia had spent aboard the *Valkyrie*, a great climax to the sunny summers of longing for her. The bitter realization that most of his marriage and his entire youth had been one long exercise in frustration had the curious effect of making death easier to face. When he forced himself to be "realistic," it seemed as though his life probably would have continued to be fairly lousy, even if there had never been a war. His dream of sailing his family's rotten old yawl around the world obviously had been a no-go from the start. Instead of doing that, he doubtlessly would have taken a job in his father-in-law's bank, moved into the little white house in the suburbs which Sylvia so craved, and divided his life between shuffling papers in an office and raking leaves at home. All the men he knew ended up like that, except his father, who sat at home carving wooden chains and puffing cigar smoke into his furnace. Terrific.

So . . . if life was all that rotten, what was so bad about dying young? This was certainly a revolutionary thought for him, but there was at least a kind of peace in it, relief from the violent rebellion he felt whenever he considered his dismal future. The trouble was, the contentment of this theory didn't last long. If he lowered his guard for a moment, memories of the way Sylvia looked when she stood in the sunlight streaming through the window by her bed possessed his mind, and he hated the thought of death so much that he began thinking of ways to evade it. If the government was crazy enough to contrive for him a doomed situation aboard a fishboat on the east coast of Greenland in winter, why accept his fate with such dumb passivity? If he put a bullet in his foot while practicing with one of the .45 automatics which the government had issued to all the officers aboard the *Arluk*, he would be transferred to a hospital and soon released from the service. Probably no one would even contend that his injury was not an accident, but there were less painful ways to earn release. He could, for instance, tell Mowrey that he loved him and wanted to go to bed with him. Christ, the old ice pilot would be sure to put up a fine howl about that, provided he didn't immediately take him up on the proposal, Paul thought with a sudden shock of intuition. . . . Less drastically, he could plead chronic seasickness to the point of disability and get shore duty, where his promotions would probably come faster than to men at sea.

Except he couldn't do that, wouldn't do that, Paul realized with a kind of surprise. Why? He couldn't quite bring himself to believe that the destiny of the United States depended on his personal bravery. A history instructor at college had once said that no nation has a much better record of morality than any other. If police records were kept on nations, every country on earth would be counted a murderer and a thief. The Germans and the Japs had not been good boys lately, but they had killed fewer people over the centuries than the Russian czars, the English kings, and the Chinese warlords, who hadn't been butchering other people much lately because they had been too busy butchering each other. If America's record was better, despite the complaints of Indians, Negroes and Mexicans, it was at least partly because her history was comparatively short, the very young instructor of history had said to his very young class. At the time Paul had been shocked and surprised that he could not refute the argument very well. He had been more shocked when the instructor had claimed that modern wars brought no benefit at all to the men who actually fought them, whether they won or lost. Almost all the men who rushed from their farms or factories to defend their country, he said, went back to poverty if they were lucky enough to live through a war, no matter what victories had been theirs. The rich, even in those countries which lost, soon found ways to recover their fortunes. The mystery was, the instructor had said, why, in view of this dismal history, governments often found it so easy to get men to fight. He'd said that since men fight without realistic hope of profit, and usually with no cause that could be shown morally superior to any other—not the case, Paul felt now—they must fight simply because they *like* fighting. Men can pretend to fight for a religion or a country they can persuade themselves to believe is morally superior to all others, despite the testimony of history, but men don't make up such elaborate excuses to do something they don't really want to do, he'd claimed. It would be more reasonable to say that one should mine coal, till the soil or labor on an assembly line for the benefit of a religion or a country, but men won't do work like that unless they're sure of immediate profit. For fighting other men, any excuse will do. Since man has evolved from those animals which outfought all the others, the all-knowing twenty-five-year-old instructor had concluded, this should surprise no one. The only question was whether or when man's mind and spirit could overcome his inherited instincts.

The class had argued indignantly with the instructor, but no one had been too convincing. Still, even while admitting that he maybe was right, Paul had hated the man and had wondered why he seemed so tense, so shifty-eyed and aggressive, as though *he* more than anyone was aching for a brawl. Why, after all, did the instructor turn his own classroom into a battlefield where no one ever talked quietly, calmly ... ?

Thinking of all this aboard the *Arluk*, Paul couldn't

persuade himself of much historic significance. But although his own people were of German stock and he had liked the few Germans he had met, he honestly did hate the Nazis, and Hitler with his murderous, irrational persecution of the Jews and anyone else who didn't agree with him. As for the Japs, they'd bombed Pearl Harbor, and whatever *their* self-styled historical necessity, Paul felt personally attacked and wanted to fight them as much as he had wanted to fight boys who punched him when he was little. Maybe . . . the Arctic bred fantasy . . . he was just a natural-born fighting man, the inevitable descendant of the great fanged apes, the Vikings and all those German ancestors of his. Well, anyway, he enjoyed learning to fight the Arctic successfully. Although his months in the Coast Guard had not been exactly idyllic, he was suddenly sure that he had enjoyed them more than he would have liked learning the ropes as a banker. He liked, even loved, the spectacular coasts of Greenland, and no doubt would love seeing any place new to him. He liked learning to earn the respect of other men and of himself—maybe that was the key to it. Self-respect had never been handed to him— he had to earn it every day of his life. . . .

Whether this was good or bad, Paul did not know, but it was an interesting discovery. Another interesting discovery started as only a suspicion, but the more he thought about it, the more he realized that at heart he didn't mind, maybe even was eager for an opportunity to fight the Nazis, the Japs, whoever was the enemy. The idea of fighting had a certain fascination—it was only the idea of losing that he didn't like, losing, being wounded and killed. Winning, he was convinced, would be marvelous, despite the fact that he would, almost without doubt, have to return to the same sort of dull job which would have been his lot if no war had rescued him. Winning, even without profit and without lasting honor, was good enough for him as an end in itself. At least for now.

Paul wondered whether he should be ashamed of this, but he was usually content with any truths he could discover about himself, finding morality enough in facing them squarely. The only trouble with discovering that winning was an end in itself for him was that it made him angrier than ever at those nameless authorities who had put him in a situation where it was almost impossible for him to win. Sending a trawler to fight German icebreakers on the east coast of Greenland was almost like sending a lightweight boxer into a room full of heavyweights.

Somewhere Paul had read that there were two great dangers in war: one was underestimating the enemy and the other was overestimating him. Some general had said that, maybe Sherman, who had said that war is hell. Certainly Paul had not underestimated the Germans. Was he right in assuming that they had many huge icebreakers on the east coast of Greenland?

Mowrey had said that when they captured Norway and Denmark, the Germans would have come into possession of many big icebreakers with experienced crews, but they had the whole of northern Europe to patrol and their resources must be stretched thin. Despite their need for weather reports, the east coast of Greenland could not seem all that important to them. Their army had already stalled in Russia, England showed no sign of giving in, and the Nazis must, at long last, be getting through their thick heads the fact that in the long run, the United States would be a deadly enemy. Those German generals who remained in possession of their senses must be beginning to see that their defeat was inevitable. Soon they would start drawing in their claws, concentrating their resources closer to home. Maybe they would forget all about the east coast of Greenland, except for sending an occasional plane over for weather reports.

All very sensible, and sooner or later it might even happen that way, but in the meanwhile, one powerful German weather ship had been sunk due to the sheer good luck of having clear skies and a flight of Lightnings overhead. The air on the east coast of Greenland was alive with German radio signals, whether or not some came from decoys, and the *Nanmak* was missing. No one, not even Paul the fighting man, could say that the Germans were not at least to be feared on the east coast during the approaching winter. If they were really desperate in the face of approaching defeat, that could make them all the more dangerous. It was somehow worse, Paul felt, to be killed by the last strike of a dying snake than to die fighting a whole nest of vipers.

In the midst of all these, as he realized, rather pompous philosophical musings, Paul was interrupted by Cookie, who loudly promised to shit in Boats's soup if that worthy didn't back up his authority over the seamen who were assigned to galley chores.

"When I say a man should be punished for doing a lousy job, Boats should do something to him. He just put a damn sailor who can't even get a plate clean, up for promotion!"

"What's the man's name?"

"Blake. He breaks more dishes than he washes. He does it on purpose to get out of the galley."

"Tell Blake and all the others that they'll need your recommendation for any promotion."

"Aye, aye, sir!" Cookie said, touching his chef's hat with his forefinger, and happily returned to his galley.

Back to reality, hero, Paul told himself.

# CHAPTER 23

The gale let up two days before they reached Narsarssuak Fjord. The sky cleared and Paul was able to pinpoint his position before he entered the ice pack. When the mountains of Greenland came into sight, he recognized the peculiar formation of the granite hills at the entrance to the fjord.

"Narsarssuak Fjord dead ahead, distance sixty-three miles," he reported to Mowrey, who staggered out of his bunk to verify this news. After staring at the distant coast for a few moments, he said, "You would have saved thirty miles if you had cut closer to the coast sooner."

At Paul's direction Nathan coded a message which gave their position to GreenPat and their estimated time of arrival at the base. After Sparks had sent it, he was told to stand by. While he waited, the crew speculated on the possibility of a change of orders.

"We can't go far without getting fuel," the chief machinist's mate said to Paul. "You better tell them that if they forget it."

After only a short wait GreenPat sent a short message which, in accordance with Mowrey's standing orders,

Sparks kept the operator repeating until Nathan had decoded it.

"Proceed to Narsarssuak Fjord," GreenPat ordered. "Render all possible assistance to DD 177, which is hard aground on southern side of entrance to fjord. Navy tanker Greenwood is standing by to take destroyer's fuel and personnel if necessary. After rendering all possible assistance, continue to this base for refueling, supplies and orders as previously given."

"Nothing I like better than pulling the damn navy off the rocks," Mowrey said when Paul gave him the message. "What the hell would all those admirals do without the Coast Guard to nurse them?"

He climbed out of his bunk, called for coffee, and began to put on his best uniform. Navy discomfort was clearly a tonic.

To Paul's mind, a destroyer was a big ship, three times the length of the *Arluk*, and more than ten times the tonnage. Studying the entrance to the fjord as they approached, he half expected this huge vessel to be blocking half the entrance. To his surprise he saw nothing, even when they were only a few miles away. It was Mowrey who finally spotted the destroyer, which looked like a tiny model of a ship at the base of a towering cliff. She was almost on an even keel with her bow pointed out to sea, and at first glance it looked as though she were simply steaming very close to shore. A small plume of smoke reached up from her stack. The radar crescent at her masthead turned slowly toward them.

"She's on the rocks in practically no water at all," Mowrey said with satisfaction as he studied the chart. "Her damn radar didn't do her much good."

"How the hell did she get in there?" Paul asked. "How did she go ashore sideways?"

"Probably she was anchored in what looked like a nice safe spot right inside the fjord, and a good foehn wind hit her. Those navy bastards never take the trouble to learn about Greenland." Mowrey continued to study the ship through the binoculars as they came nearer. "Her port anchor is still out," he said. "They probably dragged ashore before they knew what hit them."

A small navy tanker was anchored a half mile from the destroyer. Both it and the destroyer started to blink signal lights at the same time.

"Flags, get the tin can first," Mowrey said.

"I'll get the tanker," Nathan added and went to the signal light on the other side of the bridge. He could read blinker lights even faster than Flags could, a fact which rather confused Mowrey. For about two minutes the lights on the three ships flashed rapidly.

"The tanker wanted identification and then said she had taken most of the fuel off the can and was standing by to take personnel when ordered," Nathan reported.

"The can requests a tow," Flags said. "She says her stern is hard aground, but her bow is free. She's lost use of her propellers and rudder but otherwise has power. Her captain says there is good possibility we might tow her free."

To Paul this seemed unduly optimistic. When he studied the waterline of the vessel, he saw that the stern was propped higher than the bow, and the ship was canted slightly to starboard, indicating that the whole port side was aground. The still gray waters of the fjord turned brown just short of the destroyer, with several areas of a lighter brown surrounding her. Over one of these a gentle swell broke, revealing rocks. The destroyer had been swept right over a reef, perhaps when the tide was higher, and Paul wondered whether she had any bottom left.

Mowrey was at his chart table, thumbing the tide tables. "The tide's on its way up now," he said. "It will crest in about two hours. Yale, take the boat and go in there. Find out how they went aground and how long they've been there. Get a detailed damage report—I don't want her sinking the minute I get her off. Find if they've tried kedging her—her anchor is still out. The skipper is probably a commander and he'll want to be in charge of this operation. Find out exactly what he wants us to do and tell him that if we follow his plan, it's his responsibility. While you're talking to him, have Boats take soundings everywhere between us and him. I want to know where the water is and where it ain't. Have him draw up a rough chart, at least a sketch."

The spectacle of a much prouder ship in trouble and the possibility of rescuing her perked up the crew of the *Arluk*, and while Mowrey let the trawler lie dead in the water, they worked with a will to lower the whaleboat. Boats jumped aboard with three seamen carrying leadlines and a clipboard with paper for a sketch. Paul followed.

"Study the currents in there," Mowrey said, leaning over

the rail as they cast off. "Not much is running here, but sometimes it's stronger along the shore."

"Aye, aye, sir," Paul said. It seemed obvious to him that Mowrey much wanted to visit the stricken destroyer himself and to talk with her disgraced captain, but he was probably aware that his red eyes, swollen face and trembling hands would not make a good impression. Groundings were always investigated, along with rescue attempts, and Mowrey was beginning to recognize his vulnerability.

As the whaleboat approached the destroyer, a crew of seamen rigged a boarding ladder at the waist of the ship. It was very spiffy, Paul saw as they came alongside: gleaming mahogany, new white rubber with a nonskid surface on the steps, polished chromium stanchions with hand ropes of soft white cotton handsomely spliced. As Paul climbed it, he saw that the decks looked like those of a brand new ship. Everything was freshly painted, and spotless gray canvas covers with snowy laces covered the big guns which bristled everywhere. God, if we only had guns like these aboard our ship, I couldn't wait to meet the Germans, Paul thought.

Three petty officers, a lieutenant and a lieutenant commander formed a welcoming committee to greet Paul. All wore faultlessly pressed uniforms—aboard the trawler Paul had forgotten what pressing did for clothes. The gold stripes and the insignia of the officers gleamed without tarnish. The lieutenant even wore gray suede gloves. Paul, who had slept in his uniform the preceding two nights, felt like a tramp as he climbed aboard and self-consciously saluted the quarterdeck. "Permission to come aboard, sir?"

"Permission granted," the lieutenant commander said. "We're glad to see you, although I don't know what you can do. Could you come to my office?"

Paul followed him through a passage, across a wardroom that looked to him like the drawingroom of a palace, with a huge silver coffee tureen on a special shelf and a table as big as two pool tables. The office, with a sign saying EXECUTIVE OFFICER in gold letters on the door, resembled the office of a vice president of a large corporation. The tall, slender executive officer, who looked surprisingly young when he took his cap off, but every inch a patrician, sat in a swivel chair behind an empty desk, and motioned Paul toward a small leather armchair nearby.

"Coffee?"

"Not right now, sir."

"I suppose you wonder how we got in this fix."

"Yes, sir."

"We were escorting a small convoy of troop ships to the mouth of the fjord. We were supposed to turn away before entering the ice pack, but there didn't seem to be much ice."

"That wind broke it up, sir."

"So we understood. This was yesterday, not much more than twenty-four hours ago. God, it seems like years! The visibility was fine," the exec continued in an oddly detached voice. "We can't blame low visibility. We were just about six miles offshore and were planning to make our turn when it happened. We hit a growler, but nobody saw it until it bobbed up astern. We sure heard it, though. It took out both our starboard screws and one of our rudders. The damn thing wasn't much bigger than a small whale. The radar never picked it up and neither did the sonar. It wasn't deep enough for the sonar or high enough for the radar, I guess. Just a little cake of ice, so low and so much the color of the water that nobody saw it."

"We've almost hit more than one of them," Paul said.

"I never saw one like that before, ice so blue it was almost black, and so hard that our screws didn't even smash it. Anyway, it took our starboard screws and starboard rudder. We limped in here to anchor and see if we could make repairs, or wait for a tow. We let go the hook in twenty fathoms and the chart gave us good water for a mile all around. There wasn't any wind at all and the sky was clear, except for a gray overcast. We were enough inside that point to get shelter if the wind blew into the fjord, and with those mountains all around, it looked safe as a lake. The water was like a mirror when I turned in."

"But all of a sudden the wind hit you like an express train," Paul said.

"Did it hit you too?"

"Not here. We were too far out, but I've seen it. They call it a foehn wind. It just happens near shore." Paul blushed inwardly over his instant expertise, thanks to Mowrey.

"Jesus, I couldn't believe it. With our starboard screws out, we couldn't maneuver worth a damn. It wasn't exactly dark, but so much water was flying that we couldn't see

213

anything. The anchor dragged even when we gave it all the chain we had. We dropped more anchors and they all dragged. The wind was circular—a regular tornado. While we were steaming to try to take the strain off the anchors, it suddenly twisted us right around and we got the chain fouled in our port screws. That frosted it. The wind just blew us ashore sideways and there wasn't a damn thing we could do."

"I can understand that."

"All the screws and rudders are gone now. We're holed aft. She has a double bottom and it's hard to tell exactly how much damage has been done, but she's wedged so firmly in the rocks that the tide doesn't affect us a damn bit. Low tide almost gave us a chance to inspect her bottom, but it didn't drop enough for that. It must have been about halftide when we hit, but that damn wind had flooded this side of the fjord.

"I never even read about anything like it, this foehn wind. We must have been thrown up on some kind of a rock shelf. On our stern we've got eight feet of water on our port side, about twenty-five feet on our starboard side right now. As you go forward, it gets deeper on both sides. I figure the after half of the ship is hard aground. If it were a smooth shelf, you might jolt her off, but I have an idea there's nothing smooth about it. It could be just an accumulation of big boulders that have fallen from those cliffs up there."

"Seems likely."

"To be honest, I don't think we have a chance in hell of getting her off, not even if we had a dozen deep sea tugs, but for the record, we have to try."

"Yes, sir. My captain wants me to talk to your skipper about taking responsibility and other details. May I see him?"

The executive officer looked embarrassed. "To tell the truth, our skipper is taking this kind of hard. As you can guess, he had a rough night. He's just turned in and I hate to wake him up."

"I can understand that, but who's going to be in charge of the towing operation?"

"Us of course. I've got a big wire cable all ready on the forecastle. You can run a light line out with your boat and winch the big cable to your ship."

"Do you have any anchors out?"

"The starboard chain parted when it fouled our screw, and believe it or not, our winch jammed. Everything went wrong at the same time. The men are already rousting in what's left of the chain."

"My skipper wants me to tell him in some detail about the damage."

"Come on, and I'll take you on an inspection tour."

Paul couldn't believe the luxury and the formality of this brand new destroyer. Below decks there was nothing to indicate that she was on the rocks. Probably permanently. Soft music was playing from concealed speakers in almost every compartment. "The Blue Danube" was followed by "Smoke Gets in Your Eyes." The bulkheads were painted in soft pastel colors. At a soda fountain in a corner of the enlisted men's mess, a half dozen men were all faultlessly dressed, and there wasn't an unshined shoe anywhere. Paul had never before seen so much military etiquette. Unless enlisted men were eating or working, they snapped to attention whenever an officer passed. Apparently no one shouted aboard this ship. All the voices were low and respectful.

The immaculate lieutenant commander took Paul to the engineroom, where he stood surrounded by gleaming metal and white bulkheads which no smear of oil or grease defaced. The engineer, another lieutenant commander in a natty uniform, showed him a framed diagram of the ship about four feet long which had been inked in many colors. Pointing to various sections with a manicured finger, he described the wounds of the dying ship in detail.

"Smoke Gets in Your Eyes" ended on a high note and "Stardust" began.

After Paul had gathered all the information he could he went on deck and waited for his whaleboat, which was completing its soundings. A crew had taken the coverings off double five-inch guns, and was polishing them. They were beautiful pieces of lethal machinery which looked capable of blasting any German icebreaker out of the sea. Except they were stuck here.

As soon as Paul glanced at the sketch which Boats had prepared to show the depth of water around the destroyer, he knew that the sleek ship had had it. Apparently the gale and the surging seas had picked the destroyer up and dropped her not only on a granite shelf, but in the midst of a whole nest of rocky shoals. He showed the clipboard to the executive officer.

"We sent our boats out for soundings and they came back with just about the same results," he said. "Our skipper feels there's a chance of snaking us out along this route." He traced a channel with his forefinger which looked obviously too narrow and too crooked. With a rather embarrassed smile he added, "I guess we should give it the college try, anyway. For the record . . ."

"Yes, sir."

"We've notified navy salvage in Boston. They're pretty busy these days but if they could get some salvage tugs up here and maybe some devices to float her higher . . . The skipper is afraid we may not have much time. If we got another gale, or if a shift of wind brought the ice floe in here, there might not be much left to salvage. So he hopes you'll give it everything you've got."

"We'll try," Paul said, and saluted both the executive officer and the quarterdeck before descending the ladder to his boat. They towed a long light line to the trawler for pulling out the cable.

Mowrey was waiting for Paul on the bridge of the *Arluk*. He apparently was trying his best to pull himself together, and was drinking coffee with no odor of booze. Still, his hand shook as he held the clipboard with Boats's sketch and he seemed to have difficulty concentrating on the details of the operation which Paul gave to him.

"Well, I'd say we have about one chance in a hundred of doing any good, but let's get going," he finally said. "Tell Farmer I want a bridle rigged for the tow cable. Use our heaviest hawsers. And take those depth charges off the racks on the stern. Stow them in the hold."

The deck force worked energetically, and if one was not convinced that the whole exercise was hopeless, as Paul was, it all started out as highly efficient. Mowrey became his old self as he shouted instructions from the wing of the bridge and actually seemed to be enjoying the activity.

It took more than two hours to get everything ready for the towing to begin. Gradually the trawler took a strain. The heavy steel cable rose from the sea and became an arc connecting the two ships. Slowly Mowrey increased the revolution of the big screw and the arc became a straight line. The heavy manila bridle stretched and water was squeezed from it. Farmer yelled at three seamen who were standing on the fantail watching it.

"Get back, you crazy bastards!" he yelled. "That thing can break anytime."

Never before had Paul heard the old fisherman use anything approaching profanity. His warning was timely, because the bridle soon did break at the point where it had been attached to the cable. The heavy manila snapped back like a giant rubber band, and any men standing near it would have been cut in half.

Mowrey cursed the manufacturers of the manila line and ordered chain to be rigged. All day it went on. The men were remarkably willing as they rigged heavy chain with bleeding hands, and you had to admire Mowrey's refusal to give up even when the trawler had strained against the cable for hours without the slightest success.

"We're going to get her," Mowrey croaked, wearily sitting on one of the ready boxes. "If we keep taking a strain on her, something's got to give sooner or later."

Finally something did give. The cable jumped off the forecastle of the destroyer, and when they winched it in, creating a wild tangle on the well deck, they discovered that they had actually torn a poorly welded bollard off the deck of the warship. This evidence of the power of the trawler Mowrey apparently regarded as a triumph. Paul thought he might be content with that, but after more signals had been exchanged, Mowrey ordered the whaleboat to get a line from the destroyer and start the whole operation again.

The slower the men moved the more Mowrey bawled at them, and perhaps through some divine intervention, he soon began to lose his voice. His hoarse bark gradually subsided to a croak and finally there was no more than a breathy hissing when he moved his lips.

"Come on, skipper," Paul said. "You better come in and warm up. The men are worn out. We can try again tomorrow."

To Paul's surprise and relief, the old man nodded weary assent. "Anchor her," he said. "I'm going to turn in."

After making sure that the ship was secure for the night, Paul fell into a sound sleep. He was awakened only a short time later with the sensation of being choked. While trying to shake his shoulder, Mowrey's hand had blundered to his neck.

217

"Get up, goddamn it!" Mowrey was croaking thickly. "Get up!"

Paul sat up in confusion, reached up and put on the light over his bunk. Mowrey, dressed only in his long woollen underwear, was leaning over him. With his white stubble of beard, his red eyes and his swollen face, he would have looked terrible even if he had not for the first time in Paul's sight neglected to put in his false teeth.

"What's the matter?" Paul gasped.

"Get up! Got to talk to you. Important, very important!"

Because of his lack of teeth, Mowrey lisped. A lisping Mowrey!

Paul climbed out of his bunk and sat at the wardroom table, glad that he had not taken off his rumpled blue uniform. Mowrey sat across from him and picked up a glass of vile-looking orange liqueur. His eyes were wild.

"I know how to get that ship off the rocks," he lisped.

"How?"

Mowrey's expression suddenly turned crafty. "You're such a hot shot. Can't you figure it out, Yale?"

"No, I can't."

"Under those cliffs there's always a pile of big boulders that kind of slope down into deep water. She was just set up there on a kind of shelf."

"Right."

"Only her stern is really fast. There's no chance of towing her off. She's aground too hard for that, and they've lightened ship all they can. If they leave her there long, she'll be lost for sure. The first westerly will drive the ice right in here. She'll be ground to bits. So it's time for emergency procedures."

"Like what?"

"Like something drastic." Mowrey's rheumic eyes gleamed with satisfaction. "After all, there's nothing to lose."

"What do you want to do?"

"I'll blow her off!"

"Blow her off?"

"With explosives. Just the right amount."

"You'd blow her ass off and sink her right there."

"Not if we rigged double collision mats. We could place the charges right under her bilge. We could lift her up and throw her out at the same time."

218

Paul's mind was suddenly possessed by a vision of the destroyer being sort of popped to safety in one highly controlled explosion. It was beautiful, but whether it could actually work or not, he had no idea.

"There's a chance it could work," Mowrey said. "We ought to take it. The ship is lost anyway. It would be raising the dead."

"Of course we'd have to ask them."

"Go do it. Now! A westerly often follows a norther. They don't have much time."

"I'll get Nathan to get them on the blinker light."

"No! Go talk to them. You've got to see the captain himself. Nobody else can make this decision."

As Paul climbed into the whaleboat, his mission seemed almost reasonable, but the closer he came to the destroyer, the crazier it sounded. What was he supposed to say: "I request permission, sir, to put explosives under your bottom and blow you off the rocks"?

The lieutenant who greeted him as he boarded the destroyer said he could not take him directly to his captain and asked him to have a cup of coffee in the wardroom while he awoke the executive officer. The music had stopped, but the whole ship hummed with auxiliary machinery and it was impossible to think of her as a derelict. His coffee was drawn from the silver tureen by a white-coated black mess steward and was served in a handsome cup with a blue stripe. The cream pitcher and sugar bowl were silver and the teaspoon had a monogram which Paul couldn't decipher. Soon the executive officer appeared, as immaculate and unruffled as ever. He listened without any visible emotion as Paul described Mowrey's plan.

"I'll have to consult our skipper about this," he said.

"My captain wants me to see your skipper if I can."

"I'll see if that's possible."

He disappeared and Paul waited a long time. The mess attendant served him more coffee and asked if he would like a bowl of ice cream. It seemed everyone aboard larger ships asked people from a trawler, like poor relations, if they wanted ice cream. Apparently they were very proud of the stuff. It proved their ships were superior.

"The captain can see you now," the lieutenant said, and the sleepy executive officer appeared to escort him.

The captain's stateroom was on a higher deck and ap-

219

peared to Paul to be as luxurious as a penthouse apartment. Acutally, it was a suite, not a stateroom. The captain sat behind a huge metal desk with a lot of chromium trim. It looked to Paul like a Buick. Paul was not sure what he had expected, but this was a very small man, short, thin and almost birdlike. The three gold stripes on his sleeves looked disproportionately large. It was hard to tell his age. His thin, angular face was unlined, but the deep-set eyes were exhausted. He was about half bald. His bushy eyebrows and what hair he had were dark red. When he spoke, his voice was surprisingly deep and he had a slight Southern accent. It was also very flat, unnaturally calm, the way actors talk in Western movies.

"Glad to have you aboard," he said. "I wish I could welcome you in better circumstances."

"Thank you, sir."

There was a short, somehow embarrassing silence during which the executive officer cleared his throat. The captain certainly did not appear drunk, and there was no odor of booze, but he seemed dazed. Paul wondered what it must be like to have a proud command like this turned suddenly into a disaster.

"Do you have a plan?" the executive officer said.

"We think explosives might work," Paul said, and started to describe Mowrey's scheme, but the more he got into it, the crazier it sounded.

There was another long silence during which the captain stared down at his desk so woodenly that Paul wondered whether he had heard.

"My judgment is that the situation is not yet hopeless enough for such desperate action," the executive officer, Peckham, said, "and if we did decide to try it I think we should get permission from Washington first."

The captain said nothing, gave no indication that he had heard. A tic in his right cheek twitched. After another long silence the executive officer coughed and added, "My recommendation is that we make no decision on this until the salvage tugs get here."

"Yes," the captain finally said without moving his eyes from his desk. "But I'd like the trawler to stand by. It might help to keep a strain on the towline. We might get an especially high tide. I can't predict anything around here."

The thought of engaging in an apparently eternal and hopeless tow job did not appeal to Paul much, but he said he would bring the captain's request to his skipper.

"Thank you," the captain said with apparent strain. "Thank your captain for all his efforts. I appreciate them very much."

The executive officer escorted Paul to the gangway.

"Would you like some ice cream?" he asked. "Would you like to bring some ice cream to your men?"

After a moment of hesitation, Paul accepted six gallons of ice cream for his crew, two of chocolate, two vanilla and two strawberry. The navy was certainly the world's most generous soda fountain.

Mowrey was waiting for him on the well deck when Paul returned to the *Arluk*. "Do they go for the idea?" he lisped.

"I'm afraid not."

"Jesus Christ!" Mowrey said. "The crazy bastards! I could get her off, I know I could!"

"They won't let us try, not until the salvage tugs get here, at least."

"Jesus, they'll never make it in time! Haven't you noticed the wind?"

Paul had not, but now he saw that while heading into the wind at her anchor, the ship's bow was heading straight for the mouth of the fjord. The wind was from the west.

"That will bring the ice in here damn soon," Mowrey said. "It will grind her to bits."

Paul did not believe that the wind would bring the ice in all that fast, but Mowrey was too caught up in his plan of salvation in the face of acute disorder to listen to him.

"Did you talk to the captain himself?" he asked.

"I did."

"But you didn't explain to him about the wind. Damn it, I'm going in to see him myself! Bring that boat around here."

Mowrey, Paul noticed, was wearing nothing but his long woolen underwear under his parka. His teeth were still missing, and he was clutching a square bottle of triple sec in his right hand. The question of how this apparition would be greeted by the formal officers aboard that destroyer defied his imagination.

"Captain," he said, "you can't go over there like that."

"Like what?"

"You ought at least to put on some pants, and you better leave the bottle behind."

"So I've been drinking! But it isn't my ship that's on the rocks. I've never beached a ship in my life. What the hell do I care what they think?"

"Your argument might have more . . . force if you wore pants."

"All right, damn it."

Mowrey wove across the deck toward his cabin and soon reappeared in uniform and climbed into the boat, almost falling. Boats caught him by the shoulders and helped him. Still holding the bottle, Mowrey sat down heavily. "Now take me to that tin can!"

"I'll go with you," Paul said.

"You stay here, damn it! I can handle this alone. I don't need no Yale to hold my hand."

The boat was gone for more than an hour. Sitting in the wardroom drinking coffee while he waited, Paul thought he understood the intensity with which Mowrey ached for his dream of "raising the dead" to come true. Undoubtedly the old man knew or sensed that his alcoholism was catching up with him at last and that he had nowhere to go but down. The best he could realistically hope for was to be carried off the ship to a base where there was a good hospital before he got a chance to injure himself or his ship. But now there was this possibility of ending his career literally with a bang. If by ingenuity, skill and daring he saved a five-million-dollar destroyer that had been given up as a total loss, he could return to the base in triumph. No one would criticize him for being a falling-down drunk then. Instead of admonitions, he would recieve letters of commendation, a promotion and orders for some dignified "rest cure" before some cushy assignment at home. With such a climax, his whole checkered career would appear to make sense.

It was a nice fantasy, but there was little chance it could happen. What navy commander would listen to a raving drunk who wanted to blow up his ship? The only question was whether Mowrey would get back to the *Arluk* without making enough of a commotion to be reported to Green-Pat.

Paul was not to discover the answer to this question that

night. When the boat finally returned, Mowrey was fast asleep in the bottom of it.

"What happened?" Paul asked Boats.

"I don't know, sir. There was some kind of an argument, and the skipper cussed out all that navy brass but good. He was still yelling at them when we pulled away. Then he sat down and just passed out."

At least he had left the ship of his own accord. With the help of Boats and Nathan, Paul carried Mowrey to his bunk. The old ice pilot muttered, "Thank you," as they sat him on his mattress. That was all.

Paul went to the wardroom to catch a little sleep before going on watch. When he relieved Nathan at four in the morning on the bridge, Nathan stood by the wheel sipping coffee instead of going below.

"The skipper's really in trouble," he said suddenly.

"What happened?"

"He woke up about an hour ago and walked out on the wing of the bridge. 'Ring general quarters,' he said. When I asked why, he didn't answer. He just stood there staring at me, and then went back to his cabin. A few minutes later he started singing. 'One-Eyed Riley.' I think we really should do something . . . It would be irresponsible to start off on a long voyage with him. I'm really afraid he's heading into the last stages—"

"What do you think we should do?"

"Get him to see a doctor. Once the base doctor sees him, he'll be transferred to a hospital."

"I don't think we could ever get him to go see a doctor. He knows what would happen."

"Maybe we could figure out some reason to call a doctor down to the ship."

"Maybe . . . There's a chance they'd make me skipper, Nathan. Could you live with that?"

"Sure," Nathan said. "It would be a hell of a lot better than getting somebody else to yell all the time."

"You want to be exec?"

"I'd like to think about that."

There was a thump in the cabin and the voice of Mowrey could be heard croaking, "One-Eyed Riley, One-Eyed Riley!"

Paul felt a jab in his stomach.

"The man's dying," Nathan said. "I don't know why

223

people think drunks are funny. If he doesn't get into a hospital, I doubt if he lasts a month."

"I'll have a doctor come down to the ship to see him as soon as we get back to the base," Paul said. The only question was how he could get Mowrey to let a doctor see him. The old man would lock himself into his cabin, he was sure, the moment he knew a medical man was aboard.

# CHAPTER 24

Before the men had finished breakfast aboard the trawler, the destroyer signaled a request that she resume towing, "to keep a strain on the line." When Paul reported this to Mowrey, the captain groaned. "Tell him to go fuck himself," he whispered.

"Captain, I think we have to remember that a navy board of investigation will be looking for scapegoats. We were ordered to give all possible assistance—"

"I don't give a shit, I feel awful. Christ, help me up. I got to go to the head."

Paul almost had to carry him. When Mowrey crawled back into his bunk, he said, "I don't know what the hell is happening to me. I'm pissing and shitting fire."

"When we get into the base, you can get some help. They have medicines—"

"I can't even walk straight anymore. My whole body hurts."

"We can get you help."

There was a pause before Mowrey said, "You don't suppose it's the booze that's doing it?"

"I don't know."

"If the medics say it's the booze, they'll cashier me."

"You've got to get help one way or another."

"I don't care what the hell they do with me, but I hate to leave the ship."

Paul's silence spoke for him.

"Look, Yale, don't kid yourself. You're a smart kid, but

you're no captain. You don't know enough and you don't have the balls."

"Then I guess they'll assign another captain."

"Hell, they don't have no more ice pilots. Not for a trawler, anyway . . ."

"Captain, do you want the truth from me?"

"What the hell are you going to say?" Mowrey looked scared.

"If you don't get medical help, I think you're going to die, and I don't want that to happen."

"Shit, I've been drinking all my life. It's that damn sweet booze that did me in. If I had some honest whiskey . . . Do you think you could find me some . . . ?"

"I will if you'll see a doctor."

"Well, maybe. . . ." Mowrey's expression suddenly turned crafty. "You wouldn't turn me in, would you? You wouldn't want your own command bad enough to do that?"

"I don't want you to get the DT's when we're out in the ice beyond help."

"You leave that up to me. I've never had the DT's yet and I never will. You only get them when you quit drinking."

"I won't get you more booze unless you see a doctor."

"You think you're smart, you know a doctor would turn me in—"

"Maybe he could just give you some medicine."

"Listen, no Yale outsmarts me . . . I know I gave you a good fitness report, but if you turn me in, I'll turn you in."

Paul looked surprised.

"I'll report that you stole the ship's boat, falsely reported it lost, and traded it for booze. They could still find the boat. They wouldn't get me for it because I'll say I just found out about it."

"I guess we can screw each other if we want," Paul said.

"Just don't get out of line," Mowrey said.

Paul returned his stare silently.

Nathan knocked on the door. "The captain of the destroyer wants to know when we're going to commence towing."

"Right now," Paul said, and went to the bridge. A long useless towing operation somehow seemed a logical next step for him.

225

For three days they continued to stand by the destroyer, keeping a strain on the towline much of the time. Finally a seaman got his hand smashed by the cable on the winch. He screamed while Nathan bandaged it, but immediately began to boast that he had his ticket back to the States. No one sympathized with him.

Paul used this incident as an excuse to stop towing and return to the base. When informed that an accident had happened, the captain of the destroyer signaled, "Return to base at will. Thanks for your help. Well done."

The "well done" seemed rather ironic to Paul, but he was glad to see the last of that steel cable. He had no idea what he would do with Mowrey when he got back to the base, or what would happen if the old man turned him in for stealing the boat.

While they spent the day steaming up the fjord to the base, Mowrey slept in his cabin. When he learned that they would arrive within an hour, he drained the last of his bottles of triple sec, put on his best uniform and prepared to go to the officers' club for some honest whiskey.

Once more the *Arluk* received orders to anchor in the fjord until room at a wharf could be found. Mowrey ordered the boat to be launched. When he curtly told Paul that he had to go ashore on official business, Paul wondered whether he meant the officers' club or the office where he could turn his executive officer in for theft. There would be a certain Mowrey-like logic in getting rid of an executive officer, thereby making it impossible for himself to be transferred until a replacement was flown from the States.

Although Mowrey had scrubbed himself up and polished his shoes, he still looked terrible, and he stumbled on the corner of the hatch as he crossed the well deck toward the boat. I hope the son of a bitch falls and breaks his neck, Paul said to himself, a thought that would return to him because Mowrey never seemed to regain his equilibrium. Reeling from the hatch to the rail of the well deck, he started to climb into the boat. A brisk wind was making the usually quiet waters of the fjord choppy, and the whale-boat was dancing alongside.

"Goddamn it, hold that boat steady!" Mowrey roared. Then he fell. Boats and the seamen were unable to catch him. He slipped into the sea between the boat and the ship.

Paul had turned to go back to the wardroom. At first when he heard the shouting he thought that it was just part of the general hubbub which so often surrounded the skipper, but it was loud and excited enough to bring him running to the rail. Looking down, he saw both Boats and Mowrey in the water. Boats was trying to hold Mowrey up and the heavy whaleboat was pounding both of them.

"Cast off the boat!" Paul yelled. "Back it off!" Without making any conscious decision, he grabbed the end of one of the mooring lines which had been laid out and jumped over the rail. The water was so cold that it paralyzed his chest. When he got his first gulp of air, he grabbed hold of Mowrey's parka and passed the line under his arms. Boats helped him to wrap it around and make it fast. "Heave away!" Paul yelled to the seamen on the deck, and miraculously Mowrey began to rise into the air. By that time Nathan was lowering a boarding ladder. Boats, whose face had turned blue, had to be helped up, but Paul somehow made it to the deck himself. The bitter wind plastered his wet clothes to his body and he ran for the wardroom where he rushed into a hot shower before bothering to undress. While he was drying himself, Nathan arrived with hot coffee and a glass of apricot brandy.

"The skipper's alive," he said.

"Am I supposed to cheer?"

"But he's got some broken ribs and God knows what else. Flags has already told the base. They're sending a doctor out."

While trying to digest the full import of this information, Paul got into his bunk and covered himself with blankets. Despite the hot shower, his teeth were still chattering.

"I have an idea that that's the end of Mowrey as far as we're concerned," Nathan said.

"Divine intervention."

"What?"

"I never believed in it. Now I'm not so sure."

"I don't know if it was divine intervention or just a thousand gallons of booze, but I think he's done."

Nathan handed Paul the brandy and he sat up enough to drink it. His body was still trembling. A messenger came to the companionway.

"Mr. Green, a boat's coming."

Although he was still weak, Paul hurried into dry clothes.

He got to the bridge in time to see Mowrey being loaded onto a stretcher, muttering and groaning, but saying nothing.

"I gave him a shot of morphine," Nathan said.

Paul followed the stretcher bearers to the well deck. They put their burden down near the rail while they called for seamen to help lower it into their boat. Paul stood staring down into the still florid face of his captain. Suddenly Mowrey opened his red eyes and for a long moment stared back.

"You're going to be okay, skipper," Paul said.

Mowrey moved his lips and Paul had to kneel to catch his words. "Fuck you too, Yale!"

When Mowrey was loaded into the boat, the crew of the *Arluk* gathered on the well deck, their faces solemn. There wasn't a man there he hadn't abused nor a man whose life he hadn't saved in the process of keeping the ship afloat. No one waved or joked or tried to say anything as Mowrey was lowered over the side.

After the boat had pulled away from the ship, Flags approached Paul. "Sir, should I put up the third repeater? I mean, is Mr. Mowrey still captain?"

"He's still captain until someone else stands up here and reads orders changing the command."

"Aye, aye, sir," Flags said, and a moment later the little white pennant with the black stripe through its center climbed the signal mast to signify that the commanding officer was not aboard. Mowrey, if nothing else, had been a commanding officer, Paul reflected. Regardless of his weaknesses, his command had enabled a tiny fishboat with a crew of novices and hard cases from the Boston brigs to steam thousands of miles in the Arctic and to survive even when the old man himself could not. As this pennant, now trembling stiff in a rising wind, signified, the commanding officer now had gone. GreenPat might transfer Mowrey's title to him, Paul thought, but it was too bad they couldn't also transfer the old ice pilot's knowledge, his sea sense. If, on receiving the empty title, he hauled down that pennant to announce that the commanding officer had returned, Paul felt he would be exercising a sort of deception. Maybe he should cut the pennant and fly half of it to signify that a half-ass commanding officer was aboard.

# CHAPTER 25

Paul was still staring at the pennant when Nathan came up to him. "I've got a lump in my throat too," he said with his wry grin, "but damn it, I'm glad the old bastard's gone."

"Yeah."

"It was weird, how he kept calling me 'Greenberg.' You know, that really was my family name. My father changed it. I've often thought of changing it back, and now, damn it, I think I will—as soon as I get back to the States. Greenberg we were and Greenberg I'll stay."

"I think I can understand that. No matter what you call yourself, I hope you stay aboard here. With the old man gone, everything will be different."

Before Nathan could reply, Boats came up to them. "Sir, the men are all crazy to see if we've got mail."

"You want to go in and track down our mail, Mr. Greenberg?" Paul asked and allowed a smile.

"Sure. You coming?"

"I ought to go into Operations and do all sorts of things," Paul said, rubbing his eyes. "The trouble is, I feel so goddamn tired, I can hardly stand up."

"Can I report into Operations for you?"

"If you're going to be exec, I guess you can start now."

"I want to talk to you about that. Maybe we better wait till you've gotten some rest."

"No, we better get that settled. Operations will want to know. Let's go to the wardroom."

Seth was at the wardroom table beginning a long letter to his wife. Sensing a need for privacy, Paul said, "Let's go to the bridge."

Flags and a quartermaster were on the bridge. Without thinking about it at first, Paul went to the captain's cabin and sat on Mowrey's bunk while Nathan sat on the stool by the chart table.

229

"This has been a tough one for me," Nathan said. "Damn it, I'd like to be exec. The fewer people I have over me to do a lot of yelling, the better. But . . ."

He paused, shrugged and looked embarrassed.

Paul's hand hit something hard under the blankets and he drew out a bottle of blackberry cordial.

"Want a drink?"

"I could use one."

"There should be a glass in the head."

Nathan got one. Paul poured him a drink and took a swig from the bottle before replacing the cork.

"What I'm trying to say," Nathan said after his first swallow, "is that we have to face facts. This ship has a tough assignment. You and the men deserve the best exec you can get. I can't seem to lick the seasickness. I think I've learned a lot, but I still don't know anywhere near enough for the job."

Paul took another swig from the bottle. "Seasickness shouldn't be too much of a problem," he said. "You'll get over it eventually, and anyway, we'll be in ice practically all winter. And as for your not knowing enough, who does? If you won't take the job, I won't get some old salt to make second in command of a trawler. I'll just get some boot ensign who knows less than you do and thinks he knows everything."

"You mean, you really want me?"

"I think we work well together. Of course, I'm just assuming they'll give me command. They may have some old mustang waiting."

"God, I hope not. I don't want to go through that again."

"I don't think you're very smart to trust me. I don't know much more than you do . . . We're both crazy when you come right down to it."

Nathan shrugged.

"I can't get over how crazy we are," Paul said after another swig. "I've been busting my ass to get command of this ship and you've been busting yours to learn everything you can. We've both been doing pretty well, and what's the big prize? We get to take a fishboat to the east coast of Greenland, spend the winter in the ice and look for German ships which probably outgun us ten to one. I don't know why I'm so hot for this. Why are you?"

"I don't like the Germans," Nathan said quietly. He was on the point of telling Paul about the disappearance of his wife in Poland, but somehow his throat always constricted before he could get the words out. Besides, how could he expect Paul to react? If he didn't show enough shock and outrage, Nathan knew he would hate him, and what would be enough? No, Nathan thought, he probably would keep it to himself where it belonged . . . locked in him, like a series of explosions within an engine, it would drive him harder.

"If you want to fight," Paul was saying, "this is a hell of a ship for it. God, I wish we could get radar! And they ought to be able to figure out a way to give us some kind of effective guns. They say the army is developing all kinds of light stuff for fighting tanks. You know, I bet that no one with half a brain has ever thought seriously about how to make a trawler a fighting ship. They don't even give us hand grenades!"

"We could put in for radar again."

"Ah, the Coast Guard is at the bottom of the navy priority list, and the trawlers are at the bottom of the Coast Guard list. This three-inch twenty-three they've given us is what they used to fight rum runners twenty years ago! It's all a joke."

"A bad one for Hansen."

"Yeah, the Krauts were probably laughing like hell when he popped away at them."

There was a moment of silence while they both drank.

"Still, there's nothing wrong with the idea of sending small, expendable ships to spot the enemy for planes," Nathan said. "If I were the captain of a Kraut weathership, I wouldn't laugh at that."

"Except in the fog, and it's usually foggy up there."

"In winter?"

"Then it will just be dark."

"Couldn't the planes operate in darkness if we spotted the target with star shells?"

"Yeah, we'd have more of a chance in darkness than fog," Paul admitted. "If we spotted the enemy before he spotted us, we would radio his position and hide till the planes showed up. But what if he has radar and we don't?"

"In the ice floe it would be hard for a radar operator to tell a ship from the bergs if the ship didn't move."

"But we've got to keep moving to find anything."

"If we could detect his radar, it would be almost as good as having radar ourselves. We could just stop as soon as we knew he was picking us up. It's not hard to make a radar detection device. If I could just get the materials and the tools—"

"We can try. There'll be no legal way to do it. Maybe we can swap the damn boat . . ."

"I'll go visit the base radar station and their radio headquarters. A radar detection unit is really nothing but a very high frequency radio. I could build one easy if I could get the right stuff."

"Nathan, if you can fix it so we can pick up the Krauts before they pick us up . . . Concentrate on it, I'll help, but I wouldn't even know what to ask for."

"I'll do my best," Nathan said.

"If we have to buy the stuff with cash, we probably could come up with a few grand . . . Do you want me to come ashore with you? I'm a goddamn good thief."

"When I locate what I want, maybe I'll need you. Get some rest, skipper."

The title had come naturally to Nathan's tongue, but it startled Paul.

"I'm not a goddamn skipper yet," he said. "Our new Mowrey will probably come aboard any minute. Go get the mail for the guys, and after that forget everything but the materials and tools you need. Don't sleep! General quarters is ringing for you right now. Break your ass. The time to start fighting is now, not when they start shooting at us—"

"Aye, aye, sir!" Nathan gave him an elaborate mock salute. Then moving his tall, ungainly body with surprising speed, he jumped down the steps to the well deck. There was new authority in his voice when he said, "All right, Boats, get me ashore! I got some work to do . . ."

After arranging to have the mail which had been accumulating for four months trucked to the whaleboat, Nathan decided to begin his mission at the office of the commander of the Greenland Patrol. It was, after all, usually best to begin at the top. If Commander GreenPat, whom Nathan had somehow begun to visualize as an elderly Irishman, understood the *Arluk*'s need for a radar detection device and Nathan's ability to construct one, he should, if he were responsible, do all he could to get the necessary supplies. Beyond that, Nathan hoped to get some inkling of whether Paul was going to be given command of the ship. If the recommendation of another officer aboard the *Arluk* could help, he might even be able to influence that decision a little. Paul lacked Mowrey's experience, but he was at least a man Nathan could deal with. Nathan had felt withered by Mowrey's lethal combination of unreasoning contempt and righteous indignation at incompetence. Paul's faith in him, the fact that Paul actually wanted him to serve as executive officer, had released him from a nightmare. If there was anything he could do to make sure that Paul, instead of another man like Mowrey, got command of the *Arluk*, Nathan wanted to give it his best shot.

Commander GreenPat and his staff occupied a Quonset hut not far from the officers' club. A stout but immaculately uniformed lieutenant junior grade who had served twenty years as a chief yeoman looked at Nathan's rumpled uniform and said, "You must be from one of the trawlers."

"The *Arluk*, sir. We just got in."

"Are you Paul Schuman?"

"Nathan Green, sir. I'm the communications officer. Mr. Schuman will be here later. He's been on the bridge night and day for a long while."

"I understand you've had a hard time. The commander will be glad to see you."

Commander Sanders was not an old Irishman. A thin, middle-aged but careworn Yankee, he looked more like a scholar than a ship's officer, and had in fact retired from the Coast Guard five years before the war to write a doctor's thesis on polar ice and to teach at the University of Maine. He stood up behind his desk when Nathan entered his office and shook hands warmly.

"I have great admiration for you people on the trawlers," he said. "In Maine they have an expression: small ships and big men."

Since so many military people appeared to hold the trawlers in contempt, Nathan was surprised and pleased. He stopped worrying about his rumpled uniform and tarnished gold stripe.

"Thank you, sir," he said. "Sometimes we don't feel so big."

The commander laughed, then quickly sobered. "I'm sorry to hear about Captain Mowrey. I just got an initial report from the base hospital. It's not so good."

"Captain Mowrey is a sick man, sir."

"Yes, but he's a real loss. I never felt I really had to

233

worry about a ship when Mowrey was aboard. I know he gave his men plenty to worry about, but I didn't have to worry about him the way I do lots of skippers."

"Yes, sir."

"I don't know who we're going to give the *Arluk* to. She has an important assignment and a difficult one. Mr. Schuman has only had about five months of sea duty."

"But he's very good, sir. I'm sure he can handle it."

Commander Sanders smiled. "I'm glad to see he has the confidence of his communications officer."

"Captain Mowrey gave him a very good fitness report, sir. The captain told me about it."

"Mr. Schuman hasn't even been in the service long enough to get a fitness report."

"No, sir, but I think that Captain Mowrey may have known that his health wasn't good. He made out fitness reports recently. They'll be mailed to you—"

"That doesn't sound like Mowrey, but then, he's always full of surprises. Where is your friend Schuman?"

"In his bunk, sir. He's been on the bridge practically nonstop for weeks, and when Captain Mowrey fell overboard a few hours ago, Mr. Schuman jumped in to save him. He's kind of beat."

"Well, I was going to have a man flown from the States to replace Mowrey, but I'd be delighted if Mr. Schuman can take over. It's not easy to find ice pilots."

"No, sir."

"We could make you exec and find you a new ensign. There'd be less delay that way. How would that strike you?"

"That would be fine, sir. But I have a request."

"What's that?"

"Is there any chance we could get radar?"

"Not a one. Every ship in the fleet wants it. It's a brand new development and production isn't geared up yet."

"How about a radar detection device?"

"The same goes for that. Our supply guys don't even know what that is."

"Sir, if you'll look at my record, you'll see that I was in radar research and development at G.E. I could make a radar detection device if I could get the right materials and tools."

"That's very enterprising of you, but you know how the

service works. If a ship doesn't rate a certain kind of equipment, there's no way you can draw it."

"I know, but if we're going up to the east coast to look for Germans, a radar detection device could make all the difference. If the *Nanmak* had had that . . ."

"The *Nanmak* had radar, but it wasn't working."

"I know, sir. I fixed it in Argentia. It was a very primitive set, not made for marine installation. I knew it wouldn't work long. And as far as I know, she didn't have anything for radar detection."

"All this stuff is so new, we did the best we could for her—"

"I understand, sir."

There was a moment of silence before Commander Sanders said, "I guess you should know that the *Northern Light* found the *Nanmak*'s boat in the ice pack a couple of days ago. Only about a dozen men, not including Captain Hansen, were in it. The boat had been machine-gunned. No one was alive."

"Do you think that Captain Hansen and the others might be alive somewhere on the ice?"

"It's possible, but the odds are they went down with the ship, or were killed before she sank. The *Northern Light* found a little wreckage, part of the pilothouse and some splintered deck planks. They'd been hit by shell fire."

"I see . . ."

"They never even had time to get off a radio message," Sanders said bitterly. "There was heavy fog. It all must have happened fast."

"If they had been able to detect radar—"

"Yes, I understand. Look, I'll forward your request to Headquarters, mark it urgent and recommend it. Give me a detailed list of the equipment you need and I'll include it. That's all I can do."

"Aye, aye, sir."

"And tell Mr. Schuman to come up here when he gets some rest. I want to talk to him."

"Aye, aye, sir."

"Start taking on fuel and supplies. We have to get you to the east coast as soon as possible. The Germans are still sending weather signals, and I suppose there's still some very slight hope that Hansen and a few men are surviving in the ice. The Eskimos can survive indefinitely in the ice floe, and Hansen is practically an Eskimo himself."

235

"Yes, sir. We'll hurry as much as we can. If Headquarters approves of our request for equipment, how long will it take for us to get it?"

"They could put it on a plane and have it here in a few hours if they wanted to, but that's not the way it usually goes. Don't count on anything, but I assure you I'll do everything I can."

Nathan, who had not got much more sleep than Paul in the last few nights, felt a little weak as he left Commander Sanders's office. Asking the stout lieutenant junior grade if he could use a typewriter, he sat down and wrote a list of the equipment and tools he wanted. It came to two pages. After submitting the original to the commander, he pocketed two carbon copies and tried to think of next steps. He had done everything he could legally do to get the electronic supplies which he now felt were literally a matter of life and death. In his bones he also felt sure that nothing whatsoever would result, not, at least, in time to help them before they were rushed out of port. Now what were the illegal sources of such equipment? Most supply officers wouldn't even know what he was talking about. The officers in charge of the base radar and the base communications system would understand, would know how to lay their hands on the necessary stuff, and might be sympathetic to the needs of a trawler. If not, they might be bought, but who were they, and where?

"How would I find the guys in charge of base radio and radar?" he asked the lieutenant j.g. "I'm a ham operator, and I'm just curious about their equipment."

"All that stuff is army air force. We deal with a Captain Cantor at base communications. He's not a bad guy."

Well, at least he sounds Jewish, Nathan thought wryly. I better introduce myself as Greenberg. "How would I get in touch with him?"

"You can phone from here. I'll get him on the phone if you want."

Nathan tried to think what he would say. "Hey, us Jews ought to stick together up here at the North Pole. Will you help me steal a few hundred dollars worth of equipment?" That didn't sound like too promising a start. Would a base officer have any interest in a trawler resting between voyages to the ice pack? Except for most navy and Coast Guard officers, there was a romantic aura around the trawlers. Small ships and big men. Wooden ships and iron men—why hadn't the commander added that old one?

"He's on the phone," the lieutenant j.g. said.

"Hello? Captain Cantor here."

My God, he sounds like Errol Flynn, Nathan thought. "My name is Greenberg, Nathan Greenberg," he began, rather satisfied with the sound of his real family name. "I'm the communications officer of the *Arluk*, a Coast Guard trawler."

"Oh? What can we do for you?"

"I guess it's not much of a secret that we're headed up to the east coast to look for German weatherships and for one of our trawlers that went missing."

"I know about that. You won't find the ship."

"There could be survivors, so we're in a hurry. Listen, since you're with base communications and I'm the trawler's communications officer, shouldn't we meet? There's a lot I'd like to go over with you. Professionally and nonprofessionally—I'm a radio ham. Is there any chance you could have dinner with me aboard the ship?"

"I'm not sure I can be of much help to you. I'm in the administrative end, but I'd like to see one of those little ships."

"How about dinner tonight? We have a great cook. Cordon Bleu polar bear steak."

"What time?"

They met at the officers' club for a drink before boarding the whaleboat for the ship that evening. Captain Cantor turned out to be a very dashing young military man with a thin moustache and a clipped British accent with the faintest echoes of the Bronx. Nathan forced himself to keep a straight face.

"I've heard a lot about these trawlers," he said. "I wish I had your chance to get away from this base and see what Greenland really is like."

"Boy, how I envy you," he added as they rode in the whaleboat toward the *Arluk*. "Now, that's a real ship!"

The bear meat which Nathan had asked Cookie to prepare was stringy and tough, but Captain Cantor ate it with relish. Sitting at the table in the forecastle, his eyes lit up when he saw the narwhale tusks, the Eskimo paddles and harpoons which the crew had traded for canned goods and hung over their bunks.

237

"Now that stuff is really authentic Greenland," he said. "Boy, how I'd love to get my hands on some of it."

Nathan somehow had a vision of Captain Cantor fixing up his den in the Bronx like an Eskimo igloo. For the rest of his life he would probably pose as an old Greenland hand.

"I can get you all kinds of Eskimo artifacts," Nathan said. "Walrus tusks, a few soapstone carvings, even a polar bear skin. We have it all. I'm sure the boys would like to do some trading."

"What do they want?"

"Radio parts and equipment. I just happen to have a list."

Nathan took the papers from his pocket and handed them over.

"Most of this stuff is Greek to me. Like I say, I'm just an administrator. But I'll take it back to the base and see what my boys can do. They all want souvenirs. You can't come back from Greenland with nothing but beer cans to show."

# CHAPTER 26

At Nathan's prodding, the authorities at the base post office discovered a whole truckload of mail sacks for the *Arluk*. When the whaleboat brought Captain Cantor ashore, it returned with the canvas bags piled high from bow to stern. As it was joyfully tossed on deck Boats said, "Can I be in charge of sorting it out, sir?"

Nathan remembered that all these months Boats had been waiting to see whether he was the father of a boy or a girl. "You sure can help," he said. "I'm afraid that mail sorting is my job. They always mix a lot of official stuff in with the letters."

Like overeager children the day before Christmas, some of the men began to tear off the wire and lead seals at the necks of the bags. The chief machinist's mate opened one sack with a pair of pliers, and as the men tugged at it, a cascade of letters fell to the deck.

"Chief, pick those up and put them back in the bag," Nathan said. "Don't open any more bags. Pile them all in the wardroom. Mr. Farmer, Boats and I will distribute it. The fastest way we can get you your letters is to keep some kind of order."

Nathan's voice rang with new authority.

Paul, who had decided not to sleep in the captain's cabin until or unless he had received orders to be commanding officer, was awakened by the thump of mail sacks tumbling down the companionway into the wardroom. He was astonished by their number and sizes—the whole compartment was soon filled to the point where it was impossible for more than a few men to crowd into it. This did not discourage the members of the crew who wanted to watch the sacks being opened. The crowd at the companionway exerted such pressure that the first men down found themselves shoved against the mountain of mail.

"Damn it, get out of here!" Nathan roared. "Everybody but Boats and Mr. Farmer, get out! If you want your mail fast, give us a chance to work."

The chief machinist passed his pair of pliers down to Nathan. Grabbing the first sack that met his hand, he dumped a multicolored pile of envelopes on the wardroom table. Seth and Boats took a handful of letters, glanced at the address and read the names aloud.

"Blake," Boats called.

"Snyder," Farmer added.

There was pandemonium as these two men tried to bull their way down the crowded steps of the companionway.

"Damn it, form a bucket brigade and pass the letters up," Nathan said. "If we can't get order, we'll never get this stuff distributed."

He won order. A hush fell on deck as the names were read out and the letters went from hand to hand up the steps.

Lying in his bunk because there was no room for him anywhere else, Paul waited for his name to be read out. Thinking of Sylvia, he felt guilty that she had not been more in his mind of late. What had she been doing back in Wellesley? He had, he realized, never received a letter from

239

her. She had often said that she hated writing letters and in all the years they had known each other, they had never been apart for long. He hoped she would send photographs of herself. The snapshot of her which he carried in his wallet had crinkled with wear, and he had stared at it so often that like a word endlessly repeated, it had begun to lose meaning. He was shocked to realize that he ached to know what his wife looked like.

"Skipper, this is for you," Nathan said, and tossed to Paul a packet of a dozen letters in pale blue envelopes that a postmaster had tied together with brown string.

Paul opened the first envelope in the packet, noting that it had been mailed about a month after he had left Boston. He was angry at himself for seeing at first glance that the slanting sentences were written in a childish scrawl and that many of the words were misspelled. He'd always known that Sylvia had never been much of a scholar, and it was obviously wrong to judge the intelligence of a pretty girl or anyone else by the way she wrote. The fact that he was bothered by her lack of literacy made him feel disloyal, but nonetheless more protective of her than ever.

"Paul my dearest darling," she wrote, "Things are sure dull around here but I'm alright, and I don't want you to be conserned about me. We bought the adorable house I told you about in my last letter, but the papers haven't been finnished yet, and we can't start fixing it up. Mother gave a big party for Mark here when he got his navy commission. Everyone we know came, including Bill, who looks very hansome in his airforce uniforme, but I didn't drink or dance hardly at all, and you would have been proud of me. I'm trying my best to be a very good wife. Your mother sent me a picture of you and you look even more hansome than Bill in your uniforme. I kiss your picture every night before I go to sleep and now you've got lipstick all over your face the way you relly did sometimes on the boat. Remember?

"I wish I could write better letters, but I never was any good at English. How come you don't write more? The trouble is, I bet you have all kinds of escuses and I don't have any, except nothing at all is happening here. I miss you, I miss you, I miss you and I love, love, love you.

Your loving wife,
Sylvia"

Paul opened the other letters, but they were mostly concerned with her efforts to redecorate the little house which her father had bought for her on a neighboring block. She enclosed several photographs, but they were all of the house, not of her. Paul felt curiously empty as he put his letters in a drawer under his bunk. He didn't even like the house, a fake dwarf colonial, complete with coach lanterns and white wagon wheels, and that made him feel more disloyal than ever . . .

By this time all hands had received their mail. In an attempt to find privacy for reading, the men had retreated to every corner of the ship. One was on the flying bridge, one was leaning against the gun on the bow, and one had even climbed to the crow's nest. Without the usual babble of conversation, the ship was curiously quiet.

Paul went to the forecastle for coffee. Nathan was sitting at the table there, his head bent over a cup. "The men are having a contest to see who gets the most mail," he said. "So far Blake is ahead. His mother sent him more than a hundred letters. She writes him every day."

"I wonder how he can read them all," Paul replied. "How did you make out?"

As soon as he spoke he regretted the question . . . Nathan's reticence and manner whenever men referred to their wives had caused him to conclude that Nathan's marriage was troubled, or that his wife had left him. Now a muscle in Nathan's right cheek twitched as he forced a smile.

"Okay," he said, "among other things, I got greetings from my draft board. My deferment as a necessary civilian technician has been withdrawn. And a garageman whose bill I forgot says he's going to attach my car. Fortunately I sold it. Do you think I should be moral enough to pay him anyway?"

"Fuck him," Paul said with a ferocity which surprised him. "Fuck all the guys who are fucking all the girls at home. Did you see the operations officer?"

"Yeah. He's going to order the stuff I need for radar detection, but I doubt whether we get it in time. I also met a guy from base radio who might help us scrounge the stuff. He's crazy for souvenirs of the frozen north. Do you suppose we could talk the guys into trading some of the crap they've collected?"

241

"They'll trade it for beer, and we can get that for them."

"I don't know what the guy can get for us or how much he wants."

"Promise him anything. If you have to, tell him we can take him to a real Eskie settlement. I understand that there's one just across the fjord. If you tell him all that stuff that Mowrey gave us about ping-ping, he'll probably give you the whole base. Just get what you need before we have to deliver."

"I'll sure try. Paul, the commander at GreenPat wants to see you as soon as possible. I gather that the decision about a new C.O. is in the balance. I tried to tip it your way. He wants to see the fitness reports. I told him that Mowrey had made them out."

"I'll go right up there now," Paul said. "Did he tell you how soon he wants us to sail?"

"As soon as possible, I gather."

Nathan went on to tell the news about the discovery of the machine-gunned boat from the *Nanmak*, and that Hansen with part of the crew was still missing.

"They say there's a chance that Hansen still might be alive somewhere in the ice floe," he concluded. "If that's true, we ought to rush."

Paul finished his coffee silently.

"Look," he said suddenly, "I don't want to sail until you get the stuff you need. Hurrying up there and getting sunk isn't going to help Hansen. If he has survived this long, he's holed up somewhere where he can last a long time."

"If he has enough food."

"Hell, the Eskies catch fish and kill enough seals to grow fat out there. They know how to keep warm. If Hansen didn't get killed, he'll make it. I bet he wouldn't want us to go up there as much a sitting duck as he was. Do you know what I'm going to do?"

"What?"

"One way or another, I'm going to get more guns. I can't get long range stuff, but in the darkness and the ice, there's a chance we could get right on top of the Kraut. I bet I can scrounge some machine guns from the army, some mortars and at least some hand grenades. And every man aboard should have an automatic rifle."

"I'm with you."

"I'll go see GreenPat now. Maybe we can draw some of

the stuff legally. Not everybody in headquarters can really want to make us a sitting duck."

Commander Sanders was even more cordial to Paul than he had been to Nathan. After shaking hands he offered him coffee and a cigarette.

"I understand that you've been doing a fine job aboard the *Arluk*," he began. "It's only recently that I've understood that for some time, Captain Mowrey has not, let us say, been at his best."

"What have you heard, sir?"

"I've got a medical report from the base hospital, and the captain of that destroyer you were trying to rescue reported that Captain Mowrey was in bad shape when he came aboard. That complaint went through Washington and has just come back to me."

"The old guy was having a bad time, but as he said to me, he never put a ship on the rocks."

"He knew his business. But right now he's in bad shape. They're going to patch him up here as best they can before flying him back to a hospital in the States."

Paul experienced the same conflict of emotions which Mowrey always had caused, both relief and a curious sense of loss. "I hope they can fix him up," he said.

"I'm sure they will. But now the *Arluk* needs a new commanding officer."

"Yes, sir."

"Mr. Green said that Mr. Mowrey has made fitness reports."

"Yes, sir." Paul took the reports on both Nathan and himself from his pocket and handed them over. He had dated them a week ago.

"Captain Mowrey must have known he was too ill to keep on before he fell. It was good of him to make these out in advance."

"Yes, sir."

Quickly Sanders scanned the reports. "He certainly thinks highly of you two. Captain Mowrey is not always such a great admirer of junior officers."

"We all got along together pretty well, sir."

"Do you want command of the *Arluk?* Do you think you can handle it?"

"Under certain circumstances, sir," Paul heard himself say.

243

"What do you mean by that?"

"Sir, if we're supposed to go to the east coast, I think we should get radar, a radar detection device at least. I know Mr. Green has talked to you about that. I also think we should get more guns. I think that losing one trawler there should be enough."

"I agree, but are you aware of the technical difficulties involved in installing more guns? Those trawlers have too much top weight as it is, and their decks can't take bigger guns."

"I understand that, sir. But we could at least mount machine guns and some mortars. I want hand grenades and automatic rifles for all the men."

"Are you planning on fighting an infantry war out there in the ice floe?"

"Sir, there's at least a small chance that we could fight at close quarters."

"Why would the Germans allow that? Some of their icebreakers have six-inch guns, maybe a few eight-inchers."

"Sir, it's possible that we could just blunder on top of each other in poor visibility."

"We think that some of those German icebreakers may have radar."

"Yes, sir, but the Nanmak's radar was always on the fritz. Should we assume that theirs always works? And beyond that, radar is hard to read in the ice floe if the target doesn't move. We might jump from behind a berg, it's at least a one-percent chance. Hell, I might even surrender to her. Since they sank the Nanmak, they're probably overconfident. If they came right up alongside, we could keep them away from their guns with machine-gun fire, ram them or even board them. We might take them by surprise—"

"I wouldn't count on that too much."

"No, sir. But if we're supposed to follow in the wake of the Nanmak, sir, I've got to be able to give my men some hope, some strategy that could at least give us one chance out of a thousand."

"I understand that. You understand our over-all strategy on this, don't you? It was just bad luck that the Nanmak never got a chance to radio for planes the way the Northern Light did."

"Bad luck and bad visibility, sir. I guess we can expect plenty of both."

"You understand that all ships have a list of authorized armament that has been worked out by naval architects. It's hard to get permission to change that. And the Coast Guard of course doesn't have the kind of arms you mention here."

"We could draw them from the army. They must be prepared for ground attack."

"I dare say," Sanders replied with a sigh. "All I can do is forward your request to Headquarters. I'll recommend it and mark it urgent."

"Thank you, sir."

"Now, do you want command of the *Arluk?*"

"Yes, sir."

"You think that with only about six months of active duty, you can handle it?"

"Captain Mowrey was a great teacher."

"I bet that's the first time he's ever been called that," Sanders said drily. "At any rate, he certainly gave you high marks and I trust his judgment. So I'll make you temporary commanding officer of the *Arluk*, and we'll see how it works out. I'll have a yeoman type up your orders immediately." Sanders stood up with unselfconscious formality and put out his hand. "Congratulations, Captain Schuman. You are very young for a command, even in wartime."

"Thank you, sir." Paul had the errant notion that he should add, "Thanks a million." Instead he smiled and said, "If you're asking me to play David against Goliath, I hope you'll at least give me a slingshot."

"You've made your point, Captain. Now if you'll wait in the outer office, I'll have your orders ready in a few minutes. I suggest you take command formally as soon as possible. It's never wise to leave a ship long without a captain."

"Yes, sir."

Paul had turned to go when Sanders said, "Just a minute. Do you want Mr. Green as your executive officer, or do you want me to try to get someone more experienced?"

"I want Mr. Green."

"I'll have his orders made out. You can deliver them to him. I have a new ensign I can send you for communications and supply. It will be his first sea duty, but you know how things are."

"Yes, sir," Paul said, and added with a smile, "There aren't many of us old ice pilots around."

# CHAPTER 27

    With the orders making him a ship's captain (temporary) in his pocket, Paul went to the officers' club. He wanted one ceremonial drink, a silent, sentimental toast to Mowrey, perhaps. Beyond that, he hoped to make some money at poker. Probably Headquarters would not grant him guns, but even in Greenland money could buy almost anything.

While Paul was sipping his celebratory scotch, a young navy lieutenant glanced at him closely. "How's the Hooligan navy?" he asked with a smile.

"Tired from trying to get you guys off the rocks."

"You didn't accomplish much. They're giving up on that tin can."

"I'm sorry to hear that," Paul said, wondering whether Mowrey's wild plan might have worked if it had been tried.

"And I'm sorry as hell to hear about the *Nanmak*," the lieutenant said. "I always thought that all that talk about the Krauts' machine-gunning lifeboats was propaganda, but this time it happened. I talked to a guy from the ship that found the boat."

"How many men were in it?"

"About fifteen bodies, I think. He said about half the crew. Some were decapitated and some damn near cut in half by heavy machine guns. They must have caught them in a cross fire."

"The executive officer?"

"Yeah. Look, I wouldn't make a joke about a thing like this, but he didn't have any face left. Do you know how they identified his body? He'd had a medical problem . . ."

"I heard about it."

"Yeah, I guess the whole fleet did. It seemed funny in a horrible kind of way. The poor bastard."

For a moment they sipped their whiskey silently.

246

"They say gulls were eating out the eyes of some," the lieutenant continued morosely. "And one guy had a .45 in his hand. The bullets in it hadn't been fired. He never even got a chance to shoot back. When the ship came near, they probably thought they were going to be picked up."

Paul visualized the men standing in the boat while a big German icebreaker approached. Probably they were telling each other that the Krauts wouldn't treat them too bad. Then the sudden flicker of flame at the mouths of the machine guns....

"I suppose the Germans might have had a reason for not letting them go," the lieutenant said. "Christ, they might have one of their pocket battleships up there, something they really don't want us to know about. Is there any reason why a pocket battleship couldn't operate in the ice, or at least on the fringes of it, with all that armor they have?"

"I don't know."

"If a pocket battleship were sinking a lot of ships on a long cruise, they might not have room to take more prisoners aboard. I keep thinking they must have had a reason for gunning down that boat. The Krauts are white men, after all—"

Paul had to get out. "Nice talking to you, lieutenant."

Paul walked to the back of the room, where several poker games were in session. The players were baby-faced army air force captains and majors, not canny old construction men. They played with glasses of liquor on the table before them. Paul picked the table where the biggest stacks of greenbacks were in evidence. He watched quietly until an officer threw down his cards in disgust and left. Putting his hand on the back of the vacant chair, he gave his blandest smile and said, "Do you gentlemen mind if I sit in?"

Luck was with Paul that night. Not only did he win almost two thousand dollars in a few hours, but while celebrating at the bar afterward he met a colonel who, as executive officer of the base, knew a lot about the infantry weapons which the army had available. This colonel was a short fat man about fifty years old who looked more like the president of a Rotary Club—which he had been in Akron, Ohio—than an army officer. He kept wanting to sing "My Gal Sal" while Paul tried to tell him about his need for arms. When Paul said, "Nobody seems to know what they're doing when they send us up there practically defenseless," however, the man's rather piggish face sobered, and he said bluntly, "Just what the hell do you want?"

"Six fifty-caliber machine guns, six of the biggest mortars you've got, forty automatic rifles and ammo for them all. About a hundred hand grenades. I don't expect something for nothing, colonel. . . ."

"Are you offering me money?"

"Cash or anything we've got that you want. We need that stuff."

"Look, we've got warehouses full of hardware we're never going to use. I'll steal whatever you need. But I don't steal for personal profit. I'm a goddamn patriotic thief."

"Well, am I glad I met you! I was beginning to think—"

"Where do you want the stuff delivered? I can have an LCVP bring it right to your ship."

"Aren't you afraid word will get out?"

"My C.O. wouldn't question this, and nobody questions anything around here anyway. Some guys stole a B-24 last month and flew it home. Nobody here questioned it."

Paul told him where the *Arluk* was anchored.

"The stuff will be there before noon tomorrow." Finishing his drink, the colonel ordered more. Putting his head back, he sang plaintively of his wild but wonderful gal Sal.

Paul sang the chorus with him.

It was a little after one in the morning when Paul got back to the *Arluk*. The days of August were shortening and it was dark. Seeing the dark silhouette of the vessel outlined against the starry sky as the whaleboat approached, the phrase, "my ship" occurred to Paul. He had often used it, but now it was true in a new sense. Just a fishboat, a lot of people called her, but the powerful bow which had broken through so much ice, the low well deck, which was so handy for loading supplies, and the blunt stern which had risen so saucily to huge following seas looked beautiful to Paul. As he grew near, his eye caught a flicker of motion on the signal mast. The third repeater was flying, still in honor of Mowrey. Paul was surprised when the moment his foot hit the deck, Flags hauled the pennant down.

"Good evening, captain," Flags said with a grin.

Paul was going to say that the change of command wasn't official until he read his orders, but there was no point in making Flags's face fall. Rumors travel faster than orders, and undoubtedly everyone aboard had the word.

"Thank you, Flags," Paul said. "It is a nice evening at that."

The door to the forecastle was open, revealing a yellow rectangle of dim light. Too keyed up to sleep, Paul decided to see if there was any hot coffee on the stove. Glad to see that a big pot was steaming in the galley, he started to pour himself a cup. Suddenly Cookie appeared. He was wearing only his long underwear. Apparently he had just bounded from his bunk.

"Let me get you that, skipper," he said. "And how about a nice chicken liver omelette?"

"Hell, get some sleep, Cookie."

"No trouble at all."

Cookie opened the ice chest. "I'll bring it up to your cabin, captain. Mr. Green got us some beer today. Would you like a can?"

"That's good of you, Cookie, but I'm not going to drink aboard."

"Yes, sir."

Paul walked toward the captain's cabin. The idea of privacy for the first time in months was appealing, and there was no reason why he shouldn't start to enjoy it.

Someone had cleaned up the cabin and put fresh linen and blankets on the bunk. All the drawers were empty—apparently Nathan had had Mowrey's personal effects sent ashore. The only sign of the old ice pilot was his sealskin cap, which was wedged into the bookshelf over the chart table between the nautical almanac and the tide tables. Paul carefully examined it. The skin was beautifully hand-stitched with waxed sail twine—probably Mowrey had made it himself. Going to the head, Paul stared into the shaving mirror above the sink and put the cap on, adjusting it to Mowrey's rakish angle. It did not become him. He looked like a little boy dressing up. Only a real old ice pilot could wear a cap like that and get away with it. Paul put the cap back on the bookshelf. Someday, if they both lived long enough, he would try to visit Mowrey and give it back to him.

Although he was tired Paul carried all his gear from the

wardroom. Before unpacking his clothes he hung his sword over his bunk. Finally he lay down. In the engine room a generator purred smoothly and he could hear the quartermaster on the bridge telling Guns about a girl he had met in New Orleans. Nathan had set only an anchor watch. Mowrey would have demanded a sea watch at anchor here in this open fjord, but the men were tired, there was little wind and the sky was clear.

"Quartermaster," Paul called. "Keep an eye on the glass and on the thermometers. Call me if there's any change or if the wind pipes up."

"Aye, aye, sir."

Paul turned over in the unfamiliar bunk. He had hung his sword temporarily from a bookshelf, and the slight rocking of the ship caused it to sway. In the morning he would have Boats and Chief Banes put up some brackets. Mowrey apparently had never owned a sword, but Hansen had displayed his. The sword meant something, after all. Before he could figure out just what, he went to sleep.

Paul had no idea how long he slept before Nathan awoke him.

"Skipper, I'm sorry, but there's a soldier here from the army hospital. He says Mowrey sent him. The old man wants to see you right away."

Automatically Paul jumped up to his feet, hastily straightened his uniform and went to the well deck. A short, stout man in a khaki parka with a sergeant's chevrons on the sleeve was waiting for him, and a strange green plywood boat with a big outboard motor on the stern was moored alongside.

"Captain Mowrey told me to bring you in," he said, sounding as though he were taking Paul prisoner.

"All right."

Paul followed the sergeant into the green boat and soon they were skimming with surprising speed toward the base. The sergeant led Paul to a big Quonset hut with a red cross painted over the door. Inside it looked much like a civilian hospital and there was the same depressing mixture of smells. They walked through several wards before stopping in front of a room which held only four beds, three of which were empty. A stout, middle-aged army nurse stopped them at the door.

"Are you bringing him liquor?" she asked.

250

"No," Paul and the sergeant said simultaneously.

"You better not. We've got him on drugs. Liquor could kill him."

"I couldn't find none for him anyway," the sergeant said.

The nurse stepped away from the open door. Mowrey was lying half propped up in the first bed. His eyes were closed and at first glance Paul thought he was dead; his usually red face was gray. With a stubble of gray beard and no teeth, he looked shockingly old.

"I brung him," the sergeant said. "Now do I get my ten bucks?"

"Did you bring me any booze?" Mowrey did not open his eyes.

"I couldn't find none. They won't let any in here anyway."

"You bastard. I bet you didn't even try."

"I brung the officer. Now I want my ten bucks."

"Get the hell out of here or I'll call the nurse."

"You said—"

Taking his wallet from his hip pocket, Paul gave the sergeant ten dollars and the man walked out. For what seemed a long while Mowrey lay silently with his eyes closed. He did not even seem to be breathing.

"How are you feeling, skipper?"

"Like shit."

"You'll be better soon."

Mowrey opened his eyes. They were the only part of him which did not look dead. They were full of an incredibly malevolent glare.

"I ain't going to die. That's what you want, isn't it?"

"No, sir."

"Remember you're temporary. Temporary commanding officer. That's what your orders read."

"Yes, sir."

"I'll be out of here. Maybe not before you sail, but soon. I've dried out before. They'll fly me to the ship, wherever you are. I'll be back."

"That won't be my decision."

"There ain't nothing wrong with me that can't heal in a few weeks. The doc said that himself."

"I'm glad."

"I'll bet. Did you tell GreenPat I'm a fucking drunk?"

"No."

251

"You better not! If I find you put that on my record, I'll tell them you're a thief. You stole the boat."

Paul said nothing.

"I'll be back. You know why?"

"No, sir."

"Because you'll fuck up. I just hope to hell you don't sink the ship."

Paul said nothing. Taking one of his huge gray hands from beneath the blanket, Mowrey pointed an unsteady finger at him, and attempted to sit up.

"You ain't an ice pilot. You ain't a skipper. You ain't a sailor. You don't have the balls for it. You ain't even a man. You're just a fucking Yale and that's why you won't last. That's why I'll be back, sooner than you think!"

Mowrey let his head fall back on the pillow and his hand dropped on his chest. He closed his eyes. Paul stared at him for a moment before getting up and walking out of the hospital.

At the bar of the officers' club he tried to tell himself that Mowrey's words had been only the ravings of a dying old man, but in his mind there was an ineradicable picture of the *Arluk* hopelessly grounded on some Arctic shore, and a big seaplane swooping down to put Mowrey aboard. It was a fantasy which soon began to plague him even more than the one about the big German icebreaker looming out of the fog . . .

After he had had a half dozen drinks, Paul found a man with a boat, who ran him out to his ship. He made sure that he walked very steadily as he went to his cabin because he did not want the men to think that he had acquired Mowrey's weaknesses, if not his strengths. The whiskey did its job. He had no trouble going to sleep.

He did not awaken for almost ten hours, by far the longest unbroken rest he had had since coming aboard the *Arluk*. And he might have slept longer if Nathan had not awakened him. Nathan, he noted, had stopped calling him by his first name.

"Skipper," Nathan said, "sorry to bother you, but there's a landing craft alongside with a big load of guns in crates. What do you want done with them?"

"Have Seth and Guns stow them in the hold."

"God, you sure got them quick!"

"I got lucky. How you coming with your stuff?"

252

"I'm going to meet my man tonight at the officers' club. I have two more things to report, sir. An ensign by the name of Robert Williams just reported for duty. He hitched a ride on the landing craft."

"What's he look like?"

"Nothing but a college boy, sir," Nathan said with his wry grin. "Looks like he might come from Yale."

Paul laughed. "Well, it won't take us long to straighten him out."

"And there was a BuPers message in the official mail. You and I are now both lieutenants, junior grade."

"Congratulations."

"I'd feel better about it if I had earned it. It's just a block, automatic promotion. You at least have it coming."

"Nathan, will you cut that out? Anybody who has vomited as much as you have for the sake of his country deserves everything he can get."

"Damned if that doesn't sound right."

"Ask Cookie to bring some breakfast up for me, will you? Then give me about half an hour. When you get those crates off the deck, pass the word that we're going to hold quarters. I have to read my orders."

"Aye, aye, sir." Nathan did not leave. Instead he fumbled in his pocket and took out a small cardboard box. "When I went ashore this morning, I was able to pick up these."

He handed it to Paul and Paul opened it. Inside were the silver bars of a lieutenant junior grade and two sets of shoulder bars with the appropriate one-and-a-half stripe.

"God, thanks for getting me these. How much do I owe you for them?"

"Nothing, sir. The crew took up a collection. We've got the gold braid for your blue uniform too. Boats will sew it on. Can I take your coats to him?"

"Sure. Who put them all up to that?"

"I don't know who got the idea first. I don't even know how they found out about the promotion. Boats brought me a hat full of money just before I went ashore."

"The bastards are just trying to butter me up," Paul said with a grin. "Tell them it won't work. No, I'll thank them when I read my orders."

Nathan smiled, took Paul's coats from his locker and left.

Cookie served Paul croissants that morning with eggs Benedict. He also asked if he could go ashore.

"What for, Cookie?"

"I got to get supplies."

"Doesn't Mr. Green see to that?"

"Private supplies, sir."

"If you mean booze, we're turning over a new book on this ship. I think we've seen enough of booze. I'm not going to search your flour bin, but I don't want to hear about booze again. Request denied."

"Aye, aye, sir," Cookie said, looking crestfallen.

"And if you crap in my soup, I'll do it in your hat."

"Oh no, sir," Cookie said. "Thanks for warning me."

A few minutes after Paul had finished his breakfast, Nathan brought up his blue coat with a new half-stripe on each sleeve. Since the old stripe had been worn to silver, the new gold stood out.

"Thank you," Paul said. "I guess you can call the men to quarters now."

A moment later the shrill wail of the boatswain's pipe sounded. When Paul came down to the well deck a few minutes later, four rows of men stiffened to attention. In the front row with Seth and Nathan was the new ensign. He looked about fourteen years old, a short, thin chap who still had acne. Contrasted to his boyish, eager face, the other men looked bone tired, but anxious to please as they stood with their pea jackets buttoned against a chill wind.

"At ease," Paul began. "I am here to read my orders." He took them from his pocket, remembering how Mowrey had snapped his papers open only about five months ago when he had taken command. It seemed at least five years in the past. Paul was capable of no such gesture and he unfolded his orders with deliberation.

"To: Paul R. Schuman, Ensign U.S. Coast Guard Reserve—now lieutenant junior grade, as you can see. From Commandant, U.S. Coast Guard, Washington; D.C. Subject: Assignment as temporary commanding officer, U.S. Coast Guard cutter *Arluk*. Paragraph one: You will assume temporary command of the U.S. Coast Guard cutter *Arluk* without delay, pending further orders."

He folded the paper and put it back in his pocket. It had taken courage to read the word "temporary" twice instead of leaving it out. He hated that word, but tried to forget it.

"Well, men, we've come a long way together, thousands of cold miles," he began. "Captain Mowrey has taught us a lot, I think, and I'm sure we all can carry on without him."

He paused and cleared his throat. The men stared at him impassively. He could not guess what they were thinking.

"I want to thank you all for the insignia of my new rank. These insignia you have given me will be my most treasured souvenir of this war, perhaps the only one, because there's not much of it I want to remember."

This got a dutiful laugh.

"Now I'm not going to give you a speech the way Captain Mowrey did when he assumed command because you're already shaped up into a great crew and I can't tell you anything about Greenland that you haven't seen for yourself. I just have two things to say to you. First, I don't plan to offer to buy your insignia when you get promotions because I hope you all get a lot of them. I believe that anybody on the Greenland Patrol deserves all the promotions he can get just for being here. I am asking Mr. Green today to write all letters necessary for recommending every man for the next rate. I'm not sure that Headquarters will give us everything we ask, but you can be sure that Mr. Green and I will keep trying."

A cheer greeted this.

"Now one more thing. You saw some big crates loaded aboard a little while ago. They contain six heavy machine guns, six mortars, automatic rifles for all hands, ammo and hand grenades. In a sea battle that stuff might not be much good, but there are all kinds of possibilities if we meet the Germans in the ice or on the ice. A close encounter is not impossible. At any rate, I want you to know that I am doing everything I can to make this ship a fighting unit, and by that I mean a ship that can *fight*. I want this crew trained like a company of marines. I may have another few notions to help us survive whatever circumstances sank the *Nanmak*. We'll use every ounce of our ingenuity to make this little ship as dangerous to the enemy as we possibly can. For this reason I am asking Mr. Green to have a new insignia painted over the Coast Guard motto on our stack. I am taking off Captain Mowrey's personal motto, because we've all learned enough not to foul up here, and in its place I am putting a motto for the Germans to read if they ever come close enough to us. This motto used to fly on one of our country's oldest flags, way back at the beginning of the American Revolution. Mr. Green, I want a rattle-snake painted on that smokestack. And in a circle around it, I want the words, DON'T TREAD ON ME."

Another cheer.

"Dis-*missed!*" Paul said, spun on his heel and walked to his cabin. For some reason he was shaking. In his private head he splashed cold water on his face and combed his hair. After calming down, he sat on the stool in the bridge and watched Guns assemble one of the new 50-caliber machine guns. It was a snub-snouted lethal-looking instru-ment, but against a German pocket battleship, if such there actually was on the east coast of Greenland, it would be little better than a water pistol. Even so, Paul reminded himself, there was always a chance of evading the enemy until the planes could be called in. A German pocket bat-tleship would not want to betray her presence just to sink a trawler, and her captain would not fire unless he knew he had been seen. In a dark jungle a dog can run from a tiger and yap alarms to the whole animal kingdom. The rattle-snake can kill a grizzly bear, especially if he strikes before being seen. There was no need for Paul to assume he had no chance at all against the Germans. After all, they were only men, just like him, except a lot crazier.

# CHAPTER 28

The next day Paul called the chief machinist's mate into his cabin. The chief was a stout old Coast Guard regular named John Banes who had been on the point of retirement when the war broke out. Banes knew his busi-ness, knew it so well that neither Mowrey nor Paul ever worried much about engine breakdown. Despite his great bulk and knowledge, he was a curiously self-effacing man who hardly ever said anything, no matter what hardships he had to endure. His usual response to any question was a grunt, a mellow grunt for "yes," a gruff grunt for "no." He had another grunt of sheer disgust for comment on the weather, the ice, Greenland in general, trawlers and inexperienced sailors. Since he appeared to have the most limited vocabulary Paul had ever heard, he'd assumed that Banes was stupid, but with his big blunt hands he could take apart the most intricate machinery and make it work, even when the ship was rolling and pitching in a full gale. He also never got into disputes with other men. More than twenty years at sea in small ships had taught Chief Banes a thing or two.

Now the chief took his cap off as he entered the captain's cabin, looked impassively at this man half his age who had just become his commanding officer and said, "Mr. Green says you want to see me, sir."

"Yes, chief. We ought to have a talk. You run those engines so well that I tend to forget they're there."

Banes gave a pleased grunt.

"I guess you know I know next to nothing about engines," Paul continued. "You're in complete charge of the engineroom. I'll hardly ever go there except when I want to get warm."

Another pleased grunt.

"Now I guess you've heard we're going to the east coast. I suppose we could be sent home after a short voyage, but I think we would be wise to assume that we'll be up there all winter. Of course we'll be anchored or stuck in the ice a lot of the time, so fuel shouldn't be too much of a problem. Have you got all the spare parts you need?"

Banes gave his yes grunt and added, "I drew all I could in Boston and Argentia. We're pretty well fixed. I just got some spare parts Mr. Green told me to order for the gyrocompass. That's his baby now."

"Are there any repairs you want to make that would put the ship temporarily out of commission? Here's the place to do them."

"That Fairbanks-Morse will go forever. It's a good, slow-turning engine."

"That's fine. But chief, I have reason to want to delay our departure about ten days. Mr. Green is hoping to get some electronic supplies that could be important. Frankly, he hopes to build a device that can detect enemy radar. I don't want to sail until he gets everything he needs."

Banes gave his mellow grunt. "I could get a scored cylinder," he said. "We'd have to put in a new liner. That will take about as much time as you need."

"Thank you, chief."

The chief put on his cap and went to the engineroom. Paul buttoned up his parka and went directly to the Commander GreenPat office. Sanders saw him without delay.

"What can I do for you, skipper?"

"I just want to talk over our sailing date. I had hoped to be ready to go within twenty-four hours, but now my chief tells me he has to put in a new cylinder liner. We may need a week or ten days on availability."

Sanders frowned. "There's something about these trawlers. If I head their bows back to Boston, they never have engine trouble, but when I head them north—"

"Sir, the *Arluk* has a good record on that. We've never asked for availability. I'd rather take that engine apart here than in the ice."

"Of course I can't argue with that. I suppose you want a secure mooring."

"Yes, sir."

"Bring her alongside the *Redbird* at Pier Three. The navy is having a hell of a time with her. She's always on availability."

The crew of the *Redbird*, the gray navy trawler alongside of which they had lain in Argentia, greeted the crew of the *Arluk* like old friends. Upon finding that the *Redbird* had been broken down ever since reaching Greenland, the men of the *Arluk* had a fine time describing their voyage up the west coast.

"Did you see any Eskies?" the *Redbird*'s chief boatswain's mate asked.

"Sure," Boats replied with a grin. "Now I ain't going to tell you about them except they're the most *hospitable* people in the world."

To Paul's surprise, a truck soon brought another load of mail for the *Arluk*. There were a few more sacks of letters and many packages, most of which turned out to contain cookies and cakes which now consisted mostly of dry crumbs. Paul received another eight letters from Sylvia and, to his surprise, one from his brother Bill and two from his mother. He opened the letters from his wife first, quickly searching for photographs of her, but her snapshots still showed nothing but the house. Finding that her letters continued to be concerned largely with the details of interior decoration, Paul opened the envelope from his brother. Bill had enclosed a photograph of himself, a dashing young army air force lieutenant.

Dear Paul,

I finally made it through training. Boy, I tell you, it was rough! A third of my class washed out, and two crashed. You don't walk away from the wreckage of one of those advanced trainers. The Air Force saves on funeral costs—there's never much left to bury.

I thought I was off to the Battle of Britain and was all geared up to get me some Krauts, but I made the mistake of doing pretty well in my advanced training, and now, damn it, I'm a flight instructor. I still get flight pay and they say that the promotions come so fast that some guys make chicken colonel almost before they can vote, but I'd give my right arm to go where the action is. I'm doing what I can to pull strings, and maybe they'll turn me loose here after a few months.

Meantime it seems that I have danger without medals. The guys the Force is recruiting these days are so unpredictable that the death rate of instructors is worse than for combat pilots. It must be cold where you are, but at least you don't have some young cowboy trying to fly you into a tree. Sometimes I wish I had been smart enough to join the Coast Guard: Why didn't anyone tell me that flying is dangerous?

When I think of you just lolling around with the Eskimos, I get mad as hell. The Coast Guard must get boring at times, but I could sure do with a little boredom. Bring me home an Eskimo girl if you can. The girls in South Carolina have lost their magic. Man, you don't have to tackle them when you're in the air force —they tackle you, and some of them make a loop-the-loop at 400 miles an hour seem restful. I hope to get home soon and will say hello to Sylvia.

Take care—
Bill

Good old Bill, Paul thought sourly. Now there's a real operator! He gets flight pay, fast promotion, a glamor-boy uniform, stays stateside, and still gets to play the hero in mortal danger. I bet he arranges enough fast flights to combat areas to pick up a chestful of campaign ribbons without being overseas more than a month. Why didn't I have the sense to follow in my dear older brother's footsteps?

Paul's mother enclosed a picture of herself which the *Boston Globe* had published with an article on a meeting of the National Federation of Garden Clubs. It showed her in a big hat, a gray dress and white gloves. Her big news was that she had been made president of the local chapter of the League of Women Voters, and his father had entered "an exciting new period," experimenting with "canvases of abstract shape, as well as design, a marvelous marriage of sculpture and painting."

A photograph of one of these creations was also enclosed. It looked like an enormous comma, half-blue and half-black.

Nathan interrupted Paul's thoughts about this mail.

"Do you mind if I arrange the beer bust for the guys ashore today?"

"Do it as often as you can while we're here."

Nathan sat on the stool by the chart table. "I don't know whether all this mail is a good idea or not. A lot of guys got bad news. Guns found his wife has left him."

"Maybe somebody wrote her that he had been unfaithful to her with a polar bear. Do you suppose she could name a dead bear as corespondent?"

"It's no joke. He's so mad he damn near took a poke at Boats. Boats is riding high because he got the son he wanted."

"I imagine there was more good news in the mail than bad."

"But the good news may be even worse for morale. Now Boats can hardly wait to go home and Sparks is clawing down the sides of the radio shack. His wife sent him a picture of herself in the buff. He's showing it around with great pride. I must say, she has the biggest tits I ever saw. Now his mind is entirely off his work. I'd hoped that he could help me to scrounge radio parts—sometimes the radiomen are better at that than the officers. Now all he can think about is getting a picture of himself taken to send back to her. He's taken one of himself with the new ensign's camera. Do you have any idea where he can get a blue picture developed up here?"

"Love will find a way. How are you coming with your supplies?"

"It's going to be tougher than I thought. It seems that a lot of these guys who are permanently based here have built illegal ham stations to communicate with home. They've rigged up so many aerials that they call the barracks section radio city. Building this stuff is a regular craze up here, and the radio parts depot has been stolen blind. So now there's a big crackdown. My friend Errol Flynn is trying his best to help, but he says there's such a shortage it's hard to get stuff even legitimately."

Paul thought for a moment. "If you can't steal where the thieves stole, steal it or buy it from the thieves. Can't you get the equipment from one of those illegal stations? I could put up maybe three grand."

"Money isn't worth much up here, but a radio that can bring home in is valuable. And there's a lot of specialized stuff I need that wouldn't go with a ham station. My job would be a lot simpler if I knew the frequencies of German radar. I've got to build something that will cover quite a range. Without any kind of testing apparatus, it's not going to be simple."

"Can you do it?"

"Look, I believe in the can-do spirit and all that, but if I have to leave here with nothing much more than a spool of copper wire and a pair of pliers, I can't guarantee you much except all-out effort."

"Give me a copy of your list," Paul said. "I'll see what I can do."

For more than a week Paul searched out people in base radar and radio, and used all his powers of persuasion to get the material on Nathan's list. He was not used to failures of this kind and could hardly believe it when forced finally to realize that some of the key items simply were unobtainable, did not exist in Greenland except in operating radar stations which were closely guarded. He asked Commander GreenPat to repeat urgent requests to Washington so often that Sanders became angry.

"Look, I appreciate your initiative and I understand your reasons," he said to Paul finally, "but when you come right down to it, you are demanding unauthorized equipment. We're still getting German weather signals from the east coast, and the fly-boys are really putting pressure on me to get a ship up there that can do some spotting for them. The big cutters are needed for convoy duty. My other trawlers are busy on supply runs, weather patrol, or have broken down. Now if you can't take the *Arluk* up there within forty-eight hours, I'm going to have to replace you with someone who can, even if I have to take an exec from one of the big cutters."

The thought came to Paul that if he was really smart, he would let himself be replaced. Probably nothing would happen to him except an assignment to a boring but safe shore base. His emotions, however, would not agree with his mind. The *Arluk* was his hard-won command, and he was not going to give her to anyone else.

"All right, we'll leave within forty-eight hours," he said softly and gave Sanders a fairly good copy of Mowrey's sweet smile.

Paul had surprising faith in his own good luck, and he kept thinking that somehow the necessary equipment would arrive at the last minute. An hour before he sailed he sent Nathan ashore to make one last check of all possible sources. As soon as he saw Nathan return he knew their luck had run out. Nathan's gaunt body was stooped with dejection and his sad face looked more morose than ever.

"Sorry, skipper," he said, throwing out his hands in a gesture of helplessness. "I got zilch."

"Tell Boats to pipe the men to mooring stations," Paul said, and rang the engineroom telegraph to "Stand by," a signal which the chief answered immediately with a jingle of bells. Instead of calling the men to take in lines, however, Boats came to the pilothouse. "Skipper," he said, "before we go, can we send somebody up to see if any more mail has come in for us? God knows how long it will be before we get more."

"Okay—run up there yourself if you want, but make it snappy."

Boats jumped ashore and ran toward the post office. Wondering why he was really in such a hurry to start toward whatever was waiting for them on the east coast, Paul went to his cabin and studied his charts.

In only a few minutes Boats came racing back. He was carrying a rather limp mail sack, which Nathan immediately opened. After passing out the letters to the enlisted men, Nathan brought six envelopes to Paul. Five were from Sylvia and one from his brother Bill. Finding that he did not really want to learn more about the decoration of the house in Wellesley and Bill's exploits as a flight instructor right now, Paul stuck them in a drawer of the chart table and called, "All right, guys, let's get going. I want to get out of the fjord before dark."

"Skipper," Nathan said. "How about giving the guys ten minutes to read their mail?"

"All right," Paul replied, and feeling a little guilty because of his lack of eagerness for his own mail, went to his cabin and read his letters, starting with Bill's.

Dear Paul,

I don't want to get you upset or anything, but I think your girl Sylvia is getting way out of line, and I'd straighten her out if I were you. She's acting as a hostess at U.S.O. dances. There's nothing wrong with that, I guess—quite a few wives of boys who are overseas do it. Still, I was surprised when I dropped in at the Boston U.S.O. and found her dancing up a storm with some guys from my base who couldn't be trusted with their own mothers. And she goes out drinking with them after the dances. If I were you, I'd tell her to stop it. I'm not saying she's doing anything wrong. I'm saying she's giving herself too much opportunity for it. I told her I didn't like it and she got mad as hell. I imagine you'll be hearing from her about it. Sorry to stir things up, but I got to look out for my kid brother.

Things going pretty good here. I figure I'll make first lieutenant pretty quick now, but God knows when I'll get out of this instructor business. Did you ever think I'd wind up a schoolteacher? I do get plenty of weekend passes though, and get home almost every month. I'll keep in touch with things there.

Keep 'em sailing!
Bill

This letter made Paul so angry that he balled it up in his hand, walked out on a wing of the bridge and threw it overboard. Sylvia, he thought, was simply behaving much as she had before he left home, so why get upset? Return-

263

ing to his cabin, he ripped open the envelopes from her. The first two contained more details about the decoration of the house, but the third was different.

Paul darling,

I'm so mad at Bill I could kill him. I wouldn't write you about this silly thing, except I'm sure he will, and the last thing I want to do is get you all worried about me.

This is what hapened. A few weeks ago I was asked to be a hosstess at U.S.O. dances. Practically every girl I know, married and unmarried, is helping with the U.S.O. program. The Junior League is doing it. Your mother and mine are both patruns and chaperones, for God's sake. Nothing could be more respectable and it was presented to me as a patriotic duty. Boston is swarming with servicemen who have nowhere to go but the bars and we're trying to do something about it. What I do mostly is just serve coffee to the guys and let them talk. They're loanely and what they usually do is tell me about their wife and family. Not many even want to dance, and when we do dance it's right there at the U.S.O. center surrounded by chaperones. I never leave the center with the guys—even if I wanted to, which beleive me, I don't, there are strictly enforced rules against it. I'm not doing anything wrong. I thought I was doing something good until Bill came along and made something dirty out of it. He just has a dirty mind. According to him there's not a desent man in the army or navy and I should go hide myself until the war is over. Well, I think that's ridiculous and I know you will too. These are all nice boys and we're all just trying to help them keep up their moral.

I never see any servicemen outside the U.S.O. center except that Muth is working with a U.S.O. program which asks her to invite guys to Sunday dinners at home. We feed four guys every Sunday, and after the army and navy chow they get, they sure are greateful. They are more polite than anyone could imagine, and when they see my weding ring, they never ask me to go out, except to a movie sometimes, and I always refuse even to to that. Believe me, I'm faithful to you

264

and can't even imagine being anything else. Only Bill could imagine anything different.

Please don't worry about me. All I'm doing is fixing up a beautiful house for you to come home to, and trying to be patriotic.

Much love, Sylvia.

Paul sighed. Remembering the curious abandon with which Sylvia, even at the age of sixteen, had danced at fraternity parties, he could imagine her giving the boys at the U.S.O. encouragement, even if she thought her intentions were entirely innocent. The Sunday dinners with men who no doubt were much the same as the members of his own crew did not delight him too much either. How long would it be before Sylvia saw nothing wrong in accepting an invitation to see a movie, and after that—

He clenched his fists. It was all very damned childish and very upsetting. After all, his own intentions had not been too pure with the fat woman at the drunken brawl with Mowrey in Godhavn. Only circumstances, not his own morality, had preserved his so-called virtue, and he doubted whether Sylvia was much less vulnerable. How many people in this war were really able to remain chaste year after year? Maybe marital fidelity was an inevitable casualty of war, nine cases out of ten. A picture of Sylvia stretched out on a bed in some motel with an enormous man like Guns flashed into his mind and he found he was sweating. Maybe she would find someone a lot better than he'd ever been . . .

He threw his wife's letters into a drawer and jammed it shut. Right now he didn't even have time to think about her; he had no business getting himself upset. The thing to do about Sylvia was to forget her until the damned war was all over—

The shrill blast of Boats's pipe calling the men to mooring stations came to Paul as a relief, cutting off his personal life like a knife.

"All right, boys, let's get going," he said as the men took the heavy lines from the wharf. "We've got a date. We've kept the Krauts waiting for us long enough."

Ten minutes later the *Arluk* headed out of the fjord toward the open sea and the east coast. As the base faded from sight astern, Paul found himself wondering whether that was the last of "civilization" he would ever see. Somewhere ahead something that was sending German radio signals was waiting for them in the ice. What the hell, if the Germans wanted a fight he was in a good mood for it. So what if the Krauts had bigger guns? Ingenuity could overcome superiority of equipment—whistling in the dark, of course. . . . He was astonished at the cheerfulness of the men as they stowed the mooring lines and checked their pea-shooter guns. Probably the men of the *Nanmak* had been just as cheerful as they set off on their last voyage.

Nathan soon came to stand beside Paul on the bridge. Bob Williams, the new ensign, was also there, fumbling with the gyroscope repeaters on the wings of the bridge as he tried to learn how to take bearings.

"If I'd just had time or had thought about it enough in advance I could have had a friend in the States send me the stuff in my personal mail," Nathan said.

"The censors probably would have stopped it. All electronics are top secret. You could have got in a lot of trouble."

"Christ, they could have put the stuff in a cake or something. If I'd only been thinking—"

"Forget it. We'll do the best we can with what we've got. Show Mr. Williams how to use that gyro repeater before he breaks the vanes off it."

When Paul found he could see not even a smoky trace of the base astern, he realized with a sort of surprise that the ship was alone in the Arctic wilderness, and he alone was in command of it. No matter what happened, there was no one he could go to for help. Mowrey had said he didn't have the balls for such a job, and Paul wondered if the old man was right . . .

A commanding officer isn't much if he starts a long voyage looking and acting as though he was sure he was heading toward certain doom, Paul thought, and forced himself to smile a lot, his lips feeling tight and unnatural. Restlessly going to the flying bridge, he saw that Nathan had found someone to print a picture of a rattlesnake on the stack with the words DON'T TREAD ON ME. The trouble was that the amateur artist had made the snake look rather like a worm, and the motto seemed like a plea. Probably the Krauts could step on this worm without even leaving much of a smear, Paul reflected. All that had been left of the *Nanmak* had been a few scorched timbers and a bullet-ridden boat full of corpses. The idea that Hansen could still be hiding out in the ice with a few survivors was almost certainly sheer fantasy.

Paul was still unable to get his mind off these grim thoughts several hours later when they came within sight of the wreck of the destroyer. As Mowrey had predicted, the wind had driven ice into the mouth of the fjord, and several bergs bigger than the destroyer had pressed the abandoned ship higher onto the rocks, tilting her bow up so that she seemed to be climbing a high sea, with her lethal but now useless guns pointing at the low scudding clouds overhead. Nathan climbed to the flying bridge and stood beside Paul, examining the wreck through binoculars.

"I wonder if they stripped her before abandoning her," Nathan said. "Or do you suppose they left a few men aboard?"

"They'd probably signal us. Flash a light at them and see if anyone answers."

For five minutes Nathan clacked the shutter of the signal light, but there was no flash on the bridge of the broken destroyer. Picking up his binoculars he continued to study the derelict as Paul altered course to come closer.

"Maybe they're all asleep," Paul said. "When we get closer we'll blow the whistle and wake them up."

"They didn't strip her radar gear," Nathan said. "Not the stuff on the mast, anyway. Do you suppose the whole radar room is intact?"

"They might have abandoned ship in a hurry when those bergs closed in. There isn't a chance in the world of putting big stuff like that on this ship, is there?"

Nathan's face suddenly lit up. "Their big air-search radar for aircraft probably would be more than we could handle, but they're carrying a smaller antenna for navigation. If it's all still there, I bet I could make it work here."

"Hell, let's try!"

"And they're sure to have something for radar detection. But this is all secret stuff. They wouldn't just go off and leave it."

"Who the hell would steal it here, the Eskies? Probably they intend to send a salvage ship in as soon as the ice moves out. No ship could get alongside her now."

"But the whaleboat could, and it could handle anything

we need," Nathan said. "Put me aboard there, skipper, there's sure to be all kinds of stuff we can use—"

"First we better make sure there isn't a guard aboard."

After coming closer he blew the whistle—one prolonged blast. It echoed through the fjord, and there was no sign of life aboard the ship.

"Maybe they're all drunk," Nathan said.

"We'll soon find out. Get ready to go aboard. I'll anchor as close as I can. Take Guns with you. There's a nice 40-millimeter there on his fantail. Do you suppose we could find a way to put that on our well deck?"

"We might be able to hide radar when we were in port, but how would you explain an unauthorized forty?"

"The Krauts won't ask for explanations and that's all I'm thinking about right now. Do you think we could bolt that thing to a wooden deck?"

"We could probably fix it so we could get off a few rounds, anyway. Hell, if you don't mind getting court-martialed, we could steal enough here to make the old *Arluk* a regular pocket battleship!"

"Are you really an engineer?"

"I got a diploma that says so."

"So engineer me a plan to put as many guns as we can on here without turning this bucket over in the first gale. We could fill the hold with ballast to make up for some of the top weight."

"Just let me go in and see what's there," Nathan said. "I hope we don't find somebody asleep below. They couldn't just go off and leave all this stuff!"

"One thing I believe is that the navy can screw up," Paul said. "If they can let the Japs sink their whole damn fleet in Pearl Harbor the first day of the war, they can run off and leave a beached tin can. Probably the only thing they took with them is their ice cream freezer."

Paul reduced speed and took the *Arluk* close to shore, where a row of big icebergs was grounded in a hundred feet of water. He anchored behind the biggest of them. If he was going to engage in illegal salvage, he better learn to hide like a pirate.

# CHAPTER 29

      Paul ached to go aboard the destroyer, but the weather did not look settled and he decided that he better stay aboard his ship. Flags had overheard some of his conversation with Nathan, and word of their plans quickly spread through the ship. The mood of the men was exuberant as they lowered the whaleboat. Guns carried a sledgehammer, a crowbar and a huge monkey wrench tied up in a bundle as he climbed into the boat. Everyone wanted to go on the raid, and the men Paul told to stay aboard the *Arluk* smiled only when he added that they could go later.

Bob Williams, the new ensign, was one of those kept aboard, and he looked puzzled as he approached Paul on the bridge soon after the boat cast off.

"Sir, may I ask why we're sending a boat in there?"

"To see if we can find anything we can use."

The ensign looked worried. "Pardon me for asking, sir, but is it legal to take stuff from the navy?"

"Call it salvage."

"Couldn't we get in trouble?"

Paul gave him his newly acquired sweet smile. "Mr. Williams, everyone aboard this ship is in trouble. I suggest that you just get used to it."

"Yes, sir."

"But it's our business to survive trouble, and so far, we've done all right."

"Yes, sir." Looking a little more hopeful, Bob Williams went to the forecastle for coffee, and, no doubt, deep thought.

As the whaleboat steered a circuitous course through the ice, Nathan kept studying the destroyer with his binoculars. The fear that men would suddenly appear on deck to forbid all depredations grew in him, for this discovery of a goldmine of military hardware seemed much too good to be true. Nothing moved on the decks and a thin layer of snow on the top deck there was innocent of footprints. As the whaleboat found a narrow lead it could follow through the ice directly to the waist of the destroyer, Nathan could see why the ship had been abandoned. From a short distance she looked intact, but the big icebergs had pressed progressively smaller ones against her, and some flinty blue growlers had been shoved right through her surprisingly thin steel skin, ripping it open in jagged slits both above and below the waterline from bow to stern. The torn metal was already rusty, and Nathan could see why destroyers were called "tin cans." Caught between the rocks and the ice, the whole hull had been bent as though it had died writhing in a desperate attempt to escape.

The ornate boarding ladder had been left over the side, but it led only to crushed ice. Coming alongside the derelict thirty feet farther forward, Nathan told Guns to climb aboard, which he did, after tossing his tools to the deck, where they clattered loudly enough to awaken anyone sleeping below. No head appeared above a hatch as the men of the *Arluk* tied up their whaleboat and swarmed over the rail.

"Stick together," Nathan said. "We'll start aft and examine everything, first on deck and then below."

Although the light covering of snow at first concealed it, the deck was littered with articles of clothes, life jackets and other objects which had been dropped in an apparently hasty abandonment of the ship. Perhaps the ice had closed in on her suddenly in a fast midnight gale, Nathan thought, imagining how the rending of all that steel must have sounded. No boats were in the davits and the empty falls swung in the wind. Probably the boats had ferried the crew to the waiting tanker, or the salvage tugs if they had ever arrived.

The destroyer's depth charges, 600-pound monsters twice the usual size, were still on their racks at the stern. They would have been removed if anyone had taken Mowrey's drastic plan seriously. Several hatches had been left open, more evidence of panic. On the bow a short length of the steel towing cable lay in a tangle, its broken end exploded by strain into a huge cone of wire splinters. Apparently the salvage tug had arrived and had towed with all its power.

Returning to the stern, Nathan led his men down an open hatch to the petty officers' quarters, a confused mass of overturned chairs, mattresses which had slid from the upper tiers of bunks, half-packed seabags, blankets and a scattering of playing cards. Apparently there had been quite a jolt when the ice ground into the hull.

Suddenly impatient with an orderly search of the derelict, Nathan led his men directly to the bridge, which was as neat as that of a ship under way. His eyes went directly to a gray metal box on a pedestal near the wheel. A black plastic cone extended from the top of it. Nathan's heart beat fast as he ran to it and put his hands on the knobs on a control panel. Peering into the cone, he turned the set on. There was no hum of electricity, no trace of a glow on the screen. Of course the batteries and generators were dead, but the set certainly looked intact.

"Hell, we can hook it up on our ship," Nathan said. "Let's get it off here. I'll make it work!"

Eagerly the men of the *Arluk* started to help him to dismantle the set. While they were disconnecting it, Nathan went to the radar room directly abaft the bridge. The big radar set for scanning the skies for planes had been smashed with mallets, one of which lay on the deck. Before abandoning ship, all such secret equipment should have been destroyed, but in the confusion the little navigational radar had been forgotten. Nathan thanked God for the ability of the navy to foul up and began looking for spare parts. He soon found lockers and drawers full of them, and with a variety of tools.

"Mr. Green, can you really make that set work aboard our ship?" Guns asked.

"You bet your life," Nathan replied with a grin. "With this stuff, I could build a set."

"Can you keep it working at sea?" Boats asked.

"Damn right!"

"Will we have enough juice for it?" Sparks asked.

"Sure, but we'll steal a generator if we have to. Now you guys get this stuff into the boat as soon as you can. Guns, you come and help me inspect the rest of the ship."

Everywhere they went aboard the destroyer they saw equipment and supplies which would be useful aboard the trawler. The destroyer's freezers had not thawed in the Greenland air and still held enough steak to feed the *Arluk*'s crew for years, as well as countless gallons of ice cream. Cookie exclaimed in delight when he saw racks of new kitchen equipment in the galley. The quartermaster found sextants and range finders far better than anything which had been issued by the Coast Guard. The most delighted of all was Guns, who got Nathan's permission to stay on deck, examining the armament. His striker, a boyish seaman named Blake who wanted to be a gunner's mate, accompanied him. In awe they stopped by the turret of a double five-inch gun which was the size of a small automobile. The wind had loosened the lacings of the canvas cover, and on impulse Guns took it off to admire the gleaming beauty of the polished barrels.

"Boy, I wish we could get one of those babies aboard our ship," Blake said. "Then we could talk in a language the Germans understand."

Guns opened a door to the turret and went in. Blake followed and they sat in iron bucket seats, fingering the polished controls and peering through the sights.

"Could you sink a battleship with this?" Blake asked.

"Damned near, if you got close enough."

"How far can this shoot?"

"A good five miles," Guns replied, though he was not at all sure.

"Boy, I really wish we had one of these. With this I guess we could fight the devil himself."

"Come on, we got to go look at the forties," Guns said. "We actually might be able to use one of them."

"What can a forty do?"

"It's good against planes, not much else."

Guns found it difficult to tear himself away from the lethal five-inchers. Since his father had given him his first .22 for hunting squirrels in Vermont, he had been fascinated with anything that could shoot, and this was the finest engine of destruction he had ever been privileged to touch. Although he had been barely able to get through high school, his intelligence was surprisingly quick and his knowledge extensive when it came to guns of any kind. Lovingly he explored the recoil mechanism of these monsters, the machinery for pointing and training them by electricity or by hand.

"Ain't nothing really but a damn big twenty-two," he said to Blake.

After inspecting the 40-millimeter guns, which looked like toys after the five-inchers, Guns returned to his loves. With a little experimentation, he learned how to disengage the power mechanisms and train the guns by hand, marveling at the ease with which it could be done. The breech mechanisms were complex, but not really difficult for him to understand.

It did not take Nathan long to detach the radar set on the bridge of the destroyer. While he worked at that, Boats and Sparks climbed the mast and took off the revolving metal mesh crescent which emitted the high frequency waves that produced the echoes which the complex device timed to ascertain distance. They worked so eagerly that the whole job didn't take them much more than an hour.

When the radar with all its components was safely loaded aboard the whaleboat, Nathan went looking for Guns and Blake. He found Guns leaning against a bulkhead staring at the five-inch guns almost in a trance. Blake was standing nervously beside him.

"What's the matter, Guns?" Nathan asked.

"Sir, I think I've figured something out. We shouldn't bother with those forties. They're not much good against a ship. I think we could get one of these aboard."

"A gun like that would sink us," Nathan said. "It must weigh five tons."

Sparks and Boats grinned.

"Sir, will you listen to me a minute?" Guns said.

"Sure."

"The *guts* of these guns, the barrels and the breeches and the recoil mechanism, don't weigh so much. Most of the weight is in the turret and in the mechanism for pointing and training them. Our ship could stand the weight of the guts of one of these guns without the mounts."

"You want a gun you can't train and you can't point?" Boats asked.

"Boats, you ever see a fighter plane?" Guns retorted with a withering glance.

"You plan to put wings on the *Arluk* too?"

"The guns of a fighter plane are fixed," Guns replied. "You aim them by pointing the whole plane at the target. I bet we could fix the guts of one of these guns on the bow of the trawler. That could give us a chance if we ever met a big Kraut. It sure would surprise hell out of him."

"How much would the guts of one gun weigh?" Nathan asked.

"Maybe less than a ton."

"How would you hold it in place?"

"That's the hard part. But I bet we could bolt it or even

273

wire it down with steel cable secure enough to let us get off a few rounds. Even one shot could make the difference if we were fairly close."

"You might have something there," Nathan said.

"If we could lash one gun down on the head of the forecastle, we could service the breeches from the well deck. That way it would be almost invisible."

"Do you think we could find any specs on those guns?"

"I found a pamphlet in a ready box. I don't understand most of it, but I understand them guns."

"I'll come back and look it over with you when I get this radar working for us," Nathan said. "I don't know if we can make it work, but you sure got one hell of an idea."

Paul was waiting on the well deck when the whaleboat came alongside the *Arluk*.

"Request permission to bring radar aboard, sir," Nathan said with a grin.

"You got it! Can you make it work?"

"I got enough spare parts to build a set if I have to. It shouldn't take long to get the whole thing together."

It took Nathan only about four hours to install the radar set on the bridge of the *Arluk*, to hook it up with the ship's electrical system, and to install the antenna on the signal mast. When the job was done the men gathered around the pilothouse to watch him turn the set on. Bending over the hood, he adjusted the knobs. Gradually the little screen turned from gray to green. A thin beam of light turned like the sweep hand of a watch and traced a rough glowing chart of the surrounding fjord.

"Take a look, skipper," Nathan said with a smile.

Paul bent over the hood and looked with something like reverence as he imagined what this magic eye could mean in fog or Arctic night while they were chasing a German ship or being chased.

"Nathan, you've probably just saved all our lives," he said.

Nathan smiled but said, "Don't forget that the Krauts probably have some kind of radar too. What we need now is a bigger gun."

In considerable detail he explained Guns's idea about putting one of the destroyer's five-inch guns in a fixed position on the bow of the trawler. "It could work only at point-blank range," he said. "It would be like the guns on the old sailing ships."

"Look, you're the engineer," Paul replied. "Make it work if you can."

"I'd like to steal some depth charges too. I think I can figure a way to activate them with time fuses or even by radio. We might be able to set them out as mines. There should be lots of ways to use all that explosive force."

Paul nodded. "I was afraid the rattlesnake on the stack looked too much like a worm. Damned if I'm not beginning to hear it rattle."

# CHAPTER 30

With the tools they found aboard the destroyer, Guns was able to disassemble one five-inch gun, but the job of loading the barrel aboard the *Arluk* at first seemed impossible. Paul finally found a way to moor the trawler on the seaward edge of the ice pack which pressed against the destroyer. With steel cables the heavy barrel was winched over ice peaks and through ice valleys to the decks of the trawler. The men worked night and day, afraid that some passing ship would observe and report their activities.

Despite the rush, it still took them three days to secure the big cannon on the bow of the *Arluk* in such a way that it would not interfere with the small gun already there. It was Nathan who worked out a complex method of securing the barrel to the deck, which he reinforced with steel beams cut from the destroyer with one of her own acetylene torches. Chief Banes supervised the cutting and welding of steel bands and plates which were bolted to the oak. Boats also wound the barrel with steel cables that ran through holes they bored to allow it to grip the whole deck structure. No one had ever seen a gun installed like that, and they were afraid even to fire it for target practice, but they all were sure that they could get off at least a few shots in action. The gun pointed inflexibly ahead. With its slight fixed elevation it would have a range of several miles, they guessed, though no one pretended to be sure. One thing was certain: any ship coming close to the bow of the little trawler could get a surprise. The thought of that made the men of the *Arluk* feel much better.

It took two more days to cut a path over the ice pack and to roll the heavy depth charges along it to the *Arluk*. Because he was supposed to send a weekly position report to GreenPat, Paul made up a story about being caught in the ice near the entrance to the passage that led to the east coast. If they were observed before they got there by ships or planes, the results could be embarrassing.

It was the fifth of September before they were finally ready to leave the destroyer. The *Arluk* was low in the water, but her ballast of depth charges had been carefully placed, and she was perfectly trimmed. If they ran into a gale in the open sea, she would be dangerously sluggish, but Paul counted on spending most of the winter in the ice pack. Certainly there was risk in loading the ship this way and Paul realized that the chance of hitting anything with a fixed gun was slight but at least he didn't feel like an ox driven to slaughter as he finally headed the *Arluk*'s bow out of Narsarssuak Fjord.

They left at night to avoid observation as much as possible until they reached the point where Paul had already reported their position. The September gales were building and heavy clouds obscured the moon and stars. Fortunately the wind was offshore, and the sea was relatively calm five miles off the edge of the ice pack. Standing on the bridge, Paul could see nothing but blackness ahead, and it was an incredible relief to peer at the miraculous screen of the radar, which gave him his distance from both the shore and the ice pack, and warned him of stray bergs ahead. Nathan stood by the controls, occasionally adjusting them to get clear images. Several of the crew found excuses to visit the bridge and get a peek at this wondrous invention.

"Nathan, when it really comes down to helping this ship survive in the Arctic, this radar is the best thing we've got," Paul said suddenly. "We wouldn't have it without you. Damn it, next time you get down at the mouth, remember that."

Nathan shrugged, but Paul noticed that he was fighting a smile . . .

It did not take them long to get to Prince Christian Fjord, which actually was a narrow, winding pass that cut off the mountainous tip of Greenland, making an island of Cape Farewell. Glittering peaks rose steeply from both sides of the ship, and small icebergs gleamed in the light of a quarter moon in the black riverlike channel ahead. It was a splendid evening with little wind as they started that passage. Paul and Nathan stood on the flying bridge conning the ship. Suddenly northern lights, the aurora borealis, spread luminescent curtains overhead, the intensity of which pulsed in almost sexual rhythm.

"God, what a night!" Paul said.

"Very romantic," Nathan observed wryly.

Paul was full of an odd, mounting excitement. The polished barrel of the big gun on the forecastle head gleamed in the moonlight. How many miles ahead was the German ship which had sunk the *Nanmak* waiting? The duel would not be so easy for her now. At least the *Arluk* had eyes of her own that could see through fog and night. If he played his cards right, Paul thought, he could be the attacker, he could choose the time and place to strike. If they could locate a German ship and determine her future course, they could, if luck gave them just the right circumstances, circle around and sow the mines that Nathan was making out of depth charges in her path. And if they were pursued they could sow their own wake with mines. If the Germans wanted to play tag among the icebergs . . .

"We're going to get them," Paul said.

"Are you really all that confident?" Nathan asked.

"My strength is as the strength of ten, because at heart I am a dirty, tricky bastard. If all else fails I'll surrender and cry for mercy until they come within point-blank range of that five-incher."

"We better not forget that at heart they're dirty, tricky bastards, too."

"But I'm betting they'll be overconfident when they see we're just a trawler."

Paul wondered whether he too were committing the military sin of overconfidence. No, he knew that the Germans probably had at least one ship bigger than the *Arluk* waiting up there in the ice, and her armament and fire control undoubtedly were somewhat more sophisticated than a gun barrel lashed on deck. As the northern lights increased the intensity of their throbbing overhead, Paul thought about the Germans mowing down the *Nanmak*'s boatload of men. He wondered what the captain who had given the order to open fire looked like, and imagined a squat, bald Prussian officer with a monocle. Maybe he wouldn't look like a movie villain, but someone had given that order to open up the heavy machine guns on helpless men in an open boat. Paul was aware that the Germans stood accused of far worse crimes throughout Europe and Russia, but for him the whole war came into focus with the image of an open boat in a crossfire of machine-gun bullets. The men who had done that were probably only a few hundred miles ahead.

# Part III

# CHAPTER 31

After having armed and stocked his ship as best he could, Paul felt a kind of exaltation as he sailed toward the battle, but instead of meeting his enemy immediately, he just got stuck in the ice, and all the fierceness drained, leaving him frustrated as a lover whose car stalls on the way to his girl.

As the *Arluk* approached the end of the fjordlike passage through which she crossed the southern tip of Greenland from the west to the east coast, she encountered more and more ice. Even before she escaped the glittering mountains which appeared to hem her in on all sides, she was forced to push her way through small icebergs that filled the narrow channel. When she finally reached the eastern mouth of the passage it was blocked by rampart after rampart of great ice castles which had been jammed against the coast by an easterly gale and the unrelenting current. Paul finally discovered one narrow lead that twisted around mile-long islands of ice. Before long it petered out. He managed to turn the ship, but he soon discovered that the ice had closed around him, pressing him into a giant trap. Still almost under the shadow of the mountains, he could not budge one damn inch.

The ice is always moving like the hour hand of a clock, he remembered Mowrey saying, and sooner or later the wind will break it up, but now it was September and the danger of being locked in for the winter was real. If the German ship or ships were anywhere near, they too were probably paralyzed, but as long as they could send weather reports, they were still fulfilling their purpose. There was at least a kind of safety in having the enemies locked away from each other, Paul reflected, but there was danger enough in the ice, which could press the *Arluk* against rocks, as it had the destroyer. Driven by gales at the fringe of the pack, the icebergs could mount each other like great mating beasts, and pile up moving ridges that could crush and bury a ship. Even if a vessel were lucky enough to escape such cataclysms, small icebergs pressed by larger ones in current or wind could crush a hull. Modern icebreakers were built in the shape of an egg to rise above the ice when squeezed, but the trawlers, though strong, were too wall-sided for that.

Such perils were real enough, but now there was little wind and a deathlike peace pervaded the ice pack. Only the clouds above and the birds moved visibly. During this month of September the familiar pattern of nights following days of similar length was reasserted. It was too cold for the men to do much work on deck. After standing their watches, which were hopelessly dull aboard a motionless ship, they listened to radio reports of the battle of Stalingrad, won and lost their meager pay at cards and wrote endless letters, which they dropped in the wardroom mailbox for censoring despite the fact that the mail of course was going nowhere for months.

Every time the plywood mailbox filled up, Paul took it to his cabin and in his capacity of naval censor read it. This minor chore he could have assigned to one of the other officers, but he hoped that the mail would help him to understand the men better. Ever since arriving in Greenland, he had become increasingly aware of a curious fact: although they were all imprisoned together on this tiny ship with few chances to go ashore, the men in the forecastle remained almost strangers to him. One reason, of course, was that enlisted men rarely felt like confiding much to commissioned officers, and especially tried to stay away from the commanding officer as much as possible. Perhaps wisely, the customs of the Coast Guard and navy made the relationship between officers and enlisted men as impersonal as possible. Even the names of the petty officers were rarely heard aboard ship. It was hard for Paul to imagine Guns, Flags, Boats, and Sparks being called anything else. Only in the mail did Guns appear as Ralph D. Higgins, Flags as Patrick Murray, Boats as Maurice Torbot, and Sparks as George Grotsky.

Their names, of course, did not give any great clue to the nature of their personalities, and oddly, neither did their letters. Although a high school diploma was necessary for entering the service, the men of the *Arluk* were, with few exceptions, even more illiterate than Paul's own wife.

Forbidden by censorship regulations to tell where they were or anything about the operations of the ship, and aware that their skipper would read their letters, they obviously faced difficulties when they took pen in hand, but the urge to communicate with wives, mothers and sweethearts drove them to fill. over the months, hundreds of pages. They told jokes, often followed by "ha ha" in parentheses; they marveled at the good food aboard the trawler; they said "I miss you" over and over again, but rarely, "I love you." These tough men often finished with rows of X's for kisses. There was a sweetness about most of the letters, which tried primarily to stop the recipients from worrying. The men never complained about anything except boredom. Children at a summer camp might have mailed similar letters, for similar reasons.

Paul couldn't get over the fact that these gentle outpourings came from the rough, raunchy men who turned the air in the forecastle blue every time they opened their mouths. Only Sparks broke the pattern. His letters were all spelled right, were written in a firm neat hand, and were so unabashedly and imaginatively pornographic that Paul was embarrassed to find himself looking forward to reading them. Obscenity was forbidden by the censorship rules, but when Paul asked Nathan whether they should have a talk with the radioman, Nathan laughed and said that even the United States government shouldn't have a right to stop a man from talking about sex with his wife or girl.

Guns, whose wife had left him, and who did more sexual boasting than any other man aboard the ship, sent identical letters to a dozen girls in Boston and New York. These notes were short and to the point. They said: "Dearest Sally, (or Betty or Babs or Lilly), I miss you and can hardly wait to see you. I don't think about nobody but you. I'm saving my pay to blow with you when I get home. Don't forget me—Ralphie."

It was impossible for Paul to imagine anyone calling Guns, the man whose greatest boast was that he had fucked a bear, Ralphie. Somehow the mail made the personalities of the enlisted men in the forecastle more mysterious to him than ever. Once he found himself wondering whether his isolation from the men, his inability to think of them as individuals, was in part, at least, a personal problem . . . even at college he'd had no close personal friends. Nathan, he observed, talked to the men a lot—he had assumed the role of ship's doctor, and to some degree, ship's psychiatrist. In Nathan's deep-set eyes there was always sympathy, a quality that Paul was occasionally aware of lacking. But Nathan, of course, was not the captain. Paul found it convenient to forget that he had been no closer to the men when he was executive officer.

As they stayed stuck in the ice day after day the men became so lethargic that it was hard to get them to keep their quarters clean, and they were increasingly quarrelsome. When Paul lectured the crew and assigned small punishments for small offenses, he felt himself becoming more and more walled off from them. How could one really sympathize with grown men who in the face of great danger fought over the possession of a particularly soft mattress, stole clothes from each other, and kept having fistfights? How could men who endured great hardship and genuine peril month after month, and who were almost invariably skillful at their jobs, be so damned childish? Well, maybe because they didn't have his private quarters. Possessions became the man . . .

Often, Paul was aware, the men hated him. When he lined them up on the well deck to lecture them about cleanliness, when he assigned seamen to galley duty, when he punished them for fighting, he sometimes suspected that they would like to kill him. At other times, when he handled the ship well in ice, when he allowed the men to steal whatever they wanted from the wrecked destroyer or arranged a beerbust for them ashore, they almost idolized him. Which also bothered him. Mowrey often had said that a good skipper never gives a damn what the crew thinks about him, but Paul suspected that at heart the ice pilot had considered himself an actor and the crew his audience. He himself, he was embarrassed to find, felt marvelous when the men showed approval of him, and depressed when they showed contempt. One reason he kept to himself a great deal, as almost all commanding officers since the beginning of ships had done, was that he knew the nature of his job would often cause the men to hate him or love him unreasonably, which excess of emotion made him uncomfortable when he was with them.

A few of the men Paul regarded as at least equals because of their devotion to their work and their knowledge of their specialties. Cantankerous and obsequious as he was, Cookie almost never stopped working and sweating in his tiny hot galley, and obviously cared as much about preparing good food for the crew as he had for the patrons of the Ritz-Carlton Hotel. Paul and everyone else aboard regarded him simply as a miracle. Guns and the young seaman Blake had a strange passion for weapons that seemed unhealthy to Paul but a necessity now. Sparks, Flags, Boats, and Chief Banes all knew much more about their specialties than Paul did and had such pride in their work that they never needed supervision, except when they got into arguments with each other.

The days of idleness in the ice, though, increased all Paul's problems in dealing with the men. The crew soon became so edgy that his chief job appeared to be acting as judge and jury. No seaman who was assigned to help Cookie in the galley lasted more than a few days before being put on report for gross insubordination and every other crime that the fertile imagination of the old chef could invent. A running battle developed between Boats, the red-haired chief boatswain's mate, and Guns. It started when Boats began complaining about the way Guns lashed the new machine guns to the deck, and broke out again each time the two men met in a narrow passageway or at a ladder. Neither would get out of the way of the other. When Paul settled this by reminding Guns that Boats was, after all, a chief petty officer, Boats insisted that he did not want to pull rank, and that Guns just better learn to stay out of his way if he didn't want to get flattened. They asked to have it out bare-fisted on the well deck and quieted down only when Paul reminded them that the Germans would be delighted to hear that two of the best men of the *Arluk* were intent upon demolishing each other.

Paul found it hard to convince the crew that even when the ship was locked in the ice, the men on watch had to remain alert. As the temperature sank below zero, they huddled in the pilothouse or kept ducking into the forecastle for coffee. One cold midnight Paul emerged from his cabin to find no one on deck, and the two men in the pilothouse were dozing so peacefully that they started when he shouted at them. Calling all hands to quarters on the well deck immediately, he gave them a lecture about the possibility of rapid changes in the weather and of discovering the presence of the enemy nearby. Technically the penalty of going to sleep on watch was death, according to the articles of war, he reminded them. Since he did not want to go by the book quite so strictly, he would from now on sentence any man found asleep on watch or away from his station to a milder penalty: finishing his watch in the crow's nest, no matter how cold it was.

The men listened to this sullenly, their anger visible in increased snorts of steam blown from the noses and mouth. Three days later their hostility increased when Paul told them that the forecastle smelled and that all bedding and clothes must be washed in tubs made out of oil drums in the engineroom, and hung out to air.

"Captain Mowrey didn't want us to hang nothing out on deck," Boats said angrily.

"Captain Mowrey is not now in command of this ship," Paul replied, turned and walked to his cabin with his heels hitting the deck as sharply as those of the old ice pilot. Two hours later he found blankets hung over every gun and had to have them rearranged to enable the ship to remain ready for action.

The crew of a ship is as fickle as any woman, Paul realized as he received nothing but stony glances during the next week. He spent most of his time alone in his cabin devising complex strategies for beating the Germans if he ever got near them. Soon his plans for dodging behind icebergs, sowing his wake with depth charges rigged as mines if the Germans pursued him, or luring the enemy close by pretending to give up began to seem like boyhood dreams of glory. Probably they would be locked in the ice until spring, and if they ever did encounter a German, they probably would be sunk long before they got close enough to use a five-inch gun that couldn't even be trained or pointed. Since this version of reality was too painful to contemplate for long, Paul, like most of the other men aboard the ship, lay for hours thinking of the good times with his wife and the few other women he had known. It was horrifying to realize that he could not really remember anymore how a woman's body felt. He dreamed of spending weeks in bed with Sylvia when and if he ever got home, but he was uneasily aware that it wouldn't work out that way. Months of celibacy were simply slices of life that were lost, and there never would be any way he could make up for them. Thoughts of the nights his brother must be spending after training pilots in South Carolina plagued him. The soft Southern air would be full of the fragrance of blossoms. Debonair in the uniform of an army air force pilot, Bill would tour the bars of the nearest town, and as he had written in his letter, the girls in their eagerness would almost knock him down. Big-bosomed girls in tight white sweaters, girls with low necklines that showed a gold locket nestling between their tanned breasts, willow-waisted girls would smile at Bill and open their sweet mouths the first time they kissed. Where would Bill take them? The back seat of a car or a drab hotel room was not his style. Somewhere he would have rented an apartment, even if he were required to maintain nominal residence in a barracks. The apartment would have a huge bed, a bathtub and an icebox full of cold beer and wine. Even as a college boy, Bill's affairs had been more earthy than romantic. Often he had made fun of Paul for his obsession with Sylvia and had recounted tales of gymnastic nights spent with night-club dancers, shopgirls and "nice little debs who aren't really as ladylike as you think." There was probably no sexual act or position at which Bill was not proficient. In his dormitory tales, the girls had always been gasping with pleasure and begging for more. Surrounded by admiring women in South Carolina, good old Bill was probably taking them on two and three at a time. Lying in his Spartan, ice-bound cabin, Paul had a clear image of an apartment swarming with naked women, of his brother lying at the bottom of a pile of beautiful girls competing with each other to press their breasts into his face and to win possession of his cock.

Shaking his head to clear it, Paul went on deck. The sun was setting, turning the jumbled city of the surrounding ice pack to gold. Directly overhead there was a huge vermilion cloud which was almost in the shape of a woman. As he stared at it he could make out the shape of the great swelling breasts, the narrow waist and the dark groin. Looking away almost guiltily, he stared out over the ice pack and was startled to see how many icebergs had been molded by the wind into the shape of swelling breasts, some complete with nipples, and great glittering golden buttocks. My God, he thought, when a damn iceberg gives me an erection, it's time to go home, but there was of course no way to go home or anywhere else.

During those weeks Nathan was the only man aboard the ship who appeared to keep both busy and happy. In addition to bringing radar and guns from the wrecked destroyer, he and Sparks had taken possession of quantities of radio equipment. To assemble this Nathan worked night and day. When every inch of the radio shack had been used, his intricate black and gray metal boxes spread to the wardroom, which soon became another communications center.

"Why do you need all this stuff?" Paul asked.

"I got to thinking," Nathan said. "The *Nanmak* never really did preserve radio silence. She had to keep acknowledging all those messages and sending reports to GreenPat. The Krauts always must have known just where she was, and they got her right after she sent that long message to the base doctor."

"Can you figure a way to do it better?"

"Ideally we should just shut up, but of course they want weather reports from us and all the rest. So I'm setting up a system that will give any radio direction finder fits."

"How?"

"We'll be able to change frequencies so damned fast and irregularly that no one without our prearranged schedule could get a bearing on us. And we'll use frequencies that ordinary ships don't have."

"When will it all be working?"

"Most of it's working now. I'll soon be able to monitor every conceivable frequency and take bearings on it damn fast. This is one department where we're going to be better than the Krauts."

Paul grinned. "Maybe that's just the edge we need."

Except for brief naps, Nathan spent both his nights and days off watch hunched over his black boxes, turning dials. Although he used earphones, he kept a dozen loudspeakers tuned to various frequencies. Both the radio shack and the wardroom were full of hums, sharp rasps of static and the stutter of distant stations transmitting code. Seth slept with his head buried in his pillows and Sparks, who had been enthusiastic about the new equipment, complained that Nathan kept him almost continuously on watch.

"You and Mr. Green are the two most important men aboard this ship right now," Paul said to him. "You're the only ones who can get any hint of where the Germans are. So go without sleep the way Mr. Green does. If you dope off, we're all liable to sleep a long time."

Only four days after Nathan's system was in full operation, he received brief coded signals that were so faint that he guessed they must come from a very distant source.

With the rather recalcitrant help of Boats, he rigged complex aerials from the bow to the mastheads and stern. These enabled him to bring the signals in louder. By turning the ship when the ice occasionally relaxed its grip, he could use the big aerials as a giant radio direction finder. Thus he determined that the signals came from the north, probably from some point on the east coast of Greenland above the Arctic Circle. When Paul sent this information to Commander GreenPat, he was told that no Americans were near the indicated region, and the signals were presumably German.

Lying in his cabin, Paul tried to guess the nature of the German stations. Signals could be transmitted from planes or balloons, but these sources appeared to be stationary, Nathan reported. They could come from ships very near shore, but with ice conditions as they were, any vessel jammed against that rocky coast would be in danger and would not be left there long on purpose.

It was more likely that the Germans had established shore bases, Paul concluded. If he were a German commander who had been given the job of getting Greenland weather reports, he would send one ship which would establish and supply shore bases, not several ships, especially at a time when Germany probably needed all the ships she could find nearer home. In Denmark the Germans would be able to find plenty of old Arctic hands, and although the Danes rarely worked for the Germans, it would be possible to find some who would obey, either for money or to insure the safety of their families. Danes who were secretly working for the Germans would be welcomed as refugees in any of the few settlements on the east coast and could easily persuade a few Eskimos to work with them. With dog sleds they would establish two- or three-man weather stations almost anywhere on the coast where a trawler or icebreaker could occasionally land supplies.

As he studied the charts Paul realized that this could be almost anywhere. For more than a thousand miles the east coast of Greenland was an intricate maze of fjords, some of which wound more than a hundred miles inland and joined with other fjords. There were uncounted thousands of islands which were separated from each other and the mainland by endless narrow channels. There were hundreds of places where the combined navies of the world could be hidden. Most of these Arctic wastes were unex-

289

plored, and the Danish charts, which were the only ones in existence, gave few details. Only a small percentage of the islands and fjords were even given names.

Still, the countless fjords all looked navigable on the charts, though the pilotbook said that most were almost always filled with ice. Soundings were given only in the few fjords which the Danes had fully explored. If he were the captain of a German ship, he would have no more information than this. If he were trying to establish weather bases and lacked the time for exploration, he would choose places which the pilot book reported to be usually free of ice and where hidden rocks were charted. This would greatly narrow the range of possibilities.

The Danes apparently had discovered and thoroughly explored only two major deep-water ports which were usually free enough of ice to be approachable the year around —Angmagssalik, about 500 miles north of Cape Farewell, and Scoresbysund, which was another 500 miles beyond. The two biggest settlements were at those places, but they consisted of only a few dozen natives and fewer Danes who would be unable to patrol the lacework of fjords and islands which surrounded them for countless miles. The *Nanmak* had been sunk about fifty miles southeast of Angmagssalik at a point where a German supply ship bound to or from that area might have encountered her. Perhaps the whole key to the situation could be found in that region, where, according to the pilotbook, the Eskimos and ancient Norsemen had lived for centuries.

Calling Nathan to his cabin, Paul told him his theory and asked his opinion.

"That could tie in with some theories I have," Nathan said. "The real question is how the Krauts are getting their weather reports out of Greenland to Germany. If they just sent regular signals from shore bases, we'd be bound to pinpoint them soon enough, no matter what tricks they used, and bomb the hell out of them. The point is, we're not getting any strong regular signals, just occasional ones too weak for long-distance transmission."

"What does that mean?"

"They must be using a high-enough frequency for their daily weather reports to escape detection. That high-frequency stuff just travels line of sight, like light. They could be beaming it to a plane overhead, on mountain peaks to get it all the way to Iceland, where low-frequency

290

signals to Germany could be disguised in the regular flow of traffic. But they must have some kind of central base."

"What do you say we ask permission to take a look at Angmagssalik if we ever get out of this ice?"

"We might find something. And the men sure won't object."

Commander GreenPat was quick to approve Paul's request to visit Angmagssalik. Sardonically aware of his own eagerness to please his crew, Paul called the men to quarters. It was a clear cold morning when the men lined up on the well deck and snapped to attention at the captain's approach. Expecting another lecture on cleanliness or on the necessity to remain alert on watch, they looked even more sullen than was now usual.

"At ease," Paul said. "I have a bit of good news. If we ever get out of this ice, we've got orders to go to Angmagssalik, a fjord about five hundred miles north of here where there is a good-sized settlement."

A ragged cheer.

"I don't know whether the Danes will allow anyone ashore, but there isn't much military activity on this coast and the rules shouldn't be so stiffly enforced. I'll do my best for you."

This time the cheer was louder. The men puffed steam. Paul could almost feel approval coming from them. No matter what Mowrey had said on the subject, right now it felt damn good to Paul.

"I don't think there's much point in trying to make a secret of why we're going to this unpronounceable place, Angmagssalik," Paul continued. "There's some reason to suspect that Danes and maybe Eskimos are helping the Germans to maintain weather stations ashore. We're going to be looking for evidence of that and if you go ashore you can play detective with us. We are picking up radio signals from the vicinity of this place, so something is going on there. Of course the people there may be completely innocent, but we can all keep our eyes open. I don't know how long it will be before we can get clear of this ice. The fall storms ought to break up the pack before long. Until then, we still have to stay alert. This is no time and place to dope off. Dismissed."

The men ignored Paul and flocked around Nathan to ask questions. Nathan's popularity with the men had been growing ever since he brought the radar aboard. Paul was angry at himself for feeling a twinge of something like jealousy. While Mowrey had been in command, the crew had regarded Paul as their best friend.

The ice continued to imprison the ship and the anticipation of getting ashore soon made the crew more quarrelsome than ever. A machinist's mate got into a fight with a coxswain, hit him and broke his hand on his head without seriously hurting him. While Nathan doctored the man's hand, Paul looked up the procedure for a deck court.

"The guy is in pain," Nathan said. "Isn't that punishment enough?"

"I've got to stop this fighting from the start. What the hell do you think old Mowrey would do in a case like this?"

"Stamp around a lot and get drunk. He never held any deck courts."

"Maybe because he knew enough to keep the men afraid of him."

"God," Nathan said, "don't copy Mowrey. Be yourself."

"Somebody's got to have some balls around here," Paul called after him. Nathan gave no sign of hearing, and once it was out of his mouth he was glad for that.

The next day Paul reduced the coxswain to first class seaman. The man loudly complained that the machinist's mate had started the fight and had taken the first swing, a charge that the machinist's mate denied. Since there were no witnesses Paul decided to let his decision stand, but he felt he somehow deserved the angry looks the entire deck force now shot at him. In a strange way, Paul thought, Mowrey had won a victory. By making Paul afraid to show any weakness, he was making him fuck up in another way that could cost him the respect of the men.

That night Paul was unable to sleep. He was on the bridge in an instant when the bow watch reported a blinking light on the horizon. It was a little after two o'clock on a cold morning and a half moon was turning the ice pack into a vast mirror of many gleamings. Staring in the direction the lookout pointed, Paul saw a flicker brighter than the surrounding reflections. As he was studying it through his binoculars, Guns said, "Do you think it might be Captain Hansen out there signaling?"

"Hansen sank almost five hundred miles from here."

"Could it be the Krauts trying to get us to give away our position?"

"I think it's just a planet rising. It's due east."

"What makes it blink?"

"The atmosphere. Maybe there's ice between it and us that's rising and falling in a swell."

"Is it saying anything?" Guns asked.

"No," Nathan said. He too was studying the light through the binoculars.

"I'll look it up in the almanac," Paul said. "I think it's Mars."

Before he had a chance to confirm this the planet rose above the horizon, a surprisingly large red ball that left a crimson path on the ice.

"What makes it so big?" Guns asked.

"The atmosphere can have a magnifying effect," Nathan told him.

Paul returned to his bunk. He did not believe in omens, but this strangely enlarged aspect of Mars with its lurid glow on the ice would have meant all kinds of things to the Vikings, he was sure. He lay expecting the ice to part suddenly and free the ship for battle.

Which did not happen. The wind started to pipe up the next day, but it was from the east and simply pressed the ice harder around the ship. Some of her timbers groaned and even Seth's assurance that a trawler could take far more than this did not ease Paul's fears.

That night it began to snow hard, the first real Arctic blizzard they had seen. Snow filled the well deck until gusts of wind scooped it out and sent it swirling off to leeward. The wind varied from a moan to a shriek and back to low groans, sounds that the new aerials made louder than usual. At a little after four in the morning, Paul awoke suddenly. He thought he had felt the ship shudder, and sure enough, there was a definite tremor. Undoubtedly the ice was shifting. As Seth had said, a trawler could take much more than this, but Paul got up to take a look around. As he buttoned up his parka he listened to the wind, guessing by its pitch that it must be blowing close to sixty miles an hour. It was Nathan's watch. When Paul stepped from his cabin to the bridge he saw in the dim light a figure sitting on the stool by the wheel, the silhouette of a man sleeping with his face resting on the collar of his

293

parka. Good God, I don't want to catch Nathan asleep on watch, he thought, but then drew close enough to see that this was a much smaller man. Clapping him on the shoulder, he saw it was Blake, who awoke with a start.

"Where's Mr. Green?" Paul asked.

"I—I don't know, sir."

At that moment the door to the pilothouse opened and Nathan came in, brushing snow from his parka. "Morning, skipper," he said. "When I felt that tremor, I checked the engineroom and the hold to see if everything's all right. There's nothing wrong that I can see."

"Good. Blake, where are you supposed to be standing watch?"

"The gundeck, sir. I just ducked in to get warm."

"And you fell asleep."

"I wasn't really asleep, sir."

"You were asleep when I came in. Didn't you hear me say that any man who slept while on watch would finish his watch in the crow's nest?"

"Yes sir. But I wasn't really asleep, and I can't go up there, sir . . ."

Blake pulled down the hood of his parka. He was eighteen years old, still rather childlike with curly blond hair and a face that looked startlingly angelic even when scared. "I'd freeze up there, sir, and I'm scared of heights. The rigging is all icy—"

"Skipper, come in here a minute, will you?" Nathan said, gesturing toward the cabin. When Paul went in Nathan closed the door after him. "Skipper, you can't send that boy up there in weather like this."

"Nathan, you're good at radar and radio. I can't let the crew sleep on watch. So let me handle the men."

"Yes sir, but it's cruel and unusual punishment. It wouldn't stand up in court."

"Are you going to be a sea lawyer?"

"No, but Paul, I am executive officer, and we both need common sense."

Paul was surprised by the surge of anger he felt. "You just let me handle the men," he said. "Didn't you tell me you're just an electronics specialist?"

When Paul returned to the bridge he found Guns standing beside Blake.

"Sir, you aren't going to make my striker climb the goddamn mast, are you?"

"You think it's dangerous?"

"Yes sir."

"Blake, you slept on watch. That endangers every man aboard this ship. If you're not man enough to take your punishment, I'll show you how. Follow me."

Without glancing behind him, Paul walked to the well deck, padded through the snow there and jumped up to the rail by the rigging. The steel shrouds were covered with snow and ice. His heavy mittens made them hard to grasp, but Paul was angry enough to pull himself up until his boots hit the first ratlines. Then the climb was surprisingly easy, despite the fact that the wind tore at his shoulders. Glancing down, he saw the white blur of Blake's scared face. The boy had his feet on the ratlines now and was following him. Quickly Paul climbed past the crow's nest. With his feet on the last ratline he embraced the icy mast. The wind caused his parka to flap, making a sound like a luffing sail. He watched while Blake stepped into the relative security of the crow's nest, where he was sheltered from the wind up to his shoulders.

"You all right now?" Paul yelled.

"Yes sir."

"You going to freeze to death?"

"I—I don't know, sir."

Paul allowed himself to slide down the rigging until he could hook his arm around the topmost ratline. Unbuttoning his parka, he managed to wriggle out of it while holding on, first with one hand, then the other. He was concentrating on hanging onto the flapping garment so hard that he didn't even feel the cold.

"Wrap this around your shoulders," he said to Blake, shoving the parka at him. When he was sure the boy had a firm hold of it, he allowed himself to slide down the rigging to the deck. The wind was piercing his uniform and long underwear. He ran to the bridge.

"Get me another parka please," he said to Nathan.

"Yes sir." Nathan disappeared without a word.

"Guns, do you have any more ideas on how I should run this ship?"

"No sir, but he could still freeze up there inside of the next three hours."

"Give him another half hour and then send him below. Get somebody to stand the rest of his watch on the gun deck."

295

"Yes sir."

"And pass the word that my orders hold. Anyone found asleep on watch will go to the crow's nest."

Paul went to his cabin. He was allowing himself a rare drink of brandy when Nathan appeared with another parka. "Your parka, *sir*."

"You want a drink, Nathan?"

"No thank you, sir."

"You still think I should let people go to sleep on watch without punishment?"

"I don't know, sir. As you say, I'm just good with radar and radio. I'm not much of an administrator."

"But somebody has to handle the men—" Paul realized that he was asking for approval, but he didn't get it. Nathan just shrugged, turned and left.

There was no sound but the rising shriek of the wind. Paul lay down on his bunk and tried to review the whole episode. Shit, first I tried to be as tough as old Mowrey, and then I overcompensated with the big brother act. Nathan says to forget Mowrey and be myself, but who wants to have a college boy for a captain? I have to invent myself as I go along. . . .

Two days later the wind veered to the north and continued to blow hard. Paul had hoped that a north wind would free the ship, but the ice around them remained as solid as concrete. The men began to speculate about the possibility of being frozen in for the winter. Cookie said that by April they'd be down to canned beans and codfish, a prospect which oddly seemed to delight him. "Then you bastards will appreciate the food I've been cooking," he said.

Paul always had imagined that weeks stuck in the ice would be unbearably boring, but the frustrations of the crew kept him busier than ever. Sparks accused a seaman named Wollinger of stealing money from a wallet he kept hidden under his mattress, and what was worse, of taking the photograph of his nude wife, which he also had kept secreted there in its cardboard folder. Wollinger acted completely innocent. His wallet was full of bills, but no one could prove that they had come from Sparks, and no trace of the photograph could be found. Although he hated the idea of crime without punishment aboard his ship, Paul was unable to think of any way to handle this. Apparently Sparks or his friends took care of the matter, for soon

Wollinger complained that all his money had been stolen. No one could prove anything and Paul had to content himself with indignant lectures about thievery aboard a small ship.

A week after this incident, while the north wind continued to shriek through the rigging, Boats lodged a more serious complaint. It was nine o'clock in the evening when the red-haired chief petty officer knocked on the door of Paul's cabin. Taking his cap off as he came in, he said, "Sir, I want to put Guns and Blake on report."

"What for?"

"They're queer, sir. I caught them at it."

"Oh, God!" Paul rubbed his face with his hand. "Exactly what happened?"

"I went down to the hold to check the depth charges, to see if they'd shifted any. Blake was going down on Guns. They were so busy they didn't even see me."

"And you want to bring formal charges?"

"That's only right, sir, isn't it? We can't have the men going queer on us."

"Let me think about it. I'll see you in a few minutes, Boats."

Paul allowed himself a shot of brandy. Then he telephoned the wardroom and asked Nathan to come to his cabin. After hours of working with his radios, Nathan had just gone to sleep and looked haggard.

"Nathan, we got a case of sodomy," Paul began. After telling him Boats's story, Paul said, "You seem to be the great champion of the crew around here. What would you do?"

"If you bring formal charges, you'll get a dishonorable discharge for those guys and maybe twenty years in Portsmouth."

"Is it really my choice?"

"You'll lose a damn good gunner's mate and a fairly good seaman."

"But I didn't write the book. Does it really leave me any choice?"

"You want to bring charges?"

"By now Boats will have told everyone about this. Can I do nothing?"

"It seems funny."

"Damned if I see that," Paul said.

297

"Well, you don't do anything when Guns does it with a dead bear, but when the poor s.o.b. is caught with a human, he goes to prison for twenty years."

"The book doesn't mention bears."

"I suppose it mentions bestiality or some such. What happens if you just do nothing?"

"I suppose the whole goddamn crew could end up queer instead of fighting the war."

"Hell, you know that wouldn't happen. Nothing would happen, nothing different from what's already happening."

"Something could happen. Boats could press his charges when he gets ashore. Christ, he could write Mowrey about it—they were always pretty close."

"And what the hell would old Mowrey do about it? Hell, he's probably dead by this time or locked in a back ward of some stateside hospital."

"You know, the old bastard could surprise us. He could come back."

"Paul, you're obsessed with the guy. You've got to forget him. Take it from me—he's much too far gone to come back—ever."

"Okay. What would you do with this mess?"

"I'd try to talk Boats into forgetting it."

"Would that be your idea of justice? If Boats stumbled on an act of sodomy, the book says he should report it."

"Hell, this is just part of Boats's feud with Guns. Did he have witnesses?"

"Down in the hold? I doubt it. He didn't mention any."

"Hell, if the thing came to court, it would be the word of two against one. All Guns and Blake have to do is swear innocence and maybe bring countercharges. They could say that Boats had been after Blake."

"You do have an ingenious mind."

"If you tell Boats what might happen, he might drop the charges."

"Stay here with me, we'll talk to him."

Paul telephoned the forecastle and in a few minutes Boats appeared. He had put on a clean shirt and had combed his hair.

"Boats, you've brought some very serious charges here," Paul began. "If they stuck, Guns and Blake could get a d.d. and twenty years."

"I didn't write the law, sir."

"Do you have witnesses to what you say you saw?" Nathan asked.

"No sir, not down there in the hold."

"It's pretty dark down there, isn't it?" Nathan asked.

"Yes, but I could see enough, sir."

"Well, just exactly what did you see?"

"They were doing it."

"How?"

"You know. Blake was kneeling in front of Guns and Guns was making noises."

"What kind of noises?"

"You know."

"As a matter of fact, I don't know," Nathan said. "What kind of noises?"

"Sort of moans like."

"What would you do," Nathan asked, "if you got these people into court and Guns said he had dropped a crate of rifles on his foot. What if he said that Blake had knelt to see if his toe was broken and he was moaning with pain?"

"Did they say that?" Boats asked with a laugh.

"Not yet, but they might," Nathan said. "It would be the word of two against one. And Guns would bring out the fact that you two have been feuding for a long time. He could make your charge out to be an act of spite and bring countercharges. Blake might even claim that you'd been propositioning him, trying to break up his friendship with Guns."

"He wouldn't dare say that—sir, I'm telling you them two men are queer. The whole crew knows it."

"Have you been talking about it?"

"Not only me."

"If you have been talking about it and can't prove your charges, you could be up for slander."

"Why are you taking the side of these damn queers?" Boats demanded.

"I'm not taking anybody's side," Paul said, breaking a silence that had seemed long. "If you put Guns in jail, this ship loses a good gunner's mate. If he puts you in jail, we lose a good boatswain's mate. The ship can't win if you bring charges."

"And if we don't do nothing, those queers will be laughing at all of us."

"Somehow I doubt if Guns and Blake are fundamentally amused by this," Nathan said.

"Let's leave it this way," Paul concluded. "If you ever have witnesses to a queer act, bring charges and I'll back you. I don't like them any more than you do. But this time I can't do much except advise you that you may be heading into real trouble if you press charges without being able to back them up."

"Yes sir . . . well, I guess we better let it go this time. Next time I'll have witnesses and we can nail them for sure."

He left hurriedly, and there was a short silence in the cabin.

"Do you suppose we ought to give Guns and Blake some sort of warning?" Paul asked.

"The whole crew will be talking about nothing else. How much warning do they need?"

"I don't know. It seems like I should do something. If we're not careful, the whole crew will get so goosey they can't man the guns."

"Skipper, from what I read, from the beginning of time men confined on ships have done it with each other when there was nothing else."

"Not all of them, not even most, I bet. Not most *Americans*."

"No, not most. But some Portuguese fishing vessels still carry one homosexual to service all hands on long voyages, and Columbus's men were apparently very kind to each other."

"Are you in favor of all this?"

"I'm in favor of putting as few men in jail as possible and getting on with fighting the damn war. How long do you think we'll be stuck here?"

During the next three days the gale from the north continued to howl. In the middle of the third night there was a terrifying booming sound in the distance that brought all hands on deck. The ship trembled and suddenly the ice pack split, leaving a broad river with jagged edges leading toward the sea. Swimming through the clouds, the moon made the ice almost as bright as day. Hurrying to escape before the icepack again closed around them, Paul followed the lead at top speed. Within three hours they felt the roll of the broad Atlantic under them and for once it was welcome.

"Here we go!" Paul heard Guns shout to the deck gang. "Next stop, Ang-my-ass-lick. All aboard for the ping-ping express!"

# CHAPTER 32

To get completely clear of the ice, Paul kept to a northeasterly course until the *Arluk* was fifty miles off the coast of Greenland. The northerly gale which had freed them from the pack hit the trawler on the port bow, causing her to pitch and roll simultaneously. Heavy-laden with the big gun on deck and her hold full of depth charges, the little ship rose sluggishly to meet the great gray-bearded seas which, row on row, marched against her. White water often broke over her bow and seethed over her well deck, sloshing over the top of her rails.

This time only about a third of the crew was seasick. Although Nathan still had to hurry to the lee rail of the bridge frequently, he gave up his bucket, which did not seem to him to be fitting equipment for the executive officer. Paul was relieved to find that for the first time in a rough sea he felt no nausea and even was tempted to try one of Mowrey's cigars, an idea he reluctantly discarded when he felt just a touch of dizziness.

Soon after the ship began to roll heavily, Paul began to worry about the depth charges in the hold. Calling Boats to the bridge, he said, "You better check the cargo. I don't want those depth charges rolling around down there."

Ever since his accusation of Guns and Blake had been disregarded, Boats had been surly, and now he said, "Sir, when I stow cargo, it don't roll around."

"I'm sure that's true, chief, but it won't do any harm to check."

"Captain Mowrey always trusted me," Boats said under

his breath, but he went below. The ship gave a particularly vicious roll and Blake, who was at the helm, vomited, spraying the base of the engineroom telegraph.

"I'm sorry, sir," Blake said.

"Don't worry about it," Paul said. Even the smell didn't upset him too much. "Quartermaster, get Blake a bucket."

Soon Boats returned to the pilothouse. Saluting with a touch of exaggerated respect, he said, "I have inspected the cargo and have found it totally secure, sir."

"Very well," Paul said, casually returning the salute. "Get a seaman with a mop to clean up this deck before we all go sliding around." To himself he sounded like Mowrey at his sweet best.

"Aye, aye, sir," Boats said. "Begging your pardon, sir, but at boot camp we regulars are taught that there are no mops aboard a ship—only swabs, sir. Could my education be wrong, sir?"

There was a moment of silence before Paul gave Boats an extremely sweet smile and said sweetly, "In respect to nautical vocabulary, Boats, you are right and I am wrong. We reserve officers sometimes are not up to the nice points of the nautical language. On the other hand, I as a reserve officer have mastered such fundamentals as celestial navigation and ship handling without any formal training, without costing the government one cent for my education. I've also taught myself something about how to handle men and the elements of nautical etiquette. It's wrong for me to call a swab a mop and more wrong for a chief petty officer to correct the word usage of his commanding officer in front of other men. For this act of discourtesy and insubordination you are hereby given a formal warning. Quartermaster, enter that in the log. Any repetition of this offense, Boats, will get you ten days of restriction, beginning when we next hit port. Now get a man with a swab to clean up this mess. Am I speaking a proper language you understand?"

"Yes sir," Boats said, and went out the door of the pilothouse. Glancing at Nathan, who was standing just beside him, Paul saw that he was grinning, and so were the other men on the bridge, but suddenly he felt ashamed of a cheap-shot victory. So as captain of the ship he had crushed a boatswain's mate, and probably made an enemy of him for life. That certainly was no triumph in the art of handling men. Once more he had fucked up, and the sound of Mowrey's sardonic laughter seemed to ring out louder than ever.

At noon Paul took a latitude sight which indicated that the ship was making only about five knots against the wind and currents. The sextant was beginning to feel familiar to his hands and he had learned to make the mathematical computations rapidly, but he still was unable to feel any great faith in the line of position he drew on the chart. When Nathan appeared on the bridge, Paul handed him the sextant and awaited the results of his computations with interest. He felt something close to panic when Nathan's line of position turned out to be a good thirty miles from his own. In the wind he could almost hear Mowrey's contemptuous jeer. "I told you you'd fuck up."

"One of us must have made a mistake," Paul said, handing his notebook to Nathan. "You better check my figures and I'll check yours."

Neither of them had made a mathematical error. "The big variable," Paul said, "is the damn horizon. With this sea it looks lumpy as hell, and with the ship jumping all around, I can't see how we can be sure of it. When you bring the image of the sun down in the mirrors of the sextant, do you just kiss the tops of the waves with it, or do you try to guess where the horizon would be in a dead calm?"

"I've just been kissing the tops of the waves with it."

"I've been taking it a little below that. Hell, it's all guesswork and practice—there's really nothing precise about this damn navigation at all. Let's try it again and see how close we can come to each other."

For most of the afternoon Nathan and Paul took sights. Finally their lines of position came to within ten miles of each other fairly regularly, and as Paul said, if a man knew his position within ten miles, he ought to be able to make a proper landfall.

Still Paul worried as the ship slogged five hundred miles northward. In gathering clouds the tall mountains of Greenland and the ice pack disappeared and there was nothing but slate-gray sea and a sky hardly different in color. According to the charts and the pilotbook, the mountains around Angmagssalik Fjord did not look much different from any other part of the Greenland coast. During the four days it took to reach a dead reckoning position forty miles at sea in the latitude of the fjord, Paul had nightmares of finding nothing but mountains, of searching endlessly without discovering any entrance to a fjord. Standing on the bridge, he glanced at the door to the captain's cabin and almost wished that Mowrey would suddenly walk from it. Drunk or sober, abusive or sweetly reasonable, Mowrey at least had always known where he was.

Shortly after making his turn to close with the ice pack, Paul was able to get a moon sight which crossed reasonably with his lines of position from the sun. The sky was still too overcast to permit a glimpse of the stars or planets, and he could get no simultaneous lines of position that would give him a precise little triangle such as he saw in the books, but he still guessed that his estimated position probably was not more than ten miles off. If he closed with the coast and found no fjord, should he steam north or south? If he guessed wrong, he could work his way through the ice for days without really knowing where the hell he was. How would he send position reports to GreenPat and how would he explain his wanderings to the crew?

"Let's face it, men," he imagined himself saying. "We're lost. Got to be honest about it. . . ." And to GreenPat he could radio a message such as this: "U.S. Coast Guard cutter *Arluk* is now blundering around in the ice within sight of some unknown part of Greenland, we think."

Then, of course, GreenPat would send Mowrey back aboard at the first opportunity.

Paul started to sweat, despite the icy wind. Glancing at his chart, he found that they were approaching a tiny circle he had drawn to mark the spot where the *Nanmak* had sunk, or at least where her boatful of corpses had been found. According to her last radio report, the *Nanmak* had been caught in heavy ice, but now the wind had scattered the pack and only a half dozen huge bergs surrounded the empty sea where their sister ship had disappeared. Paul wondered whether he should stop to say a few reverent words over her grave, but no ship should present a stationary target in waters where the enemy might still be lurking. How had the *Nanmak* been lost, anyway? Had a huge German icebreaker suddenly steamed from behind one of those icebergs, perhaps the one that lay vaguely in the shape of a great crouched lion on the sea? Or had a Kraut submarine been patrolling the edge of the ice pack? A long-range German plane could suddenly have appeared flying low, just above the ice peaks, or an enemy trawler hardly bigger than the *Nanmak* and the *Arluk* might have demonstrated bigger guns, better fire control. There was of course no way to know. The great combers from the Atlantic rolled on, serenely erasing all tragedies only moments after they happened. Paul decided not to tell the crew when they passed the grave of the *Nanmak*.

The north wind had scattered the ice pack closer to shore than Paul had expected, and though they had to zigzag a lot, they were able to maintain full speed as they closed with the mountains. Climbing to the crow's nest with his binoculars, Paul studied every inch of the coast, trying to find the entrance to the fjord. Rust-red mountain slopes, icebergs—he might as well be approaching the west coast. Sometimes nightmares can come true, but it was necessary to press very close to this forbidding shore even to make sure that he was lost. In the mist to his left the coast seemed to fall away in what might be a bay, a fjord or just a valley between mountains. To his right there was a high point of land which seemed to extend many miles to sea, with more points vaguely outlined in the mist beyond.

"Come left slowly," Paul shouted to the bridge, glad to hear that his voice at least sounded confident. "Steady now. Steady as she goes!"

For about half an hour they twisted through the ice in the general direction Paul had indicated. The bay ahead kept deepening, perhaps to end only in a dry valley or in glaciers, but there was a glint of water between the mountains. Holding a folded chart, Paul stood in the crow's nest comparing peaks and points to the outlines on paper. Gradually everything seemed to fall into place, and as they rounded a great granite peninsula, the entrance to the fjord clearly opened ahead. Holding the folded chart in his teeth, Paul slid down the rigging and hurried to the bridge. He kept his voice casual when he said, "Angmagssalik is dead ahead."

"I can't help feeling it's a damn miracle," Nathan said.

"Just natural sea sense," Paul said with a straight face.

# CHAPTER 33

Angmagssalik Fjord was surprisingly free of ice.
Like the other fjords Paul had seen, it resembled a river at
the bottom of a great rocky canyon but it was about five
miles wide. As the *Arluk* steamed into it, a dozen kayaks
put out from shore to greet her, their ivory-tipped double-
bladed paddles flashing in the sun. They relieved any last
doubt in Paul's mind that he had found the right place.
According to the pilotbook, the only Eskimos within hundreds of miles lived at Angmagssalik.

The first kayak to reach the ship was paddled by a
diminutive Greenlander in a sealskin parka. The man had
the nearly circular copper-colored face of a full-blooded
Eskimo and long black hair streaked with gray, despite the
fact that his laughing eyes looked young. As Paul stopped
the engines, the Eskimo paddled his kayak on a parallel
course, his narrow but powerful shoulders and short arms
wielding the double-bladed paddle with astonishing skill
and force. The kayak leapt through the water. As the ship
slowed, it darted alongside the well deck. To Paul's surprise, its occupant tossed his paddle to the deck of the ship
and leapt aboard. He took the end of a bow painter with
him and speedily hauled his kayak over the rail. It all
happened in one quick blur of motion, as though Eskimo
and kayak had jumped simultaneously from the water to
the deck.

"Me Peomeenie," the man said. "Me pilot."

"Come on up to the bridge," Paul called.

Peomeenie marched to the bridge with great assurance.
The top of his head came only to Paul's shoulder as he
pointed up the fjord. "You go there," he said with authority.

The chart was on too small a scale to give details and
Paul was glad to have Peomeenie aboard when they skirted
a group of rocky islands and approached a cove. Through

his binoculars Paul could see a half-dozen of the little red houses the Danes built and more sod huts. A miniature church with a tall white steeple and the incongruous sight of a white yacht, a small ketch on the ways on a rocky beach, made the settlement look a little like a New England village.

Mr. Williams, the new ensign, who had made such an art of sort of hiding himself aboard the ship that Paul had almost forgotten about him, suddenly appeared on the bridge. He had put on a new uniform. Taking a pair of binoculars from a box, he attempted to stare at the town through them for several seconds before realizing that rubber caps still protected the lenses. When he got these off, he said, "It doesn't look like much of a town, does it, captain?"

"What did you expect, Broadway and Forty-second Street?"

Paul was ashamed of treating the new ensign almost as badly as Mowrey had treated him, but he couldn't help it. He didn't like Mr. Williams. That was unreasonable, of course, but there was something about the young man's scrawny neck and acne-marred face that infuriated Paul and almost everyone else aboard the ship, except Seth, who was fatherly toward the newcomer, and Nathan, who kept trying to teach him things, even though Mr. Williams obviously was incapable of learning even how to tie his own shoes. One of his laces always dragged. The fact that he never appeared with both shoelaces tied had begun to fascinate Paul.

"Damn it, tie your shoelace!" Paul said now. "If you trip and fall overboard, this water will turn you to ice inside of about thirty seconds."

"Aye, aye sir," Mr. Williams said. "Do you want me to send a message of arrival to GreenPat?"

"Get Mr. Green to check it before it goes out."

Peomeenie pointed to a small cove behind a point. "Anchor there."

"Boats, pipe the men to anchor stations," Paul called to the chief petty officer, who was laying out mooring lines, and the red-haired boatswain's mate gave him a murderous glance that clearly said, "Why didn't you tell me that before I got out these lines? Are you letting a damn Eskimo run the ship?"

After the trawler let go her anchor, Paul stopped the

engine. In the moment of silence that followed they all heard the distant drone of a plane.

"It's probably one of ours, but we better man the guns," Paul said. "They say the Krauts run patrols here."

Before the men had the guns loaded, the plane broke through the cloud cover and headed toward them. Clearly it was American navy, PBY. Paul's relief was swept away by the thought that it might have been sent to return Mowrey to his ship. If Mowrey recovered, as he had promised, this would be the logical place for him to be flown in the fjord made a good place for a PBY to land. Paul could almost see the old pilot arriving aboard, his uniform freshly starched, his red face blazing. The men, no doubt, would cheer.

Circling low over the trawler, the PBY dipped its wings, and to Paul's immeasurable relief headed north, following the edge of the ice pack.

A heavy black launch with a pilothouse on the stern put out from a small wharf and headed toward the *Arluk*. An Eskimo crew brought her smartly alongside the well deck and a stout white-haired man in a heavy blue greatcoat climbed aboard with such difficulty that Boats rushed to help him. Although this visitor had to be hauled over the rail almost like a sack of potatoes, he quickly recovered his dignity. Standing up as straight as his round body permitted, he said, "I wish to see your captain." Although his words were correct, his heavy Danish accent made them difficult to understand, and he had to repeat himself three times, each time louder and more authoritatively before Boats led him to the bridge.

The Dane sported a thin white mustache which looked incongruous on his fat florid face. His first words to Paul were, "I'm Swanson. I am the authority here. We do not allow enlisted men ashore, the common sailors. It is the law. Too much trouble there's been."

"I see," Paul replied icily.

"We have to protect the native population."

Paul understood that, and in his heart even sided with the Eskimos, but he also felt for his men, most of whom were already changing into dress blues. "Perhaps you can assign us a field away from the native population for recreation," he said.

"No. The common sailors must stay aboard."

"We have no common sailors here. They are all uncommon."

"What you say?"

"Let it pass."

"What you here for? You have supplies for us?"

"No supplies for you."

"What you here for?"

The Dane's tone was definitely hostile, just what one might expect if the village had Nazi sympathizers, Paul thought, and said, "We have been picking up enemy radio signals coming from this vicinity. We want to see if you know anything about them."

"Don't understand."

"How many Danes live here?"

"Just me and three families. Nine people."

"I want to come ashore and talk to them."

"All right, but no common sailors."

"I'll bring my *executive* officer, he's very uncommon."

Swanson climbed back aboard his boat with Boats's help, and with gruff thanks headed for shore without offering Paul a ride. Soon Paul and Nathan followed in the whaleboat. It seemed curious that no Eskimos rushed to meet them at the wharf and only sled dogs were visible on the beach. These dogs rushed to the end of the wharf as they approached and stood there barking and snarling. Even when Paul roared at them, they did not back away far.

"I'm damned if I'll let dogs scare me," Paul said, picking up a big crescent wrench and making throwing motions. The dogs retreated toward the middle of the wharf, but they still made the job of climbing up there appear frightening. Paul roared louder than ever. Above the snarling and the yapping he suddenly heard a woman's voice call, "Don't be afraid." Looking toward the beach, he saw a sight that was astonishing for its normality in that place. A woman wearing a tan trench coat and a broad-brimmed green hat such as one might expect to see in New York or Boston was coming toward the wharf. "Don't be afraid," she called again. "They'll run when you come close."

The dogs trotted up to her and began nuzzling her like house-pets. Paul and Nathan scrambled up to the wharf.

"I just wasn't taking any chances," Paul began.

"That was wise. Some of these dogs are dangerous." She

spoke with a British and a slight Danish accent. While petting the dogs, she added, "Can I help you with whatever you want here?"

"Can we go somewhere and talk?" Paul said above the whining of the dogs.

"I can offer you tea. I hope that Mr. Swanson didn't make you think that we all are too inhospitable. He is very protective about the Eskimos."

She was a tall, thin woman maybe about thirty years old, Paul saw as he walked closer. Her face was too narrow and angular to be really beautiful, but it was full of vitality, and her smile struck Paul as extremely sexy, a fact which he should not find surprising, he reminded himself, since he had been known to find the shape of icebergs stimulating.

"I understand about the Eskimos," Paul said.

"It seems that they've had a good deal of trouble on the west coast," the woman said with a smile, and Paul was suddenly sure that every Danish settlement in Greenland had heard of the *Arluk*'s debacle with the stolen booze.

"Our men are under a lot of pressure and sometimes they get a little out of hand," he said.

"I'm sure they're all on their good behavior now," Nathan added. "All we want is a place for them to drink beer and play baseball. We don't want them to mix with the Eskimos, either."

"Something can be arranged, I'm sure," the woman said. "Mr. Swanson is old and not very well. The reports have frightened him. He has ordered everyone to stay in the houses. He will be quite angry with me, I fear, but I often have to remind him that Greenland at least is a free territory."

With the dogs following peaceably, she led the way over a path of frozen mud to a tiny house at the end of a row of five. The middle house, both Paul and Nathan noted, had a narrow radio tower projecting from the roof, but most of the Danish settlements had radio of some kind. The dogs trotted away as she reached the front door. In a cramped vestibule like those Paul had seen on the west coast, she took off her trench coat, revealing a black and white sweater with a pattern of reindeer and a dark green skirt. When she took off her hat, Paul saw that she had dark blonde hair that was cut very short, a style that would have looked masculine if her features had been less delicate. The sweater did not do much for her—she was a lot thinner than the women about whom Paul had been dreaming.

After Paul and Nathan had hung their parkas on pegs beside her trench coat, she led the way to a small living-room dominated by a coal stove on which a tea kettle steamed. Swanson was sitting in an armchair, his big face afraid, angry, or both. Another old man got up from a straight chair to greet them and a pleasantly plump old woman came from the kitchen with a plate of pastries. They all wore conventional European clothes. The woman in the reindeer sweater introduced them. They had long Danish names which Paul found it impossible to remember. "By the way," she concluded, "I'm Brit, Brit Holstrom." Turning to Nathan she smiled and said, "Now, captain, what's your name?"

It was natural, Paul told himself, for her to assume that Nathan was the captain of the ship. Although Nathan was only about five years older than Paul, his craggy face made him appear far more mature. He was two inches taller than Paul and had much more dignity, a quality which Paul's light blond hair and boyish face made difficult to manage.

"Paul Schuman here is the skipper," Nathan said with his wry grin. "I'm Nathan Green, at your service."

He brought that little phrase off with a fine touch, Paul noticed with a twinge of envy, and Brit gave him an especially warm smile of appreciation. They all sat on hard chairs in a semicircle around the stove while the plump woman served tea.

"I'm sorry, but we have no lemon and no milk," Swanson said heavily. "Very little sugar too. I had hoped you were bringing supplies."

"I'm afraid my orders are just to check radio signals," Paul said.

"Perhaps you can explain it to me," Brit said. "I used to have a job as an interpreter."

There was no polite way to explain that he was investigating the possibility that some Danes might be radioing weather reports for the Germans. He did the best he could, concluding with "We just thought that someone who was working for the Germans might have come here under false pretenses. Have there been any late arrivals from Europe?"

"Just me and my father," Brit said. "We got here about

a year ago. Everyone else has been here for ages. I suppose you have every right to suspect me and dad. Don't be embarrassed. I would if I were in your shoes."

"I am embarrassed," Paul said. "But I have to write a routine report. Have I met your father?"

"No, but you can later if necessary. He's not well. He's in bed."

"May I ask how you came here?"

"We got out of Denmark aboard that little ketch on the ways. The Nazis strafed us. My husband and son were killed. You can be sure that we have no sympathy with the Germans."

Brit's hands fluttered in the air while she talked and died in her lap. The room was very quiet.

"I understand," Nathan said, his deep voice making it clear that he did indeed understand.

Brit glanced at his gaunt face. "Yes," she said, and glanced into her teacup.

"Let me emphasize that I never really suspected you," Paul said, his words sounding absurdly theatrical to his own ears.

"Thank you," Brit said. Getting up, she walked across the room and offered Nathan a plate of cookies. Holding it in her left hand, she touched his shoulder with her right fingers, like a curious sort of benediction, and said, "I guess that the war hasn't been so easy for a lot of us."

No one else in the room talked. There was an instant of silence before Brit said to Nathan, "For your records, I should prove what I say. I can show you where the Germans strafed my boat—not much of it has been repaired. I have the logbook and charts aboard. Would you like to see them?"

She touched his arm. To her surprise, Nathan almost flinched. His arm went rigid and his smile was a little forced when he said, "Thank you very much but I think you better ask the skipper about that. I'm just here to look at your radio equipment. Could you ask someone to show me that?"

For a moment the girl's sensitive face looked hurt, but she quickly smiled. "Of course," she said.

"I would like to see anything you have that would help me make out my report," Paul said quickly, moving to the girl's side. "It's very kind of you to offer."

Swanson volunteered to show Nathan the radio equipment. A little stiffly Nathan bid the group good-by, shook hands with Brit, and followed his guide out of the house.

The equipment that Swanson showed Nathan in the cottage with the radio mast did not have the range or frequencies the Germans would have needed. Nathan inspected it briefly and had the whaleboat return him to the ship. In ways he did not fully understand, Brit had left him oddly shaken. She did not really resemble his wife, who had been taller and had had dark hair to her shoulders, but she had somehow evoked Rebecca with startling clarity. Her hands, her hands . . . Rebecca too had such delicate little hands, with which she often gestured as she talked, and Rebecca too had often been able to send almost a shock of electricity through his arm merely by touching it. And there had been so much in Brit's face—grief, understanding, that glance of sudden rapport which she had directed at him. In Rebecca's dark eyes there had been just such immediate understanding. Eerie . . .

Since the disappearance of his wife, Nathan had been seriously tempted by no woman, and he was shocked to discover how much he wanted Brit. To him, taking another woman would mean the final acceptance of his wife's death, and he fought the temptation. Of course he shouldn't feel guilty for responding to Brit's touch with such absurd intensity, he thought. What sailor in the Arctic wouldn't tremble a little at a woman's touch?

# CHAPTER 34

Paul had noted the immediate rapport between Nathan and the girl, and had been ridiculously jealous because the girl obviously was more drawn to Nathan than to him. Although Nathan had not told him anything about his personal tragedy, Paul had sensed that there was something deeply wrong in his personal life, and when Nathan almost froze at the girl's touch he assumed that there must be a reason. He sympathized with Nathan, but at the moment he was much more concerned with Brit, who had suffered a kind of rejection, even if it all had happened so fast, and who was now turning to him with something of the same look she had at first directed toward Nathan.

"I really don't want to bother you," Paul said, "but I'd like to see your boat. The Coast Guard tries to keep a record of all vessels coming to Greenland, especially from Europe."

"That sounds very sensible," she said, and traced a sensible little circle in the air with her forefinger. Finishing her tea, she led the way to the vestibule, where he helped her to put on her trench coat, which looked much too thin for this climate.

"I haven't helped a woman on with a coat in a long time."

This time her smile was warm.

"You do it very well," she said. "You don't fumble. I can't stand men who fumble."

She led the way toward the ketch on the ways near the beach.

In the distance the little white yacht had looked ready for a Long Island regatta, but as he drew near Paul saw that she was seaworn and her hull amidships had been clumsily patched with rough-hewn planks. Without speaking, Brit led the way up a ladder to the cockpit. Stepping over splintered combing, she slid open a hatch. Following her, Paul found himself in a tiny cabin, the teak trim of which reminded him of the old *Valkyrie*. There was the same moldy smell, a chill of dampness like a tomb. A tiny stove not unlike the one aboard his father's ancient yawl stood in the galley, but it burned oil. When Brit lit it, it began to roar, and suddenly the cabin was a snug place.

Moving with quick efficiency, Brit lifted the top of a desk and took out a sea-stained notebook.

"This is the log," she said. "It's in Danish, but you could turn it in to your authorities if they want to check on us. The whole story is here." Handing it to him, she shrugged. "Of course, if I were working for the Germans, I probably would come armed with documents like this. There's nothing I can prove, is there?"

"I don't really suspect you."

"You should. I want the Americans to be smart. God knows we Danes weren't."

Rummaging in a drawer, she took out some folded small-scale charts. Spreading them on the cabin table, she pointed to a zig-zag line drawn in pencil and much smudged. "You can follow our whole course. It took us fifty-three days to get here, but of course this whole thing could be faked too."

"Is there anyone around here who could be sending radio signals for the Germans?"

"Everyone here hates the Germans even more than poor old Mr. Swanson hates the Americans. And he doesn't really hate you. He just loves the Eskimos and is scared for them. I think he's scared for me too, as a matter of fact. He's doing his best to protect us all."

She smiled. It suddenly seemed to Paul that he had never seen a mouth so beautiful. Even teeth and lips too sensual to think about, or would any woman's mouth look marvelous compared to icebergs?

"I'll keep my men aboard the ship," he said. "As a matter of fact, we'll probably have to sail in the morning. There's not much for us to report here."

"Where will you go?"

"My job is to chase Germans," he said, sounding melodramatic even to himself.

"And your orders are secret, as I'm sure they should be. Would you like some Aquavit?"

"I'd love some," he said, remembering the time he had drunk Aquavit with Hansen.

"I come down here often to be alone and try to work," Brit said, starting to talk very fast. "It's not easy to find privacy here, I've only been here about a year but sometimes it seems like a hundred."

"There's no one here near your age?"

"The Eskimos, and sometimes they begin to look taller and taller. Peomeenie is starting to look to me like your Clark Gable."

"The icebergs are starting to look like women to me."

He noticed that her hand trembled a little as she poured the Aquavit into liquor glasses.

"I've often thought of a ship coming," she said. "But I never thought one would come just for a day."

"It must be hard for you here."

"No, it's a beautiful country. I've made myself a pair of skis. I had to rip planks from my house to do it, but they work pretty well. And I've learned to drive a dog team and

315

to fish and even to harpoon seals. I love the summer but the winter is a little bad. I hate to see the days grow shorter."

"The war will be over soon—"

"How long? How long do you think?"

"Two years, maybe three."

"How nice. I'll look like an old woman by then."

"Hardly."

"This damn climate ages us fast. The Eskimos die of old age at thirty-five."

The stove was making the cabin almost too hot. Getting up, she took off her trench coat and he unbuttoned his parka.

"Do you want more Aquavit?" she asked.

"Please."

"If you think Germans are around here, you might find them anywhere. There are coves and hidden harbors all up and down the coast. Look at this chart."

There was a tremor in her forefinger as she traced the east coast of Greenland. "This is Supportup-Kangerdula Fjord," she said. "It's only about thirty miles south of here. Watch out if you go there. Supportup means 'the blower.' For some reason the foehn winds blow worse there. Do you know about foehn winds?"

"A little."

"Even the Eskimos won't go near Supportup-Kangerdula. They have all kinds of superstitions about it. They have superstitions about almost everything. Demons in the sky, all that."

"I've read a little about them."

"They're a tough people who leave their old people and girl babies out to die when food is short, but everybody loves them. I'm not sure why. They wash their hair in urine because the tannic acid in it is good for furs. They have no jealousy—they think what we call love is a disease. They just want sex from each other and help with the work of living. They love everyone. Everybody always loves them, but I'm not sure I do. God, I'm talking like a madwoman. I can't talk to the old people here. It's a relief to talk. Sometimes I get tired of Swan being so sentimental about the Eskimos, but they are a wonderful people. They know how to survive, they are the ultimate survival experts."

The cabin was growing hotter. He took off his parka and

316

she turned down the stove before taking off her sweater. She was wearing a simple cotton blouse which was discreetly open at the throat. It clung closely enough to her to reveal that she was not as boyish as he had thought. The slight swell of her modest breasts was enough to start him swallowing hard.

"I know what it's like to be lonely," he said, sounding corny to himself.

"How long has it been since you've been home?"

"Only about six months, but it seems forever."

"You're married," she said, glancing at the gold band on his finger. "Of course you're married. The Eskimos never really get married. We talk them into a ceremony, but they have no idea what it means. An Eskimo thinks that a man who will sleep with only one woman is crazy. They don't care what their women do. They have no word for jealousy."

"Maybe they're smart."

"Do you want some more Aquavit?"

"Yes."

"Do you really have to sail in the morning?"

"When we report that there's no enemy activity here, there won't be much for us to do. And my men will want to get moving. They go half crazy when they're not allowed ashore."

"I can't blame them. The Eskimos would love to have them, but they can't stand a whole crew. I heard about your ship at Godhavn or was it Godhaab? Somewhere on the west coast. War makes everybody crazy. God knows I should understand that."

They finished the bottle of Aquavit. Paul never was sure just how it started, but suddenly she was in his arms. He remembered that she helped him when his hands trembled too much to unbutton her blouse, and she said, "Now you'll be sure I'm a German spy. All the German spies try to get you into bed, don't they?"

If the beginning was hard for Paul to remember in detail, he never forgot the middle and the end. At that time in her life, Brit was not a woman who had to be coaxed up to his level of feeling. She was not the woman the sex manuals had described as a delicate violin that had to be played skillfully and gently. She was more like a whole jazz band, or ten jazz bands playing together. She was, in short, the kind of woman whom Paul had dreamed about and who, he had been sure up to this point, did not exist outside his fevered mind.

"I hope I didn't shock you," she said when they had both collapsed in exhaustion.

"It's been a long time for both of us. Give me a few minutes and shock me again."

"I should hurry back. Mr. Swanson will give me hell. He's terribly jealous, if you want the truth of it. He loves the Eskimos, but he isn't one."

"He has *hopes?*"

"Age doesn't mean much when there is no youth around," Brit said with a shrug, as she buttoned her blouse, and suddenly Paul guessed that she was Swanson's mistress. The thought of that hurt, but not as much as it would have before the Greenland Patrol.

"I think I love you," he said, not even embarrassed by the absurd abruptness of it.

"Don't be ridiculous. If icebergs could fuck, you'd love them."

She made her voice hard, but her face was as soft and vulnerable as that of a young girl.

"No," he said, "I'll never forget you, I—"

She broke into tears, covering her face with her sweater. "Don't, *please*, say you'll come back." Her voice was muffled.

"Maybe I can someday."

"Would it help if I broadcast some weather reports to the Germans?"

He laughed and they made love one more time before getting dressed and hurrying out into the dark. It was only four o'clock in the afternoon, but already the sky was black as midnight and the wind howled around the small red huts.

"I can't ask you to the house," she said. "Swan will be waiting for me."

She walked with him to the wharf. When he realized that Nathan had tactfully taken the whaleboat back to the ship, he said, "I'll need a flashlight to signal."

"I'll run you back in our boat," she said.

She started the old diesel in the heavy launch and cast off like an expert.

"What are you going to do after the war?" she asked.

"Live in a little white house in Wellesley, Massachusetts,

318

rake leaves, raise kids and work in a bank, I guess. Or maybe I'll get a boat and sail around the world. Or maybe—"

"My ketch would make it if we fixed her up." She shrugged. "I need to dream. Anyway, promise to do it with me."

"I promise."

He had time to give her only a last quick kiss before she slid the heavy launch alongside the well deck of the destroyer.

"Is that you, skipper?" Nathan called from the wing of the bridge.

"Yes."

The quartermaster stepped out of the pilothouse to take down the third repeater. Brit was already backing the launch away from the ship. Paul could hear the growl of her reverse gear, but she had already been swallowed by the night. A thought he had been holding back now possessed him: he had been unfaithful to his wife. Much had been gained, but he felt that much had also been lost. Maybe youth, he thought—I never had much innocence. Whatever he had lost, this was not the time to brood about it.

Paul slowly walked to his cabin. "Ask Mr. Green to come in," he said to the quartermaster.

Nathan had withdrawn to the wardroom, but he soon appeared.

"What did you find in there?" Paul asked.

"Nothing. Their radio transmitter looks like the original Marconi set. It couldn't possibly have sent the stuff I've been receiving. I suppose they could have hidden transmitters, but I doubt it like hell. They're just a bunch of scared old people."

"I guess."

"Do you want me to tell GreenPat we found nothing here and ask for instructions?"

"I guess we better. They don't even want to let the men ashore for a beerbust."

"Then we better get out. The men are in an ugly mood. Guns was even trying to bribe that Peomeenie guy to take him ashore in his kayak. And Mr. Williams has placed Boats on report for insubordination."

"What did Boats do?"

319

"He called Mr. Williams a fucking pipsqueak. Mr. Williams started it, he got after Boats for never saluting him."

"Jesus, I wish I could bust them both."

"I think I've handled it. I got each aside and gave each hell for being a troublemaker. I said you'd transfer them both to the same weather ship. They seemed to pay some attention."

That night Nathan sent GreenPat a message about their fruitless visit to Angmagssalik. Almost immediately a reply came: "Proceed to Scoresbysund. Look for enemy activity ashore there and remain alert for German ships."

"Scoresbysund," Paul said when Nathan showed him the message. "That's five hundred miles farther north. God, the ice will be thick there."

"I've been picking up quite a few signals from that area," Nathan said.

"Probably the Krauts have some Eskie up there with a hand crank set just to drive us crazy. All right. Have the ship ready to sail at dawn."

Paul slept so soundly that night that Nathan had to shake him the next morning to wake him.

"Dawn's breaking, skipper. Shall I get the anchor up?"

"Do you think you can take her out of the fjord, Nathan?"

"Yes, sir."

"So do it. And ask Cookie to bring me a cup of coffee."

Soon the anchor winch began to grind. Paul thought of the miles of ice and gales ahead. Probably they would find nothing but rocks and a few more old Danes at Scoresbysund. Then they would be ordered to patrol the coast all winter like the Flying Dutchman until finally, perhaps on some dark Arctic night, they found their German ship.

Paul shivered. The memory of Brit's fierce little body was still too strong in his mind to make the thought of death supportable. There were better things to do in the world than to drown in icewater. He wondered how long it had taken the Vikings to recover their taste for battle after one good night ashore.

October was not ordinarily a fall festival in Greenland, and Eskimo Summer, as a few old ice pilots wryly called it, sometimes consisted of a howling blizzard with the temperature diving to 50 degrees below zero, but during the last two weeks of this October of 1942, the weather which the

*Arluk* encountered was surprisingly mild and the ice was scattered enough to allow the ship to keep moving. As he recovered from his brief realization that life could be sweet, Paul kept reminding himself and his men that the purpose of the *Arluk* was to kill Germans, or at least to stop them from getting information about Greenland weather that helped them to bomb the cities of Europe into dust. Despite the brief deceptive peace of an Arctic calm, it was necessary to remember that they were living in the midst of a world war. News reports which Nathan had Sparks type up for the bulletin board told of the Russians still fighting for their lives after winning at Stalingrad. The British were shooting the Germans in Egypt while London burned, and in the Solomon Islands the Americans and the Japanese were killing each other by the hundreds every day. If the *Arluk* found no sign of the Germans but mysterious radio will o' the wisps all up and down the coast, her crew should be grateful, as every man aboard was aware, but contrary to all reason, they felt cheated. Even though they knew that any German ship they found probably would outgun them, most of the men were eager to fight, or pretended that they were, even to themselves. They kept asking to use the guns for target practice, a temptation which Paul resisted not only to save ammunition for some imaginary long battle, but because he instinctively felt that the *Arluk* should remain as inaudible and as invisible as possible. Sound could travel incredible distances over the ice, and the flash of guns could sometimes be seen for many miles. If a German ship was in the vicinity, the odds would favor the captain who was first aware of the presence of the other. Paul asked Nathan to use even his sophisticated radio procedures as little as possible. Because radar advertised its presence to any ship with the proper detection devices, Paul used his set only in the worst visibility, and then only as long as necessary to get his bearings.

When the radar set was on, Paul studied the small glowing chart it provided and tried to understand its implications for Arctic warfare. In the open sea there was great excitement whenever the radar picked up a target, but in the ice field the ship was of course surrounded by objects which the set duly recorded as glowing blobs. It took practice to interpret these. Rocky islands could be differentiated from even the biggest icebergs, and Nathan said that steel ships would show up more clearly than wooden ones. The only sure way to tell a ship from an iceberg, however, would be to study its motion. A ship which lay motionless in a sea of scattered icebergs would be virtually impossible to detect.

As the nights grew longer, Paul began to think of Arctic warfare as a battle between two men in a dark room. The one who stayed still and listened for the other to move would have the advantage. While trying to get to Scoresbysund, or while following orders to patrol the coast, the *Arluk* of course could not remain stationary, but at the first sign of an enemy in the night, Paul would stop his ship in defiance of naval custom, he decided. If an iceberg were nearby, he'd take cover under that, like an Indian hiding behind a rock. There he would stay as still as possible and wait for the Germans to move.

The trouble was, of course, that a weather ship would not have to go anywhere and would not have to patrol—she could just lie motionless in the ice, detectable only when she radioed her reports, and if the Germans had found a way to relay high-frequency signals, one would have to be within sight of her to pick those up. Why in this war did the advantage always appear to be on the side of the enemy? It was certainly easier to hide a radio transmitter in the vast wastelands of Greenland than to find one. Far out in the Atlantic, convoys were always easier to attack than to defend. If there was a God and if he was essentially moral, why did the inexorable laws of warfare always favor the aggressor?

Paul did not know, but he often wished he was in command of a submarine or a torpedo boat that could choose the time and place to attack, not a trawler that had to pretend it wasn't just a sitting duck trying to act like a hunter or a hawk. Yet self-deception was necessary for emotional survival. Paul refused to let himself think of the *Arluk*'s job as defending Greenland from German penetration. No, he was there to attack the Germans with any subterfuge he could invent.

Studying the chart, and trying to imagine himself as a German commander who wanted Greenland weather reports, Paul could see why GreenPat had ordered him to have a look at Scoresbysund. It was the largest harbor in navigable waters on the east coast, a great sound with many fingers extending hundreds of miles into the Arctic wilderness. Any number of small weather stations could be hidden here and supplied, perhaps only once a year, by icebreakers or trawlers. If the Germans had devised a way to send reports which radio direction finders could not pick up, they could be discovered only by accident.

The job of looking for a needle in a haystack would be easy compared to that of looking for small groups of Germans in the limitless wastes of the Arctic, but Paul found some comfort in imagining himself the captain of a German weather ship or of a vessel trying to supply shore stations. Somehow he would have to get into the ice pack and out again without being detected by ships or planes. The mysterious German method of getting weather signals out could not be perfect—in some way it must leave them vulnerable. And any ship could make mistakes, using the wrong frequencies at the wrong time, or sailing in visibility good enough to invite sighting by Eskimos, Danes, aircraft or the lookouts of the *Arluk*, if they were not asleep. The Germans must make mistakes sometimes and luck could not always be on their side. The Germans probably could find a man far more experienced than Paul to put in command of their ship, but Paul's confidence in his own intelligence and determination was growing. Who the hell, after all, did the Germans think they were? All the smart Krauts had gone to America long ago. Who but idiots would take on England, Russia, and the United States at the same time?

His job was to kill a mad dog without getting bit—but it didn't help much when he thought of the possibility of meeting a German icebreaker with eight-inch guns. The whole world was mad when one came right down to it, and the only good part of life was illegal sex.

Two days after they had left Angmagssalik, Paul took dawn star sights, was happy to find that they placed him in a tiny triangle exactly like that drawn in the textbooks, and went back to his bunk. He had just fallen into a state in which his memories of his few hours in the little cabin of Brit's ketch merged with dreams when Nathan called him.

"Skipper," Nathan said, "we see something ahead, looks like a boat—"

Paul jumped from his bunk and ran to the bridge. The sea was as calm and blue as Long Island Sound in summer, and the October sunshine was surprisingly warm. In the

323

distance to his left the ice pack glittered, and a large ice castle was a mile off the starboard bow with smaller bergs scattered in a circle around them. At first this is all he saw.

"One point off the port bow, sir," Guns said. "About halfway to the horizon. I think it's a lifeboat."

Paul adjusted his binoculars and finally he saw it, not much more than a black speck on the sapphire sea. It could be a lifeboat, a very small ship or the conning tower of a submarine.

"Sound general quarters," Paul said. "I want all guns manned and loaded."

"Can I turn on the radar?" Nathan asked.

"Yes. Track it. See if it's moving, however slowly. Seth, take visual bearings."

The klaxon horn honked with ridiculous urgency for so pleasant a morning. The men scrambled to their guns.

"Hell, we's going to get us a lifeboat," Guns said.

"The object is five point eight miles, bearing three five one," Nathan said, opening a pilothouse window. "I believe it's stationary, and I do not believe it's a steel vessel. It's very small."

Probably it is a lifeboat, Paul thought. With all those ships being sunk out in the Atlantic, a few would be bound to drift this way. The object seemed to rock slightly in the calm sea. A lifeboat, almost certainly.

"We haven't seen any signals from it," a lookout called from the flying bridge. "Shall I try to raise someone on blinker?"

"No." The thought occurred to Paul that a drifting lifeboat might be some sort of trap. Perhaps his imagination was overactive, but some smart German might leave a boat in an open stretch of sea, hide behind the nearest iceberg and wait for a ship with a captain sucker enough to stop and pick it up. If the Kraut had seen the *Arluk* coming, he might have had time to arrange that. Or the lifeboat could be booby-trapped. It could be loaded with explosives—or with dying sailors too weak to signal.

I'll have to come close enough to inspect it, try not to take any unnecessary chances, Paul decided. "Come right slowly," he said. "I'm going to circle around all those icebergs just to make sure we're alone out here. Then I'll approach to within about half a mile of whatever that is up there and let our whaleboat go in to make a close inspection."

The crew, Paul was sure, thought he was crazy as he methodically toured all nearby icebergs, like a child looking behind bushes in a game of hide and seek. No German ship was in evidence. Turning finally toward the small dark object, Paul approached close enough to make sure that it was a lifeboat. Through his binoculars he could see a standard gray double-ended hull. It could be empty, full of corpses or men too weak to sit or stand. As he approached to within half a mile and slowed, Paul saw that some objects were lashed around the sides of the boat, dark blobs that made no sense at all, but maybe they were life preservers tied there to give more stability. The boat was very low in the water. It could be heavily laden with explosives or it could be half flooded.

"All right, lower the whaleboat," Paul said as the *Arluk* glided to a standstill. "Boats, take two men armed with automatic rifles. Don't touch that damned boat—it could be booby-trapped. Just go close enough to see what's there."

The crew lowered the whaleboat smartly and Guns provided the rifles with clips. As soon as the whaleboat pulled away, Paul got the *Arluk* moving in a broad circle. Eight knots was not fast, but it was better than presenting a stationary target, and excessive precautions were better than sitting there fat and dumb.

The whaleboat slowed as it neared the lifeboat, chugged slowly around it at a distance of only about thirty feet and headed back toward the *Arluk*, which stopped her engine. Boats was standing in the stern.

As he came near he called, "They're all dead. It's full of decomposed bodies, some in lifejackets lashed all around the gun'lls—"

In his mind's eye Paul could see the lifeboat pulling away from a sinking vessel, maybe a troopship. The boat was full and the sea was swarming with men trying to get into it. They had lashed as many as they could to the gun'lls, and had all waited there dumbly hoping for rescue while they froze to death.

"Skipper, pass us a can of gasoline," Boats said. "We'll douse the bodies and we can set it off with the twenties."

"Could we read a funeral service or something?" Williams asked.

325

"No," Paul said. "We're setting no fires."

"You're just going to leave them here?" Nathan asked.

"You could see the smoke from a fire for thirty miles at least."

"It doesn't seem right," Nathan said.

"Could we give them a burial at sea, wrap them in flags or something?" Williams said.

"We'll take no decomposed bodies aboard here—"

"Skipper . . ."

"If I were dead I wouldn't want to do that to a ship's crew," Paul said. "Now get that whaleboat aboard and let's get out of here."

No one talked as they brought the whaleboat aboard.

"Captain," Williams said, "could we at least read some kind of a service over them?"

"I don't *have* any service—"

"Any Bible—"

"I don't have a Bible and I doubt if any man in the crew does."

"I have one," Williams said. "Can I read from it?"

"You can if you make it fast," Paul said. "Don't ask me to stop the ship."

Williams went to the wardroom and soon appeared with a black book in his hand. Standing on the fantail he read something as the *Arluk* passed the lifeboat, but the rumble of the screw made his quavering voice impossible to understand. The men stood hatless except for Boats, who faced the lifeboat and held a salute for thirty seconds. When Williams stopped reading, he ducked into the wardroom with his book, and the men off watch went to the forecastle for coffee.

"Could we sink the boat with gunfire?" Nathan asked.

"You can hear gunfire for twenty miles."

Boats came to stand on the bridge beside them. He was shivering when he said, "Sharks got the legs of the people in the water and seagulls were pecking at the eyes of the men in the boat. There wasn't a hell of a lot left to burn."

"They're *dead*, Boats," Paul found himself shouting. "Do you think they'd be happier in some damn bronze coffin in a churchyard?"

"No."

"Let the dead bury the dead," Paul said. "That much of the Bible I remember. Our job is to stay alive."

There was a moment of silence.

"Did you get the name of the ship that boat was from?" Paul suddenly asked.

"The S.S. *Garden City* out of New York."

"Log it. Nathan, give him the position. And don't send any radio reports about it until you can tack it on the end of something you damned well have to send."

"Yes, sir."

"And Boats, pick a shore party of twelve men who can handle rifles without shooting themelves. When we get to Scoresbysund, I'm not going to have any damned Danes telling me what I can do ashore—I'm going to search every settlement."

"Aye, aye sir."

"And don't make Guns part of that shore party. We're going ashore to look for radio transmitters, not to get laid ... Tell yourself that too, captain ... Nathan, tell Chief Banes to give us all the RPM he safely can. I want to get to Scoresbysund while this weather holds. Let's get on with it."

# CHAPTER 35

Scoresbysund turned out to be a vast almost landlocked sound, full of bays, islands and winding fjords. It was surprisingly free of ice and the smooth red granite mountains around it looked oddly warm in the short but sunny last days of October. The glittering ice of glaciers that pressed to the sea between the mountains, the odd indigo color of the water and the spectacular blazes of color at sunrise and sunset created breath-taking scenery, but the endless maze of ice, rock and water was a nightmare for anyone looking for a German weather station. The settlement there was about twice the size of the one at Angmagssalik, with similar wooden cottages and sod huts. The dozen or so Danes that Paul found were all old, but unlike the people at Angmagssalik, almost embarrassingly eager to help in any search for Germans. Paul felt ridiculous as with the aid of an armed shore party of twelve men he searched tiny attics and clothes closets in search of radio transmitters.

"Hell, any damned German would bury his equipment in the snow long before we got ashore," Paul said to Nathan. "If they have a weather station in any of these damn fjords it would be in a sod hut covered with snow. They wouldn't even have to have a radio tower. They could rig a damn aerial to the side of a mountain and take it down when they saw us coming."

"They'd have to get supplies," Nathan said wearily.

For two weeks they explored Scoresbysund. When Nathan was not on the bridge he sat hunched over his radio equipment. No signals came from the immediate vicinity, but on high frequencies he often picked up scraps of code which might have skipped from almost anywhere.

They visited two small Eskimo settlements in Scoresbysund in addition to the main one. Here the natives lived in sod huts hardly bigger than dog kennels. They appeared childlike, eager to please and ultimately inscrutable. Regardless of what they had heard about the Germans, Paul was sure that they would help any white man who arrived with a few boxes of sugar, booze and canned meat, or even if he had nothing to offer them but a smile. Apparently the Eskimos really did love everyone, but these had been told not to fornicate with sailors. When the men in Paul's shore party gave them gifts of tea and Spam and kept repeating the word, "ping-ping," the Eskimos giggled, laughed, shook their heads and retreated en masse into their huts.

Soon everyone aboard the *Arluk* felt completely frustrated, and no one was sorry when Commander GreenPat ordered the ship to go back to patrolling the coast. More radio activity had been picked up near Cape Farewell, and the *Arluk* was told to steam south.

Just as the pilotbook had warned, November marked the beginning of the Greenland winter. On October 30, low-scudding gray clouds wiped out the last scrap of blue sky, a northwesterly wind began to howl and the temperature took an abrupt dive to forty below zero. The only good part of this situation was that the northwesterly wind moved the ice pack a few miles off shore, leaving a sheltered belt of sea at the foot of the mountains in which the *Arluk* could maintain full speed. Although the clouds obscured the moon and stars, there was an eerie glow caused by the surrounding ice reflecting the slightest amount of light. The long Arctic nights were not as black as Paul had feared. With the radar turned on every hour long enough to give brief glimpses of the surrounding terrain and icescape, Paul found his job of navigation surprisingly easy.

As the ship approached Angmagssalik, Paul could not help but start toying with the idea of stopping there to see Brit. Any number of excuses could be found—he could tell Commander GreenPat that he had to put in to find a quiet spot for engine repairs, or that they were receiving more radio signals which needed investigation. For such deceptions the cooperation of the entire crew would be needed, however, and that he would not get in a port where the men were not allowed ashore. From reports of the crew of the whaleboat, the men had learned that Paul had met a Danish woman, and though neither he nor Nathan had said anything about it, they had accurately guessed why he had disappeared for three hours. If he brought the ship back to Angmagssalik without orders, their genial envy would turn to scorn, with even the possibility of official complaints from a few when they got back to the base. And although those could be handled, there was a certain code which even men like Mowrey would not break. Commanding officers were not supposed to run Coast Guard cutters like yachts, stopping at any port where a woman was available.

Shortly before they reached the latitude of Angmagssalik, the wind let up, shifted to the east and brought in heavy fog. The ice pack slowly began to close with the shore, and the *Arluk* took to twisting slowly through the bergs in search of sea room. Nathan was becoming skillful at this and was better than anyone else at interpreting the glowing masses on the radar screen. Paul spent much of his time in his bunk, trying not to think of Brit, who was now only about twenty miles away, but the strong delicate hands with which she had held his head while she kissed him were impossible to forget. Unrequited love—that was a funny old-fashioned phrase, but he felt he had suffered that all his life before meeting Brit. Maybe not unrequited love, but unrequited passion, a sense of that had eaten at him during most of his nights with Sylvia. He didn't blame his wife or tried not to, but there had been so many wasted nights, and without Brit, he might have died feeling that there was something badly the matter with him.

It was a pleasure to dream of going back to Brit after the war. He could find a pilot who could fly him in a PBY into Angmagssalik. They would anchor the seaplane off the end of the wharf and Brit would come out to meet him in the launch. The first thing he'd do when he got ashore was tell off old Swanson, tell him never to go near the girl again. Then they'd fix up the little ketch enough to sail her to Newfoundland for a complete refit. After that the world, the South Sea islands, where the wind was always warm and there was no ice outside of a highball glass.

As he thought about it, the dream began to appear like a practical plan, except maybe it would be better just to fly Brit out of Angmagssalik and buy a better vessel in Newfoundland or Nova Scotia. Maybe he could get enough money together to build a boat especially for world voyaging. In Paul's mind the design for such a vessel was quite clear. A yawl would be faster than a ketch on the wind and Brit would be good at helping him with the big mainsail. Why did he have to keep imagining Sylvia in tears? She would have her house in Wellesley, after all, and it wouldn't take her long to find a man who really wanted to become her father's helper in the banking business. No, Sylvia would not weep long, and after years of misery in Greenland, Brit would deserve a voyage to the South Seas with a man she loved. By that time he would deserve a few good years. . . . What route would they follow to the South Seas? The Panama Canal, the Galapagos, Cocoa Island and finally Tahiti—he had read a dozen accounts of small boats that had taken that route. They would rig twin headsails that would make it unnecessary to touch the tiller in the tradewinds—Paul was so lost in his dream that it was hard for him to come back to reality when Nathan called from the bridge, "Skipper, you better come here." Nathan did not shout, but there was a tone in his voice that jerked Paul from his fantasy and caused him nearly to leap from his bunk. Fog made only a small circle of gray water visible, and it was already getting dark. Nathan was peering into the hood of the radar set.

"I think we got something here," he said softly. "Whatever it is, it's big and it's moving."

"How far away?"

"Twenty-three miles, bearing two five one degrees. He's only about two miles off the edge of the ice pack. It looks like he's following it north, on a course of about zero four five degrees."

"How fast?"

"I can't tell yet. Maybe about eight knots."

"Let me see."

At first Paul was confused by the glowing masses on the screen which were reflected from the ice pack. Then he saw one small but bright blob that was crawling slowly like a luminescent bug across the glass so close to the ice pack that it seemed to be touching it. Automatically Paul went to the wing of the bridge to see it, but the fog was so thick that even the guns on the bow were only vague outlines.

"Skipper, if we both maintain course and speed, he's going to be about fifteen miles away when he's abeam of us."

"Do you think he's picking up our radar?"

"I can't tell."

"Can you tell whether he's got radar?"

"I've got Sparks working on it. He hasn't picked up anything yet."

"Stop the engine," Paul said, remembering his plan to remain hidden as long as possible. "If we stay here, how close will he pass us?"

"About fifteen miles, if he holds his course. Shall I report this to GreenPat?"

That obviously was the ship's first duty, to spot enemy ships and report them. Still, in this fog aircraft could do nothing, and the radio could warn the Germans, if that's what it was, even if Nathan was smart enough to avoid direction finders.

"What are your chances of getting through to GreenPat without having him pick you up?"

"Maybe fifty-fifty."

"Hold it for a while. Maybe it's not a Kraut, maybe it's one of our own cutters."

"They'd tell us if one of ours was headed up here."

"They're supposed to, but there could be a screw-up. Look, you better report it to GreenPat. That's doing it by the book."

"How am I going to explain that we have a radar contact when we're not supposed to have a radar?"

"Tell him how we got it. This is no time to play games."

Nathan went to the wardroom to write the message. Word of a radar contact had quickly spread throughout the ship, and men were crowding into the pilothouse.

"Clear the bridge," Paul said. "There's nothing within twenty miles of us."

It must be a trawler or an icebreaker or it wouldn't be so close to the ice pack, Paul thought. Maybe six- or even eight-inch guns. But its job was sending weather reports or supplying shore stations, and it would probably rather run than fight. Once it knew it had been detected, it would probably try to escape in this fog before aircraft could find it. Probably the skipper of that ship would try to sink the trawler that had discovered him only if that wouldn't take him far out of his way. The Germans weren't crazy enough to risk air attack for revenge. Were they . . . ?"

Hurrying to his chart table, Paul plotted the position of the *Arluk* and that of the stranger. That put the German, if that's what he was, about seventy-five miles off shore, and only about thirty miles south of Angmagssalik. Studying the chart, he saw a fjord named Supportup-Kangerdula. The ship could easily have come from there. Brit had told him that the place was known for frequent foehn winds, and that the Eskimos had superstitions which kept them away from it. Had she been trying to warn him away from it? Whether or not she knew it, had the Germans picked it for a base simply because they were aware they would not be bothered there? Paul felt suddenly certain that the German ship had just left this strangely named place. Probably it had supplied a base there for the winter before the weather got really tough and had been waiting for this fog to cover its escape to sea.

And probably the people at Angmagssalik knew about the base only about thirty miles to the south of them. Maybe they were too afraid to tell the Americans about it, afraid of reprisals, and maybe they were active collaborators. The thought that Brit might be a traitor who'd made a fool of him cut deep, but now was not the time to worry about that.

Mr. Williams suddenly appeared with a plain-language report that Nathan had written and was now coding. It started by giving the *Arluk*'s latitude and longitude. It went on to say, "We have radar contact in thick fog with unknown vessel bearing two-five-oh degrees, range twenty-three miles. Her course is about zero four five degrees, speed about eight knots. We have radar set because we took one from wreck of DD-77. Request air support as soon as weather permits and instructions."

Paul added two sentences: "Strongly suspect enemy base is established at Supportup-Kangerdula Fjord. Suggest air reconnaissance."

"Tell Nathan to send this with the addition," he said handing the clipboard to Williams.

"Are we going to close with the radar contact?" Williams asked.

"I don't know yet."

Paul wondered whether he really wanted to rush to meet a vessel that was bound to be more heavily armed. There could not be any real urgency in stopping an empty supply ship homeward bound, if he had guessed right about that, but maybe he should give it a try. Still, he'd done his main job of spotting what probably was an enemy ship and a German base. Now he should track the ship as long as he could and hope like hell for the sky to open up enough for the planes to get in their licks.

The sky gave no promise of clearing. Nathan returned to the bridge, chased Guns away from the radar set, and stared at the glowing insectlike image of the stranger, who had made no obvious change in course or speed. As he studied his chart Paul realized that the *Nanmak* had been sunk at a spot only about twenty-five miles to the south of their present position in the early summer. Maybe she had blundered onto this German while he was on his way in to build the base.

"I've got Sparks sending out the message," Nathan said. "We're using frequencies an ordinary ship wouldn't monitor, but this guy may not be ordinary. If he picks us up, he may change course and speed."

For five long minutes Nathan peered into the radarscope. "There, I'm afraid he picked us up, skipper. He's making a sharp left turn. He's ducking right into the ice pack. Damn it, he's going to be hard to track when he gets into that big stuff."

"Then we better follow him," Paul said. "Give me a course."

"Two-five-five. He's slowing down, skipper. He's not going to be able to go very fast through that ice."

"Ahead slow. Come right to two five five. Come up to full speed. Tell the chief to give us everything he safely can."

"How close to him are you going to go, skipper?"

"Close enough to keep tracking him. Hell, if he has six-inch guns and radar fire control, how close can we come to him without getting hit?"

"I'd guess we'd be safe if we stay five miles from him," Nathan said. "We haven't been able to pick up any radar signals from him yet."

"So we'll try to ride his tail. I don't want to lose him."

"Skipper, there's some scattered drift ice about three miles ahead. I may not be able to pick up all the growlers on this thing."

"Post a double bow lookout and tell them to look sharp. I want to close with him before we lose him in that ice."

It was almost completely dark now, as well as foggy. The old trawler trembled and leapt ahead as Chief Banes pushed the engine to flank speed.

"Better come right about twenty degrees," Nathan said. "There's a fairly big berg dead ahead."

Paul changed course. A few minutes later he thought he could hear the waves breaking against ice a few hundred yards to his left, but he could see nothing.

"You can come back on course," Nathan said. "We're beginning to close with him now. He's down to about four knots, and he's steering a crooked course through the ice."

"What's the range now?" Paul asked a few minutes later.

"Down to about nineteen miles. I've just lost him behind a big berg. He'll come out. I think he's trying to get back into a fjord."

"Growler," the bow lookout called. "Dead ahead!"

"Right full rudder."

The trawler's bow swung. Going to the port wing of the bridge, Nathan saw a twenty-ton hunk of blue ice lying only a few inches above the black water. It was almost within spitting distance.

"Come back to course now," he said. "Ahead half. He's not going anywhere very fast in that ice."

The distance between the two ships diminished slower now, but they still gained a mile and a half in the next hour. When the range was down to fifteen miles, Nathan reported that the edge of the ice pack was only a mile ahead, and Paul slowed down.

"I don't see any really good leads, but the stuff isn't very close-packed on the edge," Nathan said. "He got into it all right."

Paul climbed to the flying bridge, where he could see a little better. There wasn't as much fog now and there was a trace of moonglow. He ducked around the end of a huge mass of ice looming ahead and twisted between two smaller bergs. He had become skilled at maneuvering his ship through ice. Damn it, I bet no Kraut can beat me at this, he thought, and rang for more speed.

"We're still gaining on him," Nathan called a few minutes later. "He's down to about two knots now. The ice is heavier where he is."

"Range?"

"About fifteen miles."

Mr. Williams appeared on the flying bridge holding a clipboard under his arm as he climbed the ladder.

"Message from GreenPat, sir."

"What's he say?"

Williams took a flashlight from his pocket.

"Jesus, don't put that thing on! Just tell me what the bastard says."

"Sorry, sir. He just says our radar contact can be presumed enemy. He wants us to keep tracking her but not to get closer than necessary. He says he'll send air support as soon as the visibility improves, but according to his weather reports that might not be for twenty-four hours or more. Then he says that reconnaissance planes have photographed Supportup whatever-it-is fjord and found nothing, but there still could be a camouflaged base there. Then he ends with 'Proceed to investigate when present mission is accomplished. More on this later.' "

"Marvelous," Paul said. "What are we supposed to do, steam right into an enemy base?"

"I don't know, sir."

"Give the message to Mr. Green," Paul said, and called into a voice tube, "Come right slowly. I see a pretty good lead. Ahead full."

With both ships in the ice pack, Paul found he could gain on the German at the rate of about one mile an hour if he pushed the *Arluk* as fast as he could. He was in a hurry because he was afraid that if the German reached the maze of fjords which were now about fifty miles ahead she could find a niche in some ravine where she could disappear entirely. The German skipper was adept at placing large icebergs between himself and his pursuer. He often faded entirely from the radar screen, and as he zigzagged from one lead to another he sometimes popped up in unexpected places. The thought occurred to Paul that he might suddenly double back to destroy his tormentor, but the radar would give warning of that. Although the German followed an erratic course, he was obviously trying to gain the shelter of the fjords as quickly as he could.

The important thing was to keep track of his position so that he could report it to the planes, Paul knew, and the closer he could cling, the less the chance of losing him. He kept the *Arluk* barreling ahead.

At about midnight the north wind piped up, scattering the fog and occasionally blowing the clouds away from the moon. The chances for a dawn clear enough for an air attack looked good. The *Arluk* men were excited, and even those off watch stood on deck. It was a wild night, with the ice on all sides of them glittering brightly for a few minutes when the moon sailed between the clouds, and the trawler careened through crooked channels which sometimes narrowed so much that she had to push her way through. Standing on the flying bridge and shouting commands through the voice tube to the helmsman and the quartermaster at the engineroom telegraph, Paul felt curiously elated, as though he were chasing something much better than a ship he did not really want to catch. Now for a while at least, the *Arluk* was really the hunter, an avenger of sorts. No man aboard would have admitted such a thought, but they all felt something like that.

"Skipper," Nathan called suddenly at about two in the morning. "It's stopped dead. He's in heavy ice. Maybe he's stuck."

"What's the range?"

"Eight miles."

"Stop the engine."

In the sudden quiet Paul was aware that the wind was no longer blowing so strongly. The moon had retreated behind the clouds, and in the dim glow that was left he could see tendrils of fog advancing again like the scouts of a great army. He could see nothing ahead.

"The visibility is closing in again," he said. "So what? If he's stuck, we can wait him out all winter."

"Do you suppose he knows we're this close to him?" Williams asked.

"I don't know. Nathan, tell GreenPat the Kraut is stuck and get a weather report from him," he said.

GreenPat had apparently been sitting glued to his radio receiver. Without a moment of delay his answer came back. "As long as German is motionless, wait for weather clear enough for air attack. Best guess is that will be two days. Well done. GreenPat."

"Nathan," Paul said, "maintain sea watches. Let's you and me take turns on the radar. If he gets loose I want to know it right away."

"Sure, skipper. I've got it for the next couple of hours."

Paul returned to his cabin and lay down in his bunk. Well, he thought, we have met the enemy and he is stuck. So far the advantage is ours.

And suddenly Paul wondered what it must be like to be aboard the enemy vessel. She probably was not an icebreaker, the ice was not thick enough to stop a ship of that kind. She probably was a big trawler, or more likely, one of the small freighters rugged enough for light ice conditions. A freighter would make a better supply ship. He might have just left his base after having waited for heavy fog to cover his escape through the ice to sea and home. Although Paul had fallen into the habit of thinking of the Germans in Greenland as sailing big ships with huge guns that made them almost invulnerable, in the short run, at least, this German must feel like the underdog, no matter what the caliber of his weapons. Greenland was already full of American air bases which sent whole flights of Lightnings roaring low over the ice whenever the weather cleared. Darkness and fog were the only friends of the Germans here, as they were the friends of criminals everywhere. With this heavy fall fog and the long nights of winter already on them, the German must have been confident as he started home. Then suddenly his radioman must have said something like, "Captain, I think I have something here . . ." Maybe they had radar and maybe they did not, but they certainly had picked up the *Arluk*'s radio, which had been close enough to blast the eardrums of the German Sparks if he had been monitoring the right frequencies.

Had the German been scared? Had he felt that chilling

of the intestines and testicles, that foretaste of death which Paul felt when he imagined a great enemy ship looming out of the fog? Or had he thought, hell, the Americans are crazy enough just to send little trawlers up here with popguns. I'd like to eat this fellow for breakfast, but my orders say to get out before he can call in aircraft without taking the time to fight.

Maybe this German captain was the one who had sunk the *Nanmak* after managing to take her by surprise while the *Nanmak*'s radar was broken down. Perhaps he hadn't been sure whether the *Nanmak* had had time to report him, and maybe he had gunned down the lifeboat as well as the ship because he soon expected to hear the roar of the Lightnings, as the German captured by the *Northern Light* had about six months before. Fear breeds hatred and hatred produces cruelty, a chemical formula they don't teach in the basic ROTC courses. If this German captain had sunk the *Nanmak* and machine-gunned the survivors, he might feel guilt, and that might redouble his fear, his hatred and his cruelty. Even though he probably had orders to run not fight, he was probably itching to use those big guns he probably had if an American trawler were foolish enough to chase him too closely, unlucky enough to catch him.

Perhaps the Germans had debated whether they should run or fight, but then in the murk of the fog they had seen the ice pack closing around them. A freighter could not twist and turn the way a trawler could, it could not push aside even the smallest bergs. The ice would grind at her sides. If the German panicked, as even Germans might, the captain would call for all the power he had. Then a thud as he tried one turn his ship couldn't make and the bow glanced off one iceberg to hit another. He would try to back her down, but if he had hit with any speed, she would be too firmly embedded in the ice. The current and wind would soon move more ice into her wake, and she would be frozen in, stuck until the next gale broke up the pack or the spring thaw.

But of course the German could not wait for the spring thaw, and probably not even for the next gale. His position had been reported to the airbases—the first crackle of the *Arluk*'s radio had told him that. And within an hour or a half hour of the time the fog lifted, the German would hear the distant roar of the Lightnings, which would shatter his ears as they approached, guns flickering on the leading edges of their wings, tracers arching toward the motionless ship.

What kind of men were now waiting this kind of death only about eight miles away? It was nice to imagine them as movie villains, short, fat, bald Erich Von Stroheim with his monocle, the man you love to hate, or athletic wooden-faced men in Nazi uniforms giving that ridiculous stiff-armed salute, a gesture that made them look as though they were trying to push the world away from themselves. But probably they were not doing much saluting now as they waited in the ice to die. Probably they were wearing not fancy uniforms but foul-weather gear much like his own. And probably they didn't look like movie villains. In the first place they wouldn't put a senior officer in command of a supply ship bound for Greenland. He was probably some young guy. Why did Paul imagine him confident, cocky, a little taller, a little stronger than himself, the image of his brother, Bill?

Brothers, we are all brothers, Nathan had wryly observed when he had heard about the empty vodka bottle discovered by the *Nanmak*. Brotherly love—that had been a phrase which had struck Paul as ironic ever since he could remember, because his own brother had mostly loved beating him in the endless competition of their life together. But the Germans of course were not really brothers, not even distant cousins. They were simply enemies, legally declared such by the majesty of the United States government and their own . . .

Love thy enemy—had Christ himself ever been able really to do that? Maybe that was why he had been remembered two thousand years—no one else had ever been able to manage it. Carefully as he might search his soul, Paul could find no trace of love for the men who had gunned down the *Nanmak* and her helpless crew.

Love—the very word suddenly seemed to ring with irony.

"I think I love you," he had said to Brit, and she had told him, "Don't be ridiculous, you'd love an iceberg if you could fuck it." He sort of loved her for that reply, the kind of answer a woman would have to spend a year in Greenland to make.

For the first time in his life Paul found himself wondering what in the world love really was. He had, in his fashion, loved Sylvia, loved her for years, no doubt about

339

that, despite the fact that he had never really been convinced that she loved him, and their whole relationship had been mostly a study in frustration. And love or no love, he had been unfaithful to her the first chance he got. In his heart he suspected she probably would be no more faithful to him if some young officer danced with her very well at the U.S.O. and told her she was the prettiest girl in the world.

Love. Maybe the reason everybody kept talking about it so much was that it was so rare. He didn't love his enemy, he didn't love his brother, he didn't love his wife enough to remain faithful to her, and even his mistress, if that's what Brit had briefly been, had told him that talk about love was ridiculous. Had he ever loved anybody? How about his own father and mother? Once he had loved them—it was oddly comforting to be sure of at least that. When Paul had been a small child, his father had been such a warm, exuberant man. Before the great crash had knocked out his business and before the Depression had taken all hope of making a comeback from him, his father had seemed to Paul to own the world, or at least run it. Aboard his big yawl Paul's father had seemed to command the elements themselves, laughing at summer thunder squalls, always able to find his way in fog or dark of night. Paul never had been able to understand why the people of the United States weren't smart enough to kick Hoover out and make his father President. If they did that, the country would have had no problem at all. And in those early days, before the Depression had changed his father's swinging walk to the hesitant pace of an old man, Paul's mother had also laughed and hugged a lot. While they had lived in the big house on Beacon Street, she had read *Treasure Island* and *Tom Sawyer* aloud to her sons on winter evenings in front of a glowing grate of pine logs in a marble fireplace, and had played a game called Mousie which mostly had involved tickling them. . . . "Money isn't important," his mother had often said. That had been her favorite sentence, along with, "We all must love each other," but after the money had mysteriously disappeared and they had moved to the cramped cottage in Milton, love or most of its outward manifestations had also taken flight. The great lie, an affectionate deception no doubt, but a lie as hurtful as any other because it meant the truth could not be faced —the great lie about his father being an artist of genius

340

had begun, had been started more by his mother than his father, but the whole family had gone along with it. And after giving up her circle of friends in Boston, such fine Boston ladies who valued friendship until a friend got suddenly poor, his mother had become president of the garden club in Milton, despite the fact that she really didn't have a garden at all, and had gone on to more garden club triumphs, which took her mind off a husband who couldn't sell his paintings, despite his genius, and two sons who were growing more and more difficult to handle each day—

"Skipper," Nathan said, poking his head into the cabin. "We can hear a plane coming. Probably they've sent a PBY to feel out the weather."

Or it could be a German JU-88 sent to try to help its brother. Running to the wing of the bridge, Paul saw that the fog was still much too thick to give any plane a target. The *Arluk* was as safe as the German ship was. He listened hard for several seconds before he heard the drone of engines far overhead. Undoubtedly the German heard them too. Even if it was a JU-88, the Lightnings would take care of it if it stayed around while the fog lifted.

Probably the German captain was out on the wing of his bridge too, listening to the plane far above the fog banks. As Paul returned to his cabin, and told the quartermaster to have coffee brought from the galley, he wondered whether the German captain were doing that too, if they were two men bound to duplicate many of each other's actions until the Lightnings closed in to stop the game.

The plane droned away above the clouds and Arctic silence reigned again.

Climbing into his bunk, Paul wondered whether the German skipper was doing *that* too. Did he have a wife who often did not seem to love him and another girl he had briefly met in some port who made him feel marvelous?

The coffee did not arrive. Restlessly Paul walked to the galley, where he found Cookie cleaning the range.

"I'll have your coffee in a minute, skipper. Damn fool Blake let the oatmeal boil over."

"No hurry, Cookie."

The men off watch in the forecastle were playing cards, reading well-thumbed magazines in their bunks and listening to a radio announcer who was telling about German

341

defeats in Russia and in Africa. For those Germans who understood English, these American news broadcasts must sound like the voice of doom. Did they stay tuned to German broadcasts which gave them only news of victories? Did they too feel certain that in the end they would win the war?

Returning to his cabin, Paul realized that he really knew nothing at all about his enemies. If they were unlikely to resemble movie villains, they also were unlikely to be exactly like himself, despite his German blood. What must it have been like to grow up in Germany during the much worse depression that that country had had ever since the end of the last war?

Maybe the Germans were just dumb, people who did what they were told without asking why. That was one common conception of them and maybe it was true. What American really knew or much cared when the chips were down? Life was like a cowboy movie after all, and the only important question was who got the draw first.

But he would like to talk to them in their own language. "Say, fellows," he would begin, as he came wandering in from the foggy ice floe. "Let's talk a bit. Would you like to give up instead of die?"

Even if he could walk through the ice floe, such a visit would be as absurd as it seemed sensible. But why not try on the radio? The idea startled Paul. Why hadn't such an obvious move occurred to him before? Getting out of his bunk, Paul went to the bridge, where he found Nathan still glued to the radar set.

"Nathan, could you come in here a minute?"

When they were both in his cabin, Paul shut the door.

"Nathan, that Kraut doesn't have too much of a chance. He can't run and he won't fight long when the Lightnings get him."

"Maybe," Nathan said. "Don't be too confident—"

"I'm just trying to figure out the truth of it. What would you think of radioing him and asking if he wants to give up?"

Nathan's lips tightened.

"I wonder if they gave the *Nanmak* that chance? Or the men in her boat?"

"Hell, maybe this isn't even the same ship that got Hansen. Anyway, shouldn't we try to take prisoners? Wouldn't

342

that be the best way to find out about any base they've got ashore, their whole weather operation?"

"I guess so," Nathan said. "Maybe we should ask GreenPat about that. The Krauts could say they were going to give up and then clobber us when we came near. Didn't you have something like that in mind, if we could pull it?"

"Yeah, but we could wait until the weather clears and there are planes overhead. We could order them to take to their boats or walk out on the ice."

"They could still leave a few men behind to clobber us when we got near."

"The planes could sink their damn ship as soon as they'd abandoned it. We could just pick up their boats."

"Which might blow up in our faces. I'm sorry, Paul, but I don't trust the bastards."

Nathan was about to go on and tell Paul about his wife's disappearance in Poland, the near certainty that she had either been killed by the Germans or put into a concentration camp. Or a brothel—the Germans had put many Polish women into their military brothels. Nathan's whole body contracted every time that thought came to him, as it did now. How could such an emotion be shared?

"You told me once never to forget that war is a game of hard ball," he said. "If we get a chance to kill Germans, I say kill 'em. If you give them the slightest chance, they'll throw a hand grenade right down your throat."

"We could make 'em stand naked on the ice and wait for us to pick 'em up. And it would be easier to get them to tell us what they've got ashore than to go look for ourselves."

"They wouldn't tell you."

"Aren't they the ones who are so proud about being able to make people talk? Maybe they'd tell me where their harbor is mined if I put a bunch of them on the bow of my ship as I headed in."

Nathan shrugged. "Maybe," he said. "In any case, I'd ask GreenPat before making any direct contact."

"Let's do that," Paul began, and at that moment they heard the roar of a distant explosion, followed by three more. Paul's first reaction was that the Germans were shooting at him, but they were too far away for that. Had they blown their own ship up? No, of course they were trying to dynamite their way out of the ice, a maneuver of

343

desperation that had often been tried and seldom worked.

Nathan ran back to his radar set. "They're moving so much ice, I can see it here," he said. There were three more explosions. "I think they rigged up a whole string of depth charges," he said. "Look."

There were two more explosions as Paul bent over the hood of the radar. He could see blips appear for a fraction of a second to the east of the blob that was the ship. "Hey, he's starting to move," he said. "Maybe he did make it work. Have a look."

"He's got a couple of miles to go before he finds any kind of a real lead," Nathan said. "But I guess he's got plenty of TNT—"

"We better get closer to him," Paul said.

"I wouldn't want to be too close when the weather clears," Nathan said. "I don't think the aim of our fly-boys is all that good."

"Right. We better break out every American flag we have and spread them on the deck of the bridge. Those fly-boys are apt to sink us and congratulate the Kraut for spotting us."

"I'll see to the flags," Nathan said. "What will the fly-boys do if the Krauts spread out American flags too? I wouldn't put it past them."

"We better tell GreenPat to tell the pilots that the Germans have the bigger ship. Are you sure of that, by the way?"

"I'm pretty sure it's a steel ship, but I can't guarantee how big it is."

"Well, we might as well get close enough to take a look at him when the weather clears. The fly-boys rate a description of their target."

"I wouldn't really know what the range of his guns are even if they knew how big they are," Nathan said. "Sometimes I get so goddamn tired of my own ignorance—"

"Don't worry about it. There's always going to be an iceberg between him and us. Tell the engineroom to stand by. I'm going in close enough to get a damn good look at him when this fog lifts."

As Paul backed the *Arluk* out of the ice and began exploring a narrow lead that wandered in the general direction of the German, he felt he could go quite close if he wanted to. The trawler could get through ice much better than a freighter could and he was quite sure that he was dealing with a freighter, because he couldn't have caught up with a trawler. The advantages of maneuverability and power would be his. The only advantage the German probably had was bigger guns, and in a game of cowboys and Indians, cannon rarely were decisive. Rarely . . .

As Paul pushed slowly from lead to lead through the fog, using the radar to pick the areas where the pack was most scattered, he heard more explosions ahead. How were the Germans getting the depth charges, if that's what they were using, so far ahead of their ship as they inched along through broken ice? Had they rigged some sort of K-gun to throw heavy charges over the bow? If so, the charges must be fused to explode on the surface of the ice, a job Nathan had been experimenting with, and which he had found tricky, despite his ability to do almost anything with a pair of pliers and wire.

Maybe the Germans had worked out simpler solutions. A small boat couldn't get through the ice ahead of the ship, but in some ice formations men could climb up and down hills of ice, rolling or dragging heavy charges of explosive far ahead of the vessel. What a desperate effort that must be, yet it or something like it was succeeding. The German's motion was barely discernible, but the ice bridge between them and the nearest lead was narrowing.

If the German got in the clear he could still escape before the fog lifted, but the lead he was working so desperately to reach didn't go more than five or six miles before ending in a high ridge of ice castles jammed together. Maybe he didn't have radar after all, or maybe his set was as temperamental as the *Nanmak*'s had been. It was hard not to feel sorry for the men sweating out there on the ice, stumbling and swearing over the heavy loads of explosives, cheering every time a short channel was blown clear, all apparently without knowledge that they were getting nowhere.

Anyway, the Krauts were trying—Paul had to give them that. Clearly they were not yet in a mood to give up. Everything in the world might be wrong with the Germans, except they rarely turned out to be cowards. After being ashamed of his German blood ever since he had first heard of Hitler, Paul was absurdly glad to find one small enduring reason for pride. The sons of bitches didn't have any

345

idea in the world how to fight a war when it came to grand strategy, but when it came down to blood and guts, they weren't easy . . .

Just stupid, or so it seemed as the Germans kept blowing up the ice to reach a blind lead. The *Arluk* was doing fairly well in ice she could wriggle through, and the range shortened every hour.

"About six miles now," Nathan called from the radar set, and later, "Five and a half. He's just about getting to that blind lead."

"How far can he go in that?"

Instead of answering, Nathan said, "Say, skipper, something's happening here."

"What?"

"He's like a damn amoeba splitting in two. I think there are *two* ships there, a big steel one and a small wooden one that we haven't been able to pick up until now . . ."

Of course, Paul thought— a supply ship with a trawler to escort her through the ice, as the *Arluk* had escorted bigger vessels. That would explain how the depth charges had been dropped well ahead of the larger ship. Two ships would be much harder to fight if they got close enough to the *Arluk*. Two would be just as vulnerable as one when the Lightnings finally arrived, but before that there was always the possibility that the German trawler would come looking for her tormentor. In the ice she would be just as maneuverable, and might well have bigger guns, though she might have to stand by her supply ship . . .

"Stop the engine," Paul said. "We'll just stay close enough to keep them both on the scope. Nathan, tell Green-Pat that we've got two of them now."

The thought that the smaller German ship might come looking for him before the fog and night cleared sent a chill through Paul's belly, but he was quite sure now that neither ship had radar that was working. If they did, why had they labored so hard to blast their way into a dead end? Without radar they were blind in these conditions, but the blessed gray box at least enabled Paul to see.

"Get Boats up here," he said suddenly to the quartermaster.

Boats soon appeared. "Boats, we got what looks like a trawler up ahead there with a supply ship. I suppose he might leave his big baby when there's no chance to save her and come looking for us. I don't much like the idea of two trawlers close together out there in the ice—to the planes we'll look just the same. So get some red lead and paint the deck on the flying bridge and the forecastlehead red."

"Sir, it will never dry with the weather like this. The men will track it all over the ship."

"I don't give a damn. I want those fly-boys to know we're us before they get close enough to see flags. Don't paint the well deck or the fantail. We won't have to go where the paint is until it's time to use the guns anyway."

"Aye, aye, sir, but it's going to be one hell of a mess."

"Not as much of a mess as the Lightnings could make of us. Any more objections, Boats?"

"No, sir."

"Get it done before dawn. And tell Mr. Green about it so he can tell GreenPat. Tell him to tell GreenPat to tell the fly-boys."

"Aye, aye, sir," Boats said, and a few minutes later Paul heard him shout, "All right, you guys, grab paint brushes. You wouldn't believe it, but we're going to paint our fucking decks red right now."

Paul went to the radar set. It looked as though it had gone out of adjustment. Instead of giving a glowing map of the surroundings, the screen showed nothing but a crazy pattern of pulsing green lights. With growing panic Paul turned the knobs which were supposed to focus the image, but they only made it worse. Forcing himself to sound calm, he said to Flags, "Get Mr. Green up here. Tell him the radar's out of whack."

During the seconds that it took Nathan to run to the bridge Paul stared at the malevolently flashing screen and thought, of course—anything that can go wrong inevitably does go wrong at the worst possible time. The radar, like the big diesel engine, had always seemed a complete mystery to him, and it made him feel sick to realize that the safety of himself and the entire ship depended on such mechanical mysteries. He was helpless. He wished that he had been born in the years of sailing ships when there was nothing to worry about but the wind, the sea and men.

Nathan arrived, his open parka flapping, and Paul stepped aside to let him look at the screen. The gaunt face was grim as he adjusted the knobs.

"Something's the matter with it," he said. "I'll get my tools."

"Can you fix it?"

"Skipper, I'll sure as hell try."

Nathan ran to the radio shack and a few minutes later he came back with a toolbox. Word spread quickly through the ship that the radar had gone out, and a ring of men gathered to watch Nathan remove the screws at the base of the gray metal box that covered the intricate mechanism.

"Clear the bridge," Paul said. "Let him work."

The men withdrew to the wings of the bridge, where they waited in unaccustomed silence. There was a very slight tremor in Nathan's long fingers as he withdrew the screws. Lifting the box off, he turned it upside down and put the screws in it.

"You better put this on your bunk, skipper," he said.

Paul did so and returned to stare at the nest of multi-colored wires, glass tubes and a jumble of aluminum boxes projecting from other boxes. Nathan took a voltameter from his toolbox and began to probe with it. The bridge was so quiet that the tick of metal against metal sounded like a clock.

"Skipper, this may take me an hour or more," Nathan said. "There are a lot of fuses, connections and tubes to check."

"We'll wait," Paul said.

"I've got a lot of spare parts and the chances are I can fix it. Damn it, I'll build us a new one if I can't."

Reassured some, the men on the wings of the bridge drew away from the doors and a few went forward for coffee.

Watching Nathan work made Paul nervous, and he was sure that Nathan did not need an audience. He went to his cabin and tried to figure out what he should do if it took Nathan a very long time to make his repairs, or if in the end they proved impossible. Without the eyes of radar the *Arluk* was certainly in much greater danger. Her edge, in fact, was gone, all the odds changed. Faced with two enemy ships and an enemy shore base, Paul's instinct was to run or stay hidden in the ice, but now if he was to keep track of the enemy's position he would have to press close enough to see and be seen.

Still, the odds were that Nathan could fix the set. Jewish magic, Mowrey had called radar, and the old man had said, "I don't wonder that the damn thing goes out the minute you get to sea."

Nathan, Paul found himself thinking, work your magic now!

Minutes, then hours went by very slowly. Too restless to stand still or sit down, Paul went to the forecastle for coffee. The men were playing checkers.

"How's it coming, skipper?" Guns asked.

"Mr. Green is working on it. He knows his business."

"I bet he really could build a radar set," Cookie said. "He used to be in that business."

Paul marveled at the men's confidence. With a few tools and spare parts, Nathan could build a whole radar set in a few minutes, they were sure. At times like this they needed to believe that the officers they so often hated were gods. Paul was suddenly sure that now they thought even he had mystical powers. He'd better have . . .

Paul finished his coffee and carried a cup up to Nathan, who was still bent over the set. There was no longer a tremor in his long fingers. as he tightened a tiny screw, but he was sweating and paused to wipe his face and hands with a handkerchief.

"Want some coffee?"

"Later," Nathan said, and Paul gave the coffee to the quartermaster . . .

Two hours crept by before Nathan sighed and said, "I think I've got it." Paul was standing on the flying bridge.

"He thinks he's got it," Flags said, sticking his head above the top rung of the ladder.

Paul hurried to the pilothouse in time to see Nathan adjust the knobs. The screen glowed green again, flickered and suddenly snapped into focus, showing a clearly glowing little map of the surrounding ice.

"I guess that's it," Nathan said, grinning.

The men cheered and Paul found himself pounding Nathan on the back. "Do you want a drink? We can find a bottle somewhere."

"No," Nathan said.

The beaming approval of the men pleased but embarrassed him. He didn't know how to respond to it and he suddenly felt exhausted. For about an hour he had fought a growing fear that he never would be able to figure out what was wrong with the set, or that he would find a defective part he couldn't replace. In the end it had proved to be only a short circuit, a burned out connection that had taken only five minutes to fix after it had been uncovered.

With the men still congratulating him, Nathan put the gray box back in place and tightened it down. Studying the screen, he said, "Skipper, I can't see that anything has changed while the set was out but we better keep a close watch on it. I need to lie down for a while. Can you handle it?"

"I got it," Paul said. "Get a good rest. Tell Cookie to bring you anything you want. I wish I could give you the Congressional Medal."

# CHAPTER 36

Nathan walked slowly to his bunk in the wardroom and stretched out. He remembered the long days when he had lain in that bunk with nothing whatsoever to do because Mowrey had declared him incompetent, and he wished suddenly that he could tell his wife of this triumph, this discovery that he could fight the war well, better than most men. In his own way, he was strong. If Becky was huddled in some concentration camp, he was sure that she would like to know that.

The thought of his wife starving behind barbed wire was too much for him, and he caught his breath. He was shocked to find that he hoped she was dead, that he could stand the thought of death for her, but not suffering the degradation. Death, after all, came to everyone, it was part of the natural order, and so was suffering at times, but degradation was not natural, it was the ultimate perversion.

Almost certainly she was dead, he felt in his bones, because like him she would not really be afraid of death. If she was dead, dead at the age of twenty-five, her life would not be wasted any more than the life of a songbird is wasted because it is short, and beyond that, her life continued to have meaning if he could understand it, or so he tried to tell himself. But to understand his wife he had to

350

understand her family, a fact he'd been all too slow to learn. Both her parents had come to Poland from Russia in their early youth. They were the descendants of rabbis and scholars as far back as they knew, and the survivors of pogroms over the ages. They were survivors—that was perhaps the key fact about them. Her father had survived economically by learning almost twenty languages well—there was always a place for him in some university. Beyond that he had survived by retreating into his house and preserving an attitude of aloof, often humorous detachment toward the surrounding world. Perhaps to make up for the pleasures they missed outside their house, he and his wife preserved or invented a ritual of family life which was even more elaborate than their orthodox religion. When Nathan first met them he could not get over how formal and gravely polite this husband and wife were to each other. They raised their daughter as a devoted horticulturist might tend a rare rose. They'd come to America when Becky was nine years old because they were old hands at seeing trouble before it started. Their apartment in Brooklyn was nowhere near as gracious as their house and garden in Warsaw, and Brooklyn College did not treat its professors with the respect given by any Euopean university, but America, despite its noise, clash and confusion, was safe, at least relatively safe. Professor Kochalka and his wife made no attempt to make friends in America. They continued to live as though they were in a fort surrounded by savages and had to invent all the pleasures of life for each other.

There was never a child more protected, encouraged and loved than Becky, but she was not spoiled because she tried to please her parents as hard as they tried to please her. She spoke softly, as everyone else in that house did, and when her mother was ill, as she often was, Becky soon learned to cook the familiar elaborate meals for her father. Nathan at the age of sixteen was astonished to see that before she brought her father a half grapefruit for dessert, she often carved it into the shape of a little basket, as her mother did.

Becky, of course, had to go to school, and she was perhaps surprised to find that outside her familiar fort there actually were few real savages. Most people in Brooklyn treated this gravely polite little dark-eyed girl with affection. Her teachers and most of the neighbors loved her. She was quiet but her eyes danced with mischief and she got on well with other children. It was almost impossible for people to dislike her because Becky obviously was in love with the world.

"You're like the three monkeys," Nathan said to her once when they were about nineteen. "See no evil, hear no evil, speak no evil."

"What's wrong with that?"

"If you sit there covering your eyes, your ears and your mouth, you're pretty helpless, aren't you?"

"I can run. I always keep my eyes and ears open when I run. Often my mouth too."

It was true that running was always her solution to any troubles that she couldn't escape by smiling. She wouldn't even argue with other students at college if their voices grew strident. She would just smile and go.

Yet she wasn't really meek, as Nathan soon discovered. If she thought she was right she usually found ways to get her own way. She liked being the center of attention, and worked hard to earn the approval of others. She danced exuberantly and gracefully, she played the piano almost professionally, and she always dressed with a quiet elegance. Both in high school and college she was popular with groups which hardly spoke to each other.

She was transparently happy—that was always her greatest attraction. Although she was beautiful to Nathan, she was not an unusually pretty girl, but her face so often radiated a kind of delight with everything and everyone. People felt *liked* when talking to her and they were right.

The first conflict she was unable to escape concerned Nathan and her parents. Sometimes he thought that she expected him to move into her father's home when they got married, like a brother. She never seemed to enjoy their own apartment much, and could not understand why he didn't want to eat most of his meals with her parents. It was possible that the reason her father decided to go back to Poland was not only his growing homesickness, but his realization that his daughter had to learn to live without him.

But Becky was not just an ordinary bride who was too immature to leave her parents, Nathan slowly realized. The fact was that her parents' ways of life offered a kind of serenity that she needed and which she wanted Nathan to learn. The telephone was not always ringing in Professor

352

Kochalka's house—the old man had installed a switch in the wire and kept it turned off almost all the time. He had disconnected the doorbell, and there was something about the professor which did not encourage people to drop in without an invitation. The radio was never turned on in that house except for special programs chosen from the newspaper. Heavy curtains closed out most street sounds. There was always a healing kind of quiet there, unlike any house Nathan had ever known, and completely unlike the crisis center his father and mother ran.

Conversation in Professor Kochalka's house was a leisurely art. No one raged, no one tried to convince anyone of anything. The food was always prepared both to taste and look good and was served on handsome china. Although the professor was far from rich, he served good wine in crystal glasses, and the family kept drinking toasts to celebrate Becky's good marks at school, a paper her father had just published, a wedding anniversary, a birthday—it seemed to Nathan that they were forever drinking toasts to each other. Professor Kochalka and his wife were stout, middle-aged people, but they acted almost like a courting couple, jumping to do little errands for each other, holding open doors, and exchanging compliments. Nathan admired them, and if he hadn't wanted to spend most of his time alone with his wife, would have been a willing guest.

No, that was not entirely true. Nathan had been brought up in a house where people argued passionately, and where everyone was too busy to waste time over elaborate meals. He could not help himself from eating fast and trying to start political debates.

"You certainly have some very interesting opinions," the professor would say.

"Do you agree with them?"

"With many parts of them. Are you a student of Kant?"

Nathan was not a student of Kant. Almost his entire education had been technical. Professor Kochalka made him feel ignorant, immature and uncivilized, the Great American Boor.

But Becky was right—her parents had invented an enviable style of life, and it was not surprising that she missed it when they went back to Warsaw. Because Nathan had many friends and several jobs and hobbies at the same time, their own apartment was always a bedlam in contrast, no matter how much he tried to learn from the professor.

Lying in his bunk now, Nathan thought that Becky might have known more real happiness in her twenty-five years than most people experienced in a long lifetime. She had in a profound sense lived well, and had added to the happiness of almost everyone her life had touched. The fact that such a life was short did not make it meaningless.

No, but the bastards still killed her or locked her up, Nathan thought, and fury shot through him like an electric shock. The image of his wife in a grave or in a concentration camp made all his attempts to accept her loss philosophically seem ridiculous. She was Jewish and the Germans had made the cold decision that the Jews weren't really people, they could be killed like rats. And right now two German ships lay in the ice less than ten miles away.

Nathan could not sleep. He took a hot shower, shaved and put on clean clothes. Then he went to the bridge. "I've had all the rest I need, skipper," he said. "I'll be glad to take over for a while."

# CHAPTER 37

All that night Nathan and Paul took turns watching the radar. The German ships lay motionless until about two in the morning, when they made another attempt to escape. The small ship twisted her way to a lead which soon came to a dead end. It explored the situation like a rat in a maze. She could push her way, twist and turn through crevasses which stopped the larger vessel, and she kept running out a few miles in every direction, first east, then south, west and finally north as she looked for broader leads. For a half hour she was headed directly toward the *Arluk*, and Paul had his finger on the button for the general quarters alarm when she turned east again.

Tired as he was, Nathan would not leave the radar set. To prepare himself for what might be a big day, Paul turned in. He had slept less than three hours when Nathan called him.

"Skipper, I've lost the little one," he said. "She might be lying on the other side of the big one, or behind any of the big bergs."

"Could she be headed this way?"

"She might dodge from berg to berg for a while, but I'd pick her up if she kept moving for long. Both ships are playing possum, I guess. The only reason I haven't lost the big one is that I've learned to recognize her blip even when she's not moving."

They're playing a waiting game, Paul thought, but what did they have to wait for? Stepping to the wing of the bridge, he stared into the darkness. The fog was not quite as thick as before, not overhead, anyway. The moon was invisible, but a faint glow was managing to get through.

If the fog cleared before morning or on subsequent nights, the Lightnings could attack if Paul could illuminate their target with star shells. The tiny three-inch gun on his bow was the only one he had that could fire those, and he was ashamed to realize that he did not know its effective range.

"Quartermaster, get Guns up here."

When Guns arrived on the bridge he was blinking sleepily. His long hair and black beard looked as though they had not been combed in weeks.

"Guns, how close do I have to be to a target before you can put a star shell over it?"

"Well, that three-inch twenty-three ain't much good, sir. A mile maybe? I don't trust it."

"At a mile how many shells would you have to fire before you got one over the target?"

"You couldn't count on the first one, or the second. Maybe the third."

"If the enemy has six-inch guns and good fire control, we wouldn't last long if he was only a mile away, would we?"

"Not if he could see us, sir, and not if he had radar."

If there was no fog, the German would see the flash of the three-inch gun, and would be quick to respond. Why take such a chance when the Lightnings could do the job almost without risk on the first clear dawn?

Doing nothing was obviously the best course of action, if it could be called that. The large German ship almost certainly was stuck again and the smaller one was remaining motionless to achieve invisibility in the ice pack on radar. The *Arluk* remained within radar range, but too far away to hit or be hit. This was a battle without motion, without sound and without anything that could be seen, except for the glow of the *Arluk*'s radar. The weather remained the same, foggy with some small evidence of clearing overhead. The weather reports GreenPat forwarded to them every hour kept prophesying continued fog for at least forty-eight hours.

The big question in Paul's mind was how long the small ship would stick with the larger one. Would the skipper of the German trawler, if that's what she was, feel obligated to aid his charge in a hopeless fight against Lightnings to the point of sinking with her, or would he cut and run? And *when* might he cut and run, at the last possible moment, or at the first sign of clearing skies? If he cut and ran, would he try to hide from the planes, a job which would not be impossible for a well-camouflaged ship in the ice pack? Or would he try just to put as much distance between himself and the doomed supply ship as possible? Would his main objective be to escape or to attack the *Arluk* when the planes returned to their base?

Paul tried to imagine what he would do if he was the captain of the smaller German ship. I wouldn't let myself be sunk with the supply vessel, he decided—that would be pointless bravado. As soon as I saw that the weather was starting to clear I'd run and hide. I'd jam the ship between two big icebergs, cover her decks with snow and hang white canvas or even sheets over the guns. As soon as the planes had gone I'd try to kill my enemy before he got to my base.

Of course the captain of the smaller ship probably would not be the man to make the final decision. The senior officer in charge of the whole operation probably was aboard the larger ship. If he were a coward he might order the smaller ship to stand by, but it was not wise to count on a Kraut senior officer being cowardly. Stupidity, Paul felt he probably could count on, though. A stupid, brave officer might decide to let both his ships go down together in a blaze of glory.

Except of course I really don't know what the hell they are going to do, Paul thought—uncertainty is my only certainty. Right now the odds are in my favor, or appear to be, and so I just wait . . .

Nathan did not sleep at all that night. He was so afraid that some motion of the ships would not be detected by others that he sat on the stool crouched over the radar hood until he literally could not keep his eyes open anymore. He did not trust Paul to take his place for the simple reason that as captain Paul had too many responsibilities and might be called away from the screen at a crucial time. After reminding Sparks of the necessity to remain alert, Nathan turned the machine over to him and staggered to his bunk. Only two hours later he was back on the bridge, drinking coffee and staring at the screen. Nothing on it had changed. The larger ship was still motionless, the small one invisible in the ice.

As usual, the weather reports did not prove to be accurate, and they spent four days locked in this motionless struggle while the fog thickened instead of going away. Paul had never seen it so thick—from the gundeck he could hardly see the door to the forecastle. The men appeared to forget that the enemy was so near. Even Sparks, who had access to the radar images of the Germans, still kept complaining about the loss of the nude photograph of his bride when he was off watch.

"Can't you just shut up about it?" Boats asked.

"Well how would you like it if you knew some guy was drooling over a picture of your wife, jerking off?"

This really was a form of infidelity, Sparks obviously felt. He suspected Guns of stealing the picture, but the gunner's mate was too big to confront directly. While Guns was on watch Sparks looked under his mattress but found nothing. Blake reported the search to Guns, who in retaliation hid Sparks's mattress in the hold while Sparks was on radar watch. Paul had to take time out from trying to figure out what the Germans would do to make Guns bring back Sparks's mattress.

Did the Germans have such ridiculous problems while they waited in the shadow of sudden death? Paul guessed that they probably did. The possibility that they were sitting around praying was small . . .

By the fourth day of waiting Paul had the curious feeling that he and the Germans would be locked into this frozen battle forever. He went soundly asleep, leaving Nathan at the radar set, and he was astonished when Nathan awoke him to say, "Skipper, the fog looks like it's about to lift."

Paul rushed to the wing of the bridge. It was twenty minutes after ten in the morning. Heavy fog still surrounded the ship, but the rising sun was starting to burn a hole in it.

"I've got some motion from the small ship," Nathan said from the radar set. "He's been hiding behind the big one all this time, but now he's starting to work away from her to the south."

Nathan stared at the scope. "It looks like he's got heavy ice for about five miles," he said. "If he gets to that big lead he'll be free if he can beat the planes."

Paul wondered whether the *Arluk* should stay near the larger ship or chase the small one. Deciding that this decision should be left to GreenPat, he had Nathan send a message. While Nathan was doing that, Paul followed the progress of the small ship on the radar screen. It crawled toward the beginning of a lead and suddenly began to move with astonishing speed.

"Get Mr. Green up here," Paul said to the quartermaster.

Nathan arrived on the run and looked into the scope as Paul stepped back from it.

"Boy, he's really moving," he said. "What the hell is it, a torpedo boat?"

"Not in this ice," Paul said. "Quartermaster, get Mr. Farmer up here."

Seth Farmer had been keeping to himself as much as possible for a long time, almost as though he had reached retirement age aboard the ship. He arrived looking flustered, still buttoning his parka, his face heavy with sleep.

"What's up, skipper?"

"Seth, what kind of a ship can go damn fast in the ice, a small wooden ship?"

"How fast?"

"Fifteen knots, maybe even close to twenty," Nathan said.

"In pack ice?"

"Dodging through storis ice," Paul said.

"It must be a hunter-killer. No other kind of vessel could do that."

"Hunter-killer?" Nathan said.

358

"They were built for hunting whales," Paul said. "I've read about them, but I've never seen one."

"They go out with a mother ship that supplies them and processes the whales," Seth explained. "The hunter-killer has a harpoon gun on the bow, and he's designed to chase whales in the ice."

"How big a ship is it?" Paul asked.

"Not big, but it's a ship, not a boat. The hunter-killers sail in company with their mother ship."

"Do you suppose that big vessel we have on the screen could be a whaler?"

"Maybe the Krauts are using one for a supply ship. No one would be whaling out here in the middle of a war."

"Tell me as much as you can about the hunter-killers."

"Oh, maybe they're sixty or seventy feet long. Deep with the screw well down to get it away from the ice, but very narrow and all engine to get speed. They don't have to carry no cargo."

"How many men are on them?"

"In peacetime, maybe only about five."

"What kind of guns could they put on one?"

"No heavy stuff. Maybe a popgun like ours on the bow instead of the harpoon gun. Antiaircraft guns. Depth charges and maybe torpedo tubes. They wouldn't make a bad torpedo boat, though they ain't as fast as the light shoal-draft jobs."

"Have we converted any to war service?"

"The navy tried to make sub-chasers out of some. The trouble is, they can't keep to sea for long without a mother ship. They're all engine and have hardly any fuel tanks. And they're hell on their crew—a cramped, narrow, miserable little vessel, wet as hell."

"But good in ice."

"The screw is well down and they can turn to bite their own tail. They're a hell of a lot heavier built than a plywood torpedo boat."

"What would be the effective range of their torpedoes?"

"Hell, I'm not sure. Maybe half a mile if they got lucky."

"What's their top speed?"

"I don't know, but you have to go some to catch a whale and that's what they're designed to do."

The small ship had placed an ice castle between herself and the *Arluk*. She had disappeared from the radar screen. At twenty knots she'd be a hundred miles away in five hours, Paul figured, and even if she had only an hour before the sky cleared, she'd have plenty of time to hide in the ice pack, a tiny splinter of a ship in a sea of ice mountains.

"Nathan, tell GreenPat what we got out here," Paul said. "Get Williams to do the coding—I need you up here. Tell him there's no point in our chasing the hunter-killer. He's gone off on a bearing of about one seven three, speed estimated at about eighteen knots. Tell him the sun is starting to burn through. It might be clear enough for the planes in an hour."

While the message was being sent Paul went up to the flying bridge, which had been painted as ordered with red lead. With his feet still on the ladder, Paul looked around. The fog was burning off fast—there were a few patches of blue sky directly overhead, although heavy gray curtains still surrounded the ship. A whaler, Paul thought—just because the small vessel was a hunter-killer, did the supply ship have to be a big whaler? If she was really a factory ship, she might easily mount eight-inch guns and would like nothing better than to use them on the trawler which had spotted her. But there was no real reason to suppose that such a monster had been sent to establish a small Greenland base. His original guess that the supply ship was probably a medium-sized freighter might still be right.

Paul fought an impulse to push closer to the German just out of curiosity and a desire to be in on the kill. No, nothing would be gained by such risk. How strangely hard it was to do nothing! Going to the bridge, he tapped the barometer, noting that it was rising. The temperature was also rising with the sun, and was now hovering around zero, which seemed relatively warm. Now the fog ahead was really starting to thin. He could see a half mile over the bow, a jumble of icebergs about the size of the ship with veins of water twenty or thirty feet wide between them. A trawler could maintain a speed of four or five knots through ice like that. How fast could a hunter-killer zigzag through it? A new element of real danger had been added to his situation, Paul realized. At any time now, in fog or darkness, the hunter-killer could launch a torpedo attack. Of course, there'd have to be just enough visibility to allow the Germans to see their target and the *Arluk*'s radar should give warning—unless the hunter-killer darted from behind an iceberg. As long as that nimble little ship was on the loose Paul had an idea that he was not going to get much sleep. If the weather cleared quickly, the planes might find him. If . . .

The circle of blue sky overhead continued to widen. Paul imagined the officers aboard the big supply ship looking up at it, gauging the amount of time they had left before the Lightnings struck. Would they now be in a frame of mind to surrender? Should Paul ask? No, it would be dangerous to try to take them off their ship while the hunter-killer hovered nearby. If the Germans wanted to give up, they could easily initiate the process by radio. Except Paul had never heard of such a thing happening. The *Northern Light* had captured her trawler only after the planes had almost sunk it. When it was time to die, almost all crews just died without radioing any last pleas for surrender, pardon, or help, even if the odds were hopelessly against them. Naval warfare seemed as unforgiving and almost as formal as a bullfight.

The curtains of fog around the *Arluk* kept retreating and with surprising suddenness evaporated, leaving the trawler in a sea of scattered icebergs of all sizes which glistened so brightly in the sun that the men went for dark glasses. Hurrying to the crow's nest, Paul adjusted his binoculars and studied the sector where the radar reported the supply ship to be. For several minutes he could see nothing, but then dead white against ice which sparkled more, he saw the outline of a high bow, a pilothouse and a mast. The ship, a freighter, was about halfway to the horizon. At that distance she looked much smaller than he had expected, like a child's ship model discarded in the ice. Her most prominent feature was her high, old-fashioned smokestack, which the heat from a steam engine had turned dark gray. As he was squinting in the glare, a puff of smoke appeared on the bow of the ship, and a fraction of a second later he heard a sharp crack.

"They're shooting at us," Paul said, but it seemed that the distance was much too great for accuracy. "Nathan, we better go behind that big berg over there. He might get lucky."

Nathan got the *Arluk* moving. There were more blossoms of smoke from the bow of the supply ship, but no one aboard the *Arluk* could see shells landing anywhere. I guess it makes them feel good to shoot at us while they're waiting for the planes, Paul thought—probably I'd open fire too if I were in their shoes—his feeling of tolerance abruptly came to an end when a shell blew the top off an iceberg about 300 yards to his right. The next shell was coming even closer . . . he heard its high whine but didn't see where it landed.

"Full speed, let's get the hell out of here."

It took about ten minutes to gain the shelter of an iceberg big as a fortress. The taste of danger had whetted the crew's appetites.

"I wonder where the hell the planes are," Paul said.

"Sparks is down there sending out M's for them to home on," Nathan said. "That's what they wanted and that's what they're getting. They'll be here any minute. Boats, get a smoke flare ready. They want that too."

Nathan had hardly spoken when they heard in the distance an intense hum that quickly turned into a roar, more thunder than one would expect even from Lightnings. Low on the western horizon three dots hardly bigger than mosquitos materialized in the thin blue air above a ridge of ice. It was impossible to imagine how such tiny, almost microscopic objects could make such an all-encompassing noise. Rapidly they grew larger, materializing into what looked like model airplanes which had been painted an olive drab in defiance of Arctic camouflage.

"Let go the smoke bomb," Paul said.

Boats threw an object like a yellow bottle as far as he could from the well deck. As it settled on a piece of flat ice, it started to gush torrents of black smoke. Seeing it, the planes altered course slightly. Growing to monstrous size as they approached, they roared only about 500 feet above the *Arluk*, waggled their wings in recognition, and sped toward the German supply ship. Figuring that the Germans would be too busy to shoot at him, Paul eased the ship from behind the iceberg enough to see what was going on. The three Lightnings, which had been flying in a V-formation, began to play follow the leader and sped in a wide circle around the German ship. More smoke puffs appeared on her bow and little catpaws of explosive dust appeared far below and behind the planes. Her smaller antiaircraft guns opened up, sending out a few tracers like Roman candles.

"Jesus, I thought the Krauts were such hot shots," Guns said.

It's all a matter of form, Paul thought—if you have

guns you're supposed to shoot, even if the targets are flying 400 miles an hour out of range. The Germans were doing what was expected of them, just as a well-bred bull paws the ground. The odd twin-hulled planes continued to speed at a safe distance around the supply ship. The lead plane let out a few bursts to check his guns, and the two others followed suit, falling a little out of their single line formation to do so. It was all very methodical. Paul wondered what the Germans were thinking as they saw the planes warming up to execute them. Did the whole life of a man about to die in battle flash through his mind as it was supposed to do in the brains of drowning men? Perhaps not. Probably the Germans were hoping to take at least one of the planes with them and the heat of even hopeless battle was enough to burn out any rational thoughts. If the Germans were like the American sailors Paul knew, they were more apt to die cursing than praying or thinking fond thoughts about loved ones.

Suddenly the three planes went into a much broader circle, swooped down to a level only about a hundred yards above the tallest icebergs and headed toward the ship. The rattle of their guns was not as impressive as the other roars, hums and whistlings they made. Nothing seemed to happen as the three planes rocketed from the stern over the bow of the supply ship. The German guns kept blinking like signal lights in their wreaths of smoke. As the planes finished their run and turned into another wide circle, the smoke around the German's guns suddenly rose higher. At the base of the gray stacks amidship there was a ruddy glow, but still the guns on the bow and stern continued to fire, even when the planes circled almost out of sight before they came back.

On their second run the planes left the ship afire from stem to stern, but incredibly a few tracer bullets arched out of the smoke and flame in pursuit of the attackers. It was clear that men were dying on that ship and fighting heroically, but the whole scene was curiously lacking in dignity. After making each pass, the planes waggled their wings to each other, obviously an expression of sheer zest, and the men aboard the trawler cheered. Nathan stood on the wing of the bridge staring through his binoculars, his face a grim mask despite the fact that he always had been too soft-hearted, in Paul's view, whenever an enlisted man received the slightest punishment. Paul tried to remind himself that the men aboard the supply ship might be the very ones who had sunk the *Nanmak* and gunned down her boat, but somehow on this sparkling morning, the two events did not seem to be related. Well, Paul reminded himself, the Krauts have played the butcher long enough . . . "Let's move in closer. I want to take prisoners, it's the easiest way to find out about their base," Paul said.

While the planes continued to strafe the ship Paul drove the *Arluk* through scattered ice toward the plumes of smoke. It was possible that the hunter-killer was lurking near enough to make a torpedo run at any time, but Paul felt that she would stay hidden until the planes left. Then anything could happen, unless the planes happened to find the little ship out there in the ice before they went home.

Leaving the supply ship an inferno of flame and black oily smoke, the planes began flying a search pattern over the surrounding miles of ice. Separating, they each chose a sector to cross and recross, flying just above the peaks of the highest ice castles. Paul kept hoping that he would see one of them execute a little roll to announce the discovery of the hunter-killer, but they just wove back and forth between horizons, following their search pattern. Paul wondered how close they would come or had already come to the little German ship, which might even have worked her way under a projecting ledge of one of the mile-long icebergs near the coast. He'd stay there until the planes left.

I undoubtedly outgun a little ship like that, Paul thought, but he has torpedoes, and neither of us is worth a damn at a range of more than a mile. In the ability to destroy each other, we must be roughly equal. He has the advantage of speed and maneuverability; I have the advantage of being able to stay at sea almost indefinitely while he'll have to get back to his base soon before he runs out of fuel.

Suddenly Paul's strategy appeared obvious to him: instead of pursuing the hunter-killer he would hide near the mouth of his base and let him come to him. Supposing that the base was in Supportup-Kangerdula Fjord, that shouldn't be too difficult. But now was not the time to think that out. If he could rescue some survivors from the supply ship they might be persuaded to give all kinds of useful information . . .

It took Paul almost an hour to reach the burning hulk of the supply ship. As he drew near he could see that her skipper had jammed her in the ice, where she lay nearly level, still belching smoke and flame, though not so fiercely now. No men could be alive at her guns or on her decks. Paul could see no life as he studied the vessel through the binoculars. She was more of a small passenger liner than a freighter, he saw now—one of those ships which had carried both freight and passengers before the war. She carried many more lifeboats than a freighter would. Three were burning in davits on her port side, four on her starboard. Apparently only one boat had been lowered. Had all but one boatload of men stubbornly stayed aboard long enough to burn?

The one missing boat was nowhere in evidence as Paul stopped his engine and drifted a thousand yards to windward of the burning hulk in widely scattered storis ice. If the men of this ship had machine-gunned the *Nanmak*'s boat, they were more likely to hide in the ice than to rush out to be rescued. There was not much wind, and sometimes it backed enough to bring the men of the *Arluk* the smell of burning oil and perhaps, they imagined, seared flesh. The flames from the German ship made a greedy, sucking noise. The shrieking roars of the planes continuing to search for the smaller ship all around them made speech difficult. Paul climbed up to the crow's nest to see where a lifeboat might hide. The *Arluk* was surrounded by bays and islands of ice, any of which could conceal a boat.

"Skipper, when the planes go maybe we should yell that we won't hurt them," Nathan said. "I could rig a loudspeaker."

"We'll try it."

It wasn't long before Sparks came to the bridge to say that the planes were running out of fuel and were heading back to their base.

"The lead pilot called me direct," he reported. "He said they can't find a damn thing out there, but a PBY will continue the search this afternoon."

With more exuberant dips of their wings the three Lightnings went skidding low over the ice toward the Greenland coast. The sudden silence was like the end of intense pain. No sound could be heard except the licking of the flames aboard the gutted supply ship, and even they were subsiding. Sparks set up a loudspeaker on the flying bridge and handed Paul the microphone.

"I am talking to any survivors of the German ship,"

Paul called, the mechanism making his voice boom out over the sea. "We will take you prisoner and will not harm you. Throw all arms overboard and row your boat toward our ship."

After a brief silence during which nothing happened, Paul repeated the message in German, a procedure which caused a few members of his crew to look a little startled. He said it three times and had just given up when the bow lookout called.

"Boat, sir! Two points on the port bow."

Coming from behind the point of a large iceberg, a gray ship's boat came into sight. She was crowded, and the men at the oars handled them raggedly, getting them all mixed up. A man in the stern stood and shouted in German through cupped hands: "We are the survivors of the *Norway*. Are you Americans?"

"Yes," Paul said in German. "Do you speak English?"

"*Nein.*"

The boat struggled a hundred yards closer before the man standing in the stern shouted in German, "Do you promise to take survivors aboard and treat them as prisoners of war?"

"We're Americans," Paul said in German. "We do not gun down people in open boats."

The lifeboat seemed to hesitate before struggling onward. Through his binoculars Paul studied it. He could count twenty-six men. Dressed in parkas and foul-weather gear, they didn't look much different from his own men. About a third were bearded. Three were lying on thwarts and a few others wore makeshift bandages. Twenty-six men! It was at least theoretically possible that they could pull a surprise and try to take over the ship.

Paul had never thought of taking so many prisoners aboard, and realized that such a large number of men would always be a potential danger which was maybe why the Germans had gunned down the *Nanmak*'s men. The supply ship, the one enemy he had been pursuing so long was in flames, but it had been replaced by three enemies: the hunter-killer, the shore base the *Arluk* was supposed to investigate, and, potentially, at least, a whole company of Germans who would be living in their midst. Did enemies always multiply like that when you killed them?

# CHAPTER 38

As the men in the lifeboat rowed clumsily toward the *Arluk*, Paul said to Nathan, "This prisoner business could be more of a problem than I thought. Where are we going to put them all? Maybe we ought just to tow them in their boat into Angmagssalik. Then we could keep a machine gun on them."

"They have wounded aboard," Nathan said. "We could put them under guard in the forecastle. The rest are probably cold, but I don't see how we can take care of them without risk aboard here. There's not much room in the hold, and one of them might be crazy enough to try to blow us all up with those depth charges."

"We'll take the wounded aboard and give blankets to the others. In three hours I should be able to tow them into Angmagssalik."

"Do you want me to try to raise the Danes on the radio and tell them to make ready for prisoners?"

"No—I'm not a damn bit sure whose side those people in there are on. We'll play it by ear. Meanwhile, I want all officers and CPO's to wear sidearms before we let that boat alongside. Put three men with automatic rifles on the forecastle head and three on the flying bridge. Tell Guns to stand by on the well deck with the Thompson and have Boats rig a boarding ladder."

While these preparations were being made, Paul backed the trawler away from the lifeboat, a step which made the rowers and the man in the stern yell in protest.

"Just stand by," Paul called in German. "We have to make preparations."

"We have wounded," the man in the stern shouted. He was young, baby-faced despite his authoritarian voice, and had black lieutenant's stripes sewn on his gray parka.

"We'll give you what help we can, but stand by."

The rowers let their oars trail. Exhausted, they slumped

367

forward. They did not look as though they could cause trouble.

When his armed men were properly posted, Paul maneuvered the trawler close to the boat, and Boats heaved a line. It fell across the bow and the young lieutenant started barking orders.

"Lieutenant, to begin with, I just want you to come aboard for a conference," Paul called. "Tell the rest of your men to stay in the boat."

"We have wounded."

"We'll take care of them as fast as we can. You first."

The men in the boat were all talking and shouting as it was pulled alongside the well deck.

"Lieutenant, tell your men I want silence," Paul said. "We'll do this in an orderly manner."

Except for the groaning of one man who was lying in the bottom of the boat, they all quieted. The lieutenant climbed nimbly over the rail, drew himself erect on the well deck and did something so unexpected and so theatrical that the men of the *Arluk* could hardly believe it. Sticking out his arm, he gave the Nazi salute and said, "Heil Hitler!"

There was a moment of stunned silence during which Paul gave a very sweet smile worthy of Mowrey himself. Nathan put his hand on the handle of his .45 automatic, but did not take it from its holster. Williams gave a nervous giggle. Guns was the first to find his voice. "Well fuck you!" he bellowed.

The German lieutenant looked startled. His arm fell. "I am behaving correctly," he said in German.

"Get back to your boat," Paul said softly in German. "We'll have none of your Hitler shit aboard here. If it happens again, you're liable to get shot."

"I am behaving correctly," the lieutenant repeated, but without conviction. He did not move.

"Get back in your boat or we'll throw you overboard," Paul said in German. "Now."

The lieutenant scrambled back to his boat.

"Now, if you want to be correct, say, 'I request permission to come aboard,'" Paul said in German. "The next man to give your Hitler salute will finish it swimming."

The lieutenant's face flushed. "This is not the way to treat a commissioned prisoner of war," he said in German.

The men of the *Arluk* could not understand him, but

he looked so flustered that they laughed. Their nervous tension turned into gales of merriment. Nathan's face was the only serious one aboard the ship. The upturned faces of the men in the boat looked scared.

"All right, lieutenant, come aboard properly," Paul said.

The lieutenant climbed silently over the rail, his face still flushed. "I request permission . . ." he said in German.

"I'm going to send my gunner's mate aboard your boat to search your men for arms," Paul said in German. "Tell your men to throw overboard any arms, including knives, now. If we find any arms on any man of you, that man will be shot."

The lieutenant shouted at his men. Two of them discreetly poked hands over the rail and dropped knives. One dropped a Luger.

"Guns, search all of them and check out the whole boat," Paul said. "Start with the lieutenant."

"Give us a real Kraut salute," Guns said with a grin. "Hold *both* arms above your fucking little pinhead."

"He wants you to put your hands up," Paul said in German. "Now."

The lieutenant held his arms rather limply over his head while Guns roughly patted him, then unbuttoned his parka as though he were a schoolchild and ran both hands from his armpits down, and from his knees up his crotch.

"Don't be ticklish now," Guns said jovially, his stained teeth looking very bright between his glossy black mustache and beard. "He's clean, skipper. Can Blake help me check out the boat?"

"Okay," Paul replied. "How many wounded do you have, lieutenant?"

"Six."

"How many seriously wounded?"

"Four, one dying, I think. Burned."

"We'll take them aboard when we've checked out your boat. The rest of you will have to stay in your boat. We'll tow you into Angmagssalik."

"We're cold. We're all frozen!"

"We'll give you blankets and coffee. There's no room for you aboard here."

"Captain, have you ever heard of the Geneva Convention?" the lieutenant asked in German.

Paul gave him his sweetest smile. "Have you ever heard of the *Nanmak?*"

"No. I just got out here. We all just arrived on station."

"And were heading home with a supply ship? Never mind. The *Nanmak* was our sister ship. She was sunk last summer just a few miles from here, and a boatful of men was machine-gunned. There were no survivors."

"Captain, I don't know anything about that. Ask my men."

A tall old man with a stubble of white beard stood in the middle of the lifeboat. Speaking English with a strong Scandinavian accent, he said, "Captain, I'm Norwegian, not German. I'm the engineer—they took me over with the ship. Can I talk with you?"

"What have you got to say?"

"In private please?"

The Germans glowered at him but said nothing.

"Frisk him, Guns," Paul said. "Then let him come aboard. Nathan, you take charge here. Get the wounded into the forecastle. Don't take any shit."

"Don't worry about that, skipper," Nathan said.

After Guns had opened his parka and looked him over, the tall old man came aboard. "My name is Berg, captain, Olaf Berg, chief engineer, Norwegian Merchant Marine for thirty years."

"Come with me, Mr. Berg."

Paul led the way to the forecastle, the warmth of which felt good. Before they sat down he said, "First tell me one thing. Where's the hunter-killer?"

"Probably still holed up, I don't know where. He'll be expecting more planes."

Paul wished that the PBY would hurry up. The thought that the hunter-killer might suddenly pounce on the *Arluk* from the nearest big ice castle suddenly obsessed him.

"Come with me," he said to Berg, and went back to the well deck. "Nathan, have Sparks keep a radar watch for the hunter-killer. Put a lookout in the crow's nest and tell him to forget about the prisoners—just keep an eye out for the hunter-killer. Keep the twenties and the fifties manned."

"Aye, aye, sir," Nathan said.

"Come with me," Paul said. "Cookie, bring two cups of coffee to my cabin."

Paul sat on the stool by the chart table and let Berg stand. "What kind of crew does the hunter-killer have?" he asked.

370

"Eight men, sir, but she took all the brass off the *Norway*. Now she must have about twenty aboard."

"What guns does she have?"

"Just antiaircraft, sir. Depth charges and two torpedo tubes."

"Radar?"

"No, sir."

"How long can she stay at sea?"

"She only has fuel for three days, sir. Overcrowded like that, she couldn't last long."

"The Germans have a base at Supportup-Kangerdula."

"Yes, sir."

"How many men are there?"

"Only about ten when we got here. We brought about a hundred, including construction workers."

"What are they building?"

"Weather station and supply base for weather stations all up and down the coast. And a landing strip for light planes. We brought three in crates."

"Can they fly yet?"

"I don't know. They're working on them."

That was one more thing to worry about, Paul realized —even light planes could carry bombs.

"Are the approaches to the base mined?"

"No, sir. The water's too deep and there's too much tide, current and drifting ice. But they've mounted field artillery to command the entrance to the fjord."

"How big?"

"Big, but I don't know exactly. I don't know much about guns."

"How many pieces?"

"Two on each side, I think."

"Did you sail from Norway?"

"Yes. About two months ago. Our ship didn't sink your trawler, sir. The hunter-killer did."

"How many Norwegians are in the lifeboat?"

"Only three of us, sir. There were eleven of us, but the rest were killed. They wouldn't let us out of the engine-room until they abandoned ship, and the boilers went."

"How much can I count on you and the other two?"

"Nobody hates the Germans worse than we do, sir, but we have families at home."

"I'll have to treat you just like the other prisoners."

"Sir, you can trust us!"

"Can I? Sorry, you'll have to go back in the boat."

"Skipper," Sparks said. "The lookouts hear a plane. I can't pick up anything on the radar yet."

"Get back in the boat!" Paul yelled at the Norwegian. As the man did so, Paul ran to the bridge. "Nathan and Guns, you keep track of the prisoners. The rest of you man your battle stations until we get a look at that plane."

The men scrambled. Guns kept his Thompson trained on the men in the boat. Two prisoners who were carrying a wounded man aboard put him down on the well deck, and at Nathan's direction got back into the boat. Paul hurried to the flying bridge. The drone of a plane somewhere to the west could now be heard unmistakably, but there was no speck in the almost stainless blue sky. Paul was startled when the big seaplane, a PBY, came over the horizon only a few hundred feet above the ice. It seemed to float slowly toward them, almost like a balloon. When it passed overhead, it dipped its wings and began to circle in a search-pattern.

"Give me a description of the hunter-killer," Paul called to the Norwegian, who now stood in the bow of the lifeboat.

"Seventy-two feet overall. She's painted white all over. She was called the *Matador* when we had her. They call her the *Valkyrie*."

Paul looked so startled that Berg said, "You've seen her?"

"No, I've never seen her."

The coincidence of being faced with an enemy which carried the name of his father's old yawl was not really so surprising, Paul told himself. "Valkyrie" meant some kind of a German war goddess, he had always known. Still, there was something eerie about hearing that name now, as though the ghosts of his past had risen to pursue him.

"What's her top speed?" he asked.

"Better than twenty knots when she's in top shape, but her engine needs an overhaul. It won't give her much better than fifteen, and it smokes like hell."

Then they won't run the engine when planes are anywhere near, Paul thought. For the time being the *Arluk* was probably safe.

"How heavily armed are the men at the base?" he asked Berg.

372

"Lots of antiaircraft stuff. Lots of machine guns and mortars. They've put barbed wire around the base. The whole thing is so well hidden in the bottom of a ravine that planes never see it. Some have come real close."

Blake appeared. "Captain, Mr. Williams wants to know if we can knock off battle stations. He wants to get the wounded aboard."

"Tell him to go ahead, but keep the twenties manned."

Paul sent Boats to help with the wounded. He stood on the gun deck while Blake passed a stretcher down. One of the men screamed while they moved him and another kept groaning. They were so covered with parkas and great coats wrapped around them like blankets that it was impossible to see the extent of their injuries.

"Skipper, nobody in the boat has any weapons," Guns said.

"Very well. Boats, issue each man in the boat two blankets and any spare foul weather gear we have. Rig a good long line for towing it."

"Aye, aye, sir."

"Guns, will one of your fifties on the flying bridge cover that boat while we're towing it?"

"Yes, sir."

"Captain, could I at least stay aboard?" the lieutenant said. "I have many things to discuss with you."

"A good officer sticks with his men, lieutenant. Don't the Germans teach that?"

"But we have much to talk about."

"Maybe less than you think, but it will wait. Get back in the boat. Cookie, get coffee for the prisoners."

"I bet he shits in it," Guns said, and the crew laughed.

"Get them some sandwiches too," Paul said.

While food and drink was being passed to the lifeboat, Nathan took the ship's medical chest forward to administer to the wounded. Suddenly Cookie ran from the forecastle. His voice was outraged when he said, "They've given my bunk to a fucking Kraut."

Nathan followed him. "I want to use the bottom bunks," he said. "Cookie, you and the others can just sleep in the bunk of anyone who's on watch."

"First I have to get food for these bastards and then I have to give them my bunk," Cookie yelled. "What the hell kind of a war is this?"

373

The men laughed and even the Germans smiled. Apparently a few of them understood English.

"Shit, Cookie, you can have my bunk," Guns said. "Do I get the pick of the chow for that?"

"I'd rather sleep in a bear's cave," Cookie said, and still grumbling, returned to his galley.

Soon the Germans were sipping coffee from cardboard cups and munching thick ham sandwiches in the boat. They wrapped blankets around their shoulders, and suddenly looked to Paul like a bunch of firemen on a picnic. Their breath frosted as they talked to each other.

"Skipper," Williams said, "we've got a case of blackberry cordial in the lazaret. Can I give them some?"

"I'm saving that for the next beerbust ashore. It's worth fifty bucks a bottle. We're not going to give it to the Krauts."

"I have a bottle of scotch in my bunk," Williams said, "do you mind if I give that to them? Jesus, they look frozen to death."

"Do what you want with your own booze."

Williams went to the wardroom and soon came back with the bottle. The crew of the *Arluk* groaned as he passsed it aboard, but the men in the lifeboat cheered.

"Boats, stream that boat astern," Paul said. "Lieutenant, have someone steer who can keep in our wake. You're going to have about a three-hour ride."

Before getting under way Paul climbed to the flying bridge. The PBY was circling so far away that he could hear only the faint drone of her engines. Jesus, I wish he'd find the hunter-killer, he thought, still unable to think of the craft as the *Valkyrie*. If he could get that bastard, I'd breathe a lot easier.

"Mr. Williams, tell Seth to take the deck and set sea watches," he said. "We're going to Angmagssalik."

For the first time Paul realized that he would see Brit again. So much was happening that that no longer seemed important. He was not at all sure, after all, whose side the woman was on, and he had no idea how he would treat her. Going to the chart table, he drew a course to Angmagssalik. Glancing at the boat to see that the towing line was taut he said, "Ahead slow. Course three three four. Seth, build up the speed to nine hundred RPM if the boat can stand it."

"Aye," Seth said. He looked as imperturbable as if he was setting out to fish on Georgia Banks. "The boat will give us no trouble in this kind of weather."

Paul climbed to the bridge. With the binoculars he studied the horizon all around the ship. He did not expect to see anything except sky, sea and ice, and was startled when far to the south he saw a streak of fireballs in the sky, tracers. The speck of the PBY was directly above the place from which they were arching into the air. Almost as soon as he saw this Paul heard the rattle of distant machine guns.

"Jesus, the PBY has something," he called into the voice tube. "Blake, tell Nathan to get on the radio. I want to find out what's happening. Tell Sparks to stay on the radar."

Nathan ran from the forecastle to the radio shack. He had not been there two minutes before Paul saw a pale yellow bubble of fire on the southern horizon, just above a ridge of high ice castles. Jesus, the bastard got the plane, he thought, but maybe the hunter-killer had exploded. If that had happened, the plane would soon fly toward the *Arluk*, wagging her wings in triumph. No plane appeared.

Five minutes ticked by painfully. A spiral of black smoke rose from the place the bubble of flame had burst. There was no sight or sound of a plane.

"Skipper," Nathan said, running to the bridge. "Green-Pat says the PBY was attacking the hunter-killer. There's been no word from the plane since."

"Sparks, does the radar tell you how far away that ice ridge by the smoke is?"

"Thirty-eight miles, sir."

At fifteen knots the hunter-killer could catch the *Arluk* near the entrance to Angmagssalik Fjord if she knew that was the destination and if she encountered no ice. That was not likely. But she could enter Angmagssalik Fjord and torpedo the *Arluk* at anchor if Paul couldn't come up with some kind of defense.

"What are you going to do, skipper?" Nathan asked.

"Get rid of these prisoners in Angmagssalik and figure a way to hide the ship there until we can cook up some kind of plan for attacking the base."

"I have some ideas, skipper, but I've got some bad wounded up there."

"What are your ideas?"

"I can rig depth charges as mines. We could mine the entrance to Angmagssalik. Let me give these guys some morphine. One of them is dying, I think."

Suddenly Paul's and Nathan's attention was drawn to the lifeboat in their wake. The Germans, they were discovering, often acted in astonishing ways. This time they were cheering. They had seen the explosion of the PBY, they were passing the bottle of scotch back and forth. Suddenly one very young seaman who looked a little like Blake started to sing *Lili Marlene* and tried to get the others to join him. Grim-faced, Nathan stood on the stern of the trawler with his hand on his pistol in its holster, and stared at the men in the boat. The German lieutenant glanced from this gaunt man on the trawler to his crewmen, a few of whom were starting to sing, and barked an order. Immediately there was silence. Nathan took his hand from his gun and walked slowly to the bridge.

"Skipper, I've got some ideas that won't wait," he said. "Let's go to your cabin."

Paul sat on the edge of his bunk while Nathan perched on the stool by the chart table.

"The damn prisoners almost stopped me from thinking," Nathan said. "GreenPat is bound to send more planes out here to look for the hunter-killer. Our job is to keep tracking him. We shouldn't be messing with these prisoners at all. Right now we know just about where the bastard is. We should be hunting, not rescuing."

"Jesus, you're right," Paul said. "Do you want just to cut the bastards adrift?"

"We could tie them up and put them in the hold."

"I have a better idea." Paul got up, opened the door of the cabin and said, "Stop the engine, Seth. We've got a change of plan."

"What are you going to do?" Nathan asked. His voice sounded tense.

"Our whaleboat can tow that lifeboat to Angmagssalik. I'll put Williams and Seth in it with enough men to handle the prisoners. I can trust Boats to keep them in hand. You're right. We have a job to do."

"If you closed with the bastard tonight, our radar would give us the edge."

"With all this ice, we'd never be sure where he was," Paul said. "He's got twice our speed. Damn it, I haven't been thinking. He won't come after us now. He'll want fuel before he starts something like that, and he's got all the brass from the *Norway* aboard. He must be running short on everything. With a crowded little vessel like that, he'd head for his base first."

"Probably."

"I was talking to that old Norwegian about the base. Odds are he's telling the truth. He says Supportup can't be mined."

"It's too deep," Nathan said. "I looked at the chart."

"The Norwegian says they have field artillery trained on the mouth of the fjord. We could hang close outside if we can find a place to hide in the ice. We're going to have to let the bastard come to us. We'd never catch him if we go looking for him. He's like an eel out there in broken ice."

"Did the Norwegian tell you anything about the base?"

Paul gave him the information he had received from the old engineer.

"We should call in an air strike right now before the weather closes in again," Nathan said. "Hell, we know where they are. What the hell are we waiting for?"

"The base is at the bottom of some kind of a ravine. Christ, there are hundreds of ravines in there. Remember, GreenPat said the air photos don't show anything."

"They could send in big bombers to blast hell out of the whole area. We shouldn't have to go in there."

"I don't know. The main fjord is thirty miles long. They can't bomb it all."

"I'll tell GreenPat what we're doing," Nathan said.

"I'll get rid of the prisoners and head toward Supportup," Paul said. "Damn it, Nathan, we almost booted it. Our trouble is, we're still too damned soft . . ."

Paul outlined his plans to Seth and the others and told the men to hurry. It took only a few minutes to launch the whaleboat. Williams, Seth, Boats and six seamen carrying automatic rifles and submachine guns got in to take charge of the prisoners.

"Seth, when you get into Angmagssalik, tell the Danes to clear one of their damn little houses for the prisoners and post a damned good guard," he said. "Mr. Williams, find out how much diesel oil the Danes have and guard it. I don't want the Krauts going in there to refuel while we're waiting for them at Supportup."

The whaleboat cast off, took the lifeboat in tow and

started toward Angmagssalik. Seth kept the chart Paul had given him folded under his jacket. He had been in there once, he said, and could always return to a place he had seen.

The Germans kept shouting questions in German and broken English as the whaleboat headed to the northwest with them in tow, but no one answered.

GreenPat soon replied that a reconnaissance plane was on the way to inspect Supportup Fjord. Paul charted a course. In his mind's eye he saw the *Arluk* hiding in the ice where her bow guns could command the entrance to the fjord. There they would just wait, sure that their prey would show up sooner or later, no matter what the air force discovered.

After getting the ship started on the course to Supportup at full speed, Paul sat studying his chart. The shore topography was not shown enough to indicate where a base could be hidden. He started to get the pilotbook down from a shelf. Next to it was a dictionary. On a whim he looked up the word "Valkyrie."

"Any of Odin's handmaidens who hover over battlefields, choosing warriors to be victorious and conduct the souls of slain heroes to Valhalla," he read. "Old Norse: chooser of the slain."

Now why the hell, he wondered, did dad pick a name like that for a summer yawl? Did he just like the sound of it, or has he always been a warrior in his dreams?

No matter. This Kraut *Valkyrie* might think of herself as the chooser of the slain, but she never has tangled with an American rattlesnake. Handmaiden of Odin or not, she is going to get bit. Maybe the bastards can hide from planes, Paul thought, but I'm right down here in the ice with them, and I've got radar.

In these fierce thoughts Paul felt some comfort, but the knowledge that he was about to engage a ship of a type called a hunter-killer was not too reassuring. She was fast, and her torpedoes would have a better range than his own crazy five-inch gun without sights. Her skipper was smart, ruthless, and experienced—that much he had amply demonstrated. Soon he might have light planes locally based to scout for him.

"Quartermaster, tell the lookouts to keep an eye out for enemy aircraft or a small ship."

"Aye, aye, sir."

Nervously Paul glanced at the sky. Gray clouds were beginning to scud over the northern horizon, and the short day was coming to an end. Hell, it was November in Greenland. How long did he expect good weather to last?

# CHAPTER 39

The sunset that afternoon was spectacular, but in the circumstances, it struck Paul as more eerie than beautiful. The gray clouds blooming on the horizon turned to ribbons of red separated by curiously even bands of fog on the western horizon. The veils of mist parted for just an instant, revealing the sawtoothed pattern of the granite mountains silhouetted black against the great dome of the ice cap. To Paul there seemed to be something infinitely ominous about that stark coast. Nothing could be trusted here in Greenland, not the weather, not the sea, the ice, the rocky shores . . . nor the people.

The icebergs were jammed more closely together as they approached Supportup-Kangerdula. The *Arluk* twisted through a maze of crystal castles which the dying sun bathed in its ruddy glow, turning them pink and gold with flashes of crimson. As they neared the shore a great many large white sea gulls with blacktipped wings appeared from nowhere and wheeled in circles over the ship emitting melancholy mewing cries that sounded more like cats than birds. Paul had always admired the freedom of the gulls over the ice pack, but now he remembered that Boats had said the gulls had been feasting on the eyes of the corpses in the lifeboat they had discovered, and suddenly the big birds appeared to be enemies patiently awaiting their death. The black tips of their wings, which he had never before noticed, seemed to be a bad omen. Were these the real Valkyries, the handmaidens of Odin who hovered over the battlefields, the "choosers of the slain"? Had the Vikings really believed such bullshit?

Paul shivered. He did not believe in crazy myths, the

legacy of the bloody past of which the Germans were so proud. It was not the "handmaidens of Odin" who would hover over battlefields, choosing which men were to be slain and which would be heroes, it was the invisible, inaudible radar signals that would spot an enemy and give the range for the guns.

So much appeared to come down to numbers. How far offshore could the German artillery shoot? Even if he knew the caliber of their guns, Paul did not have enough expertise to know their range, and had to guess. Five miles at most? Everything in war was guesses when he came right down to it. The theoretical range of guns did not mean much in an ice field like a ruined city in darkness. Precision in war was an illusion even for experts.

When the last glow of the sun died there was an interminable hour of utter blackness until the moon rose enough to turn the clouds to silver gray and the surrounding shambles of ice to a sea of shadows. Using radar and that sea sense which he felt growing within him, Paul felt his way closer to the mouth of the Supportup-Kangerdula Fjord. As often happened, the ice thinned when he got about three miles from shore, and the radar showed a ribbon of clear water about a mile wide between the coast and the ice floe, which appeared to end a few miles to the north, where a long rocky point extended into the ice. The hunter-killer could hide in the ice or in any number of places in the lacelike coast near Supportup-Kangerdula, but if he was trying to get to his base, he would have to cross that belt of open water. Because of that long point to the north, he would probably come from the south or the east.

Paul found two small bergs lying close together in broken ice near the edge of the pack. He maneuvered his ship between them, sheltering her hull from viewers ashore, or from a ship to the east. His camouflaged bow would be hard to see from the south and because of the ice formation and the point, he did not think a ship could approach close to him from the north. The tip of his mast stuck high enough above the ice for his radar to work, and by edging the bow a little forward, he could command the entrance to the fjord and the southern sector with his forward guns. This was the best way he knew to set his trap, and the ship rested easy in her niche.

When he stopped the engine, there was nothing to be

heard but the moaning of the wind and the strange catlike mews of the gulls in the darkness overhead. Clouds soon covered the moon and he could see nothing. The mercury in the thermometers and the barometer fell as the velocity of the gale rose. Good, Paul thought—a trawler was better able to endure bad weather than a narrow, crowded little ship designed to hunt whales, not men. What was the hotshot skipper of that ship doing now?

If he's making a run for his base, he's cursing this total darkness, Paul thought. Without radar or even with it, no ice pilot, however experienced would try to grope his way into the narrow, rock-strewn entrance to Supportup-Kangerdula in utter blackness. Almost beyond doubt, the German was sitting in the ice, just as the *Arluk* was, waiting for the first streaks of dawn. It was almost as dangerous to attribute magical powers to an enemy as it was to underestimate him. Until visibility improved, the *Arluk* was fairly safe. Except for a routine sea watch, the men should get some much-needed sleep.

Everyone off watch did sleep heavily, except Nathan who between short naps kept making sure that the radar detected no motion in the surrounding ice. Sparks nodded as he tried to monitor all radio channels they thought the German might use. Nothing but static and stuttering signals from great distances came to his earphones.

Paul told the quartermaster to wake him at the first sign of dawn. The call seemed to come only minutes after he closed his eyes. Buttoning his parka tightly, drawing a knitted watchcap over his ears under the hood of his parka, and putting on heavy mittens, he went to the wing of the bridge. His ears had grown so used to the pitch of the gale that he no longer was aware of it, but now he could see snow spume being blown from the peaks of the icebergs in the gray light. The whole ice field looked curiously as though it were speeding to windward. No longer did anything appear motionless. The stiff canvas covers on the guns appeared to breathe in the wind like the flanks of animals. The rigging and the aerials vibrated like plucked guitar strings. The leather on the palms of his gloves stiffened and cracked when he flexed his hands. His face stung. Hurrying into the pilothouse, Paul checked the thermometers. The temperature was fifty-three degrees below zero, their first real taste of a Greenland winter. Good, Paul thought. If that son of a bitch tries to go fast in this stuff with a narrow, wet little ship, he'll have to keep chipping ice. No mechanism, including torpedo tubes, could be expected to work smoothly in such temperatures.

"Quartermaster, tell Guns to take the canvas off the guns."

"Aye, aye, sir."

Guns, Blake and three seamen had to cut the frozen lacings of the canvas covers and lift them off like big boxes, punching them with mittened fists to work them free. Cookie brought coffee and hot Danish pastries to Paul in the pilothouse.

"Cookie, you've got a little smoke coming from your Charlie Noble. If you can't adjust your range to get rid of that, you're going to have to turn it off."

"I fix," Cookie said, and ran across the well deck toward the warmth of the forecastle.

As the sun rose there was little change in the gray light, but the visibility increased to about five miles. Suddenly there was a high whine followed by a thunderous roar to the west and three Lightnings hurtled overhead only about a thousand yards above the ice. Apparently they did not see the *Arluk* as they descended to skim just over the tops of the tallest ice castles, seeking to avenge the lost seaplane. If they didn't even notice the *Arluk*, how could they be expected to find the even smaller hunter-killer? The PBY had been too slow to escape antiaircraft fire, but the Lightnings were too fast to make a meaningful search. They should work in teams, Paul thought. Perhaps he should radio that suggestion to GreenPat, but he didn't want to advertise his position to the Germans.

The three Lightnings broke their V-formation as they flew separate search patterns over the horizon and back again. Paul imagined the Germans in their ice-covered ship, checking to make sure they were emitting no smoke. He wondered whether he should remove the snow from his red decks to identify his ship to the pilots, but decided that the fly-boys might be too quick to attack the first speck they saw in the ice. These Lightnings were army air force. If his brother had the ill luck to be transferred from his duty as a flight instructor, he might fly one of them on missions such as this. The thought of his brother screaming overhead, or someone much like him, somehow did not increase Paul's confidence in the operation. Bill would be just the one to shoot first and ask questions later, especially the day after a PBY had been lost.

After about an hour of crisscrossing the ice field, the planes roared away to the west as quickly as they had come. Once more nothing could be heard except the howl of the wind. Paul went to the forecastle for more coffee. A dozen men were playing checkers at the big V-shaped table there. Flags, who had little signaling to do these days, had organized a tournament. He was manufacturing more sets by sawing disks off the end of a broom handle, and Blake was using a ruler to draw intersecting lines on squares of cardboard. His chef's hat tilted to the back of his head, Cookie was in the act of demolishing a row of Guns's men, and the crew cheered as though it had just won a battle.

Returning to the bridge with a mug of coffee to warm his hands, Paul sat on a stool by the wheel staring out over the seemingly speeding Arctic wastes. Now that the planes had gone, the German was probably getting under way, using the daylight to get as close as he could to his base. Probably the German was smart enough to know that the captain of the American trawler was not entirely stupid. Quite possibly he would expect the *Arluk* to try to block his return. What would he do? Try to creep in close to shore, or make a bold, high-speed dash for port after sneaking as close as possible in the shelter of the ice? Either way, he could not avoid being seen or being picked up by radar and coming within range of Paul's guns before he could duck behind the rocky points that formed the entrance to the fjord. . . . Sooner or later he will run out of fuel and have to come to me. He may fire his torpedoes, but he'll play hell trying to hit a ship as small as this when I'm coming toward him. I'll outgun him, and I'll sink him.

Maybe. Overconfidence could be lethal. Anything could happen. Guns could jam in such low temperatures, and the German captain knew this country, he might have been right in this part of the coast for the past six months or more. Maybe, like Mowrey, he was an ice pilot with a lifetime of experience. I hope the son of a bitch drinks, Paul thought, remembering the empty vodka bottle which the *Nanmak* had picked up. Dear God, let the son of a bitch get drunk.

Even to Paul that seemed a curious prayer. Studying his chart, he tried to guess what strategy the German could possibly use, but could see no way the hunter-killer could sneak past the sentry outside her door.

At noon, a fat-bellied twin-engined bomber approached from the west. Paul heard its engines first and gave the lookouts hell for covering their ears too well with their watch caps. It was clearly no light plane, however. Instead of flying out to sea, it paralleled the coast, turning to fly low over Supportup-Kangerdula several times. Undoubtedly it was taking more pictures. The army air force still was trying to pinpoint a target before sending in heavy bombers.

Twice the reconnaissance plane roared over the fjord at what would have been treetop level if Greenland had had any trees. Probably they were trying to tease the German gunners into giving away their position, but it did not work. No tracers arched from the barren rock toward the plane. It might as well have been inspecting the North Pole.

At two that afternoon three more Lightnings roared in to search the ice pack. Paul did not expect them to find the German, but at least they would make him hole up again. Soon it began to snow and the planes flashed away, disappearing into the murk over the mountains.

Gradually the wind abated, but the snowstorm developed into a blizzard. Drifts mounded the well deck and had to be shoveled away from the guns. Good, Paul thought. No need to worry about being seen now. Curtains of snow enclosed the ship in a circle hardly wider than her length. The German would play hell trying to find the entrance to the fjord in this stuff.

How long could he last out there in the ice pack? The old Norwegian had said the hunter-killer carried fuel only for about three days, and tomorrow would be his third. Of course, he wouldn't burn much while lying motionless, but even his heaters eventually would drain his meager tanks. Sooner or later he would have to come in.

All the next day the blizzard continued. Shortly after noon, Nathan came from the radio shack to the bridge, holding his clipboard in his mittened hands and a pencil in his teeth. "Message from GreenPat," he said drily, and gave the board, with its paper flaked with snow, to Paul.

"Yesterday's air photos show no, repeat no sign of any German base at or near Supportup-Kangerdula," Commander GreenPat said. "Camouflaged base is still possible.

384

When present mission completed, return Angmagssalik and organize shore party for reconnaissance on land. Try to get help of Danes and native Greenlanders. Greenland Administration officials are ordering all Danes at Angmagssalik to cooperate. Keep me informed."

Paul had a sudden vision of himself and his crew struggling in waist-deep snow, falling through crevices in the ice and trying to scale icy mountains. What the hell did Green-Pat think his Coast Guardsmen were, Alpine troops? No one aboard the ship had any training or experience in fighting ashore anywhere, never mind the Arctic. Most members of the crew were Southerners, farm boys from Georgia and the Carolinas. Even without the dangers of battle, they could not be expected to survive long ashore in the Arctic. How could the Eskimos help them flounder through blizzards in temperatures like this? It was even colder ashore than at sea, much colder. The Danes usually stayed in their little houses in winter, and how could those old people be of much use, even if they could be trusted?

The more he thought about it, the more GreenPat's order seemed to Paul like a death sentence, but now was not the time to think about it. "When present mission completed . . ." GreenPat had said. What a polite way to say, "When you've killed the hunter-killer." At least Green-Pat had said "when," not "if," as though the outcome was assured. How nice to make such plans in the warm office at the Narsarssuak headquarters.

Was it really possible for the Germans to camouflage a base so well that even the sophisticated new methods of aerial photography could not detect it? Why was Paul so sure that the Germans were based at Supportup-Kangerdula, anyway? He had come to that conclusion simply because of the presence of the supply ship and the information he had got from a Norwegian who had thrown his lot in with the Germans long ago. Maybe the Germans were doing everything possible to make the Americans think their base was at Supportup-Kangerdula, while they were building a big installation somewhere else on the coast.

Paul's doubts were rising to the point of complete confusion when Nathan knocked at his cabin door.

"Skipper, I'm getting very high frequency signals that are close. They're too high for direction-finding, but I think the base is talking to its ship. If so, the hunter-killer must be within line of sight. Maybe the Krauts have a high tower ashore or even a transmitter on a mountain, but the guy they're talking to still can't be too damn far away."

"Then they do have some kind of base near."

"There's no doubt about that. They're blasting my ears off. Short messages in code, of course."

Paul again studied his chart. The Germans were near—of that at least he was sure.

That afternoon Paul drank so much coffee that he noticed a slight tremor in his fingers. The snow fell heavier than ever, so thickly that he could hardly see his own bow. The hunter-killer couldn't find her base now, wherever the hell she was.

It was only midafternoon when darkness fell, the pure blackness of an Arctic blizzard. Paul had just lain down for a nap when Nathan again knocked.

"Skipper, their base is sending DF signals—they're making no bones about it at all. They must be trying to give their ship a bearing."

"Can you pinpoint the base?"

"Sure, it's at Kangerdula. I can't tell how far inland, but my bearing cuts right across the mouth of the fjord."

"They're trying to bring him in," Paul said. "He probably doesn't know where the hell he is out there and is running out of fuel, so he just said what the hell and requested a DF bearing."

"Looks like it."

"I was right all along," Paul concluded. "The son of a bitch is going to make a run for it. Ring up general quarters. I want all guns manned. You stick to the radar."

The men slid and a few fell on the icy, snowy decks as they ran to the guns. Nathan stood hunched over the radar set.

"I can't see anything moving," he said.

The wind howled and the men jumped up and down to stay warm. In only about ten minutes they began yelling for relief.

The German could show up anytime, Paul reflected, but on the other hand, he still might be able to delay for hours or even days. There was no point in Paul's turning his gun crews into ice statues. The lookouts couldn't see anything through those driving curtains of snow anyway. Securing from general quarters, Paul told the men to stand by below for instant action.

"Just unbutton your parkas," he said. "Don't take them off. He can flash by our bow anytime."

In the forecastle the men sat in their open parkas and took to playing checkers again. Nathan would not leave the radar set and Paul sat on a stool by the wheel staring into nothingness.

For more than two hours nothing happened. Then Sparks reported another brief transmission of homing signals from the base.

"He's getting close," Paul said. "He just wants a final check before making a run. Maybe he'll use a star shell to see the entrance to the fjord."

At about eight-thirty in the evening Paul saw a flicker of light to the east. Pushing the door to the pilothouse open against the wind, he saw a signal light flashing through the slanting snow. It looked close, but if it was a very powerful light, it could be miles away, he realized. By the time Nathan got to the wing of the bridge to read the code, it disappeared. There was no answer from the shore.

"I got a visual bearing on him," Nathan said. "Zero nine eight. The radar doesn't show anything out there but ice, fairly loosely packed. Do you want to go looking for him?"

"Maybe that's just what he wants," Paul said. "If he could get us to playing tag out there with him, he could beat us in."

"That figures."

For an hour nothing more happened. Then more lights flickered, this time to the north. Either a very dim light was being used or it was far away, perhaps beyond the rocky point.

"I think he still wants us to come out and play games," Paul said, but the thought suddenly hit him that there might be several enemy ships out there signaling to each other. No, that was not reasonable. Where would all those ships come from on a night like this in such ice conditions? The Germans wouldn't have a whole fleet of icebreakers!

Plotting the bearings they had taken on the two lights, Paul saw that one ship making only about five knots could have made both signals if he was only about three miles away. In that case he could be using an ordinary signal lamp. Did he have any purpose except to lure the *Arluk* away from the entrance to his base and to confuse?

Sparks telephoned from the radio shack to say that more homing signals were being sent from the base. They came every half hour for two minutes, Nathan soon figured. An hour of unrelieved darkness followed. Suddenly the lights flickered again to the east, seemingly very far away, but one ship could change bearings so fast only if he was very close.

"Why aren't you getting anything on radar?" Paul asked.

"He's damned good at keeping behind ice ridges and bergs, for one thing," Nathan said. "Heavy snow confuses radar and a small wooden ship doesn't make much of a blip. Wait a minute. Something's moving on a bearing of a hundred and one degrees, range about two and a half miles, but there he goes behind a berg."

The telephone on the bridge rang.

"Sparks says the base is sending steady homing signals now," the quartermaster reported.

"He's about to make his run," Paul said. "Sound general quarters. Send Guns up here."

Even the bleating of the klaxon alarm was deadened by the snow, robbed of some of its urgency. The men scrambled to their action stations and Guns came to the pilothouse. His black beard and mustache were streaked with snow, making him look curiously old.

"Guns, the Kraut has been flashing lights all around us," Paul said, "but he's got to cross our bow if he's going into the fjord in there. Forget the five-incher—he won't be close enough, and he'll go by too fast for a fixed gun. Use the three-incher, the twenties and the fifties. I'm going to close with him as much as I can. Tell the men on the guns to aim for the pilothouse and gun crews. I hope to surprise him. Good luck."

"Do you want the stern fifties, or shall I move them to bear over the bow?"

"If you fire forward from the flying bridge, you better put a pretty good man up there. If he panics, he could shoot up the men on our own bow."

"I'll put Blake up there, sir. I've trained him good."

There was a clatter as Guns moved the fifties on the flying bridge.

"He's got his bearing by now," Paul said. "He's ready to make his run. Can you see anything on the radar?"

"No," Nathan said. "Damn it, real snow makes electronic snow when it's as heavy as this."

"Hell, he's got to come to us in the end, no matter what he does," Paul said. Going to the wing of the bridge, he shouted, "I know it's cold, but stay on your toes. He's going to cross our bow any minute."

Nothing happened. The wind continued to howl in unrelieved darkness. The men jumped up and down beside the guns, slapping their mittens against their thighs. Five minutes went by, ten minutes, half an hour.

"Skipper," Guns called. "We're damn near freezing to death. How about letting half the crew warm up?"

"Okay. Spell each other. Ten minutes below and ten on deck."

After an hour of the men scrambling back and forth, this procedure began to seem ridiculous. Maybe the damned Kraut is trying to exhaust us, Paul thought.

"Guns, just have the men stand by for a quick call in the forecastle," he said. "This may go on all night. You can sleep if you stay dressed."

The men hurried through the forecastle door, cursing as snow swirled after them. Two men had to struggle against the wind to shut it. Going to his cabin, Paul studied the chart which by this time he had memorized. Judging from the last lights observed, the German was due east, hiding in heavy ice about two and a half miles from the *Arluk* and a little less than five miles from the entrance to the fjord. Now he had his bearings from his radio direction finder, and he could judge his distance offshore by the depth of the water. Sure that he was in a position to make a dash for shelter, he would probably wait until the very first streaks of dawn gave him an outline, at least, of the fjord's entrance. Dawn was not due for another eight hours. Would it be best for Paul to catch enough sleep to be alert then?

Probably, but Paul was much too tense to lie down. Returning to the pilothouse, he sat on the stool by the wheel, nodding with his chin resting on the tightly buttoned collar of his parka. Flags was standing by the helm and the quartermaster was leaning on the engineroom telegraph. In their slow Southern voices they were discussing bars they had visited in New Orleans, rating them according to the availability of women. Paul dozed. Several times he awoke with a start as the wind died a little or increased its howl. Going out on the wing of the bridge, he stared into the pelting snow, saw nothing and returned to the stool. Time seemed at a standstill. The drone of the Southern voices never changed its tempo or its subject. Paul's right toes

389

began to itch. Too tired to take off his heavy felt-lined boot and double layer of woolen socks, he stood up to stamp on his right toes with his left heel. At this moment he was stunned by two sharp reports which exploded somewhere astern of the ship. The sounds came from the north, where he had least expected action. Running to the starboard wing of the bridge, he looked aft to see a stab of fire near the horizon as another report rang out. It looked as though he were being fired at from several angles, all to the north.

It was not true that Paul panicked, as he afterward accused himself of doing. He simply assumed that the hunter-killer or another ship had worked into the ice to the north of him and was opening fire. In the light of that assumption, everything he did was logical. He rang up general quarters, called for full power astern, jerked the ship from the ice and turned her. Only about five hundred yards away there was a large iceberg, which he hurried to put between himself and the explosions. He had almost accomplished this when there was a deafening burst of machine guns from the east, the very direction he had first expected the hunter-killer to appear. Tracers were arching onto the deck of the *Arluk*. There was the sound of hundreds of bullets smashing glass and splintering wood. Someone screamed and finally the *Arluk* began to return the fire. Tracers arched back and forth. Suddenly a searchlight stabbed at the mouth of the fjord, and went out. Paul caught a glimpse of the hunter-killer speeding through broken ice toward the shelter of the land. Guns spat flame from her bow and stern. The tracers from the *Arluk*'s guns were falling short of her. The light flicked on once more for about three seconds, and the ship was gone.

There was sudden silence, broken only by the sound of someone sobbing. Flames were climbing from the flying bridge.

Paul's voice sounded reasonably calm when he called "Fire! Fire stations!"

Guns took the nozzle of a hose and started to scramble up a ladder to the flying bridge, followed by a half dozen seamen. Paul was still not sure what had happened, except that somehow they had been suckered and the German had escaped to its base. There was a lot of running and shouting on the decks. Nathan said, "We have a lot of men hurt. I'll see to them." He was just leaving the pilothouse when Paul heard a roaring scream from the flying bridge, which he would never forget. Nathan scrambled up the ladder toward it, followed by Paul. Flames in the middle of the deck there were dying under spray from two hoses. In their ruddy glare Guns stood holding a body that was almost decapitated, and which was gushing blood. From the slender size of the body, Paul guessed it was Blake who had been hit by machine-gun fire. Hugging this corpse against his chest with one gigantic right arm, Guns pushed by Paul and somehow carried it down the ladder. Cradling it in both arms he dashed across the well deck toward the forecastle. Moving almost as fast, Nathan followed him.

After making sure that the fire was under control, Paul also went to the forecastle, which was now crowded with men. Guns had stretched Blake's body on the big V-shaped table. His own parka drenched with blood, he stood leaning over the boy's head, apparently looking for a face. When anyone else tried to come near, Guns emitted a roar and shoved him aside.

"There's more wounded in the wardroom," Nathan said to Paul. "I'll take care of this."

Still in a daze, Paul walked to the wardroom. Flags was ripping up a sheet and binding the upper arm of the quartermaster. Other men lay in the bunks.

"How many wounded here?" Paul asked.

"Four sir," Flags said. "They're not too bad, but Sparks is dead. They got him right in the radio shack."

Paul went to the radio shack. Its starboard bulkhead had been perforated by machine-gun bullets. Sparks sat with his hand resting on his desk, his earphones still on. His chest dripped blood. Methodically, Paul felt his wrist. There was no pulse. Feeling lightheaded, he went to the pilothouse.

Chief Banes stood there and that was very odd because the old machinist never came to the bridge. "Two dead and six wounded, captain," he said. "I took a count."

"Thank you, chief."

"The fire's out and the ship's ready to get under way."

"Thank you, chief."

Paul stared into the hood of the radar. Nothing moved, to the north or anywhere. The illusion that he had been surrounded by ships lost its sense of reality. There had been two explosions to the north, but no shells or machine-gun fire had come from that direction. Paul sat on his stool near the wheel. Gradually his mind cleared. Apparently the

German had created a diversion to the north of the *Arluk*, maybe by leaving explosives with time fuses on the ice set to explode while he dashed in from the east, or maybe with a small boat. Paul had been suckered, like a man with a gun who had been told by his prey to look behind him. At least, that seemed the most likely explanation. Only one thing was sure: the Krauts had clobbered the *Arluk* and had made it to their base, but the old trawler was still afloat and could fight again. Right now he ached to get to sea, away from the situation he still was not sure he understood. The ship's immediate need was a safe place where she could lick her wounds.

"Is there anyone in the engineroom, chief?" Paul asked Baines.

"I got my first class down there."

"You take the telegraph and I'll take the helm. I want to get out of here. Ahead slow."

Paul steered due east. As soon as he came to a good lead, he followed it slowly into the slanting snow. He started to call Sparks to the radar, but realized that Sparks was dead.

"Chief, you take the helm," he said, and studied the radar screen himself. The lead circled north and seemed to show the way to an ice sound that probably was connected to the open sea. No noise but the steady beat of the engine and the howl of the wind could be heard as the *Arluk* beat her retreat.

Paul had just worked the *Arluk* free of the ice when Nathan came to the pilothouse. His tan parka was covered with dark stains.

"Are we going to Angmagssalik?" he asked.

"Yes," Paul said, though he had been more intent on making his ship hard to find than on going anywhere.

"How long will it be?"

"About three hours."

"What kind of medical facilities do they have there?"

"Damn little, but they must have some kind of equipment."

"We've got two men with bullet fragments and all kinds of crap in their wounds. Guns is off his rocker. I've knocked him out with morphine. Maybe he'll be all right when he wakes up."

"Sparks is dead," Paul said.

"They told me. We should get rid of the dead as soon as

possible. The prisoner with the bad burns died in the middle of all this."

"Do you want to bury them at sea?"

"I don't think anybody's up to that right now," Nathan said. "We can just put them ashore when we get in."

There was a moment of silence.

"Nathan, I'm sorry," Paul said. "They suckered me."

"Nobody blames you. As far as that goes, I was no great help. I didn't know what in hell was happening."

"I'm still not sure."

"I think I heard an outboard out there," Nathan said. "I thought I was imagining it."

"Any damn skiff could have worked around us and set off some dynamite."

"They're clever! I have to hand them that."

"But not too clever," Paul said. "They could have finished us off with torpedoes or just with gunfire. They'll find that was a bad mistake."

"What are you going to do?"

"No heroics. There was a minute there when I thought of charging right after him into his fjord. We won't fight that way."

"All we have to do is call in the planes when the weather clears."

"I doubt if it's going to be that easy. If they can hide a base they can hide a ship that small. Our first job is to get somebody in there who can see what they've got, and exactly where. That fjord is about thirty miles long. They won't send bombers until we can pinpoint a target for them."

"I'll go," Nathan said. "Just put me ashore."

"I need you here. Anyway what the hell do you know about walking around in the goddamn Arctic?"

"I can learn."

"No doubt, but frankly I'd rather send an Eskie if I can find one I can trust. Maybe an Eskie with one of our men, if we can find an athlete."

"I can walk."

"I got work for you here. Can you make mines out of depth charges that you can explode by radio?"

"Yes. I've already worked that out."

"If we're going to hang around Angmagssalik waiting for scouts and air raids, the smart Kraut might come in after us to try to finish his job. The chart shows a small shallow bay near the head of the fjord. There'd be too much ice moving with the tide for contact mines, but we could lay depth charges on the bottom if you could set them off at will."

"No problem."

"We'll lie inside a screen of charges and hope he comes after us. His only choice will be that or waiting for the planes in his damned base."

"You think the planes can wipe out the whole base?" Nathan asked.

"Maybe . . . if we can pinpoint it for them."

"In Europe they bomb the hell out of cities, but they don't kill everybody. The Krauts could go underground or beat it out to the hills. After the planes have left, they could rebuild."

"So we'll move in and mop up after the planes get done," Paul said. "I have an idea that our men are about ready for an operation like that."

"It could be rough," Nathan said. "The planes can blow up buildings, but not many trained troops."

"I promise you this," Paul said, "they won't sucker me again." He hoped they weren't famous last words.

## CHAPTER 40

After about an hour, the snow let up a little, and with the help of radar, Paul guided the *Arluk* into Angmagssalik Fjord. The wind whistled through the rock canyons there even worse than at sea. The snow from the sky was mixed with that blown from shore. In such conditions Paul did not fear immediate enemy attack. As he crept closer to the wharf, he could see the *Arluk*'s whaleboat moored alongside the Danes' heavy launch. No people were in sight and the red wooden cottages, now standing in deep snow, looked like a deserted village except for dark smoke from their chimneys and a few dimly lit windows.

"Maybe the Danes are hoping we are," Paul replied. "I said. "Hell, we could be the damned German."

"They probably don't even know we're here," Nathan was going to anchor, but it doesn't look like any boat is going to come out for us. We can unload the wounded easier if we go alongside the wharf."

As the ship slowly approached the granite pier, about twenty Eskimos came running from the village. Perhaps they had been waiting to make sure of the nationality of the ship emerging through the snowstorm, Paul thought, but their round copper-colored faces were smiling as they caught the heaving lines. One figure in a fur parka who was taller than the rest hauled in the heavy bow line, and expertly made it fast to a bollard. As he jumped aboard Paul was surprised to see that it was Boats. His gaunt face was not smiling, and his expression of anger turned to astonishment when he saw the lines of splintered holes and smashed ports left by the machine-gun bullets. Running to the pilothouse, he said, "Christ, skipper, what happened to you?"

"We got jumped. Two dead and six wounded. Are the prisoners under control?"

"They are now, but the lieutenant escaped."

"How did that happen?"

"I wanted to tie them all up before we let them get out of their boat, but Mr. Williams and Mr. Farmer wouldn't let me. The Danes and a bunch of Eskies just surrounded us while we were trying to find a place for them. In all the confusion, the lieutenant just slipped away. We didn't even find it out until we got them inside and I took a head count."

Suddenly Paul imagined how old Mowrey would react to this news, to reports of his encounter with the Germans. "Jesus, I told you you'd fuck up!"

"Maybe it isn't too bad," Nathan said. "Where the hell can he go?"

"Back to his base," Paul said grimly. "Probably with plenty of help."

"The Danes sent an Eskie after him," Boats said. "They think he'll find him."

"I bet. Where the hell are Mr. Williams and Mr. Farmer?"

"Mr. Williams is standing guard. He's pretty sore at me.

395

Mr. Farmer is sick. The Danes think he had a heart attack."

"Show me where the prisoners are."

Leaving the ship in charge of Nathan, Paul put on his pistol belt, checked his automatic and walked with Boats toward the house to which Brit had taken him. As they passed the little ketch on the ways, Paul saw that the snow had been shoveled off her deck and smoke rose from the Charlie Noble which vented her galley range.

"Mr. Williams is mad as hell with me because I said I couldn't take responsibility for the prisoners if he didn't let me tie up both their hands and their feet," Boats shouted above the wind. "He wouldn't even have tied up their hands if Mr. Farmer hadn't taken my side. Christ, there's no place to put the damned people here. They could smash their way right out of that house. Mr. Williams won't even let me lash their wrists real tight. When I said me and my men couldn't take responsibility, he took over the whole guarding operation himself."

Paul said nothing. The snow and wind cut his face as they trudged through knee-deep snow toward the village.

Harley, a tall thin seaman so self-effacing that Paul had hardly been aware he was aboard the ship, was standing or rather sitting guard in the tiny vestibule of the house which Paul had visited with Brit. He was slumped on a bench under a row of parkas smoking a cigarette with his automatic rifle propped against his knees. Seeing his commanding officer, he stood up, grabbing the rifle just before it fell.

"Don't sit down when you are on guard duty, damn it!"

Without more comment, Paul entered the livingroom of the house. It was a memorable sight. Twenty-three men were crammed together. About half stood and half sprawled on the floor. All had their wrists bound.. On a chair in a corner by the stove, Williams sat like a host, except that he was gesturing with his pistol as he talked. When Paul came in there was an instant of silence, followed by complaints in German from everyone. Their wrist bindings hurt. There were no beds. The one toilet was stopped up. Two men shouted that they were sick. Above this din Williams shouted, "Skipper! Thank God you're here!"

"Silence!" Paul bellowed in German, but there was only

396

a short lull before the voices rose again. Williams stood up and kept yelling in English for quiet. His high, piercing voice was drowned in the uproar. Pushing toward him, Paul grabbed his chair. Raising it high above his head, he brought it down on the floor so hard that it broke. The splintering crash produced a sudden hush.

"When I say silence I want silence," Paul said in German. "If you can't keep quiet, I'm going to put the stove out and see if the cold can shut you up."

The Germans stared at him, their faces stolid. The youngest looked about seventeen, the oldest about fifty. They could have been the crew of another American trawler.

"Boats, you take charge here," Paul said. "If one man speaks, shut down the drafts of the stove and open the door. Make sure you stand guard in it."

"Aye, aye, sir."

"Come with me," Paul said to Williams and led the way to a tiny kitchen adjoining the main room. As soon as he shut the door, he turned to the ensign and said, "Those men could rush you any second. You've let the lieutenant escape. This is the worst fuck-up I ever saw."

"Sir, they don't want to escape. Where the hell would they go? The lieutenant was crazy. If he's not dead by now, the Eskies will bring him back."

"Maybe, but I want them hog-tied. I want them bound hand and foot until I find a better place to keep them."

"Sir, you can't do that. Where the hell are they going to run to?"

"How do you know who might help them? Maybe that Eskie who went after the lieutenant is showing him the way to his base right now. They could take over this whole damn village if you give them a chance to think it out. Where are the rest of your guards?"

"I've got two men posted upstairs at the windows. They could shoot anyone who ran out."

"If they're awake and if the Krauts didn't take you hostage. Where are the rest of your men?"

"They have to sleep, sir. And Mr. Farmer's in the dispensary. He had a heart attack."

"Get everyone but him here. I want everyone here with drawn guns while Boats hog-ties these bastards."

"Sir, two of them are sick."

"Tough. Mr. Williams, the Krauts killed the men from

the *Nanmak* because they were too smart to take prisoners aboard a small ship. Now I haven't been that smart, but I'll get exactly that smart if I see one chance in a thousand that these people can take us over. So for their own good you better get them hog-tied until I can find a safe place to keep them."

"Yes sir."

"Now get all your men."

Paul waited until he had armed guards lining the walls of the room before he told Boats to start tying up the prisoners, hands and feet. As Boats moved toward them with his hands full of short lines, which he had already prepared for the purpose, the prisoners again started to yell. Paul went to a window, forced it open by hammering it with the palm of his hand, and fired his .45 automatic twice into the drifts outside. The reports of the gun were deafening in the small room, and they were followed by silence.

"I'll shoot the next man who opens his mouth and who doesn't hold still while he's being tied up," Paul said in German. "You people shot all the survivors of the *Nanmak*, and all I want is an excuse to shoot one of you."

The prisoners stared at him as indignantly as innocent men, but said nothing. Boats swiftly proceeded with his job, tying his knots so tightly that the men flinched.

"You'll cut off their circulation," Williams said.

"Two men aboard my ship just had their circulation cut off," Paul said. "Blake and Sparks are dead. Don't talk to me about circulation."

When the prisoners had been hog-tied, Paul had them laid out like cordwood on the floor. Leaving Boats and four armed men to watch them, he said, "Now Mr. Williams, find the governor of this place. His name is Swanson. Tell him I want to see him aboard my ship right now. Bring him aboard at the point of a gun if you have to. I'm taking over this town."

"Sir, that's not necessary. Mr. Swanson has been doing everything he can to help."

"Help who? Get him, now."

Storming out the door, Paul cringed as the snow and wind hit him, but ducking his head, ploughed toward the wharf. A dozen Eskimos followed him. There were no dogs. Eskimo settlements were almost always swarming with sled dogs. Had all the dog teams left this place, and if so, where were they going?

As Paul came abreast the ketch on the ways, he saw what looked like an Eskimo coming to meet him. He guessed that it was Brit before he saw her white narrow face. "Paul!" she said. "Thank God you're here." She put a heavily mittened hand on his arm.

"I'm not sure what side you're on—"

"I understand that, I respect it . . . I have to talk to you."

"Not now. I have wounded to take care of, prisoners, and I have to bury the dead."

"I can help you."

"From now on I trust no one but my own men. Where are the dogs?"

"Peomeenie took two teams to look for the escaped prisoner. Not many are left. The dogs usually stay with the natives over by the sod huts. We try to keep them away from here."

"Christ, I don't know whether to believe you or not."

"I won't try to convince you now. But I can tell you a good place for the prisoners."

"Where?"

"There's a little island out in the fjord with three sod huts on it. They put people with infectious diseases there. It's empty now and the huts have stoves. The prisoners could survive and they never could escape."

"Not without help, maybe."

"Your guns could cover the whole island from the shore."

"I'll look into it."

"Let me tell you about Swanson. You don't have to believe me now, but you should think about this."

"What?"

"He's not really on the side of the Germans. He's just scared to death. The Americans come and they go, but the Germans are always there, just up the coast."

"You knew that then."

"No, I didn't, not until yesterday. I won't try to convince you of that. But Swanson knew it. They told him they'd move in and butcher everyone here, Danes and natives, if they thought we were giving you people any help."

"If he'd told me that, we could have called in planes."

"Would they get all of them? What will happen when you leave?"

399

"It's a war, Brit. You have to take sides."

"That's easy for you. You have strength enough——"

"I suppose I could expect you to make a case for Swanson."

"I suppose. Come see me in my boat when you want. I'll be waiting there."

Turning, Brit ran toward the ketch, moving with astonishing speed through the deep snow.

Paul continued to the *Arluk*. Nathan met him in the pilothouse. "Skipper, I want to move the dead ashore right away. I've got them in the wardroom."

"The old Dane is coming here. I'll make arrangements."

"One of the Eskies told me they have a place to put the dead until they can dig graves. They even have a special dog sled for a hearse. They've gone to get it."

"Fine. Move the dead off as soon as you can."

Paul went to his cabin. He was chilled to the bone and his talk with Brit had left him even more tense than his dealing with the prisoners. From a drawer under the desk he took a pint of apricot brandy that he had found hidden under the mattress. He had already opened it when he was hit by the thought that he needed it too much. A man who wouldn't drink while he was playing cards had no right to touch alcohol while dealing with life and death. He poured the brandy down his sink and went to the forecastle for coffee.

The men were playing checkers again as though nothing whatsoever had happened. Two of the German wounded were watching the tournament, despite assorted bandages. Christ, even here we've got unguarded prisoners, Paul thought, and ran to the bridge. Nathan was not there. "He's in the wardroom," Flags said.

Nathan sat imperturbably writing at the wardroom table. Two bodies wrapped entirely in blankets lay crowded together like a companionable couple in the forward starboard bunk, one in the after one.

"I'm just putting their names and serial numbers in the log," Nathan said. "Sparks was a Catholic and Blake was a Baptist. I don't know what the German was—not a Jew, I presume. Do you want to hold services?"

"They have a church in there," Paul said. "They must have a minister. I suppose we should have a service of some kind." Pulling himself back to what seemed more important matters, he said, "I want to get the Kraut wounded off of here right now."

"How about our own wounded?"

"They have a dispensary up there. Check into that, but I want the Kraut wounded under guard. Christ, they're sitting up there watching the men play checkers."

"I don't think there's much fight in them," Nathan said.

"How the hell can you be sure? They could blow up this whole ship. Bring them up there to Boats and let him tie them up with the others."

"One of them is pretty bad hurt, skipper."

"I can't assign all my men to guard duty. Do you want to take chances?"

"No, you're right. I'll take care of them."

Flags appeared at the companionway. "Captain, a Dane is here to see you, a Mr. Swanson."

"Show him to my cabin," Paul said and hurried there.

Swanson climbed the steps to the pilothouse with difficulty. A fat old man who wore several sweaters under a rumpled blue greatcoat, he stood as straight as he could near the ship's wheel. Everything about him drooped—his mustache, his triple chins and his belly. A defrocked Santa Claus, he still managed to achieve the dignity of suffering.

"You wanted to see me, captain," he said in his strong Danish accent.

"I want to get a few things straight," Paul said without bothering to ask him into his cabin. "First of all you're a traitor to your own government and an enemy of mine. You knew the Germans had a base just up the coast and you didn't tell me."

"I'm sure that's the way the world will judge me." His voice was flat, beyond emotion.

"Secondly, I am taking charge of this whole area. You have no more authority. My guns say that now. We'll let our governments argue about it later."

"My own government has already told me nearly that."

"Will the Eskimos do what you tell them to?"

"The Eskimos are free, perhaps the last free men on earth."

"They won't stay free long if you don't help me fight the Germans. Are they working for them?"

"We have tried to make the Eskimos hate the Germans. It is hard for them to understand. There isn't really a word for hate in their language."

"Do they know that the Germans gunned down the survivors of the *Nanmak*?"

"We got that news on our radio. I'm not sure that the Eskimos believe it. I'm not sure they believe anything we hear on the radio these days. Who could believe it all? The Eskimos just like the radio for music."

Shouts and the snarling of dogs on the wharf interrupted the old man. Looking out the pilothouse window, Paul saw an astonishing spectacle. A fan-shaped team of dogs was towing a long black sled with black strips of cloth streaming like plumes from short staffs on each corner. The dogs were fighting with each other, and an Eskimo with a short-handled whip was lashing and shouting them into order.

"Those are young dogs," Swanson said. "Peomeenie took the trained ones."

"Do they always use that thing for funerals here?"

"Yes. The Eskimos are very good at funerals. We have had a great many lately. Measles took nineteen adults and eight children last spring. Perhaps the Germans brought it."

German measles, Paul thought, but he said nothing. He watched while the men of the *Arluk* carried the three blanket-shrouded bodies to the sled. The Eskimos tied them in place and the driver cracked his whip over the dogs. They set off at a run and three Eskimos rushed to hold them to a dignified pace. Soon they disappeared into the swirling snow. Almost immediately Nathan appeared on the well deck, pistol in hand. He and two armed seamen helped the German wounded to the wharf and marched them toward the village. When one of them fell, a seaman helped him up, put his arm around his waist and walked beside him like a lover.

"Do you have a doctor here?" Paul asked.

"Only a nurse. She is old and not very well, but good as most doctors."

"How many beds do you have in your dispensary?"

"Six with twelve more mattresses for emergencies."

"I'll send my four wounded there right away, maybe five. Your nurse can check the wounded Germans. They're with the other prisoners."

"I'll tell her."

"Have the Eskimos make the island you have for contagious diseases ready for about twenty-five prisoners. You have huts out there with stoves?"

"Yes."

"Will they hold twenty-five?"

"They have accommodated more than that, I am afraid."

"Can you get them ready tonight, now?"

"The Eskimos can. Perhaps I shall tell them that the Germans have an infectious disease. Then they will understand and move fast."

"Do you have a minister who can give a funeral service tomorrow?"

"I am a minister. What time?"

"About noon. We'll bury two Americans and one German, Protestant and Catholic. I don't care how you handle it."

"How many will attend? Your whole crew? The prisoners?"

"A third of my crew and one witness from the prisoners. I'm not going to have them making a break in the church."

"The church will be big enough then."

There was the sound of many dogs barking in the direction of the village. Soon an Eskimo came running to the ship. He called from the wharf in his language and Swanson went to the bridge to answer. They talked for about a minute before Swanson returned to the pilothouse.

"Peomeenie has returned," he said. "He caught the German lieutenant. The man is nearly frozen to death. They're taking him to the dispensary."

"The hell with that. I can't stand guard in two places. Tell your man to put him with the other prisoners. Your nurse can tell my guards how to take care of him."

"He may die, captain. Cases of severe exposure need skilled care."

"It was his idea to try to escape. Go up and have him put with the other prisoners now. My men will check on him in a few minutes."

"Yes, captain. Is that all?"

"One more thing. I hear you're afraid of what the Germans will do to your people when we leave."

"I am very much afraid of that."

"Don't be. I promise you that when I leave, not one German will be alive anywhere near here. You can count on that."

"How can you stop more from coming?"

"We'll have more and more ships patrolling this coast and more planes. The Germans will get so much kicked out of them at home before long they'll forget about Greenland. Don't you know that we're winning the war?"

"Yes, I suppose you are, but the Germans are a very resourceful, determined people. They can do a lot more killing."

"So can we," Paul said.

# CHAPTER 41

The snow looked as though it would never let up. Because the blizzard sheltered him from any possible attack, either from the sea or air, Paul was glad. He wanted to get all the prisoners moved to the island and the funeral services over with before anchoring the *Arluk* in a safer place.

An Eskimo used the Danes' big launch to help the whaleboat ferry the prisoners to the island. Paul let Nathan supervise the operation with the help of a dozen armed guards. Shortly after nine in the morning, Nathan knocked on Paul's door to announce that the transfer of the prisoners had been completed.

"Did they give you any trouble?" Paul asked.

"No sir," Nathan replied, his face grim. "For some reason they seem afraid of me."

Guns came in. The big black-bearded man was wearing only a parka and boots with no pants in between. Since Nathan had taken him to the dispensary only a short time ago, he looked at him in astonishment.

"Guns, what are you doing back here?" Nathan asked.

"I belong here," Guns replied. "Why did you take me up there with all those sick people? Why have you been doping me up? You've got me so I don't know what I'm doing."

"I've just been trying to help you get some rest."

"I don't need no rest. Where are we? Is this Angmagssalik?"

"Yes," Paul said.

404

"What are we doing here? Why don't we go in after the Krauts?"

"We will as soon as we get organized," Paul said.

"I want to go in after them," Guns said.

"You'll have your chance," Paul said.

"I want a head," Guns said.

"A head?" Nathan repeated.

"Cookie said he'd let me boil it. I'm going to clean up the skull and send it to Blake's mother."

"I'm not really sure she'd appreciate that," Nathan said.

"She'll appreciate it. I'm going to make it into a lamp. Chief Banes is going to help me."

"Well," Paul said, "you can't do much about it now. You better put on your pants or get into your bunk before you freeze your legs."

"Cookie is going to save me an olive jar," Guns continued. "When he does, can I get some alcohol from the medicine chest? I'm going to get me a Kraut prick. That's what I want for my own war souvenir."

"Guns, some Kraut will be putting your prick into a jar if you don't take care of yourself," Paul said. "Go to your bunk. If I see you out of uniform again, I'll send you back to the dispensary."

"Aye, aye, sir," Guns said. "Don't worry about me, captain, I'll take care of myself. Just take me where I can get me some Krauts." He went back to the forecastle.

"Do you think we should lock him up?" Nathan asked.

Paul shrugged. "The old Norsemen drank from the skulls of their enemies. Haven't you ever said 'Skoal!' when you touched glasses? That means skull."

"You follow your ancestral customs and I'll follow mine," Nathan said.

"Maybe that's not such a bad idea. A cold beer from the polished skull of the captain of that hunter-killer might taste pretty good."

"Are you going to ask Cookie to save you an olive jar?"

"Just remember that they'll jump you if they get a chance. Remember how the Krauts treat prisoners."

"You don't have to ask me to remember that," Nathan said softly. "There's no mercy in me at all, no forgiveness. I can't find a trace. That's what scares me, what if everybody on both sides is like this?"

405

"You better get some sleep. How long has it been since you've had eight hours?"

"I don't seem to need much sleep anymore. That nurse up there is going to clean out the wounds of the men, and I want to see if she knows what she's doing."

When Nathan left, Paul stretched out on his bunk. His watch told him it was a little before ten o'clock. It was dark outside. The long nights made it as difficult to keep track of time as had the endless days of summer. It took concentration to figure out that it was ten in the morning. Paul asked the quartermaster to call him in time for the funeral services and slipped into a deep sleep during which he dreamed of Mowrey coming back and court-martialing everybody, starting with him.

Paul was so exhausted that he found it almost impossible to get up in time for the funeral services. Let the dead bury the dead, he thought, but the crew might be upset if he did not show up, and anyway, there were many more plans he had to set in motion before getting a real rest. After taking a shower, putting on his cleanest uniform and gulping a cup of black coffee, he hurried through the snow to the church.

The chapel was so small and simply constructed that inside it reminded Paul of a tourist cabin. By the time he arrived it was already filled by all those men from the *Arluk* who were not on watch or on guard duty, a tall young prisoner who could tell the other Germans that their shipmate had had a proper funeral, his guard, who carried a .45 at his pistol belt, several old Danes and a dozen Eskimos in their furs. The heat from all these bodies and a coal stove near the altar made the room stifling, and there was a pungent, unidentifiable smell. A row of seamen squeezed together on a pew made of rough planks to make room for Paul. Glancing around he saw Brit. She was wearing the green skirt and reindeer sweater he remembered, probably her only good European clothes, and she sat leaning forward in prayer, her eyes closed. Almost as soon as Paul sat down, Swanson walked to a simple lectern. He was dressed in a black clerical robe. With his portly figure, heavy face and white hair, he looked more like a judge than a minister. Clearing his throat, he began the service in his strongly accented but correct English.

"We are gathered here to honor the memory of two

Americans who died for their country and one German who died for his. They were of different Christian sects, but all children of God. . . ."

It was rather difficult for Paul to think of Sparks and Blake as children of God, never mind the German, but as he pondered the matter, he conceded the fact that in some ultimate, inscrutable way they undoubtedly were. He was relieved to realize that he had actually liked both Sparks and Blake. How much they had endured, how hard they had worked.

"The Eskimos have a saying," Swanson continued. "On the ice all men are brothers. It must be true, for these people of the ice are the only human beings on earth who fight no wars. It makes me feel very strange to think that we who brought them Christianity also brought them war."

Pausing, Swanson pulled a handkerchief from a sleeve of his robe and blew his nose. "It gives me some comfort to realize, though, that men fight wars for ideals, however mistaken, and for love of their own kind. These men who have given up their lives have truly made a sacrifice for the benefit of others. For that we honor them and mourn them. We consecrate their bodies, sure that God understands the purity of their motives."

For a long time Swanson continued, but Paul was too exhausted to concentrate anymore. The old man read from the Bible, and just when Paul thought he had finished, he gave the whole service again in the Eskimo language. He followed that with a kind of summary of it in halting, barely understandable German, which he read from a notebook. Finally he asked the congregation to sing "Abide With Me," each in his own language. A reedy little foot-pumped organ played by a nervous old woman began the tune. The Eskimos sang exuberantly, their curiously musical language drowning out the murmurs of the others. The only white man to sing as confidently was Guns, who boomed away at the back of the church. To Paul's astonishment, he knew all the words of three verses.

The room seemed to grow hotter every minute and Paul felt grateful when he finally found himself standing outside the church in the stinging snow and wind. As he walked back toward the ship Brit fell in beside him.

"Were they personal friends of yours?" she asked.

"Not really," he replied, "but in a way . . ."

"Funerals here always make me feel very strange," she

said. "There is a Danish saying: 'to die in Greenland is to achieve immortality.' In this permafrost, the bodies lie in their graves without changing much for centuries."

"Is that really true?"

"They date some of the old Norse expeditions here by the style of the European clothes on the bodies in graves hundreds of years old."

Paul wondered what future archeologists would make of Sparks's and Blake's bullet-ridden bodies in their Coast Guard uniforms. It was curious to think that those two men might be the final witnesses of their age.

"You want to come to my boat for coffee?" Brit asked.

"I'm so tired I can barely stand and there are a million things I have to do."

"If you could only trust me, I might be able to help with some of it. I know this country and these people."

They paused in the lee of a sod hut to escape the wind. Brit's face was so lost in the fur hood of her parka and his own eyes were stinging so in the cold that he could hardly see her expression, but her voice was soft and sad.

"Is Peomeenie a good man?" he asked suddenly.

"The best. He's a pilot and a lead hunter. That's aristocracy here."

"Can I trust him?"

"To do what?"

"I'm not sure yet. He captured the German lieutenant, didn't he?"

"To Peo that was a rescue more than a capture. He would rescue anyone. I'm honestly not sure whether he would fight for you if that's what you want to know."

"Do the Eskimos have contact with the Germans?"

"Not ours. Ours have never gone near Supportup-Kangerdula. There are some rumors that others farther up the coast have been trading with the Germans. I don't know if they're true."

Paul was tempted to ask her whether Peomeenie would be a good man to send as a scout to map the German base, but he knew there was no way he could be completely sure she would not relay anything he said to the enemy.

"Thanks," he said brusquely. "I have to get back to my ship."

"I'm living in my boat now. Come if you want me."

He did not reply. He was so tired that he suddenly was not sure he could make it through the deep snow to his ship. Perhaps sensing his weakness, dogs came toward him from all directions. Brit shouted and led them away.

When he returned to the warmth of his cabin Paul allowed himself to get two more hours of sleep. When the quartermaster called him, he said, "Is Mr. Green aboard?"

"He's with the wounded, sir."

"How about Mr. Williams?"

"He's with the prisoners, but Mr. Farmer just came aboard."

"I thought he was sick."

"He looks fine, sir. Do you want to see him? He's in the wardroom."

"I'll go see him."

Seth was sitting at the table in the wardroom writing letters, a habitual posture.

"God, I'm glad to see you," Paul said. "I was worried."

"My ticker just kicked up a little. They say I need rest, but I can't stand it up there in that sickroom. Just getting back to the ship makes me better."

"Don't do any work. Just take it easy."

"I can stand my watch, skipper. Don't take that away from me."

"It's up to you. Is Boats still with the prisoners?"

"He's sacked out up forward. Can I do anything for you?"

"Where's Flags?"

"In the forecastle, I think. Can I get him for you?"

"Ring him on the telephone. Tell him I want to see him in my cabin."

Somehow Paul's brief sleep had left him more exhausted than before. His muscles ached as he walked to his cabin and he felt dizzy. It's just delayed shock, he thought. God, what will happen if I'm really coming down with something? He barely had the strength to get into his bunk.

"You wanted me, sir?" Flags asked.

"Go to the village and find an Eskie named Peomeenie. Ask him real politely to come here to see me. He's the guy who brought in the Kraut lieutenant."

"Aye, aye, sir."

"Show him here and wake me. Thanks, Flags. I'm just too bushed to go myself."

"Get some sleep, sir. I'll get him as soon as I can."

"Wait a minute. Ask Cookie to fix the best spread he can for him. Tell him this guy can really help us."

"Aye, aye, sir."

Peomeenie soon arrived. He was wearing a gray sealskin parka and britches made of polar bear skin with a big dark patch of something like mink sewn into the crotch. It made him look oddly naked in his bulky clothes. His boots were of soft white leather with geometric designs around the tops in red, black and blue. His clothes were spotlessly clean, even though he exuded the pungent odor Paul had noticed in the church. Despite his gray-streaked long hair, his round copper-colored face looked young until he opened his mouth, revealing the brown stumps of bad teeth. Completely unconscious of them, he smiled and laughed almost continuously. Paul judged that he was just under five feet tall, but he was a compact giant, not a midget. He looked as though he could punch his way through a stone wall.

"It's good to see you," Paul said, taking his tiny, iron hand. "I haven't had a chance really to thank you for bringing in the German lieutenant."

"Very nice," Peomeenie said. "Thank you, captain. Very nice. This is very fine ship."

Paul had the impression that the man had understood little and that he was repeating memorized phrases almost parrotlike. The powerful little hunter never stopped beaming. His main effort seemed to be to please.

"Let's go down and get something to eat," Paul said and led the way to the galley.

Cookie had prepared steak with mushroom sauce, a variety of canned vegetables, strawberry ice cream from the destroyer and a big chocolate cake. Peomeenie ate ravenously, but handled his knife and fork with skill. It was difficult for him to chew much, both because of his teeth and because he apparently couldn't stop smiling. He gulped his food in great chunks. When coffee was served he put five teaspoonfuls of sugar into his cup.

"Would you like a bag of sugar to take with you?" Paul asked.

Peomeenie's smile almost split his face.

"Fix up a ten-pound bag for him, Cookie," Paul said.

Back in his cabin, Paul decided not to offer Peomeenie a drink. Apparently alcohol was as bad for the Eskimos as for Indians and old ice pilots. He sat on the edge of his bunk and gave Peomeenie the stool by the chart table.

"How would you like to do a job for us?" he began. "A really important job?"

Peomeenie beamed the whole time Paul described the reconnaissance of the German base and kept nodding his head, but Paul suspected that he understood very little if anything. Obviously an interpreter was needed. He thought of getting Swanson, but guessed the old man would hate the idea of involving an Eskimo in the war, even if he were basically on the side of the Americans when he got his fear of the Germans under control. The only other interpreter he could think of was Brit. He still wasn't sure that he could completely trust her, but there might be even more danger in refusing to trust anyone.

"You know Brit, don't you? Let's go see her. She can help us talk."

"Brit, yes!" Peomeenie said and led the way to the ketch on the ways.

Paul had barely enough strength to climb the ladder to the deck of the little yacht. At the sound of their footsteps, Brit slid open the hatch.

"So you and Peo got together," she said. "Come below."

Brit offered Peomeenie hot chocolate, not Aquavit, Paul noticed, and while she prepared it, she stood over the stove and said, "Have you decided to trust me?"

"I don't think I have much choice. Look, I'm sorry. I need an interpreter."

Peomeenie smiled and nodded.

"I want him to be a scout for us. I want him to tell me what the Germans have got at Supportup. Do you think he could get in there and out without getting caught?"

"I'll let him answer that," she said and spoke rapidly to the Eskimo in his language. When Peomeenie replied he got up from the bunk where he had been sitting and stood to his full childlike height. His dark eyes flashed and he gesticulated with his small iron hands.

"Peomeenie says that he is almost as good a hunter as the old people, his ancestors, and they could move like ghosts through packs of wolves, never mind camps of men, without ever being noticed. He wants to know why you want to find out about the Germans. He says they are bothering no one at Supportup, which is inhabited only by demons anyhow."

"Ask him if he is afraid of the demons."

After a brief exchange during which the Eskimo gesticu-

411

lated with even more animation, Brit said, "He says that the old people were afraid of nothing. They killed polar bears single-handedly with a bone knife. He is not as good as they, but their blood runs in his veins." Brit paused. "Fear is not Peo's big problem," she said.

"What is?"

"He wants to know if you intend to kill the Germans."

"Tell him yes. Tell him they killed two of my men and the entire crew of a ship just like the *Arluk*."

This time there was a longer exchange of words incomprehensible to Paul.

"He wants to know how many Germans there are," she said finally.

"About a hundred on the base and maybe twenty more on a ship. I'm not sure exactly. I hope he can make a more reliable count."

After Brit had relayed this to the Eskimo, he made a brief reply. Brit smiled.

"He says he cannot kill so many Germans alone. He wants to know what help he'll have."

"Tell him we'll do the killing. I just want information, exact location of buildings and the location of big guns. I want him to draw us a map."

"He won't draw you a map, but he'll remember everything he sees in detail," she said. "He can point things out on a chart here."

"Fine, but I want him to take one of our men with him. Will he do that?"

"You don't want to ask him that. None of your men could possibly keep up with Peo, or move like a ghost, as he said. You'll have to let him do this job his own way."

"He'll go all alone?"

"He'll take a woman, a young Eskimo woman who can travel well."

"Ask him how much time he will need."

"I shouldn't ask him that. He has too much sense to answer it. The time he needs will depend on snow conditions, the weather, luck and what he finds there. Eskimos don't set time limits."

"How much time do you think he'll need? Can you make a guess?"

"At the very least, a week there and a week back—he has to go around the mountains. More probably a month, and possibly two months or even longer. If the weather gets real bad, he'll just build an igloo and hole up till it clears. Eskimos never hurry."

"But I'm no Eskimo! I'm supposed to stop German weather reports. The Germans are using them to bomb cities every day."

"I'll try to explain that to him."

This time Brit and Peomeenie had a conversation that lasted several minutes. When it was over, Brit said, "He says he'll go as fast as he can. He hopes he can be back in two weeks but can't promise."

"Would he be insulted if I offered to pay him, either in money or in food supplies?"

"No, you can bet he wouldn't."

"How much should I offer?"

"You're asking him to risk his life and his woman. How about a year's supply of canned goods and dry stores?"

"That's fine."

Peomeenie listened attentively and made a short reply.

"Good, but he also wants a rifle and five hundred shells."

"Tell him I'll give him five rifles and thousands of shells if he brings me back really detailed information."

"I don't think that's a good idea. The Eskimos are already exhausting their supply of game."

"Hell, tell him I'll give him anything he wants if he'll give me detailed information on the number of men, the location of buildings and guns, and the kind of supplies. I want to know all about the topography. I want his advice on how best to attack these people."

After another brief interchange, Brit said, "He wants your whaleboat."

"I'll try to get him one like it. If we capture German stores, he and his friends can have those."

Peomeenie grinned more broadly than ever as he listened to this.

"He wants to know when you want him to start."

"As soon as possible."

This time the interchange was very brief.

"As soon as the blizzard is over," she said. "He's going to go to choose a woman and to see to his gear now."

After Peomeenie had shaken hands and had beamingly left, Brit said, "Can I get you some Aquavit?"

"I'm so tired that it will probably put me right to sleep."

"You look exhausted. You must have had a terrible time. Can't you take at least a day to rest?"

413

"Later maybe. I have to move the ship to a safer place. When the weather clears, the Krauts may come after me with their ship or light planes."

"This snow isn't going to stop for a while. Often it goes on for a week or more."

"I have to be ready," Paul said, but he stretched out on a bunk, propping himself on pillows just enough to accept a glass of Aquavit.

"Skoal!" she said, touching her glass to his.

"Do you know what that means?"

"Skull. Let us drink from the skulls of our enemies. That's what it used to mean. Now it means 'Cheers.' Time has wrought quite a change, hasn't it?"

"The old meaning is better for these times."

"Bring me a German skull and I'll drink from it. I'd drink German blood from it. They've taken everybody and everything I had."

"And I keep thinking I'm the only one who understands this war."

"Plenty understand it, but you're lucky to be able to do something about it."

There was a moment of silence during which she refilled his glass and her own. He noticed that there was a slight tremor in her fingers again.

"But you can't think about the war all the time," she said. "You can't fight if you can't rest."

"That sounds reasonable."

"You look as though you have good Norse blood."

"German blood. I am what I hate, or a recent transmutation of it."

"Maybe it takes one to catch one."

"I'm not *that* German. The Germans are me gone mad. Maybe that's why they scare me so much."

"But you don't look scared. You seem born for your job."

"I was born to sail around the world in an old yawl. Before the Krauts clobbered me, I couldn't think of anything but taking you with me on a voyage to the South Seas."

"There isn't much we could do in the South Seas that we can't do here, except swimming."

"That's true."

"Have you ever had a Swedish massage?"

"No."

414

"A Danish massage is better. Are you too tired for me to show you?"

"I was a hundred years old when I came in here. Now I'm about forty. Give me a few minutes, and I'll be back to twenty-two."

"Is that how old you are? I thought you just looked young."

"Twenty-three next month."

"How did you ever get command of a ship so soon?"

"I traded the ship's launch for booze and stole a whaleboat from a big cutter."

"Is that the way it works in America?" She smiled a little.

"That's the way it worked in Greenland."

They were both quiet as she unbuttoned his clothes and stroked his neck, his shoulders and chest. They kissed, and then she began stroking him again.

"Your body has always trusted me," she said. "It just took your head a long time to figure me out."

"Some parts of my body are very smart."

"And strong even when you're tired. God, it's great to have a man so young."

"I'm not supposed to ask how old you are, am I?"

"Not old enough to be your mother, but nobody who's been through what I've seen is young."

"I'm about twenty years older than I was six months ago."

She laughed. "You have much time to make up for."

"I'm afraid that lost time is just lost."

"We can try like hell, but the way to do that is *not* to hurry. Hold still!"

"How come you always make me laugh? Making love was always a terribly serious matter when I was really young."

"Laughing together is what the Eskimos call it. Only the sailors call it ping-ping. The Eskimos just laugh together."

"Do they do it well?"

"Are you trying to trap me into confessions?"

"Just curious."

"I've never heard them complain about frigid women or impotent men, but then they never complain about anything. That's not their style."

"Show me how to make love like Eskimos."

"I'd rather take off our clothes. Just laugh a lot and be

kind and don't complain. Have a good time. Then you'll know how the Eskimos make love."

Paul slept heavily for five hours when the laughing together finally ended. He might have slept another ten, but she awoke him.

"The snow is letting up," she said. "Did you say you want to move your ship?"

"Yes. Thanks for not letting me sleep."

"Does this prove I'm on your side?"

"Beyond doubt."

"Will you listen to my ideas about how to attack the Germans?"

"I'll listen."

"I'll make a model of the fjord at Supportup-Kangerdula with clay. When Peo comes back, he'll show you where everything is. We'll get as many Eskimos to help us as we can. They'll lug supplies in and some may fight. I'll go along as an interpreter. What do you think of that?"

"I'll think about it—I promise you that. The model of the fjord is a good idea."

After a long kiss he hurried back to the ship. It was dark, but in the clearing sky the moon glowed behind a cloud. Nathan had rousted some depth charges from the hold to the well deck and was changing their firing mechanism. On the chart of Angmagssalik Fjord he had marked a shallow bay inside a crescent of rocky islets which he said would be a good place to defend with mines. The whaleboat had already been taken aboard, and except for the men guarding the prisoners and two of the wounded, all hands were present and accounted for. The ship was ready to get under way.

# CHAPTER 42

The relatively shallow bay which Nathan had chosen was about six miles up the fjord, west of the settlement. Just as they were arriving, the moon broke through

416

the clouds and set the snowy banks and icy mountains all around them glittering more brightly than they did during many Arctic days. The anchorage was in a semicircular cove protected by a string of smooth-backed granite islands which under snow were almost indistinguishable from growlers, small icebergs. Since the chart showed only one channel deep and unobstructed enough for even small ships, it was an ideal place to protect with mines.

"Nathan, we don't have to mess with the mines tonight," Paul said. "If he is going to come after us, he'll have to figure out where we are first."

"It's no sweat," Nathan replied. "All we have to do is drop the stuff. I have everything ready. The only thing that will take any time at all is I have to lead wire to the nearest island and rig an aerial there. I'll need the whaleboat."

"The wire goes from the aerial to the charges on the bottom?"

"That's right. It's a pretty crude rig, but I guarantee it."

"Is the wire waterproof?"

"Come on, skipper! Do you really think you have to tell me to be sure to put waterproof wire underwater?"

"Where did you get the stuff?"

"The tin can, of course. Do you think I got nothing but ice cream and steaks when I kept sending the boat over to her?"

The diffident Nathan was fast disappearing, Paul noted, and was being replaced by a man damned near as cocky as Mowrey in his own way. Nathan was getting so he wouldn't take any crap from anybody, including his about to be twenty-three-year-old skipper.

The job of laying the mines did not take much time, but the men grumbled at the heavy work involved in dropping three 300-pound depth charges overboard without fouling the wire. "Christ, they don't mess around with mines even at the big bases on the west coast," Flags said.

The aerial which Nathan placed on the icy rocks nearest the channel was as slender as a trout rod stuck in the snow and as difficult to see. When Nathan came back aboard, Paul towed the whaleboat to an anchorage as near to shore as possible. That would make the ship harder to see from the air, and he wanted to put as much distance as possible between the vessel and a total of 900 pounds of TNT. The spot he chose for dropping the anchor was about a mile from the entrance to the channel, far enough to re-duce the shock and the vulnerability of the *Arluk* to the all too well remembered machine guns of the hunter-killer if she opened fire before the mines got her.

As soon as the ship was anchored, Nathan set up a black box with an innocent appearing white button in the pilot-house near the engineroom telegraph. Paul assembled all hands to listen while Nathan explained that a touch of that button would blow up the whole entrance to the bay. A few of the men, including Seth Farmer and Cookie, looked impressed, but Chief Banes was skeptical and some of the men obviously thought it was, so to speak, going a little overboard.

Maybe his precautions were excessive, Paul thought as he toured the ship before going to his bunk, making sure that a good man and an officer would always be on watch in the pilothouse, that the red decks on the forecastlehead and flying bridge were covered with snow, that the radar would always be manned in periods of bad visibility and the 20-millimeter antiaircraft guns at the ready whenever the skies were clear. With the sound of machine-gun bul-lets smashing into the superstructure of the trawler still reverberating in his ears, it was not necessary to remind himself that there was no such thing as excessive precau-tion.

Lying in his bunk that night, Paul tried to imagine what the captain of the hunter-killer, the *Valkyrie* for Christ's sake, was like and what he would do. In his mind, Paul even gave the man a name and an image: Fat Herman. Fat Herman had succeeded in outwitting Hansen and everyone else aboard the *Nanmak*. He had been ruthless enough to gun down the survivors instead of trying to cope with the problem of prisoners aboard a small ship. He had been clever enough to sucker Paul himself for fair with his damned outboard skiff or timed charges. What was he thinking now?

Probably he's as mad at me as I'm mad at him, Paul thought. After all, I called in the planes to sink his supply ship. Fatso must be aware that I know where his base is and am just trying to figure out the best way to attack it. He must know about all the air power we've got. Probably in the back of his mind Fatso even knows that Germany will lose the war. He thinks of himself as the underdog, just like all captains of small ships do, but with far more reason than I have. Being that the blimp boy is a Kraut, he will be both brave and stupid about everything in war except the mechanics of battle. He will love the idea of a last-ditch stand, dying for his fatherland, going down in a blaze of glory. Even in defeat he will long to show how well he can handle a bloody battle ax. So he will probably attack me. He will figure that I've crawled into the nearest port to lick my wounds and plan my next move against him. He probably knows this country well, or has good charts modernized with aerial photography. He has a fast torpedo boat. What could be more to his taste than a quick dash into the enemy's fjord to catch him all unprepared at a wharf or at anchor and to sink him with a torpedo fired at point-blank range? German subs had sneaked into a great British naval base at Scappa Floe. Stealing into an undefended Greenland fjord to sink a trawler should not appear difficult to him. Maybe he had thought enough by now to be kicking himself for not finishing off the *Arluk* while he had a chance and was eager to complete his job.

When would he come? He'd plan to arrive off the mouth of the fjord in darkness, but to enter at dawn or in bright moonlight. First he would have to make sure of the *Arluk*'s exact position. If his light planes were not yet ready to fly, he might have spies among the Danes or Eskimos, or he could send a scout to Angmagssalik, just as Paul had sent one to his base. If the Germans had not made friends with any Eskimos, one of them might know enough about the Arctic to try a thirty-mile journey on the ice himself.

Of course this was all pure speculation, Paul reminded himself. Perhaps the hunter-killer was repairing her engines, perhaps she was preparing an elaborate hiding place in expectation of air attack, or maybe Herman was just drinking his Polish vodka and taking it easy for a few days. Even in time of war, nothing was what usually happened. Still, it was comforting to think that old Seth, who was now standing watch in the pilothouse, could blow up any ship that tried to get into their cove by placing one of his gnarled, arthritic fingers on a small white button.

What if the damned thing didn't work? No machinery could be counted on entirely and as far as Paul knew, Nathan had not tested his rig. Maybe Fatso would have the last laugh after all, and the last thing the men of the *Arluk* would see would be one more glimpse of that sleek, speeding hunter-killer with the machine guns blazing from her decks as a torpedo jumped from her bow.

No, machinery could not be counted on, but some men could, and Nathan would not be suckered, not in his chosen field, Paul was suddenly sure. Feeling deliciously safe, he slept the sleep of the self-deluded.

This time he was able to sleep his fill. It was dawn when he awoke, the start of a short but bright winter day. As the sun rose over the tops of the mountains, the whole fjord glittered so brightly that the crew began searching frantically to find enough dark glasses for all hands. Paul was drinking coffee in the forecastle and nibbling the end of a fresh croissant, when the general alarm went off and Flags came running in to shout, "Light plane, skipper! He don't look like he could hurt a flea, but Mr. Green said to sound the general alarm."

Paul hurried to the bridge. He could hear the drone of a distant plane as he ran, but when he first scanned the sky, he could see nothing. Looking in the direction in which Nathan pointed, he spied a ski plane that looked hardly bigger than a fly as it flew just above the silvery ridge of the mountain across the fjord. It didn't look as though it could drop a bomb much bigger than a hand grenade, but probably it was already radioing the position of the *Arluk* to Fatso and it could send high-frequency weather reports great distances.

"Can you take over, skipper?" Nathan said. "I better radio GreenPat. If he's got a Lightning in the air, it might get here in time to catch the guy."

"Give it a try," Paul said, but the ski plane had already disappeared on the other side of the mountain. When a Lightning roared in almost an hour later, its pilot had to content himself with swooping in futile circles over the frozen wastelands, the banshee shriek of his engines and wings echoing off the mountains loudly enough to rattle the dishes in Cookie's galley.

After the Lightning had gone, Nathan said, "Skipper, do you want to inspect the prisoner camp? Mr. Williams and Boats are kind of proud of the way they've set it up."

"I guess I should have a look at it," Paul said, though the idea of seeing the prisoners for some reason upset him unreasonably.

"Before we go, I'd like to do something that may seem silly," Nathan said, looking oddly embarrassed.

420

"What?"

"I'd like to practice with this damn pistol," he replied, putting his hand on the handle of the .45 automatic in the holster on his belt. "I keep carrying the thing around and I even waved it at a few of the prisoners when we were getting them settled, but I've never actually shot it. I've figured out how to put the safety off and how to change clips, but I wouldn't know what the hell to do if it jammed and I doubt if I could hit anything I couldn't practically touch. Do you mind if I get Guns to give me a lesson before we visit the prisoners?"

"That's a good idea," Paul said. "I've shot mine, but I doubt if I could hit much of anything and I wouldn't know what to do if it jammed. Let's get Guns to show both of us."

For a few minutes no one could find Guns aboard the ship and Paul wondered whether he had gone crazy enough to jump overboard, perhaps in pursuit of Germans. Finally he was located in the engineroom. From Chief Banes he had got a big flat file, the hardest steel available aboard the ship, and he was in the process of grinding it down on an emery wheel to make a murderous knife. He carried this half-finished scimitar to the well deck, and before giving his officers a lesson in the care and use of .45 automatics, demonstrated how he planned to take off a German's head with a single swipe.

After discovering that the mechanism of the pistols was not as complex as it looked, Paul and Nathan engaged in target practice, blasting away at empty bottles and cans which Cookie provided. At first they could hit nothing, and the assembled crew mixed their laughter with jeers. After firing three clips, both Paul and Nathan could sink a can at a distance of about ten yards.

"Do you want to practice quick draws?" Nathan asked Paul with a grin.

"I'm still afraid I'd shoot my foot off. I'll have a shoot-out with you, though. You take ten shots and I'll take ten. Guns, throw the cans as far as you can. Nathan, I bet ten bucks I can sink more of the bastards with ten shots than you can."

"You're on!" Nathan said. "You take the first ten. Get the cans way out there, Guns."

Guns went to the flying bridge to achieve more distance with throws. He managed to toss a big peach can so far that Paul needed three shots to sink it. Next Guns threw a catsup bottle even further.

"Catsup bottles aren't fair!" Paul said. "I can hardly see it."

"Have you got a catsup bottle for me?" Nathan asked.

"I got two left," Guns replied.

"Then we each get one catsup bottle and nine cans."

"You can't take your nine cans first," Paul said after firing and missing the bobbing neck of the almost invisible bottle. "These things are almost impossible to hit."

After the fourth try, Paul shattered the bottle. His final score was one bottle and two cans. When Nathan's turn came, he held his pistol in both hands and steadied the barrel on a rail.

"No fair!" Paul said.

"All's fair in love and war," Nathan replied.

The crew cheered as Nathan won the contest by sinking a bottle and four cans. Paul took a ten-dollar bill from his wallet and gave it to him.

They took the whaleboat about three miles in the direction of the settlement. The island lay only about a hundred and fifty yards off the end of a point, where Boats and Nathan had set up a .50-caliber machine gun to command the whole area. Fast tidal currents jostled small pieces of ice as they swirled around the island. Obviously this was a place from which no man could escape without a boat. Three sod huts with squat tile chimneys from which acrid coal smoke rose filled the middle of the island and no one was visible outside. The Eskimos had built a kind of igloo only about six feet from the machine gun on the point. They had inserted a pane of glass through which the guards could watch any activity on the island. A portable searchlight from the ship with its box of batteries was on top of this structure.

"We don't have any guards on the island at all," Nathan said. "I figured it would be too easy for the Krauts to jump them and hold them hostage. I commandeered the Danes' launch. It's tied up on the other side of the point. I can't see any way those men can escape."

Before visiting the prisoners, they stopped at the point. Boats, who had the watch, came to meet the boat and held the painter while Paul took a brief look into the ice hut. There was an oil heater there under a small hole in the roof, a tarpaulin on the ice floor, a canvas cot on which a seaman napped and packing boxes for chairs under the window overlooking the island. Six automatic rifles were stacked in a corner. The place hardly looked comfortable, but it at least was warm. As Paul and Nathan climbed back into the boat, Boats said, "I'll pipe them out to meet you." Putting his boatswain's whistle to his lips, he blew a piercing blast. Immediately a parka-coated figure came from the door of each hut.

"I've got them trained pretty good," Boats said. "If they don't come out smartly when I pipe for them I shoot a few rounds right around their damned huts."

"What do they do when they want to get in touch with you?"

"I gave them a mouth foghorn. If they want something, they send one man out of the huts, no more. We send the boat in for him and talk here. That way they don't have much of a chance to start something."

"Do they give you many complaints?"

"They did at first."

"What did you do?" Paul asked.

"I don't know. Mr. Green talked to them."

Paul decided to inspect the prisoners from the boat without going ashore.

Boats got a megaphone and yelled at the three men standing outside the huts. They came as close to the end of the point as they could to hear. In English Boats was telling them to have all hands line up on the shore of their island for inspection. They gestured that they did not understand.

"Some of them know English and some don't, skipper, or maybe they just understand when they want to. Can you tell them in German?"

Paul repeated the order in German. The prisoners ran to their huts, and soon all the men tumbled out, buttoning their parkas and pulling on mittens. A limping figure whom Paul recognized as the lieutenant who had tried to escape gave an order, and the prisoners fell into a single file facing the machine gun, behind which Boats now stood. They waited, shifting nervously and rubbing their mittened hands together while Paul and Nathan got in the boat. The water obviously was deep right up to the icy beach of the island. Circling around to approach with his bow into the swirling current, Paul found he could parallel the shore only about fifteen feet from the line of men.

Again he was struck by the fact that they resembled his own crew so closely. Most of them in their twenties, they stared stolidly at the two American officers in the boat. Neither fear nor anger showed in their faces, only discomfort from the cold. Only one man, one of the oldest and the fattest, returned the stare of Nathan and Paul with anything which could be interpreted as defiance. He stood near the end of the line, and when the boat came abreast of him, he spat and wiped his lips with the back of his right mitten.

"That one always does that when he sees me," Nathan said calmly. "I thought of having the boys throw a bucket of water on him, but what the hell. If I was in a concentration camp, I'd probably spit."

"And the Krauts would probably bash your face in with a rifle butt," Paul said. "I don't like it. I'm not in a mood for disrespect."

Paul slowed the engine enough to keep the boat stationary in the current before he called in German, "Lieutenant, bring your men to attention."

The lieutenant barked, and the men stiffened.

"Lieutenant, tell your fat man near the end of the line that if he spits again in the presence of an American officer, we'll have him wetted down with a bucket. He'll make a nice ice statue. Is that clear?"

"Yes, captain," the lieutenant said with what appeared to be respect and he shouted at the fat man, whose face became corpse-like, pale and motionless.

"Lieutenant, do you have enough food, water, shelter and heat?" Paul shouted.

"A bare minimum for survival, captain, but conditions here are intolerable. I shall have to make a complaint through official channels as soon as I can."

"You're better off than the men from the *Nanmak*. Don't give me any shit, lieutenant. You might not live long enough to complain."

Paul gunned the engine of the boat and returned to the *Arluk*. Although he did not regret anything he had said, he felt shaken. Maybe I'm too damned used to thinking of myself as the underdog, he thought. Glancing at Nathan, he saw that he too looked unhappy. The role of the victor is hard to learn, but it's better than being a loser, he thought. Still, how come there's no pleasure on any side of this damn war?

# CHAPTER 43

Paul found the men of the *Arluk* busy trying to patch up the damage inflicted by the hunter-killer's guns. Plywood was being sawed to replace shattered ports, and was being screwed over jagged holes in the superstructure. Nathan lay down to get some much needed sleep, and there wasn't much for Paul to do. Feeling almost unbearably restless, he paced the gun deck. Suddenly the future appeared disconcertingly clear to him. In a couple of weeks or so Peomeenie would come back with enough information to pinpoint the German base and artillery positions in the long fjord. This Nathan would radio to GreenPat and the army air force would send in enough bombers to blow hell out of whatever the Germans had. The Germans, however, would lie low in caves or underground shelters they had constructed for the purpose. After the planes had gone, they would rebuild at least enough of their base to enable them to send out the weather reports to their own air force in Europe. To stop that flow of important information, there would have to be more scouting to pinpoint the latest targets and more bombing raids, but there would always be enough survivors to keep the weather reports going out until men arrived on the ground to kill or imprison every last Kraut. The men on the ground were going to be the *Arluk*'s crew, because ground troops on the west coast couldn't cross the ice cap. Planes couldn't land anywhere near Supportup, and no icebreakers were available to bring in men. So the *Arluk* was on her own. Maybe some of the Eskimos could be induced to help, but the Danes here were too old. It was difficult to guess how many of the Germans would survive the air raids, but since they had undoubtedly prepared for them, quite a lot could be expected to live. Since more than a hundred Krauts were probably there now, the *Arluk*'s thirty-four men, and less now that two were dead and more wounded, might well find themselves outnumbered. Almost certainly the Germans were trained for ground fighting in the Arctic and were well armed. Some, maybe many of the *Arluk*'s men would probably die. These men were Paul's responsibility and in some profound way now, his brothers, even though he knew little about the private lives of many of them. Their survival would depend on their commanding officer's ability to outwit the Germans. Incidentally, his own personal survival was at stake too, and he wished he could think of that as an unimportant detail. He couldn't. So why was he pacing around doing nothing when he should be making a plan for attack?

There was no reason to do nothing until Peomeenie got back. Paul could guess a lot about the kind of facilities the Germans must have for a central weather base with about a hundred men and one ship which he had had ample opportunity to observe. The only real question was where in the thirty miles of the fjord these facilities were hidden. No matter where they were exactly, how could they best be mopped up after the planes left?

Surprise would be important. I must jump them the minute they come up from their shelters, while they're still dazed, Paul thought. I must have machine guns and mortars already trained on them, just waiting. That means I must establish a base near there just before the air raids, and the Eskimos can damn well help me to do that if they want to.

I'll hit them from both the land and the sea, Paul thought. As soon as I'm sure that their artillery has been knocked out, I'll bring the old *Arluk* into the mouth of the fjord with all guns firing. At the same time about half my crew can attack them with machine guns and mortars from the surrounding mountains. Hell, maybe we can roll fused depth charges down on the bastards. I'll find ways to give them hell, but in the end some of the *Arluk*'s crew, possibly many, maybe including himself, would die—of that he was curiously certain. And the thought made him exceedingly angry. Who, after all, were those crazy Germans? Why should they be allowed to take the blood of good young men? Why not ask the army to drop poison gas on their whole malignant base? Why not find some way to spread lethal diseases among them? Why fuck around?

It was a good thought, Paul concluded, but the army air

426

force would prefer to risk the lives of a few trawler men than to change the precarious rules of the war. The *Arluk's* crew would be ordered in and some would die. That's just the way things were.

And all Paul could do now, while he waited for Peomeenie to return, was to organize as much help from the Eskimos and the Danes as he could. The person with whom to begin that business was Brit. At least he'd get screwed, in the good sense of the word for a change, in the process. That was the one really good part of the war that Paul could see.

Before ordering the boat to take him ashore, Paul went to the wardroom to tell Nathan that he was leaving the ship in his charge. The tall, gaunt executive officer was sleeping so soundly that Paul hated to awaken him, but Nathan opened his eyes at the sound of Paul approaching his bunk.

"What's up, skipper?"

"I have to go ashore to see what help I can promote from the Eskies."

"I'll take over, skipper. Look, do you mind if I train Flags to replace Sparks? Flags already knows Morse."

"Fine. He hasn't had many signals to keep him busy lately."

"I can teach him enough to monitor the important frequencies right away. If I can find the time, I can finish up some kind of walkie-talkies I've started to build for the guards with the prisoners and to carry in the whaleboat."

"Nathan, you're a goddamn genius."

"I'm great at inventing things that have been in production for years," Nathan said with a straight face.

Stevens and Krater, two seamen whom Paul had never got to know well, manned the whaleboat and Paul took its helm to steer it through some fairly tricky waters to the settlement. Stevens looked as though he might have been a college boy and Krater struck Paul as though he might have been a poolroom tough before joining the service. They had become friends, however; they joked in low voices like high school boys in front of their parents and gave each other playful shoves as they sat on the middle thwart of the boat. When they came alongside the wharf, Paul said, "It's pretty cold here for you guys to wait for me and I have no idea how long I'll be. You better go back to the ship. Come and get me at two o'clock."

"Official business, skipper?" Krater asked and Stevens grinned.

"Partly," Paul said.

"Don't do nothing I wouldn't do," Krater said as they pulled away in the boat.

Turning, Paul was glad to see smoke pluming up from the Charlie Noble of the little ketch on the ways. Brit heard him coming up the ladder and met him on the deck. "The Eskimos say they saw a little ski plane this morning," she said. "I tried to get somebody in a kayak to go tell you, but they're all off seal hunting."

"I saw it. It's no immediate danger. Brit, I have something important to talk to you about."

When they went below he sat on a bunk after placing his cumbersome pistol and belt on the table.

"I'm out of coffee, but I can give you tea or hot chocolate," she said.

"Later please. Brit, how do I go about organizing the biggest possible work force from the Eskimos? Do I offer to pay them? Do I preach patriotism?"

"What do you want them to do?"

"Build a temporary base near Supportup and take guns and men to it. If I can find some Eskies who want to help us fight, so much the better."

"Swan won't let the Eskimos have anything to do with you. He doesn't want to get them involved in the war at all. He's mad as hell about Peomeenie."

"What can he do about it?"

"He'll just tell the Eskimos not to talk to you at all. They'll do what he says. They respect him."

"Can we talk him out of that?"

"Paul, Swan's whole life has been a love affair with the Eskimos. He came out here when he was twenty-one years old to bring them religion, and has never been home once since. They're his children; a few of them literally. He doesn't really give a damn about anyone else."

"So he'll fight me when I try to get their help."

"If he thought you were going to get them shot up, I think he'd kill you."

"Well, that makes it clear enough. I'll have to lock him up."

"Paul, he's an old man! He's practically a saint to the Eskimos. What are you saying?"

428

"I'll put him with the other prisoners out on the island and tell the Eskies the Krauts got him. Maybe that will make them fight for me—"

"Paul, what kind of a mind have you got?"

"A German mind. It's simple. If I'm going to save my own men, I have to get as much help as I can from the Eskies. Anyone who tries to stop me is my enemy. Any lies I have to tell to get the help I need to save the lives of my men won't bother me."

"And you don't worry about saving the lives of the Eskies?"

"I worry about them just as much but no more than I worry about my own life. I thought you knew something about war, Brit."

"I'm learning more all the time. Can't you put the old man under guard in his own house? You'll kill him if you put him out there in those huts with all those Germans."

"I can't afford enough guards to stand duty in different places. As you say, Swanson is old. I'd rather have him die than someone who's hardly had a chance to live at all."

"Well, you talk cold reason," Brit said. "I can't deny that." Her voice was cold.

She was standing near the table looking down at the pistol. "Men with guns all sound about the same," she said.

"I thought you were on my side."

"Oh, I am. I'm on your side and I hope you're on my side. I promise never to fight you. It's rather nice to have the man with the gun on my side for a change."

"Good. I'll take Swanson out to the island and leave him with the other prisoners at two this afternoon when my boat comes to get me."

"Then I better go tell him. He'll have to get ready."

"We'll tell him nothing in advance. I don't want him turning the Eskimos against me."

"You'll just grab him and march him to your boat at gunpoint?"

"Not so the Eskimos can see me. You can bring him down to the boat in friendly fashion."

"I won't do it. You're as bad as the bloody Germans."

"There's only one big difference between me and your bloody Germans. They started this war and I'm doing my bit to help finish it with as little loss of blood as possible."

429

"So you want me to trick an old man who saved my life once into letting you take him prisoner without his people knowing."

"Sorry, but I can't afford to be sentimental. I have two dead men lying up there by your church. That's enough for me."

"What will you do if I don't help you?"

"I wouldn't like it, but I'd have to put you out there with the other prisoners. If I post guards all over the place, I'll have no one to run my ship—"

"Is this a test for me, making me betray Swan? Are you doing this because I slept with Swan? Are you punishing him or trying to see if I still love him?"

"You can't understand that I don't give a damn about anything right now except keeping as many of my men alive as I can while we're killing Germans."

"I'm beginning to understand."

"Brit, if I let my personal feelings stop me from protecting my men and wiping out the Germans—"

"I understand . . . I've just never known a man like you before. I'm sure we should have had more like you in Denmark."

With her forefinger she touched the handle of the automatic, delicately caressing the roughness of its grip and the smooth steel at its edge. "We can't let my father have guns," she said. "He's been in a very bad depression ever since we left Denmark. He tried to kill himself twice."

"I'm sorry."

"My husband hated guns. He taught biology at the University of Copenhagen. He called it the science of life. He said guns are instruments of death, and he wouldn't have one in the house."

"I can respect that."

"But the Germans didn't. They shot him, without knowing it was him, of course. They just strafed our little boat because we wandered into an area where they were supposed to strafe everything. It was quite a foggy morning. When they saw that we were just a little sailboat, they actually stopped firing."

"That was nice of them."

"At the time I wished I had a gun to shoot back, any kind of a gun at all. I threw a cup of tea I happened to have in my hand at the plane. It wasn't a very effective defense."

430

"Brit, you should understand that I have to be this way—"

"Oh, I do. I guess I hate and love you for it at the same time. My country really didn't fight the war. We just gave up. A few people talked about putting up heroic resistance, but not many. So we just let the Germans in."

"The Danes had no choice. The United States is in quite a different position—"

"Yes. You have many guns and many men who know how to use them. I was brought up on your cowboy and gangster movies. I know they're only folk art, but you can tell a lot about a people from their folk art."

"We're not really so bloodthirsty. Now we have to learn how. It comes hard to us too . . ."

She picked up the pistol in its holster. "I never held a gun before."

"Believe it or not, I just learned how to shoot that thing today."

"You're better with the bigger guns on your ship, I expect. Do you mind if I take this out of its case?"

"I'm afraid I do mind."

"Why?"

"It's just a feeling. I know you'd be careful, but that's my gun. They are issued only to commissioned officers in the Coast Guard. That sounds silly, doesn't it? Anyway, I can't let anybody mess with my gun. It's just a very deep instinct."

"So it's not just a mechanism, it's a symbol. It's too important to let a mere woman touch."

"A mere civilian would be more like it. Put the gun down, Brit. Let's forget it."

"It's interesting," she said, putting the gun on the table, but still staring at it. "Someday perhaps I'll buy one for myself. Perhaps it's something every woman should have these days."

"Brit, I have to get back to business. Will the other Danes try to turn the Eskies against me when Swanson is gone?"

"They'll do whatever you tell them to. They're good at that when they're under a gun. Only Swanson would tell you to go to hell."

"How do you really think I should handle him?"

"You're right. You'll have to lock him up if you're not unkind enough to kill him. As a matter of fact, I can tell

431

you how to get him out of here without a scene that would alarm the Eskimos."

"How?"

"Tell him he can visit the prisoners on their island. He's been worried about them, not because he really sympathizes with the Nazis, but because they're people and he really is a kind of saint."

"Sort of a horny saint for an old man?"

"That's cheap. He's a Greenlander now, not a Dane, and he lives by Greenland customs. It was I who needed him when I sailed in here alone with a crazy father."

"I'm sorry—"

"Forget it . . . Anyway, he'll be glad to visit the prisoners. When he gets out on the island, you can tell him he has to stay with them. He will accept that."

"Would the Eskies understand why I had to get rid of him?"

"The Eskimos are a very realistic people, but they won't love you for making their saint a prisoner. Tell them the Germans are keeping him out there. Most of them are simple enough to accept that."

"Is Peomeenie?"

"Peo is not really simple at all, but he can be bought, as you found out. I'm afraid that many of them can be."

"Will you get them together for me tomorrow morning so I can talk to them?"

"The church is our only meeting place. Do you want to use it as a recruiting station?"

"I guess . . . you know, victory has been prayed for in every church since Christ's time, on every side, in every war. The Lord helps those, and so forth . . ."

"I'll have them come to the church tomorrow. Now do you want hot chocolate or tea?"

Suddenly conversation was difficult. It seemed to him that the most revealing thing she had said was that she both loved and hated him and he could almost see the conflict vibrating in her tense, narrow face.

"Aside from Swan, I have to admit that I myself hate to think of you leading the Eskimos into some kind of battle," she said. "It's not their war. They don't understand anything about it. It will be like you were leading some kind of children's crusade."

"Brit, I've never really known any Eskimos. Why is everyone so sentimental about them? They're not children.

432

They know more about survival than anyone. As you told me, when things get really bad, they leave their old people and girl babies on the ice to die. They sound pretty tough to me. I bet they'll understand me."

"They understand fighting the elements, not men. Hate is a luxury they can't afford."

"You think it's romantic of them to fight polar bears with bone knives, but they want guns. I bet they'll make great troops. How many able-bodied men are there around here?"

"Not much more than twenty. There used to be a hundred. You'll want to hire the women too. The men won't go far without them, and the women do all the work except for the hunting and fishing."

"So maybe I can get forty people to work for me. That will just about double the men I've got. The Germans may have close to a hundred. Do you see why I can't play games?"

"Yes, you don't have to convince me anymore . . . Paul, do you want to make love?"

"I didn't think this conversation was leading to that."

"That's what you really come here for, isn't it? You have a lot of empty time to make up for. We probably don't have much time together, so we better make the most of it."

She astonished and confused him. As she methodically undressed, she suddenly seemed as coldly purposeful as a prostitute, but after the first embrace she began to tremble and made love as fiercely as though she were fighting for her life. There was no laughing together this time. . . .

When he had got dressed, she picked up the gun he had left on the table and handed it to him with two hands as solemnly as though it were a religious article, and insisted on helping him to buckle his pistol belt. Suddenly she smiled. "There," she said. "Now you look like an American folk hero, all ready to make the Indians bite the dust."

# CHAPTER 44

After dressing herself as an Eskimo, which apparently was her usual custom, Brit took him to Swanson's house. They found the old man sitting in an overstuffed armchair which filled a quarter of his tiny livingroom.

"Swan," she said softly, "the captain here says you can visit the prisoners on the island if you want to."

Swanson was obviously surprised and pleased.

"I think well of you for this," he said to Paul in his strongly accented English. "Although you are the military authority here, I feel I still have certain unavoidable responsibilities."

"Dress warmly," Paul replied. "It's colder than you might think out there on that island."

"Captain, I respect you in many ways," Swanson said, "but don't tell me about Greenland weather. I understand it." Before putting on his parka, Swanson served them thimble-sized glasses of Aquavit and told his native housekeeper that he would be back "in about two hours."

Never in his life had Paul felt so disreputable, so thoroughly contemptible, but he was still sure that he was only doing the necessary. Military leaders should not be commissioned as officers and gentlemen, he thought. They should be required to swear their willingness to lie and cheat as well as die for their country. They should be required to put a hand on the Bible and promise to do in old men, women and children if the situation required. Why should he be feeling guilty? If the Germans were occupying Greenland, they would almost certainly shoot the old man if he opposed them. Putting him on the island with the other prisoners was a damn sight more merciful.

And it was the Germans who had created this nightmare world where it was necessary to lock up elderly saints for the very crime of saintliness, Paul thought as they trudged through the snow to the whaleboat. Hatred for the Germans was as sustaining as love, even more so sometimes. When he thought about the Germans, there was a spring to his step and he felt more alive than usual, like any young lover, or hater. If he kept on thinking about the Germans it was almost possible to forget that he was deceiving an elderly clergyman and leading him into a crowded prison camp. On the wharf several Eskimos had gathered around the whaleboat and Paul was glad that he was not taking Swanson away by force.

Paul first stopped the boat at the end of the point where the machine gun stood and went alone into the ice shack. Williams was on duty. He was sitting on a box by the window reading a paperback book which he stuffed into his pocket as Paul entered. Paul asked him to call the Germans so that he could tell them to stay in their huts until the boat left. Walking out to the machine gun, Williams took Boats's boatswain's pipe from his pocket and placed it to his lips. He had not learned to blow it at all well. It gave a thin, wavering call much like Williams's own voice, but it was still piercing enough to bring a man from each hut. Cupping his hands to his mouth, Paul told them in German that he was bringing a man to the island, and that they should all remain inside until the boatswain's pipe sounded again.

"Give them another blast from your pipe when I've left," he said to Williams and returned to the boat.

In the swift current it was difficult to hold the boat still at the landing place. Swanson was eager to get ashore, but too old and fat to jump to the ice. Finally Stevens and Krater had to help Brit to carry him, almost as though they were taking him against his will. Once on the island, the old man stood up and adjusted his rumpled parka.

"Mr. Swanson, I have to say something important to you," Paul began.

"What?" Swanson's benign face showed no trace of suspicion, but the wind made his eyes water.

"It is my duty to persuade as many Eskimos as I can to help me fight the Germans. Will you help me?"

"No!"

"Then I am sorry to have to tell you that I am taking you prisoner. For aiding and abetting the enemy. I won't

435

press charges unless I have to, but I will have to keep you with the other prisoners here until we have removed all Germans from this area."

"That is why you have bought me here?"

"Yes."

"And you, Brit? You helped him."

"Swan, I had to. I had no choice . . ." She was crying.

"Yes. There aren't many choices anymore. I'm sure we are all doing what we have to do."

Brit hugged him and they stood for a few seconds like the lovers they had been.

"Now what do I do?" Swanson asked Paul.

"Go into one of the huts. The men will come out when we leave."

Paul helped Brit back into the boat and they shoved off immediately, leaving the old man standing a few yards from the edge of the ice. Then Williams blew his boatswain's pipe. The prisoners, who no doubt had wondered what was happening, poured from the huts. They ran to the old man, surrounded him, and in a few seconds the lieutenant put an arm around his shoulders. They disappeared into the middle hut together.

"They at least will treat him kindly," Brit said.

"Probably. If he's not with me, he's with them."

"It's all so simple for you, isn't it?"

"It's just simple. Do you want us to take you back to the village? I have work to do aboard my ship."

"I don't want to go back to the village right now. Can you take me aboard your ship? I would like to see it."

"I . . . I'm afraid I don't like that idea."

"Why? Do you still think I might not be on your side?"

"It's not that. The men have no women here. And a ship is just no place for a woman."

"I sailed a boat across the Atlantic almost alone."

"I mean a warship."

"You're afraid that in these clothes I might excite your men?"

"Why do you want to see the ship so much? It's just a trawler."

"No, as you said, it's a warship with guns. Painted the way she is, she's hard to see when she's anchored out in the fjord, or even at the wharf. She looks like a ghost ship, all white and spectral. Maybe I want to know that she's real, that she won't just suddenly disappear, now that she's all that stands between us and the Germans."

Taking her aboard the ship went against Paul's instinct, but she was insistent, he of course wanted to please her, and what harm could it really do? He had a vision of the crew all whistling at her, staring and perhaps making lewd remarks, but they would not do that when a woman actually came aboard. Like Stevens and Krater now in the whaleboat, they would probably act embarrassed and stay away.

In his guess about the conduct of the crew, Paul was right. As Brit jumped to the well deck, the men came forward thinking that she was an Eskimo, but as soon as they heard her voice, they melted away, withdrew to the forecastle, the radio shack and the engineroom, there to relish the fact of feminine presence with all kinds of speculation, but inaudible to her ears, invisible. Only Nathan came forward and with his courtly manners helped Paul to show her around the ship. She spent much time studying the big guns, touching their smooth metal almost the way she had touched Paul's shoulders.

"They look as though they could sink a battleship."

"Not today," Paul retorted. "Let's go to the wardroom. Nathan, could you ask Cookie to bring coffee and something to eat?"

Cookie did them proud. In a newly starched chef's hat he served mushroom omelettes as well as croissants and Danish pastries fancier than anything the Danes had available.

"Do you always eat like this?" Brit asked in astonishment.

"Always," Nathan replied. "I can't believe it myself, but it's true."

"Only the Americans would be operating a fancy restaurant on a warship."

They laughed. The visit to the *Arluk* appeared to be exhilarating Brit more and more. She begged to see the engineroom, and after warning the men there, Paul let her take a peek at the great diesel engine which Chief Banes kept gleaming in the bowels of the ship.

"How many horsepower is it?"

"Not much for the size of the engine," Nathan replied. "These things are built to turn very slowly with great

437

power at low speeds for years, not to develop a lot of horses."

"But what is its horsepower, compared to a car?"

"I guess that depends on what car you're talking about," Paul said. "This engine is rated at about six hundred horses."

"Six hundred horses!" she exclaimed, her eyes widening. "Imagine a ship being towed by six hundred horses. Nothing could stop such power!"

In some ways she seemed as naive as the Eskimos about technical devices. She had heard about depth charges and touched those on the stern racks with the same delicacy she had bestowed on the guns. "Radar" was a word entirely unfamiliar to her ears. The equipment was supposed to be secret and Paul resisted an impulse to show it to her, but he did boast that the black box could see through night and fog.

"The old Vikings used to claim that the dragon heads on the prows of their ships could do that," she said. "The Chinese paint eyes on the bows of theirs, but now Americans can really see through anything. Do the Germans have this?"

She touched the gray box.

"I don't really know how much radar they have," Paul said. "They're supposed to be so good with technical stuff, I always assumed they had it all, but maybe not."

"Where do you live?" she asked Paul. "I mean where is your cabin?"

Nathan said that he was needed in the radio shack as Paul led the way to his cabin. Brit stepped inside, glanced around the tiny compartment and with a smile said, "So this is the seat of power."

"I've never thought of it as that."

"Aren't you aware of your power? Doesn't it give you a good feeling?"

"I don't think that many captains of these fishboats have any great awareness of power. They'd be nuts if they did . . ."

"Why? You have six hundred horses in your engineroom and guns enough to knock down buildings or sink ships. If you take the Germans at Supportup, you really will be in command of the whole east coast of Greenland . . . now that Swan's gone . . ."

"I'm more aware of responsibilities than power," Paul

438

said, sounding pretty stuffy even to himself. He thought her smile was enigmatic and wondered if she felt the same.

"I like the style of your cabin, captain," she continued. "No ornamentation at all, no bow to luxury. The way the Spartans must have lived and the old Norse chiefs."

"And the fishing captains."

She did not appear to hear him. Her eyes traveled over his narrow bunk to the sword in its brown leather case hanging over it. "How fitting," she said. "Your only ornament a sword! Or is it an ornament? Can you kill Germans with it?"

"It's just a ceremonial sword really. In peacetime officers lead parades with them."

"Can I look at it?"

"If you like. There's nothing secret about a sword."

Reaching over the bunk, he took the sword case from its brackets and handed it to her. She rubbed it like a connoisseur of fine leather. "Can I open it?"

"Sure."

Unbuckling the top, she drew out the gold-handled sword in its black, gold-trimmed scabbard. As she examined it, he felt as though he had never seen his sword.

"I wonder where the design came from," she said, touching the small improbable gold-colored metal sea snake that was coiled around the tip of the scabbard. Two other tiny sea snakes curved from the hand guard. Embossed in other parts of the metal were square knots, laurel leaves, a shield and an eagle on the pommel.

"So many symbols! The sword says, 'I am power.' Can I take out the blade?"

"Be careful. The point's sharp."

The blade made a hissing as she drew it from the scabbard, and it glittered brightly. She laid it carefully on the chart table as she studied it, tracing with her finger the embossed eagle near the handle, more stylized laurel leaves, a fouled anchor. Turning it over, she studied a flag with a trident curiously perched on what appeared to be the mast of a square-rigger, scrolls and a pattern of stars.

"But there are no embellishments on the last foot of it," she said. "The point is all business. You really could kill someone with it."

"Not today."

She put the blade back into the scabbard and its brown leather case.

"Would you give it to the enemy captain if you surrendered?" she asked.

"Brave trawlers never surrender." He put the sword back on its brackets over his bunk.

"Have you ever made love here?" she asked.

"No."

"Have you ever had a chance?"

"No, but I don't think it would be a good idea. There's nothing soundproof about this cabin."

"It would have a certain excitement. For me anyway . . ."

"No, Brit. There are men on the bridge."

"Too bad. Love under the sword—has a nice ring to it."

"A little melodramatic."

"Do you know how the expression, 'son of a gun' got started?"

"No."

"When women came aboard the old warships in the days of sail, the sailors made love to them on deck under the guns. The phrase meant a sailor's bastard."

"Where do you learn such things?"

"When I studied English at the University of Copenhagen, they had a whole course in the origin of such idioms. It was very interesting. If I should have a child by you, it would sort of be a son of a gun."

"Is that a clear possibility?" he asked a little nervously.

"No. Unfortunately I can't let myself have a son of a gun."

"Let's go, Brit."

"Will your men be talking about my being in your cabin?"

"It will be their chief topic of conversation for days. I've made them envious enough. Rank has its privileges, but they shouldn't be flaunted."

"I'm glad you're such a good captain. Are you going to take me ashore now?"

"Yes."

"But there's one thing I want to see—the galley where all that marvelous food comes from."

"That's up in the forecastle, the quarters for the men."

"I'd like to see that too. I bet they'd like to have a woman visit, even a woman dressed like an Eskimo."

440

She was probably right about that, Paul reflected, and telephoned the forecastle from the bridge to give warning.

The men of the *Arluk* quickly put pants and shirts over their long underwear when they heard a woman was about to appear in their midst, but they did not see any reason to stop what they were doing, and that was making knives out of files. Knife-making had taken the place of checkers as a forecastle diversion, and Guns had done a brisk business selling files he had bought from Chief Banes, who had stolen several sets from the wreck of the destroyer. In exchange for beer rations to be paid on the next beerbust ashore, he and Chief Banes had ground the files to a rough edge on the emery wheel in the engineroom, and now Guns was showing the men how to achieve scimitar-like perfection with whetstones provided by Cookie. In the three tiers of bunks, men lay honing a variety of picturesque daggers, dirks and curved blades. The dim light made them look like a pirate crew busy with last-minute preparations for a bloodthirsty onslaught. At the head of the table Guns, looking like Blackbeard himself, was fastening an ivory handle to his masterpiece of a scimitar.

Brit's first reaction when she saw this tableau was a sudden intake of breath. It was, Paul suspected, exactly what she expected to find aboard an American warship.

"What are they going to *do* with all these knives?" she asked Paul.

"What I'm going to do is get me a Kraut's head and make it into a lamp," Guns boomed before Paul could reply. "This baby can slice even the fattest neck like butter."

Getting to his feet, Guns demonstrated the shining arc his knife could draw in the air, almost slicing off Cookie's chef hat.

"You want coffee, captain?" Cookie asked after coolly ducking, as though that sort of thing happened all the time.

"The lady just wants to see the galley, Cookie."

"She can look from the door. I won't let nobody in my galley. I don't mean to be disrespectful, captain, but even aboard ship a chef has to have rules."

After taking a brief peek into the cramped little galley where Cookie regularly prepared such fine meals for more than thirty men, Brit fled to the deck.

"That's quite a crew you've got," she said as they reached the well deck.

441

"I think maybe they were putting on a little show just for you."

"Perhaps, but I kind of get the idea that they're not kidding either."

"No, they're not," he said.

# CHAPTER 45

The short November day had long ago died, but enough moonlight was getting through the cloud cover to make the icy sides of the canyonlike fjord appear to glow softly, and the water of the bay and channel showed clearly as black against white. Stevens and Krater, who had the boat duty that day, sat silently in the stern as Krater steered the whaleboat toward the settlement. Paul sensed that they were angry at him because they thought he had no business keeping a boat crew out in the cold just to ferry his woman. Higher pay and fancy uniforms for an officer and a private cabin for a captain were not begrudged, but the possession of a woman in Greenland was a privilege too great to be forgiven. Although Paul told himself that a good captain should not be oversensitive to the feelings of his men, the silent backs that Stevens and Krater turned to him hurt. He found that he wanted to apologize to them, but of course there was nothing he could say.

"Can you come ashore with me?" Brit asked as they neared the wharf.

"I can't keep the boat waiting, and I don't want to keep it going back and forth."

"Why not spend the night? Your Mr. Green looks as though he could handle anything."

Remembering that Brit had first taken Nathan to be the captain, Paul felt an absurd stab of jealousy. He suspected that she would have bedded any man who happened to be the commanding officer. With his courtly manners Nathan might still have a chance to join what was probably Brit's line of lovers. Hell, how long could the line be in this desolate place and why was he becoming so damned Puritanical? Paul felt miserably disloyal when Brit looked up and smiled at him, her narrow face under the hood of her parka looking oddly childlike in the shadowed moonlight, undefended, vulnerable.

"I'd like to have you spend the night," she said, taking his hesitancy as indecision.

He knew two things: that duty required him to spend his nights aboard his ship in a place like this, and that he would spend the night with Brit anyway. The fear that men would die when he finally closed with the Germans and that he would have to force himself to be brave enough to disregard his own personal safety and run more risks than any of them was building in him. The commanding officer of a ship can't go dodging behind things, assign a safe spot for himself or just lie down when the gunfire starts. He'd been tempted to hug the deck during his one brief experience at being under fire, but he hadn't let himself and it had been only luck that the bullets which had hit Blake and Sparks, who also had been too brave to seek cover, had missed him. The death rate for lieutenants, and especially for young commanding officers, is almost always higher than for the enlisted men or senior officers.

So . . . if he was about to die, it would of course be folly to spend this moonlit night alone. That wouldn't sound like much of an excuse if he made it before a board of investigation which would look into the sinking of the *Arluk* if something went wrong, but it sounded right to him. No one aboard the ship had worked harder than he had ever since he'd come aboard, he deserved to take any reasonable break he could get—

"Stop making excuses for yourself," she said. "You know you're going to do it. Just say yes."

"You already know me too well. You're right. I've made my excuses and I'm all yours. Let's get on with it, for God's sake."

After they'd climbed onto the wharf, Paul told the men to go back to the ship and get him in the morning.

"Better make it afternoon," she said. "I'm going to get the Eskimos together for you."

"Come at about fourteen hundred," he said. "I have an important meeting."

Neither Stevens nor Krater made any jokes about official

business and neither smiled as Krater saluted, said, "Aye, aye, sir," and gunned the boat away.

When they got in the cabin of the ketch, Brit turned up the fire in the range, took off her Eskimo clothes and pulled on her reindeer sweater. The fact that that seemed to be almost the only good garment she had suddenly seemed endearing and he kissed her.

"I don't think you love me anymore," she said.

"What gives you that impression?"

"The whole time I was aboard your ship, you were looking at me as though you thought I was crazy."

"I was glad to see you were so impressed by my fish-boat."

"If you'd been in Denmark when the Germans marched in, you'd know why. Oh, we had a few ships, all right, before we gave them up, but we didn't have men like yours. We were so weak that we were afraid even to hate the Germans too much. Can you understand that?"

"I think so."

"You're afraid to hate people if they have too much power over you. You have to keep imagining that there must be something good about them."

Paul remembered how hard he had resisted hating Mowrey.

"In Denmark, just before we left, a friend of my husband told us a kind of joke, if you can call it that. He said that when the war was finally all over and Hitler had been captured, the Russians and Americans tied him to a stake in Berlin. They surrounded him with dried branches sprinkled with gunpowder and they led a train of gunpowder all the way through Europe, winding across Russia, coming back through every country all the way to Norway. Have you heard this story?"

"No."

"Way up at the northern tip of Norway they lit that long train of gunpowder and all the people of Europe lined up on both sides to watch it go sputtering toward Hitler's stake. It was announced everywhere that any person, anyone in all Europe who didn't want Hitler burned at the stake could put his foot on those sputtering sparks and put them out. The sparks traveled through every country and no one tried to put them out. Everyone cheered them on until the sparks were only ten feet from the brush around

444

Hitler's stake. Then one old Polish woman stepped forward and put them out. 'Let's do it again,' she said."

Paul laughed.

"But my point is that when I first heard it, I was afraid to laugh—the Germans might get me for it. And I was afraid of the hate in that story. I felt that hate as intense as that could only result in death for everyone."

"I wish they would really burn him at a stake, but not the English way. That was really quite a quick death. Our Indians did it better. They built a ring of fire around the stake just close enough to sting a little, and they gradually closed it in. That way they could keep a man screaming for about three days."

"Isn't it nice that no one is going to report you for saying that? Even when I got here, I was afraid to let hate all out. If the Germans won the war, after all, Greenland like everything else would be theirs. I *didn't* know they were at Supportup, but I admit there have been rumors that they've been up and down the coast. Swan kept saying that after all, they're just human beings and it's wrong to hate anyone. So I bottled up my hate the way I used to bottle up my sex when I was a child."

"And now you can release it?"

"Yes. You've made me feel safe enough to hate them. Since they've taken my country and my family, I would say it's about time. I'll do everything I can to get the natives to help you. A lot of them are halfbreeds, not Eskimos, and they don't have any mystique about refusing to fight men."

"Guns and I will train them."

"Train the women too. Some of them are stronger than the men."

"We'll teach them what we can."

"So how about me? Will you teach me to shoot a gun?"

"If you really want."

"If you are going to take the Eskimos to fight the Germans, you'll need an interpreter. I've studied their language for a year. I'm writing a book on it—that's how I keep myself busy here. I'm the best interpreter you can get. It's your damn duty to take me along."

"If you can take the training, you can come."

"Now you're really making my ultimate fantasy come true, a dream I was even afraid to remember when I woke up in the morning for two years. I will kill Germans. I will cover the ground with their goddamn blood."

445

Brit's passionate desire to kill Germans was somehow connected to her desire to make love, and he soon discovered that whenever she started talking fiercely, she soon pulled him into a bunk. On this night of her release, as she called it, he wondered if she would leave him any energy for so mundane a pursuit as fighting. When he thought he was too tired ever to rise from her bunk again, she insisted on showing him a sauna which was the pride of the settlement. It was a small wing which had been added to Swanson's house, but it had a separate entrance, and Brit assured Paul that it was for the use of anyone in the settlement, though the Eskimos appeared to believe that only Danes were crazy enough to sit in fire and allow themselves to be boiled alive.

There was a tiny vestibule in which they waited while she fired up the coal stove, a dressingroom with two shower stalls and the sauna itself, a cubicle with three tiers of benches and birch paneling which had been imported from Denmark. While it heated up, they took showers. The water was only lukewarm and the stone-paved floor of the dressingroom was icy. The sauna itself was deliciously steamy when they finally entered it. At first Brit wore a towel like a skirt and he did the same. Although that was all they wore, there was something peculiarly unsexy about the sauna with its hard wooden benches, the bright electric light set in the ceiling and the heat, which almost immediately became oppressive to Paul. Spreading her towel on the second tier, Brit stretched out on her back and sighed contentedly. Her slender body was already glistening with sweat. Even in the harsh light, it had the perfection of grace and strength, though there was no hint of voluptuousness as she lay with her breasts flattened out. Without an ounce of surplus flesh but with no bones showing, she looked like a young athlete, except for a row of stretch marks across her narrow waist.

The sedentary life aboard ship and Cookie's meals had left Paul heavier than he had ever been in his life. At sea he had showered and changed his clothes so quickly and unthinkingly that now his own body looked strange to him, bulky and unlovely. Feeling her eyes on him, he was self-conscious as he lay on the bottom bench.

"You are a very powerful man," she said.

"A damn fat one, I'm afraid."

"Do you ever get any exercise aboard the ship?"

"I'm always too tired even to think of it."

"Did you exercise a lot before the war?"

"No. To tell the truth, I always hated sports. There were always too many other things I wanted to do."

"Like what?"

"Make money. Make love. Sail a boat. Read anything unless I was supposed to read it at college."

"That's interesting."

"Why?"

"You have such a powerful chest, shoulders and arms. If you weren't an athlete, they must be pure inheritance."

"So far as I know, none of my ancestors within memory were athletes."

"Within memory . . ."

He laughed. "Sometimes I like to think I am the descendant of the old Norse warriors, but I'm afraid the truth is that I come from good peasant stock. My ancestors probably developed their strength with shovels and hoes."

"My people were all intellectuals, if I can believe my father. He's very proud of that. If you're intellectual, it is almost a virtue to be weak."

"I guess there are different kinds of weakness, different kinds of strength. My grandparents were good at making money. Nobody in my family has been good at much of anything since."

The rising dry heat in the tiny room was making him feel claustrophobic. He did not understand the workings of the sauna and thought she was going to cool it down when she took a bucket of water from beneath the bottom tier and poured it on flat stones which apparently were heated by a stove beneath. Clouds of steam almost asphyxiated him.

"How much hotter is it going to get?" he asked, glancing nervously at two doors, one leading to the dressing room and one at the side of the little cubicle. His claustrophobia gave him a terrible suspicion that they might be locked and he wanted to try them.

"We're just beginning," she said with a laugh. "Do you want a cold drink?"

"Yes!"

She opened a small door built like that of a safe into a wall near her. It contained a pitcher of water, two big glasses, several liqueur glasses and a bottle of Aquavit.

447

"Say, that's pretty damn fancy."

"In peacetime the Danes up here live well. Aquavit or water?"

"First the Aquavit."

As she poured the clear liquid into the cold glass, which quickly beaded with steam, she said, "This reminds me of a story I've been afraid to think of for a long time."

The story had been told to her, she said, by a professor at her university, a Jew who had relatives in Poland. When the Germans first came into Poland, she said, they began by confiscating all the property and bank accounts of the Jews. The relatives of her friend had survived for a few weeks by selling their household effects. All their glassware, china and antiques were displayed in their livingroom, and German soldiers went from house to house looking for bargains.

"This German major came in," Brit continued. "My friend's cousin was just a young girl and she was terrified of him, but at first he was very polite. He complimented her on the quality of her crystalware, which had come down in her mother's family for generations. He particularly admired an antique decanter which stood surrounded by longstemmed liqueur glasses on a silver tray. 'How much do you want for these?' he asked. The girl named a small sum, perhaps a third the peacetime worth. The major smiled. Holding the delicate glass up to the light, he turned it slowly before dropping it to shatter on the floor. 'On the other hand,' he said, 'for an incomplete set?' "

"Jesus Christ!" Paul said.

"I don't know why, but that story makes me hate them even more than all the reports about their shooting Russian prisoners by the hundreds of thousands, and even butchering the Jews by the million. My mind won't accept all that, but the cruelty of that major dropping one glass, that really got to me when I first heard it."

"That's our brother Nordics, all right."

"That damn story upset me so when I first heard it that I kept telling myself that it was just propaganda, that it couldn't be true. The Jews kept inventing stories like that, my father said. When the Germans first came into Denmark, they looked more or less like ordinary men, even more silly than most because they tried to act so superior."

"That must be quite a burden for them," Paul said.

"The first Germans I saw struck me as rather comic. Here

they kept talking about the blue-eyed blond superior race, and most of them had dark hair and pot bellies. We Danes had the blue eyes and light hair, but we still had to hear them boast about how they were the true Nordics, the superior race."

"I don't know how they do it with a straight face."

"At first it was easier for me to think of the whole invasion as a comic opera. We didn't put up enough resistance for much bloodshed. When the Germans said all the Jews had to wear yellow stars of David on their sleeves, practically all us Danes did, and that made us real heroic, even if we only did it for a few days. It was a good joke, a fine new act in the comic opera."

"It still must have taken guts."

"Not really, because most of us couldn't imagine that the Germans would really do anything about it. When they began making a lot of arrests and people started to disappear, the yellow stars came off quickly enough. That was when Jon said we had to get out. The ketch belonged to a friend of ours. It all seemed so easy at first. We'd both been bored by our jobs for a long time and had talked of going to Greenland. Jon was a great sailor, and I've sailed all my life. We knew they patrolled the coast with boats and planes, but if we waited for fog and darkness, we didn't think there'd be much danger."

"I guess a good many have escaped."

"We almost made it without any trouble at all. We were a hundred miles offshore in international waters when the fog finally lifted. When we heard the plane, we thought it must be British or American, and Ron, my son, stood up and waved. It circled around and even when we saw the swastikas on its wings, we didn't think it would attack us. We were in international waters and we were flying a Danish flag. My father hoped they'd think we were a fishing boat—they encouraged all our fishermen to keep on working, and some of them used little yachts."

Brit paused and with a trembling hand refilled their glasses with Aquavit.

"The plane circled us twice. Ron kept waving. Then it came in low toward us and I saw that flickering on the lead edge of his wings. Jon threw himself over our boy, knocking him into the bottom of the cockpit. I did that crazy thing, throwing the cup in my hand. There was a terrible splintering sound, and then the plane was gone. My husband and son did not move, and my father was crying."

"But you still had the guts to make it over here."

"I hardly knew what I was doing most of the time. The crazy point I'm trying to make is that after a while, dad began to justify the pilot of the plane. He said it was probably a mistake. Then he said they probably had orders to attack anything in a certain sector, and the pilot had no choice. He just couldn't accept the fact that our enemy was so evil and so powerful at the same time. Can you understand that?"

"Sure."

"Lots of people in Europe and lots of Danes in Greenland are doing that right now—pretending that the Germans are really not so bad after all, they're human after all. That's what Swan kept saying. And I went along with him . . ."

"Level with me. When I first came here, did you know the Germans were at Supportup?"

"I admit I suspected it, there were all kinds of rumors of Germans landing all up and down the coast. Swan knew it, I don't know how, but he protected all of us by keeping information like that to himself. He did the lying for all of us. I don't know whether to thank him or hate him for that."

"I wish you had told me what you suspected."

"I thought of it, but can you understand when I say I couldn't imagine the Germans being defeated? When you come out of Europe, it's hard to imagine that. I thought that if you went into Supportup, they'd kill you, then come over here and kill us. In my way I tried to protect you, I tried to protect all of us. And anyway, I could have told you nothing but rumors and suspicions. I didn't really lie to you."

He said nothing.

"Except you were right to suspect me, and I'm not dead sure you trust me a hundred percent now."

"My only suspicion now is that you're trying to boil me alive."

From beneath the bottom bench she took a bucket of lukewarm water which felt deliciously cool as she slowly poured it over his head and shoulders. When he had dried his face with a towel, she gave him a glass of icy water, and poured one for herself.

"Are you comfortable now?"

"God, yes."

"Then listen to me a little more. You've taught me one thing: the Germans aren't going to win this war. There are men who can stop them. You're going to kill all those Germans at Supportup or take them prisoner. I want to help more than I've ever wanted anything in my life. I want to see it when it happens, I don't just want to hear about it. For a change I want to see how they bleed. They walked all over my country, all over Europe, and I can't wait to see how they do here. If you're going to send native Greenlanders against them, no one will be able to tell me from an Eskimo woman. I'm just as strong as they are. Give me a rifle, teach me to use it and give me one of those knives the men on your ship are making. You won't have to worry about me."

"Brit, it's brains, not simple ferocity, that's going to beat these people. I have a lot to figure out. I'll fit you in where I can."

"You look so aloof when you say that. I don't like you aloof."

With a smile she threw the icy water in her glass in his face. He grabbed her, but she twisted from his arms. From a corner she picked up three slender twigs that had been tied together and he felt them sting on his shoulders until he took them from her. In the swirls of steam she turned her back to him.

"Use them on me," she said. "It's the custom, part of the sauna."

"It's not my custom."

"It doesn't hurt. It feels good. It brings the blood up. After this we'll take a dive in the snow."

"You dive in the snow, not me."

Grabbing the twigs from him, she briskly slapped her own taut body. Suddenly she opened the side door and he saw her fling herself full length in a snowbank outside. Almost immediately she jumped up, returned with her hands full of snow and threw it on his chest. When he tried to catch her she ran outside again. He followed and for an instant they wrestled in the snow before dashing back into the sauna. After that the boiling water and the shower baths that followed made his skin tingle and every nerve respond as though he were really alive for the first time. He followed her through another door and made love to her in a big feather bed before he realized that they had entered Swanson's house, and by then it didn't seem to matter.

"I told you, it brings the blood up," she said. "Love, hate and saunas—without them we might as well be dead."

# CHAPTER 46

They spent the night in that big feather bed in Swanson's house. That did not bother him until he awoke in the morning, except there was no real morning now, only an hour or so of blurry light in the sky at noon. Staring out the frosted window into the moonlight, Paul reflected that it was one thing to lock up an old man because his beliefs made that necessary, and another thing to move into his house, drink his booze and sleep with a woman he might still regard as his in his own bed. He stirred restlessly.

"What's the matter?"

"I don't feel very comfortable here."

"I bet I can fix that," she said with a smile.

"Isn't there somewhere else we can go?"

"Nowhere with a bed like this."

She began by caressing his neck. She was impossible to resist and he did not try very hard. Never before had a woman taken the initiative and concentrated on trying to please him. He was so tired that the greatest luxury was just relaxing and allowing her to bring back his strength.

"I love you," he heard himself murmur drowsily over and over again.

"For now," she said.

"Why do you have to say that?"

"I don't know. The truth is very sexy to me."

"Would you like me to come back for you after the war?"

"I like that dream, but right now I don't need it."

"I love you," he said again.

"I wonder if you really would if you knew me?"

"I think I'm getting to know you fairly well."

"You're still mad because I was with Swan. That's why you don't like this bed."

"I can understand that you needed someone."

"You still wonder whether I was with Peo."

"I refuse to ask you about that."

She gave a rueful laugh. "I used to be the kind of girl you want. I think you want me to pretend I still am."

"No . . ."

"That is a very weak no. Of course I should pretend, but I have my own needs and maybe truth is one of them. Lying isn't sexy at all for me. Telling the truth is like taking off the clothes."

"You haven't lied."

"I want you to know what I am, what I've been through. Try to imagine Denmark when the Germans came in."

"I can't really."

"My husband and my father kept saying things wouldn't be too bad. They said we shouldn't antagonize them."

"In that situation . . ."

"But Jon loved his job. He had a record as a liberal. He used to give speeches. And my father went into his depression. He wouldn't leave his bed. Someone had to cope."

"You don't have to tell me . . ."

"You don't want to hear, do you?"

"I don't like seeing you in pain."

"The pain is in keeping it all in. Even Swan wouldn't have understood."

"You worked with the Germans for a while."

"How do you think we got gas and food for the ketch? Everything was rationed and expensive. How do you think we got out of the harbor at all? Someone had to be looking the other way."

"So you did what you had to do."

"For the sake of my family—that excuses everything doesn't it?"

"Yes."

"I told myself that, and the guilt went away, most of it. When you see people die, it's hard to worry about sex much. You take help where you can find it and give what you must."

"Yes."

"The Eskimos know. They always convert everybody who comes here to convert them."

"They sure understand necessity."

"They understand truth. They don't swear undying love to anyone. They think what we call fidelity must be a joke. Why should laughing together be made so complicated?"

"That wouldn't work for me."

She laughed. "It *is* working for you."

"I guess I like the practice but can't buy the theory. Not as a way to live forever."

"You want me to promise to stay away from poor old Swan after you've left?"

"I hope you will."

"And when Peo takes me out to teach me how to hunt seals, you want to ask him to build separate igloos for us?"

"You're laughing at me."

"You want me to keep myself pure for you after you've gone, even if I know damn well you'll go back to your wife? Even if the war lasts years and years?"

"Well, it's a nice thought—"

"No, it's an ugly pretense."

"What do you want me to say?"

"I want you to love me as I am. Isn't that what everyone wants?"

"I guess."

"I want to love life without having to pretty it up. Prettying it up ruins it. Can't you love yourself without prettying yourself up?"

"What do you mean?"

"You're not discovering the great love of your life that will make you leave your wife. You're just a lonely sailor in Greenland."

"Can't romantic hopes be good too—?"

"As good as what we've *got*? In the long run, they'll just make you hate to think of me. I'd like you to remember me as an honest woman."

"*That*, I will."

"So don't ruin the laughing together with serious talk. You taught me how to hate honestly."

"Maybe I don't even feel so great about that."

"I know. We're supposed to fight wars without hating

and to make laughing together respectable we have to tell a great many lies. Don't you get sick of it?"

"Sometimes."

He still didn't know how to tell her that her realistic talk left him feeling curiously empty . . . "Are you always going to hang onto the Eskimo idea of love?" he asked. "Will it always just be laughing together, nothing more?"

"How many couples do you know in America who have more than that? How many have less?"

"I never made a count."

"Don't count and let's have no more talking. If I've made it hard for you to laugh, I'm sorry."

She began to tickle him and it wasn't long before he began to laugh. He was surprised when she quickly led him to finish the love-making and began to get dressed.

"I think I could laugh a little more with you," he said.

"We have work to do. Don't you want me to get the Eskimos together for you in the church?"

"How long will that take?"

"I want to visit each hut and explain a little what's happening. Give me about an hour."

Before leaving she fixed him a breakfast of small seabird eggs, smoked herring and hot chocolate, Swanson's usual, he guessed. While waiting for her he sat in Swanson's huge overstuffed armchair, glanced at his books, which were mostly theological discussions and anthropological studies of Eskimos, and tried to avoid picturing the old man now, huddled on the ground near the stove in one of those overcrowded sod huts. Probably the Germans, despite the atrocities they had worked on others, would be good to him, and he would be more sure than ever that all men are brothers, including murdering Germans.

When the meeting started, there was just enough daylight in the church to make the stained-glassed window, a primitive picture of Christ on the cross, glow. The stove had just been lit, and as the Eskimos filed in, their breath frosted in front of their mouths like speech balloons, and he wished they could be filled with English words. In this frigid air, the Eskimos, who could never wash their bodies in the eternal chill of their sod huts, did not smell. It was only the temperature created by white men which made them offensive, he realized. They brought many children

455

with them, and as they crowded the benches, they looked like a furry PTA meeting. The round copper-colored faces of the full-blooded Eskimos and all the gradations of inter-breeding with the whites were impassive, waiting for the next surprises from the new white men. They talked together hardly at all. The women cuddled their fur-clad babies and the men caressed the toddlers too. Paul had read that in Eskimo communities no one knew or cared who the father of a child was. The children were the sons and daughters of the whole group and were loved by all as long as there was enough food to feed them.

Paul stood next to Brit beside the lectern. She said, "I have explained that you want to talk to them about the Germans. Just speak slowly and give me time to translate each sentence."

He tried to keep his speech as simple as possible. "The Germans are a people who look just like the Danes and the Americans, but their hearts and their minds are very different," he began. "In Europe they have killed millions of people—"

"They don't have a word for millions," Brit said to him. "I'll say, 'The dead they left in Europe are as many as the snowflakes here.' "

The Eskimos looked incredulous.

"They have sunk an American ship just like mine," Paul continued. "They shot all the survivors in an open boat. They have killed two of my own crew, and their bodies now wait for burial in the shadow of this church. More than a hundred Germans—"

"They don't have a word for 'hundred,' " Brit said, inter-rupting her translation. "I'll say 'more than ten times our fingers and toes,' but try not to use numbers."

"Many of them, more people than we have here, have settled at Supportup-Kangerdula," he continued. "They will kill us if we do not kill them."

The Eskimos again looked incredulous.

"I need your help," he said. "I have many guns, large and small, but I need your help to get them near the Germans. I need your dog sleds and your knowledge of how to hunt in Greenland."

While Brit translated their faces were impassive.

"I will pay for your help," he continued. "I will give you guns and ammunition which you can keep when I go. I will give you canned meat, sugar, coffee and tea."

Now they all smiled and he knew he had them. Somehow he felt as disappointed and guilty as he did relieved. In one respect he had lied to them—he did not think the Germans actually would kill them if they minded their own business. But without their help, he was sure that many more of his own men would die and he would rather let a few of these strangers die instead. That was the truth of it, and he had to live with it.

When Paul had finished, Brit gave a long, impassioned speech in their language. He heard her use of the word "Germans" frequently and guessed that with the fervor of a new convert, she was teaching them to hate. This seemed to be an ironic sacrilege in a church, but he reminded himself that even a prayer for victory cannot really be without hate.

"I told them what happened to my husband and son," she said when she had finished. "And I told them that Swan was out on the island trying to teach the Germans the error of their ways. They would expect that of him. Wasn't that a good idea?"

"Fine."

The Eskimos now put their hands up like good pupils and asked questions. They wanted to know exactly what they should do. Paul said he would soon send men in to give them guns and explain their use. They would make plans together. Through Brit he thanked them, praised them for their understanding. Then he hurriedly left.

"What time do you have to go back to your ship?" she asked.

He glanced at his watch. "A little more than an hour."

"How about some lunch? I can fix you a sandwich on the boat."

She rummaged in the bottom of a locker in her little galley and came up with a small can of Danish ham which he guessed she had been saving for a special occasion. He sat down on a bunk and watched while she sliced both the ham and a homemade loaf of bread very thin.

"I'm afraid you'll never find a woman who can do as well as the cook on your ship," she said with a smile.

Arranging a pillow, he lay comfortably back. Her knife poised over the bread, she appeared to be studying him.

"I'm trying to imagine you in civilian clothes," she said. "I can't. What did you usually wear before the war?"

"Gray flannel slacks and a tweed coat."

457

"You were a student?"

He found he had caught some of her desire to be loved as he was, or at least understood. He told her how he had supported himself by selling clothes, playing cards and taking out charter parties on his father's old boat.

"You were a poor, penniless American student with a yacht?" she said with a smile.

"During the Depression we couldn't sell her for anything like she was worth. I at least made her pay her expenses."

"What is your wife like?" she asked, her voice so casual that it was disarming.

"That's not fair."

"You mean, women like me aren't supposed to ask about wives?"

"No, it's just a damn confusing question."

"Is she a student?"

"No."

"What does she do?"

"She decorates a house and she dances at the U.S.O. to improve the morale of our country's fighting men."

"I don't know what that means. You sound so bitter!"

"Probably I have no right to be, but I do get angry at her sometimes. I don't think I've ever admitted that. Do you think that the wife of a soldier overseas should entertain the troops at home?"

"Are you afraid she's unfaithful to you?" Brit asked, arching one eyebrow a little.

"I've worried about it. She used to be sort of wild. It must be hard for a wife to be left alone for so long. The war bitches everything up."

"How long have you been married?"

"Not much more than two years."

"Were you happy?"

"I don't think I really know what that means. Things were pretty mixed up. No, damn it, I wasn't happy. I never admitted that before either."

"Do you have children?"

"No."

"Don't have any until you're sure where you're going. Marriage shouldn't trap people, but children can."

"I believe that."

"I'm too old to dream of your coming back for me, so I'm not speaking selfishly."

"I know."

458

"I don't read palms, but I'm not bad at reading character. You're kind of shocked by me and by yourself with me, aren't you?"

"Maybe a little."

"You've never done anything like this before. I'm afraid I'm sort of the end of a dream for you, a terrible crack in your American idealism."

"Am I really all that naïve?"

"I admire you for it. My husband was like that. He couldn't imagine being unfaithful to me. He told me that often."

"And you?"

"For a long time, but as you say, the war bitches everything up."

"To be honest, I don't think that Sylvia and I were headed for much happiness, even if there had been no war. I have never been able to face that."

"What do you think was wrong?"

"I don't know. I never felt I was satisfying her."

"Sexually?"

He felt his face start to burn. "Among other ways."

"She made you feel that you were no good?"

"Sometimes, and maybe I made her feel she was no good."

"I used to be a rather difficult young girl myself, and I think I've learned a little about you."

"I'm afraid to ask what."

"All last night you kept asking me if I was satisfied. That seemed a great worry for you."

"I'm *sorry*." This time his face really was burning.

"Don't be sorry," she said, coming to stroke his face. "That's a rather charming worry, especially for a man so young. I meant it when I said I was fine and you're fine. You don't have anything to worry about."

"Thank you," he said. "Probably it's silly, but I'm very glad to hear that."

"Do you want me to prophesy your future? My husband used to say I was a witch."

"Maybe I'm afraid to hear it."

"I don't know if you will work out your troubles with your wife or not, but you're not the kind of man who will let a woman destroy your self-confidence for long. My guess is, you'll know lots of women before you find one that will let you be as idealistic as you want."

"Maybe."

"I wish I were twenty years younger and could meet you about five years from now. When you'll be old enough really to settle down."

"I guess this sounds corny, but I'll never find anyone like you—"

"Not as old, not as cynical and not as *educated*," she said with a laugh. "Now eat. If we hurry, we'll have time for laughing together one more time before you have to go back to your ship."

The whaleboat took Paul back to the *Arluk* later that afternoon. The men greeted their captain stonily. Only Nathan was friendly. They went to Paul's cabin to talk and Cookie brought coffee which tasted good after the sweet hot chocolate ashore.

"Skipper, I've been thinking a lot about our whole situation," Nathan began. "The only thing that's happened here is that that ski plane showed up again today with the sun. He just took a peek over the mountain at us and disappeared again. Maybe we can deduct something from that."

"Like what?"

"The Krauts probably are not in radio contact with people here. If they were, they wouldn't need to take a peek at us every day."

"Sounds reasonable."

"And maybe they're more afraid of our attacking them than they are anxious to send their ship over to attack us."

"How do you figure that?"

"They've known where we are now for some time. The weather's been good enough for them to attack. If they had been smart they would have hit us before we got the prisoners organized and got over the pasting they'd already given us. If they're smart enough to have done some of the other things they've pulled on us, they'd be too smart to let us get all ready for them. I know we can't be sure, but I think the odds favor some such interpretation."

"Their main job is of course to defend their own base, and maybe they think they can do it better by preparing a real hot reception committee for us than by trying to get us here," Paul said. "They must know we're cooking up something, now we know where they are. Maybe they're concentrating on making a place where their ship will be safe from aircraft, or just building up their defenses. When you

460

come right down to it, they may be just too smart to walk into the trap we've set for them here. The bastards always seem to be one ahead of us."

"I have some suggestions that might let us catch up," Nathan said. "In the first place, we ought to get that damn little plane of his. I don't like letting him keep track of us so easily. He seems to show up just about two minutes after sunrise every day. If we got a Lightning to time its arrival just right tomorrow, it might catch him."

"Tell GreenPat that."

"I've got a message all ready to go. Now do you mind if I talk for a minute about some ideas which might help our overall strategy?"

"I've got a few. What are yours?"

"I've been studying the charts and the pilotbook. The fjord the Krauts have is just about like this one—it's different only in detail."

"As far as we know," Paul said.

"Peomeenie will probably be able to tell us more, but for the time-being let's assume that the two fjords are very much alike. We can assume that with prepared positions, most of the Krauts can survive any air attack, and will be ready to fight like hell when the planes go."

"That's the assumption I've been going on."

"One thing we could do is to ask for not just one air strike, but several. There's a chance we might bomb them into surrendering. That would save a lot of lives."

"But I don't think it will happen. Their primary job is to get out weather reports. If they've prepared underground shelters, enough could survive any number of air attacks to keep a weather station in action."

"All right. Surrender is unlikely but still possible if we make things tough enough for them. So our job is to hit with the greatest possible shock while they're still dazed by the bombs."

"My idea is to sail right into the mouth of that fjord with all our guns firing. We'll have a land force ready to hit them from behind the minute they start shooting at the ship."

"How many Eskimos do you think you can recruit?" Nathan asked.

"Thirty or forty anyway. They're not so hard to persuade. And we can let about half our men go with them."

"If only half the Germans survive the planes, and if they

461

are trained troops, they could kill us. They could find cover from the ship's guns—remember, we'll be fighting in their back yard. They'll concentrate on the land force and wipe it out. There won't be much the ship can do. If the hunter-killer is still in action, you'll have your hands full without even worrying about the men ashore."

"What else can we do?"

"The greatest power of this ship is in all those depth charges in the hold, something like three tons of TNT. Our problem is to put it where it will kill Germans."

"How are we going to throw three tons at them?"

"We have the Danish launch and the whaleboat. Figuring a way to steer them in there by radio might be a little too fancy to be reliable, but if we figured the tide and the current right, we might be able to drift them in. I can rig all kinds of fuses."

"If we could blow those boats up near them, it would make a hell of a diversion, even if we couldn't get them close enough to do any real damage."

"We'll have to see how close their installations are to the bank of the fjord and how far in. An Eskie might even take one in under cover of darkness, moor it and escape in a kayak. I'm just mentioning possibilities. There's another one that may prove more practical. If the Krauts' main attempt has been to protect their base from air attack, they probably have put it at the bottom of a ravine, where Lightnings can't come in and strafe really low. That would be effective against planes, but leave them highly vulnerable to caveman tactics."

"You want to throw rocks at them?"

"No, I want to roll stones, or in our case, depth charges."

"I've thought of that. If the terrain really turns out to be right. . . ."

"We could work out variations on the theme. In certain kinds of situations, we might let a sled loaded with fused charges coast down a slope."

"Or we could get Eskies to plant charges down there ahead of time at night."

"That would be risky for the Eskies, but it might work. Okay, we should be able to deliver charges so that we can ring the bastards with really massive explosions the minute after the planes disappear. That should confuse the hell out of them. Then if you sail in the mouth of the fjord with all guns going and a ground force attack from the other

462

direction, we might produce the kind of shock that actually will get them to surrender. There's at least a chance that we can pull this thing off without losing a man."

"O.K. That's good, Nathan. Now we got to set all this up—"

"We don't want just to wait for Peomeenie to come back. All he's going to tell us is details. Our main job will be to move men and all those heavy charges thirty miles over the ice where we can lie waiting for the planes to strike. If the weather's bad, we might have to wait days. We'll need advance bases."

"The Eskies will help us do that."

"Then there's a technical job of rigging all those fuses, figuring out the exact times. No one can do that but me."

"I can't quarrel with you there."

Nathan took a deep breath. "Skipper, the law requires you to stay aboard your ship during a battle. I want to be in charge of everything else."

"All the ground forces?"

"Yes."

"I was planning on putting Guns and Boats in charge of the land force."

"A commissioned officer should be with them."

"I was planning on sending Williams—"

"He can't rig fuses. Neither can Guns or Boats."

"Can't you prepare all the gear in advance?"

"I may have to guess the amount of time it takes a depth charge to roll down a cliff, and set the fuses accordingly. I'll have to be there."

"I'm not sure I want to run this goddamn ship all alone."

"You'll keep enough crew to man the guns. The whole thing will probably be over, one way or another in about ten minutes if we set it up right."

"You want to be in charge of training the Eskies?"

"I want this to be my baby, right from the start."

There was a moment of silence while Paul drained his coffee mug. "I've got to put it bluntly," he said finally. "You're a smart man, Nathan, but I'm not sure you're too good at handling men."

"I have an idea that the Eskies might respond better to someone who isn't too damn military."

"How about Guns and Boats? Can you handle them?"

"Yes. I've grown up a little."

"How are you going to handle Guns if he tries to fuck

463

every man, woman and child ashore instead of training anyone?"

"Tell him you'll break him down to seaman and give him permanent galley duty if I don't give him a good report. Don't let him have any booze, not even a beer. And give me three seamen who can tie him up if he gets really out of hand."

"I think you're getting the idea. All right, the whole shore operation is your baby. I don't mind saying the ship is all I want to worry about. I'm a sailor, not a marine."

Nathan laughed. "One of my big ideas was to join the marines. They turned me down. I have an idea they didn't think marines should be Sheenies with PhD degrees."

"Looks like they missed a good bet. If I were a real Kraut, I don't think I'd want to be up against a Sheenie with a PhD and three tons of TNT."

"I don't want to get cocky. Maybe none of this stuff will work. But Paul, for the first time I can see how I can really fight. Maybe it's corny, but I'm getting a sense of power. I don't feel so much like a victim anymore."

"Don't let it go to your head. What's your first step?"

"I'm going to get GreenPat to send a Lightning to go after that ski plane."

"And after that?"

"I want to go ashore and stay there until I get the Eskies organized. I want them ready by the time Peomeenie gets back."

"Get Brit to find you a place to stay—maybe Swanson's house. Take any five men you want with you, including Boats and Guns. Can Flags stand routine radio watch?"

"He's smart and I've shown him enough to get by."

"Take some rifles and as much canned stuff as Cookie can spare you. The Eskies should get a taste of their pay. Use Brit as an interpreter. She's so much on our side now that she damn near scares me. She wants to kill all the Krauts single-handed."

"I'll give her one," Nathan said without a smile. "The rest are mine."

# CHAPTER 47

Before Nathan went ashore, he got confirmation from GreenPat that a Lightning would arrive at Angmagssalik at dawn the next day to try to catch the ski plane. Word of this spread quickly to the forecastle. The men of the *Arluk* had named the ski plane "Hans" and began to bet on how long he could survive attack by one of the Lightnings, which had eight guns to his one if he had any at all, and which was at least four times as fast as a light plane. Some bet that Hans wouldn't last ten seconds, while Cookie maintained he might survive for ten minutes by ducking in and out of narrow ravines. The meeting of the two planes, if it actually occurred, promised to be a memorable spectacle. A half hour before daybreak the next day, the crew gathered on the forecastle and the flying bridge, coffee mugs in hand. The betting now was on whether either plane would actually appear, or which plane would show up first, and on whether the Lightning could locate the ski plane and pounce on it before it could make a getaway, perhaps by making an emergency landing on some snowy slope on the other side of the mountains.

As the first streaks of dawn turned the edges of a ridge of dark clouds low on the eastern horizon to gold, excitement ran high. Paul stood on the starboard wing of the bridge after making sure that the antiaircraft guns were manned to guard against the possibility of the ski plane making a last desperate dive into the ship. Deep down he felt that nothing would happen, as it usually did. Fat Herman had disappointed him by failing to sail his hunter-killer into a well-prepared trap, and now Hans would probably prove to be just as shrewd. Paul was surprised when he heard the faint drone of the light plane's engine, and saw it appear, no bigger than a fly, just above the ridge of the mountains. He was even more astonished when a few seconds later he heard the roar of an approaching Lightning. For once everything seemed to be working right.

The Lightning came in low over the ice cap, swerved sharply up to clear the mountains, saw the ski plane almost at once and hurtled toward it. Hans swerved as though in panic and headed back to his base, but even before he had a chance to finish his turn, the Lightning swooped down on him like a hawk on a sparrow. The men on the *Arluk* could hear the rattle of her guns and see tracers stab out from her wings. The men who had bet on a quick decision cheered, but Hans dived, swerved to the left and leveled out over the water in the fjord instead of crashing. Carried by its 400-mile-per-hour momentum, the Lightning disappeared into the clouds before completing a wide circle, and returning to search for its tiny antagonist. Catching sight of him headed out to sea only a few feet above the highest icebergs, the Lightning dived to attack again.

The planes were so unevenly matched that it took discipline for Paul not to start cheering for David and jeering Goliath. As the Lightning flashed by the tiny plane, Paul realized that its speed, which could not be reduced enough, was its greatest handicap. No sooner had the pilot of the Lightning got Hans into his sights than he had to swerve to avoid crashing into him as he rushed by. The far tighter turning circle of the ski plane enabled Hans to reverse direction with startling suddenness, while the big Lightning kept zooming out of sight before hurtling back with the necessity of locating its prey before trying another attack. Of course Hans had no guns or fired none, and the final outcome of the battle seemed beyond doubt, but for twenty minutes the two planes swooped and circled over the mountains, through the fjord and above the ice cap.

At first Paul thought that the jerky movements of Hans meant that he was panicking, but his completely unpredictable course made him almost an impossible target. The pilot of the Lightning clearly was becoming more and more angry as his frustrations continued. In an effort to follow the intricate maneuvers of the ski plane he forced the big fighter into aerial acrobatics which almost made him lose control. When he should have been slowing almost to landing speed, he poured on the power and banked so sharply that his plane flipped onto its back and did a complete barrel roll, narrowly missing a mountain peak before it straightened out. Hans used the seconds the Lightning lost to head north along the coast, just skimming the ice pack, and dodging into every cove and mountain notch. The Lightning circled high over him before catching a glimpse of the little plane as it hopped over a long granite point that extended into the sea. With its wings and engine screaming it dived, missed again, and began circling Hans, a procedure that enabled him to keep his prey in sight but made shooting him almost impossible. As the men of the *Arluk* watched, the two planes disappeared between two snow-covered mountain peaks. There was an instant of silence, followed by the sound of a sharp explosion in the distance. A bubble of yellow flame rose from the notch between the mountains.

"Well, he finally got the bastard!" Flags said, and a ragged cheer came from the men of the *Arluk*. Before it died, they were astonished to see the ski plane reappear. It waggled its wings before scooting over the ridge of mountains to its base. There was no sign of the Lightning except a plume of black smoke in the distance.

"Now how the hell did that happen?" Flags asked.

It seemed obvious to Paul that the rage of the Lightning pilot had caused him to dive too fast to pull out, or had blinded him to the sides of the canyons around which the ski plane was ducking.

"The guy flying that Lightning must have been one of the pilots my brother trained," he said in disgust. "Damn it, we're getting to be a whole nation of fuck-ups." Perhaps that was no joke. Paul was beginning to fear that the Germans really could not be beaten, even when they were hopelessly outclassed. And the escape of the ski plane meant that it would still be there to observe Nathan's ground troops when they finally started toward its base.

When Nathan returned to the ship, they sent a message to GreenPat, explaining the debacle. GreenPat merely acknowledged the information, but at dawn the next day a PBY showed up. The big sea plane was slow enough to float astern of a light plane while she gunned it down, but not fast enough to catch it. At the first sight of the PBY, the ski plane disappeared over the ice floe.

After that the ski plane gave up its regular dawn patrol, and GreenPat soon tired of sending planes to try to catch it. On bright moonlight nights, though, Paul could still hear the drone of the little engine, and on one cloudy dawn he caught a glimpse of it just before the last rays of sunlight died on the horizon.

Nathan and Paul felt that no supplies could be moved toward Supportup until Peomeenie returned, presumably with some information about the location of the ski plane's hidden base. The whole operation would have to start with the Lightnings' putting an end to Hans on the ground. Nathan guessed that after that at least a week would be needed to move his men and supplies up and make all the necessary preparations for the final attack.

Paul had hoped that Peomeenie would return within two weeks, but by mid-December there was still no sign of him. Brit kept saying that Eskimos never hurry and that even an additional two weeks of delay would be nothing to worry about, but Paul and Nathan began to wonder what they could do if Peomeenie and his companion just never came back. Maybe the Germans had taken them prisoner or had shot them. It was all very well for an Eskimo hunter to boast that he could walk like a ghost through a wolf pack without being detected, but the Germans were beginning to seem to Paul as though they had magical powers of their own. Nothing was going right. Why should he expect one lone Eskimo and a woman to handle people who had captured all of Europe?

Nathan looked for more Eskimo men who could start another scouting expedition, but none was interested. They all apparently assumed that Peomeenie would return sooner or later in all probability, and if he did not, there was small enthusiasm for following in his footsteps. Nathan began trying to learn enough about Eskimo methods of travel to undertake the journey himself.

One night when Nathan came aboard to report the progress of his efforts ashore and to help Flags with any radio traffic, his tall, stooped body was identifiable amongst six Eskimos he brought with him only by its shape and size. He had on the whole native Greenlander outfit: sealskin parka with hood, sealskin blouse with the fur turned in, polar bear pants with a dark slice of fox fur or otter in the crotch, and *kamiks*, the soft sealskin boots with geometric designs around the top. He even had Eskimo mittens with slits to permit him to poke out two fingers to bait hooks and Eskimo sun glasses—a strip of polished driftwood with two slits instead of lenses.

"Call me Nathan of the North," he said as he climbed from the whaleboat to the well deck.

"How about Lawrence of Greenland?" Paul asked.

"Hell no. I'm Green of Greenland. Greenberg of Greenland."

"You'll need to leave long diaries. Don't leave out all your sexual exploits with the natives."

There was a look on Nathan's face then, just a momentary flinch before he said, "I don't think I'm exactly in Guns's class yet." He then began talking seriously about going to Supportup himself with three natives if Peomeenie didn't show up soon.

After discussing that and drinking many cups of coffee in his cabin, Paul said, "Where did you get Eskie clothes big enough to fit you, anyway?"

"Brit had some of the women make them up."

So Brit is really taking care of him, Paul thought . . . dammit, was he always going to be jealous of every woman he knew?

"They look good," he said. "Have you got those Eskies so they can shoot yet?"

Dismissing Nathan as soon as possible, Paul stood watching the boat take him back to the shore. Since Nathan had been spending most of his time working with the natives at the settlement with Brit as his interpreter, a close relationship between them was inevitable. Perhaps it was almost as inevitable that Brit should see nothing wrong in teaching Nathan the native custom of laughing together without guilt. If Nathan became a willing student of Eskimo philosophy, who could blame him?

I could, Paul thought, and was surprised at his own intensity.

"Lesson one: don't take the skipper's girl," Mowrey had said to him once long ago at Godhavn. Perhaps it was time to give Nathan a lesson in such elementary seamanship, a more basic kind of philosophy than anything he would learn from Brit or the Eskimos.

The strange thing was, Paul could not imagine having such a conversation with Nathan. His gaunt face with the deep-set eyes was somehow above or beyond such simplicisms. He would look hurt or give Paul a glance of that smoldering anger he usually kept for the Germans. It would be impossible for Nathan to have a lighthearted affair, even in Greenland with Brit, Paul suspected. Nathan

469

would be torn by guilt over infidelity to a wife he never talked about and who, Paul supposed, was giving him some kind of trouble. He would feel more guilt about taking his skipper's girl—no, Nathan was not the man for a carefree fling with anyone.

But was he a man who could turn Brit down on a December night in Greenland? Perhaps. Paul found himself hoping so, but the possibility seemed less and less likely the more he thought about it. A good commanding officer, he reminded himself grimly, never asks a man to do anything he can't do himself.

If he had any sense, Paul told himself, he would dismiss his suspicions, or convictions, as a bad joke. What Nathan and Brit did was their own business, wasn't it? Certainly Brit had gone out of her way to avoid making any promises to him. To let a woman with a kind of free-floating Eskimo heart disrupt his relationship with his executive officer just before attacking the Germans would be ridiculous. Definitely, if he had any sense he would forget the whole thing.

The trouble was, in this area Paul did not seem to have much sense. Since Nathan was now spending most of his time ashore, Paul's duty clearly was to remain aboard the ship. Brit never visited him. Perhaps she had felt herself unwanted aboard the trawler, and she had no boat since the Danish launch had been taken for the use of the men guarding the prisoners. Still, if she had wanted to see Paul, she could have sent out a message with the crew of the whaleboat.

The more Paul brooded about it, the more it seemed that Nathan's request to train the Eskimos ashore had been rather clever. Now that he was living in Swanson's house, the sauna and the big feather bed would always be handy. Nathan was probably teaching Brit to shoot all kinds of guns, and her new release of hatred for the Germans was probably mixing with love for her new tutor in her inimitably explosive ways.

Damn him, Paul thought, god *damn* him . . . Which made Paul feel rotten, but it was the sum of his emotions when he woke up late at night in his narrow solitary bunk after dreaming that he only had to move his hand an inch to touch Brit's smooth warm skin.

Damn it, he thought, why couldn't I meet a real Danish girl instead of a goddamn white Eskie? The Eskie philosophy may be fine for them, but it can get white men to killing each other if they don't watch out . . .

Paul spent hours trying to reconcile himself to the probability that Brit of course had included Nathan in her love for all mankind, and then trying to convince himself that Nathan was just "too decent a guy" to do such a thing. He even was able half to convince himself that Brit was "too nice a girl" to take on two American officers from the same ship. Somehow none of this helped much. No matter what she was doing, he was hungry for her. The small icebergs in the fjord and the clouds overhead were beginning to take on the shape of women again. His memories of her lovemaking kept repeating themselves in his head, making it impossible for him to concentrate on the books about gunnery he was trying to study.

Finally Paul gave up and decided to send Stevens ashore with a note, asking Brit to come to dinner. Worried that she would bring Nathan, he added, "I've learned the Eskimo philosophy from you, but this Eskimo is dying of loneliness. I want to see you alone, if only for a few minutes."

When the whaleboat returned to the trawler, she was standing between Stevens and Krater in the stern, laughing with them. Dressed in her Eskimo outfit, she jumped lightly to the well deck. Feeling the eyes of his crew on him, Paul shook her hand with curious formality and said, "Thank you for coming out. There are a lot of communications we ought to work out together."

At least she had the good grace not to laugh at that. She followed him toward his cabin. The quartermaster and Guns were standing near the wheel talking about New Orleans again. They left and stood on the port wing of the bridge as Paul opened the starboard door for Brit. As soon as they got into his tiny cabin, he shut the door and kissed her.

"I thought you didn't want to make love here," she said a few minutes later.

"The hell with it. But keep as quiet as you can."

The discipline of trying to maintain silence somehow intensified their passion. He was constantly afraid that someone would knock at the door and hurried. Eskimofashion, they did not take off their clothes . . . When they'd finished, she lay in the bunk staring up at the sword on its brackets while he rearranged his uniform. "You certainly have some fine ideas about working out communications," she said.

He did not want to, but the damn question came out in spite of his better sense . . . "Have you been working out communications with Nathan?"

"Don't ask that," she said, looking startled. "Paul, for God's sake don't make him feel worse than he already feels."

"What does that mean?"

"I mean that he's so full of guilt and sorrow about his wife that—"

"What about his wife?"

"You don't know? He never told you?"

"He never talks about her."

"That's hard to believe. He never talks to me about anyone else. I thought you two were friends."

"Should I know about her?"

"Paul, if you care anything about Nathan, you damn well should know. His wife disappeared in Poland. She went back just before the war to try to get her parents out. He hopes she's gone into hiding but he believes she's probably in a concentration camp, or dead."

"Oh, Lord," Paul said, rubbing his eyes. "I guess I always sensed there was something, but not that."

"Maybe he was afraid to talk about it. He kind of broke down when he told me."

"It makes me feel strange—all this time I thought I knew him so well and I didn't know the main thing—"

"He's all right now. There's nothing weak about him."

"That's for sure. Funny how little you can really know about somebody even when you're all locked up aboard a little ship . . ."

"Maybe it's just that men don't usually talk about their wives much, even with their best friends. Did you ever discuss yours with him?"

"No. I don't have all that much to discuss."

There was a short silence.

"How do I stand with you?" he asked finally. "I mean, are you really tied up with Nathan? I don't blame him and I don't blame you, but I should know."

"Paul, you have me when you have me. We're all blind people here, stumbling around trying to help each other in the dark. No rules apply here. Now, didn't you ask me out

472

for dinner? I can't wait to see what that cook of yours is going to give us."

Cookie had prepared roast lamb with appropriate fixings. It was good, but Paul didn't feel at all hungry. He thought of Nathan wrapped up with worry about his wife while old Mowrey was hounding him and he was seasick all the time. No wonder his gaunt face had that look of tragedy, even when he smiled.

"There's one more thing I want to tell you," Brit said when the dishes had been cleared from his cabin. "Nathan said he'd talk to you about it, but it would be better if I did."

"What?"

"I want to get out of here and get my father out. Nathan says planes go to the States from the west coast every day, and if I could get the proper authorization . . ."

"We can radio for permission. I don't know what they'll say."

"We still have an embassy. If you could get in touch with the right people—it was Nathan's idea."

"We'll do what we can. I should have thought of it myself."

"I didn't really level with you. I'm going crazy here and my father's already crazy. Paul, we have to get out."

Soon she asked to go ashore and he had the whaleboat take her in. When it came back, he saw Nathan standing in the stern. The tall, gaunt man in the Eskimo furs stepped awkwardly to the deck.

"Could you come up to my cabin for a minute?" Paul called from the bridge.

Nathan came up the steps. Paul met him in the pilot-house.

"Nathan, Brit told me about your wife," he said, and to his own astonishment, found himself hugging his executive officer. He had never before hugged a man in his life, not even his brother or father. Embarrassed, he stepped back.

"Thanks," Nathan said. "You know . . . well, we've always understood each other anyway. You know . . . we don't have to talk."

"Not about that. But send a message to GreenPat and see if we can find a way to get Brit and her father to the States. I wish I'd thought of that myself."

"I'll take care of it, you've been busy."

Turning, Nathan almost ran out of the pilothouse. Paul climbed wearily to the flying bridge. It was a bitterly cold night, but a half moon was breaking through the windswept clouds as though it were fighting for life.

# CHAPTER 48

As the ninth of December wore on, the days became shorter and shorter until finally sunrise merged with sunset and there was only a few minutes of ruddy red glare on the icy mountains to mark high noon. That would be time enough to allow the bombers to do their work and on clear nights the stars and the moon made that white world surprisingly light without the sun. The trouble was, there were few clear nights. One blizzard was quickly followed by another, and what the Eskimos called good weather was any wind less than fifty miles an hour and any temperature above fifty below. Still the fjord, with its swift-running currents and great tidal rise and fall, did not freeze, and the ice pack off shore was so driven by winter gales that it formed a less formidable barrier along the coast than it did in summer.

Driven by the knowledge that they must soon attack the Germans, the crew of the *Arluk* worked as it had never worked before. Every man who was not needed to guard the prisoners and the ship unloaded the heavy depth charges from the hold and carried them in the whaleboat and in the Danes' launch to the settlement. Because a dog sled could carry only one of the great charges at a time, Nathan and Brit decided that the Danish launch could carry a load of them to a point just short of Supportup, where they could be landed on the coast and dragged up low cliffs there with ropes. This operation awaited only the return of Peomeenie. Paul should not be surprised by his long absence, Brit still kept saying. In every blizzard Peo undoubtedly would build an igloo out on the ice shelf that extended from the shore for thousands of yards into the sea. The proximity of relatively warm ocean currents there cut the cold in the shelter of an igloo, and by hacking a hole in the ice Peo could catch enough fish to last out the winter if necessary. With his whale oil lamp glowing in his crystal dome, he and Ninoo, his companion, could laugh together until the sun came back to stay.

"I should have told him I wouldn't pay him unless he got back here fast," Paul said.

"When you come right down to it, what's the hurry?" Brit asked.

"While your friend Peomeenie and his damn Ninoo are laughing together, the goddamn Krauts are sending out weather reports, and with those their planes are bombing the bejesus out of every city from Moscow to London," Paul said. "We're supposed to break that up. *That's* what the hurry is."

"But not even an Eskimo can go far in a blizzard," Brit said. "And Peo is very thorough. You kept telling him you want to know where every gun emplacement is. That means he has to cover both sides of the fjord. He'll have to go inland for miles before he can cross it. I'm sure he's doing his best and no one in this world could do better."

Paul was not convinced. His fear that Peomeenie might have been captured or killed was growing. The moaning of the wind and the ruddy glare of the sun during its brief appearances on the horizon seemed to be setting a scene only for disaster. While everyone else worked to maintain the ship, guarded prisoners or drilled with the Eskimos ashore, Paul actually had very little to do, and the long hours he spent idly in his bunk made him feel obscurely guilty. Flags reported that radio signals in a variety of frequencies were pouring from some place nearby to the south, presumably Supportup. Obviously the Germans were carrying out their mission. Perhaps it had been only cowardice that had caused Paul to make these elaborate preparations, instead of sailing into their fjord and just attacking as best he could. Each day Paul checked off on his calendar in the nautical almanac seemed a personal defeat.

There was not a book aboard the ship he'd not read and his memories of the past did not offer much comfort in introspection. For a long while he had avoided thinking about his wife. Sometimes Sylvia came to him in dreams, voluptuous, golden-haired and more eager for love than she had usually been, but such visions just made him wake up hornier than ever and when he was in that mood, he had to be careful not to get furious at Brit and Nathan. He felt peculiar now every time Nathan knew he was alone with Brit and every time he knew she was alone with him. Damn it, they weren't Eskimos, no matter how much they all respected and needed each other and so forth . . .

The more Paul thought about his situation, the more ridiculous he appeared to himself. He was an unfaithful husband who brooded about both his wife and mistress being unfaithful. He admired the Eskimos' freedom from jealousy and possessiveness, but needed at least the ideal of one man and one woman pledging themselves to each other forever and meaning it. Temporary love affairs in time of war were probably inevitable, maybe even necessary to stay alive sometimes, but in the future he wanted at least to hope for something more. He could accept Nathan's need for Brit and her desire to comfort him, but he found that he did not want to daydream anymore of coming back to her after the war. He didn't want to ask her to sail around the world with him. Perhaps it was only a white man's craziness, but if he took a woman on such a voyage he would not want to worry about her running off with any man who needed her, or who offered a jolly hour of laughing together without jealousy or a sense of betrayal. It seemed, in short, that he was hopelessly himself . . .

Suddenly he began to dream of Sylvia again. Forgetting his hard times with her, her disappointing letters, and his worries about her as a USO hostess, he remembered the day she had dived from the top of the old yawl's mast. A girl who had done that certainly could grow up to sail a small boat around the world. He remembered the flamboyant way she danced, the vitality of her face, and wondered how he had ever been interested in anyone else. After the war was over she would have outgrown her few disturbing ways and they would sail the South Seas together. Sometimes he would realize that this was an unlikely dream, but he felt that it was one he *needed* . . . men in the Arctic tended to create their own women, weaving memories into fantasies. Almost no man on the Greenland Patrol remembered an ugly or nagging wife.

The future with Sylvia would be wonderful, he was sure, but the truth was that he would have no future if he did not find a way to attack the German base efficiently. If he messed up that operation, he would die in the snow or in the freezing sea.

Strangely, the most comforting fantasy of all during those long, long nights of waiting turned out to be one of victory in battle, not love. In his imagination Paul could see the plans he and Nathan had devised working in magnificent detail. First the planes would bomb hell out of the fjord. Before the smoke had cleared, Nathan would explode three tons of TNT in a ring around the bewildered Germans. At that point the *Arluk* would make her magnificent entrance into the mouth of the fjord with all guns blazing. She would find the hunter-killer, this new Valkyrie, already afire, but would finish her off with one blast from the big bow gun. Then he would rake the Germans, who would be trying to set up their machine guns ashore. Before they even opened fire, Nathan, Guns and thirty well-trained Eskimos would attack them from the rear with automatic rifles, hand grenades, and finally, those murderous-looking knives the men had made. More depth charges would explode all around the Germans. They would give up—they would have no choice. They would beg for mercy, kneeling in the snow . . .

Somehow the fantasy stopped there—Paul did not want to figure out now exactly what he was going to do with all those prisoners. The fantasy picked up again when Paul sailed back to his base on the west coast, to Narsarssuak. There Commander GreenPat would congratulate him, would put him up for a promotion, for command of a full destroyer, and for medals. He would be flown home for a hero's welcome. Sylvia would come running into his arms. They would take a honeymoon suite at the Ritz-Carlton Hotel for a month. A second honeymoon much better than his first would be his prize for heroism . . .

Impatient with those fantasies and almost frightened by their ability to take his mind off any kind of reality, Paul kept his men at gun drill aboard the ship, made sure that Williams was adequately guarding the prisoners and watched Guns show his furry troops how to shoot mortars while Nathan kept an eye on him and Brit tried to teach the natives enough numbers to understand the concept of a weapon's range.

Finally everything was done that could be done before Peomeenie's return. Hans still piloted his ski plane for a peek over the mountain on clear moonlit nights. If it had not been for him, Nathan would have started to move his depth charges up the coast toward Supportup, but he did not want to take any chance of giving up the great advantage of surprise. For a week there was very little to do but wait. Using clay from supplies, which had been sent from Denmark for the native children, Brit constructed a model of the fjord at Supportup-Kangerdula on a table in the schoolroom next to the dispensary for the sick. She used all the information she could get from the charts, the pilot-book and from Eskimos who had been near that place, but the model was badly lacking in detail.

"Peo will be able to finish it," Brit said. "He sculpts beautiful things from soapstone and walrus tusks. He'll be able to make a model better than he can draw a map."

Now all sentences began with "When Peo gets back . . . When Peo got back, he would be led immediately to the clay model. As soon as he had shown exactly where the Germans were, that information would be radioed to GreenPat, with a request that the place where the light planes were kept be bombed and strafed immediately. If Peo had been able to locate the position of the hunter-killer, she too should be attacked. Nathan had this message already coded and tacked to the bulletin board in the *Arluk*'s radio shack. Its last paragraph said, "Except for attacking ships and planes, please delay final bombing of base until our ground forces are in position of attack as soon as planes leave. We do not want to give the enemy a chance to dig in again. Amount of time needed for this operation will depend on the weather. Our best guess is a week if conditions we can work in. All our preparations have been made."

This message was rewritten several times as Paul and Nathan refined their plans. In their initial attack, the Lightnings and bombers should try to take out all German artillery which protected the fjord, as well as the light planes and the hunter-killer, if they could. As soon as this had been done, the *Arluk* could move into the fjord without waiting for the ground force to arrive. Without getting close enough to take losses from machinegun or small arms fire, the *Arluk* should tease the Germans into readying all their forces for an attack from the sea.

After consultation with Paul, Nathan gave all these detailed plans to GreenPat in advance. They were promptly approved. Even GreenPat started sending messages which began, "When your native scout returns . . ."

"I'm beginning to think we're waiting for the Second Coming of Christ," Paul said. "It seems to me that our whole fucking war is coming to a standstill and breathlessly waiting for one damn Eskimo and a woman named Ninoo to quit laughing together and get down to business."

On a clear moonlit night two days before Christmas Peomeenie and Ninoo drove their dog sled back to the settlement at Angmagssalik as casually as though they had been on a brief Sunday excursion. They were more concerned with greeting relatives and friends than with hurrying to bring their information to the Americans, and Brit might not have known of their arrival for hours if she had not heard the excitement of the dogs. She and Nathan ran to the Eskimo settlement and found Peomeenie in one of the sod huts which was so crowded with his welcoming friends that no one could get in a word edgewise. Peomeenie and Ninoo were ravenously eating a feast of nicely rotted raw seal meat which had been awaiting them.

"For God's sake ask him what he saw," Nathan said.

Brit had to push through the tight rings of Peomeenie's admirers before she could catch his attention. He grinned at her with his mouth full before gulping his food and answering the questions that she kept repeating. They shouted back and forth in the Eskimo language. From Peomeenie's grins, Nathan guessed that his trip had been successful, but Brit looked astonished when she turned to him and called above the din, "God, I don't know what's happening. He says the Germans are all going home. He says not many are left!"

"Going home? *How?*"

After more excited questions from Brit and more laconic replies from Peomeenie, who continued to grin and eat, Brit said, "He says the little planes and the ship have been taking many Germans out."

Hell, Nathan thought, the bastards aren't going home—they're evacuating a base they know will be attacked and setting up small weather stations all down the coast. That of course is what they came here to do in the first place, and we've been sucker enough not to stop them.

"Where's the ship now?" he called to Brit above the babble. "Ask him where the ship was when he left."

479

After a brief exchange, Brit said, "The ship is in Supportup Fjord now. They are loading her with many oil drums."

"She's the one who's going home," Nathan said. "Her job's done. Now she'll load up with their brass and get the hell out of here. Jesus, we've been suckered again. Get Peo out of here. We've got to take him to see Paul. We still might catch that goddamn ship."

It was difficult for Brit to give Peomeenie any sense of urgency. If the Germans were going home, he kept asking, why was there anything to worry about?

The first that Paul knew about any of this was the sound of the whaleboat approaching the ship in the darkness. With mixed emotions he saw Brit and Nathan standing in the stern as it came alongside the well deck, and then he saw Peomeenie standing beside Brit. He ran from the wing of the bridge to greet them.

"Christ, everything's a mess," Nathan began. "The Krauts are evacuating. Their planes and their men have probably spread men all along the coast, and when Peo last saw their ship three days ago it was loading oil drums on deck."

Paul's head felt as though it were spinning. All their carefully laid plans were for nothing. While they'd been sitting fat, dumb and happy with their great strategies, the goddamn Germans had indeed suckered them again.

"How many Krauts are left?" he demanded.

"Peo says he saw no more than twice twenty—not more than twice his fingers and toes," Brit said. "There may be more underground. He says they live like foxes. And he said their ship is crowded with men."

"It sounds like it's getting ready to make a dash for home now," Paul said.

"We might still catch them," Brit said.

"Wait a minute," Paul said. "Peo, come with me."

He led Peo to his cabin and showed him a chart of Supportup Fjord. Unhesitatingly Peo pointed to one of several narrow ravines branching out from it, and showed where the airstrip, the hidden hangar and the hunter-killer were. After quickly jotting down these positions, those of the field guns and the rest of the base, Paul gave them to Nathan.

"Radio these positions to GreenPat. Tell him to start bombing. We'll get under way and wait off the entrance of the fjord for the air strike. If Fatso is already at sea, we'll never catch him, but if he's still there, we'll get him when he comes out."

Nathan ran to the radio shack, Paul to the bridge. The shouting on the well deck had already brought most of the men from the forecastle.

"Captain," Boats said, "do you want me to pick up the whaleboat now, or do you want me to take the civilians ashore?"

"Pick it up," Paul said. "I'll stop at the wharf on the way out. That will be quicker."

"You can't put me ashore," Brit said. "Peo and I can help."

"Don't argue," Paul said, and called, "all right, let's get the anchor in. Take the boat aboard."

"Paul!" Brit said, tugging at his arm. "You should hurry. Putting us ashore will be a waste of time."

"Do what I say. Wait on the well deck with Peo. When I come alongside the wharf, jump fast. I'm not going to tie up."

"Where's Nathan?"

"Now don't go bothering Nathan! Brit, I don't have time to argue with you. If you and Peo don't jump ashore fast as soon as we get alongside that wharf, you'll be thrown ashore. Now don't give me any more crap."

"Are those your famous last words to me?"

"Oh, for God's sake—"

"You'll never be back, you'll go right back to the west coast. Mission accomplished."

"Brit, I got no time for this. I'll try to get in touch later. Now get off the bridge and wait on the well deck. *Please.*"

Brit looked at him, and left the bridge.

"We're over the anchor," Boats called.

"Break it out. Secure that boat as fast as you can."

Paul conned the *Arluk* down the fjord at her top speed. He approached the wharf at the settlement with a reckless dash Mowrey himself might have admired, paused there for the instant it took Brit and Peomeenie to jump ashore, and headed out of the fjord. Nathan appeared suddenly on the bridge.

"GreenPat says the planes should wait for dawn," he reported. "That's just about five hours. They'll be here then."

481

"Good. That will give us a chance to get there. If their ship hasn't already left, the planes will drive it out."

Raising his voice, Paul told the men on the well deck that they would be off the mouth of Supportup Fjord in about three and a half hours, and that planes would attack the place at dawn. "If their ship hasn't already left, we can expect her to make a run for the open sea as soon as they hear the planes coming. I'm going to close with her as soon as I can."

The men had been geared up for action and were obviously confused by the prospect of more hours of waiting. After loading the guns, they stood hunched against the cold wind, talking and laughing. Cookie passed out mugs of hot coffee and the men started back to the forecastle.

Paul too felt a letdown after a sense of violent urgency. It was a little before seven in the morning. A three-quarter moon was riding high in the sky, so bright that no stars were visible near it. The recent gales had left only a thin scattering of icebergs near the coast. A belt of gleaming back water separated the icy mountains from the main ice floe, which glistened about three miles offshore. Changing course to steam down the middle of this, Paul said, "Nathan, can you get the mouth of Supportup on the radar?"

"I got it. Nothing's moving, but we couldn't pick up a little wooden ship like that until we're damn near on top of her."

"Just hope that she's not already on her way to Germany."

"Skipper, do you really want to close with her? How close?"

"Close as I can get."

"Machine guns at point-blank range? Can't we do better than that?"

"How? We can't aim that five-incher worth a damn. The three-incher can't hit anything until we're right on top of it. We got two twenties and five fifties. We outgun her."

"We'll take a beating. Two small wooden ships with machine guns at close range could blow each other up."

"What would you suggest?"

"Track her and call the planes down on her if we can."

"If she gets out in the ice pack again they'll never find her and she can outrun us."

"We could stay just beyond range of her light stuff and give Guns a chance with our three-incher."

"If we screw around too much she's liable to get away. I'm going to take her this time, I don't give a damn what happens—"

"Just give us a chance with the three-incher first. If that doesn't work, close with her."

Paul knew he was right, but for some reason that made him angry. "Damn it, I'm going to do this my way," he said. "After this, you leave the grand strategy to me—"

"O.K., *skipper*. But don't forget that I want him as much as you do. I just want to take him on our terms, not his. Don't forget he's got torpedo tubes."

"You think he can hit a trawler with those?"

"I wouldn't give him a chance unless I had to. With the planes and big guns on our side, we shouldn't have to get near him."

"Right from the beginning, we've been overcautious. You know that, Nathan? We've been fucking chicken. One way or another I'm going to finish this thing today if he's still in there. I'm not going to let him get away."

"I'm with you," Nathan said, and meant it as he turned back to the radar set.

Everything continued to be curiously peaceful as the *Arluk* cleared the land and turned south through widely scattered ice floes. Even the wind had reduced its moan to a whisper. It was warmer at sea than in the fjord, though the mercury hovered near thirty below zero. The barometer was dropping, Paul saw as he tapped it. Before long another blizzard was bound to hit. Such good weather in December couldn't possibly last long.

If one of those narrow little ships designed for hunting and killing whales loaded enough fuel to try to cross the Atlantic and took on all the people she could cram below decks, she wouldn't have much speed left, he figured. Maybe he's no faster than I am now. And if an overloaded little ship like that hit a full gale out here, he'd have his hands full without worrying about me. He'd ice up, and roll over or be swamped. Maybe he wouldn't head straight for home. Maybe he'd try to find someplace to hole up in the ice while he waited for his own weather stations to tell him when to make his break. If he has a deck cargo of oil drums, he sure wouldn't want to get machine-gunned. Maybe he'll try to hide instead of running or looking for a fight tonight . . .

Except who the hell could be sure of anything? For the most part, his clever deductions had led him unerringly to the wrong conclusions for months. Who the hell knew whether the damn ship was in its fjord, three days out to sea or in between?

God, let him still be in his base, Paul found himself thinking. Let me have him, I *want* him. I want his blood. Now what the hell kind of prayer was that?

It was at least an honest prayer. Paul was a little astonished to realize that at the moment, all he wanted to do was fight. The fears that had been making him doubt himself ever since he could remember had disappeared. The idea of spotting the German ship for the planes and letting them attack it was infuriating, and he didn't really want to try to sink the German with his three- or five-incher while staying safely out of range of his machine guns. No, if he obeyed his instincts he'd simply charge the enemy with all guns firing, bring the five-incher to point-blank range and ram the bastard if he stayed afloat. Reason told him that the German machine guns were sure to kill many of his men in such a battle and that he stood a good chance of dying himself, but after months of this dancing around it really was time to fight. Now. Only the delay was hard to take and the thought that the German might already have gotten away. I want him, Paul kept saying to himself, I want him and this time I'm going to have him. Please, God, don't let him get away—

Except this was crazy. With all the odds on his side, why get a bunch of men killed?

Paul shook his head to clear it, as though he were drunk. Nathan was right—he should close with the German only as a last resort. This was no time to pull an Errol Flynn.

"Get Guns up here," he said to the quartermaster.

Almost immediately Guns appeared.

"If I can, I'm going to stay just beyond the range of this guy's machine guns," Paul said. "Do you think you can get him with the three-incher?"

"We'd have to be pretty darn close," Guns said. "I can get him with the three-incher at two thousand yards if you give me time for enough shots."

"We'll try it," Paul said. "If it doesn't work, I'm going to steam right down the bastard's throat."

Guns nodded. "We'll get him, sir. One way or another. The crew is ready."

The moonlight was so bright that they could see the glittering humps of the mountains around Supportup Fjord while they were still twenty miles away. The ice pack had pressed closer to the coast there, the radar showed, and there were several large icebergs in the two-mile strip of relatively open sea between the mouth of the fjord and the main floe.

"We're going to have to go in close," Paul said to Nathan. "If we don't stay right on top of the mouth of that fjord, he could get away."

"If he's loaded deep, he couldn't have too much speed."

"But we don't know how much and we don't know if he'll try to run north, south or east when he gets out."

"There's a good-size berg about fifteen-hundred yards just off the mouth of the fjord," Nathan said, studying the radar. "If we hid behind that we might have some surprise going for us."

"If they have lookouts on the shore they'd spot us before we got in that close."

"Do you suppose their field guns could get us out there?" Nathan said.

"If that damn Eskimo was right, they're further in the fjord. Hell, we got to go in close. Any other way, he could duck us."

As they neared the mouth of the fjord, the bleak white mountains and the rocky coast looked so barren that it was difficult to imagine that a base of any kind could be nearby. No light, no wisp of smoke, no mark in the snow showed anywhere. Paul brought the ship slowly toward the iceberg which was less than a mile off the entrance to the fjord. It was about three times the size of the *Arluk* with a slanting flat top like the roof of a big shed. The sea had eaten away its waterline, producing a ledge about ten feet wide which ran around the edge of it like a skirt. Keeping the iceberg between the ship and the shore, Paul stopped and drifted with his bow only about fifty feet away from it.

"Can you see over it from the flying bridge?" he shouted through the voice tube.

"No," Krater answered.

Paul went to the flying bridge and jockeyed the ship until he could see over the slanting top of the iceberg. All but a few feet of the bow of the *Arluk* and the mast were hidden from the shore. When he stopped the engine, the men could hear a gentle groundswell sloshing under the snowy skirt of the iceberg and the strange catlike mewing of gulls with black-tipped wings that swooped around them. Paul glanced at his wristwatch. Twenty minutes after ten, about an hour and a half before dawn.

"Here we wait," he called to his men. "The planes should hit soon after the first streak of dawn, and if our little friend is in there he should come out and play. You guys better get warmed up while you have a chance."

Standing in the pilothouse to get the ache out of his own feet and hands, Paul tried to imagine what was going on now aboard the German ship and at their base. Since the Germans had no way of knowing that Peomeenie had visited them, they would have no reason to suspect that an attack was this imminent. Probably all but a few men on watch were asleep in underground bunkers or in houses buried in the snow. If their ship had already loaded a deck cargo of oil drums, she was probably ready for sea and waiting for a good weather report for the run across the Atlantic. If she planned to carry a lot of passengers, including most of the German brass whom she had saved from the supply ship, she would probably have to wait for them to come aboard when she got the first warning of enemy planes approaching. Big brass wouldn't be apt to sleep aboard a crowded little ship until the last moment. But sure as hell she'd try to get out at the first sound of planes.

Then which way would she go? Paul went to his cabin to study the chart. To the south the land fell away in a long shallow bay full of small islands and rocks. To the north the mountains plunged almost vertically into the sea. The German would probably head right for the ice pack at first, but when he saw the *Arluk* blocking his way, he could run either way, or choose to fight it out on the spot.

"Nathan, does the radar show any leads into the ice pack near here?"

Nathan turned a knob and studied the screen closely before answering. "The stuff is pretty closely packed out there. About ten miles to the south there's something that might be a good lead."

"But he doesn't seem to have radar, so he couldn't know that."

"That's right."

"Funny that they don't have radar, isn't it? I always just sort of assumed that they did."

486

"That's what they get for kicking all the brains out of Germany before they even started their war."

"What do you think he'll do when he comes out?"

"I think he'll try to get close enough to us to use his torpedoes."

"If I keep my bow to him, he won't have a ten-percent chance."

"But it will be just about his only chance to sink us."

"If he has any speed left I bet he'll run. Would you want a fire fight if your decks were loaded with oil drums?"

"No, but I'm not suicidal. The Krauts are. That's the only explanation of everything they've done."

"I don't know."

"I do . . . it's only a question of how many poor bastards they'll kill before they get what they really want—a fiery death, the last act of a bad opera. They love it."

"Well, we'll soon see."

Restlessly Paul climbed to the flying bridge. The catlike calls of the seagulls with black-tipped wings which were wheeling all around suddenly infuriated him. The seagulls, after all, were in no danger—they were just interested spectators, and after the battle was over they would feast on the eyes of Germans and Americans with equal relish. He had an impulse to take out his pistol and shoot at the gulls, probably would have except that they were close enough to shore for even a .45 to be heard. The moon was only a little above a low ridge of clouds on the western horizon, clouds that seemed to be growing, and Paul suddenly was afraid that they would spill over the whole sky and ground the planes before any action began. That was ridiculous. Even in Greenland in December bad weather didn't build up that fast. He went to the pilothouse and tapped the barometer. It was still falling, but dawn should break in about forty minutes. At Narsarssuak Fjord on the other side of the ice cap the big bombers would be already warming up. Their pilots were probably having a last sip of coffee. To them the prospect of bombing a German weather base in Greenland which now had been pinpointed for them would appear to be just a milk run.

As the moon set behind the clouds there were a few minutes of utter darkness during which the whole coast of Greenland disappeared. The stars on the eastern horizon glowed brightly, much larger than they appeared at home. Invisible now, the gulls continued to mew like hungry cats.

The first sign of dawn was the gradual disappearance of the faintest stars. Then there was a murky gray line on the eastern horizon, made jagged by the intervening icebergs. Without orders the men trooped to their guns. They checked the breeches and trained them restlessly around the horizon.

Paul went to the voice tube to the engineroom. "It's starting to get light," he said. "We could have action anytime."

"Standing by," Chief Banes said.

Paul went to the flying bridge. The snowy coast of Greenland was beginning to emerge from the gloom, pristine white slopes which looked as though they had never been touched by man. Veils of gray cloud now obscured the highest peaks. Through his binoculars Paul studied the entrance to the fjord. The sea was black where the current and tides had prevented it from freezing. The German's white camouflage wouldn't help him when he came out.

By now the planes should have taken off, Paul thought. Jesus, I hope they don't find some way to screw up . . . "Nathan, is Flags on the radio?" Paul called through a voice tube to the bridge.

"Yes, they'll tell us if there's a change of plan."

At first the sound of the approaching bombers was so faint that Paul was not sure that he heard it. He turned the collar of his parka away from his ears. The men at the guns started to cheer as the distant drone grew to a roar. Suddenly, like plump geese, three fat-bellied bombers appeared in a V-formation above the ice cap. They circled high above the fjord, trying to make sure of their position.

*Now* the bastards in there know what's coming, Paul thought. That hunter-killer is trying to get under way. I bet everybody is running, trying to jump aboard . . . if the son of a bitch didn't sail three days ago . . .

This suspicion that the German had already escaped was the worst of it. Paul gripped his binoculars so hard his hands ached as he studied the mouth of the fjord. Overhead the bombers continued to circle lazily. Suddenly the lead plane sloped toward the fjord. It dipped down, leveled off just above the sides of the icy canyon, crossed it and circled away. Paul had seen no bomb drop and had heard nothing, but a plume of heavy black smoke suddenly climbed from the edge of the fjord.

So now the target is marked, Paul thought, and almost immediately heard gunfire as antiaircraft batteries along the ridges of the fjord opened fire at the planes. The bombers circled far above the puffs of smoke. Paul had to force himself to keep a watch on the entrance of the fjord instead of the planes.

He's pretty damn slow getting under way, Paul thought, and now a conviction that the German ship had already escaped began to grow. *Damn,* he thought, and at just that moment he saw a tiny white object move just inside the rocky entrance. It was much smaller than he had thought the hunter-killer would be, even at that distance.

"He's coming," Paul yelled, and slid down the ladder to the wing of the bridge.

"I've got him on the radar," Nathan said, his deep voice sounding almost matter-of-fact. "Range, sixteen-hundred yards, bearing two six three."

"Guns, open fire with the three-inch at will," Paul called, and repeated the bearing and range.

The crack of the small cannon answered almost immediately. Paul rang for flank speed. As soon as he was clear of the iceberg he said, "Come right slowly and steady on the mouth of the fjord. Can you see the ship coming out?"

"Aye," the helmsman said.

The three-inch gun kept firing at about five-second intervals.

"Can you see if he's hitting anything?" Paul asked Nathan, who was studying the oncoming ship through his binoculars.

"I can't even see where the shells are landing."

There was another report. "That one's way short," Nathan said.

Paul did not need his binoculars now to see that the hunter-killer was still heading straight toward him. No guns were flickering from her bow. Smoke was pouring from her high stack. Gray drums of fuel oil were lashed all over her deck. The *Arluk's* three-inch gun continued to fire and one shell burst just off the target's left bow.

"How much more do you want to close, skipper?" Nathan said.

"Till we hit him."

"We're getting into his range."

"He's not shooting yet."

Paul had hardly spoken when he saw a flicker of fire on

the bow of the hunter-killer, and tracers arched toward the *Arluk*. They fell about a hundred yards ahead, looking like rain on the water.

"Left full rudder," Paul said, wondering whether he was a coward, fighting with the impulse to keep barreling closer.

"He's turning too, skipper," Nathan said.

Paul saw that the target was indeed making a sharp turn to the right and was starting to run parallel to the shore only a few hundred yards off the coast. The little ship was very deep in the water and was throwing a huge stern wake. Paul maneuvered the *Arluk* to parallel her course.

"Nathan, take bearings on her. Is she outrunning us?"

There was a pause while Nathan peered into the radar. The three-inch gun continued to fire and a shell burst just ahead of the hunter-killer.

"Not by much, skipper," Nathan said. "Maybe a little."

"If we don't hit her pretty soon—"

The next shell from the three-inch gun narrowly missed the stern of the hunter-killer. To Paul's astonishment she turned abruptly and headed for the center of the shallow cove.

"She'll run aground in there," Paul said.

"Maybe he's got his own charts."

"Anyway, we've got him. He can't run from us in there."

The three-inch gun continued to fire, but the stern presented a narrow target. Shells exploded on both sides of it.

"I think he's trying to beach her," Nathan said. "That way most of them might get off . . ."

Close against the icy shore, the white ship was difficult to see. She zig-zagged through some low-lying small islands of rock. Slowing to make a sharp turn to the south, she suddenly stopped.

"She's aground," Paul said. "She's only about two hundred yards from shore."

He headed the *Arluk* toward the stationary vessel while he studied her through the binoculars. The *Arluk*'s three-inch gun continued to crack. Paul was astonished when flames suddenly blossomed on the bow of the hunter-killer.

"Jesus, we've got him," Paul said. "Cease fire."

"I just got the range!" Guns said.

"He's aground and afire. Let's see what happens."

Nathan and Paul studied the German ship through the binoculars as the *Arluk* sped closer. The hunter-killer's bow was tilted up on rocks and she was listed about twenty degrees to port. Smoke and fire climbed from the bow. Her stern was alive with men.

"They're launching rubber rafts," Nathan said. "If they get ashore they may be able to make it to one of their weather stations."

"Like hell," Paul said. "Guns, open fire."

The next shot toppled the smokestack. Paul was about to order another ceasefire when a machine gun on the stern of the German opened up. The *Arluk* was barely within range, but Paul heard bullets falling on the flying bridge and the splintering of wood.

"Give them everything we've got!" Paul yelled. "Ahead full. Let's finish this."

As all her machine guns opened up, the whole hull of the *Arluk* shook. And almost immediately the hunter-killer burst into flames.

"Cease fire," Paul yelled, but he had to repeat the order twice more at the top of his lungs before the guns were silent. The oil drums on the whole length of the hunter-killer's deck were blossoming into flame. From her stern men were crowding into two large rubber boats. A few had paddles, and they frantically moved away from the burning ship while men were still trying to jump into them. About a dozen men were splashing in the water between the stern of the ship and the rubber boats.

Suddenly the machine gun on the stern of the burning ship again started to fire. Without being told the men on the *Arluk* opened up with their machine guns. The stern of the hunter-killer exploded. In the instant of silence which followed, a white-clad figure gave one piercing shriek, stumbled and fell on the well deck of the *Arluk*. Boats and two seamen ran toward it. Boats kneeled by the head.

"It's Cookie," he yelled. "He's hit bad."

Paul started to run to the well deck, but Nathan said, "Skipper, hold it. Those bastards are going to make it ashore if we don't act quick."

Paul stared toward the burning wreck. The two crowded rubber boats had made it halfway to shore. At least a half dozen men were paddling in each.

"Guns," he said, "take out those boats. The twenties ought to be able to do it."

The two 20-millimeter guns began their staccato stutter. Tracers arched toward the rubber boats. A few men dropped their paddles and tried to stand before they were hit. The guns kept on firing until there was nothing but smoke on the water . . .

"Cease fire," Paul said. He was aware only of the fact that he felt absolutely nothing. Not the exaltation of victory, not pity, not horror. Nathan was studying the bow of the hunter-killer, which was sending up a tower of flame.

"Burn, damn you," he said softly.

An explosion that made all the others seeem like nothing suddenly made the men on the *Arluk* look toward Supportup Fjord. The bombers had turned the middle of the rock canyon into an inferno. Great oily funnels of smoke full of angry red flames were boiling from it.

"God, I can't see how any of them could live through that," Nathan said.

"Well, we'll soon see," Paul said. "Our real job is just beginning. I bet that plenty of them will still be waiting for us in there."

While Paul conned the ship toward the entrance of the fjord, which was now almost hidden by smoke, Nathan went below to see if he could help Cookie. He found the chef screaming in his bunk while Seth Farmer, who seemed more shaken than he was, kept offering him a glass of apricot brandy.

"I don't know how bad he's hurt," Seth said.

Cookie lay with his knees doubled up and kept alternating shrill screams with fierce curses. Nathan got morphine from the medicine chest and gave him an injection. When his moans became drowsy, he knelt by his bunk and opened his clothes. Cookie had not been hit directly by a bullet. One had hit the oak cap rail of the trawler about six inches from him and had sprayed the whole front of his body with oak splinters, some of them six inches long. As far as Nathan could see, no one of the wounds was necessarily fatal, but there were perhaps a hundred of them. Nathan ran to the bridge.

"Captain, I got to work on Cookie," he said. "Can you get along without me for an hour?"

"I got to wait for some of that smoke to clear before we go into the fjord anyway. Where did Cookie get it?"

"Wood splinters, all over."

As Nathan ran back to the forecastle Paul climbed to the flying bridge and studied the burning fjord through his binoculars. The bombers had disappeared but roiling black smoke full of red flames was still climbing from the center of the fjord. They must have dropped incendiaries, Paul thought, but what did they hit to keep such an enormous blaze growing? Diesel oil—only that could make such dirty smoke, and the smell of it filled the air. But why so much of it? Perhaps the Germans had been prepared to supply their submarines as well as a string of weather stations. Were they trying to fight the fire now or were they digging in for a last-ditch stand when a ship or ground troops appeared? It was hard to imagine how anyone could have survived such a conflagration but he was sure some had, and even a half dozen men with machine guns could take a helluva toll. Well, I can call in more planes or go back and bring in some armed Eskies, Paul thought—I'm not going to let them hit any more of us. But first he would have to investigate the place. There wasn't any way around that, and he found he was looking forward to the job . . .

When the *Arluk* neared the mouth of the fjord Paul could hear the sucking of the flames. Smoke enveloped the places where he had reported field guns. The wind veered a lot, making the tallest column of smoke twist like a snake trying to strike first in one direction, then another. It looked as though it could burn for days, and Paul was surprised when it began to die almost as rapidly as it had bloomed. In that blaze and the winds it created in the deep, narrow fjord, even thousands of barrels of oil couldn't last long.

Now we ought to move in, before they have a chance to get over the shock, Paul thought, and rang up general quarters. The men, many of whom had been standing on the forecastle head and the flying bridge, moved toward their guns with curious nonchalance.

"We're going in there," Paul said. "Keep an eye on both banks of the fjord. Shoot anything that moves if it doesn't have its hands up."

Hurrying down the ladder from the flying bridge, Paul entered the pilothouse just as Nathan came from the forecastle.

"You can stay with Cookie for a few more minutes if you want," Paul said.

"I've done about all I can for now." Nathan looked shaken and his hands trembled slightly as he adjusted his binoculars and looked at the mouth of the fjord.

"How is he?" Paul asked.

"Bad. Thank God for morphine."

Paul ordered full speed ahead.

As they neared the mouth of the fjord Paul kept expecting a German field gun which had survived the planes to open fire, but no sound broke the Arctic silence. Scared away by the noise and smoke, even the gulls gave no hint of motion or life to the white mountains and the long, black smoldering scar on the snowy banks of the fjord which they saw after passing the first headland. The continuing silence seemed eerie, unnatural and dangerous. Paul had a vision of men waiting in an underground bunker, sighting their guns on his ship. The snowy banks of the fjord looked completely untouched right up to the beginning of the burned area. Melted snow made the black ashes glisten in the last red rays of the setting sun. Soon it will be darker in here than the bottom of hell, Paul thought, and told Guns to keep some star shells ready. Some twisted metal girders lay in the center of the strip of ashes, but that was the only sign that men had ever been there. Suddenly the starboard 20-millimeter gun opened fire, its rapid reports echoed and magnified by the steep icy sides of the fjord. After only a few seconds it stopped.

"I thought we saw something move in there," Guns said.

Paul studied the spot at the edge of the charred wreckage the tracers had been arching toward. A sled dog bounded from a crevice and dashed toward the bank of the fjord, barking at the ship.

Suddenly a signal light blinked from a bank of snow at the edge of the wreckage.

"Hold your fire," Paul called as the *Arluk*'s guns swung toward it.

Nathan studied the light through his binoculars. "He's blinking S.O.S.," he said.

"They could just be trying to suck us in here," Paul said. "Tell him—"

His words froze in his mouth as figures suddenly appeared around the edges of the ashes. It was not necessary to use the binoculars to see that they were wounded men, their faces and clothes blackened, their clothes hanging in shreds. Some held up their hands as they approached the edge of the fjord, some were too weak to do that and hobbled along, leaning on other apparitions. One tall man carried a torn white shirt on the end of a stick. He cupped his hands as he shouted in English with a strong Scandinavian accent, "Everyone here surrenders. I am Danish. Can I come aboard to talk?"

Paul stopped his ship in the middle of the fjord and kept all his men at the guns while he sent the whaleboat in with four armed men to get the Dane. When the boat landed at the jagged edge of a concrete wharf that had been built in irregular curves as part of the camouflage, a horde of ragged men pushed toward it and tried to get aboard. Of course the survivors were dying of exposure, Paul realized —the temperature was 40 degrees below zero and there was a sharp wind in the fjord that kept swirling the last of the smoke from the embers of the wreckage. Across the still black water he could hear the sound of coughing. The boat had orders to bring back only the Dane and its crew pushed the ragged men away. They limped back to their holes in the ground as the boat returned to the ship with the tall Dane standing in the stern.

"My name is Carl Peterson," the Dane said as he stepped to the well deck. Although his parka and face had been blackened by oily smoke, he was clearly a handsome man, and he stood very straight, trying to achieve dignity but looking more like an actor struggling with a very bad part. "I am a Dane brought here by the Germans very much against my will."

"We'll get to that later," Paul said. "Is anybody in there going to fight?"

"No. May we get out of the cold to talk?"

The man was shivering. His parka was sheathed with ice. Paul led the way to his cabin. He was about to tell the quartermaster to ask Cookie to bring up some coffee when he remembered that Cookie had been hit. Peterson slumped wearily on the stool by the chart table.

"How many men are in there?" Paul asked.

"About fifty. Most of the officers left on the ship."

"How many are wounded?"

"Almost all. They tried to fight the fire. The wind changed suddenly. Many are burned."

"You're sure that none are still underground?"

"They all came out to fight the fire. Thank God you got here, captain. A lot of them got wet, they're freezing to death."

"I'll go alongside the wharf. I want you to make an announcement. Tell them that if one shot is fired at my men we'll machine-gun everyone here before moving out."

Peterson was so weak that he needed help as he climbed to the flying bridge. After bringing the ship close to the wharf Paul gave him a megaphone and he made his announcement in German which was even more accented than his English. The ragged men who were waiting at the edge of the wharf stared dumbly. When Paul ordered them in German to hold their hands over their heads as the ship came alongside, only a few had the strength to comply.

As soon as the ship touched the wharf, the freezing Germans hurried to climb aboard.

"Guns, keep order down there," Paul said. "Line those men up and search them for arms before you let them aboard. I don't give a damn if they're dying—no one gets aboard here without being searched."

Guns and Boats pushed the prisoners into a line.

"God, they really are dying," Nathan said. "What the hell are we going to do with them all?"

"Put the worst ones in the forecastle and the rest in the hold. We'll take them into Angmagssalik."

Most of the *Arluk*'s crew changed quickly from fighting men to rescuers, and without any sense of irony—they were too exhausted and shocked by the sight of so many Germans dying from burns and exposure to be conscious of their own emotions. It was impossible to keep order as prisoners collapsed on the well deck and were carried to all available berths. Boats spread tarpaulins in the hold for the overflow. In the midst of this great groaning, cursing confusion, only Guns remained military. After organizing five seamen to search all the prisoners, he came to the bridge.

"Skipper, I think I ought to take some armed men ashore and make sure that no more of them are hiding out there."

"Take six and make it fast."

Moments later Guns led six seamen ashore. They were carrying automatic rifles, hand grenades and knives as they began to circle the charred wreckage of the base. Paul stood on the wing of the bridge watching them. He was conscious mostly of the fact that his feet were very cold, and he stamped them. The well deck was still swarming with the prisoners and the men trying to help them. There was so much confusion that Paul kept trying to insulate himself from it by concentrating on immediate plans . . . I've got to get them to Angmagssalik, he kept repeating to himself. What then? How could so many wounded men be treated there? This was a question without an answer, and Paul just stood watching Guns and his men prowl through the smoking ruins. They were, he saw with astonishment, collecting souvenirs, filling a seabag with German pistols, helmets and caps.

"Captain, we got to do something," a bewildered voice said.

Paul turned and saw that Seth Farmer had come up behind him. The old fisherman appeared to be in almost as much shock as the prisoners. His face was white and slack. "They're all dying," he said. "The whole ship is full of dying men."

"We're doing everything we can," he said. "You better go down and get some rest yourself."

"But they're all burned, so terrible burned," Seth said. "Can't you help?"

"Jesus, what the hell do you want me to do? Go and lie down before you pass out."

Seth wandered dazedly toward the well deck. A moment later Paul saw him helping Flags carry an inert body to the forecastle.

Paul went to the bridge to warm up and stood at a port where he could watch Guns and his men circle the wreckage, pausing at every hole. Then he went to his chart and methodically charted a course to Angmagssalik. He felt dizzy and was confused by the fact that he really felt no emotions at a time when everyone else seemed so excited. He just felt half-dead. His hands were so heavy he could barely handle the parallel rules. I'm in shock too, he thought dully. I have to compensate for that. I'm one person who can't crap out now. Suddenly he felt a surge of irrational anger at the Germans. What right did they have to swarm aboard his ship begging mercy and turning it into chaos? It would not really be difficult for him to order them all thrown ashore or even overboard, to rid the vessel of them, cleanse the ship and release his crew from this awful mess. He knew he should feel guilty for even thinking of this, but he was too tired.

Suddenly he felt sick and went to the head to vomit. After that, still feeling nauseated and weak, he went to the wardroom, where he found Nathan surrounded by more wounded men who sat huddled with blankets over their shoulders. The bunks were full of motionless bodies. Nathan was applying a tourniquet to a man on the table whose thigh was gushing blood.

"Seth just died," he said.

*"What?"*

"Heart. Nothing can be done. We got to get these men ashore as soon as we can. You better get everyone aboard and get under way."

Paul went back to the bridge. Guns and his men were still prowling through the ruins ashore. They were digging at the foot of a charred mound. When Paul gave five short blasts of the *Arluk*'s whistle and motioned to them from the wing of the bridge they came trotting back toward the ship. Guns carried a bulging seabag on his shoulder, and their bodies were hung with German rifles.

Paul watched them dully as they jumped aboard the ship. Guns went to the galley and a few minutes went by before he came to the bridge. "No one alive is left in there that we can see," he said. "Plenty of bodies—the bastards didn't all get away."

"Good," Paul said dully.

"Look what I got," Guns said, and from his pocket took his olive bottle, which he had filled. When he held it out, Paul at first did not notice its contents. Then he took his pistol from his holster and brought the barrel of it down on the big man's wrist so hard that Guns screamed. The olive bottle dropped to the deck, but did not break. It rolled into a scupper. Squinting his eyes to avoid looking at its grisly contents, Paul picked it up and threw it overboard.

"You can't do that," Guns said, holding his wrist against his stomach. "It's mine—"

"Get below," Paul said.

"You're not going to take my head," Guns said. "Nobody's going to . . ."

He ran toward the forecastle. For a moment Paul was too bewildered to understand what was happening. Then he followed him, too tired and disgusted to hurry. When he got to the galley he found Guns standing with three other men staring into a huge pot that was already steaming on the stove.

"Throw that thing overboard," Paul said.

Instead Guns grabbed the pot and ran toward the door, except it was so hot that he dropped it in the forecastle.

Gray water and a cloud of steam spilled out, together with a head, which lay on its right ear. The open eyes, the gaping mouth and the stump of the neck had already been boiled colorless. Guns scooped it up, and holding it under his right arm like a football broke through the encircling men and dashed to the deck. Paul followed in time to see him jump ashore.

"*Boats*," Paul called. "Take some men and bring him back."

Boats, followed by a half dozen seamen, went in hot pursuit. Paul went to the wing of the bridge and stood watching them zig-zag through the charred ruins, like men playing football. His sensibilities were still too dulled for him to feel much. The fact that Guns was running with a head under his arm did not seem a great deal more surprising than any other part of what had overwhelmed him here . . .

Finally Boats tackled Guns and the other men piled on top of them. Slowly they stood up, leaving the head on the ground. Two men were holding Guns's arms, and he was shouting, "Goddamn it, let me go, what's the matter with you bastards—?"

"What do you want us to do with . . . this?" Boats called to Paul.

For a moment Paul wondered whether he should hold a funeral service for the head. Should he bury it at sea, rolling it off a plank? And how about the rest of the body and all the other corpses in those black ruins? Clouds of scavenger seagulls were already circling around, waiting for the smoke to clear. No doubt he should bury the bodies and read some words from the Bible, but it was more important to care for the wounded and to guard the prisoners. All his men were so exhausted that they hardly had strength even for that. "Leave it there," Paul said. "Bring Guns back aboard."

Guns appeared perfectly normal by the time the men let go of his arms. They walked aboard like a group of old friends. Guns came to the bridge.

"You don't understand, skipper," he said. "I promised Blake's mother. I promised I'd make her a lamp."

"You wrote her a letter?"

"Oh, I knew you'd censor that. But I promised her in my heart. I was going to take it home to her myself."

499

Paul sighed. "I'm sorry, but mutilating corpses is . . . well, it's against regulations. Lay below. Boats, pipe mooring stations. We're going to get out of here."

"Can't I handle the bowline like always?" Guns asked.

"Yeah, okay, go to your mooring station. Let's *go*."

While Paul was automatically giving orders to get the ship under way he wondered what he should do about Guns. If he logged the incident with the olive bottle and the head and brought charges he'd have to keep Guns a prisoner and eventually the man would be sent to a mental hospital in the States, maybe for a very long time. Everyone would be horrified by him, all the more so, perhaps, because he stood for a kind of ferocity that the war made many people feel but damn few wanted to admit. Somewhere Paul had read that soccer was an ancient game that had started when warriors celebrated a victory by kicking around the head of an enemy chief, and that football was a derivative of that. War had not really changed much—except now it involved so many people that it had to be prettied up. Paul wondered whether Guns really was crazy, so crazy that he shouldn't be turned loose except in battle. He'd have to watch him, he decided wearily, he'd just have to watch him. He didn't want to see the poor bastard get locked up in a place that was bound to make him crazier than he already was. . . .

When they worked their way into clear water Paul set a course for Angmagssalik. It was beginning to snow and he could see almost nothing. Only the dimly lit compass card and the glowing green eye of the radar screen made any sense.

To Paul and everyone else aboard the ship that three-and-a-half hour voyage seemed endless. Shock had the good effect of reducing emotion, but it also had the effect of making time appear to stand still. Paul stood on the bridge, concentrating on the simple task of conning the *Arluk* through widely scattered bergs as she churned north between the mountains and the ice floe. Before the moon came up there were only scattered stars to prick the darkness and he steered mostly by radar. On the well deck he could see dim shapes moving and realized that Boats was piling bodies under a tarpaulin there to make room in the bunks. When the moon climbed above the icy eastern horizon, he could see gulls wheeling all around the ship and wondered whether "those damned flying cats" could smell blood.

Paul's eyes felt heavy, and he concentrated mostly on staying awake. He asked for coffee and once more had to remind himself that Cookie could no longer bring it. Why did the thought of Cookie riddled with oak splinters bother him more than the groans of so many dying men?

As Paul changed course to enter Angmagssalik Fjord he tried to concentrate on the details of moving the wounded up to the Danish houses. If he radioed for a doctor could a PBY bring one in? Probably there was too much small ice in the fjord for a seaplane, but couldn't they parachute someone in? Except why should a doctor risk his life for the Germans? Paul had no answer for that, but God knew they needed a doctor, if only for Cookie. Nathan should get on the radio.

"Captain," the quartermaster said, "is anyone getting the names of all the prisoners for the log?"

"Forget it."

"We're supposed to log everyone who comes aboard."

"Forget it, I said. We'll get the names later. Tell Boats to make some kind of stretchers for carrying the men ashore."

Paul felt a sense of urgency as he approached the wharf at Angmagssalik. He wanted to moor and get the wounded ashore as fast as possible, but his mind wasn't working right, and he got the ship broadside to the current, backing off just in time to avoid slamming into the wharf. Slowly he circled and came alongside properly. As soon as the ship touched the wharf, a small fur-clad figure jumped aboard and ran to the bridge. It was Brit.

Somehow Paul was very surprised to see her.

"What happened?" she said, out of breath. "I saw the smoke."

"We wiped out the base," he said wearily.

"Did you get the ship?"

"Yes."

She hugged him. "I knew you would."

He could think of nothing to say.

"Are any of your men hurt? Is Nathan all right?"

"He's all right. Look, I got about fifty wounded prisoners. Burns and exposure. We got to get them up to the houses. Cookie's hurt bad."

Already wounded men wrapped in blankets were gathering on the well deck. Brit stared at them and suddenly the look of pleasure on her face died. "Fifty!" she said. "Good God. I'll get the Eskimos down here with sleds and try to get ready for them."

She ran up toward the settlement. Paul went to the wardroom to look for Nathan. He found him helping a boy about eighteen years old to get his burned hands into the sleeves of a dry parka.

"You got to get on the radio," Paul said. "Have we told anything to GreenPat yet?"

"I haven't had time."

"He must be going crazy. Tell him what happened. Maybe he can parachute a doctor and medical supplies in here."

"All right," Nathan said, and staggered up the companionway. Soot from the burned clothes he had been handling had streaked his gaunt face so that he looked like a walking corpse himself.

Paul went to the pilothouse. He watched Boats and four seamen make stretchers out of strips of tarpaulin and rifles lashed muzzle to muzzle. "Boats, come up here . . ."

Boats walked quickly to the bridge. Still alert and brisk, he seemed curiously untouched by the confusion around him. "What can I do for you, sir?"

"How many of the prisoners are well enough to make trouble when they get a little rest?"

"I haven't checked them all, sir. They all look pretty beat, those I've seen."

"There must be some who aren't wounded at all. Find out how many. I want them put out on the island with the other prisoners."

"It's already pretty crowded out there, sir."

"There are more prisoners here than there are of us. I don't want them even to think about taking over."

"I'll see to it, sir."

"Can I talk to you, captain?" Carl Peterson asked. He was standing on the well deck, wrapped in a blanket.

"All right. Come up here."

Hoisting his blanket above his knees to avoid tripping, Peterson hurried to the bridge. Apparently he had already recovered from much of his shock.

"Captain, can I go ashore?" he asked. "I know some of the people here. I can help."

"You're a prisoner. You were working with the Germans."

"Captain, I had no choice. They just grabbed me in Copenhagen because I'm an ice pilot and marched me aboard their ship."

"I suppose there will be hearings of some sort to figure all that out. Until then, you're a prisoner."

"But meanwhile, can't I help? We've got to find a way to feed all these people in there. I at least can set up a field kitchen."

There was a pause. "All right, go and help," Paul said wearily.

Peterson jumped ashore, his blanket fluttering, and hurried into the darkness toward the houses. Paul heard the sound of dogs, and a team with a sled surrounded by a crowd of Eskimos arrived on the end of the wharf. Brit was shouting orders at them. The Eskimos began to help the *Arluk* crew put the wounded on stretchers and carry them ashore. Paul saw her pause over one German who was moaning and tuck his blanket around him more tightly. She too had changed instantaneously from victor to rescuer, also probably without being aware of it.

Damn it, they ought to get Cookie ashore first, Paul thought, and hurried to the forecastle. Cookie was lying in his bunk, his eyes open but so opaque that Paul thought he was dead. Still drowsy with morphine, Cookie managed a weak smile.

"We're going to get you ashore," Paul said.

"No!" Cookie sounded terrified.

"You'll be more comfortable up there."

"Let me stay here. Mr. Green will take care of me."

"I'll let him make the decision," Paul said. "Is there anything I can do for you?"

"Who's going to cook?"

"We'll find someone."

"The men have to eat . . ."

"We can live on K-rations. You go to sleep."

Nathan was busy in the radio shack. Paul returned to the bridge and sat watching while the crew and the Eskimos moved the wounded ashore. Boats lowered the whaleboat and set off for the island with eight unwounded prisoners.

Nathan suddenly appeared on the bridge. "I got Green-

Pat," he said. "The bastard wanted to know every last detail. He finally said he'd try to parachute in a medic and some supplies."

"Good."

"He wants us to stand by until things are under control and then take all the wounded who can make it back to Narsarssuak."

That was too much for Paul to think about at the moment. "Cookie doesn't want to be taken ashore," he said.

"I can take care of him here. I'm saving the last of the morphine for him. He needs a doctor quick."

"We got to figure out a place for them to parachute a man in and have Eskimos there to get him. Where's the best flat land?"

"Brit will know. I better get her to arrange it and tell GreenPat."

"Jesus, you must be dead on your feet."

Nathan wearily shrugged. "I don't know, skipper. If winning is like this . . ."

"I guess it's better than getting beat."

Nathan went ashore. When the last of the prisoners had been carried to the houses the *Arluk* crew returned to the forecastle and sprawled in their bunks. Krater lit off the galley range and began emptying cans of soup into a large pot. Paul came and sat at the big V-shaped table with the others while it warmed. Stevens was gathering up soiled blankets and throwing them in a pile on the well deck. The whole forecastle still smelled of sickness, wounds and scorched flesh. Everyone was too tired to talk as Krater handed out coffee mugs full of lumpy tomato soup and the last of the fresh bread that Cookie had made.

"Cookie, you better get well damn soon," the quartermaster said, but the old chef did not answer. With a surprisingly delicate, long-fingered hand covering his eyes, he slept in his bunk.

The soup revived Paul a little. He had a compulsion to inspect the ship, to see what damage had been done by the gunfire they had taken, and perhaps to seek reassurance from his men as much as trying to give it. As his mind reached back, trying to reconstruct the events of the past day, he began to realize that the ship would not have been hit at all and Cookie would not have been wounded if he'd had enough sense to keep out of range of the enemy's machine guns. Any sense of victory remaining to him was now wiped out by guilt. He was surprised and grateful when Flags, who had the watch on the bridge, smiled at him and said, "Well, skipper, you must be feeling pretty good."

"Better than the Krauts do, I guess."

Better than Fatso did when he died, he thought, and wondered what kind of man the captain of the hunter-killer had been. Had he been killed aboard, or had he been in one of those rubber boats? The image of the men trying to stand as those rubber boats disintegrated under the 20-millimeter gunfire was still sharp in Paul's mind. About that, at least, he felt no guilt at all.

The wardroom was the last compartment Paul inspected. The table there was covered by a tangle of soiled blankets. In a starboard bunk a body lay completely covered by a rumpled sheet. That must be Seth, Paul thought, but had no inclination to make sure. Jesus, he was a good man—old enough to be the father of all of us, and never a word of complaint. I guess I should write to his wife . . .

And Sparks's wife, and Blake's mother—I should write them all, he thought. All the women should get letters telling them how brave their brave men were . . .

Paul put his hand on the wardroom table to steady himself. The tangle of blankets there stank. They should be thrown overboard, but then there would be no blankets. They should be washed and dried in the engineroom. First thing in the morning, as soon as the men got some rest . .

Without thinking Paul began to pick up the blankets and fold them neatly, then carried them to the well deck and shoved them under a tarpaulin. Staggering a little, he went to the bridge and tapped the barometer. It was still falling. Soon it would snow and blow like hell. Stepping to the wing of the bridge, he looked at the sky. Clouds had already obscured the moon. They better hurry with their medic, he thought. I ought to tell them, but hell, they have more weather reports than I do.

The thought of a big blow coming made him get a flashlight and check the ship's mooring lines. They should be doubled up, but everyone was too tired. The manila was still fairly new and should hold.

He walked slowly back to the bridge. Guns, his wrist wrapped in a bandage, was talking to Flags about the girls in New Orleans.

"Skipper, we're just about out of ammo for the three-incher," he said, perhaps to find out if he had been forgiven, or to prove that he was ready to forgive.

"I'll get some as soon as I can," Paul said. "You did some good shooting, Guns."

"I shouldn't have taken so long to get on target, but with a short-barreled gun like that—well, hell, we won. That's the important thing, isn't it?"

Paul went into his cabin and shut the door. Suddenly he wanted a drink and wished he hadn't thrown out all the booze he had found in the drawer under the bunk. There were a few bottles of sweet liqueurs still locked in the lazaret, where they were being kept for a beerbust ashore. Now on this night of victory he should get them out and share them with the crew. The trouble was he was too tired to get out of his bunk and all but the two men on watch were asleep anyway. Victory made a man very tired.

Paul slept for more than ten hours. He was awakened by Nathan.

"I'm sorry to bother you," Nathan said, "but a hell of a lot has been happening."

"What?"

"They got a medic in."

"Has he looked at Cookie?"

"I made sure that Cookie came first. He's a living pin cushion, but it looks like he'll make it."

"Did you get any sleep?"

"A little. Look, we've got orders."

"What the hell are we supposed to do now?"

"We're to take aboard all the worst wounded who can make it and bring them to Narsarssuak. Also, all the most able-bodied prisoners who might make trouble here."

"We'll be loaded like a slave ship."

"GreenPat knows we can't take everyone. The number is up to you. He'll send another ship to get the rest as soon as he can."

"He'll probably have us going back and forth all winter. How the hell are we going to handle able-bodied prisoners?"

"Boats is making the hold into a brig. He'll be done in a few hours."

"I'll sail as soon as you're ready. How are we going to guard prisoners in the hold?"

"I've made up some stuff that will act as tear gas. If they act up, we can drop some in."

"Keep their hands tied anyway. I don't want to take a cruise to Germany. And don't take too many. Leave enough men to guard the rest on the island."

"Boats will take care of that . . . Brit wants to see you—"

"Why? You're taking care of her, aren't you?" He couldn't keep an edge from his voice.

"I'll pretend you didn't say that."

"You're trying to get her out of here. Well, don't ask me to take her without authorization—"

"She's changed her mind about that. I better let her talk to you. She's in the forecastle now."

"Send her up."

"Paul, I don't know how things are between you and Brit, but she's been a hell of a big help. She's been running everything ashore. Without her—"

"I know, you don't have to tell me about her. Just send her up."

When Nathan left, Paul went to the head and washed his face in cold water. He did not have time to shave but combed his hair and put on a less rumpled blue coat. Soon he heard a light knock on his cabin door.

"Come in."

She was wearing her green skirt and the reindeer sweater. She had recently brushed her short hair but her face looked exhausted, her eyes dark and enormous. She shut the door behind her and kissed him lightly on the cheek.

"I won't pretend," she said. "I've come to ask a favor, a big one."

"Nathan says you've changed your mind about wanting to get out of here."

"There's too much for me to do here now. With Swan gone . . ."

"What do you want?"

"What are you going to do with Carl Peterson?"

"He's a prisoner. He can stay with the others."

"He's a Dane!"

"He was working with the Germans and still would be if we hadn't captured him."

"He had no choice. He has a family in Denmark. Do you know what the Germans would have done if he hadn't worked with them?"

Paul sighed. "That's not my business. Somebody else will have to figure that out. To me, he's got to be just a prisoner."

"We need him here. Why can't you just leave him with us?"

"How would I ever explain that?"

"Who would ever ask for an explanation?"

"I should report that I captured him—"

"Why? They could keep him locked up for years until they figure out what I know now. If I thought he was a traitor do you think I'd beg for him?"

"Have you known him before now?"

"Yes. He taught courses about Greenland at the university. He's a fine man who got dragged into this war like everybody else. Can't you just forget you ever saw him?"

There was a pause before Paul said, "All right, Brit. Carl Peterson will be my sort of a going-away present to you . . ."

"Don't say it like that."

"I feel it like that!"

"Will you always be bitter about me, your whole life?"

"No. Hell, I don't like to lose you. I can't share you. Can't you understand that?

"We don't have any choices. Can't *you* understand that?"

"I guess . . . Brit, am I any different to you, or are we all just men who happen to need you?"

"You are the only man I ever knew who I think will somehow always win . . ."

"Win *what?*"

"Anything. And winning is important, believe me . . . you have to lose to learn that."

"I understand . . . Jesus, Brit—"

"I'll remember this cabin," she said, "and laughing together, so silently, under that sword."

"I'd give it to you as a souvenir, but I'm afraid it would make all your other friends jealous." He didn't smile.

"Jealous men I don't want. I'd like to have your sword. I'd hang it on the wall to remind me that it's not always necessary to lose."

He took the sword in its leather case from its brackets and handed it to her.

"Does this mean that you surrender to me?"

"I did that a long time ago, and you know it."

"I have something to give you in return. I'll send Peo

508

down to the ship with it before you sail, but I'll tell you about it now."

"I'd like a picture of you."

"I'll send that too, but my real gift is a narwhale tusk, the biggest I've ever seen. Do you know about narwhale tusks?"

"Not much."

"The Greenlanders for centuries have sent them to Europe and Asia, where they think they come from a unicorn. Old men grind them and drink the powder as a love medicine."

"You think I need that?"

She touched his face. "Not for sex, Paul, but maybe for love."

"I guess you're right."

"No, I don't mean that . . . Just take the narwhale tusk and hang it over your bed and if anyone asks, say it comes from a unicorn. And if anyone says that's a mythical beast, just say, 'How could it be? Here's its horn.'"

He laughed, and kissed her, and then Guns was knocking loudly at his door and saying, "They're bringing the wounded aboard, sir, and Mr. Green is going to have funeral services for Mr. Farmer up in the chapel."

Brit went with Paul to the funeral services. No clergyman was present, but almost all the members of the *Arluk*'s crew were there and many Eskimos. The old woman played the organ while they sang "Abide With Me." Mr. Williams read a service from his Bible that Paul somehow did not want to hear, and then Nathan said, "I think the men would like to hear a few words from you, Paul."

He felt curiously weak as he made his way to the lectern. He looked at Brit's tired face, at Nathan's haggard one and at the exhausted faces of the *Arluk*'s crew and suddenly he was terrified he'd break out into tears and not be able to say anything.

"I don't know what to say," he began. "Seth Farmer died while he was helping to carry a wounded German below. He had a bad heart, and a great one. Most of you knew him as well as I did. He never complained . . ." For about five minutes he praised the old fisherman, but his words didn't seem to make much sense to his own ears, though they were all true enough. The church was much too hot . . . "What I guess I'm trying to say is that Seth was part of the *Arluk* and part of us, whatever we are. I think

509

we're important, but I don't know how. We've been through a lot together, and now we're burying one of our own. May God have mercy on his soul and on all of ours."

He paused and was grateful when the organ began to play "Rock of Ages." He returned to his pew and stood beside Brit while everyone mumbled the hymn. Afterward he followed her out of the church.

"I suppose Greenland will preserve Seth forever, with all the rest of her dead," he said of her.

"Nothing really dies here," she said. "Nothing changes. I told you that."

"After the war is over, will you stay here?"

"I don't know. I don't think ahead. Paul?"

"What?"

"I have to go now. I mean really go. And so do you."

He nodded.

"It isn't only bodies that Greenland preserves. Memories too. Nobody ever forgets anything that happens to him here."

"I believe that."

She brushed his cheek quickly with her lips before turning and running toward her small ketch. . . .

When he got back aboard his ship Paul found that Peomeenie had delivered a magnificent narwhale tusk in a sealskin case. Over six feet long, it had been polished to the consistency of a candle, and the intricate spiral weave of the ivory was just as ancient writers had described the unicorn's horn. It exactly fitted the brackets which had been built for Paul's sword above his bunk.

The *Arluk* did not get stuck in the ice on the way back to the west coast, but an almost continuous gale and blizzard slowed her, and the voyage took two weeks. Because Nathan was occupied with the wounded and the other prisoners, Paul stood watch most of the time himself, snatching only brief naps while Flags and Boats took over the watch on the bridge. His exhaustion protected him from feeling too much as the ship crammed full of dazed sick and wounded men rolled and pitched in the endless darkness. Most of the time he had to navigate without a sun, without a horizon and without stars. But he still had radar, and with that he paralleled the coast, keeping a good thirty miles out, located the mouth of the passage which led across the tip of Cape Farewell and headed up the west coast. When he finally gained the shelter of Narsarssuak Fjord, the rolling and pitching of the ship mercifully stopped, but the quiet waters of the inner fjord had frozen into smooth ice unlike the Arctic, more like a pond at home. It made a sound like continuously breaking glass as the *Arluk* ploughed through it and slowed her to a bare four knots. It was snowing, it was always snowing, and the steep white sides of the fjord were invisible. Flags gave Paul almost continuous radar readings, his voice so hoarse that he whispered.

"Get Nathan up here," Paul said to the quartermaster.

Nathan arrived, so exhausted that he stood supporting himself on the engineroom telegraph. "When are we going to get in?"

"About four hours. Give GreenPat an ETA of six o'clock. Have ambulances meet us and trucks with guards for the prisoners." There was a pause before Paul added, "I have an idea that old Mowrey will be waiting for us, all ready to take his ship back."

Nathan smiled. "That's a private nightmare of yours, skipper. The old man was done when he left here."

"Maybe," Paul said, "and maybe I'd half like to see him come back. When the old bastard was sober he at least knew what he was doing."

"You haven't done so bad," Nathan said. "All you need is some rest—about thirty days leave. You'll be raring to go again."

As soon as the ship was moored alongside a wharf at the base in Narsarssuak, Paul toppled into his bunk and slept for twelve hours. He might have slept much longer, but he was awakened by Nathan.

"Skipper, Commander GreenPat wants to see us."

"Have the prisoners all been taken ashore?"

"Yes . . . the commander is here. He came aboard to see us. I think that's supposed to be some kind of an honor."

"Where is he?"

"Up in the forecastle drinking coffee."

Paul struggled to a sitting position in his bunk. Nathan had shaved and either because he had no clean clothes left or because of pride had put on his Eskimo outfit.

"You go talk to him," Paul said. "Talk Eskimo to him. Tell him you forgot all your English."

"He wants to talk to you. He's been waiting about a half hour."

"He probably wants to send us right back to Angmagssalik. Tell him we need availability for engine repairs. Banes will think of something."

"He's sent a brand new icebreaker up there. She's already left."

Paul climbed from his bunk. "I wish to hell I had an Eskie outfit. This uniform looks like I slept in it for about six months."

"Keep your parka on," Nathan said. "Come on, I think the commander might have orders for us. Maybe he'll send us home."

Commander Sanders, the curiously scholarly personification of GreenPat, was drinking coffee and talking to Boats when Paul entered the forecastle. He stood up and held out his hand.

"Good to see you, captain," he said with his Maine twang. "You must have had quite a time of it. Well done."

"I think the Germans still established weather stations all up and down the coast."

"A few maybe, but without their base, their ship and their planes, they won't be able to supply them. They won't last too long."

Paul's body felt stiff and he was terrifyingly weak. He sat down and Krater brought him a mug of hot coffee.

"Thanks," he said. "Commander, did you ever hear what happened to Captain Mowrey?"

"They sent him back to the States and retired him. Apparently there was a lot of trouble before he left the hospital here. Somehow he got hold of some booze, and I understand that he decked the nurse who tried to take it away from him."

Krater, who was pouring more coffee, laughed, but Paul said, "I'm sorry," and meant it.

"The veterans' hospitals will take care of him . . . Now let's talk about you two and this ship. How long before you'll be able to sail?"

"Where to?" Paul said, his voice dull.

"Back to Boston for a refit. You better get her in shape because that can be a rough voyage this time of the year. To be frank we just lost a trawler in Davis Strait. We think she just iced up and rolled over. We're going to send you on a more southerly route, away from the Labrador coast. You should give the crew a rest, but the weather's going to get worse, not better. Do you think you could sail in about a week?"

"If we're going to Boston, the men will take her out tomorrow," Paul said.

"Make it a week. In Boston they'll need about a month for the refit, and then they'll be wanting to send her back here. We're still mighty short of ships that can work in the ice."

"Yes," Paul said, his mind too tired to think that far ahead.

The commander looked around. Krater had withdrawn to the galley and they were alone in the forecastle.

"Captain, you'll probably be getting orders," the commander said to Paul. "I'd like to make you permanent skipper of the *Arluk*, but as soon as a man turns out to be a good skipper of a trawler they move him up to a bigger ship."

"Right now, all I can think about is getting home," Paul said. "Will we get leave?"

"Thirty days. I'll make sure of that."

"Who'll take over the *Arluk* if I leave?"

"Do you have any recommendations?"

"Do you want her, Nathan?" Paul asked.

"Do you think I can handle it?"

"What do you think?"

"If I'm lucky . . ."

"He can handle it," Paul said to the commander.

"I'll recommend him. I don't make the final decisions, but I raise such hell when they send incompetent skippers up here that they don't entirely ignore me."

The commander stood up and shook hands with the two officers. "You both deserve medals of some kind, but I can't even make Headquarters understand we're fighting a war in Greenland," he said.

"Just make sure we get leave," Paul said. "And if I get orders, how about giving me a ship in the South Pacific? I'm damned tired of ice."

As the commander was going, Chief Banes came in. "A whole truckload of mail just arrived," he said. "The men are crazy to have it sorted."

"I'll take care of it," Nathan said.

Paul went to his cabin. He felt nervous, and almost

513

didn't want more letters from his brother and Sylvia. Sylvia's letters were always hell on his fantasies of her. He was still exhausted and lay down in his bunk but couldn't sleep. For a long time he had tried not to worry about Sylvia, just to remember his best times with her. Probably he would now get only some cheerful letters about her beloved house ... he should understand her need for a home of her own. It was absurd of him to worry about that business of serving as a hostess at the U.S.O. A lot of very respectable women did it, didn't they? Brit and the Eskimos were right —jealousy was a crazy disease. ...

A half hour later he heard a knock at his door and Nathan's deep voice saying, "Letters for you, Paul."

This time there were only three letters from Sylvia and one from his brother. He opened the letter from his brother first because he knew that if there was bad news, Bill would give it to him straight.

Dear Paul:

There's no way around it—I can't make this nice. They say we shouldn't send bad news to you guys overseas, but this is a situation that you have to do something about.

The simple fact is that Sylvia ran your car into the back of a truck around three o'clock in the morning on Commonwealth Avenue in Boston on New Year's Eve. She was going fast. She was hurt but not killed— she's in the hospital with broken legs and maybe her back is hurt but the doctor says she'll eventually get well. Now brace yourself because that's not the worst. A guy was with her, an air force captain, and he was hurt worse, although they say he'll get better too. I'm afraid that lawsuits may come from this. Sylvia was driving and the cops say she was drunk. The truck driver was pretty badly shook up, although he's out of the hospital. Some shyster lawyer got hold of him and the air force guy, and I've hired a lawyer for you— the car is in your name. Fundamentally, you have nothing to worry about—they're not going to hang you for being overseas while all this happened.

I don't know what's going to happen to Sylvia and frankly I don't give a damn. She of course claims she only had a couple of beers and she has all kinds of explanations of why she was driving around Boston at three o'clock in the morning with an air force captain. You can believe her if you want, but I have to tell you that she's been running wild practically ever since you left. You have to face the fact that she's a tramp. I didn't want to spell it all out, but this accident can't be kept a secret. Among other things, I think you should cut off her allotment. I have a lawyer who may represent you for free, but I hate to think of you sending most of your pay for her to spend on other guys. She keeps a party going practically all the time in that new house her father bought for her, and it's always full of free loaders.

I know this must be very tough on you but . . .

There were two pages more, but Paul did not read them. He started opening the letters from Sylvia. The first had been written before the accident and was all about decorating the house. The third was written in a wavering scrawl:

Paul dearest,

I hate to bother you with this but I had a stupid accident. I'm not badly hurt and the doctor says I'll get completely better. I wouldn't bother you at all with it, except the thing was in the papers. Bill saw it, and you know he's always had it in for me. I'm sure he'll tell you terrible things and I just want to explain that they're not true at all.

I was driving a guy to a hospitle. It was an emergency. He's an air force captain I met at the U.S.O. strickly in the line of duty. He'd just come back from flying fifty missions overseas and he got terribly drunk. He and some other guys got in a fight and he fell and hit his head. I was terribly scared and tried to get him to the hospitle as soon as possible. This stupid truck driver jammed on his brakes right in front of me and there wasn't a thing I could do. The air force guy was carrying a bottle in his pocket and the stuff went all over me, so the cops thought I was drunk, but I'd hardly been drinking at all.

Bill won't believe me—he's really being horid about this. That forces me to give you the real reason, although I never wanted to. The truth is that Bill has always been after me and when you sailed off he got to be a real problem. I slaped his face hard and he's never forgiven me. Now he's trying to get even by making you hate me. Paul, darling, I know you won't believe him. What we have together . . .

Paul couldn't read any more. He didn't trust her and he didn't trust his brother. The only thing he was sure of at that moment was that he wanted to get drunk, drunker than old Mowrey had ever been. Cramming his letters into his pocket, he walked out of his cabin. Nathan, who was trying to bring order to the arrival of more mail sacks, saw him run across the well deck and jump ashore. After one glimpse of his face, Nathan followed him. He caught up with him on the road that led from the wharf to the officers' club, where Paul was slowing to a fast walk.

"Where are you going?"

"I need a drink."

"Mind if I come with you?"

"Christ, let me alone!"

There was such a look on Paul's face that Nathan fell back, but he still followed him to the club at a discreet distance, then stood at the other end of the crowded bar. He saw Paul order a scotch, toss it off and order another. After Paul had downed four drinks as fast as he could get them he sat bent over his glass. Nathan walked over and sat next to him. Paul gave no sign of noticing him. At the other end of the bar a group of men started to sing, "You are my Sunshine, my only Sunshine . . ."

"Give me another scotch," Paul suddenly called to the bartender, his voice oddly shrill.

After eyeing him coldly for a moment, the bartender poured him another drink.

"I'll have one too," Nathan said, going to his side.

Paul turned and stared at him for a moment, almost as though Nathan were a stranger.

"So something bad happened," Nathan said. "Whatever it is, believe it or not, it's really not the end of the world."

Paul stared at him. He mumbled, "Not the end of the world."

"Do you want to talk about it?"

Paul thought about that for a few seconds before putting his hand in his pocket and handing him the crumpled letters. "Letters from home . . ."

Nathan read the letters. The lines in his mournful face seemed to deepen.

516

"Ah, shit," he said, finally. "You don't deserve this."

"I don't know," he said. "Maybe I do. It's crazy. I guess she hasn't done anything I haven't done, but I still want to kill somebody. I want to take my damn pistol and go home and wipe them both out."

"You won't feel that way long."

"What *will* I do?"

"You'll try to understand whatever happened and eventually you will—"

"I already understand this . . . I never want to see those people again. I want to begin over with somebody else—"

"That would be one solution—"

"What do *you* think I should do? Go home and try to patch everything up with the little wife?"

"I don't know if that would be possible. I just know that anger like yours doesn't do much good . . ."

"You're lucky, you can be angry at the Germans and you've already helped to kill a few—"

"I was angry at my wife too. I didn't want her to go back to Poland to get her parents. I thought it was crazy and I told her so. We had a fight, we had lots of fights. Maybe that's the real reason she went off."

"But what happened wasn't your fault."

"Which doesn't help much. Guilt or innocence—sometimes in the long run they don't much count."

"What does?"

Nathan shrugged. "Survival for one thing, and I guess kindness when possible . . . you're too good a man to let this sour you for long . . ."

Paul felt embarrassed. "I don't know, for the first time in my life I've no idea what to do."

"For a while, how about nothing? Let the days go by."

"I don't know what I'll say when I see her. I don't know what I should write."

"Write nothing, say nothing. Just let the days go by."

"I don't want to go home. Do you think I could get transferred to a ship that's going to stay here?"

"Probably GreenPat would arrange that for you, but this isn't a time to make decisions . . ."

"Yeah, I'm tired of making decisions, I've never been more tired in my goddamn life."

They had more drinks. Then Nathan called the motor pool and was able to get a jeep to take them back to the ship. Paul staggered up the steps to his cabin, grabbing at

517

the rails the way Mowrey used to do. Nathan helped him into his bunk and took off his shoes.

"The truth is," Paul said with startling clarity, "the truth is, I loved her for no damn good reason I could understand. And now I don't love her, not anymore, even though she's probably no worse than I am. That isn't reasonable, is it? There's nothing about it that makes sense."

"Who always makes sense?"

"I never want to see her again. I don't want to hurt her, I just never want to see her again."

"Just let the days go by," Nathan said. "Do nothing as long as you can. It's what you need."

The next day Paul felt calmer, in spite of his hangover, but he still hated the thought of going back to Boston to see his wife and brother. He seriously considered asking GreenPat to transfer him to a ship that was going anywhere else in the world, but Nathan talked him out of it.

"Damn it, I'm not ready yet to take the *Arluk* on a long voyage alone," he said. "Anyway, GreenPat will think you're ice-happy if you tell him you don't want to go home. He'd probably be afraid to give you another command. You're liable to end up as exec under some other crazy bastard like Mowrey . . ."

So Paul stayed aboard the *Arluk* and helped to get her ready for the long voyage home. The winter weather on the North Atlantic was even worse than usual that year, but by this time Paul had enormous confidence in the old trawler, her men and in himself as a sailor. He spent hours on the flying bridge as the ship drove before a full gale, and there were moments when he felt a kind of serenity not like anything he'd known before. At such times he felt himself freed from anger at Sylvia, his brother and even himself. He realized that he didn't really know what had happened, what Sylvia and Bill had done or not done. Probably he never would know for sure and he wasn't at all certain he wanted to find out. He had no desire to ask a lot of questions and play detective. Sylvia was Sylvia—he had rarely been able to be sure she was telling the truth, and maybe that was why he could no longer love her. Maybe lying was the worst part of infidelity. Brit at least had never gone in for that. Maybe his love for Sylvia had always been a little crazy, as everyone in his family had kept telling him.

Maybe the Arctic seas, Greenland, Brit and Nathan had helped him become sane, to grow up, and he would finally escape Sylvia, but there was no reason to do it with a lot of fireworks. Ashore or at sea, dramatic—melodramatic—action was usually a mistake, and when things were worst it was most important to stay almost casual, as though nothing was happening at all. There was no *reason* to attack Sylvia for being whatever she was. He would visit her in the hospital, if that's where she still was, try not to increase her pain and leave as soon as possible. If he had to see his brother, he would say little, listen for as short a time as possible and get out. Soon he would be given another assignment, a much bigger ship, perhaps, and that was good to think about. The war would go on, God knew how many years, and when it was over, if he was still alive, he could make up his mind whether to go back to Sylvia. As Nathan had said, sometimes it's wise not to make decisions . . . he'd let events make them for him. For now, anyway.

Unfortunately these moments of calm were often swept away by gusts of rage. Why did all this have to be happening to him? Why couldn't he come home, a conquering hero, like he'd often imagined, and be met by his faithful admiring wife with sighs of love? Certainly that sort of thing must be happening often to men no more deserving than he. At least half the men in the forecastle were waiting for it to happen to them, and not all of them would be disappointed.

Well . . . if I'd picked a saner wife and had been saner myself I could expect better rewards, he lectured himself, but in some ways I'm a damn lucky man . . . For one thing I'm alive and unhurt. Hansen, Sparks, Seth, Blake, Cookie, the living pincushion—if he thought about them it was hard to feel sorry for himself. . . .

As they neared Boston a heavy blizzard enclosed them in the now familiar curtains of snow, but with the help of the radar Paul found his way into the harbor without difficulty. Just before dark he nosed the *Arluk* alongside a wharf in the same shipyard where they had first boarded her less than a year ago. It seemed a lifetime. There was no one ashore to catch their heaving lines, but Guns jumped from the forecastle head, and the ship was quickly moored.

"Finished with engines," Paul said, and Nathan rang up the signal.

"Liberty party requests permission to go ashore!" Boats called from the well deck.

"Permission granted," Paul said, and the men, who had been wearing their dress blues for hours, scrambled over the rail.

"I've given Mr. Williams the duty aboard tonight," Nathan said. "I'll be around tomorrow. There's no reason why you can't take off."

"You got any plans?" Paul asked.

"I'm going to have a drink at the Ritz bar."

"I'll join you before I make my telephone calls."

They both put on rumpled khaki uniforms because they had no clean blue ones, and they felt out of place at the Ritz bar with beautiful women and sleek-looking men laughing all around them. They said very little as they downed two drinks, and then Paul, with a rising sense of dread, walked to a telephone booth. He decided to call his parents first to see where Sylvia was. His mother answered.

"Paul! Where are you?"

"Home."

"I'm so glad! I've been so worried about you. I'm so sorry everything happened the way it did. You've heard about it, haven't you? Bill is just furious at Sylvia. He told me before he left that he hopes none of us ever have to see her again."

"Where did he go?"

"Didn't you get our letters? They sent him to England, and now I'm so worried about him. He volunteered to go even though he could have stayed as an instructor here."

Well, Paul thought—at least I won't have to see him . . . "Is Sylvia still in the hospital?"

"Yes . . . she's really in very bad shape, I hear. Bill says she's mental. She's got more than broken bones. I'm so sorry. It's such a terrible thing for you."

"I'm all right," Paul said, got the name of the hospital, promised to visit his parents as soon as possible, quickly hung up and walked slowly back to the bar.

"One more drink," he said to Nathan. "I've got to visit a hospital."

"Want to come back here afterward? We could have a late dinner."

"That would be good," Paul said. "I shouldn't be long."

He took a taxi to the Massachusetts General Hospital. A

receptionist gave him the number of Sylvia's room. He walked through endless corridors, all of which seemed to him to be full of the smells and sounds of sickness and death. As he approached the open door of Sylvia's room he heard her laughing exactly as she used to do at parties. She was sitting in bed with one leg propped up in a plaster cast, and she was talking to two white-coated young interns who were drinking from paper cups. Vases of flowers filled every level surface in the room.

Aware that his sudden arrival might come as a shock to her, Paul hesitated by the door.

"You're just saying that!" Sylvia said. "You're just trying to cheer up a poor cripple."

"No, I mean it," the taller intern said.

Sylvia's glossy dark blonde hair had been brushed over the shoulders of her pink bed jacket. She was wearing, as usual, a little too much makeup, but in her face there was that familiar vitality, the same old excitement, and her eyes sparkled as she laughed with the interns. Paul walked slowly toward her. From the doorway, he said, "Hello, Sylvia."

She jerked her head to face him, and went so pale that her lipstick and rouge seemed to brighten.

"Paul! My God! You're *back!*"

She held out her arms and the interns hastily brushed by Paul on their way out. Leaning over the bed, he kissed her on the forehead and gave her a quick hug before stepping back.

"What kind of a greeting is that? Oh Paul! Are you mad at me?"

"No."

"I wish I wasn't like this. I wish I could ask you to jump right into this bed with me."

He smiled.

"Oh, Paul, sit here on the edge of the bed and hold my hand. I have so much to tell you about. I want to explain the whole thing, so you don't have any reason to be mad at me at all . . ."

She talked very fast, often contradicting herself and her letter, making him almost embarrassed for her as she strained to explain why she was driving around the city at three o'clock on the morning after New Year's Eve with an air force captain and why she had been charged with drunken driving, but she managed to give a certain plausibility to her protestations of innocence, except for the fact

521

that she now had the air force captain a terrible man who had practically kidnapped her.

"It all must have been very hard on you," he said.

"It wouldn't really have been more than a stupid accident if it hadn't been for Bill. I haven't wanted to tell you this about your own brother but . . ."

According to her, Bill had been pursuing her for years and had almost raped her only a week after Paul had gone to Greenland. Paul was sure that she exaggerated this, but also suspected there was some substance to it. He was very glad that Bill was three thousand miles away.

"I'm sorry about all this too," he said, "but there's not much we can do about it now, is there?"

"No, but I just want to be sure you believe me. I haven't done one single thing wrong."

"I'm not judging you, Sylvia. I'm not in very good shape for judging anybody . . . but I can't stay long. I have to go—"

"Where? Why? Chris said you'd get a thirty-day leave when you came home."

He thought of confessing his sins and asking her honestly to confess hers, but the thought appalled him, and he was sure that after the whole messy scene was over he would still want to get away from her. There was no point in putting her or himself through all that.

"I have to go," he repeated. "Sylvia, you and I need time to figure things out. Let's just do as best we can until after the war is over. Then we'll see where we stand."

"You are mad at me then, aren't you? You don't believe me!"

"I think we both need time to see where we are and what we are."

She looked scared. "You're not going to cut off my allotment, are you? Bill said you would."

"I won't do anything like that. Get better and don't worry. We both have to sort things out . . ."

He kissed her on the lips this time and quickly turned to go. She broke into tears, and, damn it, he was strongly tempted to go back. He was also pretty sure that that would turn out to be the worst decision in his life, and by now he was something of an expert in the mistake line. He went out of the room so fast that he jostled a cart full of trays in the hall, spilled one, and was shouted at by an angry nurse. "Why don't you look where you're going?"

Some way to talk to a hero ...

By the time he got back to the Ritz bar, his calm had deserted him, and he realized that he was almost in shock. His hand trembled as he reached for a drink.

"You're not as terrible a man as you think," Nathan said with his crooked smile.

"I don't know. She's sick and I just walked out on her. She was crying. Maybe she really was telling the truth."

"Do you really believe that?"

"No. But maybe that shouldn't matter."

"Maybe."

"But in the long run it would. Damn it, I want to get out of this town. I don't want to see her again and I don't want to see my parents. They'll just keep telling me how terrible she is."

"Why don't you go up to the district office tomorrow and see what orders they're cooking up for you? I met a commander here at the bar a few minutes ago, and he said they're sending practically everybody to some kind of school in Florida between assignments."

"You mean *now* they're going to send us to school?"

Nathan laughed. "That figures, doesn't it?"

The next day Paul found that he was indeed slated to go to Advanced Officers' Training School in St. Augustine, Florida, for six weeks. After that he would be given command of one of many small ships which were being built for service in the southwest Pacific. The thought of palm-fringed islands pleased him. Until then he had not realized how much he dreaded going back to the Arctic. The personnel officer told him that there was no reason why he could not go to Florida right away and take his leave there before reporting to the school. A month of lying on the beaches in a place where no one would expect anything of him seemed to Paul to be just what he needed. No matter how much sleep he got, he still felt exhausted. ...

When Paul was detached from the *Arluk* Nathan was given orders making him commanding officer of the trawler. Paul was packing his clothes when Nathan came to his cabin to show him the mimeographed papers.

"Aren't you going to get any leave?" Paul asked.

"Later maybe. I want to be here to make sure that the refitting goes right, and I've got to train practically a whole new crew."

523

"I bet you turn out to be worse than Mowrey," Paul said with a straight face.

"I can't really believe I'm skipper," Nathan said. "When we first came aboard here, who in the world could have imagined that?"

"In war everything changes fast, including us."

"You mean the Coast Guard has made men out of us?" He smiled.

Paul closed his footlocker and strapped it to Brit's big narwhale tusk in its sealskin case. "Maybe you'll see Brit again," he said.

"I doubt if we get over to the east coast again, but maybe."

"Give her my best."

"I will. Do you want me to have some of the men carry your gear out to the street?"

"I'd appreciate it. You better read your orders to the men as soon as I've gone. They should know who their skipper is."

The petty officers who appeared to take Paul's footlocker were new hands. All the men Paul knew were on liberty or had been transferred. There was no one to say good-by to, but before leaving he walked through the wardroom and up to the forecastle, which was strangely deserted. Nathan followed him. They stood by the gangway for a few moments, oddly embarrassed about saying good-by.

"Take care of yourself," Paul said, taking Nathan's hand.

"Let's get together after the war."

Paul clapped him hard on the shoulder, turned and walked ashore.

A few moments later he turned to take a last look at the *Arluk*. Nathan had hurried to the signal halyards and as Paul watched, the third repeater fluttered toward the top of the mast to signify that the commanding officer was not aboard. Standing by the foot of the mast, Nathan made the halyard fast, turned and raised his hand in a salute that ended in a wave. Paul waved back, and then, acting on impulse, gave the ship a formal salute before turning and hurrying toward the street, another ship and another war.

# EPILOGUE

Nathan and Paul did not meet again for thirty-seven years, and then it was by chance. Before that they often thought of each other and considered trying to get in touch, but like many men they were perhaps afraid to attempt to carry a wartime friendship into peacetime. Neither of them was a jovial backslapping type who enjoyed meeting people for old times sake. Perhaps they thought that some memories that were good, almost hallowed as time went by, could be ruined by an awkward reunion. Besides that, they were both unusually busy men who lacked the time for sentimental excursions into the past.

Still, Nathan often wondered what had happened to Paul in the Pacific, whether he went back to his wife and whether he found a way to be as effective in, say, business as he had been aboard the *Arluk*. And Paul wondered how Nathan had managed aboard the *Arluk* back in Greenland, whether he had seen Brit again, whether he had ever found out what had happened to his wife in Poland, and whether he had found a career suited to his unusual talents. Their memories of each other were like stories with the last pages missing, but that was the way most wartime friendships looked in retrospect. Both Nathan and Paul were thoughtful men, and they concluded that the fragment of each other which they possessed had a certain completeness in its own right. The past belongs to the past and was often ruined when dragged into the present. . . .

Nevertheless, Paul was delighted one morning in May, 1979, when he picked up a copy of the New York *Times* in his office and saw a small headline which said, "DR. NATHAN GREENBERG TO ADDRESS N.A.M. ON SOLAR ENERGY." A photograph of a craggy-faced, balding man in his sixties removed any doubt that this was indeed Nathan of the North and Paul was not surprised to see that he had changed his family name back to Greenberg. The article said that Dr. Greenberg was a professor at M.I.T. who was considered a pioneer in developing solar energy, and it added that his address was going to be given at the Hilton Hotel at three that afternoon.

On impulse Paul called the hotel to see if Nathan was registered there, and when he found he was, telephoned his room. Nathan's deep, "Hello" seemed to echo unchanged across the chasm of thirty-seven years.

"Nathan, get your ass up on the bridge!" Paul said. "The fog is closing in. I need some radar bearings."

"Paul! My God, that voice of yours still makes me jump. Where in hell is the bridge these days?"

"I'm not more than a dozen blocks from you. I'll come over to see you any time you're not too busy."

"Come now. I'll order coffee and I'll see if I can get some croissants or some Danish pastry like Cookie's best."

Nathan's suite was as impersonal as most hotel rooms, but he had arranged a feast on a fake marble table that would have done justice to Cookie himself. There was even a bottle of Aquavit. Paul found himself studying this before allowing himself more than a glance at Nathan. Stooped and gaunt even in his youth, Nathan had not aged well physically, but his craggy face, especially his eyes, still had the vitality of youth. He was dressed in a blue serge suit almost as rumpled as their uniforms aboard the *Arluk*, but his white-on-white shirt, his maroon tie and his shoes all looked expensively tasteful. He looked, Paul decided, more like Abe Lincoln than ever.

Nathan, too, found it hard to get accustomed to the appearance of his old commanding officer. Paul was fat—not grossly so, but he was huge. His full head of hair was white and still refused to stay combed. His face, though heavy, still retained a certain boyishness. He wore the clothes of a successful businessman—dark gray silk, a club tie of some sort, a delicately striped shirt, polished black shoes almost like jackboots.

The two men shook hands awkwardly and sat down on a couch by the coffee table. Nathan poured coffee, but they did not interrupt their words with food.

"I'm not going to beat about the bush," Nathan began. "Damn it, I want a full report. What happened to you out in the Pacific?"

"I had a gas tanker. We were hit. It wasn't too much fun. How did you make out with the *Arluk*?"

526

"Mostly we just made milk runs up and down the west coast but we rescued some men from the *Dorchester*, and the crew of a wrecked plane. That made us feel pretty good. We never got back to the east coast."

There was a moment of silence before Paul said, "Did you find out what happened to your wife in Poland?"

"She died at Buchenwald. I found the records." There was a pause before he added, "I married again, a great Brooklyn girl. We have two sons."

"I'm glad. I married again, twice, I'm afraid. I'm still lucky at cards. Still, I have a good son and two daughters who spoil me."

"Do you mind my asking what happened to Sylvia?"

"She fell in love with a major from Texas while I was out in the Pacific. She wrote me a classic 'Dear John' letter and I wished her well. I understand that she's a real Dallas duchess these days."

"So the world made your decisions after all."

"One way or another . . . I was worried about my brother, and he was shot down over Germany just a few days before the end of the war . . ."

They both were silent a moment before Paul said, "Did you ever hear anything from Brit?"

"I was over in Denmark about twenty years ago and I made some inquiries at the headquarters of the Greenland Administration about her. She came back to Copenhagen after the war, but after that they had no record of her. She wasn't in the Copenhagen phone book. I suppose she married and has a different name."

"Did you ever hear anything about Cookie or any of the other men?"

"Not a word. Cookie must be an old man now. I hope he's retired to the Alps with a restaurant of his own."

"Yes. He was one hell of a fine man."

"I'd say they all were," Nathan said.

They sipped their coffee. "Now let me guess what you're doing now," Nathan said with a smile. "You're a banker. You have a big yacht on Long Island Sound."

"Is that what I look like?"

"A rather raffish banker. I'm not sure I'd trust my money with you. You might sell one of the branches to buy booze for the president."

Paul laughed. "You're partly right, but I don't have a

yacht. I got my fill of the sea when I had to drink about half the Pacific."

"But you are a banker?"

"Sort of. I have a little investment company that specializes in risk capital. It's no big deal, but I like to feel we help to start new kinds of business."

"How about solar energy? God knows we need risk capital in that."

"We're actually doing some research on it. Maybe we can help each other."

"I sure would like that. It would bring us full circle."

"Don't forget that if I put money in something, I want control of it," Paul said with a grin.

"You bastard, I should have figured that. You'll have me saluting you all over again. No thanks, I can raise my own capital."

"Maybe we can talk about it. I'll listen to your speech."

"I'll send you some books that will tell you more. By the way, do you have any pictures of the *Arluk?*"

"Not a one. I wish I did."

"I got some from the archives at Coast Guard Headquarters, and I even got copies of her blueprints. My sons and I made a model of her. If you give us time, we might make one for you."

"I'd like that."

Nathan put his coffee cup on the table. "It's surprising how much I think about the old days," he said. "There's a whole section of my mind that's still Greenland. Sometimes when I wake up suddenly I still think I'm surrounded by all that glittering ice."

"Me too.

"And the funny thing is," Nathan went on, "I keep dreaming about something that never happened at all."

"What's that?"

"I keep seeing myself dressed up as Nathan of the North, leading my Eskimo storm troops to the top of the mountain overlooking Supportup Fjord. I have whole piles of depth charges piled on the highest ridge. With freezing hands I adjust the fuses with fiendish cleverness and roll them down on the Krauts. I blow up the whole base with an explosion bigger than an atom bomb."

"Still the Germans fight desperately," Paul picked it up. "Then you lead your Eskimo storm troops in a magnificent charge while I bring the old *Arluk* into the fjord with all

528

guns blazing. One blast of that monstrous five-incher on the bow wipes out the Germans to the last man."

"Yes," said Nathan with his still-familiar smile. "That was the way it was. That, no question, was our finest hour."


That afternoon Paul went to hear Nathan's speech. There was a big crowd of important people and it was an impressive presentation of all the known facts about solar energy, including a great many that Paul couldn't understand at all. After the last question had been asked Paul went up to Nathan at the podium. "Could we get together some night? My children would like to meet you. They've been hearing stories about you all these years. They'd love to meet Nathan of the North."

Nathan laughed, and they went to the hotel bar.

"You're famous in my household too," Nathan said. "My sons know that if you hadn't seen that iceberg dead ahead that night before we got the radar, they wouldn't exist."

"I've often said that without the radar you brought aboard, we would have gone missing like the *Nanmak*. In lots of ways we saved each other."

"We survived," Nathan said. "You know, of all the things I've ever done, I'm really proudest of that. We beat the Krauts and the ice."

"And our own damn ignorance."

"And seasickness," Nathan said. "That was my real victory. But it's nothing I can explain to anybody. My wife understands everything about me except the way I feel about Greenland."

"Greenland can't be explained," Paul said. "I finally quit trying." There was a pause before he said, "Would you and your family like to come to dinner some night? How about tomorrow? I'll round up my kids."

Nathan smiled and there was some of the old hesitancy in his voice when he said, "We can't tomorrow. I have a meeting in Cambridge. But we'll make it soon. I'll be in touch."

They exchanged home addresses, but somehow Paul had a feeling right then that the dinner for their families would never happen. The past was past and there was too much risk in trying to drag it further into the present. Like sunken iron cannon, memories could disintegrate when taken away from the sea. Old war stories should stay old war stories without having the heroes played by modern actors who could not possibly now have any resemblance to the originals. Perhaps Nathan and he were afraid that they could not live up to each other.

Paul did not think he would ever hear from Nathan again, and he was surprised when a few days later a messenger delivered a large cardboard box to his New York apartment. An envelope was taped to the outside of it and Paul opened that first. On M.I.T. stationery, Nathan had written:

Dear Paul:

As I said, my sons and I made a model of the *Arluk*. Building it was really even more fun than owning it, and we kept all the blueprints. We can build another. Meanwhile, here's our first effort at shipbuilding. You gave the original to me. I never would have got command of her without you.

It's a very real pleasure to give you this model. If you can ever figure out how this little fishboat took us so far in so many ways, let me know. This model always seems to me to be the real *Arluk* as seen through the wrong end of a telescope. Be careful. I found that sometimes when I stare at it, she keeps seeming to grow bigger and bigger. Hell, you were aboard her less than a year, and I served aboard her only about two years, a tiny part of our lives, but such a part! I guess it's true that Greenland preserves the past the way it preserves dead bodies. When I made this model, I found that I hardly had to glance at the blueprints. I wish I understood the rest of the world as well.

As ever,
Nathan

Paul opened the cardboard carton. He found a mahogany base under a glass box which had been elaborately wrapped in padded paper. In it the model of the *Arluk* rested on a cradle. The blue and white hull was only about twelve inches long, but had been wrought in such infinite detail that when he held it up to the light he almost felt as though he would find Mowrey there, Guns, Sparks, Cookie and all the rest. The ice camouflage glistened in the sun from the window. The five-inch gun barrel they never had fired still rested on the forecastlehead beside the three-inch twenty-three, which finally had sunk the German hunter-killer. The radar antenna was in place above the flying bridge. On the signal mast there was a tiny pennant, a little bigger than scale, but still Paul had to put his glasses on to see it clearly. It was of course the third repeater. The commanding officer was not aboard this ship.

Paul carried the model toward the mantelpiece in his living room. For a moment he had the curious sensation that he had grown to almost godlike size and was holding his ship in the palm of his hand. It was true that the ship seemed to grow larger as he stared at it. Soon he imagined that he could almost hear the rattle of the anchor chain and the voices of the men.

"Yale, Yale, where's that bastard Yale?" Mowrey shouted. "Where is that son of a bitch?"

The bitter wind was howling over the ice pack, and Paul was young again, young, ignorant, and scared to death, but finally, for a little while at least, victorious.

He put the model on the mantelpiece. It certainly was a nice thing to have.